SEXTON BLAKE

YVONNE'S VENGEANCE

A Collection of 8 Classic Tales

Beyond Reach of the Law
When Greek Meets Greek
On the Brink of Ruin
Settling Day
A Minister of the Crown
The Detective Airman
The Missing Guests
By Right of Possession

George Hamilton Teed

ROH
PRESS

The Teed Files: Volume 1
Sexton Blake: Yvonne's Vengeance

George Hamilton Teed (1886-1938)
Beyond Reach of the Law, Union Jack #485, 1913
When Greek Meets Greek, Union Jack #488, 1913
On the Brink of Ruin, Union Jack #492, 1913
Settling Day, Union Jack #495, 1913
A Minister of the Crown, Union Jack #498, 1913
The Detective Airman, Union Jack #501, 1913
The Missing Guests, Union Jack #505, 1913
By Right of Possession, Union Jack #509, 1913

Cover: Adapted from *Beyond the Reach of Law*, by Val Reading, 1913 and *Wanted!* by Eric Parker, 1933

Illustrations by Val Reading

ISBN: 978-1-998879-02-1

Typos and Text

Each story has been meticulously edited to give you the best reading experience possible. However, sometimes the odd typo or two may have slipped through. If you spot one, please let us know and we'll fix it immediately. You can contact us at: rohpress@gmail.com. One last note: the original tales in this series were published between 1913 and 1917. While these stories have many entertaining elements, in some cases there are uses of language, instances of stereotyping, and attitudes expressed by the narrator or the characters which modern readers may find objectionable. It is not possible to separate these stories form the histories of their writing. They are presented as originally published with some minor language amendments of extremely offensive terms to make it more suitable for the modern reader.

www.rohpress.com

A Note from the Publisher

Sexton Blake Meets His Greatest Female Foe!

"What a wonderful woman!... What a brain—what thoroughness! Truly, my unknown friend, you give the chase a decided zest!" ~Sexton Blake, *Beyond Reach of the Law*

Mademoiselle Yvonne Cartier. Yvonne the Adventuress. The Princess of Mystery. Whatever her title, most fans agree her first appearance changed Sexton Blake's world forever. No female adversary before her matched her in style and daring, no one before her captured the detective's heart so thoroughly. She quickly became a fan favourite and appeared in Blake adventures for thirteen years, at first matching wits with the great detective and then later fighting alongside him.

Yvonne's story begins with an act of betrayal. Towards the end of the Edwardian age, the Cartiers are swindled out of their land in Australia. Yvonne swears vengeance upon the eight men who destroyed her family and begins to go after them one by one. Her exploits were wildly popular, the public enthralled by the tale of a young woman righting wrongs in the vein of a female Count of Monte Cristo.

The 'Vengeance Series' ran in the *Union Jack* from January to July 1913 and was comprised of the eight titles collected in this anthology: *Beyond Reach of the Law*, *When Greek Meets Greek*, *On the Brink of Ruin*, *Settling Day*, *A Minister of the Crown*, *The Detective Airman*, *The Missing Guests* and *By Right of Possession*. Of special note: *When Greek Meets Greek* also marks the debut of legendary Blake foe Dr. Huxton Rymer. You'll find out more about him in our second Teed anthology *Sexton Blake: Rymer and Wu Ling*.

This is the first of fourteen anthologies that collects G. H. Teed's most popular works from 1913 to 1917. Each edition includes all of the original illustrations! Enjoy!

Nico Lorenzutti
Editor
www.rohpress.com

Author Spotlight

George Hamilton Teed (1886-1938) was a Canadian author who wrote under the pen names G. H. Teed, Hamilton Teed, Louis Brittany, Murray Hamilton, Desmond Reid and Peter Kingsland. He specialized in adventure fiction and detective stories but also wrote science fiction and romances. Teed wrote close to three hundred Sexton Blake tales over the course of his twenty-five-year career, more than any other author.

Teed was born in Woodstock, New Brunswick and studied at McGill University, in Montreal. After completing his studies, he travelled the world, trying his hand at various jobs, including overseeing a banana plantation in Costa Rica, and sheep-farming

in Australia. His writing career began by chance. While sailing to England from Australia in May 1912, he met Mrs. Margaret Sempill, the widow of Michael Storm, (Ernest Sempill, 1862-1909) a popular author of Sexton Blake tales. He convinced her to allow him to ghost her late husband's stories for part of the fee. Over the summer, with Teed at the typewriter and Mrs. Storm making the sales, the pair produced four works which they sold to the Amalgamated Press. He made his debut in November 1912 with *Dead Men's Shoes.*

Legend has it that after falling out with Mrs. Storm, he approached the editors of the Amalgamated Press and declared himself to be the true author of the Michael Storm tales that they had published. The editors, of course, did not believe him, but when challenged, Teed sat down at a typewriter and banged out the first few chapters of a new tale. The editors, impressed, bought the story on the spot and Teed became a regular contributor for *Union Jack* and other Amalgamated Press publications.

It was in 1913 that the 'Teed era' truly began. That year saw the creation of three of his most legendary characters: Mademoiselle Yvonne Cartier, a beautiful, multi-skilled Australian adventuress who sets out to avenge crimes against her family; Dr. Huxton Rymer, a world-renowned surgeon who turns to a life of crime, and Prince Wu Ling, a member of the Chinese imperial family bent on world domination. They were among the founding members of what would eventually become a large pantheon of master criminals: highly talented men and women who matched wits with Blake in every corner of the world.

Teed had a great talent for creating lifelike characters, and his emancipated, complex, female master criminals almost single-handedly changed the way women were portrayed in British detective story papers. He also specialized in creating thrills in exotic locations, drawing from his own travels, observations, and personal experiences to create authentic atmospheres that had readers clamouring for more. These two traits set him apart from many of his contemporaries. Of the two hundred authors who penned Blake tales, Teed is considered by many to be "the master of them all."

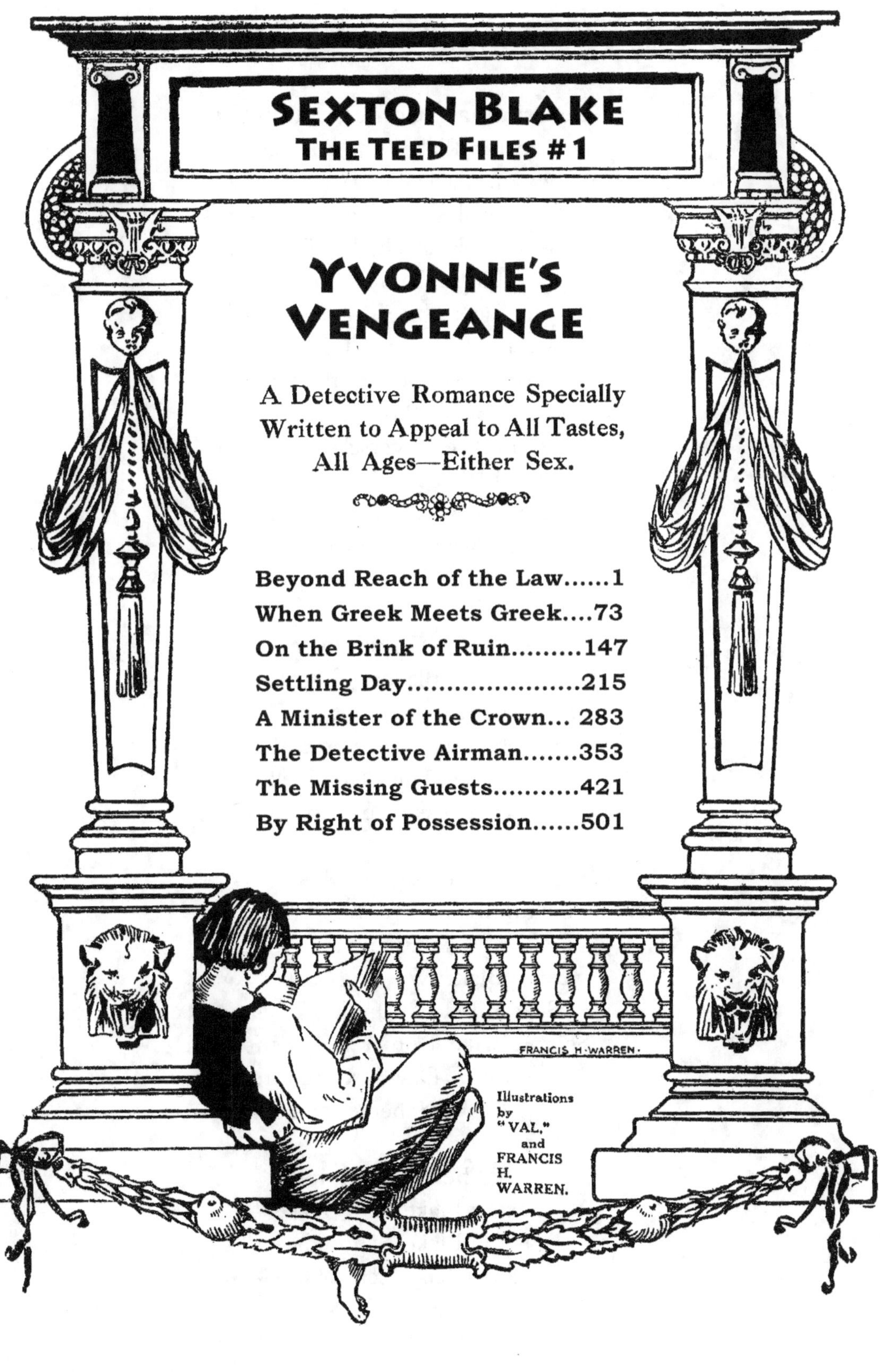

YVONNE'S VENGEANCE

A Detective Romance Specially Written to Appeal to All Tastes, All Ages—Either Sex.

Beyond Reach of the Law......1
When Greek Meets Greek....73
On the Brink of Ruin.........147
Settling Day.....................215
A Minister of the Crown... 283
The Detective Airman.......353
The Missing Guests..........421
By Right of Possession......501

Our Anthologies
Collections of Classic Works of Fiction

The Criminals' Confederation Series
Sexton Blake: The Bat Files
Sexton Blake: The Bat Files #2
Sexton Blake: The Bat Files #3
Sexton Blake: The Bat Files #4
Sexton Blake: Confederation Rising
Sexton Blake: The Sinister Island Saga
Sexton Blake: Yvonne Joins the Fight
Sexton Blake: Beware the Shadow
Sexton Blake: Plots and Intrigues
Sexton Blake: Reversals of Fortune
Sexton Blake: The Rival Presidents
Sexton Blake: Reece's Republic
Sexton Blake: Twists in the Trail
Sexton Blake: Final Curtain

The Golden Age
Sexton Blake: Spy Stories
Sexton Blake: The Ferraro Files #1
Sexton Blake: The Three Murrays
Sexton Blake: The Claire Delisle Files
Sexton Blake: Spy Stories #2

The Teed Files
Sexton Blake: Yvonne's Vengeance
Sexton Blake: Rymer and Wu Ling
Sexton Blake: Wu Ling Strikes Again
Sexton Blake: Cunning Schemes
Sexton Blake: Palmer and Beauremon
Sexton Blake: Dawn of the Great War
Sexton Blake: Schemes and Scandals

The Great Serials
Sexton Blake: Schooldays #1
Sexton Blake: Schooldays #2
Sexton Blake: Schooldays #3

THE UNION JACK. 1d.

BEYOND REACH OF THE LAW
OR: · A · WOMAN'S · REVENGE ·

NO. 485. NEW SERIES.]　　　January 25th, 1913.　　　[EVERY THURSDAY.

Prologue
The Great Mining Swindle

THE afternoon sun was dipping behind the hills of an Australian mining camp. Silhouetted against the deep-blue sky were the derricks of the mines which lined the ridge, looking frail and flimsy in the distance. The cable wheels still spun round on most of them, bringing up rich loads of quartz to be swallowed by the smelter.

The line of mines followed the visible outcrop, stretching away in the distance, and against the tool house of one in particular—the Jig Saw—leaned two men.

They were both bearded but while one was dressed with immaculate care, the other bore marks of toil, and his garments were rough. An intimacy evidently existed between them, for they spoke in confidential tones, and looked warily around from time to time.

"I'll tell you, Pearson, now is the time," the city man was saying. "If we bring it to a head while they are out here, we can get things wound up at once. On the other hand, if we wait until they return to England—well, it means correspondence, and we don't want any more of that than is necessary in a deal of this kind."

"Maybe you're right, Ike," responded the man called Pearson. "What do the others say?"

"They're all agreed. I tell you, Jim, now is the time."

"All right, if all of you think so, I'm agreeable; but I would have liked another three months to get the stone out of this saddle formation. The gold is fairly sticking out of it, and if anyone got down on that level they'd twig in a minute."

"Oh, Mrs. Cartier won't send anyone down! She doesn't know anything about mines or business, and the girl knows less. Things will go beautifully. You'll see. I'm no fool at money juggling," Ike grinned. "And when Ike Vineburg takes on a thing it usually goes through. This means a cool million[1] amongst the eight of us, and, from what you say, the mine ought to show another."

"It'll do that all right," grunted Pearson. "I've been in a good many mining districts—from Alaska to Chile—but this beats any prospect I've ever tackled. It's simply reeking with the stuff!"

Vineburg's eyes glittered with greed as he listened, and his tongue moistened his lips with anticipation.

"I'll go ahead with the deal," he said briskly. "You know, your part. Don't on any account let anyone you don't trust down the mine."

"Leave that to me. I didn't go in on this without careful consideration, and I'm taking no chances. When do you start to knock the price down?"

"I'll get things going tomorrow," answered Vineburg. "The others will start dumping their shares on the market in big blocks, and I'll circulate the report that the mine has petered out. People will come up to you, as the manager, and ask for a confirmation of the news. You tell them the yarn we arranged, and that means in twenty-four hours all the small holders will rush to sell. I will buy every share up quietly as it comes on the market, and when the bottom has dropped out, I will wire Mrs. Cartier to run down from the station."

"Do you think she will turn over the station as security to float a loan?"

"Of course. Before Cartier died he told her the Jig Saw was the richest thing in sight, and when I tell her we simply must borrow to carry on further working, and provide new machinery, she will bite beautifully. You leave that to me. I can handle her; she's as simple as a baby, and will do just what I say."

"It seems to me it'll be risky transferring to ourselves the shares and deeds of the station afterwards," remarked Pearson, dubiously.

"I've arranged for that. I'll provide dummies to loan us the money on the deeds, and when the further work fails, we will tell her the mine has snuffed out entirely. All she can do is to swallow the medicine. As we will apparently be heavy losers as well, she won't suspect anything. Ten to one she'll go back to England at once, and then we can make the transfer back to ourselves."

"I guess you've got a shrewder brain than I have," said Pearson, with an admiring glance. "I couldn't have engineered a deal like that in a thousand years."

---

[1] £1,000,000 in 1913 is worth £116,000,000 in 2020

"I haven't been a bookmaker for twenty years for nothing," laughed Vineburg, in a self-satisfied manner.

"By the way, Ike," went on Pearson, "what's going to win the cup this year? Anything strong favourite yet?"

"*Tragedy Prince*," came the prompt reply. "Put your socks and boots on it—it can't lose. And I don't tell you that because I own him, neither. He's the best piece of horseflesh in Australia today."

"I guess I'll leave it alone," grinned Pearson. "I don't think I'll risk much with you on the betting game, Ike. It's poor business, judging from the thousands Cartier lost with you."

"Cartier was an easy mark," replied the bookmaker, with a contemptuous snap of the fingers. "He'd trust anybody. As for me, I wouldn't take my own brother's word, on oath, on the race track."

"I don't blame you, Ike," returned the other, acidly. "I've heard it wasn't worth much."

"I didn't speak literally!" snapped Vineburg, flushing. "But take the tip, or leave it. I wouldn't take your money on *Tragedy Prince* in any event. I'm putting a fortune on him myself."

"All right, Ike," smiled Pearson, good humouredly. "Don't lose your temper. If you back him yourself, maybe, I'll put a couple of thousand on him. But about this other matter. Will you start smashing the price tomorrow?"

"Yes," replied Vineburg, in a modified tone, "I'll get along now, and tip off the boys. Have your story ready, Jim. And, for Heaven's sake, don't let anything leak out from this end!"

"I tell you I can trust every man I've got!" snapped Pearson impatiently. "You handle your end, and I'll guarantee nothing leaks out here."

"Very well. I'll slip up again in a week or so, and let you know how things go."

"Right!"

A few seconds later Vineburg was scrambling down the side of the hill to a buggy which waited below, and Pearson turned away to enter his rude quarters.

***

The day following the conversation between Pearson and Vineburg was a memorable one on the small mining exchange, which transacted business in the shares of the surrounding mines.

Soon after it had opened for the day's business, disturbing rumours crept about that all was not well with the Jig Saw. The famous saddle formation from which the mine had secured so much gold, and the discovery of which had boomed the price of the shares, was reported to have petered out. Later rumours seemed to confirm this, and further details gave a minute description of how shafts had been driven in all directions to try and pick up the "legs" again, but that they had ended in nothing.

The price of the shares had dropped, and fluctuated unsteadily at the first report; but later news had sent them down helter-skelter.

They firmed a bit when Todd and Kelly—two of the biggest stockholders, appeared on

5

the floor, for it was reported that they had come to deny the rumours. But when, instead, they threw large blocks of shares on the market, the smaller holders, who had been hanging on desperately waiting for official news, lost their nerve, and rushed to sell.

Several brokers were buying up the shares at bargain prices; but where they could afford to hold for the reaction, the small holders could not.

Men had rushed off to the mine to ask the manager if the report was true, and when they returned and fought madly for a sale, the panic grew general.

Early in the morning the price had stood at nearly five pounds per share, but on the close of business they were offered at five shillings, and holders were hopeless of receiving even that. Further selling orders had come in from Melbourne, Sydney, and Adelaide on the news which had been telegraphed to these centres, and the outlook for the next day was black.

The worst anticipations were realised, for further large blocks were thrown on the market wholesale, and on the evening of the second day Jig Saw shares stood at two and six, which meant no value.

On the same evening a lady stepped from the train at the little station. She was small, and delicate-looking, and dressed in mourning. A heavy, black veil obscured her features; but as she raised it to greet a man who came up to her, the light from the platform lamp shone on a sweet, gentle face, which must have been very beautiful in its youth.

"Ah, Mrs. Cartier," exclaimed the man effusively, "I trust your journey hasn't been very tiresome?"

"How do you do, Mr. Vineburg?" she replied, in a clear, sweet voice. "No; I was too worried to notice the discomfort. I came immediately on getting your telegram. Are things any better today?" she asked anxiously.

"I'm sorry to say, Mrs. Cartier, that they are much worse," answered Vineburg, in a gloomy tone. "I have done all I could to stem the tide; but my pocket has a bottom, and I had to give it up. I hardly dare reckon my losses."

"But is the report true, Mr. Vineburg, that there is no more gold in the mine?"

"I'm afraid it is, Mrs. Cartier. It is a big blow to us all, and I regret exceedingly that your husband is not alive. I had great faith in the Jig Saw; and we might save things yet, if he were here."

"Save things! How do you mean, Mr. Vineburg?" she asked eagerly. "I know my husband had every confidence in the mine. I don't know anything but what you tell me about such things; but if it is anything I can do, let me know what it is. I know Mr. Cartier would do almost anything to save the Jig Saw."

Vineburg's eyes gleamed as she spoke; but they assumed a sorrowful expression as he turned to answer.

"I'm afraid you don't understand, Mrs. Cartier. You see," he went on, as one speaking to a child, "there is only one direction left in which we can drive to try to pick up the vein. It will take a great deal of money, and the credit of the mine is gone now. I would gladly put up all I have, but I have already done so, and the other directors have done the same. We would need to borrow a great deal of money to go ahead. Mr. Cartier would have saved the situation; but I am afraid we must swallow the loss." And he sighed admirably.

"I am afraid I'm very stupid, Mr. Vineburg. Tell me what would Mr. Cartier have done?"

They had been walking down the main street as they talked, and had arrived at the entrance of the hotel. The light from its entrance shone across the footpath, and Vineburg stopped in the shadow to reply.

"Well," he laughed, "it won't do any good to tell you; but I feel sure he would have arranged the loan for us by putting up the necessary security."

"Security!" she echoed. "What security?"

"He had such perfect faith in the mine that I feel positive he would even have temporarily pledged his station—temporarily, you understand."

He gazed beneath lowered lids as she gasped:

"But, Mr. Vineburg, that is all I have left now, since the shares have gone. Do you think he would have pledged it?"

He nodded, without speaking, for he knew the value of silence at such a time.

"I'll—I'll think over it tonight, Mr. Vineburg, and let you know in the morning. Good-night! Are you sure my husband would have done that, Mr. Vineburg?" she turned back to ask. "If he would—why, I suppose I ought to as well."

Again he bowed silently, and then, bidding her goodnight, hastened down the street. As he turned the corner a triumphant smile flitted across his face, for he knew she would do it.

Ike Vineburg had not been a bookmaker for twenty years without knowing the tricks of the game and the gullibility of human nature.

II
Bad News

IT was six months after the panic in Jig Saw shares.

Binabong Station preened itself proudly in the warm rays of the sun.

Its fertile acres, freshly green from the tender shoots of young grass, stretched for miles in every direction.

The giant trees threw their welcome shadow at intervals, and here and there a large clump had been left where the ground was swampy.

The house was a low, rambling structure, covered with vines, and its corrugated roof threw back the sun's rays with a trying glare. Canvas curtains shut in the verandah from the persevering rays, and several sheep dogs lay listlessly in the shade.

The surrounding garden was, however, unaffected, for its stalks were still vigorous with the life of spring.

To the left of the homestead was the horse paddock, while in the rear stretched a vivid patch of lucerne, forming a foreground for the anxiously cared-for field of ambercane, which would make rich fattening food for the aged ewes in the summer when the grass was sparse and dry. From the right came the refreshing murmur of a huge overshot dam, fed by the towering pillar of the artesian spring. Shearing was in progress, and from the sheds came the steady hum of the machines as the heavy fleeces dropped to the floor. Stretched over the home paddock were hundreds of newly-shorn sheep, looking ridiculously naked, while from the yards surrounding the sheds came the mournful bleat of those still waiting their turn. The sharp bark of a dog sounded, accompanied by the shrill cries of the stockmen as they drove some of the waiting sheep into the pens as a finished mob poured out at the other end.

Inside the shed all was bustle. Men, stripped to singlet and trousers, sweated over sheep which lay helpless between their knees. Occasionally the blade would go deeper than intended, and a red patch would appear, vivid against the new whiteness. A loud call of "tar" brought the tar boy on the run, and the red patch was soon changed to black by the application of the brush.

Other men rapidly gathered up the fleeces as they fell to the floor from the last snap of the shears, and threw them dexterously on the large tables, where others quickly "skirted" them around the edges, the fleeces going into their proper piles according to class, and the skirtings going to swell the rapidly increasing pile of "locks," "bellies," or "pieces," as the case might be.

Further on, the wool-press rapidly pressed the finished fleeces into large bales, which a boy branded as the pressman finished sewing and released them.

A slow moving team of bullocks loaded up as the completed bale was rolled aside, removing them to a high-floored shed where they were safe from the dampness.

Half a mile away, in a large paddock, a traction-engine "chugged, chugged," followed by two large disc ploughs. Behind came a fine-cutting disc harrows, and sharp diamond-tooth harrows brought up the procession, for the overseer of Binabong believed in fallowing, and fallowing well.

Riding a big chestnut with the grace of the born stockman, was a slim, bronze-haired young woman. A broad-brimmed felt hat sat carelessly on her head, and the neat, divided skirt dropped in straight lines to the small feet booted in heavy tan. Her face was flushed with a warm colour, and her lips were parted in a happy, unconscious smile as she cracked a long stock whip, and sent a shaggy sheep dog flying around the mob of ewes which she was mustering.

To the casual observer the scene on Binabong Station that beautiful day presented an ideal picture of industry, peace, and prosperity, with consequent happiness. No cloud, either figurative or literal, obscured the horizon, but a tiny speck which appeared in the distance, and which rapidly grew larger as it approached, was to obscure the happy scene with a startling swiftness.

As it grew more distinct it resolved itself into a horse and jinker, in which were seated two dusty men. The driver turned toward the house as they reached the home paddock, and the jinker rattled over the soft turf, to the accompaniment of the fierce barking of the dogs which, tired from mustering, rested in the shade of the verandah.

As the sound of the dogs reached her ears, the young woman lifted her head, and, shading her eyes, looked intently in the direction of the house. A puzzled line appeared between her deep, serious eyes, and she turned with a sharp exclamation to the boundary rider who accompanied her.

"Strangers, Jerry. I'll have to go to the house. Take over the mob, and keep the dog."

"All right, Miss Cartier," replied the tanned stockman and, winding up her stock-whip, she rode at a clinking pace for the house.

The strangers had already disappeared through the wire door when she arrived, and, tossing the bridle rein to a black boy, she hastened in after them, for she imagined her mother would be asleep, and there would be no one to welcome the new-comers.

She was right, for the visitors sat alone in the cool gloom of a wicker-furnished reception-room, wiping their wet foreheads.

They rose, and bowed, as she entered.

"I'm sorry," she began. "I saw you arrive, and came as quickly as possible. Did you wish to see my mother? She usually rests in the afternoon."

"It is our turn to apologise—Miss Cartier, I presume," replied the darker of the two; and, as she nodded, he went on: "We are sorry to disturb Mrs. Cartier, but the maid insisted on calling her. We could have waited until her usual time for appearing. Besides, this room is delightful after the sun." And his teeth flashed as he smiled at her.

"But allow us to introduce ourselves. My companion, Mr. Morgan—Miss Cartier. My name is Vineburg," he added, with another flash of the white teeth.

The young woman bowed, and replied:

"Mother wouldn't mind being roused, but she has been ill lately, and I am very anxious about her. However, I expect she'll be here presently, and if you'll excuse me I'll order some refreshment for you. It is hot in the sun."

They bowed their thanks, and resumed their seats as she left.

"By Jove, Morgan, isn't she a stunner!" whispered Vineburg. "Did you ever see such hair?"

"Oh, you're caught by every pretty face!" growled Morgan. "Now, I——" But he broke off as Mrs. Cartier entered.

She looked pale and tired, and held out her hand to Vineburg with a listless gesture.

"This is a surprise, Mr. Vineburg," she smiled; "but, nevertheless, you are welcome."

"Thank you, Mrs. Cartier," returned Vineburg suavely. "Believe me, madam, I would not have come if it hadn't been urgent. But permit me to introduce Mr. Morgan. You have heard me speak of him as one of the directors of the Jig Saw," he explained, as Mrs. Cartier acknowledged the introduction.

"Yes, I remember," she murmured, as she sank into a chair; "but you speak of urgent business, Mr. Vineburg. I trust you have no further bad news about the mine?"

The conversation was interrupted by the entrance of Miss Cartier, accompanied by a maid carrying a tea-tray. General topics were discussed while the travellers refreshed themselves, and presently Miss Cartier rose to leave, but her mother put out her hand.

"Don't go, Yvonne! It is business about the mine."

"All right, mother dear," replied Yvonne, resuming her seat. "But are you well enough to talk business this afternoon? Can't it wait?"

Yvonne in her native element.
TINKER GASPED IN ASTONISHMENT AS HE SAW THE BEAUTIFUL WOMAN WHO ENTERED

"No, dear. Mr. Vineburg says it is urgent, and now, if you don't mind," she added, turning to Vineburg, who seemed the spokesman of the pair, "please let me hear what it is?"

"Well," answered Vineburg hesitatingly "you must prepare yourself for bad news, Mrs. Cartier. The fact, is—er———"

"Go on, please!" cried Mrs. Cartier, in an anxious tone. "Don't keep me in suspense! Have we lost more money?"

"Yes, that is the case," replied Vineburg hurriedly, as though anxious to get the words out. "We've lost a lot; in fact, Mrs. Cartier, the Jig Saw Mine is a total failure."

Yvonne jumped up and rushed to her mother's side. She was only twenty-three, but she could see tragedy in the eyes which she held so dear, and the protective instinct, which she had inherited from her father, quickly asserted itself. She passed her arm around her mother's shoulder, and turned toward the men to speak, but Mrs. Cartier gathered her strength together to reply.

"And that means?" she whispered.

Vineburg's eyes fell before her terror-stricken gaze, and Morgan shifted uneasily in his seat.

"It means," replied Vineburg, clearing his throat, "that the collateral must be forfeited to the creditors. They are clamouring for their money."

"I—I think I understand, Mr. Vineburg," faltered the stricken woman. "It means Binabong must go?"

Her eyes dwelt with a despairing intensity on her face, and as he bowed his head in silent assent, she dropped to the floor with a low moan. Both men jumped to their feet as she did so, but Yvonne waved them back. Picking the frail body up in her strong young arms, she stumbled from the room, her eyes blinded with tears, and went down the corridor to her mother's chamber. Tenderly she laid her on the bed, and hastily sponged the hot temples.

"By Jove!" muttered Morgan. "I've got enough decency left in me to be disgusted with myself for being in this!"

"Oh, shut up!" replied Vineburg. "We've started on it, and it must go through. If you are so squeamish you should have said so." But he held his eyes averted as he spoke.

Inside the chamber, Yvonne worked feverishly. She finally heaved a sigh of relief as the unconscious woman's eyes opened.

"Oh, mother, mother dear, don't take it so hard! It won't make any difference to us. We'll go back to England, and be happy there again. Don't—please don't worry about it, dear!"

Her mother's eyes stared straight ahead, and Yvonne's filled with an unknown terror as she saw the lips moving, but knew they were not speaking to her. She bent her head to listen, the tears falling thickly on the coverlet.

The sick woman seemed unaware of the young woman's presence, and seemed to be addressing someone else.

"Forgive me John!" she whispered. "I did it because I thought you would have me do it. The mine was dear to you, and that made it dear to me. You told me, John, to be careful.

"Oh, Yvonne!" she wailed, turning to the young woman. "Your father suspected before he died that he was being swindled, and he took measures to protect us, and now when it is too late I see it all. Those two villains and their confederates have deliberately ruined us! They have everything! And now—now, my poor child, we are penniless! Oh, Yvonne, my dear daughter, what will become of you, all alone and penniless, amongst——"

But the frail body gave way under the strain, and the weary spirit fled.

It had only kept on under protest ever since John Cartier had died, and since then its only tie with earth had been its passionate love for Yvonne, for she typified in a feminine degree all the self-reliant virtues of her father.

The mother dropped back before Yvonne was aware what had happened. She gazed in horror for a moment, then feverishly she called into the deaf ears, and madly she pleaded with the still lips to speak.

She pressed her head to the shrunken breast, but no throb sounded from the still heart, and as she lifted her head, she realised for the first time the awful truth.

Her eyes hardened, and, turning, she staggered from the room and up the corridor to where the visitors sat.

They stared in amazement at the wild look in her eyes, and started to speak, but she silenced them with an imperious gesture. Her voice came with a strange, husky sound, but cleared as she went on. She spoke slowly and emphatically, and her words fell like icy drops in that dim room.

"I am unaware," she said, "of the exact details as to how you have succeeded in your dastardly and cowardly purpose! I knew when my mother came back from her trip to the mine, and said she had turned over the station to you as security for a loan, that you were taking advantage of her ignorance of business matters! But now I know that you swindled my father, and that he suspected you, and that you have deliberately swindled my poor mother and myself out of everything we had! If the law will reach you, rest assured it shall! But I imagine you have been clever enough to carry out your dastardly schemes within the fringe of the law! First you cheated us out of the mine, and now out of our home!

"For the money or the station I don't care; but my dear mother,"—and her voice broke pitifully for a moment—"lies dead—dead—do you understand?—in the next room, and you your dastardly schemes have killed her! Hear me now, and mark well what I say! I swear I will never rest until I have caused each and every one of you to suffer as you have made her suffer! Don't say to yourself that it is the raving of a grief-stricken young woman—it isn't! Now go! Go quickly, before I call the dogs to drive you from the place! In a week's time you may send your jackals to take possession of the station!"

All Vineburg's suave confidence had departed under the stinging lash of her words, and, picking up his hat, he slunk through the door with Morgan following.

When the sound of their steps died away, Yvonne turned and went back to the still figure in that other room. As her eyes fell on the cold, stiff features, her tense body relaxed; she staggered weakly to the bed, and fell prostrate across her mother's body in a raging torrent of grief.

***

Yvonne found, on going through her mother's papers after the funeral, that, there was no doubt about the swindle.

Her shrewd young mind read between the lines what her mother had failed to see, and when she left the station at the end of the week, penniless and alone, her heart was filled with bitter anger against the men who had ruined them.

She laid the case before a lawyer in Melbourne, but after going into it he shook his head.

"It's no use, Miss Cartier," he said. "There isn't the slightest doubt but that you and your mother were swindled out of the mine and the station, but they have done it too cleverly for the law to reach them.

"That is the fault of the law, and the innocent must suffer. It is unfortunate that such is the case, but we cannot alter it."

Yvonne rose wearily and passed out. As she gained the street, heedless of the passers-by, she raised her hand, and said:

"I swear I will not rest until I have tracked down and ruined everyone who had a part in our mine!"

III
Vineburg Takes on a New Hand

"IKE" Vineburg, bookmaker and owner of many racehorses, was in good humour as he walked into his training-stables, one clear, bright morning shortly after his rather undignified departure from Binabong Station.

From his own point of view he had reason to be, for the previous afternoon had seen the end of the business connected with the transfer of the station and the Jig Saw Mine back to its old owners.

In a few months, when things had blown over a bit, they could announce another rich discovery of gold, and the shares would boom. And in the meantime—well, the station was showing a big profit under the new management, and his "book" had been doing particularly well of late.

His horses had also won several minor races; and *Tragedy Prince*, the apple of his eye, was shaping even better than he had dared to hope, and if it continued to show such form, it looked certain that his colours would be carried to victory in the Melbourne Cup in November. He flushed as he remembered his last visit to the station.

Heavens, she did go off pop, but her words were only the ravings of a girl. Besides, she had left the station a month previously, and he had heard nothing of her since. Chances were, she had returned to England. "She'd cool off a bit when she got down to pounding a typewriter for a living." And he grinned, for the picture pleased his fancy.

He greeted Lee, his trainer, with particular affability, and astonished that worthy man by offering him a cigar. For Ike Vineburg had never been known to give away very much.

"How is *Tragedy Prince* this morning?" he asked.

"Splendid, sir!" answered Lee. "If he keeps like he is now, there's no question about the Cup!"

"Good! Don't let him get stale, Lee."

"Indeed I won't, Mr. Vineburg!" responded the trainer. "I'm out to get the Cup for you this year, and we've got the horse that can do it."

"By the way," went on Vineburg, "have you succeeded in getting anybody interested in *Firefly*?"

"No, sir; and I'm sorry. His reputation as a vicious horse is too well known. It's a pity, too. He's only eating his head off here since they brought him from the tracks."

"H'm! Well, let's have a look at him. I feel pretty fit this morning, and if he doesn't look too vicious, I'll try him around the stable-paddock for a bit."

"I would advise you not to, Mr. Vineburg," remarked Lee. "He'll kill you, or try to, anyway!"

"Oh, I'm not afraid of him!" laughed Vineburg. "I'm no dab in the saddle. Thrash him into submission. That's my motto."

The trainer reluctantly led the way to a stall where a black gelding stood. It had for some time been barred from the racecourse on account of its vicious habits at the barrier, and as the trainer approached, it lashed out savagely.

"Saddle him up, Lee," said Vineburg. "I'll try him."

Lee knew from experience that argument was useless. Picking up a saddle and bridle, and watching his chance, he dashed in beside the gelding; he succeeded in putting them on, and backed the horse out. The two men led it through the stable to the rear, where the trainer held it for Vineburg to mount.

As the bookmaker did so, a slim, red-headed boy appeared from round the corner of the stable and stood watching the performance. It would have been hard to recognise in the ragged boy, the young woman who, only a month before, had been the happy Yvonne, but such it was. Her disguise was perfect, and her natural slimness assisted her immensely.

Vineburg started around the paddock, but before he had covered a hundred yards the gelding began to show temper.

Vineburg may have found his motto, "Thrash him into submission" a successful one with men, but when he applied it to the black gelding that morning he made a mistake. He brought his whip down with a vicious cut as the horse showed its temper. It was like a match to a cask of gunpowder. The gelding reared on its hind legs, its mouth opening viciously as it felt the sting of the whip.

Vineburg held his seat, but when the horse dropped back, and, turning, bit savagely at his leg, he lost his nerve. When again it reared he clawed madly for a moment at its neck, and then rolled with a cry from its back.

The gelding dropped to the ground, and leaped forward, and Lee gave a gasp of horror as he saw one of Vineburg's feet still sticking in the stirrup. Those flashing, plunging hoofs would surely beat his brains out!

The trainer dashed forward in an endeavour to catch the maddened animal; but as he did so, a slim figure passed him. It was the ragged boy who had been watching the performance, and Lee stopped in amazement as he watched the lad.

Over the turf bounded the boy, and as the horse and fallen rider approached, he watched his chance.

Springing, not for the horse's head, but for its back, he succeeded in clutching the saddle. The horse shied wildly and bit at him, but the boy held on; evading the snapping teeth, he vaulted with all his strength, and, although the horse again plunged, the boy landed safely. He grasped the bridle-reins, and the battle began.

Every moment it looked as though the horse would bring its feet down on the head of the now unconscious Vineburg, but the boy with marvellous skill kept it clear. While he kept the horse busy, the trainer, who had followed, dragged Vineburg free.

It is needless to go into the details of the battle which followed. It was fierce and desperate, and many times in a half-hour, which seemed like an eternity, the boy barely saved himself from falling beneath the plunging hoofs.

Vineburg had recovered, and as the boy pulled up the conquered horse, he approached and held out his hand, but the boy did not seem to see it, for his own remained occupied with the horse. Vineburg unsuspiciously pulled his back, and spoke.

"You have saved my life, my lad, and I wish to thank you."

"Oh, that's all right, sir!" answered the boy.

"You don't look too prosperous," continued Vineburg, "and if you will come into the stable, I will see what I can do for you. By the way, you can ride all right. How would you like a job here?"

"I'd like it first rate, sir. I came to see if you needed a boy."

"Well, that's fortunate! What weight are you?"

"About eight stone, sir."

"And your name?"

"Tom, sir,"

"Tom what?"

"Just Tom, nothing else."

"H'm! Yes—well, you'll have to take a second one to ride under. Now, go along with Mr. Lee and get fixed up."

Again thanking the boy, he turned on his heel to go and change his mud-stained clothes.

He would have been a very astounded man had he seen the veiled look which followed him, for he would have seen a great resemblance to a look he had received from an angry young woman at Binabong. But, unfortunately for him, he didn't know, and Yvonne followed the trainer to her new quarters.

That look of Yvonne's had been an expression of her intention. On leaving the lawyer's she had racked her brains in an endeavour to devise some form of revenge against the men who had ruined her home. Vineburg was close at hand, and her funds were low, consequently she decided to start on him first.

Again she racked her brains for a scheme to follow, and there it was that her magnificent gift of riding aided her. Her plans once formed, she had quickly put them into effect, and luck had favoured her, for now she had the position she desired in the very stable of her enemy.

"You can bunk in here, Tom," said the trainer, throwing open a small door which led into a dark box of a room. "If you're hungry, go up to the house and get something."

"Thank you, sir," replied Tom; and such was Yvonne's entrance, as the jockey Tom, into the stable of Ike Vineburg.

Vineburg was right when he said Tom could ride.

The new jockey got his first mount at an important meeting at Aspendale, and got home an easy winner. A string of successes at Sandown, Williamstown, Moornee Valley, and Caulfield tracks followed, and Tom's "percentages" having been carefully saved he now had a snug account in the bank.

It was after a specially brilliant win at Caulfield that Vineburg came to him and promised him the mount on *Tragedy Prince*, for the rapidly-approaching Melbourne Cup.

Cup Day dawned warm and sunny.

Business in Melbourne was practically suspended for the day, and the streets swarmed with visitors from every part of the Commonwealth, as well as a fair number from England, for the Melbourne Cup is world famous.

By midday a steady stream started in the direction of Flemington, where the race is run, and by half-past one the beautiful course presented a lively appearance.

The crowd was enormous—well over a hundred thousand people. On the lawn were congregated a dazzling array of feminine beauty, vying with each other in the advantageous display of beautiful and expensive gowns.

Beyond, under the trees in the betting-ring, the strident tones of the bookmakers were just starting to call the odds, and still further on a steady stream poured into the birdcage to gaze on the horses which were being either led about, or carefully attended, in preparation for the coming events.

The jockeys scattered about lent a tinge of colour to the scene, and many an anxious-faced punter hovered near, waiting for a word which would send him scuttling away to put his money on.

Behind the main grandstand on the hill, the more moderate-priced crowd thronged as densely, and the steady stream of arriving flat patrons straggled out for half a mile or more.

But whether in the paddock, the hill, or the flat, the ever-present tipster rushed about, recklessly dealing out valuable information on sure things and moral certainties which the owner, "a close friend of his", had told him as a special favour. Such was Flemington on "Cup Day."

As the betting settled down, and particular horses were mentioned, *Tragedy Prince* was made a strong favourite.

Vineburg had not adopted any secrecy, for as soon as the betting opened he had sent his men through the ring, placing his money in all directions. The result was that the *Prince* soon firmed from the nominal opening price of eights down to threes.

The Viennese, who had shown great promise in Sydney had opened at almost the same price as *Tragedy Prince*; but as the money came in thousands for the stallion, she drifted to twenties, *Trafalgar*, the idol of the people, shortened in price, coming to the multitudinous small bets of the general public, and remained firm at sixes. *Aurifodina* came next at sevens, and the rest of the numerous field trailed along until, any price was offered against some.

The first two races had been run, and the weighing-out bell for the Cup had rung, when a sudden stir occurred in the betting-ring. Punters, who had held their money until the last thing, hurried after several rushing figures which had invaded the ring to listen to their bets. A gasp of amazement went up as thousands were laid on *The Viennese* as the emissaries were known agents of the stable, a general rush took place to get on; and the mare shortened quickly to fives, and then, when still more money came, she went to fours. *Tragedy Prince* eased a point, and when the horses went to the barrier, both the mare and the stallion went out equal favourites.

Only three people on the course knew the real reason for the sudden popularity of *The Viennese*—two were the owner and the trainer, and the other was Tom Fair (Yvonne had taken the name Fair to ride under), who was riding the other favourite, and real choice of the punters, *Tragedy Prince*.

That reason had emanated from a private conversation which Tom had had the preceding evening with Morrison, the owner of *The Viennese*. Tom had sounded the owner carefully, and, the latter, guessing at the lad's meaning had arranged an interview. There he put the question plainly to Tom. Would he pull up *Tragedy Prince*, and permit *The Viennese* to win over him? Tom had passed his word, and Morrison was a very astounded man when Tom refused any money for doing so.

Morrison naturally became suspicious that a double game of some sort was on, for he had been prepared to go as high as a thousand for a guarantee that *Tragedy Prince* would be "dead"; but his suspicions were quickly allayed when Tom, who had come prepared, passed over to Morrison every penny he had saved, which amounted to a very respectable sum, with the percentages he had won in minor races.

Morrison took the money, and promised to put it on *The Viennese* at the longest price possible, and, consequently, he had waited confidently during the betting until his horse drifted to twenties before he made a single bet.

The barrier flew up, and the horses got away fairly well together. *Roseboy*, a stable mate of *Tragedy Prince*, took the lead, setting the pace for the field. *Auriodina* was second and *Trafalgar* third, *Tragedy Prince* fourth, and *The Viennese* fifth. From that on, the field bunched in twos and threes, the unreliable *Caro* bringing up the rear.

In this order they passed the stand, accompanied by the excited urgings of their backers, and from the "flat" *Trafalgar*'s name predominated, showing the shillings and half-crowns of the patrons there had evidently gone on the old favourite.

As the string pulled around to the back, *Roseboy* dropped out, and *Aurifodina* took the lead. *Trafalgar* shortly went back to fourth place, and, on passing the Abbattoirs, *The Viennese* came with a fine spurt, and secured a lead of nearly a length.

The excitement was intense. A momentary hush fell as the horses swept into the straight, and a deafening chorus of yells and hysterical feminine shrieks greeted the on-coming animals.

"*Tragedy Prince—Tragedy Prince*! He'll do it! No! It's *The Viennese*! Come on, *Trafalgar*! *Tragedy Prince*! Look at him coming up on the outside! He'll do it yet! Wake him up Fair! Give him the whip! *The Viennese—The Viennese*!"

On swept the horses, *The Viennese* still holding the lead, *Trafalgar* next, and *Tragedy Prince* coming up rapidly on the outside. Tom brought him on with a sudden slash of the whip. The stallion leaped forward, and, as they went past the judge, he seemed to have won it by a nose from *The Viennese*, with *Trafalgar* third. But Tom knew he had just lost. He was too good a horseman to have left his spurt even that fraction of a second too late, if he wanted to win. And when the numbers went up giving the race to *The Viennese*, with *Tragedy Prince* second, a mingling of groans and cheers went up from the spectators, according to whether they were on the winner or not.

Probably not one rider in a hundred could have made such a show of trying to win, and intentionally lose by as close a margin as had Tom. But he had calculated to a nicety, and when the numbers went up not one of the eagle-eyed stewards knew that *Tragedy Prince*, in being placed second, was placed just exactly where his rider had intended him to be placed.

Tom had a strenuous half-hour with the disappointed and angry Vineburg at the stable that night, and in the early dawn he faded away as mysteriously as he came.

A run of luck as a punter increased his already large banking account to a very substantial sum, and three months later Yvonne sailed for Europe.

Mr. Ike Vineburg was mystified on receiving a note, couched in the following terms:

"A very small credit has been placed to your account. The balance of the account will be collected at another time. —Yvonne Cartier."

Vineburg knit his brows in an ugly frown as he read the note; but his temper had not been of the best since he lost the cup, and he tore it up in a rage, cursing the young woman for trying to play some practical joke upon him.

It never occurred to him to connect his former rider, Tom, with the writer of that note.

IV
The Compact

THE tropical sun blazed down with a fierce intensity. The sea rolled in oily laziness, while the surf flung itself in a never-ending rainbow-coloured assault over the coral reef of the little South Sea Island.

Inside, a deep-hued lagoon lapped against the beach; the cocoanut-palms and banana-trees forming a vivid background to the attractive picture.

Riding gracefully at anchor in the lagoon lay a rakish, white yacht, with the speedy cut of a racehorse, her shining brass catching the sun, and throwing it back in dazzling streaks. White-garbed sailors worked busily about her deck, endeavouring to find a soiled spot on her already spotless paint.

A large awning was stretched across the stern, and in its cool shade a beautiful, bronze-haired young woman stretched gracefully in a wicker deck-chair. Beside her, on a small wicker stand, was a long glass of lemon cordial, in which the ice still clinked, and face down in her lap lay a large volume.

Reclining opposite was a middle-aged man in white flannels. He had just been speaking, and wore a cynical smile as he awaited her reply.

"Yes, I'm quite ready to descend upon society, as you put it, Uncle Jack. When mother was stricken down by the machinations of those scoundrels I vowed vengeance, because I felt they had robbed her.

"Possibly I would have been satisfied with my youthful revenge on Vineburg at the Cup; but, afterwards, as you know, I found those papers amongst my father's belongings, which really pointed to Vineburg and his crowd as a gang of clever rascals. Since then, as you know, I have toiled almost night and day for revenge, and six years of preparations have left me as resolved as ever."

"Yes, I understand," drawled the man. "But why not do as I suggest? You've got the brains and the shrewdness, and together we can make a nice thing out of society. Personally, I've got to do something, for, to be frank, I'm stony. I admire the success of rascals like Vineburg, but loathe their methods; but with forethought we can work in perfect safety, particularly if you bring into use some of the latest scientific discoveries which you say you are able to apply."

"Well, uncle, I'm almost inclined to agree with you. Every man on the yacht is safe, for they have been chosen for that purpose, and, as you know, Captain Vaughan lost his ship, and was unjustly blamed. He is quite prepared to wage a war upon society. But if I agree to extend my ideas from the men I had in mind to society in general, it will be on a strictly business basis. It must be clearly understood that I am the sole head, and that my word is law. Moreover, that none of the circle make any attempts of any kind without submitting them to me, and that everything is to be planned and executed according to my ideas. If you think you can live up to that—well, we will talk it over tonight with Captain Vaughan and Hendricks, the mate."

The eyes of Graves, her uncle, gleamed with satisfaction as Yvonne spoke, and he rose with a sigh of relief.

"Excellent! I can see my troubles are at an end. *Au revoir* until dinner!" And the wayward brother of Yvonne's gentle mother went below humming gaily to himself.

Yvonne remained alone, gazing in brooding silence over the tropical sea.

Beyond, through the trees which lined the lagoon, appeared a solitary light from the luxurious retreat which, the far-seeing Yvonne had built for herself in case of need.

The boy came to announce dinner, and, with a heavy sigh, the young woman rose, and descended the companionway. On reaching the lower deck, she bent her footsteps towards the after part.

Yvonne passed through the saloon and followed a short passage which opened into a broader one stretching the whole width of the yacht. She pulled a tiny brass key from a chain round her neck and opened a door, turning a switch as she did so.

The light revealed a large saloon covered with a thick carpet, on which her feet made no sound as she carefully closed the door and moved across the room.

The sloping sides of the yacht each formed a wall, which was covered with books. Opposite the door, and stretching from side to side, was ranged the most complete laboratory equipment the most exacting professor could wish. Strange brass and steel instruments of every conceivable shape and size filled every available space in the room, and over the long, glass-covered worktable were hundreds of bottles and test-tubes, containing mysterious powders and liquids. Overhead was a maze of different sized wires—some as large as one's little finger, and some as delicate as a thread.

Yvonne glanced lovingly about as she moved to a small crucible in which was a greenish-coloured liquid. She carefully poured in a few drops of another liquid, and returned to the door.

Again looking about her, she paused before opening the door, and her lips moved.

"At last—at last! Six years of studying, working day and night. But I can move at last. Vineburg first, then the other seven."

Her eyes hardened, and her hands clenched as she spoke the words to a whisper. Turning slowly, she switched out the light, and passed out, emerging a moment later with a smile into the brilliantly-lighted saloon, where the gleaming silver twinkled against the snowy table linen, and the delicately-upholstered furniture contrasted with a pleasing dignity against the cedar and black palm woodwork.

The First Chapter
The Pearl Fraud

I T'S certainly a magnificent affair, but I'm afraid it's I more than I wish to pay."

The speaker was a tall, middle-aged man, immaculately dressed, and his words were addressed to Bechstein, the proprietor of the famous Bond Street jewellery establishment.

They stood near the window in the latter's private room, examining a beautiful string of pearls which the customer held in his right hand. From his left dangled a walking-stick with a gold filigree handle, and he swung it carelessly to and fro as he made the remark.

Bechstein rubbed his hands, and smiled in an insinuating manner. The customer's demand to see a finer assortment of pearls than were displayed in the outer shop had brought the proprietor himself hurrying to handle the fastidious customer, and they had gone into the private room, where the jeweller pulled forth several exquisite strings from his private safe.

"It is a fair price, but not too much for the stones, sir," he replied. "See the exquisite colouring, the unrivalled purity; it is impossible to match it in Europe. And fifty thousand[2]—it is money, yes, but the pearls! Ah, sir, they have not their equals! But what was that?" he broke off to inquire. "Ah, yes, the sunlight on the gold of your stick. I saw the flash, but did not notice the stick before. But, as I was saying, sir, these gems are second to none."

"I know—I know," replied the other, laying them back in the tray with a sigh. "But it is a lot of money. However, I will think it over, Mr. Bechstein, and let you know. By the way, I will leave you my card."

"Thank you, Mr."—the jeweller paused as he read the name engraved on the card—"Mr. Morris. I will be pleased to do anything I can to suit you; but hadn't you better reconsider your decision? Say forty-eight thousand cash—that's as much as I could really afford to take off."

"No, I won't decide today," said Morris, turning towards the door. "I'll be in again in any event, and if I purchase at all will do so here."

"I'm sure that is very kind of you, Mr. Morris," remarked the suave Bechstein, as he bowed his guest out to the accompaniment of much hand washing. "It will be a great pleasure to me." And he again smiled with oily politeness as the customer nodded and departed.

Bechstein returned to the tray of gems as the door closed, and, after glancing with genuine admiration at the beautiful string which had been the subject of the conversation, he carefully locked them away.

"He'll come back," he muttered. "He's dead taken with it, and means to have it. Probably didn't intend to go so high, and wants to realise on some securities. But it's worth the money. It's the finest thing I've seen in the five years I've been here. Nice mess, the countess going bankrupt and leaving it on my hands. I'll have to do something with it soon; can't afford to let that amount be idle in the safe."

He moved toward the door, grumbling to himself, but on emerging into the outer-shop his suave smile returned as he went forward to greet more customers.

Some days passed, and in the press of business the jeweller had given little thought to the man who had admired the large necklace. But he had need of a large sum in a few days, and as he sat in his office one foggy afternoon planning ways and means, his mind reverted to Morris.

"Never came back," he muttered, "I should have persuaded him to pay a deposit. He's probably cooled off, and decided the price was too stiff. Wonder who he was, anyway? Talked a bit like an American. However, I've got to have money by the first of the week, and I don't see anything for it but to get the bank to loan me on the pearls. I hate to do it, but——"

His musings were interrupted by a knock at the door, which opened to admit a lady, followed by an assistant.

---

[2] £50,000 in 1913 is worth about £5,800,000 in 2020

"This lady desires to see something in necklaces, more valuable than we have outside, sir, so I thought you would desire to show her some yourself," said the assistant.

"Certainly—certainly!" smiled Bechstein, rising. "Won't you be seated, madam, and I will show you some very fine gems."

"Thank you!" replied the lady, in a low, sweet voice, lifting her veil as the assistant retired.

Bechstein's observant gaze saw a beautiful face, surmounted by deep, serious eyes, and beneath the broad hat was visible distracting waves of gleaming bronze hair. Her garb was simple in the extreme, but the jeweller was judge enough to know that it was from an exclusive and expensive establishment. He glowed with satisfaction as his quick eyes noted the fact, for the suave Hebrew liked dealing with wealthy ladies. He had an almost uncanny knowledge of their weaknesses, and he played on the strings of their vibrations with the skill of a great musician.

He opened the safe, and drew out a tray of glittering gems, in the centre of which reposed, like a queen surrounded by her women, the magnificent necklace of pearls. He knew the value of first impressions, and cleverly placed the tray so that the light fell at just the right angle on the stones, throwing into bold relief the central string.

The fair customer gasped as she saw the fascinating display, and the jeweller dropped his eyes to hide his satisfaction as her hand involuntarily went out and was quickly withdrawn.

"They are exquisite—exquisite!" she murmured rapturously. "That beautiful one in the centre; it is perfect! Don't touch it, I beg of you!" she cried, as the jeweller reached for it. "Let me admire it for a moment first. The light falls so perfectly on it."

Bechstein had quickly pulled back as she spoke, cursing himself for being too precipitous. She was evidently a finer-tuned instrument than the average feminine customer, and would need delicate handling. But he smiled inwardly with satisfaction, for her every detail breathed affluence, and he considered a sale as good as made.

"Oh, how lovely!" she breathed again, putting forth her hand, and this time picking up the gems. "But I suppose it is very expensive?" And she looked inquiringly at the jeweller.

"It is listed at sixty thousand,[3] madam," replied Bechstein, "but for an immediate sale, I would let you have it at almost cost—say fifty thousand net. It was made for the Countess of Brent, but was left on my hands. Every stone is a picked one; it hasn't its equal for beauty and purity."

"Yes—yes, it is exquisite; but the price is far, far more than I can pay. I only wish for something moderate."

She laid it down with a sigh, and picked up a smaller string. "How much is this one, please?"

Bechstein was disappointed, but he concealed his chagrin, and smiled in his usual manner as he replied. He had not yet lost hope.

"That, of course, is much smaller, but I can guarantee every stone to be absolutely perfect. It is worth four thousand."

---

[3] £60,000 in 1913 is worth about £6,970,000 in 2020

"I am sorry you showed me the large one now," she said, with a silvery laugh. "This is nearer the price I wished to pay."

Fifteen minutes were spent in examining the other contents of the tray, but at the end of that time the customer returned to the smaller of the pearl necklaces.

"I think I'll decide on this one," she said. "If you will make it thirty-five hundred I will take it with me. The other is far beyond my means."

"It is impossible to take off that much, madam, but I will make it thirty-seven fifty. I am sorry you won't consider the large one. It is an unparalleled opportunity."

"Perhaps I will return with my uncle in a few days, and try to persuade him to buy it. A thing like that is just the same as saving the money, isn't it?" she asked innocently. "However, I will leave it today, and take the other."

"Any bank would be glad to loan a good sum on the large one," replied the jeweller. "I would suggest you brought your uncle in as you mention. I am sure he would endorse my statements."

"I am sure he would," she murmured, as Bechstein turned to get a case for the small string which she had purchased.

She counted out the notes, and a few moments later rose to depart with her purchase in her bag, the jeweller deferentially accompanying her to the street entrance.

He bowed low as she climbed into a large red motor, and almost forgot his poise in astonishment as she entered the driver's seat and took the wheel, the car having no chauffeur.

"It's a pity," remarked the jeweller to himself, as he hastened back to his private room to put away the gems, which he had for the moment forgotten.

"I'll give her three days to come back, but I'm afraid she won't. If she had intended taking the big one, she wouldn't have bought the small one. If I don't sell it in three days, I'll have to borrow on it, that's all."

He had reached his private room, and heaved a sigh of relief as he saw the gems were just as he had left them. It was careless of him, as customers in the outer shop were near the door of the private room.

He locked them away, and sat down once more to figure ways and means.

For five years had Bechstein been the proprietor of the jewellery establishment in Bond Street. That he had borne the name Vineburg in Australia, was known only to himself. A hasty departure had made it impossible to realise on as much as he might, had he had more time at his disposal. On his arrival in 'Frisco, he had taken the name of Bechstein, and arriving in London a short time later, had taken up his old profession of dealing in precious stones.

Every available penny had gone to purchase the Bond Street business, and trade having been bad the past few months, he had been financing himself by strenuous measures.

The throwing back on his hands of the expensive necklace, which had made a heavy drain on his available funds, had been a tremendous blow, and his financial condition presented a gloomy aspect at the present moment.

As the jeweller feared, the fair customer did not return, and four days later he placed the necklace carefully in his pocket and left the shop.

He would go to Isaacs first. Isaacs was a large diamond merchant and knew the value of stones. He would probably loan more on the pearls than would the bank. He hailed a taxi, and twenty minutes later sat in the private office of the busy diamond merchant.

Bechstein wasted no time in preliminaries, and rapidly stated his request.

"Thertainly, thertainly, my friend," repeated Isaacs, with a strong Hebrew accent. "Have you the stones with you?"

"Yes," answered Bechstein, pulling out a velvet case and opening it. "The finest lot I've ever seen."

Isaacs took it from him, and looked at it with admiration.

"Beautiful! Beautiful, Bechstein! Vonderful purity! Vonderful colouring!"

He turned and placed them on the desk in front of him, picking up a glass as he did so.

"Just a formality," he laughed apologetically, as he bent to examine them, and Bechstein smiled serenely, knowing the value of the great string.

"Isaacs must be a careful customer," he decided, with an inward grin. "He takes long enough to test them."

"Are you frightened they are false?" he said aloud, in a joking manner. "Here! What——" he began, half rising, as Isaacs deliberately picked up a small hammer and cracked lightly at each pearl.

Bechstein's eyes widened in speechless horror as each pearl broke, and a thin covering fell off, leaving nothing but a common glass centre.

Isaac's jaw set grimly, and his eyes glittered angrily, as he gathered up the pieces and passed them back.

"Is this a practical joke, Mr. Bechstein?" he said icily. "If so, I must say it is in exceedingly bad taste!"

"Good heavens! You don't think I knew they were false, do you?" almost screamed Bechstein frantically. "I swear to you I don't understand it! I got them specially from Craig's for the Countess of Brent, and they haven't been out of the shop since!"

"I believe you, Mr. Bechstein. You have evidently been the victim of a very clever fraud. They are the finest imitations I have ever theen. If it hadn't been for a tiny crack in one of them, I vould have passed them as genuine. I vould advise you to put the police on the matter at vunce."

Bechstein sat in a huddled heap. His voice had deserted him, the sweat stood in great beads on his forehead, and his eyes stared in fascinated horror at the pieces of the necklace in his hand.

"No, not the police!" he moaned. "Keep it quiet, Isaacs! I have heavy payments coming on, and if this got out my credit would be ruined! What will I do—what will I do? Fifty thousand pounds!"

The mention of the money caused a fresh convulsion of his features. He jumped to his feet, muttering incoherently as he jammed his hat on his head and dashed wildly out the door, clutching in his hand the broken pearls.

Isaacs turned back to his desk with a shake of the head.

"Poor Bechstein!" he murmured. "I'm afraid he'll never trace the man that did that job!"

The Second Chapter
Sexton Blake is Called In

BECHSTEIN entered his private room and locked the door. Sinking into a chair, he dropped his head on the desk. His brain was in a whirl, and his reasoning power was stunned by the shock of the discovery.

"Good heavens!" he whispered. "Fifty thousand pounds just when things are critical!"

He crouched motionless, heedless of the passage of time. The assistants had come from time to time and knocked timidly on the door, but the jeweller paid no attention, and they went away, not daring to knock again.

Hours passed and still he sat motionless, and not until night closed down did he move. He stumbled wearily to his feet and smoothed his hair. Gathering himself together he unlocked the door and entered the outer shop, where the assistants were packing away the trays of jewellery preparatory to leaving for the night.

The head assistant came up, and Bechstein spoke, his voice husky in spite of himself.

"I haven't been very well this afternoon, Ford. Anything of importance?"

"No, sir," replied the assistant. "I knocked once or twice, but as you didn't answer I thought you must be feeling unwell. Can I do anything, sir?"

"No, thank you, Ford. It's only a bad headache. I've got some writing to do, and will remain for a while. Just put the spring-lock on when you go."

"Very good, sir." And as the assistant hastened away, Bechstein returned to the private room.

"It's a mystery to me," he muttered, dropping wearily into his chair again. "Only Ford has a duplicate key of this safe, and he is absolutely beyond suspicion. I've only had it out three times—once when I showed it to Sir George Wellington, once when that American Morris was here, and again when I sold the small necklace to that woman three days ago. It hasn't been out of my sight for a moment, and—— But hold on, I did leave it for a few moments when I went out with the lady to the street; but it couldn't have happened then."

He picked up the pieces of the imitation and looked closely at them.

"Perfect in every detail, even the filigree work on the clasp is exact; and the stones themselves, they're marvellous! No, it didn't happen then! The person who made this imitation would need detailed drawings to scale to execute the work. It's uncanny, even the small bend which the original had in its clasp has been reproduced. Is it possible it has been done while it lay at Craig's, and that they have been duped?"

A gleam of hope lit up his eyes for a moment, but despair soon succeeded again. "No hope there!" he muttered. "But the question is—what am I going to do? If I put it in the hands of the police it will get out, and with things in such a critical condition it would send me to the wall.

"No, that won't do. If I only knew—ah! Wonder if I could get that chap Blake? They say he is a marvel! I'll look him up in the phone book and see if he is on the line."

He found Sexton Blake's number, and made the call, being answered by a clear, boyish voice.

"Is that Mr. Blake's residence?" inquired the jeweller.

"Yes. Who is speaking, please?" came the reply.

"Bechstein, the Bond Street jeweller. This isn't Mr. Blake speaking, is it?"

"No, sir. I am Tinker, his assistant. But I'll call the guv'nor. Just hold the line, please."

Bechstein waited impatiently for some moments until a deep, distinct voice came over the wire.

"Yes, Mr. Bechstein, this is Sexton Blake. What can I do for you?"

"Are you very busy, Mr. Blake?"

"Well, yes, I am rather. Is it anything important?"

"It is of the utmost urgency. A very serious thing has happened, and I would like your advice. I would go up to your residence, but perhaps you would prefer to come here where I could better explain?"

"I can spare an hour or so, and will come straight along," replied the famous detective; and Bechstein felt a little less hopeless as he hung up the receiver.

"From what I've heard he can ferret the thing out if anyone can," he muttered, pacing the floor restlessly as he waited Blake's arrival.

He hastened quickly to the door as the detective rattled it and led the way to the private room.

"Now, Mr. Bechstein," began Blake briskly, "just what is the trouble?"

He dropped into a chair with his back to the light, and faced the jeweller, who walked up and down nervously.

"The trouble is, Mr. Blake, that I've been robbed of a fifty thousand pound string of pearls, and if I don't get it back quick, I'll go to the wall with a ruined credit!"

Blake's eyebrows went up almost imperceptibly.

"That is certainly a serious loss, Mr. Bechstein. Supposing you give me the facts, and then I will let you know if I can spare the time to take the case. Firstly though—have you informed the police?"

"No!" replied the jeweller heavily. "That would mean publicity and consequent ruin, which I'm trying to avoid."

"I see," nodded Blake. "Well, what are the facts?"

"As far as I can see, Mr. Blake, there are no facts," jerked out the jeweller.

"Keep yourself in hand, Mr. Bechstein," said Blake, seeing the jeweller was labouring under strong emotion. "You say you have been robbed. That in itself is a fact, consequently there must be other details."

The jeweller collected himself a little under the influence of the calm voice of the detective.

"I'll tell you all I know myself!" he cried desperately. "But I can't see for the life of me where you will find anything to help you solve it. Some weeks ago I ordered Craig's, the big importers, to pick up a number of the choicest pearls for me which they could find. Three weeks later they sent word that they had secured the number I needed. I took a run down to their place, and was very pleased with the selection. A few days later they delivered it, and I put it in the safe. I had got it for a special order for the Countess of Brent; but, as you know, she lost everything through the failure of Green & Co., and it was left on my hands. Since then I have only had it out on three occasions—one to show it to Sir George Wallington, the second time to show it to an American by the name of Morris, and the third time when I sold a cheaper string to a lady."

"What was the lady's name?" asked Blake abruptly.

"The receipt was made out in the name of Miss Cole. Here is the imitation," went on the jeweller, handing the pieces to Blake, who thrust them carelessly on one side.

"I never dreamed there was anything wrong until I took the one you see to Isaacs, the diamond merchant. As I told you, I am temporarily in need of funds, and intended borrowing from Isaacs, giving the necklace as security. He examined it, and discovered by a tiny mark on one of the pearls that the whole thing was false, otherwise, it would have passed the keenest judge. It is the most perfect imitation I ever saw. Every detail is exactly like the original—this filigree clasp, this bend in it, the chain, everything. That is the story, Mr. Blake."

The great detective had sat motionless as the jeweller told his story. From outside appearances he seemed to take no interest in the narrative; for he had thrust the necklace aside when Bechstein passed it to him, and he had not even glanced around as the jeweller pointed out the similarity in the workmanship. Only a tense look in the eyes indicated that the brilliant mind was working with lightning-like rapidity—every word the jeweller said being either tossed aside as useless, or carefully stowed away for future investigation. Rapidly the keen reasoning power started on the construction of the circle, and if the jeweller didn't see the meaning of the questions which Blake rapidly asked, it mattered not to the great detective.

"Now, Mr. Bechstein, listen carefully, please! We will start at the beginning, and please answer my questions as clearly as possible."

"Very well, Mr. Blake, I will do my best," replied Bechstein, sinking wearily into a chair. "Go ahead!"

"We will eliminate Craig's for the moment," continued Blake. "There is, of course, the possibility that the substitution might have happened there, and I will look into that point later. Now, to start from the day you received it from them, and placed it in your safe. Firstly, has anyone else a key of the safe besides yourself?"

"Yes, Ford, my chief assistant; but he is beyond suspicion, Mr. Blake. Besides, it would take hours to make the detailed sketches according to scale, and no one else had the opportunity. I am here all day nearly, and a watchman has been on at night ever since the robbery in Regent Street, two months ago."

"You say you showed the pearls first to Sir George Wallington?" went on Blake.

"Yes."

"How long had you had them here when that occurred?"

"Nearly a week."

"Where were you at the time?"

"Right here. He sat where I am, and I lifted the tray out, and laid it on the desk in front of where you are sitting."

"How long was he here?" asked Blake.

"Not over five minutes altogether."

"You noticed nothing at all out of the ordinary?"

"Yes. He just remarked that it was a deuced fine thing, and, after admiring it a bit, laid it back on the tray. I immediately put them back, and we went out together."

"How long after did this American—Morris—look at them?"

"About ten days."

"Was it in here also?"

"Yes. He sat at first in the same chair in which Sir George had sat; but when I passed him the necklace, we walked over to the window."

"Did you notice anything at all out of the ordinary while he was here?"

"No, nothing. I do remember remarking once about the sun reflecting from the gold on the end of the handle of his stick; but I don't suppose you mean trifles like that."

"Nothing is a trifle in a matter of this kind, Mr. Bechstein," remarked Blake quietly. "Did you have your eye on the pearls all the time he was here?"

"Yes, every second. I'm very careful that way. I'm positive on that point. He didn't stay more than a few minutes either."

"And you say the next time was when you took it out to show a lady—a Miss Cole?"

"Yes."

"She bought a small string?"

"Yes, and paid cash for it."

"How much did it come to?"

"It was four thousand, and I let her have it for thirty-seven-fifty cash."

"Anything out of the ordinary with her?"

"No. She admired the big string, as women will, but put it down. She looked over everything in the tray, but, finally decided to take the small one."

"Did you lose sight of it at all?"

"I did for about two seconds; but the necklace was in exactly the same position when I turned back. Even if she had been able to substitute, I would have heard her movements. And besides, how could she have an imitation? It would take hours to sketch it, let alone the days of expert work afterwards."

"Did she stay long?" went on the detective.

"No, not long. I went to the door with her. She got into a big, red car, which she drove herself. The few minutes I spent in going to the door with her was the only period in which the necklace was out of my sight. I had neglected to put them back; but everything was undisturbed when I returned, and I wasn't more than three minutes altogether."

"Where was Ford when you returned—do you remember?"

"Yes. He was serving a lady out near the door. It would have been impossible for him to get in here and back in the time."

The great detective did not reply; but sat buried in deep thought for some time. Bechstein watched him anxiously, hope and despair alternately chasing themselves across his face. He jumped nervously as Blake suddenly broke the silence.

"I will take the case, Mr. Bechstein. It presents some most unusual features, and, at the present moment, nothing is very clear. But I will go ahead on it at once."

"Thank you, Mr. Blake!" replied Bechstein, his voice husky with relief. "It means failure to me if you don't succeed; but I know if anyone can, you can."

"I will do my best," answered Blake. "By the way, is Ford, your assistant, interested in photography do you know?"

"I don't know; but I don't think so!" exclaimed the jeweller, in a surprised tone. "Why?"

"Oh, I just asked!" laughed Blake. "Have you the addresses of all your assistants?"

"Yes; they are in the ledger."

"I would like them, from Ford, down to the night watchman. You don't know the address of either the man, Morris, or the woman, do you?"

"No. Morris just had his name on his card, and Miss Cole only gave me her name when I wrote the receipt."

"I see. You said she was driving a large red motor-car? Am I to understand there was no chauffeur?"

"Yes. She was all alone."

"I know Sir George Wallington, and, of course, he is out of the range of suspicion," went on Blake. "Just give me as close a description as possible of the two."

Bechstein did so, and the detective took the details down in his book.

A list of the addresses of all the employees was made up, and Blake thrust it into his pocket, with the pieces of the imitation necklace.

"I can't say when you will hear from me, Mr. Bechstein; but knowing how urgent the matter is, rest assured it will be as soon as I have anything definite to report."

"Thank you, Mr. Blake! It is of the greatest urgency. Don't let expenses stand in the way of pushing things."

Blake smiled as he held out his hand; but when he had gained the street, his brow knit in deep thought.

"From present indications," he muttered, "I can see no mistakes. The master brain behind this is unknown to me. Is it possible that what I have always expected has come—a scientist who practises crime as I practise its solution? If so—well, it will be a great chase."

The Third Chapter
The Nun—Blake is Puzzled

AS Blake walked along absorbed in his thoughts, he was unaware of a veiled feminine figure noiselessly following him.

He hailed a taxi, and gave the driver his order, and, as the unsuspicious detective headed for Baker Street, the woman also hailed a cab, and followed closely.

Could he have known the tenor of her thoughts; he could that night have made a move which would have saved him from endless complications; but, unfortunately for him, and fortunately for the woman, he did not, and little did he dream he was the subject of these thoughts.

The woman wore a heavy veil; but, had she raised it, the reader would have recognised the young woman of the yacht, for it was Yvonne.

Her eyes were thoughtful as she peered ahead through the window of the taxi.

"He looked like the pictures I have seen of Sexton Blake," she muttered to herself. "If Bechstein has put him on the case, I'll have to go warily. They say he is the cleverest-known detective; but it will take a cleverer man than you to trace me," she added, with a vindictive look at the front taxi. "I'll have to try to gain an entrance to his rooms on some pretext, in order to know more about him, for he must have assistants. It will be risky; but it's got to be done, and I'd better try tonight before he knows anything of me."

She sank back, only peering out again as they turned corners; but when the cab swung into Baker Street, she sat up with a jerk as the street sign caught her eye. She hastily took the speaking-tube from its hook, and signalled the driver.

"If the other cab stops, keep right on," she ordered. And a nod from the chauffeur told her he understood.

She was not a moment too soon, for barely had she returned the tube to its hook when the other taxi pulled into the kerb, and, as she went swiftly by, she saw the tall, slim figure of her quarry descending.

Once again Yvonne had recourse to the speaking-tube, and in obedience to her directions the chauffeur swung around a corner in a dark side street, coming to a stop a short distance up.

Yvonne dismissed the man, and stood motionless in the shadow until he was out of sight. But for herself the narrow street was vacant, and she moved slowly along, still keeping in the shadow.

A large house loomed up on her left, and the numerous placards, which decorated the front, told her it was to let. She tried the iron gate which led into the area, and muttered a word of relief as it yielded to her pressure. She glanced sharply up and down the street, but she was still the only wayfarer, and, again turning to the gate, she pushed it open. The gloom swallowed her up, but it was evident that she did not need light for her purpose, for she worked in silent haste, only a soft rustle betraying the presence of anyone amongst the shadows.

A few moments later there emerged from the area-way on elderly nun, who acted very peculiarly for one of that Order, for she glanced cautiously up and down the silent street before stepping forth.

With downcast eyes and slow step, the aged-looking Sister made her way towards Baker Street, and five minutes later rang the bell in front of Sexton Blake's apartments.

Something of moment disturbed her as she looked down, for she started visibly, and lifted her left hand quickly, but as the door was opened by the landlady she dropped it as quickly, and held it, with bent fingers, against the voluminous folds of her skirt.

Whatever she had intended doing had been prevented by the sudden opening of the door, and no other chance seemed to present itself before she was ushered a moment later into the consulting-room of the great detective.

Blake was sitting in his big chair before the fire as the nun was announced, while Tinker sat opposite, and Pedro lay between with one great eye open. All three rose as the Sister advanced into the room, and Blake bowed.

"I expect you are rather surprised to see one of my Order at nine o'clock at night," said the nun, with the slow enunciation of age, "but I know you are a busy man, Mr. Blake, and as I was in Baker Street I took the liberty of calling."

"I am accustomed to callers at all hours, Sister," smiled Blake, as he offered her a chair. "I trust there is nothing serious the matter?"

"Oh, no, indeed!" smiled back the nun, sinking into the chair. "Perhaps I shall not be so welcome when I tell you the object of my visit. I know you have a kind heart, Mr. Blake, and as we are making special efforts to send a large number of children to the seaside this summer, I am going to ask you to help us."

"With great pleasure," replied Blake, pulling out some notes. "Will ten pounds[4] be of any use?"

"Yes, indeed, Mr. Blake," answered the nun, reaching for the notes. "You are very good. It will give a great deal of happiness to several poor children. And now I won't detain you any longer. I know you are a busy man, and must be tired," she added, as she rose and held out her hand.

"Not so busy as all that," laughed Blake, as he took her hand. "I trust you are successful in your endeavours. Poor children, they don't get much happiness, I'm afraid. Ah, a thousand pardons!" he exclaimed, as he knocked against a small tabouret, which fell over against the nun.

Tinker and Pedro had been silent listeners to the conversation, and the lad's eyes widened with surprise as the accident occurred, for Blake had had plenty of room to pass, and Tinker had never before known him to be clumsy.

The nun deprecated the matter as Blake straightened the tabouret, and, with a smile which included all three, she bowed and departed.

"I say, guv'nor," began Tinker, as the door closed behind her, "that was———"

"S-sh!" warned Blake, holding up his hand, and standing motionless until the nun's footsteps died away in the passage. "Get your cap and follow her, Tinker!" he ordered. "Be quick!"

Tinker sprang to his feet with a wondering stare, but he had been trained to obey orders without question. Blake spoke hurriedly as Tinker got ready.

---

[4] £10 in 1913 is worth about £1,200 in 2020

"Don't lose sight of her for a moment. I'm not certain yet whether she is young or old. If she is young it is the most perfect disguise I have ever seen. But this I know, she is not a nun."

"Why? How——" began Tinker in astonishment.

"Hurry!" interrupted Blake. "She had forgotten to remove a ring from her left hand. She had evidently remembered it when too late, and I noticed that she kept her hand buried in the folds of her skirt. I wondered why, and thought it might be from habit, but in order to make sure I knocked over the tabouret. As I expected, she involuntarily lifted her hand to stop it, and I saw the ring on her finger. Nuns don't wear rings, and although she may be only a begging swindler, it is just possible—— I'll explain that later," he broke off, as Tinker buttoned his coat. "You have plenty of money?" And as Tinker nodded, he went on: "Leave Pedro with me, for if she turned round she'd recognise him."

Tinker departed silently, and Blake moved to the desk with an expression of profound meditation.

"There's hardly a chance," he muttered, as he fingered a paperknife. "No one would be so bold. I'm afraid I'm rating the perpetrator of the Bechstein robbery too high, but it certainly bears the marks of a great brain."

The thing was so unlikely that he could hardly consider it in his deductions, but it was typical of his great analytical mind that every suggestion of his instinct should be investigated. Many times had his brilliant reasoning advanced certain conjectures which, to the average mind, would seem meaningless and without connection, but scientific calculation told Blake that every abnormal happening might have a bearing on a subject, and the nun's visit was certainly to be classed as abnormal.

He resolved to wait up for Tinker's return, and, picking up a journal on photography, returned to the fire and began to read. Pedro sat up, and rested his head on Blake's knee, and the detective stroked the long ears as he read. Truly it was a scene of peace and comfort, but it did not last long. As Blake finished one article and turned to another, he suddenly stopped stroking the hound, his eyes grew tense with concentration as he hastily read the lines on the page before him.

It seemed a harmless article enough, for it dealt in a simple, forceful manner with advanced experiments on long distance photography, but it apparently held a deep interest for the detective.

"Extraordinary!" he muttered. "I didn't know there was anyone but myself working on that particular line of investigation. It shows a deep knowledge of the matter. It can't be Professor Greeley, for he is working on other lines. I'll write to the editor and ask who contributed the article."

Suiting the action to the word, he rose and moved over to the desk.

He wrote rapidly, and a moment later, with Pedro at his heels, he picked up his hat and went out to post the letter at a nearby pillar box.

Blake sat for some time after his return, smoking his pipe, in deep thought. At intervals he rose and paced the room, followed by Pedro's watchful eyes. It was evident that a new thought was receiving consideration, and time passed unnoticed as he turned it over in its every phase.

Pedro's rising and stretching of his great legs recalled the detective, and he saw, with surprise, that the clock pointed to one o'clock.

"Tinker ought to have been here long before this," he muttered, as an anxious frown appeared. "I trust nothing has happened to him. But he's probably had a long chase. I'll wait up another hour———" But he broke off as he heard a ring, and knowing the landlady would be in bed he opened the door of his consulting-room, and moved down the passage to answer it.

He opened the door, and gazed with surprise as no one was visible, and, glancing down, he saw a folded piece of paper at his feet.

He bent down and picked it up. His eyes contracted, and his jaw set grimly, as he opened it, and saw the same ten-pound note which he had given the nun. It was unaccompanied by any writing whatsoever, and had been evidently thrust under the door by the person who had rung the bell.

"Every move shows a master mind," he muttered, as he scrutinised the note. "The extraordinary care taken to return this note proves it. A less clever mind would keep it, but this shows———"

The sudden jar of a starting motor sounded from some distance down the street, and Blake's teeth came together with a snap as two quick, decisive blasts on the horn told him he had been watched.

He dashed out to the kerb, and peered intently after the vanishing motor. As it passed under the light of a street lamp he saw that a solitary figure was driving, and from where he stood the colour of the car seemed to be—red!

The Fourth Chapter
Tinker Captured by the Enemy

TO return to Tinker. When he started out to follow the nun, he stood in the shadow as he reached the street, and was just in time to see a black-robed figure turn a corner.

With silent swiftness he sped after, and treaded warily as he reached the corner. No one was in sight as he cautiously peered around it, and thinking the nun had entered one of the houses, he was about to move along and endeavour to discover which one, when a dark figure emerged from an archway a short distance on, and turned in his direction.

Tinker hastily withdrew around the corner, and sank into the friendly gloom of a nearby doorway.

Hardly had he done so when the dark figure appeared, and a puzzled frown wrinkled the lad's face as he saw it was a stylishly-dressed woman, heavily veiled, and, from her walk, apparently young.

She passed without seeing him, and as she walked at a pace, Tinker had to think quickly.

"She's not much like the nun," he thought, "but I'll bet it's the same woman. She never had time to get any further up the street than where this one came from, and how she has changed so quickly—if it is her—I don't understand. However, I don't dare risk losing sight of her to investigate, so I'll chance it and follow."

He kept to the dark part of the footpath where the buildings threw long shadows, and followed at a safe distance.

His quarry seemed to have a definite idea in mind, for she walked quickly, turning corners in rapid succession, and Tinker had his work cut out to keep up with her and not be discovered.

The chase led for several blocks, and Tinker looked in dismay as a solitary taxi appeared and his quarry hailed it.

He cast his eyes rapidly about for signs of another, and raised his arms quickly as one appeared around the corner. The other had already started, and was quickly gathering speed as he ran to meet the one he had hailed.

"Follow that taxi!" he gasped, as he threw open the door. "A half sovereign over your fare if you keep it in sight!"

The chauffeur needed no further inducement, and almost before the door slammed behind his fare he had thrown in the clutch and was speeding after the other.

Tinker leaned forward, and closely followed the progress of the chase, which led rapidly until the other taxi turned into Piccadilly. Up Piccadilly it went, and past Hyde Park Corner to Knightsbridge.

Swinging around into Sloane Street, it slowed down, and Tinker hastily signalled his driver to keep on as the other drew into the kerb.

He looked back, and heaved a sigh of satisfaction as he saw the veiled woman get out and proceed in the same direction as he was taking.

His driver was still going at a good pace, and when several blocks had slipped by, Tinker signalled him to stop.

Slipping out as the taxi reached the kerb, he paid the man, and dismissed him. Far up the street he could see the dark figure of the woman still coming in his direction.

A hedge-lined street led off near at hand, and Tinker sought its shelter as the quick footsteps drew near.

As they came opposite and passed on, Tinker emerged from his hiding-place and once more took up the chase.

Through Chelsea they went until the leading figure turned down a narrow, dark street.

Rapidly the lad followed, and, turning the corner, he just had time to see a large motorcar standing a short distance up the street, and to notice that the woman had suddenly vanished, when he heard a soft rustle behind him, and he turned to find himself gazing into the shining barrel of a revolver which was held by the steady hand of the veiled woman.

"I wouldn't advise you to move," came a clear voice. "If you do, I will shoot without hesitation. I might inform you that this revolver is fitted with a new silencer, and the sound doesn't carry more than a few feet. Walk on, please, as far as that motor."

The crestfallen Tinker had nothing to do but obey; for the revolver was held in a very business-like grip, and the voice had spoken with decision.

"I'll watch my chance," he muttered, as he walked on with his captor uncomfortably close behind. "Maybe I'll be able to turn the tables. Heavens, what will the guv'nor say when I tell him I was fooled by a woman?"

He broke off to glance about for a chance of escape; but his heart sank as the tall figure of a man rose from the tonneau, where he had evidently been lounging on the seat cushions, for his head had not been visible from the rear.

"Hallo!" he exclaimed, as Tinker and his captor approached. "You're late. Who is this with you?"

"He is a persistent young man who has been following me. I tried to shake him off, but found he was too quick, so I brought him along, since he seemed so anxious for my company." And she gave a low laugh, which even Tinker, angry and disgusted with himself as he was, couldn't help but admire.

"What on earth are you going to do with him?" drawled the man, as he descended from the car. "He'll be an awful nuisance!"

"Oh, I'll take care of him all right!" she replied. "Just get those straps from under the seat, uncle, please, and tie him securely. Then put this in his mouth to keep him quiet." And she pulled a silk sash from under her jacket as she spoke.

The man followed her instructions, and a few minutes later the discomfited lad lay bound and gagged in the bottom of the tonneau.

He had kept his ears open as they talked, but noticed that they made use of no names.

"Well, anyway," he grumbled, as he nearly choked from the gag, "I know their relationship anyway. She called him uncle."

They had started to converse again, and Tinker strained his ears to listen, but the voices were too low for him to hear. As they ceased speaking, and the sound of departing footsteps reached him, he judged they were those of the man; and he was right.

He was ruminating on this point, and wondering what would happen next when he felt a quiver, and the car moved off. He tried to gain some idea of the direction by the turnings, but found it impossible, and, finally, gave it up.

He judged it to be fully half an hour later when the car came to a sudden stop, and he heard the driver descend and walk away. He knew positively then that it was the man who had left previously, for the present steps were the short, rapid ones of a woman.

As they grew fainter he struggled with his bonds, straining with all his strength; but they had been too cunningly tied, and again he sank back in despair. He had no idea where he was, and, as no sound of passing vehicles came to him, he judged he was either in a quiet side street, or in a suburb.

Little did he know that Blake was at that moment opening the street door not very far away, and that the panting figure which scrambled into the car at the same moment had just come from that door.

Two short blasts of the horn sounded as once more the car moved ahead, and Tinker wondered why the woman in the front seat laughed as she changed gears.

"I WOULDN'T ADVISE YOU TO MOVE". CAME A CLEAR VOICE.
"I SWEAR I WILL NEVER REST UNTIL I HAVE CAUSED EACH, AND EVERY ONE TO SUFFER, AS YOU HAVE MADE HER SUFFER."
"ARE YOU VERY BUSY MR. BLAKE?"

On they sped, and from the way in which they took corners, Tinker judged his captor was expert at driving. Two hours must have passed before she again brought the car to a stop, and Tinker wondered if they had reached their destination when the door of the tonneau opened, and his captor entered, and rapidly bound another silk sash around the captive's eyes, and, slamming the door again, started. They stopped in a few moments, and Tinker heard the sound of whispering as the tonneau door opened, and he was dragged to his feet. His legs were released, and he was led along blindfold. He was conscious of walking up some steps, and judged he was in a house or building of some description. His guide came to a halt, and the lad felt a current of air blow against his face as they started again.

"Look out, you're going down some steps!" growled his guide. And Tinker knew that the woman had turned him over to a man.

He felt his way cautiously as he descended, counting the steps as he went, and found, on reaching the bottom, that there were twenty-eight. Another journey followed, until once more his guide halted. He released the bandage from Tinker's eyes, and the lad blinked as a brilliant glare hit them. As the blurred picture cleared he looked about, and rapidly took in his surroundings.

He seemed to be in a small room, about twenty feet square. No windows of any description were visible, and his heart sank as he saw that the floor and walls, and even the ceiling were of stone. He looked towards the door; but no ray of hope lay in that direction, for it was of massive steel. The room was comfortably enough furnished—containing a small brass bed, covered with snowy linen.

A few rugs lay on the stone floor, and a well-filled bookcase lined one wall. In a corner stood an attractive desk, lit by the rays from an overhanging electric light. From the centre of the ceiling hung more lights, and in another corner was a marble wash-basin, with shining, nickelled faucets. Truly it was an impregnable prison—if prison it was.

As he finished his rapid survey of the room he looked at his guide, who was untying his bonds.

He had expected to see a ruffianly-looking fellow, and he opened his eyes wide as the man straightened up. He was dressed in a neat, blue uniform, with brass buttons, and had a distinctly nautical air about him.

He laughed as he saw the lad's look of surprise, and when he spoke it was with a suave intonation.

"Well, my lad," he smiled; "these are to be your quarters for some time. And, although there are no windows to admire the view, still you will find many entertaining books in the case—one in particular you ought to enjoy. It is a book of some of Sexton Blake's adventures. You won't be asked for your parole———"

"I wouldn't give it if I was," interrupted Tinker.

"As I was saying," went on the man imperturbably, "you won't be asked for your parole, because any efforts to escape are useless. Food will be served regularly to you, and you will remain here until further instructions are given regarding you. I might add"—and the man's eyes narrowed a trifle—"that if you do attempt to escape, I have instructions to deal summarily with you."

He moved to the door as he spoke, and Tinkers heart sank as the great steel barrier crashed to, and the bolts were shot.

The Fifth Chapter
The Mysterious Photograph Articles

WHEN Blake saw the fast-disappearing motor, he immediately connected it with the presence of the ten-pound note under his door.

He stood with knit brow watching it as it turned a corner.

Pursuit was out of the question. There was no taxi in sight. And besides, one of those low-geared cars would stand little chance of overtaking the big roadster.

The detective returned slowly to his room, and stood thinking deeply.

"Is it possible?" he muttered. "Red motor at Bechstein's—red motor tonight. The call of the nun, and the return of this note. Then that article in the journal. If there is a connection, I think my unknown antagonist must feel they have made a pretty safe retreat to dare to snap their fingers at me as the return of this note indicates. I can do nothing tonight. I'll leave the light for Tinker, in case he returns, and in the morning— well, my unknown friend, you have made the first move in the game." And his jaw set aggressively. "We'll see who calls checkmate. And by the way," he muttered, as he turned to seek his room, "if my deductions are correct, it proves that my unknown friend knew I was at Bechstein's, and had taken the case."

Blake was up betimes the next morning, and before sitting down to breakfast phoned for the big, grey car to be sent round.

He hastily perused his letters, and ran through the papers. He was depressed and worried over Tinker's non-appearance, and, as he donned his coat, Pedro looked at him with questioning eyes, and moved to the door ready to accompany him.

"It's all right, old chap!" said Blake. "We'll give him until tonight to return. He may have had a long chase; but if he isn't back, then we'll start to look for him."

Pedro wagged his tail in trustful understanding, and they descended to the waiting car.

Half an hour later Blake entered the office of the *Amalgamated Photographer*, the well-known journal on advanced photography.

He was ushered into the office of the editor, who greeted him warmly.

"Well, well, this is an early call, Mr. Blake. Be seated. Have you brought us an article? It's some weeks since we received anything from you, and, strange to say, I was about to write you and ask you to let us have something, if you were not too busy."

"I'm afraid I must disappoint you," laughed Blake. "I have really been too busy to write lately. But I see you have another contributor supplying you with articles on the same subject. I read one last night, and it interested me, as it showed the writer was following the same line of investigation which I am following. And that is really what brought me in this morning. Have you any objection to telling me the author's name?"

The editor's eyes had held a twinkle in them ever since Blake had entered; but as the detective made his request, he burst out laughing.

"You are fond of a joke, Mr. Blake. One would never think it, either. But I'll give in. Name your price, and I'll have the cashier write you a cheque for them."

"Fond of a joke—name my price! I don't understand!" Blake said, with a puzzled look: "I assure you, Mr. Gordon, I am not joking in any way."

"Do you mean to say," asked the editor, sobering suddenly, "that you haven't been sending in those articles on long-distance, and embossed colour photography anonymously?"

"I assure you on my solemn word that I have sent in no anonymous articles," replied Blake.

"Well, I'm blest!" answered the other. "We've had four of them—bang up good articles, too! I thought all the time you were sending them in, and having a joke with us by not signing them. When you came in this morning I kept it up, pretended not to know they had come from you; but what you tell me is very surprising. Someone has been sending them in, and evidently they don't desire payment, for no name has come with them."

"As I have already said," remarked Blake, knitting his brows in deep thought, "I know nothing of them, and I have a particular reason for desiring to know who wrote them. Were the manuscripts typed?"

"Yes, all of them."

"I wonder if anyone in the office remembers what postmark was on the envelopes?" queried the detective.

"I hardly think so," replied the editor. "But I will see, if it is really important to you."

"I will be greatly obliged if you will—it is important."

"All right! I'll have Judd, the cashier in. He put the articles down to your credit, and may possibly have noticed the postmark; he's an observing old dog."

Gordon rang for the cashier.

He was a tall, thin elderly man of nondescript appearance, except for a deep-set pair of keen grey eyes.

"Good-morning, Mr. Blake," he began, his eyes lighting up with pleasure. "I suppose you have dropped in to have the laugh on us, but we were too smart for you; we've credited them all up to you." And he shook his grey head as he chuckled.

"I'm afraid you are doomed to disappointment, Judd," laughed Blake. "Sorry to spoil the old man's pleasure, but I honestly didn't write those articles. I've just been telling Mr. Gordon."

"What?" gasped the cashier. "You didn't write them? Why——"

"No; we've made a mistake, Judd!" broke in the editor. "But Mr. Blake is very anxious to discover the author of them. You don't by any chance to remember the postmark?"

"Come to think of it now, I do remember. When the first one came in without any name, I naturally looked at the postmark. It was posted from Barnesley, in Surrey. I didn't notice the others, for you said they must have come from Mr. Blake, and that he was probably having a joke with us. I just credited them up to him."

"Good! Good!" exclaimed Blake. "Judd, you ought to have been a detective. It isn't much to go on, but it may help. I'm a thousand times obliged for the information."

"Not at all, not at all, Mr. Blake!" smiled the pleased cashier. "I'm glad if it is of any use."

"If any more come, I'll note the postmark, and let you know," said Gordon, as Judd withdrew. "Not professional jealousy I hope," he laughed; "but honestly, they were fine articles."

"No, something entirely different," replied Blake, rising.

"But you're right, I would say—yes, I would certainly say they emanated from a very brilliant mind."

"They certainly did; and I could do with a few more of them. By the way I hope you will send us something soon."

"I will, shortly. And now I'll be getting along. Don't forget to note the postmark if anything else comes from your mysterious contributor, and do me the favour to say nothing about it, will you?"

"Right, I suppose, as usual, you have some unfathomable reason; but I'll say nothing."

Blake hastened to the street and climbed into the waiting car, where Pedro had remained on guard.

The detective threw in the clutch and threaded his way through the traffic of Fleet Street and into the Strand.

He stopped at a telegraph-office on the way and sent several messages.

He then turned the car towards Baker Street, little dreaming of the surprise that awaited him there.

The Sixth Chapter
Yvonne's Underground Retreat

WHEN the steel door clanged to, making Tinker a prisoner, he went over to it, but no sound penetrated through its thickness.

He sat down and considered things from every point of view, but his brain was too tired to solve the riddle.

He hadn't the faintest idea where he was, or what was the identity of the mysterious veiled woman. All he knew was that she was undoubtedly the same individual as the nun, and that he had followed the right person. Beyond that, and the fact that he was probably some distance out of London, he was all at sea.

Who his captors were—what they proposed to do with him, or in what way they were connected with Blake's investigations, he could not guess. He knew the detective was working on several cases, but Tinker did not know the details of the Bechstein robbery, as the nun had called so soon after Blake's return from Bond Street.

It was very late, and he was very tired; so, giving up the riddle for the time being, he undressed and slipped between the snowy sheets.

On the other side of the steel door was a scene which would have enlightened Tinker could he have witnessed it.

Yvonne sat in a large, stone-walled room, before a large mahogany desk. In another chair sat the man who had conducted Tinker to his prison. He was a clean-cut man, and it was obvious from his attitude that he was paying close attention to Yvonne's words.

The room was furnished as a mixture of laboratory and study. On one side were hundreds of technical and scientific books in glass cases, while on the other ranged the laboratory equipment. Wires of all sizes stretched across the ceiling, and instruments of brass and steel abounded everywhere. A large pillar rose from one corner, and on it was what looked like a very delicate instrument, for several very fine wires ran from it and disappeared through tiny holes in the stone walls. Yvonne consulted this instrument frequently, and she had just returned from one of her visits of inspection when we look in upon her.

"I don't think he'll come tonight," she remarked, as she resumed her seat before the desk. "If he had been able to get a car in time to follow, he would have been here by now."

"I don't imagine he will come at all," replied the man. "But you are marvellous. Miss Cartier!" he went on, with a deeply admiring glance. "I never thought I'd turn criminal; but honestly, it's a pleasant surprise to find it so interesting. I always had an idea that criminals wore a hang-dog look and were coarse ruffians, but without doubt the world moves."

"I have certainly been fortunate in finding a reliable ally like you to take charge of the yacht and assist me, Captain Vaughan," answered Yvonne, with her silvery laugh. "But I promised to explain to you tonight the workings of the 'ear instrument.'" And, rising again, she led the way to the instrument in the corner which she had been consulting with such regularity.

"I will give you the necessary technical notes which will explain it thoroughly," she went on. "But roughly, the idea is this."

She then proceeded to describe in detail the delicate instrument which was the product of her brilliant mind, and certainly no one would have thought the beautiful, bronze-haired young woman, who stood talking with such a profound knowledge of science, was probably the cleverest, and for that reason the most to be feared, criminal living. She had started with a strong motive, but the fascination of the game had seized her, and she pursued it now for the love of it. She had developed into more than an adventuress. Her wonderful brain had studied incessantly with extraordinary patience until she ranked with the greatest scientists of the day. This knowledge she brought to bear on her operations, and everything was planned with mathematical precision and detail before she embarked on it.

"So, you see," she said, as she finished her demonstration, "that is really on the same lines as Marconi's invention for ships. These wires carry the waves outside for a radius of sixty feet in all directions. Any moving object in that radius comes into contact with the waves, and the movement is reflected back on this register. That is the reason I had all the trees cleared away in order that the moving of the branches would not reflect on the register. Consequently you can see how I could easily discover if anyone approached the house."

"Marvellous!" murmured her companion. "It makes a remarkable watchdog for you!"

"It does, indeed," smiled Yvonne, as she returned to her seat, "Yes, I feel quite secure in my retreat. The cleverest man in the world could roam over the house above, and he would never discover my underground apartments. But this man Sexton Blake must be stopped!" she went on, her eyes hardening. "He is unlike other detectives, and has a wonderful mind. I think I have planned my retreat too well for him to discover me; but at the same time, one never knows when he may stumble on something, and for that reason he will have to be watched."

"What, will you do?" asked Taylor.

"I'm going to take the bull by the horns and invade his rooms. He will have made notes, and I may be able to get a look at them."

"But that will be impossible, won't it?" protested the captain.

"No, I'll manage it all right. If I am discovered—well, society will lose one of its most shining members, for I wouldn't permit Sexton Blake, or anyone else, to interfere with my plans. And now, captain, I want you to slip in and see if my captive is asleep. If he is, bring all his clothes out to me, for I will need them."

The mystified captain did as he was bid, and returned a few moments later with Tinker's clothes in his arms.

"He was sound asleep!" he chuckled, as he dropped them.

"He'll be surprised in the morning when he finds his clothes gone!"

"You'd better take in some of uncle's, and leave them for him," remarked Yvonne, "and then go to the yacht. Tell uncle to come up here, and you'd better keep steam up. If things come to a crisis between this man Blake and I, I might need to get away quickly."

"Very well," he replied. "I trust you won't come into conflict with him. He's a dangerous man."

"I'll take care of myself all right," she laughed, but her companion wore a worried look as he departed.

Immediately he had gone, Yvonne closed the door and moved to the mirror. She uncoiled her beautiful bronze hair, and reaching for a jar, applied some greasy substance to it.

Its thick, wavy folds clung together as though wet, and when she tucked it under a close-fitting, flesh-coloured skull-cap, it lay down flat.

"Let me see!" she murmured, as she walked over to a large cabinet. "He has brown hair, hasn't he?"

Opening the cabinet, a large stock of wigs of all shades were displayed, and, choosing one of a brown colour, she placed it on her head. She next moved to the door, and opening it, hastened down the passage to the room where Tinker slept. Softly slipping the bolts and switching on the light, she entered, and moved over to the sleeping lad. She earnestly studied his face, feature by feature, and, apparently satisfied with her scrutiny, she left as noiselessly as she had come.

On her return to the laboratory, she went again to the mirror. A few touches here and there, and a rearrangement of the wig changed her fresh, girlish face into the more boyish duplicate of Tinker's. Slipping off her dress she struggled into Tinker's garments, and five minutes later glanced at her reflection with satisfaction. And well she might, for she stood a perfect reproduction of the sleeping lad.

"It wouldn't deceive Blake," she muttered "but it will get me past the landlady all right. I hope the dog isn't there, it might be awkward."

She placed Tinker's cap on her head, and switching out the light, left the room. She went through the stone passage, turning off the lights in several luxuriously-furnished rooms as she passed, stopping for a moment in one to pick up a revolver, which she slipped into her pocket. Up a flight of stone steps she went, and on reaching the top, turned out the last light.

She pressed a button, and a huge, stone door swung back noiselessly. Passing through as the door swung to behind her with a soft click, she emerged into a wide, old-fashioned fireplace such as are common in ancient houses. It opened into a small, meagrely-furnished cottage sitting-room, and through an open door could be seen a cottage parlour, its quaint furniture looking ghostly in the just breaking dawn.

It was a harmless-looking cottage, and might have belonged to any small farmer. Little would one think such a luxurious retreat lay beneath it.

The old stable, to which Yvonne directed her steps, was equally innocent-looking. The floor was half-covered with empty bins, but what was not known to casual observers was that on the bottom of each bin was a small, innocent-looking metal strip which lay over the big spikes in the rough-looking planking.

A curious mind would find it quite possible to move the bins freely about, but he would not know that through those spikes at times caught a high current of magnetism, which held the bins firmly to the floor on certain occasions. And this was one of the occasions, for as Yvonne entered the door she reached her hand up to a small nail in the wall, and gently pressed.

One side of the floor dropped, while the other rose, and the bin-covered farm floor turned completely over on a pivot, bringing into view a smooth steel floor on which was a large red motor held to by clamps. The whole movement could not have been heard ten feet away. It was ingenious, to say the least, and certainly Yvonne had gone to great pains to secure a safe retreat.

She released the clamps which held the motor in place when the floor had been upside-down, and, pressing the starting button, backed out of the stable. She sprang out, and once more pressed the small nail on the wall, and again the rough, bin-covered floor appeared, the current which had held them being cut off as the floor swung back into place.

Springing into the driving-seat, she threw in the clutch, and, with a last parting glance at the innocent-looking farm cottage, headed for London.

The Seventh Chapter
Blake Draws a Blank

YVONNE reached Baker Street about eight o'clock, and swung the car up a side street, where she pulled up. Springing out, she strolled casually to the corner, and a gleam of satisfaction came into her eyes as she saw a large grey car a short distance up the street.

She hastened back to her own car, and, after looking carefully around the quiet side street, she reached forward and turned a small button. A quick "slushing" sound followed, and the red coat which had thrown back the morning sun flashed up and out of sight like the cover of a roll-top desk, leaving a dark-blue coloured body instead.

"I might need to change twice," she muttered, as she reached once more for the button. Again the slushing noise followed as the blue coat disappeared under the overhanging rolled edges, and a grey appeared. With the driver so much like Tinker, it did not look unlike Blake's machine, and Yvonne smiled to herself as she noticed the similarity.

Once more she strolled to the corner, and loafed casually for some time.

As Blake appeared and entered his car, she hurried back to her own, and bent over out of sight as Blake swept past the corner.

She straightened after he had flashed by, and climbed into the seat.

Patiently she sat, and the occasional passer-by never looked twice at the whistling boy lounging in the seat.

Half an hour passed before Yvonne made a move. She slipped from the car and walked to Baker Street, quickening her footsteps as she turned the corner. Pulling from her pocket a small bunch of keys which she had taken with Tinker's clothes, she rapidly tried them one after the other, and heaved a sigh of relief as the lock yielded.

She hastened down the passage, and opened the door of the consulting-room where she had been the previous evening. She wasted no time, and moved at once over to the desk, but stopped as her eye fell on the photographic journal which lay uppermost on the table where Blake had thrown it the previous night.

Quickly snatching it up, she turned the leaves, and her eyes narrowed as she saw the pencilled criticisms which Blake had made in the margin.

"So, he's up in that, is he?" she muttered. "You're cleverer than I thought, Mr. Blake, but I guess you're not clever enough to find the author of that article or to connect it with Mr. Bechstein."

She carefully replaced the magazine as she had found it, and continued towards the desk. Rapidly she ran her eye over the contents, and she was reaching for a small notebook when the sound of a motor stopping outside came to her ears.

Yvonne swung round, and crept softly to the window. As she peered through the curtain she saw a big grey car from which Sexton Blake and Pedro were just descending.

Her heart stood still for a moment, and she cast about rapidly for a place of escape. Rushing to the door, she opened it and looked up and down the passage. No one was in sight, and she closed the door behind her and sped down it as her eye caught sight of a small door at the lower end. It looked like a cupboard, and she was right, for as she pulled it open and sprang in she stumbled over a pile of linen.

Yvonne just had time to close the door when the click of a key sounded at the street entrance, and she heard Blake's steps come down the passage and enter the consulting-room.

Blake made straight for the photographic journal as he entered, intending to read the article over again, but paused to glance curiously at Pedro, who was running about the room, sniffing excitedly.

"What is it, old chap?" asked the detective, puzzled by the dog's unusual actions.

Pedro only pounded his tail, and kept on sniffing. Blake turned sharply as the hound suddenly lifted his head and dashed at the closed door.

"Better give him his head and see what bothers him," muttered Blake, moving across and opening the door. As Pedro dashed out, the detective followed, and as he did so he looked up the passage as he heard the street door click.

"Strange!" he muttered, as Pedro dashed down the passage to the cupboard and back to the front entrance.

"Somebody must have gone out, and, from Pedro's actions, whoever it was must have been in the consulting-room. It wasn't the landlady, for Pedro never pays any attention to her. I wonder——" He broke off, and, dashing to the door, threw it open, and hastened out to the footpath. The figure of a lad running caught his eye, and he gasped in amazement as he took it at first sight for Tinker, but as it turned the corner he called back Pedro, who had started in pursuit, and jumping into the car, which stood at the kerb, started after.

"Good heavens!" he muttered, as he threw in the clutch and turned recklessly. "I could almost have sworn it was Tinker except for the run. The lad never ran like that, but one thing is certain. There is some deep game on, and Tinker has fallen a victim to it, for I'll swear those were his clothes. I'm up against a shrewd antagonist, for whoever it is has dared to enter my flat and search it."

He turned the corner as his musings reached this point, and increased the speed as he saw the imitation Tinker leap into another grey car and dash off at breakneck speed.

Blake was more convinced than ever of the clever brain against him, and he settled down over the wheel for the chase with a savage gleam in his eye. It boded no good for the fugitive ahead if he were caught, for Blake was irritated by the boldness of his unknown enemies; and, to make matters worse, he was so far completely in the dark as to their identity.

He had, of course, his ideas on the subject, and was working on those lines, but he had started without a clue of any sort in the real sense of the word, and the slender threads on which he was working would have seemed ridiculous to anyone else. He knew, however, that he was up against a big hidden force, and no doubt remained in his mind that it was connected with the Bechstein robbery. He knew every move he made was probably watched, and his eyes grew anxious as he thought of Tinker in the hands of the enemy.

"I'd give something to know who is behind it all!" he muttered, as he followed the other car, which was going in violation of all speed laws. "But I won't rest until I do, and when I know—well——" And the detective's jaw finished the thought.

On dashed the two powerful grey cars, and Blake risked a further increase of speed as he saw the quarry head for the Strand.

"If I don't keep close I'll lose it in the traffic," he thought.

The leading car eased up as it entered the narrow, crowded Strand, and Blake did likewise. He was gaining, however, and trusted to his power with the traffic police to get him through if a blockade occurred.

He sent the car forward, and swung around as the other turned a corner. As he did so his brow knit in puzzlement, for ahead of him, it is true, was a big motor, but it was not grey like the one he had been following, but blue, and instead of a boy at the wheel the driver appeared to be a man, for he was wearing a black bowler hat.

The amazed detective pulled up as he came to the entrance of a courtyard, and, jumping out quickly, surveyed the inner enclosure. His examination was fruitless, however, and he dashed back.

"It's a poser," he muttered, "but it must be the same. Another proof of their cleverness. I'll have a job to overtake it," he thought. He sent the car forward again, and followed on. There was only one turning, and it led to the left and thence round to the Strand again. Blake followed, and as he reached the street he saw a blue car just speeding towards the Law Courts. It had a solitary driver, and although he now wore a soft hat, Blake swung after.

As the detective threaded his way through the thundering buses, his already exasperated temper would have blazed had he seen a big red motor enter the Strand shortly after from the same street from which Blake had come, for the wily Yvonne had seen the blue car, and, risking Blake's following it, she had circled right around the way she had come, and, pressing the button, threw down the red coat before she emerged.

She chuckled as she saw Blake driving after the other, and, turning, headed swiftly in the opposite direction.

Blake overtook his quarry as he reached the Law Courts. As he came up behind he took note of the number. He had been unable to catch the number of Yvonne's car, but as he memorised what he thought was it a doubt filled his mind, for the back of the driver's head looked vaguely familiar.

He pressed the horn sharply, and, as the other involuntarily turned, Blake gasped in disgusted amazement as he recognised the well-known profile of Inspector Kelly of Scotland Yard. Rapidly he pulled alongside, and signed to the inspector to stop.

"Hallo, Blake!" called the inspector, as he pulled up. "Did you wish to speak to me?"

"Yes, for a moment," replied Blake. "Which way have you just come?"

"Straight up Whitehall, and through the Strand. Why?" asked the inspector, in surprise.

"Did you leave the Strand at all?" continued Blake.

"No. As I told you, I came straight along. Anything wrong?"

"No. I took you for someone else," answered Blake. "Sorry to have troubled you."

"He seems savage," grinned the inspector, as Blake turned and drove off. "Wonder what bothers him? Maybe someone has given him the slip. If that's the case, and he followed me in mistake, no wonder he's wild. Ha, ha! That's a good one on him if it's so! I'll pass it on to the chief." And the inspector, still chuckling, continued on his way.

Blake returned direct to Baker Street. His face was set sternly as he entered the consulting-room. Pedro took up his place by the fire, and watched his master with anxious gaze as the latter paced rapidly up and down. The detective lunched lightly, and afterwards carefully re-read the article in the photographic journal.

Bechstein rang up on the phone soon after, and the detective told him shortly to drop around in two days' time as he was moving in the matter that night.

During the afternoon several telegrams arrived, in answer to the ones he had sent early in the morning, and all were of the same tenor.

"None of the employees interested in photography. That settles it," he muttered, as he read the last.

He filled his pipe, and not until the shadows lengthened did he move.

Rising, he donned a heavy coat and cap, and, slinging a revolver in his pocket, told the disappointed Pedro to watch things, and left the house. His face was still grim as he climbed into the car, and headed the powerful monster for Surrey.

The Eighth Chapter
On the Trail

IT was a chilly evening; but Blake was too absorbed in his thoughts to pay any attention to the weather. Mechanically he drove the delicately-tuned car which had been through so many adventures with him, and where the road was clear he put on full speed.

The detective's deductions were, it is true, based on a very slender thread, but beyond this slender thread absolutely no trace of a clue existed. Three people had inspected a certain necklace in a certain jewellery establishment in Bond Street. None of them had had it in their hands for more than a few seconds. It had only been in the establishment for about three weeks, and yet, strange to say, when it was examined at the end of that time it was discovered to be a forgery. And what a forgery—every tiny detail had been reproduced perfectly, even down to the bent filigree clasp.

On first thoughts it would seem unlikely that the false necklace could have been reproduced while the genuine one lay at Bechstein's. Consequently, the step would lead back to the point from which it originated. Blake had naturally followed that line of reasoning, but had discarded the hypothesis after a conversation with Craig, the head of the big firm which had supplied the necklace to Bechstein.

"No," Mr. Craig had said, "there would be no possibility of the article being duplicated here, Mr. Blake. I myself selected the pearls as they came in, and my brother drew the design for the settings and clasp. Both gems and designs were kept in the private safe, and until they were brought out to set, no one had access to them but my brother and myself. The setting was all done by a man who has been with the firm for over thirty years, and each night he brought everything to be put back in the safe, for even with us this was a good-sized order, and we gave it every care. The very day they were finished they were delivered to Bechstein, so any duplication must have taken place while they were at his place."

Blake ran over the conversation as the car pounded over the quiet country roads, and again he eliminated the possibility of the duplication at Craig's. It would require a long time to make the design for the settings and the filigree clasp, let alone the pearls, which require even longer. As far as Blake could see the whole thing could hardly be done in three weeks. He had carefully investigated the possibility of any of the assistants having sufficient access to the safe, but Ford was the only one, and the investigation of his affairs had yielded nothing bearing the slightest suspicious element.

From that point the circle narrowed to two elements—one of which was the possibility of Bechstein having duplicated the necklace himself—but that also had been cast out by the detective, for mathematically it was not possible. Bechstein's distress had been too genuine, and he would not willingly cut his own throat financially, and Blake's investigations of the jeweller's financial affairs had yielded the fact that Bechstein spoke the truth when he said, if the necklace was not recovered in a few days he would go to the wall.

No; only one thread remained, and as has been said, it was so fine that even Blake's keen reasoning barely grasped it. But his system of analysing had cast out any others, and, true to his nature, he seized the only thread exposed. Whether it was strong enough to connect up and tie the loose ends of the circle remains to be seen. In any event, he would follow it until it led to something else, or broke in mid-air to use his own expression.

But he frankly acknowledged to himself that the whole matter presented less material to work on than any case he had ever had. He still persisted in his theory that no criminal, no matter how clever and scientific, was capable of organising and committing a crime, and making a retreat without a single mistake. He stubbornly held to that, although the present case seriously jarred his theory.

Tinker's disappearance worried him, and proved that a strong unknown force had started to work against him from the moment he took up the case. Certainly every detail bore the stamp of a master brain, which used methods compared to those of the ordinary criminal, as the automatic pistol is to the ancient blunderbuss.

But he would stick to the chase until he either succeeded or was beaten and the steady look of his eyes made it obvious that that would be only when life departed.

With this culmination of the working of his mind he entered the village of Barnesley.

Barnesley was a mill village, and, consequently, the individual dressed as a mill-hand, which quietly slipped out of the back door of an inn, and entered the bar an hour later created no curiosity, as he freely mingled with the other customers.

One of their many grievances was being aired by a talkative individual, and the disguised Blake, anxious to gain all knowledge he could without causing comment, listened as he carelessly sipped a glass of beer.

"I says as 'ow it ain't fair," the speaker was saying, in a slightly thick voice. "'Ere we hare workin' like blessed slaves for wot? I ses for wot?"

His companions seemed more interested in their beer than in his meandering, and no one volunteered "wot" they were working for. But the speaker was not discouraged by the lack of interest, and kept on, himself supplying the answer to his question.

"I'll tell yer for wot," he hiccoughed. "For a bloomin' 'ard bed, and bloomin' little food, and bloomin' little beer, and——"

"Sounds like a rose garden with all your bloomin's," put in a facetious listener, but the orator waved his remark aside with a contemptuous snort, and continued unabashed.

"Yuss, an' wot do them for who the likes of us works get? I arsk you, brethren?"

"Oh, shut up, and have a beer!" growled a burly good-natured looking man on a form. "We gets paid for our work, and I know at the present time if higher wages had to be paid the mill would have to shut down."

"Again I arsk you!" persisted the inebriated one. "Wot do they get? Look at the man wot drove that big, grey car today. Does 'e work as hard as we do? I'll bet 'e don't know wot work is. Prob'bly the gilded son of some useless rich man."

Blake smiled into his glass at this description of himself, while the orator leered with satisfaction at his own words.

"An' look at all the other idle rich wot do nothin' but run round in motor-cars, and 'unt. There's that party wot dashes through the village in 'er big, red car as though we was all dogs, to go scampering out of her way. Only tonight she drew up the road to the station, and I had to move bloomin' quick to save myself. I tell yer again."

But what he was going to tell them again ended in a gurgle as the big man on the form reached forth a mighty hand, and unceremoniously dragged the speaker down, where he lay in undignified discomfiture.

In the general laugh which followed none of them saw the gleam in the eyes of the strange mill-hand when the drunken orator spoke of the "red car an' 'er." Quietly he finished his beer, and unobtrusively slipped out while the laugh still kept on.

"I wonder—I wonder," he said softly, as he quickened his steps and hastened in the direction of the railway-station, "if this is a lengthening of the thread, or only a profitless chase?"

He swung up the road leading to the railway, and almost ran as he heard the whistle of the evening train. He was too far away to see if anyone descended, and stopped in the shadow as the train quickly started again. The purr of a motor had come to his ears, and he sank back still further as the brilliant headlights shone down the road. A moment later it swept past him at high speed, but not before Blake had seen that it contained three occupants—one of whom was at the driving-wheel, and it looked like a woman, and he also saw that the colour was red.

Hastily he gathered himself up as the motor sped on, and he started on a run in pursuit, not stopping until he had reached the top of a hill. Here he paused, and gazed intently through the night until he saw the lamps appear on the main road below. He watched them until they reached the cross-roads, and turned to the left, and not until then did he relax his tense attitude.

For a man who seemed as interested as he had been in the appearance of the motor, Blake descended the hill at a strangely-leisured pace.

He walked with apparent indifference down the main street of the village, pulling up as the solitary constable appeared.

"Good-evening!" remarked Blake, as that worthy passed. "A fine evening!"

"None o' yer smartness," growled the constable. "You mill fellers are getting too cheeky to the law." And he drew himself up with puffing dignity as he delivered himself of the words.

Blake laughed, and, turning, strolled along beside the other. He spoke a few words to that individual as they walked along, and the policeman turned to reply sarcastically when he paused as he saw the look in the mill-hand's eyes.

"You're bluffin'——" he began.

"I don't blame you for doubting," interrupted Blake; "but come with me to the inn, and I will prove it."

"I'm sorry, sir," apologised the officer, as he recognised the ring of authority in Blake's voice. "You see, sir, these fellows of the mill are always trying to put up a game on me, and I have to be careful. But I'm mighty proud to meet you, sir—that I am," he said, his eyes lighting with pride. "But no one would ever know you in that get up, sir. I've mixed with these mill men all my life, and I'd never have known the difference."

"All right, officer!" laughed Blake, good-naturedly. "Come along to the inn! I'd like some information from you!"

A few moments later Blake and the policeman entered the inn by the side door, and went quickly to the detective's rooms.

If the policeman had any lingering doubts as to Blake's identity they were dissipated on Blake's return in usual garb from his bedroom, where he had gone at once on entering.

He quickly put the now embarrassed constable at his ease, and, offering him a cigar, lit one himself.

"Now, officer," he began, "I'm down here on a little private investigation, and if you care to assist me, you won't be the loser by it. By the way, what is your name?"

"Hobbs is my name, sir; and I'd be proud to work with you without any reward for it," replied the constable. "Anything I can do, Mr. Blake, I'll be glad to do."

"Thank you," smiled Blake. "But remember, please, that for the present everything I say is strictly between ourselves."

"I understand, sir," replied the flattered constable.

"Did you see the big red motor-car which was in the village?" asked Blake.

"Oh, yes, sir!" answered Hobbs. "It often comes in."

"Do you know who owns it?"

"I can't say I do, sir. Sometimes a lady drives it, and sometimes a man—middle-aged he is. I'd know their names if they lived in my district, but I think they must live over Colby way. Hanson has that district, but he makes Creighton his headquarters."

"Why, then, would they come here instead of to Creighton?" asked Blake.

"I imagine, sir, because the London express stops here and doesn't at Creighton."

"I see," mused Blake. "Do you know Colby well?"

"Oh, yes, every foot of it!" answered Hobbs. "I've often relieved over there."

"You'd know, then, all the residents, of course?"

"Yes, indeed. I got to know it pretty well during the Granger murder there six years ago. I was at the Granger Farm for some time during the investigation."

"You wouldn't know, of course, at what place those people live in the Colby district?"

"No, sir, I wouldn't. I've always imagined they must be on a visit. I don't know of any vacant places or any that have changed except the old Granger Farm, and, of course, these people wouldn't live at a place like that. Besides, no one will go near it since the murder."

"I see!" again muttered Blake. He subsided into silence, and puffed his cigar thoughtfully for some time.

"Well, Hobbs, as I said, keep quiet for the present. In the meantime I'll think over things tonight, and will communicate with you in the morning."

"Very good, sir," replied Hobbs, rising to leave; and as the door closed Blake threw himself into a chair, and smoked in deep absorption over a road map until long after midnight.

The Ninth Chapter
Blake is Captured

BLAKE was astir early the next morning, and started in the big car for Colby village.

He had left a note for Hobbs telling him to keep quiet until his return.

His ideas might be without foundation, but he decided to test them, and, with that end in view, had made an early start.

He reached Colby village early in the afternoon, and an hour later left the inn dressed in tweeds and a cap. He struck across country, and as the afternoon waned and dusk closed down he came in sight of the deserted Granger farmhouse.

It looked desolate and cheerless, but that evidently did not detract from its interest for Blake, for he dropped into some thick bushes, and turned his gaze on the old place.

Over two hours passed, and still the detective did not move. Darkness had shut down some time ago, and the house was now invisible, but he still kept his gaze in its direction. Another half-hour passed, and the silent figure stirred as a sudden light flashed and disappeared. It came from the direction of the house, and Blake leaned tensely forward as it appeared the second time. The light moved along for a short distance, and again disappeared. Two minutes later two brilliant lights gleamed forth, and Blake smiled in grim satisfaction.

"The motor!" he breathed, as he stood up in the shelter of the trees, and watched the lights as they swung round and headed away from the house. When they had disappeared, he sank back, and watched patiently for another half-hour before he moved.

"I'll try it now," he muttered, as he rose. "They may come back at once, and, on the other hand, they may have gone to London. It's a funny place to hang out, and it's a risky proposition to investigate it alone, but it's got to be done. Who knows, poor Tinker may be in that house. It's a flimsy place, and if it belongs to whom I think it does it doesn't seem in order with their usual cleverness!"

Unfortunately for Blake, he did not know at that time just how clever his unknown antagonists really were, and although he knew he was running a great risk in investigating that lonely place by himself, he didn't dream of the complete system and luxurious retreat hidden away under that lonely farmhouse.

He crept cautiously, picking his steps, and noiselessly parting the branches as he went.

Dropping to the ground as he reached a large clearing, he could just distinguish the black bulk of the house and stable.

"It doesn't look very inviting," he thought, as he took a careful reconnoitering look around before proceeding.

"Seems deserted, too. Perhaps there's nobody at home. However, here goes!" And he began to creep stealthily forward over the open ground.

Little did Blake know that as he crawled through the short grass toward the creepy blackness of that desolate house, that almost underneath him, in a luxuriously-furnished stone-walled apartment, sat an alluring bronze-haired young woman with narrowed eyes and scornful smile, intently watching a small machine set in one corner, on which a delicate needle was quivering, registering every movement the detective made.

The watching woman muttered a smothered exclamation, and rose to her feet as the needle swung round half-way.

"I wish uncle and Hendricks would hurry," she muttered, as she went over to the desk and picked up a revolver. "It may be only some prowling tramp, but, on the other hand, that man Blake may have stumbled on something. However, I'll have to chance it!"

Switching out the lights, she slipped off her shoes, and, gripping the revolver, stole noiselessly along the passage and up the stairs. She turned out the passage lights as well, although it was a needless precaution, for not the faintest ray could penetrate from that perfectly-built retreat.

Yvonne stood listening for some time, but as no sound came from the interior of the cottage on the other side of the stone door, she pressed the releasing button, and the perfectly balanced door swung silently open.

Creeping through, with infinite caution, Yvonne dropped flat, and lay, scarcely breathing, as the almost imperceptible click of the closing door sounded behind her. Holding before her the hand which held the revolver, she crept out of the fireplace and across the floor to the door of the room. Softly she turned the latch, and caught her breath with a jerk as it made a very slight noise which sounded like the report of a gun to her taut nerves.

Again she lay still, listening for sounds, but none came, and she continued her creeping progress. Over the short grass went the dark figure, ever keeping the revolver pushed in front, until the black shadow of the stable loomed up. On reaching one comer she dropped back and held her breath. Her teeth showed for a moment as a slight shuffling sound reached her ears. Slowly, and feeling cautiously every inch, she crept into the dark entrance. From inside came no sound; now and again she dropped to the ground.

Silence still reigned from inside the stable, and she dared not move, for she knew not in what direction the intruder might be creeping.

The intruder had a very good reason for keeping silent, for his instinct, almost as soon as his quick ears, had realised the presence of another being somewhere in the surrounding darkness. He also had dropped down, and lay scarcely breathing, for he was as yet uncertain whether the sound emanated from somewhere inside the dark stable or came from the outside.

It was one of the strangest positions in which either had ever found themselves. Only a thin wall separated the cleverest detective of crime and the cleverest female perpetrator of crime that the world had ever known. Both of those brilliant brains were working rapidly to devise some scheme to make the hidden foe make the first move, and in the meantime the deadly sinister silence reigned, heavy with the portent of the coming struggle.

As is usually the case, the woman's mind worked more rapidly. Its decisions are not always the soundest, but in this case it was a brilliant stroke.

To fully appreciate the situation, it must be remembered that, as usual, the bin-covered side of the floor had been swung back into place as the motor departed, and it was in this confused array that Blake lay. He was on foreign ground, and up until now had carried on his investigations by darkness, as he had considered it unsafe as yet to use a light. And in that moment he congratulated himself on his forethought, but, alas! it only saved him for the moment.

Outside lay Yvonne within a few feet of the open door. Only the thin wall of the stable separated them, and where they lay they were only a few inches from one another. Yvonne acted quickly once she had made her decision. Regardless of noise, she dashed to her feet and bounded madly for the open door. As the dark figure entered, Blake lifted his revolver, and suddenly, seeing the shape of the figure, hesitated to fire, for in the dense gloom he thought, and rightly, it looked like a woman. He could not fire, but he could take her prisoner forcibly, and, stuffing his revolver in his pocket, leaped forward.

But Yvonne's fingers had found the small nail in the familiar wall. Feverishly she pressed it, and sprang back, firing into the darkness as she did so.

As the bullet whistled past Blake's head, he felt the floor suddenly sink from under him. He reeled and stumbled, then gathered himself together on his hands and knees, gripping wildly in the dark for something to hold on to. Lower went the floor, a brilliant light flashed, giving him a lightning view of a tangle of gold bronze hair above a white, gleaming skin, and as the floor swung still lower and turned completely over he dropped into the void below, passing into unconsciousness to the sound of a silvery, mocking laugh.

The Tenth Chapter
Yvonne Proceeds

TINKER had spent two miserable days in his prison.

True, he had been served very good food at intervals by a woman, who pushed it through a cunningly-devised opening in the steel door, and the bookcase was filled with many interesting volumes.

He had been getting around in a suit of clothes about five sizes too big for him, and he could only judge the time by the regular arrival of the meals. Otherwise it was impossible to tell whether it was day or night, for no windows were let into his stone prison. How the place was ventilated Tinker had been unable to discover, but a pure current of air flowed through constantly from some invisible source.

He was disgusted at his capture by a woman, and worried on Blake's account, and at the end of the second day he paced the room in his big, loose garments, with his brow wrinkled savagely. He was certainly in a very unpleasant frame of mind, and, from his point of view, he had reason to be.

It is hard to guess what his feelings would have been had he known that at that moment Blake was creeping over the ground within a very short distance of him.

The lad had seen none of his captors since his arrival with the exception of the woman who handed in his meals, and all attempts to draw her into conversation had failed.

Consequently, although he knew not the reason, he was relieved to hear the bolts spring back in the door, and he swung round as it opened.

He gasped in astonishment as he saw the beautiful woman who entered, and his fascinated gaze barely noticed the two men who followed, bearing an apparently lifeless body.

He tore his gaze from the woman, and every thought but one fled from his mind as he saw that the body was Blake's. He gave a strangled cry as it was laid on the bed, and, rushing over, knelt beside it. Feverishly he felt the cold wrists, and pressed his ear to the apparently still heart.

He gasped with relief as he heard it beat faintly, and, springing to his feet, swung on his captors. He recognised the elder of the two men as the man who had descended from the motor the night he was captured. The other man was dressed in nautical uniform, but he was not the same who had conducted Tinker to his prison.

The lad was burning with deep distress and indignation, and he almost choked as he blazed out at them, but he did not notice the curious look in the woman's eyes as he spoke.

"If any evil befalls the guv'nor from your fiendish schemes, I'll—I'll kill you all, if it takes me all my life to find you!" The lad's voice broke as he struggled manfully to control the sob of distress that would break out. But he gazed in surprise as the beautiful woman spoke.

"Don't worry, my lad," she said gently. "Your guv'nor, as you call him, will have his life spared this time. He took his life in his hands when he came to this place, and I had intended making it cost him that life. But this time—and remember it is only for this time—I will spare it. I have memories," she added, more to herself, "See what you can do, uncle, to bring him round; and you, Hendricks, go, please, to the laboratory and bring me the blue jar in the left-hand corner of the top case."

She moved to the brass bed as she finished speaking, a look of brooding sadness in her eyes. Her thoughts were far away in a grief-laden, ranch house in sunny Australia; but as they swung round to the people who had caused her to adopt the kind of life she led, she almost regretted her momentary generosity.

Long and earnestly she gazed at the strong, still face beneath her.

She knew she ought to violently hate the man who was doing his best to spoil her carefully-planned scheme. True, she admired him as being the only force she had to really consider seriously in her calculations, but that would not prevent her from hating him. Wisdom told her to put him forever out of her way, for something whispered to her that the unconscious man on the bed would keep on, like an unrelenting Nemesis.

But a curious contraction stirred her heart-strings as she gazed at the strong features. What caused it she knew not, but instead of hatred against him she felt the hot blood surge into her eyes. Confused and at a loss, she turned away, not knowing why her pulses throbbed with such exquisite pain. Her tense gaze had possibly recalled the wandering consciousness of the prostrate man, for he opened his eyes and gazed vaguely about.

Tinker gave a cry and sprang forward. The deep eyes gleamed with momentary joy and relief as they recognised the lad's; they swung again and gazed steady for a moment into the strangely-softened eyes of the woman, but unconsciousness again stepped in claiming them, and they dropped as the reeling mind once more wandered.

Yvonne stumbled with a strange dizziness from the room, passing the returning Hendricks as she did so.

"Give him one of the tablets in the jar every ten minutes until he has had six," she said thickly. "He will sleep deeply, and in the morning be none the worse for his fall."

Hendricks nodded. He was surprised at her voice, which was usually so clear, but although an indulgent and kind mistress, Yvonne ruled with a stern hand, and he dared not question her. He hurried in and found the elder man bending over Blake with a cynical smile on his thin lips.

Tinker was still kneeling beside the bed, chafing Blake's wrists, and paid no attention as Yvonne's uncle spoke.

"I thought my niece the one exception among women," he drawled cynically, as Hendricks approached the bed. "But alas! I see she has wandered from the strictly safe paths."

"How do you mean, sir?" asked Hendricks.

"My boy," drawled the other, "she is falling in love with our attractive-looking friend on the bed! She doesn't know it herself yet, or it wouldn't have shown in her eyes; but she will find it out before long. I think—yes, I decidedly think—Hendricks, I should be doing a very wise thing if I took matters in my own hands and assisted our prostrate friend on his journey to the other world, but—well! I have seen my adorable niece in a few tempers, and I don't think I'll risk it. Give him the stuff as she directs, Hendricks. Perhaps she may persuade him to join us—who knows?"

He strolled from the room with the cynical smile still on his lips, and languidly drew out his cigarette-case as he finished speaking.

He had spoken in an inconsequent drawl, but his eyes hardened when he got into the passage, and his jaw set firmly as he quickened his steps and hastened to the laboratory.

Yvonne sat before the desk, her chin resting on her hand and a far-away look in her eyes.

She glanced unseeingly at her uncle as he entered, but the expression of his face drew her quickly back to the present.

"What is it?" she asked, reading the look in his eyes.

"You've made a big mistake!" he snapped, as he dropped into a chair opposite her. "It's a mistake you'll live to regret! Mark my words!"

"To what do you refer?" she asked coolly.

"Why, to this man Blake, of course. Are you so confident of your own powers that you think you can turn him loose again? If you are, I'm not; and I think you should consider me and the others in the matter. You yourself laid down the strict discipline and rules by which we should operate, and on that basis I threw in my lot with you. But what is the result—you yourself are the first one to break them."

"In what way, might I inquire, have I broken any of the rules of the circle?"

"By allowing this man to live, of course. Also keeping that boy here. You don't seem to realise that this man Blake is the cleverest detective living. He solves problems in the same way in which you create them. For Heaven's sake can't you see the risk?"

"Listen, uncle," replied Yvonne calmly. "Don't get excited. As for breaking any rules I may have made, I haven't done so. Be good enough to leave matters in my hands. I assure you, I know what I am doing. As for this man Blake—poof!"—and she snapped her fingers in disdain—"he's not half as clever as you think. Everybody weaves a halo around his head because he had been successful; but wait, he hasn't had methods like mine to combat. I haven't any intention of allowing him to go free—nor the boy, either. What I shall eventually do with them I don't know yet; possibly I will follow your suggestion, but in the meantime I propose removing them from here to the yacht, and will take them to the island. Afterwards I will decide."

"Very well," replied Graves moodily. "Of course, you do as you think best; but again I say he ought to be put aside while we have him. When will you take him to the yacht?" he continued.

"In a day or two. I'm going to London tomorrow to make another attempt to go through his desk. He must have notes, and I want to know if possible, just what Bechstein's condition is. My information led me to believe he would be forced into bankruptcy, but he is still holding on. I will dress as the boy again. It seemed to work pretty well last time," she smiled.

Meanwhile, Hendricks had been working over the unconscious Blake, whose regular breathing indicated a natural slumber.

He administered the last tablet, and after carefully locking the steel door, joined the others in the laboratory.

Tinker pulled up a chair, and with anxious eyes watched the rise and fall of Blake's chest all through the long hours of the night.

***

About ten the next morning a big, grey motor pulled up in Baker Street, and the driver, who descended, looked extremely like Tinker.

At any rate, the casual observer would have thought so, for he ran up the steps and quickly fitted the key to the lock, throwing open the door with a familiar air.

He hastened down the passage and into the consulting-room, but pulled up sharply as he saw the figure of a man sitting in a chair.

Before the lad had time to speak, the visitor had swung round, and the disguised Yvonne's heart jumped as she recognised Bechstein.

"Did you wish to see Mr. Blake?" ventured Yvonne, in as good an imitation of Tinker's voice as was possible.

"Yes," replied the jeweller. "I had an appointment with him this morning. But who are you—his assistant?"

"Yes," answered Yvonne, realising from his question that he had never seen Tinker, and, that if she was careful she might gain valuable information from the unexpected encounter.

"He has been unavoidably detained," she went on. "But can I do anything for you, sir?"

Bechstein grunted.

"I don't imagine you know anything about the matter!" he snorted ungraciously. "My name's Bechstein, and Mr. Blake said he might have some progress to report this morning."

"On the contrary," said Yvonne boldly. "Mr. Blake confides fully in me. He is working on your case, Mr. Bechstein, but I am sorry to say we have nothing definite as yet. Er— it was rather urgent, wasn't it?"

"My heavens—yes," groaned Bechstein, mopping his brow. "He knows I can't hang out much longer if it isn't recovered soon. Have you any idea when he'll be back?" he asked, his face breaking into anxious lines.

"No, not exactly," replied Yvonne, dropping her lids to hide the gleam of satisfaction in her eyes, as she saw her victim squirm. "You see, he's working on it now, and won't be back until he has something definite to report. Perhaps he will be back this evening. You might ring up on the phone, in any event."

"All right, I will," grunted Bechstein moodily, as he rose.

Yvonne turned to the desk as the door closed behind him. She had really gained, by a fortunate accident, the information she needed, but would run through Blake's papers while she had the opportunity. Another such chance might not occur again. She had reached the desk, and was leaning over it when the bedroom door opened. Her head dropped as she looked up, but she gasped with relief as she saw the intruder was only the big hound. She would send him back to the bedroom.

Moving over to the dog, who stood gazing at her, she leaned down and patted his head.

Pedro sniffed the clothes in a curious manner. That they were Tinker's he knew, but the one who wore them he knew was not his young master. The intelligent beast worried over the master, and, lifting his head, gazed with a puzzled expression at Yvonne.

He was unable to solve the mystery, but his instinct evidently told him there was something wrong.

He resisted Yvonne's efforts to push him in the bedroom, and gently and firmly forced her back to a chair. Yvonne grew nervous as she saw the dog's persistency. She had her revolver, but dared not use it in the room. Leaning down, she laughed and patted Pedro, rising as she did so. Pedro submitted to her strokings, but when she rose he put up one big paw and pushed her back.

Yvonne realised the situation was desperate. She must do something soon to outwit the dog. If anyone came they would at once see something was wrong, and complications might arise.

Again she tried to get up; but as the dog once more pushed her back her face paled as the sound of a motor came from outside, and a moment later hurried footsteps came down the passage.

Who could it be? If it was someone who knew the real Tinker, the fact that Pedro was holding her forcibly in the chair would at once give her away.

Pedro also heard the steps. With a deep bay he dashed to the door as the handle turned.

It was a slender chance, but Yvonne seized it. Jumping up, she dashed madly for the bedroom, and just managed to close the door as Pedro bounded back.

She stood panting, and looked for some way out. Voices reached her from the outer room, and as Yvonne recognised them, her eyes dilated with fear.

Feverishly she turned like a hunted animal. On came the footsteps straight towards the bedroom, and, with a sharp cry as the handle turned, she dashed for the half open window, and half rolled, half fell through it to the street.

The Eleventh Chapter
Blake and Tinker Escape

YVONNE'S tablets had worked as she had prophesied, and Blake woke early the next morning feeling almost his old self. His head was still sore where he had hit it in falling, but, otherwise, he felt fairly fit.

Tinker's eyes were drooping with weariness but the tired lad forgot his weariness, as he saw Blake smile in the old rational way.

"I thought it was a dream, Tinker," he said, sitting up. "How did I get here? Ah, yes, I remember falling! I seemed to remember seeing you afterwards, but I'm not sure. But where are we? What place is this?" he added, darting his eyes about the room as he spoke.

Tinker detailed all that had happened to him up until Blake had been carried in unconscious.

"But how did they get you, guv'nor?" he asked, as he finished.

"It was my own fault," replied Blake savagely, as he explained to the lad how he had arrived at the Granger Farm, and what happened after. "I should have known such clever criminals would not depend on a flimsy old farmhouse for a retreat. I imagine we are in underground apartments," he went on, rising and making a tour of the room. "Yes, yes, stone walls, ceiling and floor; no windows, electrical ventilation. Very complete indeed; no hope here," he muttered, as he examined the massive steel door. "How many are there?" he asked, as he swung round.

"I don't know, guv'nor," answered Tinker, "I didn't see anyone, except the woman who brought the meals, until last night. There were two men and a woman there, but I know there is another man, because I saw him the night they brought me here."

"Ah," exclaimed Blake, nodding, "I remember now the woman—yes, I remember. Tinker, my lad! It is hopeless to try and break out of this prison; but we've got to get out some way. Things are serious—very. I begin to see things more clearly, and can now gauge the force we are up against."

"Yes, guv'nor—but how!?" inquired Tinker.

"We'll have to try strategy, that's all; and it may mean a big struggle. If there are only the two men we stand a chance, if we get them before they shoot, and, on the other hand, if there are more, or they shoot quickly, we are done for. However, that is a chance we've got to take."

The detective sank into a thoughtful silence, and Tinker waited patiently until that keen mind had devised some way out of their predicament.

"I've got it!" exclaimed Blake, breaking the silence. "Now, listen, Tinker!"

Rapidly he explained his plan, and Tinker nodded in understanding.

"It's risky," wound up Blake; "but it's the only way. If one of us gets through, he mustn't wait for the other, but must go as quickly as possible for help."

They shook hands silently, and Blake again lay down on the bed while Tinker prepared to carry out the scheme.

Blake closed his eyes in apparent unconsciousness while Tinker raised an unearthly din by banging at the steel door with a heavy, oaken stool.

Through the stone passage reverberated the noise, and a few moments later the slide was pushed open, Graves's face appeared in the opening, anger written on his countenance.

"Here what the——" he began; but Tinker cut him short.

"Quick!" he cried. "The guv'nor is not breathing like he was last night! There's been a big change!"

All of which was strictly true, but not in the way Graves thought. "Come and see what is the matter, please!"

"Oh, all right!" snapped the man. "I'll be back presently!"

He returned in a few moments with Hendricks, who carried the blue jar of tablets, and impatiently threw open the door.

"This man Blake is a nuisance," muttered Graves, as he walked over to the bed. "My advice should have been taken in the first place."

Neither of the men noticed Tinker walking quietly behind, still carrying the heavy, oaken stool, and still grumbling. Graves leaned over the bed.

He gave a startled cry as the apparently unconscious man seemed suddenly to turn into a galvanic battery.

Up shot his arm like a bar of iron, gripping unerringly at Graves's throat. Quickly Blake's body followed his arm, and, as the other gathered his wits together they gripped in deadly silence. Hendricks' jaw had dropped in astonishment at the sudden attack; but almost before Blake had seized Graves, Hendricks had instinctively turned.

He was just in time, for Tinker was leaping for him, the oaken stool upraised ready to strike.

Without a moment's hesitation Hendricks hurled the heavy blue jar at Tinker. Had it hit the lad it would have killed him at once; but glancing off the stool, it caught him in the side of the head. He staggered with the shock, and, as Hendricks leaped forward, Tinker found it was too close quarters to use the stool.

Dropping it, he grappled as the other reached him, and down they went, rolling over and over in the struggle until they brought up with a jerk against the other struggling pair.

Silently the quartet fought. Graves was a powerful man; but Blake's muscles were like steel springs, and it was evident that the detective was slowly overpowering his antagonist. But with the other two fortune lay the other way.

A sailor's life had made Hendricks accustomed to fighting, and he was a much more powerful man than the lad. Although Tinker fought gamely, he was still dizzy from the effects of the blow from the jar, and he gasped as he felt himself slowly giving in.

The struggle still hung in the balance. If Blake overpowered his man before Hendricks subdued Tinker, he could go to Tinker's assistance, and the day was theirs.

On the other hand, if Hendricks succeeded in beating Tinker before Graves gave in he could attack Blake, and thus win the day. All four combatants realised this, and none more so than Tinker, who, knowing he must inevitably go under, devoted all his remaining strength toward retaining his senses, and keeping Hendricks occupied until Blake could come. Graves was doing the same on his part, and the grim race went on as the panting men struggled for the mastery.

But hard as he fought, Tinker felt the iron grip tightening on his throat. His eyes blurred as he choked. Valiantly he gave one more supreme effort; but the ever-tightening grip did not relax. Slowly his head dropped; everything reeled madly around; his eyes closed, and he was dimly aware of a crushing weight falling on him as he sank into unconsciousness.

That weight which Tinker vaguely thought was his death, was in reality Hendricks crashing down, as Blake, having overcome Graves, leaped to Tinker's assistance. Hendricks released his hold on Tinker's throat, and turned and grappled with Blake; but the latter had a steel-like grip of the sailor's throat, and, as the detective planted his knee in the small of Hendricks' back, he sank with a fierce cry of pain.

Blake was taking no chances, and, before attending unconscious Tinker, he securely bound and gagged Graves and Hendricks, ripping up the sheets for his purpose.

After being satisfied that they were now incapable of mischief, he turned to Tinker, and soon had the lad on his feet.

"Crikey, guv'nor, that was a close one!" said the lad, ruefully rubbing his neck. "I thought he had me—certain."

"He nearly did," laughed the still panting Blake, "But come, we have no time to waste! Others may arrive soon, and Heaven knows how long it may take us to get out of this place!"

"What will you do with these two?" asked Tinker.

"We'll leave them here for the present, and lock them in. If, as I think, the steel door locks with a secret combination, the serving woman won't know what it is, and, as they are well gagged, they can't tell her. You don't look very presentable in those clothes," he smiled grimly; "but I hope to be able to personally secure your own ere long. We have still got the chief one to get yet, and I think I can guess where that one is, since she isn't here. What a wonderful woman!" he muttered to himself. "And what a pity!"

As Blake had thought, the steel door was worked by a combination. Hastily examining it he closed the door, and swung it round.

"That will hold them until we come back," he said, as he changed the combination to a different cipher.

The detective made a rapid survey of the different rooms as they made their way down the passage, and his eyes were filled with admiration when they reached the stairs leading up to the stone exit.

"Marvellous!" he muttered. "And to think she has conceived all this without my being aware of her existence! What a brain—what thoroughness! Truly, my unknown friend, you give the chase a decided zest!"

A short examination by Blake discovered the button which released the stone door. He pressed it, and located the outer one before allowing the big stone to swing to.

Making for the door he led the way over the open into the woods, and kept on across country at a rapid pace until Colby was reached.

It was the work of a few moments to secure the big grey car and start the engine.

Tinker refrained from speaking as Blake sent the machine forward at a bound, for he knew the detective's moods too well to break in on his line of thought when the deep eyes held the look they did at present.

Blake certainly never drove more recklessly than he did on that journey to London.

Through villages he dashed, utterly indifferent to speed laws or the indignant remarks the outraged farmers shouted after him.

Turning into Baker Street, Tinker expected to see him slow up, but the sight of another grey car outside his apartments only spurred him on. He did not slacken speed until within a short distance of the door, and, sharply throwing out the clutch, he put on the brake, skidding wildly into the kerb and stopping a bare inch from the other car.

Without a word he dashed out and up the steps, followed by Tinker.

Down the passage went the hurried steps, and, for once disregarding Pedro's demonstrations, he headed for the bedroom door, the handle of which his keen eyes had seen move as he entered the consulting-room.

"Quick, Tinker; follow me!" cried Blake, as he opened the bedroom door and saw a figure disappear through the window.

On he rushed, following the fugitive through the window, with Tinker and Pedro tumbling after him.

Yvonne, for she was the fugitive, dashed on, and gained her car, the engine of which was still running. She swung the wheel and started to move as Blake gained the sidewalk and came on in pursuit.

"Stop!" he cried, pulling out a revolver and levelling it; but Yvonne leaned low as the car gained speed. Swinging it straight into the road, she sat up and pulled out her own revolver.

Blake was firing low in order to try and hit the tyres, and Yvonne could hear the lead pattering on the machine. Swinging around, she took careful aim, and through luck or cleverness, her bullet reached her mark in one of Blake's tyres.

With a muttered exclamation Blake dashed to his car and began to rapidly unbuckle his spare wheel. Tinker was filled with amazement at the astonishing reproduction of himself in the other car, but, as he hastened to assist Blake, he refrained from asking questions when he saw the detective's jaw, as, for the second time in twenty-four hours, a silvery, mocking laugh floated back.

The Twelfth Chapter
Blake and Tinker Again Prisoners

BLAKE had spent a small fortune in having a motor built according to his own designs, and many times had the wisdom of his action been proved, but never more so than at the present time, for no ordinary car could have withstood the racking pace at which the detective started in pursuit.

As the new wheel had been clamped home, he turned and ordered Pedro back to watch the house, and jumped, without further word, for the wheel, leaving Tinker to get aboard as best he could. Into the tonneau tumbled the lad, and when his tangled legs had separated, climbed over the seat and sat beside Blake.

For perhaps the first time the lad realised that they were on no ordinary chase.

He had never remembered seeing quite such a steely look in Blake's eyes before.

Back over the road which they had travelled a little earlier went the big car.

Once again the villagers gazed after the flying monster with astonishment and anger, but Blake was indifferent to everything but one idea.

The slender thread which he had followed had developed into a strong cord with amazing rapidity, and his sole object was to run to earth the mysterious power which had flouted him several times since he had taken the case. He was not accustomed to such things, and the fact that he felt confident it was a woman's brain which had devised such baffling methods made matters worse.

But even in his tense condition he smiled in grim admiration. His opponent was worthy of his greatest skill, and never before had Blake played the game with greater zest. The boldness of snapping her fingers at him by returning the ten-pound note had put Blake on his mettle, but those two silvery, mocking laughs had gone deep. Nothing now would make him stop until he had the author of them under his hand.

It was early afternoon when they pounded through Colby, and Blake kept on, without stopping, toward the Granger Farm.

They were fully a mile from the road which led up to it, when Blake, gave a smothered exclamation as a grey motor turned out of it into the main road. It contained three occupants, and Blake knew Graves and Hendricks had been released. They had evidently caught sight of Blake, for they looked back steadily for a moment.

If the leading car had been an ordinary motor, Blake would have felt easy about overtaking it; but he had been only a few moments clamping on the new wheel, and the fact that it had reached the farm so quickly showed that it must be of high power.

If it was possible for his own car to go any faster, it did so, and, outside of Brooklands, probably there never was such a race between two powerful motors as took place that day between the two grey cars.

Through the afternoon that race kept on. Both drivers were giving their cars all they could stand, and it said much for the equality of both machines when three hours left them almost as they had started.

Blake had gained a trifle, but only a trifle. He could have perhaps gone a little faster, but man and machine, through constant association, had become almost one, and the detective knew any more strain on this finely-tuned engine would send it flying to pieces in all directions.

Tinker sat in silent intensity through that long chase, and not until dusk shut in did he move.

Reaching down, he pressed the button which lit the brilliant road lamps, and a gleam ahead told them the others had done likewise.

Then he refilled the petrol tank, which was under the seat.

As the darkness fell the houses grew scarcer, the country wilder, and a salt tang told them they were near the sea.

Another hour passed before the sea appeared, but when it did it met them with a rush.

Over the brow of a hill raced both cars, and as they did so, below them appeared a small bay. Close in shore lay a brilliantly-lighted yacht, and, on drawing nearer, Blake saw that it was moored to a tiny wharf.

A sudden stop ahead brought Blake up with a rush beside the leading car. Quickly throwing on the brakes, he leaped out, followed by Tinker.

He saw the reason of the stop as he drew near, for one of the tyres had a gaping hole in its flattened surface.

Both Blake and Tinker knew they must act quickly if they were to secure their quarry, for the sound of shots would bring assistance from the yacht to their enemy.

"Shoot to hit!" jerked out Blake, as he levelled his own revolver and fired. A cry rang out; Hendricks dropped. Tinker fired, and a crash told them his bullet had gone wide, hitting the windshield. But Graves and Yvonne were now firing rapidly. Yvonne had secured the revolver with a silencer attached, and its bullets whined past in sinister silence.

"Catch her arms and hold her!" cried Blake, as he dashed forward with bent head.

Tinker did as he was bid, but Yvonne was too elusive for him. Tinker had secured many women since he had been with Blake, but never one like this, and he gasped as his hands clutched the empty air.

Once again that maddening laugh rang out, and Blake sprang with extraordinary savageness at the still shooting Graves as he heard it.

Graves had had quite enough experience of Blake's powers as a fighter at the farm, but the detective came with such a rush that he was forced to drop his revolver and grapple. As man to man, the result of that fight was a foregone conclusion. Yvonne dared not shoot, if she could, for fear of hitting her uncle, and now it was impossible, for Tinker had succeeded in gripping her arms.

Blake sank his fingers into his antagonist's throat and pressed them deep with a savage grip. He intended wasting no time in subduing Graves, and he was on a fair way to succeed, when Hendricks, who, up to now, had lain quiet where he had fallen, stumbled to his knees. Tinker gave a cry of warning as the sailor picked up his revolver and gained his feet, but it was no avail. As Blake turned to meet the new danger, Hendricks struck, and the detective dropped like a stone.

Tinker left Yvonne, and dashed forward, but he was soon overpowered and bound.

The two prisoners were packed into the tonneau of Blake's car, and Yvonne drove it at a slow pace down to the wharf.

As they were carried aboard, Tinker recognised the man who had conducted him to his prison at the farm. Several others, dressed in seamen's uniforms, stood around, but he had no time to see anything else. They were quickly carried down a companionway and through a brilliantly-lighted saloon to the door of a cabin.

One of the uniformed sailors threw this open, and the captives were tossed unceremoniously into the bunks.

Blake appeared still unconscious, but Tinker lay back gloomily as the door closed and the lock clicked.

***

Outside in the luxurious saloon, Yvonne leaned against the table while Hendricks' wound was attended to.

When it had been bound up and his arm strapped to his side—for it was in the shoulder—two of the sailors assisted him to his cabin.

Captain Vaughan had retired to the bridge to get the yacht under way, and Yvonne and her uncle were left alone in the saloon.

"Well," drawled Graves, "I trust you are satisfied? If you had done as I wished this would never have happened. It's the closest shave I ever saw, and if Hendricks hadn't come to just in time we would all have been prisoners in the tonneau of this confounded Blake's car."

"I had no chance to express my opinion of your intelligence when you told me in the car how he escaped," replied Yvonne icily. "But I will do so now. You and Hendricks must be about as clever as a piece of wood. Oh, you babies, to be taken in as you were!"

"You would have been yourself!" snapped Graves sulkily.

"You know better than that, uncle," replied Yvonne. "Heavens, what madness to go in as you did! You who held him up as such a wizard, to trust yourself that way. Did you forget who he was? Didn't you know if there was one chance of escape, Sexton Blake would seize it as soon as he awoke? You see now that he did. But I shall take it upon myself this time to see that he doesn't get another chance."

"What do you propose doing?" inquired Graves.

"I'm going to offer him the chance of joining us. With him we could achieve anything. If he refuses—well, he'll have to go. He's too dangerous to be free!"

"You'd better marry him," drawled Graves, his old manner returning. "You'd make a nice king and queen. I'd certainly——"

"Stop!" exclaimed Yvonne, going deathly pale. "Don't take a liberty, uncle! I won't permit it!"

Graves flushed as she spoke; for although he was older, and her uncle as well, he stood in awe of Yvonne, as did all who surrounded her. She dominated her associates by sheer force of character, and her word was never questioned.

"Well, don't get wild," replied Graves, "I didn't mean anything."

"Very well; but kindly remember not to make such a remark again. And now leave me, please," she added wearily. "Send two men to bring Sexton Blake here, and don't allow anyone to disturb me until I have finished."

Graves departed to do her bidding, and Yvonne sank into a deep chair and awaited her prisoner's arrival.

The Thirteenth Chapter
Yvonne's Offer to Blake—The End

TINKER had fallen into a deep sleep, and did not hear the cabin door open to admit the two sailors who had been sent for Blake.

They carried the still unconscious detective outside, and entered the saloon.

He came round under the invigorating effect of some raw spirit, and blinked around dazedly as the brilliant lights hit his eyes. His hands were tied behind him, but otherwise he was free to move. He leaned against the table as the sailors took their departure, and not until then did he see the woman in the chair.

Long and silently did those two look at one another.

All about them was the magnificent saloon, its further corners softened by shaded lights. Only over the gleaming white of the silver-covered tablecloth did the lights shine with unrestrained brilliancy. The beautiful oak and black palm woodwork gleamed somberly amongst the rich upholstering, and underfoot the deep carpet increased the restful atmosphere of the saloon.

The beautiful, bronze-haired woman, sitting in the deep chair was a fitting decoration to its harmony, and the lack of a single jarring note reflected credit on the woman who had designed it.

Overhead sounded the occasional sound of feet as the sailors obeyed the commands of the captain, but both occupants of that deep-toned saloon were too intent on the coming test of wits to hear.

Yvonne's eyes dropped as she rose and walked toward the detective.

Stopping in front of him, and placing her hands behind her back, she smiled; and Blake, as he looked into her eyes, was compelled to smile in return.

"I must congratulate you," he said, bowing. "You have succeeded, so far, most admirably."

"Why the emphasis on the 'so far'?" she smiled back.

"Do you consider the game played out yet?" inquired Blake, also smiling.

"Not quite," she replied. "But I'm afraid you must confess the next move lies with me, Mr. Blake."

"At the present moment I must confess it does. But one never knows when the tide may turn," answered Blake.

Had she seen his hands stealthily reach out behind him and pull towards him one of the shining knives which lay on the table in anticipation of the coming meal, she would have seen that, as usual, he had seized the first opportunity of turning the tide.

"I'm afraid there is little chance of it turning this time," she replied saucily. "But I wish to make a serious proposition to you, Mr. Blake."

Blake glanced in puzzlement, as Yvonne half turned away, her face changing from white to red, and back to white again. He kept silent, however, and awaited her reply, although his hands were all the time cautiously working as industriously as his bonds would allow.

Again Yvonne began to speak, and her voice was strangely unsteady for one of her assurance.

"I—I——," she began hesitatingly. "Oh, it is very hard to say!" she went on hurriedly. "But, believe me, I have never before talked to any man, or permitted any man to talk to me in such a way. But you must realise that now I have you in my power I cannot permit you to go free and always menace my plans."

Blake's look of wonderment deepened as she spoke, for he had no idea of what was to follow.

"You must be put out of the way!" continued Yvonne, her head still averted. "But there's one alternative."

"What's that?" asked Blake quietly, as she paused.

"It is that you join us—join us in every sense of the word! Wait, hear me out!" she cried, raising her hand as Blake started to reply. "They had not erred in their estimate of your cleverness," she continued; "but I am clever, too. I have already made a large fortune, but with you we could have anything we wished, and who would say 'Nay'? I am lonely! Oh, can't you understand?"

Yvonne turned away in shy embarrassment. Blake forgot the criminal, and saw only the lovely young woman who had offered herself to him.

"I am sorry," he said gently, "but it is impossible! My duty lies in stamping out crime, not promoting it. And my wife—if I ever have one—must not be on the side of crime."

Yvonne swung round sharply as Blake spoke the last sentence. The blood departed from her face, leaving it like marble. Her wonderful eyes gleamed like flashing points, her breast heaved with pent-up emotion.

"You—you—I hate you!" she said, in a voice of deadly calm. "Do you know what you have done? I have humbled myself! I a woman of birth, wealth, brains, humbled myself to you, and you throw my gift back in my face! For that, if even for nothing else, you will die!"

Blake stood like a carven piece of granite as she spoke intensely. It was an uncomfortable position, but he deemed silence the wiser plan; and besides, he wasn't so sure about being put aside so easily as he felt the cords drop from his hands.

Yvonne approached nearer. Every moment she seemed to be getting angrier at the blow her pride had received. Finally verbal chastisement failed to satisfy her, and she leaned forward, lifting her hand to strike the detective. Through the air swished the white, jewelled arm, but it never reached its mark, for an arm of steel shot out and grasped the white wrist, and before the astounded Yvonne could cry out Blake's other hand covered her mouth as she struggled in his arms.

"Be quiet'!" he breathed. "I've got the whip-hand, and I mean to use it! You claim to have brains, if so, you must use them. You are a woman, and I don't want to use force. Pass me the word you will not give the alarm, and I will release you."

"I promise!" she nodded; and Blake, knowing she would keep her word, released her.

"That's better!" he exclaimed, as she dropped into the chair. "Now we can talk comfortably. Firstly, by the way, I haven't the honour of knowing your name. Permit me to formally introduce myself although it seems unnecessary, as you already know my name—Sexton Blake, mademoiselle, at your service," smiled Blake bowing.

"Charmed!" replied Yvonne rising, and returning the bow with mock politeness. "Mademoiselle Yvonne is honoured!"

"Am I not to know the other name as well?" asked Blake.

"Not yet!" she replied maliciously.

"Well, that's too bad," he went on again, smiling, "It forces me to the exertion of finding it out."

'HELLO! BLAKE! CALLED THE INSPECTOR. "DID YOU WISH TO SPEAK TO ME?"
"LONG AND SILENTLY DID THOSE TWO LOOK AT ONE ANOTHER."
"AH! A THOUSAND PARDONS". BLAKE EXCLAIMED.

"And I believe you will!" cut in Yvonne viciously.

"Well, we will let it pass. As I said, firstly Mademoiselle Yvonne, I arrest you, in the name of the King, for the robbery, from a Bond Street jewellery establishment, of a valuable pearl necklace!" and he added, in mock seriousness "Let me warn you, that anything you say may be used against you!"

"Thank you!" replied Yvonne, "But how do you propose to take me to prison?"

"Easiest thing in the world," answered Blake. "You'll see when the time comes!" he added, dropping his bantering tone.

"Tell me, please, how did you trace me?" asked Yvonne.

"It would be very foolish for me to tell you my methods," laughed Blake. "You might turn detective when you get out of this and take all my clients away."

"I cannot see where I left any tracks," mused Yvonne.

"You didn't; at least, none that could possibly be eliminated," broke in Blake.

Silence reigned for some moments.

Yvonne was sunk in pensive thought, while Blake's mind worked rapidly, devising some plan to free Tinker and get past the sailors with his prisoner. A plan had just occurred to him when Yvonne spoke again.

"I wonder if you'd care to hear why I took up this profession?" she asked.

"I would, indeed," replied Blake; "if it won't take, too long."

"It won't. I'll be brief."

Rapidly she ran over the story of the mine swindle which had killed her mother, and sent her into the world, her heart seething with the thoughts of revenge.

Blake listened silently as she unfolded the story, and his lips shut in a straight line as she reached the time when she landed in England prepared for her work.

"I had kept track of Vineburg all these years," she went on, "and when he left Australia after a crooked deal on the racetrack, I followed him. He took the name of Bechstein, and with the money he had made bought a jewelry establishment in Bond Street. For five years I watched him while I perfected my training, and when I was ready to strike, I struck. I took him first because he was the chief mover in the deal."

"I'm astounded at your story!" remarked Blake. "And I believe it. Bechstein came to me, and asked me to take up the case. Naturally, I did so; but had I known his full history, I would not have done so. But having started off on the case, I must finish it. You have done wrong, and have broken the law. I am not a preacher," he smiled; "but it is not for each man to take the law in his own hands. If that were the case, anarchy and chaos would reign. I don't doubt that Bechstein has done you a great wrong; but if he kept within man's law—well, rest assured he will one day be fully punished. However, after what you tell me, I will not arrest you. The actual crime part is for Scotland Yard to take up. I will not start them on the case; but if Bechstein does, I must give evidence. That is all I can promise you. What I must insist upon, however, is the return of the necklace. That I insist on, for I cannot permit myself to enter the word failure in my index."

"What if I refuse?" asked Yvonne, looking up.

"You won't," answered Blake quietly. "But if you did, I'd have to re-arrest you, and take you with me."

"Do you realise that as soon as some supplies arrive, the yacht will at once put out to sea?"

"That makes no difference. I will take you back, nevertheless."

"I believe you would," she muttered softly. "We'll call a truce, Mr. Blake," she added, rising, "I'll return you the pearls, and for tonight we will be friends."

"With pleasure," smiled Blake. "But I must ask you to pledge your word you will communicate with no one while you go to fetch the pearls."

"Would you take my word for that?" she asked curiously.

"Yes; in your case."

Yvonne departed, and returned shortly, with the magnificent string of gems.

"Here they are," she laughed.

"Thank you!" answered Blake, as Yvonne moved to the table, and poured out some wine.

"To our next meeting!" she flashed, lifting her glass.

Blake took the challenge, and drank the toast.

Five minutes later, with the released Tinker following, he strode through the hostile stares of astonishment of Yvonne's associates, and passed over the side.

He pulled up the motor at the top of the hill, and gazed back.

Below the brilliantly-lighted yacht was backing slowly from the tiny pier. Overhead the stars shone in pale splendour, and all around the trees banked in a sombre background.

"What a pity!" he muttered, as the yacht's head came round. "What a brilliant mind, and what a detective she would make! To our next meeting—eh?" he breathed softly. "It promises well, mademoiselle." And, strangely stirred, Blake threw in the clutch; and sent the car bounding toward London.

***

"Tell me, guv'nor," asked Tinker, as they sat before the fire several hours later, "how did you pick up the trail of the pearls. I've puzzled over the points you told me, but I couldn't make anything of it."

"You hardly could," laughed Blake. "It was a case strictly out of the normal; but it proves what I have always contended—that the present-day investigator of crime must keep ahead in every line of science. But I'll show you how I followed it up.

"You remember," went on the detective, puffing thoughtfully at his pipe, "how I told you the case narrowed down—either Bechstein, or one other thing?"

Tinker nodded, and Blake continued:

"Well, I had to eliminate Bechstein from the matter, and only the other thing remained. You remember only three people had examined the necklace. It stood to reason that some time must be spent if designs were to be prepared for a substitute. Everything pointed to that being an impossibility. How then could a design have been obtained? you ask.

"Only one way is known which will give an instantaneous reproduction of an article, and that is photography. But ordinary photography would not do, and, besides, a camera would be too bulky. The next point was—what kind of photography would do? Only one, and that was so new to science as to be still in the experimental stage. It was hardly probable that any criminal would know enough, and adopt it. Still, after hours of deduction, everything pointed to that.

"True, it was a weak thread to work on, but in the absence of any other it had to be utilised. Consequently, working on that hypothesis when, if so, had the necklace been photographed? As each of the three had only visited Bechstein's once it was obvious that two of the three had been working in collusion—one to take the embossed photograph, and one to make the exchange.

"Sir George Wallington was beyond suspicion. Only the other two remained, and it was necessary to search every detail of their visit.

"Bechstein's office, where the necklace was viewed, is fairly dark, and for a detailed photograph, an artificial light must be used. The camera, in order to be invisible, and yet handy for use, must be secreted in a place which would hide it, and yet bring it freely into play. Bechstein accidentally noticed what he thought was a flash of sun on the gold head of the supposed American's walking-stick. I read a different meaning. What better place could be devised for the purpose than the handle of a walking-stick?

"In it could be placed a small camera suitable for embossed photography made specially for the purpose. The sudden flash was the artificial light used for the purpose. That, naturally, was a risk, but not as great a risk as one would think, for, unless one was looking straight at it, the flash would be over so soon that it would be hard to locate it exactly. And, of course, there are now several different methods of applying a flash without the attendant smoke of the old powders, which would be out of the question in a case of this kind."

Tinker's eyes glistened with excitement as Blake paused to relight his pipe.

"Then," continued the detective, "we have in support, the fact that the man was the second caller. Then came the woman. Did she get an opportunity to make the exchange while there? Yes, if she were clever enough; for to allay any suspicion she went to the trouble of purchasing a fairly expensive necklace, and while the jeweller turned his back to get a box for it, if she were quick, and had the nerve, she could do it. And you have seen whether she has the nerve or not," he added grimly.

"The next step was to trace the identity of both man and woman. There I was at a loss. The nun's visit puzzled me, and I did not connect it with the case at first. I thought she might be a masquerading swindler; but when you went in pursuit and did not return, and later in the evening I found the ten-pound note under the door, I knew I had been watched, and that some powerful, unknown force was working against me.

"What had been puzzling me about the embossed photograph of the necklace was how it could be enlarged to the exact scale of the object photographed. I had been working on this same line myself, but as yet had discovered no method.

"In a photographic journal I came across a most exhaustive article on this point, and saw that it was entirely possible. Could there be any connection? Hardly. Still, it must be followed up. I told you of my interview with the editor, and how the trail led me to Barnesley in Surrey. From that point, you know the rest, and can see the line I followed. But we should not have fared nearly so well, and the chase would have lasted much longer if Pedro hadn't taken a hand."

The big hound raised his head as Blake spoke his name, and rising, struck his cold muzzle against the detective's knee.

"Yes," he went on, "it was evident to me that Pedro had been keeping her here by force, for otherwise, he would not have bayed as he did."

"I wish I had my clothes back," remarked Tinker.

"You'll get them," laughed Blake. "Mademoiselle Yvonne promised to send them, and she'll keep her word."

"Bechstein will be glad to get his pearls back, won't he, guv'nor?" continued Tinker.

"Yes, I imagine he will," replied Blake curtly, for he had not told Tinker what Yvonne had confided to him. "I see he has been here tonight," he added: "I noticed his card on the desk as I came in. He probably came to inquire what progress we had made. And now, my lad, let's to bed. We will call on Bechstein early in the morning, and give him the pearls."

Rising, they turned out the lights, and Tinker did not hear the muttered remark which Blake made as he passed into his room. Had he done so, he would have wondered as to its meaning, for it was:

"To our next meeting."

***

But Bechstein was not to receive the pearls. The next morning when Blake and Tinker arrived they found a curious crowd about the door, and, on forcing his way through, Blake was informed by a policeman that Mr. Bechstein had shot himself in the night, and from a short note which he had left they had gathered that it had been caused by financial worries.

Blake and Tinker turned away, and left the place to the police.

Blake's idea, which happened to be correct, was that Bechstein had called to see if anything had been discovered about the necklace, and, not finding Blake at home, had given up hope. Had he waited, as Blake had told him to do until the banks opened the next day, which was Bechstein's final day of grace, he would have weathered the storm, for Blake and Tinker had arrived at Bond Street long before the time.

But Fate had decreed otherwise, and by Bechstein's own hand had Yvonne been revenged.

The UNION JACK. 1d
SEXTON BLAKE
YVONNE-THE ADVENTURESS
WHEN GREEK MEETS GREEK
OR, THE BULLION THIEVES
NO. 488. NEW SERIES]
February 15th, 1913.
[EVERY THURSDAY.

<table>
<tr><td>With this issue is presented No. 2 of our wonderful soul-stirring new series of Yarns which open to public view Sexton Blake's startling adventures, while opposed to that mistress of science—Yvonne.</td><td></td><td>These Yarns are confidently recommended for readers of <u>all</u> ages and of <u>either</u> sex! Every care has been taken to make them equally attractive to Old and Young alike, and the Skipper is satisfied that they really are so!</td></tr>
</table>

Prologue
Dr. Huxton Rymer Tries His Fate—His Success

IF you know Puerto Costa, that dirty, smelling, sandy, fascinating tropical port, which boasts a really fine harbour, you will know the main street which runs at a distance parallel to the moon-shaped harbour, the proudest possession of the tiny republic of Salvarita.

If you know this street, you will know, if you have poked beneath the surface, the disreputable district which stretches between street and harbour, and if you have gone very deeply into the submerged life of the cosmopolitan port, you will also have more or less knowledge of those unspeakable dens of iniquity which fringe the harbour—their ever-open doors, throwing a constantly beckoning light to the newly-arrived sailor, and their dark, surrounding alleys forming a convenient spot into which the victim is tossed when its night-born vultures have finished with him.

In one of the lowest and filthiest of these dens, if there is any grade in them, sat a big, strong-jawed man. His seedy appearance created no desire in the many sinister, appraising eyes of the other occupants of the den.

He was silently cursed as a hated Gringo, but although his soft felt hat almost covered his face, his visible jaw created respect amongst the dusky horde, and he was left in peace.

For several nights running had the man occupied the same seat in the same den.

The first night of his arrival, a big black man had questioned his presence in no uncertain terms; but one piercing look of contempt from the Gringo's intensely peculiar eyes had sufficed to silence him and send him slinking away with a sickly grin.

Since then he had been unmolested, which evidently suited his purpose.

Such was the appearance of Dr. Huxton Rymer on a certain night in Puerto Costa.

On this, the fifth night, he had ordered his drink of "white eye," that fiery, maddening drink of the native and the black, and had sat immovable as the motley, ever-changing crowd moved about him.

All nationalities were there, but blacks and *mestizos*—those of mixed Indian, Portuguese, Spanish, and African ancestry—predominated.

Idly they loafed from den to den, their bestial eyes seeking for an "honest man." Their quest was not for the same type of honest man for whom Diogenes searched, and they used no lantern to guide them. In their case an honest man represented one with money in his pocket, and brain-stealing "white eye" in his stomach.

Rymer sat unmoved throughout it all, his ears deaf to the quarrelling voices and the tinkle of a broken guitar, his eyes cast, apparently, into his half-filled glass.

But, though they knew it not, no man, no matter his origin or the colour of his skin, entered or departed than those all-seeing eyes did not search him absolutely with a glance of lightning rapidity.

For Dr. Huxton Rymer was decidedly "up against it." A little affair in New York had caused him to seek a more hospitable climate, especially after one Sexton Blake had arrived in the great American city.

Rymer, with his natural gift of "sangfroid," had taken the first steamer regardless of her destination. She happened to be bound for Salvarita, but not for the legal port of entry.

A large consignment of innocent-looking cases, marked "sewing machines" and "farming implements," had been landed at a solitary spot on the coast.

A sudden desire for agricultural pursuits seemed to seize a large portion of the populace, for they gathered at that lonely spot in large numbers, and eagerly seized upon the cases of ploughs, etc.

The shippers seemed to have made a sad mistake, for on being opened, the cases were found to contain many Mauser rifles and a large supply of cartridges.

But the peace-loving people had nobly swallowed their disappointment, and had shared the arms amongst themselves.

When the solitary passenger, Rymer, had seen their noble restraint in the face of disappointment, he had joined them.

Since they had guns, it seemed a pity not to use them. Consequently, a little shooting-party was organised, with the Government as the target, and, naturally, having shared their disappointment, Rymer had shared their deal.

Unfortunately, the shooting-party ended rather abruptly, for the Government had strenuously objected to being used as a target, and their reply had been very much to the point.

The noble-minded rifle-party had broken up in haste, and consequent on this, Rymer, almost penniless, had drifted to the river dens, there to seek fresh pegs by which to again, ascend to the roof of luxury which he loved so well.

Not until two half-drunken Spaniards entered did Rymer move. As they sat at the next table, he shifted carelessly, but when he had resettled himself, his head was sunk in obviously drunken slumber upon his drink-stained chest, albeit his ear was in a straight line with the adjoining table.

The two Spaniards called in loud voices for drinks, and their following conversation was more picturesque than interesting.

Rymer was looking upon his elaborate movement as wasted time, when the conversation veered to a topic which caused him to listen.

"So, Señor Alvarez, you will grace the president's ball with your presence tomorrow night?" remarked the elder of the two, a short, stout-bearded individual.

"*Si.* I go surely. I know none in the city but you, Señor Gomez, and I would meet some of the women for which it is famed."

"*Caramba*, you are sly dogs, you men from the *haciendas*! You have, then, a card?"

"*Si.* In my district, I am a strong supporter of the Government. I receive cards every year, but not for years have I been in Puerto Costa."

"Ha! Well, *amigo*, I trust you will enjoy it. For me, I am too old for such caperings. But come, we will make a night of it tonight. Let us go to the cards."

"Bueno!" grunted the younger, rising heavily.

Arm in arm they passed out of the door, but hardly had they been swallowed up in the sinister shadows before two of the villainous *habitués* of the den followed them. They, too, disappeared, and Rymer, stumbling to his feet, reeled out after them.

As the gloom enwrapped him, he dropped his staggering gait, and quickened his footsteps, closely dogging the pair ahead.

"It's a hundred to one chance," he muttered, "but you never can tell. Those two cut-throats had mischief in their eyes, and, who knows, something might fall my way, and, Heaven knows, I need it! Any way, it can't make things worse and in a week I'll be stony. Curse Sexton Blake. If ever I get him where I want him, Heaven help him!"

His eyes gleamed savagely in the darkness, and so absorbed was he that for a moment he did not notice that his quarry had disappeared. He hurried on, and coming to a dark, narrow lane, peered up. Far along hung a solitary red lantern, symbol of a gambling den, and against its dim reflection, Rymer could see several dark forms. Even as he looked, a smothered cry floated down to him, and the noise of a scuffle followed.

Drawing his revolver, and breaking into a run, Rymer dashed up the lane. As he had thought, the two men had left the den with the intention of attacking the two Spaniards, and had seized upon the dark lane as an opportune place.

The Spaniards were already on the ground when Rymer arrived, and the thieves were bending over them. The new-comer did not stand upon ceremony. Springing forward, and using the butt of his revolver, he struck with all his strength at one of them.

The thief had turned and risen in alarm, and Rymer's blow caught him with crushing force between the eyes. He dropped, and none too soon, for his companion, with a snarl, had drawn a knife, and was coming for Rymer.

Rymer dared not shoot except as a last resort, for a shot would bring dozens of the human vultures on the scene, and he would stand small chance of getting clear. He acted quickly and silently. His left hand shot forward, and grasped his adversary's wrist. Evading the man's attempt to retaliate by doing the same with his free hand, Rymer again brought the butt of his revolver into play. Twice he struck before the blow affected that hard skull, but his second attempt achieved his purpose, and the man dropped.

Sinking on his knees, Rymer opened the coat of the nearest Spaniard, A few moments' manipulation of the expert fingers sufficed to transfer the belongings of the unconscious man to himself. He could just make out the features of the man called Alvarez, and was turning his attention to his companion, when he heard footsteps approaching.

The police rarely ventured into that district, and when they did, it was in force and well armed. Their inspection was of the most cursory nature, and was made merely as a matter of form. This night had evidently been chosen for one of their mock inspections, for in the swinging lantern light, Rymer could make out the police uniforms on the men coming up the lane.

With a silent curse, he stole silently away, quickening his footsteps as he turned down another black tunnel.

"Just my luck," he muttered; "but, anyway, I got something, and it may not be such a bad haul after all. Another five minutes, and I'd have cleaned out the other. It's a toss up if the police don't relieve him before they take the pair back to their hotel."

The police did take the pair back to the hotel, where they awoke the next morning sadder but wiser men, and the gay Señor Alvarez lost no time in taking the first train back to his *hacienda*, vowing that never again would he favour Puerto Costa with his presence.

Rymer held his revolver ready for action, as he hastily wended his way out of the black hole, but beyond one encounter with a seedy-looking man whom he settled summarily, he reached his miserable lodgings in safety.

"By Jove!" he muttered, his eyes glittering as he emptied the contents of his pockets on the table, and looked them over by the feeble candle light. "A thousand pesos. Not much, but enough for a time—two rings, worth a hundred quid, anyway; watch and chain, not worth much; scarfpin, solitaire, must be worth forty pounds; and a handful of gold; and, what's this? Oh! Yes, the card to the president's ball!

"Huxton Rymer, my boy, I believe the wheel has turned at last. You are certainly in luck tonight, anyway. I wonder if I dare risk using this card tomorrow night. Yes, by Jove, I'll do it! When luck turns, follow it up. It's hard to tell what I might run into tomorrow night."

And with these pleasant reflections, Dr. Huxton Rymer sought his bed, and sank into an untroubled sleep.

II
The Palace Ball—The Unbidden Guest

THE small republic of Salvarita, like many of her sisters, has seen many vicissitudes; but when this story opens, the little republic had completed her fifth year without any revolution of note, with the exception of the fiasco which Rymer had joined. Perhaps the reason of this was the firm hand, which controlled the course of events.

That hand belonged to one James Pearson, a foreigner, who had drifted into the republic five years previously.

The country had been torn by dissensions at the time of his arrival, and his keen, organising mind had seized the opportunity presented.

He had identified himself with the landed party, and six months later a vigorous policy had evolved a semblance of order out of the chaos which reigned.

Where he had come from no one knew, and his unheralded entry was forgotten in the reflected glory of his court—for President Pearson knew his people, and the exact value of a glittering spectacle with them. Consequently, the past five years had seen many gorgeous demonstrations, not least among which was the annual presidential ball, to which the leading lights of all parties were bidden.

Pockets were strained in order to ransack Paris and London for suitable gowns, and if they were twelve months behind the fashions of those centres, what mattered it?

To this glittering spectacle had the unfortunate Señor Alvarez received a card of invitation.

A prosperous coffee-planter, he rarely came to Puerto Costa, and, in fact, his present unfortunate journey was his first for some years.

And it was to this same spectacle that Dr. Huxton Rymer betook himself in his one remaining suit of evening clothes, with the card of the coffee-planter in his pocket.

All the best of Puerto Costa were there that night, and President Pearson, big and coarse, with heavy grey beard and iron-grey hair, received his guests with a pleasant smile, and a genial handshake.

The big ball-room at the palace was decorated with a mass of luxurious, trailing, tropical plants, their heavy odour ascending on all sides. Over the windows, and along the walls were draped flags of the republic, and at one end, framed in smaller flags, was a picture of the popular president.

The decorator had cunningly banked the thick green, so that many secluded *tête-à-tête* spots abounded in its shelter. For the present they were deserted, all the guests being in the thick of the entertainment in the main room; but afterwards, when supper was over, and hot, Southern heads were made hotter by wine; very few of the secluded nooks would remain unoccupied, and the heavy, twining plants would hear many flowery speeches of mercurial Spanish love.

The evening was well advanced, and the president had retired from the reception before Rymer risked an entrance into the thronged ball-room.

His knowledge of Spanish was passable, and a small, black moustache, with a military imperial, gave him a decidedly Spanish appearance.

He had passed the guards carelessly, the footman barely glancing at his card, and he presented a picture of distinguished nonchalance as he leaned against a bedecked pillar near the door.

His eyes roamed around the brilliant gathering with a bored expression, and little did any of that gay company think that the man who lounged so carelessly against the pillar was using an exceptionally clever brain to utilise some of them for his purposes.

After an hour's survey of the dancers, Rymer, with a barely concealed yawn, wandered aimlessly through the room, and sought the buffet.

The many green-banked aisles confused him for a moment as he entered their heavily-scented shelter, and he paused to turn and seek another way out.

He stood for a moment with a natural appreciation of the surrounding beauty, when something caught his eye which caused him to step softly back into the concealment of a spreading palm.

Through the heavy tangle in a neighbouring nook, he could just distinguish a slim, beautiful, bronze-haired young woman.

She was alone, but it was not that which created such interest in the watching man's eyes. Rather, it was her occupation, and truly it seemed a strange proceeding even in that land of strange happenings.

In her hand was a delicate, jewelled, ivory-handled fan, which she held end up.

As Rymer watched, she pressed a spring in some invisible part, and the end of the round handle flew open. Into this the young woman dropped a glittering diamond pendant and chain, and closed the top with an almost imperceptible click.

This done, she opened her fan, and languidly moving it to and fro, left the secluded spot, the while she hummed a lilting French *chanson*.

"Curious performance, my dear young lady!" murmured Rymer, as he also turned. "I'll just keep my eye on that little fan. What luck!" he chuckled. "Who would think that ivory handle contained a small fortune. She's probably frightened of losing it," he added to himself, as he once more entered the ball-room.

Rymer sought his old position against the pillar. Not for a moment did his eyes leave the bronze-haired young woman.

"She was evidently someone of consequence," he mused, for he noticed that the highest officials and the brilliantly uniformed officers struggled in friendly rivalry for the opportunity of dancing with her.

Supper was over, and the weary dancers had again scattered, when a loud gong brought them all with wondering eyes back to the ball-room.

An elderly Spaniard, evidently one of the high officials of the Government, held up his hand as the last couple returned.

"I regret to say," he began, in a loud voice, "that Señora Alfreda, the wife of our honoured Secretary of State, has lost her diamond pendant. It needs no description, for you are all familiar with it, the pendant being the one which the people of this republic presented to the Señora in recognition of her services to the wounded during the trying times of five years ago when our beloved president came amongst us.

"It is inconceivable that anyone bidden here would retain the jewel if he found it, and I ask you as loyal Salvaritans if you find it to return it to the Señora."

Loud exclamations of astonishment greeted the statement, and the guests looked nervously at one another.

A personal search of that fiery-natured crowd was out of the question, and the philosophic natures settled the matter off hand.

"If it was lost, it would be found and returned. If it had been stolen—well, it was a matter for the police, and it would teach the Señora to guard more carefully the tokens of esteem presented to her by the people."

Half an hour later it had been forgotten by most of them as the evening went merrily on, but one among them was far from forgetting it.

That one was Dr. Huxton Rymer.

His lids had dropped to hide the exultant gleam in his eyes as the loss was announced, but not so much that he was unable to surreptitiously watch the face of the bronze-haired young woman.

She stood beside a uniformed captain of cavalry, carelessly swinging the ivory-handled fan. Her attitude altered not a whit as the old official spoke, and her brows lifted with just the proper surprise. She turned with a smile to her companion as the music again started, and a moment later her small, blue-slippered feet were flying over the floor as though such a thing as a diamond pendant did not exist.

"By thunder," exclaimed the watching Rymer, with a look of intense admiration, "you're the coolest hand I've seen for a long time! Ye gods, what luck I'm in!" he chuckled. "My little, bronze-haired señorita, who would think you were so clever! Huxton Rymer, my boy, your star has certainly risen again.

"And now to introduce myself to my future partner, and future partner you are going to be, my child, although you don't know it yet!"

With self-congratulation, Rymer sought the refreshment table, and fortified himself with the sparkling wine which flowed with reckless prodigality at the president's entertainments.

Had Rymer known the identity of the young woman whom he proposed to make his future partner he might have gone ahead with perhaps a little less assurance.

Sexton Blake could have enlightened him, for in the bronze-haired young woman he would have recognised Mademoiselle Yvonne, the temper of whose steel he had tested.

III
When Greek Meets Greek—Yvonne Takes a Partner

THE señorita looks tired. Perhaps she might care to rest in the quiet of the palms yonder?"

Mademoiselle Yvonne looked up, and her eyes narrowed a trifle as they met those of the man bending over her.

"I think you have made a mistake, sir!" she replied icily.

"Hardly," returned the man urbanely. "I must be rude enough to confess that, for the moment, your name has slipped my mind, a matter which is easily rectified by your own charming lips. But a mistake, no, señorita, don't be cruel enough to call it a mistake."

"Sir, you are insulting," responded Yvonne. "Leave me, or I will be compelled to call someone to my assistance."

"I don't think the señorita will do so," answered the man. "Pardon my presumption, what an exquisite article!"

Deftly he secured the ivory fan which lay in her lap, and before the angry young woman could speak, he continued:

"Yes, it is truly an exquisite piece of work. Fifteenth century, is it not? I am a keen collector, señorita, so you will forgive my enthusiasm. Did you ever examine some of the old fans one can pick up in Venice? Really, they give quite an insight into the secretive natures of the old Venetians. Quite an education, I assure you. Most of them have the most fascinating secret springs, which send the end flying open, and, presto! we have a splendid hidden receptacle for secret letters, compromising papers, or even jewels. Now, if this is genuine, as it seems, I wouldn't be surprised if it also had a secret spring. Did you ever try to find out, señorita?" he asked, bending down with a smile.

"Who *are* you?" whispered Yvonne tensely.

"But, as I remarked before, señorita, you look tired. Won't you reconsider your cruel words, and rest for a little amongst the palms?" he inquired suavely, ignoring her question.

Yvonne was white with anger and mortification at the unknown man, but his appropriation of the fan had seemed significant. True, his words were coolly impersonal, but a dry glitter in those mocking eyes indicated a deeper meaning to the words.

Yvonne did not know the meaning of fear, and she was probably far superior in subtlety to the man who addressed her. But for the moment he had the advantage of her. In some way, he must have a knowledge of the contents of the ivory-handle of her fan. Was he detective, or was he thief? She did not know, and in humouring his desire to retire to the palms, she would move warily and endeavour to discover. Consequently, her words were tempered to her decision as she replied to the smiling question.

"Very well, señor," she smiled, rising. "I will adopt your suggestion, but first, my fan, please!"

"Presently, señorita—presently. Do not, I beg you, deprive me so soon of the pleasure of carrying it," answered Rymer, in a mocking tone.

Yvonne bit her lip, and allowed him to lead her to the seclusion of a palm-enclosed nook.

"Now, señorita," went on Rymer, bowing Yvonne into a seat, "we can talk in comfort. Perhaps you would prefer to rest in silence, or would you care to renew the discussion of ancient fans?"

"I will be glad if you will drop this trifling, and come to the point," said Yvonne coldly. "You sought me out apparently with a purpose, and I await some enlightenment."

"Certainly, if the señorita wishes; but as yet I have not the honour of the señorita's name."

"We will waive that formality for the present. Please proceed."

"Very well, señorita," replied Rymer, dropping into the seat beside her. "But first, permit me to tell you a very brief story."

"Keep to the point, please, and tell me why you sought me out."

"But my story contains the point," smiled Rymer.

Yvonne resigned herself to listen, and Rymer brought his eyes to bear on her as he began.

"Once there was a man, señorita, and he was very poor. Why, has nothing to do with the story. Unfortunately, he desired many things which he had been accustomed to, and which his poverty could not supply him. He was very clever; and when he called himself clever, it was not from conceit, for only one man in the world had succeeded in getting the best of him, and that man is the cleverest detective in the world. But, señorita, the man's time will come, and when it does——" And Rymer finished, with a significant shrug of the shoulders.

"Ah!" interrupted Yvonne. "And has this detective a name?"

"Yes, señorita; we will give him a name, and although it is well known, you may not know it. We will call him Sexton Blake."

Rymer glanced down at the fan in his hand as he spoke, and did not see the expression in Yvonne's eyes as he mentioned the name.

"To continue," he went on. "As I said, this man was very clever, and consequently, when he found himself without money in a foreign country, he looked around for a chance to retrieve his fortunes. Fate led him to a brilliant reception one night, and while there he saw a beautiful young woman doing a most extraordinary thing. She stood behind a bower of palms—and, by the way, señorita, it wasn't unlike this one—and, lifting a beautiful ivory fan, she pressed a secret spring. The top flew open, and into the hollow of the handle, señorita, she dropped a beautiful diamond pendant. She closed the top and went back to the dancers.

"The man thought the beautiful young woman owned the gems, and was in fear of losing them. He watched her as she danced with the most prominent of the guests, and he was sure his deduction had been correct. As she seemed to have plenty of this world's goods, señorita, the poor man decided to relieve her of the fan and its contents, but before he found an opportunity a strange thing occurred.

"The wife of one of the most prominent guests lost a very valuable diamond pendant, and a search failed to reveal it. The man, señorita, immediately thought of the one he had seen the beautiful young woman drop into the handle of her fan. He listened to a conversation, and the description he heard tallied exactly with the one he had seen.

"Consequently, señorita, he changed his ideas about the beautiful young woman. Instead of taking the fan from her, he would join forces with her. Working together, what could they not achieve? Therefore, he sought out the young woman, and told her of his desire. What do you think her answer was, señorita?"

"Your story is very interesting, señor," replied Yvonne coldly, "but I really fail to see the point."

"This is the point! señorita," interrupted Rymer, pressing the secret spring, and catching the glittering gems which tumbled out. "You see," he continued, "the beautiful young woman was clever enough to secure the pendant, but, unfortunately, she failed to retain it. The poor man succeeded in getting it, but it was really a small thing compared with what they might have had if they had worked together, for doubtless the beautiful young woman belonged to one of the upper families, and could gain an entree wherever she desired."

"I must confess, señor," answered Yvonne, with blazing eyes, "that the point of your story is clearer. If she were an ordinary young woman, she might be tempted to permit the man to keep the gems since he needed them so badly; but, being what she is, she will trouble him for them quick!"

She spoke in a quiet voice of deadly calm, and Rymer looked up in amazement, to find himself gazing into the barrel of an extremely business-like-looking revolver.

"Quick!" repeated Yvonne, as he hesitated. "As you can see, my 'clever' friend, it is fitted with the latest silencer, and the sound doesn't carry a yard."

"Señorita," murmured Rymer, with barely concealed chagrin, passing over the stones, "I admired the young woman of my story, but I evidently rated her too low. I bow to superior odds, and much more than ever would I desire to work with the beautiful young woman."

"Listen, señor!" answered Yvonne, as she dropped the gems back into the handle and thrust the fan into the bosom of her gown. "I will tell you a story as well. Perhaps you will be cleverer at seeing the point than I was.

"Once there was a young woman, and she went to a brilliant ball. She was not an ordinary young woman, and she had not been long in the country. In fact, she had only arrived a few days previously, and was living aboard her yacht, which lay at anchor in the harbour."

"Ah!" exclaimed Rymer. "I can already see, señorita, that you are far superior at story-telling than I; but pray proceed."

"While at the ball she was watched by a man who, thinking to take advantage of what he saw, approached her, and made certain proposals. He foolishly imagined that she was a simple young thing, who had managed to find a diamond pendant. But it took her best abilities to secure that pendant, señor, and she meant to keep it. While the floor was crushed with dancers, she had reached forward and secured it, and her greatest skill had to be used in order to avoid discovery. So you can see, señor, she was hardly the type you thought her. In reality, she was something very different, as she proved to the man later. She led him on, to see just how far he would go, and when she was quite ready she demanded back her gems, and she got them, señor. This man, señor, in his arrogance, kindly offered to take the young woman as his partner. The young woman, señor, shares her supreme power with none; but she took pity on the man, and decided to admit him to her confidence, and give him an equal share on certain conditions."

"I am interested to know the details," murmured Rymer.

"The details, señor, were that he should never question her authority. She needed a really clever associate; one to be equal to herself in all but final authority. You mentioned a very clever detective in your story, señor. Sexton Blake you called him. Well, my story also contains a detective, and, strange to relate, he has the same name. It might interest you to know, señor, that this detective was offered the same thing which the young woman of my story offered the man in the palm bower, but the detective preferred the other side of the fence. What do you think the man's answer would be, señor?"

"I would say, señorita," drawled Rymer, "that the man's answer would be 'yes,' with all the conditions agreed to."

"Shall I finish the story, señor?"

"Decidedly!"

"Very well. The man of the story accepted the woman's offer. She then invited him to her yacht in the harbour at ten o'clock the following morning. There she would discuss with him the details of the agreement, and outline to him a particularly big proposition which was being entered upon at the time, and in which he could share."

"I would say the man accepted the invitation with extreme pleasure," remarked Rymer. "But how did the man in the story know the young woman meant all she said?"

"He was not in the position to be able to choose but trust her," replied Yvonne coolly; "but if he doubted her word, he might consult the detective whom we previously mentioned. Sexton Blake is the young woman's enemy, but he would accept her bare word under any conditions."

"For once I think the man would do well to emulate the admirable detective," laughed Rymer. "He accepts her word, señorita."

"Very well, señor; and now your name, please?"

"Dr. Huxton Rymer, señorita. Ah, I am flattered! I see my poor fame has reached your ears."

"Yes. I have heard of you," replied Yvonne, studying him closely. "And now I am tired. Come to the yacht in the morning, and ask for Mademoiselle Yvonne," and she smiled maliciously as she saw the look of consternation on Rymer's face as he heard the name of the famous adventuress.

"Good heavens!" he muttered, as he followed her from the nook. "To think I took her for a simpleton. She certainly played with me to perfection. But, Huxton Rymer, my boy, you are certainly in luck. Tomorrow—tomorrow, to begin again. And you, my charming partner, will lend a decided zest to the game."

IV
Yvonne Grows Confidential—The Plan

D R. Huxton Rymer expended a large portion of his remaining funds early the next morning on a new outfit. He felt the occasion warranted the expenditure, and at five minutes to ten he entered a small boat at one of the wharves.

He was resplendent in new white ducks, white canvas shoes, and a broad, white helmet. Sticking from his pocket was the watch-fob belonging to the unfortunate Señor Alvarez. One of that gentleman's rings adorned Rymer's finger, and his scarfpin also did duty for the occasion; for to Rymer it mattered not from whence they came so that they did come.

TINKER WAS LIFTED UP AND A MOMENT LATER WAS FLUNG OVER THE RAIL.
RYMER FOUND HIMSELF GAZING INTO THE BARREL OF A REVOLVER.
BLAKE CAUGHT THE CHINAMAN IN A THROTTLING GRIP.

He recklessly threw the native boatman five times his fare, and ascended to the deck with a jaunty step.

Yvonne was reclining in a large wicker-chair on the shady side, and she presented a picture of dainty freshness in a yachting costume of white serge.

"You are punctual, my friend," she smiled, giving Rymer her hand. "Be seated. You sent your boat back?"

"I did, mademoiselle," smiled Rymer, in reply.

"That was right," answered Yvonne. "We will talk alone until lunch, and then I will introduce you to my uncle and the other members of the circle."

"That will suit me admirably," rejoined Rymer. "May I smoke a cigar while we talk, mademoiselle?"

"Certainly," laughed Yvonne. "I will join you with a cigarette." And she lifted a tiny silver reticule as she spoke.

Rymer lit his cigar, and settled himself to listen to her words. The sailors were working on the lower deck, and as far as he could see they were quite alone where they sat.

The sky was a deep blue, and the blinding glare of the overhead sun was broken by a cool canvas awning. The atmosphere was pleasantly languid, and Rymer's blood coursed in pleasant anticipation as he cast an appraising eye at the white paint and shining brass of what he hoped was to be his future home for some time. For luxury abounded on every side, and luxury was the chief aim of Rymer's life. Not for him the smaller but honest rewards earned by the sweat of the brow. Others could have that, but he—he would take advantage of the present opportunity, and this time he would achieve the permanent reward of brains, which until now, Sexton Blake had always snatched from his grasp.

Yvonne spoke slowly and clearly, and the blue wisp from her cigarette ascended into the still air.

"Have you an intimate knowledge of Salvarita, Mr. Rymer?"

"No, not intimate, mademoiselle. I only landed here a few weeks ago. But I know every foot of Puerto Costa, and also the coast-line for some miles. You see," he added, with a grin, "I landed here unheralded; but, unlike the popular president, I joined the wrong side."

"Ah! Yes, I remember reading of the sudden ending of the revolution a short time back. You know something of President Pearson, then, do you?"

"Only what I picked up here," he replied.

"Do you know anything of the inside of the Government?"

"Yes, naturally," he replied. "Monero, who came over to the rebels, was in the Government, and he told me a lot. It was inside news that influenced me to join them."

"What was the inside news, might I ask?"

"Only a matter of a loan which the Government is negotiating in London for a matter of two millions. It would have been very pleasant, to have a share in the expenditure of that loan, and as it is based on the customs receipts for fifty years, it wouldn't matter to the lenders who was in power, for the agreement provides that they shall place their own man in charge of the customs."

"I see you do know something of their plans," remarked Yvonne, "for your information about the loan is quite correct. But what would you say if I told you that you might yet share in that two millions?"

"I would say it is too good to be true," answered Rymer, his eyes lighting at the thought.

"It may be; but, at any rate, we are going to have a try for it."

"Good heavens!" exclaimed Rymer, sitting up. "Is that a fact?"

"I never state anything else!" said Yvonne drily.

"And is that the big thing you spoke of last night in which you said you wished me to join?"

"Exactly," smiled Yvonne, lighting another tiny cigarette.

"Then, mademoiselle," he cried, "you can count Dr. Huxton Rymer very much into it."

"That is settled, then," remarked Yvonne. "And now I will give you the details.

"You perhaps don't know that the loan has been definitely arranged for the first of next month?"

"No, I didn't know that."

"Well, it has. But you, of course, know that the new Government bank which our friend Pearson is building is still unfinished?"

Rymer nodded.

"Well, I have it on most excellent authority that the two millions will be shipped from London in bullion by special steamer. It will arrive here between the fifteenth and the seventeenth. I also have it on excellent authority that until the bank is finished, the whole amount will be placed in the president's palace for safe keeping. A guard of ten men will stand over it night and day, and the work on the bank's vault will be rushed forward in order to receive it. For extra safety, it will be stored in the room adjoining the president's bed-room.

"That, my friend, is the situation, and you can rest assured it is correct in every detail. Now, for the rest of it. That two millions is all in gold bullion, you understand. It will arrive safely, and will be stored safely. But I have decided that we can find a much better use for that two millions than the Government of Salvarita. I hate to deprive those worthy ministers of the chance of feathering their nests for life; but, my friend, we are going to get that bullion."

"Good heavens," gasped Rymer, "it is so enormous it seems almost too big to try for! But, by thunder, what a scheme!"

"Wait, you have not heard all," continued Yvonne. "It is big—yes, but we have unlimited funds to draw on, for—pardon me for the remark—I seem to have been a bit more successful than you. We also have plenty of willing hands, for every man on this yacht shares pro rata in the circle. For that reason, it is not too big for us, and my plans have been most carefully thought out. No trail will be left by me, and I trust you have done nothing by which you can be traced."

"No, I assure you nothing," answered Rymer.

"That is well, and now for the rest. In addition to the bullion, we are going to take their president as well. Suspicion will naturally fall on him, and the search will be for him, not us. I have a place in the South Sea Islands to which we will take the bullion and the president. I might inform you that the securing of the president is as important to me as the bullion. For the money alone, I would not bother at the present time, but I have a personal score to settle with President Pearson."

"It is magnificent, magnificent. Mademoiselle, I bow to you. It will be a pleasure to work with one whose ideas are so stupendous, and who has the brains and money to carry them out. Is it a strictly personal affair you have with the president?"

"Yes, and that remains my secret. It is of old standing, and I have watched him for years. My chance has now come, and I will take it. More than that, it is not necessary for you to know. We will get under weigh tomorrow, and cruise about until the arrival of the bullion. My uncle is the treasurer of the circle, and you can draw on him freely for any amount you need. I might say that at the meeting of the circle this afternoon you will be elected vice-president, and I trust you will be loyal to the circle."

"Mademoiselle, I am deeply grateful for your offer, and I swear to you I will be absolutely loyal to the circle."

"And now I will leave you," she said wearily. "I am tired, and desire to rest before lunch. Enjoy yourself here until the gong goes, and then I will introduce you to your future associates over whom you will have direction."

Rymer rose as Yvonne departed, and when she had disappeared down the companionway, he sank back in his comfortable chair, and dreamed pleasant dreams until the luncheon gong sounded.

Below, in her state-room, Yvonne lay face down on the small brass bed which she had had placed in her cabin.

Her eyes were closed, and her lips moved in a whisper.

"On—on, always on. But I have taken up the plough, and must follow it to the end of the furrow."

She rose as the gong sounded, and the smiling, clear-eyed Yvonne, who entered the luxurious saloon, was radically different from the weary young woman who had lain face down on her bed a few moments previously.

None of the circle knew of the weariness of Yvonne's solitary hours. They only knew the iron-willed, dominating young woman, who directed them and led them with marvellous success, and to only one man had it ever been given to know her in any other way. That man was Sexton Blake.

The next day the beautiful white yacht sailed gracefully out of the harbour of Puerto Costa, and dipped her dainty nose into the blue rollers of the Atlantic.

End of Prologue

The First Chapter
Arrival of the Bullion—Yvonne and Rymer Take a Hand—The Capture

PRESIDENT Pearson, although he wore outwardly his usual stern expression, was in a jubilant frame of mind.

He sat before his desk in the executive-room at the palace, and sighed with satisfaction as he signed and sealed with the arms of the republic the last document before him, and passed it to the waiting secretary.

"Just hand this to the agent in charge of the bullion, Cortez," he said, turning to his secretary, "and pass the word to the guards to be in readiness to escort it up from the wharves."

The Spanish secretary hastened away to do his bidding, and as the door closed, the president leaned back in his chair and lit a cigar. He permitted his features to relax as he puffed contentedly at the mellow Havana, and his lips moved, his murmured words indicating his train of thought.

"Not so bad, by thunder! Two millions,[5] and I need it. The army hasn't been paid for six months, and the guns are terribly out of date. A little railway up to Santa Rosa, and that land of mine will be worth a handsome figure. A good reserve for the new bank to work on, and I'll clear up a fortune out of that."

And truly President Pearson had cause for self-congratulation. Five years previously he had landed in Salvarita, penniless and unknown. The revolution which was in progress had turned the wheel of fortune for him. He had joined the landed party, and threw himself heart and soul into the campaign. The timely death of the general commanding had made it necessary to elect another. By pulling the proper strings, and by sheer force of character, Pearson had secured the vacancy.

More than ever did he vigorously prosecute the campaign, and on the victory of his troops, the presidential chair had been a natural step for him. The army stood by him to a man, and if the chief office had not been offered to him he would have again taken the field. Whence he came, none of his confrères knew, but had inquiries been made throughout the mining districts of Australia his identity could soon have been established.

An unfortunate occurrence in Melbourne in which he had been mixed up had caused his sudden departure from that city, and Salvarita had been chosen as his destination, not so much on account of its climate, as the fact that no extradition laws existed.

Consequently, considering the conditions of his arrival, Fate had certainly used him kindly.

As yet he had remained unmarried, but his intimate friend and partner, General Mendoza, the Salvaritan Minister in London, had a charming daughter, and rumour said that

---

[5] £2,000,000 in 1913 is worth about £232,000,000 in 2020

the señorita would soon become the president's wife. General Mendoza was the wealthiest of the Salvaritans, his fortune being estimated at something like five millions.[6] His daughter was his only child, and Pearson had a comfortable sensation in the region of his heart when he thought of the inevitable journey of that fortune on the general's death. In the meantime, the general was to settle a round million[7] on the señorita when her marriage took place.

President Pearson's thoughts broke off, and his face assumed its wonted sternness as the door was opened by the returning secretary.

"Everything is arranged, sir," he said. "Captain Alameda is taking ten of your bodyguard to escort the bullion to the palace. They will remain on guard until midnight, when Lieutenant Sandra, with ten more of your guard, will relieve him. They are placing it in the room next to your bedchamber, sir, and I have sent word to Lieutenant Sandra to keep his men quiet during the night in order not to disturb you."

"Very well, Cortez. Thank you," replied the president. "Did you find out what progress is being made on the vault at the bank?"

"Yes, sir. The contractor hopes to have it ready for use by the end of the week."

"Very good. I am calling a Cabinet meeting this evening, Cortez, to ratify my proposals about the increase of pay to the army and the payment of all back allowances. I will be glad if you will notify the members, and meet me at the council chamber at eight."

The president had a highly successful meeting that evening. Substantial increases were voted for the army, and an order was passed authorising the treasurer to pay all back allowances. The president's proposal to spend a good sum for new weapons was received with enthusiasm, for he had taken care to have a majority of the military in his Cabinet. Other expenditures were tentatively discussed, and as the president rose he was greeted by long and enthusiastic cheers.

He received their ovation with smiling dignity, and sought his chamber next that which contained the bullion; but he stopped to have a word with Captain Alameda, and to glance with satisfaction at the valuable cases which would make things so wonderfully pleasant.

He dropped a discreet hint as to the resolutions of the evening, for it would be well to have the information disseminated through the army as soon as possible, and he had no doubt as to the rapid spread of such welcome tidings.

He passed on to his bed-room, and retired. A hard day had made him tired, and before the guard changed at midnight, the president lay in a deep slumber.

***

While things were running so smoothly at the palace this evening, other events were happening at a lonely spot on the coast some fifteen miles away.

---

[6] £5,000,000 in 1913 is worth about £580,000,000 in 2020

[7] £1,000,000 in 1913 is worth about £116,000,000 in 2020

A rakish, white yacht, with all lights doused, steamed slowly up and down a short mile from the white, sandy beach.

As eight bells struck, several dark figures emerged from below.

They hastened to the davits, and at a signal from the captain lowered away two large flat rafts, on each of which reposed a long, roomy motor-car.

Slowly and carefully they worked until the rafts reached the water, when they stood waiting further commands.

Yvonne appeared from below, followed by Rymer and Graves—her uncle.

"It's fortunate the sea is so smooth," remarked Yvonne, "otherwise we would have been compelled to utilise the wharf at Boro, a few miles along, and that would be more risky."

"Yes, things seem to be working well," answered Rymer, as he puffed at a cigar. "I suppose we'd better be getting along now, hadn't we? You say the guard is to change at twelve, and we will need to have a good look around before going ahead with the plan."

"Yes, we'll start now," answered Yvonne. "You take one lot, and I'll take the other. My uncle can go with you, and Hendricks with me. Captain Vaughan will remain in charge of the yacht. That will give you seven men, counting yourself, while I will have six. Three to remain with the captain will be sufficient."

A few minutes later the two rafts were being propelled towards the shore, and in half an hour they grounded gently on the sloping beach.

No time was lost in getting the cars ashore, and the men, filing silently into the cars with all lights out, headed at a moderate pace for Puerto Costa, Yvonne driving one, and Rymer the other.

It was eleven o'clock when they reached the town, and Rymer took the lead as they entered its environs, heading by a little-used road, until he pulled up in a thick wood in the rear of the palace.

The palace stood practically alone on a high hill, and for their purpose the lack of surrounding buildings suited them well.

Silently the two parties descended, and leaving one man to guard both cars, struck across through the woods in the wake of Rymer.

A few minutes' walk brought them to a deserted spot on the main road leading from the palace to the town, and here they dropped silently to the ground.

The silence was broken a little later by the rattle of vehicles, in which the members of the Cabinet were returning to the town; but as the sound of their wheels died away in the distance, silence again reigned for some time.

It still lacked a few minutes of midnight before anything else occurred to disturb the quiet of the night.

The regular sound of marching feet came up the dark road, and not until then did the silent watchers stir.

Swiftly and silently did Rymer arrange his men.

Half he sent across into the deep shadow of the other side of the road with whispered instructions.

"Ten to one they'll be marching in pairs. Pick your man, and use your sandbag before he can cry out."

They had barely assumed their positions when the marching footsteps grew close, and as the little band appeared, they stopped in stupefied amazement as several dark figures leaped at them from each side of the road. Their surprise had been calculated upon by Rymer and Yvonne, and before a cry could be uttered the sailors were at work with their sandbags. It was over in a moment, and Rymer congratulated himself on its swiftness and lack of outcry.

"Hurry!" he whispered. "Put on their coats, belts, and caps, and take their rifles. Your own dark trousers will pass. Then bind them and gag them with the things we brought."

He himself appropriated the coat and sword of the lieutenant in charge, and so quickly had the operations been carried out that it still wanted a minute to midnight as the uniformed party entered the palace gates, Yvonne and her uncle following at a short distance in the rear.

Two men were on guard at the gate, but before they could cry out they shared the fate of the others. The clock over the palace just started to boom the hour of midnight when Rymer and his men entered the main door and ascended the staircase.

Down the passage they went, and the subdued clink of arms in a neighbouring room told them the guards still on duty were preparing for their release.

Rymer knocked at the door with the handle of his sword, and as it opened his eyes gleamed with satisfaction on seeing the dim lights. That fact meant, perhaps, ten seconds of advantage, and in the present position those ten seconds would be of immense value.

Captain Alameda, who opened the door, looked surprised as Rymer and his men entered.

"Why," he said, lifting his brows, "I expected Lieutenant Sandra. Why hasn't——"

But the captain got no further. With a lightning spring, Rymer was upon him, and before the astonished captain could cry out, Rymer's fingers had closed on his throat.

The mock guard had taken their cue from Rymer, and each picking his man, leaped for him.

The hardy sailors were used to a rough and tumble fight, and knowing things would go hard with them, if the alarm were raised, they wasted no time in preliminaries.

As quickly as one guard was overcome, he was bound and gagged, and Yvonne barely reached the room when the panting men straightened up, the last guard secured.

Captain Alameda lay senseless on the floor where Rymer had thrown him. One of the sailors bound him, and thrust his own handkerchief in between his teeth, and the job was done.

"You have done well, my friend," whispered Yvonne to Rymer. "And now let us lose no time in securing the president."

The scuffle had not been without noise, but President Pearson was a sound sleeper, and still lay in slumber as Rymer, with three men, softly opened the door of the bed-chamber and entered.

A small nightlight was burning, and the outline of the president's form was visible under the coverlet of the great four-poster bed.

With a panther-like tread Rymer crossed the room, and the president awakened from his golden dreams a moment later to find four men in the uniform of his own guard bending over him.

He started to sit up but found himself securely held, and as he opened his mouth to give the alarm, a silk handkerchief choked the sound.

Silently he was lifted out, and his clothes put on him.

His eyes glared in blazing anger at his captors, but he had no choice but to submit. He made an attempt to struggle, but a sudden twist of his arm reduced him to quietness.

His clothes on, the three dusky sailors hoisted him up, and followed Rymer out.

Rapidly, they carried him to where the motors were, and returned to help their comrades in removing the bullion.

The last box had been placed in the car, and still the palace lay wrapt in the unknowing slumber when the engines were started and the cars headed for the sandy beach fifteen miles away.

The Second Chapter
Sexton Blake Reads the Paper—The Sequel—The Chase Begins

SEXTON Blake apparently found something of interest in the morning paper, for he replaced his cup in his saucer, and devoted both hands to holding the sheet.

Twice he read the article which had caught his eye.

"Here, Tinker," he remarked to the lad who sat opposite him at the breakfast-table, "read this article, and tell me what conclusions you come to."

He passed the paper across, his finger pointing to the paragraph, and with a thoughtful look proceeded with his breakfast, while Tinker read the article which stared at him in bold outlines:

"EXTRAORDINARY SITUATION IN SALVARITA! PRESIDENT PEARSON DISAPPEARS! TWO MILLION POUNDS IN GOLD BULLION ALSO DISAPPEAR! GREAT EXCITEMENT IN PUERTO COSTA! MARTIAL LAW PROCLAIMED! THE ARMY IN A FERMENT!

"Cables have been received describing an extraordinary state of affairs in the Republic of Salvarita.

"President Pearson, who has been the chief executive for five years, has mysteriously disappeared, leaving no trace.

"Two million pounds in gold bullion has also disappeared with him. This large amount had just been landed from England, and was a loan arranged with Messrs. Crick, Field & Co., the well-known London banking firm.

"The Opposition accuse the missing president of decamping with the bullion, and demand the immediate resignation of the Cabinet.

"The army still believe in foul play, and the finding of the palace guards bound and gagged lends weight to their argument.

"The Opposition, however, insist that it is part of an elaborate plan.

"In the meantime, the army controls the situation, but matters are reaching a critical stage.

"An interesting point is that just before his disappearance, President Pearson carried several proposals involving large expenditures for the benefit of the army. This fact probably accounts for the attitude assumed by them.

"President Pearson was shortly to be married to Señorita Mendoza, daughter of the wealthy Salvaritan Minister to London.

"Further developments will be anxiously awaited."

(Later.)

"Further details are at hand regarding the disappearance of President Pearson.

"A fisherman states that in the early hours of the morning he saw two boats leave the beach about fifteen miles from Puerto Costa, and proceed to a yacht, which was cruising about with all lights out.

"The Opposition point to this as evidence of President Pearson's guilt, and the army, after holding out for some time, have given in.

"The Cabinet has resigned, and Señor Martina, the leader of the Opposition, is temporarily at the head of the Government.

"Our representative called upon Señor Mendoza at the Salvaritan Embassy, but was unable to obtain an interview.

"Messrs. Crick, Field & Co. have as yet no further information than ourselves."

"Looks as though the president had made a pretty clean 'get away' with the bullion, guv'nor," remarked Tinker, as he finished reading.

"I see you agree with the article that he is guilty," laughed Blake.

"Why, yes," responded Tinker. "Don't you, guv'nor?"

"Well, looking at it casually it would seem so," replied Blake; "but let us look into it. We have a few minutes to spare, and the matter interests me, for you will remember it was in Puerto Costa that I ran Barnes, the big forger, to earth."

"Oh, yes; I remember, guv'nor. Then you know Puerto Costa."

"Quite intimately," laughed Blake, rising and entering the consulting-room.

"Now, Tinker," he continued, walking over to the bookcase, "I will just refresh my memory by referring to my Index. Ah, here it is!" he exclaimed, turning to the letter "S."

"'Salvarita—South America. Population 700,000.' Then follows a long string of figures relating to the customs, receipts, foreign debt, etc. 'Capital, Puerto Costa, has a fine harbour. Form of government—Republic, governed by a president and legislative council. President: President Pearson, who is also commander-in-chief of the army.' There are a lot of notes quite beside the question," said Blake, skipping a paragraph. "Ah, here we are again.

"Unknown generally from where President Pearson came. Arrived in Salvarita five years ago. Rumoured engagement to Señorita Mendoza, daughter of Salvaritan Minister to London.'

"That is all," he remarked. "Now we will turn to "M." Here it is:

"'Mendoza, Jose. Salvaritan Minister to London. Extensively interested in plantations, etc. Rated by Braddun at five millions. Age about 60. Has one daughter, aged 25, his wife being dead.'"

Blake closed the Index, and, returning it to the shelf, walked over to the window.

"Well, guv'nor, what do you think of it?" asked Tinker, "Doesn't it look as though the president was guilty?"

"It looks that way, Tinker," answered Blake; "and it is possible it was intended to look that way. But it has points of very great interest. I would like to know what Señor Mendoza—Why, hallo! Isn't that—yes, it is Señor Mendoza coming up the steps!" jerked out Blake, returning to his seat. "He looks in a dickens of a hurry, and if I'm not mistaken, we'll hear more of this case."

Blake lit his black pipe, and stretched himself out in his chair. Hardly had he done so when Señor Mendoza was announced.

He was a small, dark-skinned man. His hair and moustache were grey, and his dark eyes were filled with worry.

"Come in, Señor Mendoza," smiled Blake. "I see you are quite convinced of his innocence, and believe in the theory of foul play. I don't know but what I agree with you."

"What—how?" gasped his visitor, sinking into a chair. "I don't understand, Mr. Blake. How did you know I came about President Pearson, and that I believe in his innocence?"

"Very simple," laughed Blake. "President Pearson in his five years of office has undoubtedly acquired a fair amount of property in Salvarita. Then he becomes engaged to your daughter. She is your only child, and will eventually get all your fortune, which is in the neighbourhood of five millions. President Pearson mysteriously disappears, and with him two million in bullion.

"Had he anything to gain by doing that, when he would have control of the spending of it in any case? Would he leave a place where he ruled with almost absolute power, and was honoured and respected, to go into hiding when it was not necessary?

"He had more to gain by remaining.

"Then you come to me in a state of great agitation, señor. If you believed in his guilt, you would have stirred up the police in every capital in Europe, unless the Government has already done so. But the fact that you come to me at all proves you believe in his innocence and wish to find him."

"Extraordinary!" gasped the Minister, his mouth agape with astonishment. "Mr. Blake, they have not overrated you. I have come for your assistance, for I know it is impossible for him to be guilty; but alas! besides myself and my daughter who is prostrated, I am afraid no one else believes him guiltless."

"Suppose you tell me a little more," suggested Blake.

"Very well; I will. What I know, but what no one else knows, is that Pearson owned lands alone in Salvarita which will be shortly worth as much as two millions. They are held in my name, and he was not generally known as being interested in them. In addition, I had promised to settle a million on my daughter on her marriage, and he knew they would get at my death the balance of what I had.

"That is why I know he is guiltless, Mr. Blake. My idea is that some of his enemies have done this, and that he is held a prisoner in the mountains of Salvarita. But your statement makes my explanation much easier than I thought it would be, and I beg of you, Mr. Blake, to take the case and find the missing man.

"Unlimited funds will be placed at your disposal, and needless to say, I will pay anything to have his innocence established, for, as I said, my daughter is prostrated, and I would pay any price to bring smiles back to her eyes. Will you take it, Mr. Blake?" he ended, looking anxiously at the detective.

Blake smoked in deep thought for some moments. Finally, rousing himself, he said:

"Yes, Señor Mendoza, I will take the case. It interests me on account of several features. I will start at once."

"Oh, thank you, Mr. Blake!" answered the Minister, springing to his feet and almost throwing his arms, in his effusive Spanish way, around the detective's neck.

"Don't spare money; all you need is at your disposal. In anticipation of your acceptance, Mr. Blake, I have hired Lord Cardby's yacht for an unlimited period. I thought if you accepted the case you might wish to leave for Salvarita at once. But in any event she will have steam up constantly awaiting your orders."

"Ah, that will be very satisfactory!" replied Blake. "I may decide to leave at once for Salvarita, and can make faster time than by the ordinary route. But one word, Señor Mendoza. Not a word to anyone—not even to your daughter—that I am working on the case. Let her think, if necessary, that I have refused it. If President Pearson does happen to be innocent, as we think, it points to a great force behind the affair, and you can see the necessity for strict secrecy if I am to work to advantage."

"Certainly—certainly, Mr. Blake; anything you say I will do. And you can trust me to keep the secret, for that is one thing at least in which we diplomats excel."

"Very well, that's settled, then!" rejoined Blake, rising. "I will communicate with you at intervals—if not personally, by my assistant."

And he indicated Tinker.

"Good! And now I'll be getting back. I wish you every success, Mr. Blake, for my beloved child's happiness depends on it."

Blake bowed, and a moment later the street door slammed behind the anxious little Spaniard.

The Third Chapter
Alone in Mid-Ocean-Tinker's Peril

"WHAT do you think of it, guv'nor?" asked Tinker, when some time had passed.

"It would be futile to form any theory yet," answered Blake, rousing himself. "Of one thing I feel convinced, and that is that President Pearson did not disappear of his own free will. Naturally, many theories present themselves, and I may start on several false tracks; but they must be followed until they lead somewhere, or bring up against a blank wall. But now to business, my lad!"

Blake walked to the window again, and gazed out. Something caused him to suddenly withdraw behind the shelter of the curtain, and he peered cautiously through its thick web.

"We'll postpone arrangements for a bit, Tinker," he softly said, backing away. "There is a man on the other side of the street whose elaborately careless attitude makes me think this house is the object of his attention, for it is the only one at which he is not looking. It is just possible that he has followed Señor Mendoza here, and it may have something to do with the object of his visit. I am going to walk along in the direction of Oxford Street. Wait a few moments, and then follow. If he shadows me, keep him in sight, and see where he goes, for I will shake him off, if possible."

"Right, guv'nor, I will," answered Tinker, creeping cautiously to the window, and peering out. "He'll be easy to follow, for that light coat of his will be visible in any crowd."

"Don't depend too much on that," replied Blake, as he put on his hat and picked up his stick. "You yourself have often had on a light coat which you have rapidly changed to a dark one in the space of a few seconds, and our friend outside may possibly know that wrinkle."

"All right, guv'nor; I'll be careful," answered Tinker.

Blake, closing the street door, stood on the step, and carelessly lit a cigar before starting out. The utter indifference of manner of the man across the street convinced the detective that he was being watched, and he glanced from the corner of his eye as he strode down Baker Street.

He swung around a corner, and hailed a taxi, and the appearance of his man, who also hailed a taxi, proved the truth of his suspicions.

Blake directed the driver to go to Oxford Street, and, on reaching that crowded thoroughfare, he pulled up before one of its large emporiums.

"Here, cabby," said Blake, tossing the man half a sovereign; "wait on the rank for about ten minutes and then drive away! Be sure and wait at least ten minutes."

"Right, sir!" answered the driver.

And as Blake entered the big store he saw the following taxi pull into the kerb.

He hastened through the building, and out at the back. Hailing another taxi he drove to Cockspur Street, and the absence of any following cab told him the ruse had worked.

"I hope Tinker won't lose him," he remarked to himself, stepping from the cab. "It's just possible, though, that he may spot the lad."

Blake crossed the footpath and entered the office of a steamship company. He emerged a little later, and in his pocket was a ticket for the Republic of Salvarita on a steamer sailing the following day.

He returned to Baker Street, and awaited Tinker's return, early afternoon had come before the lad came back.

"Well, did you find out anything?" asked Blake.

"No, guv'nor," answered Tinker ruefully. "I'm sorry, too, but he must have spotted me. I followed him until I saw you enter the store in Oxford Street. He went in after you, but came out a little later frowning, and I knew he had lost you. He jumped in his cab, and I followed in mine. I don't know just when he knew I was following, but I saw he had spotted me when his taxi started driving up one street and down another in an aimless fashion. Well, we finally got into the Strand. A block in the traffic stopped me, but he got through, and before I could jump out to follow he was gone."

"Never mind, Tinker," replied Blake kindly. "He was probably a shrewd fellow, and if I succeeded in shaking him off, it is no discredit to you to have been shaken off by him. But the events of this morning have caused a change in my plans. I am entrusting you, my lad, with one of the most important matters which has come under my hands, for I am going to send you alone to Salvarita."

"Jiminy, guv'nor! It's jolly decent of you to trust me so much. I realise the importance of the president of a country disappearing, and I promise you I will use all my endeavours to follow your instructions."

"I know you will, my lad. But let me impress upon you one very important thing. Watch yourself and everyone about you day and night. I am quite convinced that the man who gave us the slip this morning had followed Señor Mendoza, and that an attempt will be made to watch every move we make, for they will know as a matter of course that he came to see me in order to get me to take the case. It stands to reason that there must be a particularly daring band at work, and that they will spare no efforts to counteract any move we make."

"I'll remember, guv'nor," rejoined Tinker earnestly. "When do I start for Salvarita?"

"Tomorrow morning," answered Blake. "While you and your unknown friend were playing hide-and-seek this morning I slipped down to Cockspur Street and got your ticket. The *Orinoco* sails at ten, but it will be wise for you to go aboard tonight. And now for your instructions."

Blake filled his old black pipe, and Tinker settled himself to listen carefully to his instructions.

Inwardly the lad was filled with pride, for Blake was showing great confidence in him to entrust him with such a weighty mission.

"You will go to Salvarita," began Blake, sending forth clouds of smoke, "and present a letter I will give you to Señor Martina, who is now at the head of the Government. He, being the leader of the Opposition, will naturally believe in the president's guilt, but that needn't bother you, for he won't have any idea of your mission. In fact, no one must know. But I did a bit of a favour for Señor Martina a few years ago, and he was more grateful than perhaps the occasion warranted. Consequently, he will do everything in his power to make things pleasant for you, and that is what I want.

"Puerto Costa will naturally be in a very excited state, and it will be difficult to get about freely. An authority from him will assist you to do so.

"Now, from the facts at hand, the case presents two lines of thought which we must follow. Firstly, has President Pearson been seized by native Salvaritans and taken prisoner to the mountains, as Señor Mendoza thinks, or, secondly, has the attack come from an outside source?

"If the second theory is correct, the yacht which the fishermen saw will be found to have played an important part, for the shipping reports show no vessels of any description have left Salvarita for five days.

"Of course, a third hypothesis, based on the theory of hidden facts yet to be discovered, may show both lines of thought to be incorrect, and that President Pearson is guilty.

"It would need a very strong hidden motive to make him take such a step, but I will be able to weigh this point more clearly when I have traced his life previous to his arrival in Salvarita.

"That is the case as it stands now. You will endeavour to find out all you can, and pay particular attention to the yacht which the fisherman saw."

"Yes, guv'nor, I will," answered Tinker earnestly. "But how about you? Aren't you going to take it up yourself yet?"

"I'm going to see how you make out," laughed Blake, in a noncommittal manner. "I'll take a hand when the time arrives. I see you looking at Pedro," he continued, holding out his hand to the big hound. "Well, he's to remain with me for the present. You will be playing a lone hand, my lad," he added seriously, "and perhaps I am wrong to send you on such a mission alone; but the events of the morning have made it absolutely necessary."

"Oh, I'll be all right, guv'nor! I'll watch out carefully. What identity shall I take?"

"Well, I think the same as on your last trip to New York. Travel as a young man of leisure. You will, of course, have unlimited funds to support it. Communicate with me here at all times, but in case anything should happen that I shall have to leave suddenly, I will leave a sealed letter with full details with Señor Mendoza. He will deliver it on presentation of our code, a copy of which I will give him so that it won't fall into strange hands. And now, we have a lot to do before this evening, when I will give you final details."

***

The *Orinoco* was berthed at Tilbury, and Tinker went aboard at ten that night, as Blake had suggested. He had taken elaborate precautions to avoid being followed, and, for safety's sake, had parted from Blake at Baker Street.

He sought his berth early, resolving to keep to his cabin until the steamer sailed, and as he crawled into his bunk flattered himself he had got aboard unobserved.

The average steamer is usually held up for some time after her advertised time of sailing by the tag end of the freight, but the *Orinoco* slipped her moorings on time.

Tinker did not come on deck until they had reached the Channel. He spent the day sizing up his fellow-passengers, who were few in number at this time of the year, and all one class, for the *Orinoco* was a small steamer, and passenger traffic to Salvarita was light, even in the best season.

An elderly planter and his family, a young Spanish lady and her duenna, two lads about Tinker's age, going out as pupils on a coffee estate, a middle-aged, hatchet-faced woman, who looked as though she might be going on a solitary expedition to the wildest part of the Andes, but who in reality was a mild-natured missionary, and a husky-looking clergyman made up the party.

Tinker rapidly made friends with the two lads, and the captain and officers, seeming a very decent lot, Tinker looked forward to an enjoyable trip.

The second day the lads were busy organising sports to while away the time. Land dropped away from sight, and by evening they had settled down like old acquaintances.

A cold, driving rain came on during the evening, and those who had not gone below from sea-sickness sought the saloon's genial warmth.

Tinker found the atmosphere stifling, and, slipping down to his state-room, got his macintosh and cap.

He ascended to the deserted deck, and moved to the wet side, for he liked walking with the driving rain in his face.

He had been the sole occupant of the deck for some time, when he saw the big clergyman make his appearance.

The reverend gentleman stopped as he reached Tinker, and, swinging about, kept pace with the lad.

"Rather a dirty night," he remarked, as they walked towards the stern. "I see you, like myself, are fond of the rain."

"Yes, I am very fond of it," answered Tinker. "It clears the cobwebs away!" he laughed.

They had reached the stern, and were turning to go back as he finished speaking.

Suddenly, without warning, the big clergyman swung on him with blazing eyes. Springing for the lad, his huge hands closed on Tinker's throat.

"Oh, you do like the rain—eh? It clears the cobwebs—eh? Well, Mr. Sexton Blake's assistant, since you like water so much, we'll see if the ocean clears your brain, for into it you are going pretty quick!"

Tinker struggled fiercely in his assailant's grip, and once almost twisted free, but those huge hands held him with a deadly hold.

He reproached himself deeply at that moment for not being more careful; but really there was some excuse, for the so-called clergyman had conducted prayers with a most sanctimonious air. But Tinker realised with horror that the man's eyes were filled with a deadly purpose. It was not a question of avoiding being followed, but a fierce struggle for life itself.

His hands sought a grip on the man's body, but his antagonist was too powerful for the lad, and his brain whirled with despair as he felt his lungs bursting under that awful, choking pressure.

Everything swam before his eyes, his mind reeled. He gave one last, despairing struggle. His arms dropped, coming into contact with something. Tinker grasped it, to use it as a buffer between him and the man, but he was too far gone. Again his arms dropped. He felt himself being lifted up, and a moment later, still clutching his useless weapon, he sailed over the rail and sank with a splash into the cold, black depths, while the steamer ploughed her way through the dark, stormy night.

The Fourth Chapter
Pedro's Warning

HARDLY had Tinker left Baker Street to go aboard the *Orinoco* on his ill-fated journey when Blake hastened to his room and rang the bell.

Telling the landlady, who appeared in answer, to pack his bags, he returned to his desk and wrote many letters.

It was after midnight before he finished, but he had yet much to do.

A telephone message brought the big grey car around, and half an hour later, with Pedro and his bags in the tonneau, he threw in the clutch and headed for Plymouth.

Night still lingered over the water when he brought the car to a stop at the docks.

Around the harbour were dotted the lights of vessels at anchor, but it was impossible to make out any particular shape in the gloom.

Blake was turning to re-enter the car and await the coming dawn, when an early boatman passed.

"Good-morning sir!" he remarked cheerfully. "We'll have rain before another twenty-four hours."

"Good-morning! Do you think so?" replied Blake.

"Yes, sir. It's almost certain. Be you waiting for friends, sir?"

"No," answered Blake. "By the way, I wonder if you know where Lord Cardby's yacht—the *Corsair*—is lying?"

"Oh, yes, sir! She lays where you see those twin lights off yonder. Be you wanting to go out to her?"

"Yes. Do you want the job?"

"Certainly, sir. I'll have the boat ready in two minutes."

Blake sent the car back to London with the man, and entered the small boat.

Dawn was just breaking as he climbed the ladder to the deck of the beautiful yacht which had made a name for her speed.

A word sent one of the watch to notify the captain, who happened to be on the bridge.

"Come up, sir!" he called down to Blake. "I presume you are Mr. Blake?" he said, as Blake gained the bridge. "I hardly expected you so soon, but if you want to get away I'm all ready. By the way, my name is Pentland."

"Thanks, captain; I do, if you can manage it," replied Blake.

The captain was a slim, pointed-beard man of the Naval College class, and Blake could not help but admire the finished manner in which he issued his orders and secured their carrying out.

"Now, Mr. Blake," he said crisply, as the throb of the propeller sounded, "Mr. Ross, the chief officer, is relieving me in a few minutes, and if you care to remain up here until then, I will show you your apartments myself."

"Thanks, captain," answered Blake, lighting a cigar; "I'll do so. It will be a relief to get some of this beautiful morning air after London, although I got a good dose coming down."

"You didn't come by train?" inquired the captain.

"No; I motored down."

The yacht swung round as Blake spoke, and the morning sun, appearing above the horizon at the same time, shone with golden splendour on her gleaming brass.

Mr. Ross, the chief officer, appeared as the yacht got under way, and Blake liked him at once.

He was a young, smooth-shaven man, with keen eyes, and greeted Blake warmly as his eyes lighted with pleased admiration, for he had heard much of the famous detective.

He took the bridge, and Captain Pentland conducted Blake to his apartments.

They proved to be a sitting-room and huge sleeping-cabin, stretching clear across the after part of the yacht.

"I hope you'll be comfortable, Mr. Blake," said the captain, throwing open the doors. "I'll have a steward detailed to look after you, and if there is anything lacking, don't hesitate to ask. The whole yacht is under your orders, and if you tell me to go to the South Pole, I'll attempt it."

"I won't ask that, captain," laughed Blake; "but I'm glad to know I can depend on you. I can see I am going to enjoy my trip with you immensely. If you will send my steward to me I'll be obliged. And I will ask you to excuse me from appearing today, for I am dead fagged, and will sleep."

"Right, Mr. Blake! I'll do so."

Blake began wearily to undress as the captain departed, and the steward spreading out his pyjamas, the worn-out detective was soon fast asleep.

Perhaps he would have dropped into one of his concentrated moods instead of seeking his bed had he known that barely had the yacht left the harbour when a throbbing motor pulled up, and the driver gleaned from a loitering boatman the fact that he had only a short time before taken a gentleman out to the white yacht which was disappearing in the distance. Much more would Blake have kept awake, and probably his instructions, which had been to sail for Salvarita, would have been altered had he seen the motor turn and proceed to a cable office, where a message was despatched to that chaotic republic.

But he did not know these things, and consequently he appeared at dinner that night, refreshed from his sleep.

He found the captain and Mr. Ross all he thought them. The chief engineer, Mackay, was a crusty Scotsman, with the heart of a lion, and the captain raised his brows in astonishment as the usually taciturn man thawed perceptibly under Blake's magnetic manner.

On the second night the driving rain, prophesied by the old boatman, duly set in, and the quartet gathered in the luxurious saloon for a game of bridge, the first of many to be on that voyage, which was to toss them all over the globe, and lead them through many perils before they again saw England.

Blake and the engineer were partners, and the detective, who found little opportunity for relaxation, threw himself completely into the spirit of the game.

How different would he have felt, and how his heart would have tightened, had he known that out on that black waste of waters Tinker, who was so much in his lonely life, lay struggling for life against the monstrous waves which were fast overcoming him.

Pedro, who had accompanied Blake, and lay under the table, raised his head at that moment, and all four men started nervously as the great hound emitted a deep baying wail.

The superstitious Scotsman raised his eyes nervously.

"I'm thinkin' soom mon has this moment gone to his death," he said solemnly.

A weird feeling came over the detective as Pedro got up and placed his head on Blake's knee, looking at his master with great pleading eyes, which seemed almost to burst in their endeavour to make the man understand.

"What is it, old chap?" said Blake in a reassuring voice. "You're not getting nervous of the sea after all these years of travelling, are you?"

But Pedro was not to be comforted. He paced restlessly about the saloon, finally casting himself down at the door, where he lay gazing into nothingness, with his great eyes wide.

The four men proceeded with the game, but the spirit had gone out of it after Pedro's strange wail, and they broke up early.

Blake called the dog as he went below, but although the faithful fellow pounded his tail in acknowledgment, he did not get up, and all Blake's coaxing failed for once to make him rise.

The Fifth Chapter
The Stabbing of Sexton Blake

BLAKE, with the exception of the one evening when Pedro had acted so strangely, enjoyed his trip immensely.

As he had expected, he found the captain and officers most congenial companions, and before the yacht arrived at Salvarita there was not a man on board, from the captain to the cook's boy, who would not go through anything for the detective.

In addition, the voyage benefited him greatly, for the previous months had been very hard ones, and little rest or recreation had entered his busy life.

But although Blake enjoyed his rare opportunities for relaxation, his active mind was not content for long to only puzzle over bridge problems, and consequently, when Captain Pentland remarked that another twenty-four hours would show the coast of Salvarita, Blake once more put everything from his mind but the business he had come on. Typical of his brilliant mental system was the complete manner in which he remarshalled all the points of the case, as though they had all been tagged and laid away for a few days.

He held a consultation with the captain that evening, and it was decided that the yacht should cruise about until nightfall the following day. Then she would draw closer to the shore, and a small boat would land Blake at a lonely spot on the coast. The yacht would then put to sea, and return a week later. A small boat would be sent ashore again at the same lonely spot, and if Blake desired to come aboard he would be there. If not, she was to put to sea again, and return in three days, when he would in any event be at the rendezvous.

This plan was put into operation, and the following night Blake, who had garbed himself as a dilapidated sailor from the wardrobe of the yacht, landed on the sloping beach of a small cove, and was soon lost to view of the returning boat in the dense tropical growth lining the shore.

According to the captain's chart, it was about seven miles from Puerto Costa, and as Blake gained the road he set out at a brisk walk for the town.

He was unaware that the appearance of the *Corsair* had been closely looked for, and that a stealthy figure dodged along the silent road behind him.

Had he taken Pedro, the hound would have scented the following man at once, but for the time being the faithful fellow had been left aboard the yacht.

On reaching the town Blake took himself to the disreputable district in the lower part.

He had been twelve days at sea, and although the *Corsair* was equipped with wireless, and they had picked up messages from passing steamers, nothing had been received referring to the situation in Salvarita, and consequently Blake was not aware of the latest developments.

That the country was still in a very excited and unsettled condition he quickly saw on reaching the town, and as he approached the water-front, the signs of disorder were more accentuated.

The whole underworld of that, at any period, evil district, seemed to be about.

The narrow streets, lined with the gambling and drinking dens, threw an extra stream of light into the murky surroundings.

The harbour was dotted with vessels, and the roaring, drunken songs, bellowed forth in every language, indicated the fact that the crews were on shore-leave.

All the side-streets were in darkness, their narrow blackness leading to mysterious retreats, and secure in their shelter, sinister figures lurked and watched for their prey.

The motley cosmopolitan parties of sailors in every stage of drunkenness, reeled, and staggered from one noisy den to another, greeting with maudlin familiarity the drink-sodden *habitués* of the dens.

Woe to any who passed alone from den to den, or got separated from his companions, for the watching vultures in human form made short work of their prey. Were he very drunk, brawny arms would seize him in a choking grip, and before his muddied wits could make sense of what was happening, he was hustled up a dark alley. A crack on the head sent him to the ground like a log, and a dexterous hand relieved him of his possessions.

But whether drunk or sober, the new arrival took his life in his hands when he entered those sinister tunnels, and no man possesses a record of the "reported missing" who never returned.

And it was into this abyss of crime and loathsome evil that Blake ventured.

He knew his way about the underworld of Puerto Costa, for he had passed through its darkest spots some years ago in his chase for the famous forger Barnes.

He saw things had not altered for the better since his previous acquaintance with it, and, in fact, as he got deeper he found that several new dens had started, and were apparently doing a profitable trade, to judge from the sounds of ribald merriment that came through the doors.

Cautiously Blake picked his way along. He had a definite object in view, for he passed many of the brightly lit places, and headed towards the darkest part of the district.

He made his way to a dark, uninhabited-looking building, and knocked in a peculiar manner upon the door, repeating it twice at intervals.

Some moments passed before a cautious whisper in Portuguese descended from somewhere above.

"Who knocks?"

"One who desires an audience!" replied Blake.

"Do you bring the pass-word?"

"Yes. Of the upper grade!"

"Name it."

"Todos!" whispered Blake.

"A moment, and I will admit you!" and a faint, shuffling sound came, followed by the cautious opening of the door.

When Blake had been in Puerto Costa before, he had, as mentioned previously, been the means of saving Señor Martina, the present head of the Government, from an extremely compromising position.

His movements at the time had led him into strange perils, one of which had forced him to take part in a terrible riot in the underworld. A quick shot had saved the life of the man fighting next to him, and the latter's gratitude had known no bounds. He had presented Blake with a beautiful emerald, and had conducted the detective to one of the strangest places he had yet been in. Blake had discovered the man he had saved to be as strange as the surroundings.

He was a wizened native, who was the head of a secret society. The old man had boundless wealth, drawn, Blake suspected, from some hidden mine in the interior. He ruled like a potentate, and although the outside of his den was dilapidated, the inside was in the most luxurious style imaginable.

Blake had been made an honorary member of the society, and this fact had been of great advantage to him previously.

Consequently he had sought out the old man this time, for he knew he would know every occurrence which took place in that mysterious underworld.

His guide led him along a dark, evil-smelling passage, and down a flight of steps.

Pausing, he knocked in the same manner as had Blake, and an invisible door swung open.

A flood of light gushed out, and Blake's eyes rapidly took in the scene, which looked exactly the same as it had five years previously.

The walls were hung with rich silks from China, a rare Turkish carpet that would have delighted the heart of a connoisseur, covered the floor—in the centre stretched a magnificently-carved table with attendant, comfortable leather chairs for the members. Huge copper lamps lighted the room, their brilliancy dying away in the silken folds on the walls.

But incongruous as did the room look for such a place, even more so as regards the room did the wizened, dark-skinned figure appear, who sat on a raised dais at the further end. His parchment-like countenance looked more Chinese than South American Indian, and Blake had often suspected that such was really the case.

He was dressed in a flowing yellow robe, and was smoking a "hubble-bubble" pipe. His eyes were deep-set and were the most remarkable feature in his face—all the wisdom and mystery of the ages seeming to congregate in those ancient orbs.

Blake bowed as he entered, but a wave of the hand motioned him to a seat at the foot of the dais.

"It is long since you were here," remarked the old man, in a soft, melodious voice.

"Five years, Giver of Light!"

"You have done well since then," continued the old man whom Blake had called by the grandiloquent name of "Giver of Light." "You have had great success, and the good wishes of the 'Source' have been with you."

"You have followed my doings?" asked Blake, in a surprised tone.

"Naturally," replied the old man. "I broke all precedent when I admitted you to the Source without knowing more about you, but I felt you were worthy. My confidence has been doubly repaid, for I have followed with satisfaction all your doings. But you have come for something. Shall I tell you what?"

"If you can," smiled Blake.

"You have come about the missing president."

"Quite right!" answered Blake, knowing his admission was perfectly safe. "And I have come to you, O Giver of Light, to ask you in your great wisdom a question."

"What is it? If I can I will answer."

"My reasoning tells me he is not in Salvarita," went on Blake. "Am I right?"

"You are. He is not in Salvarita!"

"Can you give me any further information?"

"That I cannot, and for a certain reason. I am in a hard position, my son. Only this can I tell you. Great and powerful interests are against you, and members of the Source themselves are in it. Between you, I must, by the rules, remain neutral. I regret that I cannot help you more, but I tell you, my son, give it up. The odds against you are too big, and you will never find your man!"

"I am sorry," answered Blake, rising. "I quite see your position, and thank you. As to the odds and not finding my man, that remains to be seen," he added grimly. "And now, with your permission, O Giver of Light, I will retire, for I have much to do."

"Peace go with you!" answered the old man, returning to his pipe.

Blake was disappointed at the result of his interview. He had counted on getting valuable information from the old man, and knew from his words that he was fully aware of all the details of the president's disappearance.

"Well!" he muttered, buttoning up his sailor's jacket, which he had opened when in the room. "I've made a certainty of one thing, and that is, the importance of the other side. I'll have to take a shot at some of the dens, and find out something about the yacht if I can."

Blake started down a black side-street in the direction from whence he had come. As he passed an even darker alley, he heard the lapping of the water, and was changing his course in the direction of the water's edge to reach the dens more quickly, when that dark, silent figure which had followed him ever since he landed, seized his opportunity.

Blake had his hand on his revolver, and looked about him warily as he walked; but it was intensely dark in that locality, and, although he could not see another being, he knew that all around him sinister eyes were watching his progress.

These vultures he was on guard against, but not until too late did he hear the stealthy steps behind him.

He swung round quickly, and struck out fiercely in the dark, but he was too late, for the assailant lunged heavily, the long blade of his knife sinking deep between the detective's shoulders.

Blake's arm dropped, and with an almost imperceptible moan, he fell unconscious, his life's blood ebbing rapidly.

His assailant made off silently, not stopping until he reached a cable-office far up in the town.

Then he filled in a form, and a few minutes later the following words were speeding over the wires to London.

"*Orinoco* completed. B. finished tonight. All clear. Report to headquarters and advise any other instructions here."

The Sixth Chapter
Yvonne's Revenge—President Pearson's Fate

TO return to Yvonne and her associates who had put Salvarita in such a predicament. The old fisherman had been quite right when he said he had seen two boats put off to a yacht which was cruising with all lights doused.

The captors of President Pearson had arrived at the beach safely, and had lost no time in transhipping their captive and the bullion to the yacht.

Yvonne gave orders to proceed to sea at once, and barely had the captured president been conducted to the cabin which was to be his prison, than the *Fleur-de-Lys*, her lights once more burning, put to sea.

She laid her course towards the south, and about the time Tinker met his fate in mid-ocean, and Pedro displayed his uneasiness on the *Corsair*, the *Fleur-de-Lys* was forging along at a rapid pace towards the Straits of Magellan.

A stop was made at Valparaiso, where Yvonne received a cable which had been forwarded from London, and which read as follows:

"*Orinoco* completed. B. finished. All clear. Report to headquarters and advise any other instructions here."

Her eyes filled with an intense weariness as she tossed it to Graves, who read it with satisfaction.

"Ah, that's good news!" he remarked. "We have been fortunate in our choice of agents. I can breathe more freely now with Sexton Blake and that assistant of his out of the way."

"I am sorry it was necessary," replied Yvonne; "but Sexton Blake seemed fated to cross our path, and since he refused to join us—well, he had to go."

But she rose as she spoke, and descended to her cabin, and certainly her associates would have marvelled had they seen her cast herself on her small brass bed and burst into a passion of weeping.

But none knew of the interview she had once had with Blake, in which he had refused the offer of her hand, and although she felt positive the old proverb relating to a "woman scorned" fitted her case, she realised since receiving the report of his death that her feelings had never altered.

Rymer was equally as elated as Graves on hearing of the end of Sexton Blake and his spirits went up considerably.

"At last," he thought, "I will be able to achieve something. That cursed Blake won't be stepping in again to spoil my game, and lay me by the heels!"

President Pearson had been kept in close confinement since leaving Salvarita, but as beautiful, wicked Valparaiso dropped away behind, he was brought on deck previous to an interview with Yvonne, for she felt that now was the time for her triumph.

After dinner that night she dismissed all from the saloon, and sank into a chair awaiting the arrival of the prisoner. He came a few moments later, and glanced in amazement at the beautiful woman in the faultless evening-gown.

"So it's you, mademoiselle, to whom I owe my thanks for this unexpected hospitality. When you came to Salvarita with letters of introduction, which I see now must have been forged, I did not know in receiving you at my palace that I was nursing a viper, as it were."

The president had spoken in slow, measured tones, attempting to remain dignified in his galling situation; but he started visibly as Yvonne replied.

"As to whether I am a viper or not, we will let that pass," answered Yvonne, coolly lighting a cigarette. "But as to my hospitality, I am afraid you will have to put up with it for some time, Mr. James Pearson, one-time manager and director of the Jig Saw Mine in Australia, and one-time defrauder of innocent women!"

"What do you mean?" gasped Pearson, paling. "Who are you?"

"You may well ask," returned Yvonne. "If your former partner, Mr. Vineburg, alias Bechstein, were alive, he might be able to tell you; but as he isn't, I will condescend to inform you. My name is Cartier. Perhaps that will enlighten you somewhat."

"The daughter of John Cartier?"

"The same. I see your memory is quite good."

"But—but why have you abducted me and ruined me?" he asked dazedly.

"Do you need to ask?" answered Yvonne coldly. "Is it nothing that you and your associates swindled my mother and myself, first out of the mine, and not content with that, out of our home? Is it nothing that the shock of your schemes killed my mother, and sent me into the world a penniless and friendless young woman? Have you forgotten my vow to be revenged on you and your companions?" she asked bitterly. "That vow I have kept. Yes, you were very clever, you and your 'honest' companions! You took good care to keep within the law in your swindles on two helpless women, and you thought my threat of revenge was the idle ravings of a grief-stricken young woman. Well, you have seen whether that is so.

"Your friend, Vineburg, alias Bechstein, has met his fate. I ruined him, and his suicide followed. You were the next on the list, James Pearson, and I have already accomplished your ruin. Every paper in the world is ringing with the tale of the absconding of former President Pearson, of Salvarita, with two millions of the country's money!"

"My heavens!" gasped Pearson, sinking into a chair, and mopping his brow in an agony of suffering. "Have you done that?"

"I have saved several papers, and will give them to you to read. You can see for yourself that I have done it. It might also interest you to know that Sexton Blake, your only hope, was sent in search of you. Well, that hope is gone, for he has been stabbed in Puerto Costa."

"Will you never be satisfied?" asked Pearson bitterly. "I ask no favour from your hands for myself. It would be a waste of time to tell you that I was never in sympathy with the deception practised on your mother. But is your nature so hardened with revenge that all womanly feeling has died?

"I ask you to consider Señorita Mendoza, my affianced wife. Keep the bullion, strip me of my honour, and send me into the world a broken man if you will; but I ask you to spare her. A line from you assuring her of my innocence in this affair. I assure you I changed my life, and threw off old companions, and have worked hard to build up the prosperity and honour which I achieved. Isn't that sufficient revenge for you? Will you have pity on the señorita, who has never harmed you?"

"Did you and your associates have pity on my mother, who never harmed you, but, on the contrary, as she thought, befriended you? Did you have pity on me when you forced me into the world to punish where the law wouldn't reach? Oh, I have suffered, don't make any mistake about that!

"What has my life been since then? To achieve my purpose, I was compelled to build up a machine—a well-organised circle—and now even if I would release you I couldn't. Since the members of that machine have stood by me, they must have their reward. You it was, you and your companions, who forced me outside the law, and I have no doubt you will gloat when you know that the one being on earth I cared for, the man who started to search for you, was against me, and I have been compelled to agree to his removal.

"But that additional suffering will react on you and the rest of your associates, James Pearson, for it will increase the spirit of my revenge. Everything have you deprived me of, and as I have sworn, so will I do.

"As for the Señorita Mendoza, I will think it over. I have no desire to send a woman through the suffering through which I have gone. Now leave me. I will let you know my decision."

Pearson seemed to age under the lash of her tongue, and on being dismissed, he stumbled from the saloon, almost tottering from the realisation that he was a ruined, broken man.

Yvonne sat in deep thought after he had departed, and her eyes were filled with an aching sorrow. With a heavy sigh she rose and approached the exquisite mahogany desk, stopping before a long mirror on the way.

Long and earnestly she looked at her reflection.

"Yes, I am beautiful," she muttered. "I could have been a devoted wife to some good man. My brains would have assisted him to a high position. Instead, I am sent into the world, an adventuress. Forced to live a life I hate, and receive only the admiration of men whom, in other conditions, I would not wipe my feet on. Had things been different, even Sexton Blake, cold as he is, might have thawed. And then they ask pity."

She turned wearily away, and sat down at the desk. Picking up a pen she wrote, her hand travelling slowly over the paper.

Only a few lines, and the note had neither beginning nor ending. She read it over, and the text was as follows:

"Señorita Mendoza is informed that the missing president, whom the writer understands is the affianced husband of the señorita, is guiltless of the charge of absconding. But the señorita is further informed that he is receiving just punishment for actions of his earlier life. He is unworthy of the señorita's love, and she would do well to forget him. The señorita is warned that if this note is made public, it will be immediately known, and the president will meet with a swift fate. The writer has no desire to injure an innocent woman, and writes, in answer to the president's plea, in order to ease the señorita's mind."

Yvonne seemed satisfied with the contents, and, folding it up, she addressed it.

Typical was it of her nature that she refused to give Pearson any definite answer on the matter, but her yielding had its own reward in the mitigated suffering of the grief-stricken señorita.

BLAKE BOWED AS HE ENTERED.
THE WOMAN DREW BACK IN FRIGHT - AS A HUGE HOUND DASHED IN FOLLOWED BY TWO MEN.
BLAKES ARM DROPPED. AND WITH. A MOAN. HE FELL UNCONSCIOUS

The Seventh Chapter
The Spanish Woman—Her Reward—Blake Resumes the Battle

WHEN Blake had dropped to the ground in the dark street where he had been stabbed, it will be remembered that he had immediately sunk into unconsciousness.

When he came to himself he was lying on a mattress in the corner of a dim, rickety room.

He tried to raise himself, but sank back in surprise on finding his muscles refused to support his effort.

His eyes grew puzzled in an endeavour to elucidate the reason of his being where he was. He was laboriously piecing together the events leading up to his departure from the house of the Secret Society, when the door opened and a woman entered.

She hastened over to the corner on seeing the detective's eyes open, and as she bent down, Blake saw the shattered remains of a once dusky beauty.

"The señor is better," she said, in soft Spanish. "I am glad."

"Where am I?" asked Blake weakly.

"You are safe, señor, and will now, soon be better. You were stabbed, and once I thought you were dead; but the señor is blessed with a wonderful constitution, and the wound is now nearly healed."

"Ah! I remember!" answered Blake, the memory of his attack returning to him. "But you say it is nearly healed. Have I been here, then, some little time?"

"Over ten days, señor, and always your mind was a blank."

"Over ten days!" echoed Blake, in amazement. "Then——" And he broke off, in anxious thought, as he remembered his arrangement to meet the yacht at the latest at the end of the ten days.

"What day is this, then, señorita?" he asked.

"Wednesday, señor. I brought you here on a Monday."

Blake knit his brows in worried calculations. Two days since he should have been at the meeting-place. What would they think? Where was the yacht? What was Tinker doing? And what was the situation? All these thoughts chased rapidly through his mind, but he could find no solution to them.

"The señor must not worry," said the woman, speaking again.

"I am perplexed, señorita," answered Blake, gazing up into her dark eyes. "But I evidently owe my life to you and your care, señorita. I wish to express my gratitude."

"No, no, señor! Don't!" she replied tensely. "If you knew all you would not thank me!"

"How do you mean?" asked the puzzled Blake.

"Oh, señor," she said, turning away her eyes, her dusky face turning yet darker with a flood of shame, "you owe nothing to me. I saw you leave the house of the society, and followed you to take advantage of you. A man reached you first, señor, but he left you without taking the contents of your pockets.

"I picked you up and dragged you in here, to take what you had and let you die; but I couldn't, señor. I know not why. Bad—terribly bad—have I been, and many men have been sent penniless from this place, but I could not bring myself to let you die. I dressed your wound, and—and I got interested in my work, señor. All your belongings are safe. See!" she said, rising and going to a small chest of drawers. "Only a few pesos have I taken, and that was to get things, for you. Not a penny have I touched for myself, señor."

"I quite understand, señorita," replied the amazed Blake, gently. "I owe you my life, and am deeply grateful to you. That it has in some way changed you I am glad, and your reward will be my care."

"I don't want a reward which you will give, señor," she said, in a low tone. "Of money I have enough. But you have talked too much, and must rest. Have you any friends? Can I——"

She broke off, and started up as a sudden noise came from without, and, as a deep bay followed, she sprang to the door, snatching up a revolver as she did so.

Blake raised himself, with a new-found strength, as he heard the sound.

"Don't shoot, señorita!" he exclaimed. "Open the door. It is my friends."

The woman lowered her arm and pulled open the door, drawing back in fright as a huge hound dashed in, followed by two men.

It was Pedro, with Captain Pentland and Mackay, the engineer.

Recklessly Pedro bounded over to the corner where Blake lay, his huge tongue licking the detective's hands in an ecstasy of delight.

"Thank Heaven we have found you!" exclaimed the captain, hastening over and shaking Blake's hand. "Mackay and I, with the dog, have been searching these cursed dens for two days and nights for you! But you are ill! What has happened? Is it serious?"

"Someone took enough interest in me to bury the blade of a knife in my back," smiled Blake, as he dropped the captain's hand and reached for Mackay's.

"Good heavens, you'll meet your death, Mr. Blake, if you go alone into these dens!" replied the captain.

"They nearly got me this time," laughed Blake, rubbing the ears of the hound who had snuggled close against him, his pounding tail and panting sides visible tokens of his joy. "The señorita found me and took care of me," he continued; "and but for her they would have succeeded. But I'll tell you all about it later. In the meantime, can you make arrangements to get me out of here secretly? I don't want it known that they failed in their purpose."

"Yes; I will make arrangements," answered the captain.

"We will get a carriage and transfer you to the hotel tonight. But no one would know you with that growth of beard. And now," went on the captain, shifting nervously, "I'm afraid I've got bad news for you, Mr. Blake. Do you feel strong enough to withstand a shock?"

"Yes—yes. What is it?" replied Blake. "Tell me, captain."

"Well, it's this way, sir. Captain Brown, of the *Orinoco*, arrived in port last week. He reported on his arrival that a lad by the name of Gates, travelling alone, had been lost overboard in the North Atlantic two days out. As you told me your assistant was travelling under that name, I thought you ought to know."

"My heavens!" gasped Blake. "Are you sure?"

"Quite, Mr. Blake. I'm sorry to bring you such bad news, but of course, there is always hope that he may have been picked up."

"No—no!" muttered Blake, his eyes filling. "There is little chance of such a thing! Pardon my emotion, gentlemen, but that lad was very dear to me, and I am still a bit weak. But leave me now, and return tonight for me. I wish to be alone."

Slowly they withdrew, the taciturn Mackay furiously blowing his nose. And as the door closed, Blake turned his face to the wall, and, with Pedro's head under his arm, gave himself up to horrible thoughts.

"Poor lad!" he muttered to the dog. "He was such a help and such a companion! What will I do without his sunny ways to cheer me? He had grown so much into my life, and now he leaves it—sent to his death by me!" He groaned involuntarily at the thought. "I've only got you, now, old chap, but together we will avenge him, Pedro! It will go hard with his murderers, for murder it was. Tinker never fell overboard! He was forced over!"

The Spanish woman, who had withdrawn on the captain's entry, returned to the room, and, seeing Blake's dejected attitude, hastened to his side.

"Is the señor feeling worse?" she asked. "Has the visit been too much for him?"

"No, señorita," answered Blake sadly. "My friends brought me sorrowful tidings. One whom I dearly loved is gone from me."

"Was she the señor's wife?" asked the woman.

"No, señorita. I have no wife. It was a young Caballero—a lad."

"I am very sorry, señor!" she replied.

"Thank you! And now, señorita, I must prepare to leave you. My friends come for me this evening."

"Very well, señor. I will lay your things out, and send a lad to help you with your clothes."

The woman left the room, and a few moments later a young dark-skinned lad entered.

Blake had to rest many times before the last garment was on, but he finally managed it. He tossed the lad a peso, and, sinking into a chair, buried his head in his hands.

The news of Tinker's death had been a great blow to him, and, weak as he was, every move was an effort. Pedro was very dear to him, but Tinker had been a great deal in his life, and he looked forward to the future with an aching heart.

He sat buried in his thoughts until the swift, tropical night had fallen and the woman returned.

She prepared him a strengthening drink, and he had barely finished it when the soft rattle of wheels sounded in the dark, sandy street.

"Well, señorita," said Blake, rising stiffly, "I hardly know how to express my gratitude to you. I wish to reward you for your care for me, and later, when the present blackness of my life has cleared a little, I would do something for you."

"No, señor; I have told you I wish no reward. But listen, señor, before the others come," she went on, speaking rapidly and turning her head. "You, señor, are great and good. The greetings of your friends show me you are honoured among your fellow men. Señor, I might have been a better woman had I been born in a different atmosphere. You are the first good man I have known. I know that to you I am as nothing; but, señor, there is one reward you can give me, if you will."

"What is it, señorita?" asked Blake gently. "Believe me, if it is possible, I will gladly give it."

"It is this, señor," she whispered, moving closer to him. "I would have you kiss me once before you go."

Silence reigned for a moment before it was broken by Blake's low voice.

"Señorita, permit me," he said softly, and, bending, gently touched his lips to the woman's forehead.

The wheels stopped as the carriage pulled up at the door, and the captain entered.

"Good-bye, señorita!" Blake said, as he moved away.

"Good-bye, señor! God guard thee! You have been most generous!"

As the door closed, she stumbled to the mattress in the corner and cast herself down in an agony of bitter remorse.

***

Blake rapidly gained in strength, and much he needed it, for the days following his departure from the tumble-down house were strenuous ones.

He had a secret interview with Señor Martina, the present head of the Government, and that gentleman had given him the name of the old fisherman who had seen the two boats leave the beach on the night of the president's disappearance.

A conversation with that individual had elicited only one new fact. He was cautious about admitting it, but Blake's tact secured it after an hour's battle of wits. It was that the yacht, in the opinion of the old fisherman, bore a great resemblance to one which had lain in the harbour of Puerto Costa a few weeks previously. He had been chary about admitting the fact, for those aboard the yacht had been intimate with the powers that were, and he did not wish to risk getting himself into trouble.

Blake followed up this point, and had another interview with Señor Martina.

"By the way," remarked Blake, in a casual tone, "I hear there was a yacht in the harbour a short time back. I had some acquaintances cruising in these waters, and have been wondering if it were they."

"Ah! Yes, we had some charming people in port!" replied the old statesman. "A Mr. Grant and his niece. Very wealthy people, I believe. They brought splendid letters with them, and I think we managed to make their stay pleasant."

"Ah! The niece—let me see—I seem to have forgotten her name," murmured Blake.

"Mademoiselle Carston," answered Martina. "A beautiful young woman."

"Yes—yes! She is, as you say, a beautiful young woman. They still have, then, I presume, the same yacht—The *Viking*—if I remember rightly?"

"Ah, no. They must have secured a new one, or altered the name, for it was called the *Fleur-de-Lys*."

"Why, of course! How stupid of me!" laughed Blake. "I remember now. I got the name mixed up with that of another. I am sorry I missed them, but may yet run into them."

And the old statesman, not knowing the double meaning of that last sentence, smiled in answer.

Blake hastened from that interview to the office of the British Consul. There he secured copies of the shipping reports for some weeks back.

It was a long and tedious search, but his eyes lit up with satisfaction as he saw the following item:

"Valparaiso, Chile; Yacht *Fleur-de-Lys*; Vaughan, master; arrived."

And, dated two days later, was:

"Valparaiso, Chile; Yacht *Fleur-de-Lys*; Vaughan, master; cleared for Suva, Fiji."

Blake hastened back to his hotel and gave orders to have his bag packed at once.

"Grant—Carston. It may be only a coincidence; but, by heavens, I don't believe it! If Mademoiselle Yvonne isn't at the bottom of this I'll be greatly surprised! And my idea is strengthened since I have discovered that Pearson came from Australia. What on earth is she doing in the South Pacific, and where is she heading for?"

Before he left the hotel, Blake despatched a heavy sealed envelope to Señor Mendoza, in London, and it was addressed to Tinker.

"It's probably useless," he muttered sadly; "but I can't help clinging to the hope that he has been picked up and if he returned to London he would go at once to Señor Mendoza on finding me gone."

Sadly he left the hotel, and quietly joined the *Corsair*. Captain Pentland had full steam up, and five minutes later the speedy yacht was cutting her way in a southerly direction on what was to be one of the longest chases Sexton Blake had ever had.

The Eighth Chapter
Tinker is Picked Up—He Returns to England—Where is Blake?

WHEN Tinker had felt himself dropping through the rain into the dark waters of the Atlantic, he had, as has been said, mechanically clutched his useless weapon. His senses had been too near the borderland of unconsciousness when his assailant threw him over to distinguish the character of it. But as the air rushed back to his lungs he realised that in his effort he had grasped a lifebuoy. Dodging under it, he came up through the hole, and, resting his arms on the circle, gazed about him as he battled with the waves.

Now far ahead were the lights of the fast-disappearing *Orinoco*, and even as he gazed she was swallowed up in a heavier deluge of blinding rain.

"This is a pretty situation!" he gasped to himself, as he fought for breath. "What a fool I was to be taken in by a clergyman's outfit, and after the guv'nor warned me so carefully, too! I'll have my work cut out to keep afloat, and it looks like a small chance of being picked up, especially if this rain keeps on. But I don't want to die!" he gasped, as he struggled on. And he was right. He did have his work cut out to keep his head above the waves.

How long he had battled in that tossing, black water he did not know, but a sudden hope grew in his breast as the lights of a ship appeared quite near.

He yelled frantically, but the blinding rain beat down his voice, and as the ship kept on, unheeding, he sank back in despair.

It was perhaps as well for Tinker's nerve that he was unaware that on board that brilliantly-lighted steamer were Blake and Pedro, and that the faithful hound had in some way heard his call for help. Had he known, his despair would have been almost overpowering.

Minutes passed that seemed like hours, hours passed that seemed like an eternity, and still the brave lad battled with the relentless waves.

He lost all count of time, the strain of his constant battle in the cold water was fast numbing his senses.

As dawn broke, he saw what he thought was a sail, and frantically called. His voice came in a hoarse croak, and he sank back with a sob of despair as he saw his reeling senses had enlarged the wings of a gliding seagull to the sail of a ship.

The morning wore on, and Tinker sank into a stupor. Thirst claimed him, and, try as he would, the salt waves found their way into his mouth. Mechanically he battled for breath, but as he sank deeper into a delirium the weary muscles gave up the unequal fight, and he lay back heedless of the green monsters which swept over him.

***

Captain Masters, of the tramp-steamer *Annabel*, had been at one time one of the smartest captains in the passenger service.

Fate had dogged him, however, with unrelenting steps, and the loss of his ship had reduced him to his present berth.

The wreck was not his fault, and all hands had been saved by his individual efforts, but the loss of a ship is an unpardonable sin in shipping circles, and after a year's total suspension he had been given a seedy tramp-steamer.

But his seamanship had not been impaired, and his keen eyes—perhaps grown keener since the tragedy of his life—searched the sea with their accustomed keen scrutiny.

For that reason, when a small object caught his eye just before dusk shut in, he looked earnestly at it. Reinforcing his naked sight with his telescope, he grunted as the glass confirmed his opinion.

Quickly he sang out an order, and the tramp swung round, heading for the object of his attention.

Again he grunted as they approached it, and lowered a boat.

The sailors returned on deck with the limp figure of a lad, which they laid at his feet.

The captain wasted no time, but went quickly to work. He poured raw spirit between the cold lips, and one of the sailors worked the arms up and down, while another removed the lad's shoes and chafed the cold ankles. Their efforts were rewarded by a faint stirring in the heart region, and as it grew stronger the captain rose.

"Take him up, and put him to bed in the cabin adjoining mine. Give him another dose of spirit, and have the cook prepare hot blankets. He was about gone, but will come round all right now."

He picked up the lifebuoy as they carried the unconscious figure away.

"*Orinoco!*" he muttered, reading the name painted on it. "She's in the South American trade. Well, I don't know how he got in the water. Perhaps the *Orinoco* has gone down. In any event, he's going a long distance away from his destination, for I can't land him until I reach Cape Town, and as this magnificent liner isn't equipped with wireless, his friends will have to wait for news."

Tossing aside the lifebuoy, the captain returned to the chartroom, and entered in his log the occurrence which had just taken place.

Tinker, for he was the lad who had been rescued, did not awaken until the following day.

Captain Masters came to see him in the morning, and Tinker gave him a full account of his adventure, concealing only the fact of his real identity.

The kindly man supplied him with extra garments, and before another day had passed Tinker was well enough to come on deck.

His mind was anxious, for he knew Blake would be expecting word from him, but he was very thankful for his escape, and considered himself very fortunate in being rescued at all.

It was nearly three weeks later when they entered Table Bay—that beautiful harbour, guarded by the impressive bulk of the mountain from whence it derives its name.

Tinker thanked the captain earnestly for his goodness, and as he hastened into the town resolved to get Blake, if possible, to use his influence in securing for the captain a better berth, for Tinker had wormed out the story of the captain's life, and his heart had filled with sympathy for the kind-hearted skipper.

Tinker kept the cables warm with his messages.

That night he got only one reply, and it was from Mrs. Bardell, the housekeeper at Baker Street.

"S. B. LEFT SAME NIGHT YOU LEFT. HEARD NOTHING SINCE. GREATLY WORRIED ABOUT YOU BOTH."

Tinker sent an answer to the good soul, and sought the steamship office, his mind full of misgivings about Blake.

He inquired about sailings, and returned to the Grand, where he found another answer. It was from Señor Martina, and read:

"PARTY MENTIONED HAD BAD ACCIDENT. RECOVERED, AND SAILED FOR UNKNOWN DESTINATION."

"What had I better do?" muttered the lad. "And I wonder what accident the guv'nor had? He must be on the track, though, and he will be nearly crazy about my disappearance. The best thing I can do is to get back to London as quick as I can, and see if he has sent any advice to Señor Mendoza as we arranged."

Rising as he spoke, Tinker hastened back to the steamship-office, where he purchased a ticket.

The next day he was a passenger on the *Denley Castle* for England.

The Ninth Chapter
The Reunion—Blake's Message—Tinker Takes a Journey

LITTLE less than three weeks later Tinker hastened into the Baker Street apartments. Mrs. Bardell met him, and her relief at his safe return found vent in a voluble conversation.

Tinker gathered from her stream of talk that nothing had come from Blake, but that there was a cable addressed to Tinker, which she had laid on the desk.

Tinker dashed into the consulting-room, and over to the desk.

It was piled high with the correspondence which had come during Blake's absence, and on the top was the cable.

Tearing it open, he read the terse sentence:

"GO TO S. M."

And before the astonished landlady could speak again he had dashed out on a run.

"Well, I calls it strange goings on!" she gasped, as she hastened to the window and saw Tinker hail a taxi.

"They both disappear, and one of 'em comes back looking as though he'd been in the wars, and where the other one is goodness only knows. Now he goes off again, before he's been in the 'ouse five seconds; and when he'll come back again I don't know. They'll both be killed one of these days, I know they will! And what's the use of a woman worryin' her head about them, when they just won't take care of themselves?"

The kindly soul wiped the corner of her eye as she spoke, and moved about trying to find a spot of dust in the already spotless room.

Tinker took the letters "S. M." to mean Señor Mendoza, and although the cable was unsigned, he knew it must be from Blake.

Señor Mendoza was not at his office in the Embassy, but was in his private apartments.

"Ah, señor," he smiled, as Tinker was announced, "I remember you! I have been expecting you for some days," he said. "And now let me present you to my daughter."

Tinker bowed to the beautiful, dark-eyed young Spanish woman who sat on a large divan, and the lad could not but sympathise with her as he saw the haunting look of sorrow in her eyes.

Turning to the Minister he stated the reason of his coming, and handed over the cable.

"Yes, I have a letter for you, but must ask you for the code."

Tinker supplied it, and the Minister handed over the letter.

"Leave us, Carmen, please," said Señor Mendoza, to his daughter. "I have some important matters to talk over."

The young woman rose as he spoke, and, bowing gracefully to both of them, retired.

"If you will excuse me, señor, I will read my letter," said Tinker, as the door closed. "I think it is of importance."

"By all means," replied the Minister, lighting a cigar.

Tinker broke the seal, and hurriedly read through the many closely written sheets, which, he saw, were in Blake's handwriting.

"Well, señor, I hope I am not impertinent in surmising that your letter is from Sexton Blake?"

"Not at all, sir," answered Tinker. "It is from Mr. Blake, and in it he says if I receive it I am at liberty to tell you the contents."

"Ah, thank you!" exclaimed the Minister. "I should be very glad."

The letter was long, the first part being Blake's fears as to Tinker's fate, and, with shining eyes, the lad skipped this portion. Rapidly he gave the Spaniard the gist of what followed, which was a detailed account of Blake's movements, and also the particulars of his chase after the yacht.

"He says here, sir," Tinker added, "that he will put in at Valparaiso for an hour, to see if there is any news to be picked up, and then he will continue the chase to Suva. He says if I get this I had better cable to Suva and travel to Port Said and await instructions. Of course, he fully thinks me dead by now, but he always considers every detail, and it happens I can go tonight without wasting any time."

"I see," remarked the Minister, as Tinker finished. "I agree with you, he is a very thorough man, and has done wonderfully well to pick up the trail so soon. But I wish to show you something. Naturally you understand it is confidential," he added, opening a drawer in his desk and taking out an envelope. "Read that, señor!"

Tinker took the envelope and read the enclosed note. It was the one written by Yvonne to Señorita Mendoza, and Tinker's eyes opened wide as he read it.

"By Jove, sir, it's a cool hand that wrote that! How long since you received it?"

"It only came yesterday, and it proves Mr. Blake is on the right track. Now you will remember he forbade my telling my daughter he was working on the case, but in my opinion, things have altered since then, and I want your permission to tell her."

"Well, I don't know———" began Tinker.

"Wait, señor," said the old statesman, raising his hand. "I vouch to you on my honour that she shall not breathe a word, and in addition, I am going to ask you to let us accompany you to Port Said. Then you can cable Mr. Blake we are with you. If he objects, we have nothing to do but return. If not, we will continue on to where you meet him. It is for my daughter's sake I ask, for this strain is nearly killing her."

"Well, in that case, señor Mendoza, I am sure Mr. Blake would endorse what I do, and I consent with pleasure."

"Thank you, señor," said the Minister, with deep emotion. "I quite realise why you hesitate. And now, when can we start?"

"I will cable Mr. Blake to Suva immediately, and we will catch the Continental train from Charing Cross tonight."

"Good! My daughter and I will be ready. How about joining us here for tea at the Embassy, and we can all leave together?"

"Thank you, sir. I will be delighted," answered Tinker, rising.

Shaking hands with the Minister, he hastened away with a lighter heart to cable Blake.

***

That night Tinker, Señor Mendoza, and the beautiful señorita left Charing Cross for the Continent.

At Port Said, Tinker received a long cable from Blake expressing his deep joy at the lad's safety. It was sent from Melbourne, and went on to say they were clearing for Hong Kong. Tinker was to catch the first steamer and hasten on. Blake confirmed Tinker's action regarding Mendoza, and told him by all means to bring them along.

They were fortunate in securing a steamer to Colombo at once, and by the reckless use of money, Señor Mendoza got in touch by cable with the captain of a Hong Kong steamer in the Ceylon port, and arranged to have it held for their arrival.

It was a seedy steamer which they joined there, but Tinker was in high spirits at the early prospect of again seeing Blake, and even the saddened señorita seemed to brighten a bit under the lad's sunny ways.

He spent many hours of that journey telling her of former deeds of Blake's, relegating himself modestly to a very unimportant share.

Consequently it was a fairly cheerful party that steamed into Hong Kong, and Tinker could hardly contain himself when he saw Blake and Pedro on the quay.

It was a memorable meeting between them. Señor Mendoza and the señorita turned away as the lad rushed to the waiting pair, and their eyes wet when they turned back to greet Blake, who was presented to the señorita.

It was a happy reunion on the yacht that night, and none of that cheery party knew of the cloud so quickly to descend again.

Many explanations had to be made. Tinker had to give a detailed account of his adventures, and then Blake took up the conversation.

"The reason I kept my departure for Salvarita from even you, Tinker, was because I knew we had been watched from the moment Señor Mendoza came to see us. I intended to reach Salvarita before you, and meet you there, but as we know events happened to both of us which forbade it."

Blake then recounted his experiences in Puerto Costa up to the time he had started on the chase for the *Fleur-de-Lys*.

"We headed the *Corsair* at full speed for Valparaiso," he went on. "I had Captain Pentland stop in there for an hour, but discovered nothing new. I was clinging to the hope that there might be something from Tinker, but I was doomed to disappointment, and needless to say, I took up the chase again with a heavy heart.

"The *Fleur-de-Lys* had cleared from Valparaiso for Suva, and we sailed at once for that port. Naturally, I had no hopes of overtaking her by then, but I hoped there to pick up the trail.

"Well, you can imagine my surprise on our arrival, when I discovered she had only reached there four days before we had, and had cleared for Melbourne only the day before. Unfortunately we were held up by some necessary repairs to one of the bulkheads, and when we left Suva, the *Fleur-de-Lys* was four days ahead.

"I had been unable to glean any information in Suva, so of course all we could do was to keep on the trail until we overtook her, and then take steps to find out if our quarry was really on her, or whether we had been on a false trail from the very start.

"On arrival in Melbourne, we discovered she had taken on some electrical material, and had cleared for Hong Kong. The next day we were after her, and when we arrived here found she had left the day previously for Batavia.[8] I discovered here that they endeavoured to secure some electrical supplies, which they were unable to do, and have gone to Batavia for that purpose. For certain reasons, which at present I cannot tell you, I feel more convinced than ever that the people I am after are aboard the *Fleur-de-Lys*. I know pretty well what their next move will be, and you might be surprised to know that I think we would soon see them if we returned to Suva.

"But on the other hand, I have to guard against unknown details, and for that reason we will sail in"—and he pulled out his watch—"just twenty-two minutes for Batavia. We had to wait an extra day for your arrival, so that gives them two days' start."

"Hadn't you better show the guv'nor that note you showed me, sir?" asked Tinker, turning to Señor Mendoza as Blake finished speaking.

"Ah, yes, certainly! In my interest I had for the moment forgotten it."

He took the note from his pocket, and passed it over to the detective.

"Ah!" exclaimed Blake, when he finished reading it. "I see my deductions are perfectly correct. This endorses them entirely. I now have positive proof that I am right," he said, handing it back.

"Is it asking too much to inquire if you can tell me who is the writer of this?" Señor Mendoza asked.

"I am sorry, but I must disappoint you for the present," replied Blake. "All I can tell you is this. The writer of that note is the cleverest individual with whom I have ever

---

[8] Batavia now Jakarta, Indonesia

crossed swords. Some day, señor, I may tell you that individual's history, and I promise you it is an interesting story. I have been confident all along that such a gigantic coup could only be carried out by one or two persons, and after reading that note, I have all the proof I desire. And now, señorita and gentlemen, I hear the propeller starting. Let us adjourn to the deck and get our last view of Hong Kong."

The Tenth Chapter
Tinker Disappears—Blake Takes a Hand—Blake and Tinker on Board the *Fleur-de-Lys*

HONG KONG forms the tip, and beautiful, dirty, cosmopolitan Batavia, the other extremity of that treacherous, hand-like stretch called the China Sea, of which the Gulf of Siam forms the thumb, and the Java Sea the wrist.

Into the harbour, twisting its way through the many dirty craft and the kaleidoscopic life of the teeming East, steamed the *Corsair* a few days later.

Blake and Tinker stood on the bridge with Captain Pentland, and the former's eyes lit up with satisfaction as he saw a graceful white yacht standing out from its surroundings, on the bow of which was painted in gilt letters "*Fleur-de-Lys*."

"The scent grows warm, Tinker," he murmured softly. "And now to ascertain if our quarry is on board, or if we have come on a wild-goose chase, which I think is not likely."

"I say, guv'nor," said Tinker, in an eager tone; "how about my slipping over there after dusk, and trying to discover if they are on board?"

"Well, my lad," smiled Blake; "if you are very careful, I don't mind. But look out they don't handle you as they did before."

"I'll be careful, guv'nor," promised the lad. "I'll be glad of the chance to get back at them for tumbling me into the Atlantic."

"Very well, Tinker; but not a word to the others. For the present I only wish ourselves to know the identity of our quarry."

That evening when the night life of Batavia had begun its course, Tinker slipped quietly over the side, and made his way across the harbour to where the *Fleur-de-Lys* lay. He was not aware that hardly had he done so, when Blake slipped over after him and followed.

Tinker kept in the shadow and moved cautiously, stepping with great care as he got near the yacht.

Several bales were scattered about the dock, and behind these he took refuge.

Half an hour passed before anyone stirred on the yacht, and then it was a stout Chinese man who waddled down the gangway and disappeared up the dock.

Tinker judged it to be the yacht's Chinese cook going into the town, where he would probably spend his leave in the opium-clouded atmosphere of some Chinese den; and he was right.

Although the brilliant streams of light came through the saloon portholes, over another hour went by, and still no movement occurred on deck.

Tinker raised himself, and started to make his way cautiously along and endeavour to reach the silent deck, when a soft movement behind caused him to turn.

He gazed into a pair of angry eyes set in a face which was distorted with rage. It was Dr. Rymer, although Tinker did not know it.

Tinker dodged, and started to run, but Rymer shot out his arm, and caught the lad a staggering blow behind the ear.

Tinker had desired to get away without being recognised, but he saw that it was now hopeless. He turned and sprang at his assailant, but through the dark came crashing the heavy butt of a revolver, and he dropped.

Quickly Rymer picked the lad up, and, swinging him over his shoulder, disappeared with his burden up the gangway.

Blake had seen the struggling figures through the gloom, but he had been some distance away when it happened, and when he arrived at the scene of the encounter both participants had gone.

He was positive it must have been Tinker, and was strongly tempted to return to the *Corsair* and get a party and storm the *Fleur-de-Lys*. But if by chance he had made a mistake, it would look rather peculiar to go racing aboard a strange yacht with a dozen armed men at his heels.

But he must do something, for if the yacht did contain the people he was after, and if it had been Tinker whom they had captured—well, if they discovered who Tinker was, his plans would all be upset, and Heaven only knew what their next move would be.

Rapidly he thought, and finally a daring plan came to him.

He had seen the fat Chinese cook go ashore. It would be late when he returned, and probably only the watch would be around. They would know where the cook had been, and would pay no attention to him, thinking his mind would be clogged with opium.

Blake would hasten back to the *Corsair*, and get his own Chinese disguise. This, with the necessary windings to make him as fat as the cook, would serve.

He would watch for the man's return, and attack him. It would only take a moment to make his face a counterpart of the cook's, and with the latter's clothes he would pass.

Once he had elaborated his plan Blake moved quickly. Softly he hastened back to the *Corsair*, and got the necessary things.

Captain Pentland had gone into the town, and Señor Mendoza and the señorita had both retired, Ross was in charge, and Blake told him he would be gone for two or three hours as he hurried over the side.

Quickly he made his way back to the *Fleur-de-Lys*, and, sinking again behind the scattered bales, settled down for a long wait.

All was still and quiet aboard the yacht, and he noticed that during his absence the saloon lights had been extinguished.

The glow of a cigar on the deck told him someone was sitting in its dark shelter.

He dared not light a match and look at his watch, but he calculated an hour must have passed before the glowing cigar-end sailed over the rail into the water, and a scrape and the sound of footsteps indicated the moving away of the invisible smoker.

Another long period passed without movement, and Blake judged it to be near midnight when his quick ears caught the soft shuffle of approaching steps.

"That must be him at last," he breathed to himself as he crept around the bale, and as he gained the other side he crouched low, ready to spring, as through the darkness loomed up the stout, shuffling figure of the Chinese cook.

Blake waited until the Celestial got opposite him, and then, like a panther he threw himself through the air.

He caught the unsuspicious cook in a throttling grip around the throat. The man squirmed and wriggled under Blake's hold, but the detective was taking no chances of discovery. Pressing his knee in the small of his adversary's back, he jerked backwards, and, with a gasping gurgle, the Celestial yielded and dropped at his feet.

Blake dragged the body to the shelter of a shed some distance away. He hated to treat the man in this way, but Tinker's life was in danger.

Pulling out a small electric torch, he propped it up with its circle of light shining on the unconscious man's face.

Rapidly Blake worked. A few lines here, a puffing there, a darker shade, a squint to his eyes, the shape of the brows changed, and so perfect had his work been that he could easily have passed in daylight as the unconscious Celestial on the ground.

He quickly appropriated the cook's clothes and slippers, and when he had bound his body to the correct size and had put on his Chinese wig and his victim's hat, he was an exact replica of the senseless man before him.

Extinguishing the light, he bent down and hastily bound and gagged his victim, and a moment later he started down the dock towards the *Fleur-de-Lys*, his feet shuffling along in a perfect imitation of the Chinese cook's stride.

Blake was pleased at the success of his plan so far, but, nevertheless, he kept his revolver in a handy place as he shuffled up the gangway of the yacht.

He had only a vague idea where the cook's quarters were situated, but that was a risk he would have to take.

He was moving along the dark deck in the direction where he thought them to be when a dark figure loomed up and a harsh voice spoke. Blake's heart leaped as he recognised Rymer's tones, but he acted warily, for he knew, with the odds against him, he would have short shrift were his masquerade discovered.

"Here, John!" came Rymer's harsh voice. "This is a nice time to be getting back from leave! We've been waiting for your return to get under way for two hours. I've a good mind to rope-end you! Get below!"

Catching Blake by the shoulders, Rymer hustled him along and sent him sprawling with a kick to the lower deck.

Blake picked himself up, his fingers itching to get at Rymer, but he realised the madness of such a proceeding at the present moment. Bottling up his wrath, he walked to the side and gazed over, his mind working rapidly over Rymer's remark.

"Waiting two hours to get under way!" he muttered. "That means they will soon start, and if I am to do anything I'll have to work quickly. But, my friend, you will suffer for that kick!" he added savagely.

His thoughts broke off, and he looked up as he heard the clang of bells and the sudden churning of the propeller.

"Heavens, they're going now! What a situation! Here am I aboard and Tinker, too! If they discover who we are the game is up. Dare I—can I bluff it out until I get a chance to move? Impossible, but there's nothing else for it. Why didn't I get a dozen men from the *Corsair* and risk a raid? If they find things out, it will be a quick end for both of us this time."

Swiftly Blake hastened to the other side. There were already several yards of black water between the yacht and the dock, and moving further along, he gazed along the docks, his eyes following the line they would take in leaving the harbour.

"By heavens," he muttered, "we'll pass close to the *Corsair*! wonder if I dare risk it?"

A sailor passed at that moment, and threw a curse at the Chinese cook, but Blake paid no attention.

He moved as quick as he dared towards the fo'c'sle, and muttered with relief as he came to the cook's galley.

Two more sailors passed, and Blake snuffled audibly as they went by.

"Oh, you got back, did you?" growled one. "A nice temper you have put the skipper in. You'll get that pigtail of yours pulled tomorrow for you!"

"Me velly solly!" answered Blake, in a sing-song voice. "Velly many fliends in Batav."

"You'll wish you didn't have so 'velly many fliends'!" growled the sailor, as he hastened on.

But Blake knew the sailors would not annoy him too much, for, whether it be windjammer or liner, the cook is a personage to treat with respect, particularly at sea, where another cannot be secured. Once more alone, Blake opened the door of the galley and shuffled in carefully closing it after him. Lighting a match, he searched until he found a candle. This lighted, he darted his eyes around his new quarters.

Fortunately his predecessor had been neat, and in that moment Blake blessed him for his neatness, for he could not discern what he hoped to find, and time was more than precious.

That which he was searching for was a piece of paper, and he grunted as his eye caught an old piece of brown wrapping paper in the wood box behind the galley stove.

He set the candle down, and smoothed out the crumpled paper. Pulling out a short piece of pencil, he rapidly wrote:

"Captain Pentland,—Tinker captured. Myself caught on board as yacht sailed. Make for S—Will endeavour communicate with you there. In greatest haste.—S. B."

"It's a slim chance that we will pass close enough to the *Corsair* to send this over, but I'll have to take the chance," he muttered.

Feeling in his pocket, he drew out a couple of spare revolver cartridges, and carefully wrapping the note around these, extinguished the candle, and stole outside.

Overhead the stars shone in brilliant tropical splendour. The dainty *Fleur-de-Lys* was rapidly gaining speed, her sharp bow cutting the water and throwing it out in gleaming phosphorescent foam.

On all sides lay the medley of native craft, over which silence reigned.

Blake crept noiselessly to the bow, and strained his eyes ahead watching for the *Corsair*.

There she lay far ahead, silent, and unsuspecting of the fate of her two passengers.

Hardened as he was, Blake gasped as the *Fleur-de-Lys* swung around several points, for he knew if he failed to send his message to the *Corsair*, he and Tinker had a slim chance of escaping. Even if his message did reach its destination, things would probably reach a crisis long before they could be overtaken.

But it was a chance, even though it was so slim, and that chance he had to take.

Even supposing they did pass close enough for him to throw the note, his greatest fear was that in the darkness it would fall short or go too far.

His taut nerves relaxed again as the yacht swung back, and he saw that the change in her course had been made to avoid a native sampan.

The *Corsair* was growing more distinct as they swept on, and Blake leaned tensely forward as she drew nearer and nearer.

Would they go close enough? Yes, they would! No; again the *Fleur-de-Lys* changed her course—no, it was hopeless! Ah, but wait; she was coming round again! Yes, they would pass fairly close! Nearer, nearer—just another cable's-length! As they came opposite, the crouching Blake drew back his hand. Aiming with all his care, he brought his arm forward with all his strength, and released the lead-weighted message.

It sailed through the air, and the detective landed forward, listening tensely for its fall. It came. But was it a flop in the water or on wood? He could not tell, and his heart sank at the torturing thought that it had fallen short.

But he had no more time to investigate, for several sailors tumbled out of the fo'c'sle to take the watch, and the Chinese cook left the rail, and stole noiselessly back to the galley.

The Eleventh Chapter
Sexton Blake, Chinese Cook—Tinker Walks the Plank—
Chan to the Rescue

BLAKE discovered he had tackled one of the biggest propositions in his life, when he went aboard the *Fleur-de-Lys* disguised as the cook.

He had cause, it is true, to congratulate himself on the perfection of his disguise, for as yet it had created no suspicion, but that was small comfort in the circumstances.

It was the second day out, and as yet he had failed to discover any signs that Tinker was aboard.

One thing, though, he had gained, and that was the proof that his quarry was aboard, and he puzzled his brains over the partnership of Yvonne and Rymer.

Hitherto, they had always worked separately, and Blake had no idea they knew each other.

One had been quite enough to tackle, but with both working together, and on the high seas, with a captain and crew in complete accord with them—well, if his disguise was penetrated, his life shouldn't be worth a minute's purchase.

His only hope was that their suspicions would be killed by the thought that Blake had been put out of the way by their agent, but he knew the slightest thing might bring discovery.

About Graves he did not worry much, for he knew the full extent of any danger to be apprehended from him, Yvonne's uncle ranked far below Yvonne herself in natural shrewdness, and Blake knew it. His methods were less delicate than the woman's, but Blake knew if his disguise were to be penetrated, Graves would be the first to demand his instant death, and would probably gain his point.

Of the missing president he had seen nothing, and, although he had kept his ears open, the sailors' gossip told him nothing.

He was, for the time, in a very dangerous situation, and absolutely helpless in the camp of the enemy—an enemy who would not hesitate to put an end to him, if necessary.

Little time had he, however, for conjectures, for as has been said, he had tackled a tremendous proposition.

Lucky it was that Blake was an expert cook, for his studies had given him a thorough insight into all methods of cookery. And well he needed it, for he was kept on the jump.

Up at five every morning to prepare the sailors' breakfast. Then at night, the saloon breakfast had to be prepared.

At eleven, beef-tea for the upper deck. Twelve brought the sailors' dinner-time, and one the saloon lunch.

Hardly had he cleared up from this, when afternoon tea had to be served on deck, and the stewards kept him busy. The sailors' supper came at five-thirty, and the saloon dinner at seven, after which a cold supper had to be served at nine.

Truly he had tackled a proposition if you will, and although he was prepared to do anything to run down a quarry rather than write the word failure in his book, he was heartily sick of the situation at the end of the second day.

He smiled grimly, as he thought of the situation, for, dangerous as was his position, he had to confess that it contained an element of humour, and his smile still broadened when many rough compliments were thrown at him from the fo'c'sle on the improvements of his cooking.

To complicate matters, his first morning had brought to light an unexpected inheritance from his predecessor in the shape of a young Chinese "cookee," whose English vocabulary extended to the one word "allight," which he monotonously emitted, when the sailors addressed him. Luckily, Blake knew Chinese, and he spent half an hour with the astonished boy in strenuous diplomacy, for the young Celestial had discovered at once the difference in accent. But when he had finished, Blake had secured a firm adherent who eventually proved a useful ally.

Blake had not seen any signs of Tinker for a very good reason, but the evening of the second day was to bring him those signs, and their coming was to send the detective through a sharper and swifter agony of mind than he had ever experienced.

When Tinker had been carried aboard by Rymer, he had been conveyed to a cabin, and unceremoniously tossed into a bunk. For two days the stress of affairs had prevented the investigation of his conduct, as it was thought he had been only a curious loafer. Rymer had carried him aboard merely to be on the safe side, and little did he dream that he had captured the lad whom he thought at the bottom of the Atlantic. He would not have recognised Tinker if he had seen him; but Yvonne, Graves, and Captain Vaughan knew him well, not counting Hendricks, the mate.

Consequently, he had been left undisturbed, except for the visits of the steward who brought his meals.

Tinker was aware they were at sea, but his porthole only showed a weary stretch of waves, and for that reason he welcomed the gruff command to come to the saloon. It would at least be a break in the monotony; but, brave as the lad was, he would have clung to that monotony as a haven of delight had he known the fate in store for him.

The saloon was brilliantly lighted. Yvonne sat lounging in her favourite chair—Graves was smoking in another, while Rymer loafed restlessly about.

Tinker's conductor left him at the door, and the lad blinked his eyes as he stumbled in.

Yvonne and Graves threw off their languid attitude, and sat up with a jerk as Tinker walked over and stood in front of them. Rymer, seeing something unusual was in the wind, stopped prowling about, and walked closer.

"So," said Yvonne, "we meet again, my young friend. I thought you were safely at the bottom of the sea by now."

"It is no fault of mademoiselle's that I am not," retorted Tinker, as evenly as Yvonne had spoken.

"Your spirit has evidently not suffered," she went on. "Are you of the feline tribe, that you have so many lives?"

"As to that, mademoiselle, I will leave you to guess. As for my spirit, you may bend it, but you and all your associates cannot break it."

"Truly, my lad, your late master had reason to be proud of you," returned Yvonne, her eyes softening. "Come, I will give you freedom, give you wealth, and give you life, if you will join us. What do you say?"

"Look here, Yvonne," said Graves, "you're too chicken-hearted. We evidently failed the first time, and this time he must go!"

"Don't interfere, please!" replied Yvonne coldly. "I trust I am still at the head of affairs. As yet I have not been responsible for the taking of a life, unless it be Bechstein's suicide, a fate which he deserved. You issued the instructions to have Sexton Blake and this lad removed, and when it was too late to alter matters I countenanced it.

"But I do not believe in assassination. If I had met Sexton Blake in fair fight, and his removal had been essential, I would have taken the necessary step—but to knife a man in the back, no; nor will I permit any member of the circle to do it. Now, my lad," she added, turning to Tinker, "what do you say, will you join us?"

"Mademoiselle," answered Tinker, "it is impossible! Believe me, Sexton Blake had a high respect for you, and I am glad to hear that you were not responsible for the attacks on us. I am young, mademoiselle, and don't wish to be impertinent, but instead of my joining you, I would suggest you come over to the side of the law. I have heard Sexton Blake say you would have made a great detective."

"You speak boldly, my lad," answered Yvonne, "but you conjure with a powerful name. You are too young to understand how, but enough—if you won't join us, you will have to remain a prisoner! Now leave me, and I will consider your case."

She rang as she spoke, and sent Tinker away with the man who answered.

Rising, she bowed coldly to her uncle and Rymer, and swept away to her own cabin.

She did not see the blazing look of jealousy in Rymer's eyes when she told Tinker that he had conjured with a powerful name when he used that of Sexton Blake. Nor did she know that those words had created in Rymer a deadly enmity against Tinker.

For Rymer had fallen hopelessly in love with Yvonne, and her coldness towards his advances had only added fuel to the flame. Some instinct had told him that Sexton Blake had received her love, and the remark she had made had brought his jealousy to fever heat.

He had concealed the tempest of his emotions as Yvonne rose and departed, but as the door closed he turned with a snarl to Graves.

"It seems," he said, "that you are right. Mademoiselle is getting chicken-hearted!"

"Yes; and it's a big mistake!" growled her uncle. "If I had my way, I'd get rid of him while we have him in our clutches. Experience ought to have taught her the danger of not doing so. But she will ruin herself and the whole lot of us with her quixotic notions of honour."

"I agree with you," replied Rymer. "Why shouldn't we take the law into our own hands? I am vice-president, and you are secretary and treasurer. Surely our own mutual decision for the good of the circle ought to go?"

He leaned forward and gazed craftily at Yvonne's weak uncle, and the latter, always yielding to Rymer's dominating will, gave in.

"Gad! There'll be the deuce of a row when she finds out!" he muttered.

"She'll come round all right," replied Rymer confidentially, seeing he had won. "I tell you I won't rest until every sign of Sexton Blake is swept from my path!" he added savagely.

"How will we do it?" inquired Graves.

"I've thought it all out," answered Rymer. "Listen! Mademoiselle has gone to retire. We will give her half an hour, and then we will take our young friend on deck. And this time, believe me, there will be no mistake. We will put out a plank, as the pirates of old used to do, blindfold him, and bind his hands, and he will walk that plank! I guess that'll send him under to stay this time."

Graves nodded, and the two silently left the saloon.

Yvonne, it is true, was against the laws of society, but her outlawry was confined to what she considered the meting out of just punishment to those who had ruined her mother and herself. She had accepted all the conditions of such a life, and when necessary, would in fair fight, countenance a killing.

Perverted and wrong her ideas certainly were, but it had been the fault of those whose punishment she was now endeavouring to bring about. But she had a strict code of honour and scrupulously lived up to it. It was that which claimed such a deep admiration from Sexton Blake, and it had been an additional shock to Yvonne's proud nature when Blake had refused her hand.

His heart would have softened towards the wayward young woman had he known the intense suffering she had experienced since she believed him dead. But we sum Yvonne up best, perhaps, when we say she ran straight, and with the exception of her wrong ideas of taking the law into her own hands, her honourable and upright nature would have been a credit to many on the side of the law and order.

But the two men who had just quitted the saloon were not troubled by any such ideas; but in acting as they did, in direct defiance to Yvonne's orders, and the underhand methods they used, they broke the salient law which holds criminals, as well as other orders, together—honour with each other, and the breaking of which invariably spells ruin.

Tinker had breathed easier at Yvonne's words, and his heart had filled with a great sympathy toward her. Consequently, he got a rude shock when the door of his cabin opened, and he was roughly seized and his arms bound behind him. His captors, two husky seamen, dragged him on deck, and led him along to the after port.

He gasped with sudden dread as he saw the plank sticking out over the dark waters, and read their fiendish purpose.

To do him justice, he never for a moment suspected Yvonne had gone back on her word, and had issued orders for his death. He knew that in some way her lieutenants had taken the law into their own hands. If he could attract her attention, he might yet be saved. Opening his mouth he started to yell, but a heavy hand descended, choking it off in a low gurgle.

Swiftly they bound a handkerchief around his mouth, and another over his eyes.

Tinker gritted his teeth, and brought all his manhood to bear and keep his nerve and die bravely. But he had had one awful experience in the ocean, and dreaded another. Then, he had had a fighting chance, but now he must die like a dog. His thoughts raced back to Blake and Pedro, and he struggled valiantly to suppress a choking sob, for life had been very dear to him since he had lived with Blake, and he was young.

But no relief came to him, and with a fervent prayer for courage to hang out he set his foot on the plank.

Slowly, and with an awful agony of suspense, he shuffled along the plank, but before he had covered half its length the men at the side of the yacht tipped it up, and the helpless lad dropped into the shark-infested waters.

Blake was sitting in the darkness of his galley when the unusual stir told him something out of the ordinary was happening.

He had cautiously slipped along the deck, crouching low as he saw in the glare of a lantern the circle of men at the rail.

He gasped in horror when he saw Tinker led up and bound. The plank told its own story, and the beads came out on the detective's forehead as he saw the lad's impending fate.

He worked his way back to the bow, and searched feverishly until he found a long coil of rope.

Shouldering it, he whispered softly to the Chinese boy, to whom he spoke rapidly in guttural Chinese.

The boy nodded as eagerly as his nature would permit, and the celestially-attired pair crept back along the deck, Blake carrying the long coil of rope.

He had counted on the interest of the men at the rail in their occupation to assist his purpose, and he calculated rightly, for, absorbed in their fiendish work, they did not see the gliding Orientals who crept by on the opposite side and made for the stern.

Rapidly Blake uncoiled the rope, and secured one end firmly to the rail, the other end he tied around the boy's waist.

"You are sure, Chan, that you are a sufficiently strong swimmer?"

"Oh, yes, master! Many years have I dived in the waters for pearls."

"Very well, my lad. I would go myself, but you would not be strong enough to pull me back. Chan, don't miss him!" he added, the sweat breaking out again on his forehead. "If you succeed, your reward will be great; and if you fail—well, I swear I will destroy every being on this yacht."

Solemnly he whispered the words, and a moment later Chan went over the side ready to slip into the water.

Blake crept up, and stared back tensely, and gasped as he saw the helpless, blindfolded Tinker start on his awful journey.

Hastening back, he stood at the rail, and never had Sexton Blake passed through the eternity of agony through which he went that moment.

It seemed a year before the splash came, and he had no need to give the signal to the Chinese boy; for he also had heard it, and his slim body cut the water like an arrow as he dived silently.

Blake grasped the rope, gritting his teeth to control himself. He heaved back as he felt a tug, and gazed with intensity at the black water. But no head showed above it, and his heart contracted with fear as he looked for the sign of success or failure.

Chan had dived in order to try and grasp Tinker as he went past. But it would be very easy to fail in that black water, and, as the yacht was travelling at high speed, if he failed once, the helpless lad would soon be far astern in those shark-infested waters.

Blake's jaws worked as he saw Chan's head come up, and he momentarily raised his eyes in a great wave of thankfulness as the boy's laboured struggles told him he had a burden.

Desperately he pulled in on the rope until the boy was underneath.

A great length of the slack rope now looped along behind, and the resourceful Chinese boy soon had it looped around his burden.

Blake pulled again, his arms straining with the dead weight. But he had the strength of two men that night, and the strong man gave a dry sob of relief as he drew the inanimate Tinker over the rail.

He tied the rope to the rail, and Chan rapidly squirmed up it hand over hand.

Silently they bent over Tinker. His would-be murderers had not known when they tied the handkerchief over Tinker's mouth that it would eventually be a help to the lad, but such it was, for it had helped to keep the water from entering his lungs. Blake worked rapidly, and breathed easier when Tinker's lids fluttered, and finally opened.

He stared in amazement at the Chinese man bending over him, but his eyes filled with joyous tears as Blake whispered a few words.

It was a long and dangerous trip from the stern to the cook's galley in the bow, but the little band managed it.

Blake gave Tinker a dry outfit, and concealed him in the privacy of his own galley, where, unless something out of the ordinary occurred, he would be moderately safe.

He gripped Chan's hand in deep gratitude as the Chinese boy departed, and then sat down to bring his keen mind into full play in an endeavour to solve the problem.

And well was it for Sexton Blake that he had the asset of such a mind in such a position.

The Twelfth Chapter
The Mystery of the Water Tanks—Blake Makes a Purchase—Blake Captures the *Fleur-de-Lys*

SEVERAL days passed safely, and the detective began to breathe easier.

Blake expected every day that the concealed Tinker would be discovered, but his predecessor had evidently impressed the sailors with the fact that he would not have them in his galley, for, with the exception of their trips at meal-time to have their plates filled, they gave the galley a wide berth.

What was their destination he had no idea, but he was able to form a rough notion of their position from the talk of the sailors.

In this way he had known when they passed through the Torres Straits, and likewise a few evenings later he heard one of the sailors remark that New Caledonia lay off the starboard side.

That night Blake spent several hours in deep thought.

He had discovered for a positive fact that President Pearson was not aboard, and the problem was where and when had he been set off?

He went over the steps of the chase point by point. He could place every movement of the *Fleur-de-Lys* with the exception of one period.

Her journey from Valparaiso to Suva had consumed an extraordinarily long time, for, although she had over two weeks' start from Salvarita, Blake had reached Suva only four days after her arrival. That pointed to a blank time to be filled up by some movement of the yacht. He figured it was almost certain that she had stopped somewhere between Valparaiso and Fiji, but the point was where?

That stoppage would give the necessary opportunity for disposing of the president and the bullion. What strengthened the detective's theory that she had stopped somewhere was the fact that she had continued on to Melbourne, Hong Kong, and Batavia, and in each place had taken in heavy supplies. Then, instead of proceeding to Europe, she had started back toward the South Pacific, and now Fiji lay just ahead.

Certainly it pointed to some destination in the South Pacific. The detective had no idea as to whether Captain Pentland had received his hastily-written note. If he had not Blake was in a hard situation. He must get word to the captain in some way, but the problem was how?

Long and persistently he turned the problem over and over in his mind, and finally adopted a plan which, though risky, seemed the only one with a chance of success.

Late that night, when all hands but the watch were wrapped in slumber, the stout Chinese cook would have surprised his shipmates by his athletic actions. He seemed to be performing stealthy feats of agility in the neighbourhood of the water tanks, and the result of his midnight journey was demonstrated at breakfast-time the next morning.

The first sign came from the sailors. One and all they spat out their coffee in disgust, and an indignant deputation waited on the cook.

"There," growled the spokesman of the party, poking his cup under Blake's nose. "Wot do yer call that mess?"

"Cloffee—vely good cloffee!" replied Blake, with an expansive Celestial smile.

"Oh, it is 'velly good,' is it? Well, just you taste it, and see how 'velly good' it is!"

The sailor thrust the cup at Blake, who tasted it, and hurriedly spat it out.

"Velly bad—velly bad!" he answered, in a sing-song tone. "Sailor quite light! Me no undelstand."

"Well, you'd better jolly quick understand!" growled the sailor, partially mollified by the cook's acknowledgment as to its badness.

"Me no undelstand!" sang Blake. "Me make it same as all time. Come, I show you!"

The sailor entered the galley, and watched Blake rapidly mix fresh coffee. He poured it out as he finished, and handed the cupful to the sailor. That worthy put it to his lips, but a comical look of disgust came over his face as he set it back hurriedly and hastened outside.

"You see," said Blake, "it is not my fault."

"Well, give me a cup of water until I wash this taste out," growled the sailor, "and then we'll see Captain Vaughan."

Blake did as he was bid, but, as the sailor took a deep draught, getting the full benefit of the awful acid taste, it was the last straw.

Dashing the cup to pieces on the deck, he fairly danced with rage.

"It's the water, you bloomin' ol' fool. Wot in blazes 'ave yer put in it?"

"Me put nothing," protested Blake innocently.

"Well, it's rotten!" gasped the sailor, "Come on, boys, and investigate it."

The sailors hurried to the water tanks, and drew off a pailful from each. But their efforts were barren of success, for every tank was tainted with the peculiar acid taste.

The party of seamen hastened to the captain and informed him of the state of affairs.

Captain Vaughan himself descended and investigated the tanks, but his results were the same as those of the seamen.

He hastened away to inform Yvonne, and, returning a few moments later, informed the seamen that they would head at once for Suva to have the tanks overhauled and take in fresh water, and that in the meantime they would all have to get along on distilled water for the time being.

"It is a mystery how the water has become tainted," he wound up. "Someone may be playing a practical joke on us, but if I find out who it is I'll show him the joke of a rope's-end. Now, get on with your work, boys, and as quickly as I can get some water distilled I will have the cook prepare you a breakfast. In the meantime, you will all be served out an extra round of rum."

The sailors cheered, and returned to their work; and in the cook's galley the stout Chinese cook smiled, for he had gained his point, and they would stop at Suva.

The yacht made Suva the next day, and the cook found it necessary to obtain leave to go ashore for a few things for the galley.

He explained matters to the concealed Tinker, and, leaving Chan on guard, hastened over the side.

Blake made his way to the British Consul, and binding that astounded gentleman to secrecy, left a letter with him to be delivered to Captain Pentland on his arrival, for a perusal of the shipping news disclosed the fact that the yacht *Corsair* had cleared from Batavia bound for Suva, Fiji, and he knew his first note had miraculously landed on the deck.

In the note he explained his suspicions to Captain Pentland, and told him to remain at Suva, where the detective would endeavour to communicate with him later.

It would have simplified matters wonderfully if Blake could have had Yvonne and her companions arrested at Suva; but, unfortunately, he had no positive proof as yet that they had abducted President Pearson, and, besides, Salvarita had no extradition law with Great Britain.

Consequently, all he could do was to stick to the trail until he discovered the missing president, and in the meantime, give every attention to details.

On leaving the British Consul's Blake made his way to a chemist's, and there purchased a box of harmless-looking white powder. Then, making a few purchases as his excuse for being ashore, he hastened back to the yacht, his box of white powder concealed in the flowing sleeve of his capacious jacket.

Tinker was still undiscovered when Blake returned, and that evening, with her tanks cleaned and replenished, the *Fleur-de-Lys* once more got under way.

Three days later a dark cloud appeared on the eastern horizon, and as the day wore on the sailors clustered eagerly in the bow.

Blake left the galley and moved to the rail, his eyes inscrutable, his ears open for any remarks.

"I'll be jolly glad to get back to the island!" remarked a sailor near him.

"So will I!" answered another. "It means a rest and good food and a jolly good time."

"We ought to make the lagoon about eight," returned the first.

"Not much," replied his companion. "I heard the captain say we'd drop anchor at ten."

Blake turned casually, and returned to his galley. At least he had definite information, and a move must be made soon.

As the afternoon wore on he started preparing the evening meal, and, strange to say, in all the food, both for the saloon and the fo'c'sle, he put a large portion of the white powder he had purchased in Suva.

He did not wish to have it affect the sailors before dinner had been served in the saloon, as suspicion would be aroused and his plans upset.

Consequently, the sailors' supper was not ready until six that night. But the seamen were in a good humour at the prospect of early release, and only a few mild curses greeted the cook's unpunctuality.

Seven arrived, and dinner was sent into the saloon promptly on time. Half-past seven came, and for men who had not had a hard day, the sailors seemed to be suddenly seized with an extreme weariness, for first one and then another started yawning prodigiously.

Those who were not on watch gave in to the demand of their heavy lids, and sought the fo'c'sle, where they threw themselves out on their bunks.

Almost before they had settled themselves they were in a heavy sleep.

Those on watch battled valiantly to overcome their sudden sleepiness, but first one and then another succumbed and dropped helplessly to the deck.

Blake smiled as he saw the effects of his powder, but he looked for quicker results in the saloon, for he had made their dose particularly stiff, and had given less to the sailors, in order that they should not succumb before the saloon dinner had been served.

He had not long to wait, for a few minutes later a scared-looking steward dashed out from the saloon, and headed for the cook's galley.

"What in blazes have you done?" he gasped as he reached Blake. "Everyone has gone to sleep at the table."

His answer was a sudden spring from Blake, and to render him helpless was the work of only a moment.

Blake dragged him into the galley, and there hastened to release Tinker.

"Now, my boy, we've got our work cut out for us," he said, as he passed Tinker a revolver. "There are five more stewards to settle yet, for they haven't had their supper, and will be unaffected. Then we've got Hendricks, the mate, who is on the bridge, and the mate at the wheel. The engineer and his assistants can wait, for they won't be up yet for another half-hour. Are you ready?"

"Yes, guv'nor, you bet I am! Crikey, but you have scored!" he said, with a look of admiration at the detective. "But just let me get at them! I've got several scores to settle with them!"

Blake smiled grimly, as he led the way to the saloon.

Yvonne sat with her head resting in her hand, fast asleep. All around sat Captain Vaughan, Rymer, and Graves in a similar condition.

But Blake and Tinker lost no time. Two stewards were endeavouring to awaken the sleepers, and their hands went up quickly as Blake levelled his revolver.

Tinker quickly bound them, and they proceeded to find the others.

Two were getting the cabins ready for the night, and these received the same treatment as their fellows. As they went along the passage the last steward appeared with his arms full of linen, and he also was bound.

"Now for the bridge, Tinker!" jerked Blake.

They hastened up the companionway, and along the deck to the bridge companion.

They crept up softly, but Hendricks and the man at the wheel were as yet unsuspicious.

The mate was pacing up and down, and his eyes opened in amazement as he saw the supposed Chinese cook with a levelled revolver in his hand.

"Here, you wretch! What do you mean?" he snapped angrily. "Get below at once!"

"Not just yet, Mr. Hendricks!" answered Blake coolly.

Hendricks' eyes dilated as he heard Blake's voice, but that was mild compared to the look of horror on his face as he saw Tinker appear.

Up went his hands, for he saw they meant business; and Tinker's uncanny appearance, when by all calculations he ought to have been at the bottom of the ocean, took his breath away.

"Now walk to the wheelhouse, Hendricks!" snapped Blake. Hendricks did so, his hands still aloft.

"Now, Tinker," continued Blake, "go below and get Chan! Then get some rope, and tie up every one on the yacht, with the exception of mademoiselle! Carry her to her cabin, and lay her in her bunk. Then lock her in. After you have done that, go on guard at the entrance to the engine-room, and the first man who appears secure him! Don't run any risks. If he fights, disable him. You will know how," he added grimly. "I will attend to this pair myself."

"Right, guv'nor!" responded Tinker. "I promise you I'll settle them this time!"

"Now, Mr. Hendricks," snapped Blake, pulling out a cigar and lighting it with one hand, "you will keep on in exactly the same course! You will instruct the man how to enter the lagoon, and if you don't do just exactly that in every detail, I promise you I will deal with you in a way you won't like! And you know whether I mean what I say or not."

"Oh, I know when I'm beaten!" growled Hendricks surlily. "I'll take you into the lagoon all right. But I'd like jolly well to know how you've overpowered the whole crew."

"I don't mind in the least telling you," answered Blake coolly. "They had a sudden desire for sleep, which, strange to say, invaded the saloon as well. They succumbed to it, that is all. And now, Hendricks, no more talk, please!"

The man at the wheel had gazed in open-mouthed astonishment at the "hold up," but on Blake's ordering him to keep the yacht's head as she was, he swallowed his fear and curiosity and attended to the wheel.

Blake leaned against the rail, his revolver ready for business.

Two hours later Tinker came up to report that all hands had been secured, and that one of the engineer's assistants had also been secured on making his appearance on deck.

As the lad finished his report the yacht swung into the opening of the lagoon.

Hendricks, at Blake's orders, signalled the engine-room to stop and she floated ahead by her own impetus. Blake, leaving Tinker to keep the wheelman covered, forced Hendricks at the point of the gun to the lower-deck, and compelled him to release the anchor.

Calling Chan, he ordered the Chinese boy to bind the mate, and that grinning individual seemed delighted at the job, for he had received many kicks from Hendricks in days past.

Blake ascended again to the bridge, in order to secure the wheelman, after which the triumphant trio made their way to the engine-room.

The astonished engineer and his remaining assistant, however, were not to be taken without a fight, and picked up heavy wrenches as weapons.

But Blake was in no mood to lose any time, and his revolver spoke sharply, disabling the engineer's arm. The assistant, seeing the fate of his chief, gave in, and a moment later the last of the yacht's company lay helpless on the engine-room floor.

Blake, Tinker, and Chan returned to the deck, and Blake heaved a sigh of satisfaction as he surveyed the scene of his success.

The Thirteenth Chapter
Yvonne Completes Her Revenge—Blake Finishes the Chase—Unmasked—The End

BUT Blake and Tinker were by no means out of the wood yet.

Through the trees fringing the shore of the lagoon came the gleam of lights.

"That's their hiding-place," remarked Blake, "and the question is, Tinker, how many have been left in charge?"

"It doesn't seem as though they would leave many, guv'nor," answered Tinker.

"No, it doesn't, my lad; but, on the other hand, we don't know. It is true, the island may be uninhabited; but in that house yonder they have probably got the missing president, and there must be, at least, half a dozen in charge. It is strange no one has appeared to meet the yacht, but as we came in without lights, and did not whistle, they may not have noticed us yet. However, we've got to investigate, so let's get along."

Rapidly they worked the davits, and a moment later the small boat hit the water. The three skimmed down the ropes, and cast off.

Chan was an expert at the oars, and he pulled noiselessly over the dark stretch between the yacht and the shore.

They grounded silently, and Blake led the way through the trees in the direction of the lighted house.

As they approached, they saw moving figures in what they judged to be the dining-room, and Blake crept forward to investigate.

He gave a start of satisfaction as he saw a man with iron-grey hair at the table whom he knew to be President Pearson.

A man was serving him, and another man with a rifle stood near the door.

Blake crept back to his companions, and told them what he had seen.

"My idea is to make a rush for the front door, and take them by surprise. They will think it is only their returned companions, and we stand a chance of succeeding."

Leading the way, Blake walked up on the wide balcony, and opened the front door.

Tinker and Chan came close behind, and they got clear to the open door of the dining-room without being challenged.

"Hands up—quick!" snapped Blake, as he entered.

And the rifle of the astonished guard fell with a clatter to the floor as his hands went up. The serving-man dropped the plates he was carrying, and followed suit, while the president gazed in amazement at the stout Chinese with the levelled revolver.

"It's all right, President Pearson," smiled Blake. "Permit me to introduce myself. I am Sexton Blake, and must confess I have had a long chase to find you. But later for that. Can you tell me how many more there are?"

"Yes, Mr. Blake," replied the relieved president. "There are two more, I think. But allow me to thank you for your success in finding my whereabouts."

Blake smiled, and, picking up the fallen rifle, handed it to the president.

"I don't suppose you will object to keeping guard over these two while we find the others," he remarked.

"That I won't!" answered the president. "And if they move a hand, Heaven help them!" he added, grimly.

They found the remaining two in the lower regions of the house, and, securing them, dragged them to the dining-room.

The guard and the serving-man were then bound, and Blake and Tinker, who were weary and hungry from the strenuous evening, joined the president at the table.

Chan investigated the kitchen, and served a very passable meal to the victors, and while they ate Blake heard the president's story, but what he did not hear from that gentleman was the reason of his abduction.

After dinner they worked late into the night transferring to the yacht the prisoners and the bullion, which they found still intact in a large vault.

Blake sent the president into the engine-room with Tinker to help him. The detective himself, who had carefully studied the yacht's chart of the lagoon entrance, took the wheel. Chan reigned supreme in the cook's galley. As dawn broke in golden splendour over the palm-fringed lagoon Blake rang the starting bell, and the *Fleur-de-Lys*, clipping her dainty nose into the pearly waters, headed out of the lagoon, manned by her small but victorious crew.

Blake headed the yacht for Fiji, and at the end of the first day he entered the wireless-room to endeavour to get in touch with the *Corsair*. He was not able to do so until the following morning, but shortly after daybreak he got a clear answer.

Rapidly he sent the message, informing Captain Pentland of his position, and instructing him to put to sea and meet them in mid-ocean.

An affirmative reply came back, and early the following evening the two yachts met.

Captain Pentland sent the *Corsair*'s second officer and a prize crew aboard to take charge of the *Fleur-de-Lys* and her prisoners, but before turning them over officially to President Pearson to be taken to Salvarita for punishment, Blake had two interviews.

Yvonne had been released at once on her recovery from the effects of the sleeping-draught which Blake had administered. She had passed her word not to attempt to hinder his plans nor to release her companions, and once again Blake had accepted the young woman's word.

She had been dumbfounded at seeing Blake alive, and, regardless of the peril in which she stood and the apparent failure of her plans, she was filled with a reckless gaiety caused by her deep relief that he still lived.

Blake had invited her to a place opposite him at the table, and as the president did not have his meals at the same hour, Yvonne was free from the restraint of his presence.

The consequence was that in her reckless mood all her innate charm came to the surface.

It was hard to realise that their positions were those of captor and prisoner, and when her shapely bronze head disappeared through the door Blake marvelled at the deserted air of everything, and the odd sense of loneliness which came over him.

Just before they met the *Corsair*, Blake called Yvonne into the saloon and spoke to her.

"Mademoiselle," he said, "I find that although you planned the abduction of the president and the removal of the bullion, that you were not responsible for the attempt on my life and that of my assistant, and, on the contrary, you forbade the use of violence the second time Tinker fell into your hands. For that reason, mademoiselle, I wish to say that I can offer you freedom, but not that of your companions."

Yvonne drew herself up as she replied.

"Thank you, Mr. Blake," she said quietly. "But I do not desire my freedom. I have stood by my companions and will do so to the end. It would be cowardly and dishonourable for me to accept your offer and to leave them to suffer the punishment. I thought you knew me better than that."

"I took it for granted, mademoiselle," answered Blake "that such would be your answer. I admire your sense of honour at the same time regretting it should have to be brought into play under such circumstances."

"I know you will never see my point of view," she replied. "But as for the second attempt on the life of your assistant, I do not plan murders. Had I known in time it never would have happened. How you saved him I don't know; but both Rymer and my uncle would have suffered for that act on my arrival at the island. Rymer I would have put in irons, and landed in Europe or South America at the first opportunity; but, as things have turned out, I will stick by them. We are not in the Salvarita prison yet," she added saucily, "and I promise you I will endeavour to release my companions as soon as you turn us over to the president. If I succeed I will drop Rymer at once, for I don't desire a member of his calibre. Besides," she added, dropping her eyes, "his attentions were getting altogether too persistent."

And Sexton Blake, man of ice, for some unaccountable reason, felt a sudden desire to drop violent hands on the absent Rymer.

"I am glad you offered me my freedom before you turned me over to Pearson," went on Yvonne. "For the present I cannot explain, but I will do so before you leave. You said, I think, that Señor Mendoza and his daughter were aboard the *Corsair*?"

Blake nodded.

"Very well; I wish to ask as a favour that you will bring the señorita over to the *Fleur-de-Lys* and arrange a few minutes' conversation for me. I would like you to be present, and, above all, President Pearson."

"I think I can grant your request, mademoiselle," smiled Blake. "You have been a very good prisoner, and deserve a reward."

Thus it came about that after the prize crew had taken charge of the yacht, Yvonne, the señorita, Blake, and Pearson met in the saloon.

Yvonne leaned against the table facing them, and wasted no time in beginning.

"You all wonder, perhaps," she began, "why I have requested you to grant me these few moments—all, perhaps, except you, James Pearson."

Pearson opened his mouth to speak, but Blake silenced him with a gesture.

"My reason is threefold," continued Yvonne. "One is my desire that you, Mr. Blake, shall understand why I abducted the president; the second, that Señorita Mendoza shall understand exactly the kind of man he is; and thirdly, that you, James Pearson, will suffer still more for your sins."

"I protest!" cried Pearson. "Señorita, I beg of you to refuse to listen to the tales of this adventuress!"

Again Blake silenced him, and Yvonne, looking at Pearson with contempt, went on:

"Adventuress; yes, perhaps! But who made me one? Listen, señorita, and I will tell you who the noble President Pearson is!"

Rapidly Yvonne told the story of how Pearson, with Vineburg, and the other directors of the Jig Saw Mine in Australia, had ruined her mother and herself by their swindles, causing her mother's death from shock. Of how the law would not reach them, and how she had been driven into the world penniless and her heart full of bitter desire for revenge; of how she had made money, backing horses, and how she had started on her campaign of retribution; how she had picked Vineburg as the first to be revenged upon, and how he having changed his name to Bechstein, had committed suicide. Then how Pearson was the next on the list, and the result of the attempt on him.

"Now, señorita," finished Yvonne, "if you still desire to marry him, I wish you joy of your bargain. You may think me cruel to tell you this, but it is for your own good."

Blake had heard the tale from Yvonne when he had captured her in the Bechstein case, and he had had a shrewd suspicion that Pearson may have been mixed up in the deal.

He turned and looked with contempt at the big, loose-jointed man, who stood with beads of perspiration on his forehead.

"Don't believe her, señorita!" he snarled. "I swear to you they are all lies!"

The señorita had not spoken as she listened to Yvonne's indictment of Pearson, and only the laboured heaving of her breast told of her intense emotion.

As Pearson spoke she looked at him, and then turned to Blake.

"What do you say, Señor Blake—are they lies?"

"I have never had any occasion to doubt mademoiselle's word," answered Blake quietly, "and I see no reason to doubt her word now."

The señorita turned to Pearson, her dark eyes flashing with anger.

"It seems, señor," she said, in a tense voice, "that I gave my trust and love to a contemptible cad! My one hope is that I may be able to wipe every recollection of you from my mind, for what was once love has now turned to loathing! A swindler of women, and you dare to offer marriage to a Mendoza! Mademoiselle, I thank you! Permit me to retire!"

Bowing, the disillusioned and angry señorita swept from the saloon, and Yvonne turned to Blake, a wistful look in her eyes.

"Now you understand, do you not?"

"Yes, I understand, mademoiselle," he replied softly. "Again I offer you immunity before I turn the yacht and prisoners over. It is now an unpleasant duty, but it is my duty, and must be done."

"I thank you, but I cannot accept it. James Pearson," she added, turning to the president, who had sunk into a chair, crushed by the señorita's contempt, "I and my companions are now your prisoners, but watch us well," she said, in mocking tones, "for we will escape if we can!"

Blake left the *Fleur-de-Lys* with a strange tug at his heart-strings. The wayward mademoiselle, with her wistful eyes and fascinating manner, had made a deep mark on the unimpressionable Blake, and although he had brought to a successful conclusion one of the most dangerous cases in his experience, he felt no sense of triumph as he was pulled across to the *Corsair*.

Señor Mendoza had heard from the señorita the truth about Pearson. He had refused to go over and see his old partner, and was only anxious to get started for London, when he could begin steps to separate his interests from those of Pearson.

Pedro's joyful reception brightened Blake up a bit, but as the yachts parted company that night, one heading for London and the other east for South America with her freight of prisoners, he walked to the rail and gazed over the misty water. Once again he murmured, as he had done months before, "What a pity!"

***

Some weeks later the returned Blake, Tinker, and Pedro sat once more at breakfast in the cosy Baker Street rooms.

Blake was reading the morning paper, and Tinker looked up as the detective uttered a sharp exclamation.

"What is it, guv'nor?" he asked.

"Listen to this, Tinker," he replied. "I will read it to you. It is a cable message from Salvarita, and you will find it of interest:

"'News is at hand of the return of President Pearson on board the yacht *Fleur-de-Lys*. With him he brought the missing two millions of bullion, and, most extraordinary of all, a whole cargo of prisoners. President Pearson was at once interviewed, and gave a vivid account of his capture, and ended by ascribing his release and the capture of his captors to the famous British detective Sexton Blake.

"'The people gave the returned president a rousing welcome, and great excitement reigned as he was carried to the palace and installed in his old apartments. His cargo of prisoners have been kept aboard the yacht to await punishment.'"

"Gee, guv'nor, he got a great reception, didn't he?" remarked Tinker.

"Yes, my lad; but wait. There is more yet. This is a later message:

"'Typical of the rapid changes in some South American republics is the following message received as we go to press.

"'A climax has been reached in the affairs of Salvarita. Señor Mendoza has cabled from London his resignation from the Ambassadorship to England, and has also cabled a long denunciation of his former friend and partner, President Pearson.

"'Señor Martina proceeded to the palace to inform the president. As he approached the council chamber he heard a shot, and a man rushed out with a smoking revolver in his hand. Señor Martina feared something serious had occurred, and endeavoured to seize the man, but failed.

"'Calling to the guards to warn them, he hastened in to the council chamber, and found his worst fears realised. President Pearson lay on the floor already dead, adding another to the long list of the assassin's bullet. The guards succeeded in catching the assassin—one Gomez—who proved to be a soldier recently discharged in disgrace from the army. To complicate matters, the prisoners on the yacht *Fleur-de-Lys*, who were awaiting trial for the abduction of the late president, and the stealing of the now famous bullion, have overpowered their guards and recaptured the yacht.

"'The guards were set adrift in the harbour in small boats, and the last seen of the yacht was the smoke from her funnel as she disappeared over the horizon.

"'Our representative has interviewed Señor Mendoza, who confirms the above.'"

"Crikey, guv'nor," exclaimed Tinker, "things have certainly been moving in Salvarita, haven't they?"

"They certainly have," smiled Blake. "It looks as though I might again run up against the charming mademoiselle," he added to himself, "And it's a curious thing Fate has intervened and given her her revenge, as it did with Bechstein."

"Well, Tinker, let's to work," he continued aloud, rising; and they entered the consulting-room where so many exciting trails had their origin.

***

On a dreary, foggy night, not long after the events just related, a white yacht, looking ghostly in the creeping mist, stopped her engines and lay to off a lonely spot on the English coast.

The name *Fleur-de-Lys* was painted on her bows, and a slim, bronze-haired young woman in a heavy coat stood on the bridge.

"This will do, captain," she said, turning to Captain Vaughan. "Have them lower the boat here."

The captain turned to issue instructions, and a few moments later four sailors took their places in the boat.

"Bring up the prisoner!" commanded Yvonne.

Two more went below. They appeared shortly with a man in irons, and the man was Rymer.

"Knock off his irons and land him there," continued Yvonne.

Once released, Rymer turned and began to demand a reversal of her decision, but Yvonne's teeth came together with a snap.

"No; it is impossible! What I have said, I have said. You came here on the understanding that my word was to be law. You deliberately broke the rules, and attempted to murder the boy. You have thrown away wealth and success, but that is your own fault. Leave now, please."

Rymer, seeing further argument was useless, turned and descended the ladder.

Swiftly the boat set him ashore, and a few moments later the yacht turned and headed through the fog for the sunny South Sea island.

Yvonne went below early, but before undressing she gazed long and earnestly at a rough pencilled sketch on the wall.

It was a sketch of Sexton Blake, and had been made secretly by Yvonne when she was for three days his prisoner, and, strange to say, a happy one.

The End.

MY CHUMS,—

If you have enjoyed this splendid Yvonne and Sexton Blake yarn, please give a non-reader chum a chance to enjoy it as well. Remember, that another Yvonne and Blake yarn appears in three weeks' time, entitled:

"On the Brink of Ruin."

Please mention this, and tell your chums.

THE SKIPPER.

Next week's Grand Yarn will be entitled: **"ON THE BRINK OF RUIN"** and will introduce charming Yvonne Cartier, the beautiful young woman who has caused such a great sensation in publishing circles on account of her wonderful popularity in so short a time.

Seldom has a new character "caught on" so quickly and effectively as has Yvonne, and the hitherto large army of "U. J." readers has welcomed many thousands of recruits, and these, in their turn, are bringing in many more.

I am satisfied that there is no call for sweeping reforms in the great *Union Jack* Army, and no seductive inducements need be held out to non-readers!

All that is necessary is for them to read a Yvonne yarn, and they will be loyal chums from that moment on.

So, if anyone knows of a non-reader, will they kindly lend their copy of next week's "U. J."? The result is assured. Just play up next week, my chums, and do the "good old Skipper" a turn, and read **"ON THE BRINK OF RUIN".**

It will tell in a most dramatic manner how Yvonne obtains her revenge on one of the old Jig Saw Mine Swindle Ring, now the owner of a successful mill. Do not miss it, chums!

The Skipper

The UNION JACK. 1d
ON THE BRINK OF RUIN
Or, THE MYSTERY OF THE MILL
"Hands up!" cried Sexton Blake sternly.
NO. 492. NEW SERIES
March 15th, 1913.
[EVERY THURSDAY.

DR. HUXTON RYMER

RETURNS IN

THE TEED FILES #2

The Diamond Dragon
The Great Mining Swindle

Prologue
The Plot

BEFORE the fire, in a luxuriously-furnished sitting-room of a private suite, at King's Hotel, sat Mademoiselle Yvonne Cartier. On the other side lounged Graves, her uncle, languidly smoking a cigarette and watching Yvonne's occupation. On her knee rested a small pad of paper, on which was a column of names.

A line was drawn through the two that headed the list, and a close examination would have revealed the fact that the top one was Vineburg, and the second, Pearson.

The third name was Todd. It had as yet no line through it, but even as Graves watched, Yvonne placed the point of her pencil opposite it and made a tiny cross.

Graves flicked the ash from his cigarette, and spoke in a drawling tone as he did so.

"Which is the favoured gentleman this time, Yvonne?"

"Mr. Mortimer Todd, and I think he will find it less amusing than you seem to," replied Yvonne, her white teeth coming together with a click.

"I thought you were going to turn your attention to Kelly next?" continued Graves.

"I was, but I got wind that Todd was in England, and while I was here it seemed a pity to lose the opportunity. That is why I sent for you to meet me here at once. I am investigating, and I expect a full report tonight."

"Might I ask what character your fond uncle is to assume this time?" grinned Graves.

Yvonne smiled.

"If I carry out my present intentions, you will glory in the name of Cyrus Harmon, American millionaire. As it will be necessary to keep up the role in a financial way, it ought to suit you right down to the ground."

"Right you are, my dear. I must confess that I am a trifle tired of the yacht, and the prospect of shore life under such a pleasing role strikes me very favourably."

"Before we get through, it might not be so delightful as you anticipate," replied Yvonne grimly.

"My dear, I am quite content to leave things to your guiding hand. I must say, though, that I think it would have been wiser to have got rid of Sexton Blake when we had the chance."

Yvonne opened her mouth to reply, but changed the words to "Come in!" as a soft knock came at the door.

It opened to admit a man in a long coat and soft hat. It was difficult to see his features as his collar was turned up, and the hat pulled down over his eyes.

But as he advanced into the room he took off his hat and threw open his coat, revealing the fact that he was a high caste Chinese, in evening clothes.

"Oh, Dr. San Lo!" said Yvonne, waving him to a chair. "See you are prompt. Permit me to introduce you to my uncle—Mr. Graves."

The newcomer bowed gravely to the astonished Graves and seated himself, drawing from his pocket an envelope as he did so.

He was tall and thin, and might have been anything between thirty and fifty. His face was less seamed than the average Celestial's; his eyes were those of a deeply intelligent man.

If he felt any surprise at Graves' presence, no sign appeared on that inscrutable countenance. When he spoke it was with an almost imperceptible accent.

Only on his "r's" did he slur at all, and it created rather a pleasant impression than otherwise.

"I have here the report which you desired, mademoiselle. It is as you thought, the same. I also have the financial information which you desired."

"Oh, that is good news. Thank you," she added, as he passed it over. "If you will both excuse me for a few moments, I will run through this. Uncle, pass Dr. San Lo the cigarettes."

She opened the envelope as she spoke, and drew out several folded papers covered with small, neat writing. Rapidly she ran her eyes down the pages, her eyes gleaming with satisfaction as she finished.

"You have been thorough in your work, Dr. San Lo," she remarked, looking up and smiling. "It is extremely satisfactory."

"I am glad, mademoiselle," replied the Celestial, smiling for the first time. "We have a saying, mademoiselle, which I think you also have in English. It tells us, if a thing is worth doing at all, it is worth doing well."

Yvonne rose and went over to the table, where she picked up a newspaper. Returning to her chair, she opened it at a page containing classified advertisements, and then turned to her uncle.

"Now, uncle, I will explain everything to you. Firstly, Dr. San Lo is from now on a member of the circle. You weren't here, otherwise I would have explained things before, but I preferred you to meet him first. His real name is Dr. Li Hoang San. He is a graduate of Oxford, and under that name was secretary at the Chinese Legation under the monarchy. He is the best known authority in the world on radium, and it was during my experiments in that line that I came in contact with him.

"I met him at the Scientific Institute, in Paris. His wife is the Princess Ling, who is kept prisoner from him, and he himself is exiled from China. He had, in some way, heard of me, and seemed to think enough of my poor ability to ask me to help him find and rescue his wife. I have agreed to do so, but first am going to finish my own affair with Mr. Mortimer Todd.

"That is all. Are you quite agreeable? If not, don't hesitate to say so, for Dr. San Lo— as he chooses to be called—won't mind, I know, as naturally I admit no new members without the full consent of the circle."

"Why, no! On the contrary!" answered Graves. "I have heard a great deal about the doctor, and, as far as I am concerned, am quite agreeable that he should join us."

"Very well, that is settled. And now I will outline my plan. Listen while I read this advertisement: 'For immediate rent—charming Tudor mansion, at Bournmill, Lancs. Residence of Sir George Waltham. Moderate price only for immediate lease, as owner is leaving for Africa. Apply personally, at Bishop's Club, Piccadilly.'"

"That's Waltham, the big game-hunter, isn't it, Yvonne?" remarked Graves.

"Yes, and it was this ad. which decided me to proceed against Mortimer Todd, for he is now the proprietor of a large cotton mill there, and I have been watching my chance for some such opening."

"I see. Well let's have the plan."

"Here it is," went on Yvonne. "You are to adopt the role of Cyrus Harmon, American millionaire. I am to be your niece. Tomorrow, you will go to the Bishop's Club, and lease this place for a year, if possible, from Sir George Waltham. At the same time mention that a few letters from him to his neighbours would be desirable, and, from what I have been able to find out about him, I think he will readily agree.

"Dr. San Lo has been investigating Todd and his business, and, from the report, I see he is really shaky financially, but that fact is not generally known. But, on the other hand, several other mill-owners at Bournmill owe him money. By the way, I have explained to Dr. San Lo that Todd was one of the men who ruined my mother and myself in the Jig Saw Mine swindle in Australia.

"After we take the house in Bournmill, Dr. San Lo is to go down as a Chinese merchant, and purchase a large quantity of cotton. He will get Todd to sign a contract to deliver by a certain date to Dr. San Lo's London agent.

"Now, as you know, in my radium experiments, I have been able to create a shower of radium molecules from the smallest part of a grain. But what you don't know is, that these molecules destroy any cloth with which they come into contact. When I discovered Todd was at Bournmill, in the cotton milling business, with the assistance of Dr. San Lo, I at once experimented with the molecules on cotton.

"We discovered the effect varied on different colours. On white and grey several purple patches appeared; on red the effect took a bluish tinge; on yellow it was the same as on the white, but on purple the effect was absolutely invisible. We then tested a large roll of purple cotton, and the experiment was a perfect success—the cotton rotting quickly, without visible signs. Consequently Dr. San Lo will order purple cotton.

"Now perhaps you see my plan. As you know, every mill in the country is at present behind in their output, owing to the last strike. When Dr. San Lo receives his big consignment from Todd, he will apply the radium to each bale, and in twenty-four hours the cotton will be rotten. He will then repudiate the goods, and, at the same time, demand heavy damages or an immediate replacement of the goods. Todd won't dare go to his bank and tell them all his output has been thrown back on his hands in a rotten condition. To fulfil his contract he will have to put every machine to work, and, in addition, go into the open market and purchase cotton where he can.

"That is where we come in. It will be our part to cultivate Todd's friendship as Cyrus Harmon and his niece, the wealthy Americans. Todd will be at his wit's-end for money, and if we succeed in getting very friendly with him, he may come to us for assistance. But that point will develop later.

"As soon as Dr San Lo succeeds in ruining the cotton, I will manage to spend a night in the mill, and—well," added Yvonne grimly, "when I get through, the machinery will be pretty poor security for a loan. That, I think, will about finish Mr. Mortimer Todd. Dr. San Lo will be in touch with us all the time in case of complications; but I think I have considered every detail. It will be difficult and extremely risky to treat the machinery, but I have anticipated that, and, as far as I can see, the punishment of Mortimer Todd will go through without trouble."

"There is one detail which perhaps you have not considered," drawled Graves.

"What is that?" asked Yvonne sharply, knitting her brows.

"Sexton Blake," replied her uncle laconically.

"Ah!" murmured Yvonne softly, closing her eyes for a moment. "I have considered that. No, I have not forgotten Sexton Blake."

II
The Recognition

THE London "season" was drawing to a close, and the effects of a strenuous society campaign showed on the weary faces in the boxes at the "Royal."

Only a great singer, long absent, could bring tired society out so near the end of the season, but such a singer was appearing at the "Royal" for one night only, and every box and stall was filled in consequence.

Tier upon tier of jewelled women and black-coated men chatted, nodded and smiled. Anxious-eyed matrons, scanned the audience closely, endeavouring to pick out in the jumbled mass of people, the men who, all through the season, had eluded their carefully laid plans to make them sons-in-law.

Through the medley of colour and sound came the strains of the orchestra, just finishing the overture, and as they died away, the chattering crowd grew hushed.

Just before the lights were lowered, a lady and two gentlemen entered a box, which, until then, had remained vacant.

The lady was young, and her features showed no traces of the tiredness which sat on most of the countenances there.

She was faultlessly dressed in a gown of shimmering green—its soft tones harmonising with the heavy coils of her gleaming bronze hair.

She wore very few jewels. An exquisite emerald blazed in solitary splendour on her hand—its deep colour contrasting perfectly with her gown. A magnificent necklace of the same deep stones encircled her neck, and an emerald studded ornament in her hair completed the harmony.

On many women the combination would have either struck a harsh note, or a dead note, but against the white skin and perfect colouring of the finely cut features, it struck a note of reserve and simplicity.

It breathed the true artist! And true artist, indeed, was the woman who had conceived it, for it was none other than Mademoiselle Yvonne.

Her companions were duplicates of their black-garbed, white-fronted fellows.

The taller of the two was Sir George Waltham—evidently well-known, to judge from the numerous nods and bows which he returned. The other was a clean-shaven man of middle age—languid in manner, and drawling in tone.

Sexton Blake, the great English detective, would have recognised in him the features of Graves—Mademoiselle Yvonne's uncle and lieutenant in her undertakings, but at present he was known as Cyrus Harmon—American millionaire.

Mademoiselle Yvonne smiled demurely when addressed as Miss Harmon, niece of the wealthy magnate, and little did the unconscious baronet dream of the real identity of his guests.

An easy-going man, spending every other year shooting big game, and whose sojourn in England was divided between his clubs and polo-ponies, he accepted his fellows at their face value.

He was about to leave on one of his periodical trips to Africa, and consequently, when he had learnt that Cyrus Harmon, American millionaire, whom he met at his club, was looking for a place in the country for twelve months, he jumped at the chance.

Over lunch the details had been arranged.

Harmon and his niece were to take over Sir George's place at once, and Sir George would write personal letters to his friends, to call and make things pleasant.

No time was lost signing the lease, and this evening at the "Royal" was a little courtesy shown by Sir George to his future tenants.

Had he been told that the beautiful bronze head beside him contained one of the most brilliant brains in Europe, and that the demure Miss Harmon had waited patiently for months for a vacant estate, and proper introductions to Bournmill, where Sir George's place was situated, it is doubtful if he would have given it a serious thought.

As he was leaving England on the following day, he excused himself when the curtain fell on the first part, and sought out his more intimate friends in the neighbouring boxes.

As the door closed behind Sir George, Miss Harmon turned her head and addressed her uncle in a low tone.

"Did you arrange matters all right?"

"Yes! It was very easy, I offered him references and all that, but he pooh-poohed the idea."

"Did he write the letters to his friends?"

"Yes, at the club. He wrote half a dozen, and you will be pleased when I tell you that one was addressed to our man Mortimer Todd."

"Ah!" breathed Yvonne. "That will simplify matters. We will go down on the afternoon train, tomorrow. I think the best plan would be—Good heavens!" she broke off in a startled tone. "Uncle, get your hat and coat, quick! Hand me my cloak, and open the door. We must get away at once quick!"

"What is the matter, Yvonne?" asked Graves, agitated at her startled tones.

"I have been seen, and I am sure I have been recognised. Quick, hand me my cloak! You will have to apologise in some way to Sir George tomorrow."

"What is it? Who has recognised you?" whispered Graves anxiously, as he snatched their wraps and opened the door.

"Sexton Blake! I'm sure he recognised me!"

Down in the stalls sat Sexton Blake, the great English detective and Tinker, his assistant.

Having brought a stiff case to a successful issue, and feeling the need of relaxation, Blake, taking Tinker, had thrown aside all cares for the evening, and had come to the "Royal" to hear the famous singer.

He had arrived after the curtain went up on the first scene, and as yet, had had no opportunity of scanning the audience. But as the curtain rolled down and the exodus to the lobby began, Blake's scrutinising gaze embraced the lights of society.

As he brought his all-seeing glance around, he suddenly stiffened, and spoke sharply to Tinker in a low tone.

"Don't look up now, Tinker," he said, the movement of his lips barely visible, "but run your eye casually over the stage box on the left."

Tinker glanced about him in a careless fashion, finally sweeping his eyes past the box indicated by Blake.

"Why—why, guv'nor, isn't that—yes, by George! It is our old friend, Mademoiselle Yvonne. What do you suppose she is doing in London, guv'nor?"

"That is just what I have been wondering myself," murmured Blake. "It is unlikely that mademoiselle is here without a purpose, and—ah! Tinker, quick my lad, follow me! She has spotted us, and, foolishly, I allowed my glance to rest a moment too long in that direction. We'll have to hurry! She is already leaving the box."

Blake jumped up, and followed by Tinker, hastened out. Unfortunately, their seats were well down front, and, the audience now returning for the second scene, hindered their rapid progress.

Reaching the lobby, they hurried on, and Blake gave a sharp exclamation as he saw the ruffle of a green dress and a dainty green slipper, disappear into the taxi, followed by a man whom he recognised as Graves.

Another taxi pulled up into the kerb, and Blake hastened towards it. He was anticipated, however, for another man in evening clothes reached it first, and as Blake glanced at the successful one, he saw the features of a high-caste Chinese gentleman, whose eyes looked into his with an inscrutable expression.

The other taxi, containing Blake's quarry, had already gained headway, and unless the detective could start in pursuit at once, the attempt to follow it would be useless.

As he turned to hail another taxi, as a forlorn hope, the Chinese gentleman spoke.

"If you are in a hurry, sir, you may take this car, and I will secure another. I have the whole evening at my disposal."

Blake returned the Celestial's look with one equally inscrutable; but his mind was working rapidly.

"Curious," he thought. "Where on earth have I seen this man before? Was it in China, or here? His voice is more familiar than his face."

But he had no time then for such conjectures. Hardly had the thought flashed through his mind when he replied to the Celestial's remark.

"Thank you, sir! I am rather in a hurry, and will gladly take advantage of your kindness. I am slightly late for an appointment."

Which remark was strictly true, although Blake had only made the appointment a few moments previously, and the persons with whom he had made it seemed not too anxious for him to keep it.

The gentleman bowed gravely and drew back, standing at the edge of the kerb near the rear of the cab, as Blake, bowing also, leaped in, followed by Tinker.

He directed the chauffeur to drive on quickly, intending to give him further directions when they would not be overheard.

As the cab left the kerb, the Chinese gentleman withdrew his left hand from his coat-pocket, where he had carelessly thrust it. Taking his cigarette from his right, he knocked the hot ash off, the shower of ashes and sparks falling on the tyre of the near-side wheel of the taxi as it started.

Returning his cigarette to his right hand, he hailed another cab, and, entering, was soon speeding away.

Blake pointed out to his driver the fast-vanishing taxi which held Yvonne and her uncle, and ordered the man to follow, promising him half-a-sovereign over his fare if he succeeded in doing so. He leaned forward to watch the chase.

The man risked being stopped by the police, and dashed on recklessly. And, as Blake saw they were gradually overhauling the leading cab, he heaved a sigh of relief.

"I thought we would be too late, Tinker," he remarked, pulling out a cigar. "But I think we will do it yet. Our friends—— Hallo, what is that?"

A loud hissing sound had come from the back of the taxi, followed by a bumping, and a sudden stoppage.

Blake leaned out as the driver descended, and hurriedly examined his tyres.

"I'm sorry, sir," he said, coming to the window where Blake leaned out; "one of my rear tyres has gone."

Blake muttered in disgust as he threw open the door and jumped out.

"Well, it can't be helped, my man. What is it—a cut? It wasn't a 'blow out,' for there was no report."

"I'm blest if I know, sir!" returned the driver. "It's the funniest puncture I've ever seen, and I've been driving for several years."

"How do you mean?" asked Blake.

"Well, sir, just look here!" And, as he spoke, the driver loosened a lamp, and threw its glare on the flattened tyre.

Blake told Tinker to hail another cab quickly, and, as the lad hastened to do his bidding, the detective bent over the wheel.

"Bring the light nearer, cabby," he said, bending closer.

Something seemed to interest the detective exceedingly, for he studied the tyre closely for some moments, finally, drawing out a magnifying-glass, and making an even closer examination.

The tyre was covered with a multitude of purple patches, and, even as Blake made his examination, several of them grew, a hole in the tyre-cover appearing as they did so. Several which had already opened had caused the air to escape, but it was to those which had not yet done so that Blake turned his attention.

"Where have you been tonight, cabby?" asked Blake, straightening up.

"On the rank ever since seven, sir. You were my first fare."

"Ah, do you know if your tyres were all right when I got in?"

"Yes, sir; I'm sure. Before I went on the rank I slipped into a garage, and had all of them filled, and I know they were all right then. What do you make of it, sir? I've never seen a puncture like that before. It looks as though the tyre had been riddled with a charge of shot."

"Yes, it does look that way, my man," laughed Blake. "I can't say what is the matter—— But here, I will give you the half-sovereign I promised you, although the taxi I wished to follow has disappeared. Will you get a new cover put on tonight?"

"Oh, yes, sir! I've already got the Stepney spare wheel on the off-side front."

"Well, if you bring me that old one, my man, I will give you another sovereign."

"Right you are, sir! I'll be glad to do so. What name, sir?"

"Sexton Blake," smiled the detective.

"Oh, I know the address, sir!" grinned the man.

Tinker arrived at that moment with another taxi, and Blake entered.

"Drive to Baker Street," he ordered, and sank back, his eyes brooding in deep thought. "Strange—strange," he muttered. "I start after mademoiselle, and my tyre suddenly goes flat. That in itself is not remarkable, but the appearance which it presents certainly is remarkable. It will bear investigation. I wonder if my Celestial friend could enlighten me as to the cause?

"Those marks on the tyre certainly look as though a chemical had been applied. But what was it, and who applied it? As soon as I get the cover I will make an exhaustive test, and then—— Well, mademoiselle, who knows, it may even be the means of once more bringing us together."

True to his promise, the taxi driver turned up two hours later with the tyre-cover, and Blake at once retired with it to the laboratory. Many were the tests he applied to read the meaning of those peculiar purple spots; but many hours passed, and still he was baffled.

Almost every test he knew had been applied, when he finally reached up, and drew down a volume as a last resort. He did not anticipate success, but true to his thorough methods he left no stone unturned. The volume was thick and technical-looking, and was labelled with one simple word.

That word was "Radium," and even as the first grey streaks of dawn crept through the window of the laboratory Blake opened it, and buried himself in its intricacies.

III
Jack Fenwick Views a Rosy Future

BOURNMILL is marked on the map by a very small dot, and, as far as the world generally is concerned, is not of vast importance. But throughout the import and export world it ranks as an important centre in the purchase of raw cotton, and the subsequent shipment of manufactured cloth.

It was during the previous generation that Bournmill was chosen as the location of a cotton mill. In those days only a ramshackle old mill, driven by a water-wheel, leaned in an alarming manner over the waters of the Bourn River, but today, what a change!

The first cotton mill proving a success, others had been quickly established, and now Bournmill, formerly a not very prosperous farming centre, teemed and clattered to the buzz and rattle of the modern octopus.

If a sudden stoppage of the mills should occur, and the huge buildings be dismantled, the now busy town would see a radical change. Like the Arabs, fully nine-tenths of the population would, figuratively speaking, fold up their tents and depart. Nothing would remain but the silent mills and empty cottages, and once more Bournmill would rank as a not very prosperous farming community. Not until such a serious event occurred, would the present landowners really appreciate the value of the mill population, for long familiarity had made a matter of course the teeming, buzzing, clattering life of the mills.

Not for them the shrieking call of the hooter, while night still reigned over the dark waters of the Bourne. That was for the workers who made up the many cogs of the mighty machine of toil, and to them it was a remorseless master—all their comings and goings being regulated by its watchful voice.

Clustered within a stone's throw of each other were the mills, the smaller buildings nestling in the shadow of the giant chimney, were dotted the cottages of the workers.

There, as the first warning of the mills pierced the blanket of night, lights appeared. Small wisps of smoke ascended into the growing greyness.

Yawning lads and lasses, tired fathers, and often mothers, and even stiff age stumbled into the tiny kitchens, and ate the hurried breakfast.

Another warning hoot, the noisy clatter of clogs in the narrow, smoky streets, the slamming of doors as laggards hurried out, and on swept that great human stream, born at morn to rush on to the great red ocean which absorbed it, shifting as each jerkined man and boy and shawled, clogged woman and girl sought their respective mill.

Laughing sallies, and moody surliness floated about in the human current, accompanied by the rattle of starting machines, the shrieking, buzzing clatter from every floor, and the last warning hoot which spurred the laggard on.

Through the gates poured the stream of human beings, swallowed at once in the great maw of the mill, seeking and scurrying to their proper rooms, and another day had begun.

Such was Bournmill. And of its many prosperous inhabitants, probably the most powerful and influential was Mortimer Todd, sole proprietor of the largest mill, formerly known as the Creighton Mill.

Six years previously, when the cotton industry was struggling through a heavy depression, and mills were closing their gates, some not to reopen, Mortimer Todd had arrived in Bournmill.

Like many others, the large Creighton Mill was tottering on the brink of ruin, and the worried directors had jumped at a cash offer from the new arrival. Many heads had wagged in gloomy prophecy at the venture in the teeth of the conditions which governed at the time; but a strong reserve fund carried Todd through the depression, and his keen, organising mind had built up a sound, and profitable business.

It was later, when money was coming easily, that he made mistakes, and gambled heavily on the Stock Exchange, but no one but Mortimer Todd knew of that.

In the six years which had passed, he had become a power in the mill-town. Whence he had come none knew; but his generosity and charities and his readiness to meet the demands of the workers had made him popular.

In a word, Mr. Mortimer Todd was a desirable citizen, and none thought so more thoroughly than Jack Fenwick, assistant in the dye-room of Todd's Mill.

From the lowest rung had Jack Fenwick worked his way up, carefully accomplishing his work each day, and studying at night to rise still higher.

An orphan, he had had a hard fight as a lad; but clean grit had carried him through, and now at the age of twenty-five he was looking forward to a bright future which contained a certain brown-eyed young woman, who, with a widowed mother, resided in a cottage on the outskirts of Bournmill.

On the morning in question, Jack Fenwick whistled cheerfully as he worked amongst the colours, his eye alternating between a bulge in his coat and the hands of the clock.

As ten o'clock came round he wiped his hands and slipped on his coat.

For Jack had worked diligently at an improvement in the present system of dyeing, and both his experiments and common-sense told him it was practicable. He would show it to Mr. Todd, and solicit the mill-owner's assistance in giving it a trial under actual working conditions. Then—well, when Jack reached that point his mind went off to rosy clouds, for it meant success and wealth.

Knowing the great man would have finished reading his letters, Jack hurried through the main office and knocked at the door marked "Private."

A booming voice bade him enter, and the mill-owner looked up inquiringly as Jack closed the door.

"What is it, Fenwick?" he asked.

"May I have just a few minutes of your time, sir?" asked Jack, approaching the desk.

"Yes, but be quick. What is it—a complaint?"

"Oh, no, sir, I wish to show you these." And Jack opened the envelope as he spoke.

"What are they? I don't understand."

"They are the particulars, sir, of an improvement in the present system of dyeing. I have been working at it for months, and I am positive it will cause a revolution in the present method. I thought, sir, you might help me to give it a trial."

"Hm! I don't imagine it amounts to much," replied the mill-owner bluntly. "All inventors have the same idea, and nine times out of ten they are worthless. However, open them up. If it shows promise I will consider it."

Jack unfolded the papers, and was soon deep in a technical explanation of the details. So absorbed was he in his explanation that he did not see the look of undisguised interest which crossed the man's face, and which was followed by a cunning look of calculation. As he finished and looked up he saw only an expression of mild interest, and he waited breathlessly for Todd to speak.

"Your idea has some good points," remarked the mill-owner picking up the plans. "How it would work in practical use I don't know. Have you patented it yet?" he asked carelessly.

"No, sir," replied Jack. "I wanted your opinion on it first."

"H'm; I see. Well, Fenwick, if you care to leave these papers with me I will go into it more thoroughly when I have more time, and see what it is worth. If I think it is of use I will finance it for you."

"Oh, thank you, Mr. Todd!" answered Jack. "It is very good of you to take an interest in it."

"Oh, that's all right," smiled the mill-owner genially. "I'll just stick these in the safe. I'll take it up, as I said, and let you know my decision."

Jack rose as Mortimer Todd spoke, and, again pressing his thanks, was turning to go, when the mill-owner called him back.

"By the way, Fenwick," he said, "I like to see industry, and believe in encouraging it. I will see the cashier about giving you an advance."

And Jack left the office with a springy step.

Once alone, Todd returned to the safe and drew out the papers again. Spreading them out on the desk, he pored over them for some time, emitting a grunt of satisfaction at intervals.

"It's great!" he muttered, folding them up. "The young fool will be as well satisfied with his rise in salary. This thing is worth a fortune, and with finances in their present condition it will just put me on my feet. I must lose no time in making a copy and taking out a patent for it."

He rose, carefully locked the plans away, and returned to his letters with a smile on his face.

*****

As the shriek of the hooter signalled the dinner-hour Jack slipped on his coat and hurried out, joining the clattering stream of workers which poured from every floor.

The machines grew silent, a strange quietness seeming to reign even over the clatter and chatter of the workers. The belts ceased to flap, and for a brief hour the tireless jaws of the regular rows of cogs would stop. Jack was carried through the lower door in the crush, and as he tumbled down the steps to the mill-yard he elbowed his way along until he reached the gates. Some of the workers from outlying districts still remained in the now silent rooms eating a cold lunch; others clustered against the mill wall in the sun, while others hurried along to the nearby cottages. But Jack Fenwick did none of these things.

Pulling a packet of sandwiches from his pocket, he started at a rapid pace for a little cottage at the edge of the town.

For Phyllis Cameron, the brown-haired young woman, must be told the good news at once, and he would just have time to tell her and get back before the hooter again sounded.

Phyllis saw him coming, and ran to meet him. As Jack told her the good news they hurried into the cottage, where it had to be repeated all over again to the delighted Mrs. Cameron, with whom Jack was a great favourite.

*****

The evening of the day of Jack Fenwick's good fortune was the same evening on which London Society turned out in force at the "Royal."

No visible connection existed between the brilliantly-lighted theatre and the tiny cottage on the outskirts of Bournmill, and yet Fate was at that very moment weaving a tangled web which would connect them closely—a web which would seem to baffle all efforts to unravel it.

End of the Prologue

The First Chapter
The Outrage at the Mill—Yvonne Makes a Capture

CYRUS Harmon and his niece had been welcomed by the neighbourhood with open arms.

Sir George Waltham had been as good as his word, and barely had the new arrivals got settled when callers descended upon them.

Three months had passed, during which time the Harmons had given several dinner-parties, these, under Yvonne's guiding hand having been a series of triumphs.

On the night on which this story opens they themselves were dining out, their host being none other than Mortimer Todd, the wealthy mill-owner.

A bachelor with no desire for matrimony, he had only entertained at rare intervals, but since the beautiful Miss Harmon had arrived he was to be seen out wherever she appeared.

It was patent to all that he greatly admired the charming American, and as she was the niece and sole heiress of her wealthy uncle it would be a desirable match.

Only Mortimer Todd himself knew just how desirable the Harmon fortune would be, and he had reason to hope that his suit would meet with success, for certainly Miss Harmon had not discouraged his advances.

Up till now pressure of financial obligations had left little time for other matters, but the previous day had seen the last shipment of the biggest order the Todd mill had ever turned out, and the temporary relief he anticipated from the payment of it would give him more time to push his suit.

With that end in view, he was giving a strictly informal dinner this evening, the Harmons being his only guests, for Todd was a good general, and knew every move to make in such a campaign.

But had he known that Cyrus Harmon and his niece were the famous Graves and Mademoiselle Yvonne, and that the young woman had waited and planned patiently to meet him, instead of seeking them out he would have done better to have sought the ends of the earth.

Harmon applied himself as usual to his plate, only making a drawling remark from time to time. But his niece was a brilliant conversationalist, and never did she sparkle more than on that evening.

Todd was fascinated by the vivacious and scintillating personality, and when the conversation swung round to mill matters he himself talked well, not aware that his brilliant guest was drawing him out.

"You must take me over your mill, Mr. Todd," remarked Yvonne. "I have never yet been over one."

"With pleasure, Miss Harmon. Any time you care to come I would be only too happy."

"It must be quite a model place," she laughed. "I hear such glowing accounts of you on every side."

"Oh, I don't have much trouble," he smiled. "It's always best to meet the union half way. Then you get better work out of your people. I am bringing in an improvement that will revolutionise older methods. It will make far cheaper production, and the workers will make even more than they do at present at a less rate of pay. I venture to predict that it will be adopted by every mill in the country inside twelve months."

"Oh, that is wonderful!" exclaimed Yvonne. "Is it an invention?"

"Yes—a very simple but very potent one."

"You must be awfully clever!" flattered Yvonne blandly, "I should like to see this invention."

"I'm afraid you wouldn't understand much about it," smiled the pleased Todd, "but when you come down I will explain it to you from the plans."

"Thank you! As you say, I don't imagine I shall understand it, but I will try. Are you hunting on Saturday?"

The conversation branched off to hunting topics, and no more was said about the mill.

Dinner over, the guests departed early, and as Mortimer Todd closed the door he returned to his library feeling optimistic about the future.

Yvonne and her uncle returned at once to Waltham Hall. A telegram lay on the table, addressed to Miss Harmon, and, picking it up, Yvonne tore it open and read:

"SHOWER IN LONDON TONIGHT. DUST COMPLETELY LAID."

It was not signed, but no signature was needed, for as she passed it to her uncle she spoke in a low tone.

"The doctor has succeeded. I think it will be wiser to make the move here before his letter of complaint arrives at the mill."

"Yes, I think that would be the best plan. Will you go alone, or do you wish me to help you?"

"No, I'll go alone. Watch for my return, and have the motor ready in case anything happens. I've made a pretty fair study of the mill, and I think I can manage all right. There is only one night watchman, and I can handle him."

She hastened to her room as she finished speaking, and, calling her maid she slipped out of her gown, and, approaching the mirror, she worked rapidly. Her hair was flattened down, and concealed by a close-fitting skull cover. Over this she put a wig of short, black hair. From a trunk she took a suit of male attire, and a pair of heavy boots, into which she slipped. A few touches to her face, and a cap on her head, and the lad who now stood before the mirror bore not the faintest resemblance to the beautiful young woman who had stood there a few moments before.

She again had access to the trunk, from which she took a very small black bag, a small electric torch, and an automatic revolver, fitted with a silencer. Thrusting these in her pockets, she switched out the lights and descended the stairs.

Entering the library she gave a few whispered directions to her uncle. And midnight was just striking as she opened the door, and stole silently down the drive.

On reaching the road she turned, and bent her steps in the direction of the town.

She kept in the shadow, and hurried through the silent, narrow streets until she stood before the huge, black bulk of the Todd Mill.

Only a solitary light gleamed forth, and while she stood in the shadow it moved in a swinging manner past the row of windows.

"The night watchman," she muttered.

As the light approached the further end of the building the dark figure drew itself up to the top of the gate, and dropped silently to the ground on the other side.

Stepping softly she crept across the dark yard, stopping before a window in an angle of the building. Pulling out the small, black bag, she drew out a tiny instrument. A further search brought forth a pot of greasy material, and a small, circular piece of paper.

Reaching up she rubbed the grease over the window near the top of the lower sash. Over this she placed the paper, and then brought the instrument into play. Swiftly and silently she ran it around the edge of the paper, and on the completion of the circle the paper dropped toward her, bringing with it a circular piece of the glass.

She placed the glass, paper and instrument back in the bag, and, inserting her hand, threw back the catch. Noiselessly she pushed up the window, and slipped through into the dark interior.

Pulling out her torch she pressed the button, and found she was in a large office. She crept across and opened the door entering a passage, which ended in a flight of stairs.

As she did so, a sound on the floor above caught her ear. She put out her light, and sank back into the shadow of the stairs. The footsteps approached, and began to descend, the swinging light of a lantern being thrown almost on the concealed Yvonne.

It was the night watchman making his rounds, and, as he reached the bottom, Yvonne gathered herself together.

Turning the torch around in her hand she sprang forward, silently bringing down the heavy end on the back of the watchman's head.

The lantern dropped with a clatter to the floor as he reeled and fell, and Yvonne thrust the torch back in her pocket as she saw another blow was not necessary.

Picking up the lantern she hastened through a door into what proved to be the weaving-room. There she secured several heavy strands, and returned to the prostrate figure of the night watchman.

He was still unconscious, breathing heavily, and Yvonne wasted no time in binding his arms and legs.

She rolled up some of the strands into a yielding ball, and this she thrust into his mouth, tying his own handkerchief about his face to prevent it coming out.

She had worked quickly, for if the open window should be seen, her position would be dangerous. She had not closed it on entering, for if the night watchman had proved too much of a handful, she would need to make a hasty retreat.

But fortune had dealt favourably with her, and, picking up the watchman's lantern, she returned to the weaving-room.

Carefully closing the door after her, she set the lantern on the floor, and again had recourse to the little black bag. From this she drew forth a long, narrow glass tube, in the top of which a rubber stopper had been fixed. With this in her right hand, and the lantern in her left, she moved through the room, stopping for a moment at each machine.

That room finished she entered the next, going through the same performance. From there she ascended the stairs, visiting every machine on each floor. Into the vital parts of each machine she dropped a few drops of the contents of the glass tube, and when she returned to the passage where lay the night watchman, every machine in the building had been treated.

Sexton Blake and Tinker's thrilling fight for mastery —over Graves and his— Chinese companions.

The watchman still lay unconscious, and, stepping over him, she proceeded to the office. She extinguished the lantern, and drew out her torch as she entered and moved softly across to a door marked "private." It opened into the mill-owner's office, and Yvonne directed her steps to a large safe in the corner.

Once more the black bag was brought into use, and her eyes gleamed with satisfaction as she saw the safe was operated by a key, and not a combination.

With her expert outfit the lock presented no insurmountable difficulties, and she laughed softly as the big door swung back.

The lower part was filled with large books, and these she passed over. On each side above them were cash-boxes, and in the centre a small, iron door.

Yvonne turned her attention to this first, and a few moments sufficed to force it open. Inside lay several bundles of papers, and, running through them quickly, she again laughed softly as a folded packet of plans caught her eye. Thrusting them into the inside pocket of her coat, she turned her attention to the cash-boxes. On being opened these proved to contain more papers, and in one were several banknotes. She bundled everything into her pocket, and again peered closely into the dark interior of the safe.

Four large bags of coin rested on a shelf, and she pulled them out. She untied the strings, and smiled on finding them full of gold.

"Evidently preparing for pay day," she muttered. "Well, my friend, I'll just take it, and credit it up to you."

She suited the action to the word, and emptied the contents of the four canvas bags into the little black bag.

Another search of the safe revealed nothing of further interest. A hasty examination of the desk proved equally barren, and, with a last look round, she put out the torch, and silently slipped out into the main office.

She crossed to the window and peered out, uttering a gasping cry as a dark figure suddenly loomed up on the other side of the sill.

She found herself gazing into a pair of surprised eyes, and her hand moved stealthily for her revolver.

The man on the outside was as astonished as was Yvonne, and several seconds passed before he collected himself.

"Here you, what are you doing in the mill?" he asked, sharply starting to clamber in.

"Hold on, my friend, not so fast!" answered Yvonne, coolly swinging up the revolver which she had secured. "Who are you, and what are you doing here, might I ask?"

"I work here," was the reply. "And I saw a light in the private office. You haven't any business here, and you'll have to come with me!"

"On the contrary, my friend, you will have to come with me!" snapped Yvonne. "If you make a move, believe me, it will be at your peril. This little silencer which you can just make out in the darkness will make it perfectly safe, so don't do anything rash. How did you get in?"

"I opened the gate," growled the new-comer. "But you'd better not go too far with this. You'll find yourself in prison."

"Will I, my young friend?" laughed Yvonne softly. "If you knew to whom you were speaking, you would realise how foolish your remark is."

She hopped over the sill as she spoke, and stood beside the other whom she discovered to be a young man.

"Now, my friend," she went on, "you are going to come with me."

"No, I'm not!" growled the other, risking all, and leaping forward.

Yvonne did not hesitate. She lifted her arm, and an almost imperceptible click followed. A smothered cry came as the reckless young man stopped, and grasped his left hand.

"That is just a lesson," said Yvonne coolly. "I aimed for the thumb of your left hand, and I think you will find that is what I hit. Perhaps you understand now that I mean what I say."

The other was busy tying up the wounded thumb with his handkerchief, and did not reply.

"By the way, what is your name?" went on Yvonne.

"Fenwick," growled the other.

"Well, Fenwick, turn round and take hold of my left arm. Now watch carefully. You see how I put my right hand inside my coat? Do you feel the barrel of the revolver against you?"

"Yes."

"Very well. You will remember that if you make one false move it will speak again, and this time it won't be your thumb. Do you understand?"

"Yes. I know when I'm beaten," growled Fenwick. "What do you want of me?"

"You'll discover soon enough. Now march! If we pass a policeman, I wouldn't advise you to make any sign, for I assure you I will shoot at once if you do!"

In this manner Jack Fenwick and Yvonne moved arm-in-arm through the gate, and along the dark, silent streets.

He had no idea as to the identity of his captor. All he could see was that it was a young man, and a very determined one.

The barrel of the revolver, pressing against his side, forbade any move for freedom. For the moment he was helpless to do anything and could only watch his chance.

Through the silent town they went without meeting anyone, and the lad's eyes grew puzzled as his captor headed for the open country. For a mile they continued, and Jack grew still more puzzled as they entered the drive of Waltham Hall.

His captor led him to the front door, where a soft whistle brought a middle-aged man, whom Jack recognised with surprise as Mr. Harmon, the American millionaire.

As the door closed, and he was led down to the basement, his mind whirled in an endeavour to elucidate the mystery. But it was totally beyond his understanding.

On reaching the cellar, his captor released him and thrust him into a stone-walled room without windows. The door slammed, and a key turned, leaving the anxious and mystified lad in the dark.

The Second Chapter
Mortimer Todd Receives Several Shocks

MR. Mortimer Todd was awakened long before his usual hour by a sharp knock, and the entrance of a sleepy servant. It was still dark, and he sat up with a vague feeling that something was amiss.

"What is it, Gordon?" he asked sharply.

"Please, sir, the foreman of the mills has called up on the telephone, and says he must speak to you at once. He says it is very urgent, sir."

Todd hopped out of bed, and, without waiting to put on his dressing-gown, hastened out of the room and down the dark staircase.

When he returned, his face was as grey as the coming dawn, and he lost no time in getting into his clothes.

Always a stickler for appearances, and knowing their value, he dressed with his usual care, but the drawn, grey expression still rested on his face as he climbed into his motor and headed at full-speed for the mill.

The last hooter of the other mills came shrieking through the morning air as Todd threaded his way through the last of the hurrying workers. But the hooter of his own mill was silent. No rattle of belts and buzz of machines came from the towering buildings. In the mill-yard stood the employees of the Todd Mill, wondering expressions on their faces, at the still closed doors.

They stood aside and allowed the mill-owner to pass, and when he reached the steps, he turned and faced them.

Silence reigned as he held up his hand and spoke.

"The foreman has telephoned me that there is a breakage in the machinery," he said, in a loud tone. "I don't know yet how serious it is, and I trust it will not hold us up for long. As quickly as I make an examination I will post a notice."

A buzz of remarks followed as he turned and hurried into the mill.

The foreman met him in the passage, and Todd led the way into his private office.

"Now, Allen," he said, turning to the man as he closed the door, "just what is the matter?"

The man's face was even greyer than Todd's, and his hands twitched nervously as he answered his master.

"I'm almost afraid to tell you, sir!" he gasped. "It seems like a nightmare!"

"Quick, man, get to the point!" snapped Todd. "Tell me just how serious it is."

"Well, sir, every machine in the mill is ruined!"

"My heavens! What do you mean?" asked Todd, sinking weakly into a chair.

"That's all I know, sir. When I came this morning, I found the night watchman lying, bound and gagged, in the passage. I untied him, and he told me what had happened."

"Go—go on!" said Todd hoarsely, as the man stopped and wetted his lips with his tongue.

"Well, sir, he said that he was attacked last night by someone, but he didn't know what they had done afterwards, as he had been knocked unconscious. We came in here first, sir, thinking naturally they would go through the safe, and the door of your safe was open, and it looked as though it had been rifled. I closed the door, sir, but touched nothing else."

With a groan of dread, Todd jerked himself to his feet and hurried to the safe. His hand shook as the handle turned, and the door swung open, telling him the man's story was indeed true. As he looked inside and saw how complete had been the rifling, he collapsed on the floor, and great beads stood out on his forehead.

Feverishly he dragged out the books and remaining contents of the safe; but as the full realisation of his dread hit him, he groaned again, and his jaws moved noiselessly in an effort to speak. White and shaking, he got slowly to his feet and tottered to the chair.

"Tell me—tell me all!" he whispered. "What about the machines?"

The foreman's eyes had grown frightened as he saw the effect of the news on his master, and he hesitated to add to the blow, but as the mill-owner's voice came again in a high, almost hysterical, command, he spoke.

"Well, sir, when we saw what had happened here, I was going to the phone to let you know at once, when the hooter sounded. I knew the hands would soon be coming, so I went first on my rounds to see that everything was ready for starting. When I got to the card-room—— Again he stopped and wetted his lips.

"For heaven's sake, man, go on!" almost shrieked Todd.

"Well, sir, I found this on the floor!"

The foreman put his hand in his pocket and drew out a small shiny bit of steel as he spoke, and passed it to his master.

"Ah!" gasped Todd, snatching it and peering at the gleaming row of teeth. "What else?"

"I picked it up, and as I did so, I saw another under the next machine, and then another and another, until—— Oh, Mr. Todd," he gasped, "I can hardly believe it, but I found one of these pieces under every machine on the floor! I ran up the stairs to the other floors and back to the weaving-room. Every room had something wrong, sir; and when I finished, I found some part of every machine in the mill had broken off in the night! I—I don't know what to make of it, sir! It's awful!"

Allen wiped his brow and sank into a chair, and so great was the mental strain of both men, that neither noticed the action, which at any other time he would never have thought of doing.

Todd slowly collected himself, but his voice still shook as he spoke.

"Do the workers know yet what the real trouble is?

"No, sir. I only said there had been a breakdown, and I kept the doors closed."

"Where is the night watchman?"

"He is in the weaving-room, sir. I told him to wait and say nothing until you came."

"That was right. Allen, you have done well. Call him in and I will speak to him."

The foreman hastened away, and returned in a few moments with the night watchman. Todd found the man's story threw no further light on what Allen had already told him. Rising, he led the way, and with the two men made a rapid examination of the mill.

He found the foreman's story all too true. Every machine had some part broken, and the completeness of the ruin made it evident that it was the result of a carefully-planned outrage. If any doubt had existed, the attack on the night watchman and the rifling of the safe settled it.

Todd returned to the office and sat down, the foreman and night watchman standing nervously before him. The mill-owner was breathing hard, and it was evident that he was labouring under an intense emotion.

"See here, men!" he said in a low tone. "For certain reasons the real nature of this outrage must not get out. Who has done it, I haven't the faintest idea; but I will have detectives put on the matter at once. Can I depend on you to see it goes no farther?"

Both men, who felt partly responsible for the safety of the mill, were only too glad to agree.

"Don't let a whisper get out!" went on the mill-owner. "You, Allen, post a notice on the door saying there has been a slight breakdown, which will necessitate a few days' stoppage, but that half-pay will continue right along. State also that there has been——"

He broke off, as a hasty knock came at the door, and it swung open to admit a stout, middle-aged woman.

"What do you want?" said Todd testily. "What do you mean by coming in here when I am engaged?"

"I'm really sorry, Mr. Todd, to disturb you, but I won't keep you long, sir."

"I can't talk to you now, my good woman. I——"

"I just want a word, sir," interrupted the woman. "I want to know, can you tell me where Jacky Fenwick is?"

"How should I know where he is?" snapped Todd. "I suppose he is at his home, or in the mill-yard with the rest of the hands."

"No, sir, he's not, and hasn't been home all night."

"What's that?" gasped Todd, sitting up. "Hasn't been home all night?"

"No, sir. He went out about seven last evening to Cameron's, sir. He be courtin' Phyllis," explained the woman. "He lives with me, and when he didn't come home, I got worried, for he's always in by eleven. I waited up all night, and when he didn't come I went over to Mrs. Cameron's, thinking perhaps she had been took ill, and he had stayed there. But she was all right, and Phyllis said he left there at half-past ten, sir. I thought maybe he had come back here to do some special work, sir, and came to make sure."

Todd had sat motionless, his eyes tense, and his hands clenched tightly as the woman spoke. His eyes held a steely glitter, and he laughed harshly as he replied.

"Yes, you are right. I think Fenwick was doing some special work last night. But you will see him soon, don't worry about that."

"I'm sure I'm obliged to you, sir," said the woman, in a relieved tone, and curtseying. "It's taken a great load off my mind."

She bowed, and withdrew; and as the door closed, Todd turned and spoke sharply to the foreman.

"I don't think we need look farther for the perpetrator of the outrage and the thief of my papers!" he said grimly. "Add in your notice, Allen, that some money has been stolen as well, and that Fenwick has disappeared. Say that, if anyone harbours him they will be in danger of the law as accessories."

"But, sir!" stammered the foreman. "Surely Fenwick couldn't do this terrible thing, sir! He——"

"Do as I say, Allen!" snapped Todd. "I'm the best judge of that; and don't forget what I said. On your lives not a word about the damage to the machines. Do you understand?"

Both men fervently said they did, and Allen hastened away to post up the notice.

Mungall, the night watchman, was also turning to go when the mill-owner stopped him.

"You, Mungall," he said, "were responsible for the safety of the mill. I don't think you were in any way an accomplice in this; but if you were, it will come out."

"Oh, Mr. Todd," pleaded the man, in a trembling tone, "I swear to you, sir, that I wasn't!"

"As I say, I believe you at present," returned Todd; "but, I expect you to do all in your power to help find Fenwick. In the meantime, go and bring the police, and remember, not a word to them about the machines."

As the door closed on the night watchman, Todd got up and crossed the floor. Turning the key in the lock, he returned to the desk, and again sank into his chair.

Every ounce of strength the man possessed had been utilised to keep up before the others, but as he found himself alone, he gave vent to all the utter despair which filled him.

His hands rose and fell weakly, his face worked in an agony of suffering, and his lips moved as he muttered brokenly:

"My heavens—my heavens!" he moaned. "Ruin—utter ruin! Could that young fool Fenwick have done this? Has he discovered in some way that I was getting a patent for the process? Has he stolen the plans, robbed me, and ruined the machines in revenge?

"Ruin—it's worse than ruin! It's everlasting disgrace. Surely he couldn't commit such a wholesale outrage! Thousands of pounds' worth of damage in one night! My heavens, what shall I do? Even if I do catch him, it won't help any!

"But, by thunder, I'll make him suffer! I'll keep the damage to the machines quiet, and push him for the robbery of the money. If I can get the papers back quickly, perhaps I can borrow enough yet to save myself. If the bank knew of this they would put me into bankruptcy in a minute. And that big overdraft must be paid in ten days. Thank heaven, I will have the cheque from that big Chinese contract to meet it. It ought to be here now."

Todd bent over as the thought occurred, and picked up the pile of letters on the desk. Quickly running through them, a faint glimmer of relief appeared in his eyes as he came to a large blue envelope. Tossing down the other letters, he tore it open.

"This will be it," he muttered. "I will be able to fix up that overdraft, anyway, and———"
He stopped, and searched the envelope feverishly. A folded sheet of paper was there, but
no cheque, and a fresh dread seized him as he unfolded the paper and read:

Dear Sir,
The consignment of cotton ordered from you by my clients for shipment to China
has been received by me and inspected here as per contract.
I regret to inform you that every bale is rotten, the cloth falling apart in the hands.
I am surprised that you should have attempted to dispose of such goods to my clients,
and am today returning the whole consignment at your expense.
In accordance with the authority received from my clients, I herewith give you notice
that I shall expect the contract filled inside of one week from date. If not, I shall at once
take proceedings for damages and breach of contract.
I am, sir, yours faithfully,
HAN Wo
Commission agent
London.

Never did a more frightful expression appear on a man's face than did Todd's assume
as he finished reading the curt letter. His eyes rolled, he grew ashen grey, and he babbled
idiotically.
Ruin had stared him in the face before, but now it crouched with a strangling hold on
his shoulders.
He had no recollection of the half-hour but from the chaos of mind in which he
struggled only one thing shone forth as a ray of hope.
If he could keep his position secret, and persuade Miss Harmon to marry him, he might
yet be saved. He would go at once and try. She would be surprised, but he could explain
in some way. Ah, yes!—he would say he found he had to leave soon for Italy on a business
trip, and that he hoped to make it a honeymoon trip as well. Yes, that would do.
Gathering himself together, he stumbled across the office and unlocked the door.
He summoned all his strength to appear natural as he walked through the still loitering
mill-hands, and, acknowledging their sympathetic remarks with a bow, climbed into the
still waiting motor.
He gave the chauffeur his directions, and leaned back in an endeavour to grow calm
and appear natural before Miss Harmon.
He had moderately succeeded by the time they turned into the drive leading to Wal-
tham Hall, and his bearing was fairly natural as he ascended the steps and rang the bell.
A maid answered almost at once, and Todd forced a genial smile as he inquired for
Miss Harmon.
"Oh, sir, she went up to London this morning with Mr. Harmon. They are to be gone
two weeks, sir."
"Up to London? Did they leave an address?"

"No, sir; they said they didn't know where they would stay, and that they might run on to Paris. But what is the matter—are you ill, sir?"

But Todd did not answer. He turned and staggered down the steps, and was helped into the car by the astonished and frightened chauffeur.

As the motor-car sped down the drive, a gleaming row of white teeth appeared, as the trim, dark-haired maid smiled and spoke, and, strange to say, it was Yvonne's voice which issued from between those smiling lips.

"Trick number one, Mr. Mortimer Todd—and from the look of things it won't need another one to finish you!"

The Third Chapter
Sexton Blake's Visitors

SEXTON Blake pulled up his big grey motor in front of the Baker Street apartments and descended. Tinker and Pedro tumbled out of the tonneau and followed him, the famous trio springing up the steps vigorously, for they had been for a brisk run in the country, returning invigorated by the pure morning air.

They entered the consulting-room, and Blake paused as he saw a slim, girlish figure almost lost in one of his huge armchairs, a look of pathetic appeal in her frightened eyes.

"Good-morning!" exclaimed Blake, cheerily holding out his hand.

"Good-morning, sir. Are—are you Mr. Blake?" asked the young woman nervously.

"Yes," smiled Blake. "Pray be seated, Miss—er———"

"Cameron. Phyllis Cameron is my name."

"Ah, thank you. And now, Miss Cameron," went on Blake, drawing up a chair, "I see you are in trouble, and you evidently consider it serious, to come all the way from Manchester to consult me."

"Why—why, how did you know that?" gasped the young woman, her eyes opening wide.

"Very simple," laughed Blake. "But I will go even further. I would say you lived outside of Manchester, probably in some small town, and, to make a pure guess, I would say a mill-town."

"You are perfectly right, Mr. Blake," answered the amazed young woman. "How you know I can't imagine, for last night was the first time I have been in Manchester in my life."

"Well, suppose you tell me what your trouble is?" smiled Blake kindly. "You can speak freely before my assistant."

And Tinker blushed as the young woman turned her eyes in his direction.

"I will tell you, Mr. Blake, but first I must tell you that at present it is impossible for me to pay you. My mother said no detective would help us without being paid, but I have read so much about you and your kindness, and I feel so desperate, that I took every penny I had saved and came to London to see you."

The great detective again smiled in a kindly manner.

"That was right, Miss Cameron. If you are in trouble and it is really serious enough to demand my help, I will assist you. As for the money, we will not worry about that."

"Oh, thank you, Mr. Blake; you have given me hope, for now we are not alone."

"Begin at the first, and tell me all," said Blake. "And if I am to help you, you must tell me everything."

"I will—I will, Mr. Blake," answered Phyllis earnestly. "It is about a—a friend of mine. His name is Jack Fenwick."

"Ah—your fiancé?" inquired Blake.

Phyllis blushed and nodded.

"We were to be married soon, and were so happy, but now— oh, I don't know what is the matter!"

"You haven't come all the way to London to consult me about a lovers' quarrel, have you?" asked Blake.

"Oh, no; it is much more serious."

Rapidly Phyllis spoke, telling Blake the simple history of herself, her mother, and Jack Fenwick. Of how Jack had toiled for months on his great process which was to revolutionise the present system of dyeing; of how he had given the papers to Mortimer Todd, and his subsequent high hopes and rise in salary; of how months had gone by without Todd mentioning the matter again, and Jack had lately become worried about it. Then how he had spent the evening with them two nights ago, and his following disappearance; of the robbery at the mill, and the issue of a warrant for Jack's arrest.

Phyllis was sobbing now, and her words came brokenly.

"He—he couldn't do it, Mr. Blake; I know he couldn't do it! He is the soul of honour. Somebody else has done this, and some accident has happened to Jack."

"Exactly when did this happen?" asked Blake quietly.

"The night before last, sir."

"And you say this Mr. Todd, the mill-owner, has issued a warrant for Fenwick's arrest?"

"Yes, sir. I tried to see Mr. Todd, but couldn't."

"How much money was stolen, do you know?"

"No, sir. There are all kinds of reports about, but no one seems to know exactly. There has also been some accident to the machinery, but no one knows what."

"H'm! Rather a mysterious occurrence all round," remarked Blake, rising and pacing up and down.

Phyllis watched his face, fearfully awaiting the word which would either give her hope or send her to despair.

"The case presents some interesting points," said Blake, coming to a stop in front of the anxious young woman, "and as the next few days are not filled with very important matters, I will run down to Bournmill and look into this affair, Miss Cameron."

"Oh, Mr. Blake, thank you!" cried Phyllis, taking the detective's hand in a grasp of gratitude, the tears falling on it as she did so.

Blake, slightly embarrassed by her thanks, lifted her up, and frowned over her head at the grinning Tinker.

"That's all right, Miss Cameron. You return at once, and if I am to be of any use, remember no one must know I am going down, or that you have been to see me."

"I will keep it from everyone," she promised. And, with a few last instructions, Blake opened the door for her to depart.

As he returned to his chair he smiled at the still grinning Tinker.

"You rascal!" he said. "She might have seen you."

"I couldn't help it, guv'nor," answered Tinker. "When she grabbed your hand I wondered what Mademoiselle Yvonne would say, and——"

But a book sent at his head made him break off and dodge for safety.

"But I say, guv'nor," went on Tinker, picking himself up, "how on earth did you know she came from Manchester, or near there?"

"Oh, that was very plain," laughed Blake. "Her umbrella was perfectly new, and on the inside was a label stamped with the name of Robbins, Manchester. Her boots were also new, and were of the type which is found in small towns, and particularly in mill-towns. Her face told me she was in trouble, and it was safe to assume that she had come specially from Manchester to see me."

"Well, I'll be——" began Tinker, but broke off as a knock came to the door and a big man entered. His eyes were drawn and haggard, and his step dragged. If ever a man was worried, Blake's visitor was that man, and the detective carefully noted every detail as he waited for his caller to speak.

"Are you Mr. Sexton Blake?" asked the new-comer in a hoarse tone.

Blake nodded.

"My name is Mortimer Todd, and I have a case which I wish you to take up, Mr. Blake."

"My time is pretty full," answered Blake, concealing his surprise at the announcement of his visitor's name, "and I am afraid——"

"Wait, wait, Mr. Blake," interrupted Todd. "It is a matter of life and death to me. Don't say you can't help me. It will mean ruin to me—absolute ruin."

"Be seated, Mr. Todd, and tell me the facts, then I can better decide," said Blake. "Have a cigar; it will calm you, and if the case is as serious as you say—well, perhaps I can arrange to take it up."

Mortimer Todd took the cigar and sank into a chair.

"It's such a terrible outrage, and such a mystery," he began, "that I doubt if you will credit it. But I think I know the perpetrator of the deed, and I want you to find him, Mr. Blake."

"Why don't you call in the police?" asked Blake.

"I have, but for certain important reasons I can't tell them all the facts, and I want you to find the man before they do."

"H'm! I hardly understand, Mr. Todd."

"I'll explain. To begin with, I am a mill-owner in Bournmill, near Manchester. Er— how about this lad?" he broke off to inquire, glancing at Tinker.

Tinker rose to leave, but Blake held up his hand.

"Sit down, Tinker," he said quietly. "You can speak freely before my assistant, Mr. Todd," he added, turning to the mill-owner. "He has my full confidence."

"Oh, I didn't suggest that he didn't," remarked Todd, colouring slightly, "but what I am going to say is very private, and I wished to be quite sure it was safe. As I was going to say, Mr. Blake, my present financial position is very critical, and the night before last things occurred which make it worse than critical. In fact, ruin is before me unless you can help me. Yesterday morning I was sent for from my mill. When I arrived there I discovered that during the night someone had bound and gagged the night watchman, rifled the safe, and ruined every machine in the building."

"Ruined every machine? How do you mean?" inquired Blake, knitting his brows.

"That I don't know. A vital part of every machine was broken off. How it was done I can't tell you. But done it was, and here is one of the pieces."

He drew out a shining piece of steel as he spoke, and passed it to Blake, who thrust it carelessly in his pocket.

"Proceed, please," he said briefly.

"Well, that alone means ruin to me," Todd went on, "but not content with that, the person or persons who ruined the machines rifled the safe. In it, I had a large sum for pay-day—nearly two thousand pounds in notes[9] and gold. But, worse than that, the thief took all my private papers, amongst which were papers relating to a new dyeing process which I have discovered, and which alone are worth a fortune."

"Ah!" said Blake quietly, although his eyes narrowed slightly. "Can't you make fresh papers of the process? It shouldn't be hard."

Todd stared at him for a moment, but quickly collected himself.

"Oh, er—yes, I can, but hardly in the time-limit which stands between me and ruin."

"I see," answered Blake.

"At the bank," continued Todd, "I have a big overdraft. I made heavy purchases of cotton three months ago, and the bank financed me. It was a profitable order, and less than a week ago I shipped it to London, where it was to be inspected and a cheque in full sent at once on approval of the goods. That cheque would tide me over at the bank for a few days longer, as I could secure another overdraft, but yesterday morning, just after the discovery of the outrage at the mill, I looked over my letters, and found one from the consignee of the cotton."

"Well, and was the cheque enclosed?"

"No, and, worse still, here is the letter I received."

He drew out a blue envelope, from which he took an enclosed letter.

Blake ran his eyes down the lines which had spelled additional ruin to the man opposite him, and as he finished looked up.

"May I keep this letter for a short time?" he asked.

"Yes. What do you think of that? Isn't that enough to put a man in the asylum? Three thousand pounds[10] worth of stuff ruined."

---

[9] £2,000 in 1913 is worth about £233,000 in 2020

[10] £15,000 in 1913 is worth about £1,742,000.00 in 2020

"But how, if you bought the raw cotton, and manufactured it yourself, could it be rotten?" inquired Blake.

"I haven't any idea. The cotton was a new season's crop, and I examined it myself before accepting it, and there is nothing wrong with my dyes. I tell you, the whole thing is a mystery to me, and I'm pretty nearly mad over it."

"Do you trace any connection between the rotten cotton and the outrage at the mill?" asked the detective.

"Oh, no—none. Even if I did have the money, and could go into the open market, and buy cotton in order to fill the contract, I don't know where I could get that amount of purple goods. It's an off colour."

"Purple!" exclaimed the detective sharply. "Was the consignment purple?"

"Yes, every yard of it. It was to go to some of the back provinces in China."

"Ah! Let me have the rest of the details, Mr. Todd. You interest me."

"That's nearly all," replied Todd. "There was a young fellow working for me in the dye-room. Fenwick is his name—Jack Fenwick. Well, he has disappeared—hasn't been seen since the night of the outrage, and I figure he is at the bottom of it, although I can't imagine why he would ruin all the machines, unless out of revenge."

"Revenge—why revenge?"

"Oh, he might have some imaginary grievance. But anyway, he's got the papers of my dye process. If I can get those back in ten days, Mr. Blake, I can borrow enough on them to save myself. They are worth a fortune. I haven't told the police about them nor about the machines, for the reason I said—publicity at present would ruin me. Now you know the facts. Will you take the case, and try to find this fellow Fenwick? Those papers are my only hope, and if you succeed you won't find me ungrateful."

Blake did not reply at once. He sat in deep thought, his eyes glittering with the dry, hard glitter which always appeared when he was concentrating deeply. Finally he roused himself, and his voice was level and expressionless.

"Yes, Mr. Todd, I will take the case. I promise nothing, but if I can possibly secure those papers within the necessary time I will do so, and will have much pleasure in returning them to their owner. You suspect no one else but this Fenwick?"

"No, no one. I'm sure he has them."

"It seems a most colossal outrage, and on its merits alone I would have said only a very deep brain, coupled with extraordinary daring and cleverness, could have conceived and executed it. And one doesn't look for such a brain in the poorly-paid assistant of a dye-room. However, I will know better after I make an examination. Since you desire secrecy, Mr. Todd, it is hardly necessary for me to impress you with the fact that no one must know I am working on the matter."

"Certainly—certainly: I understand," replied the relieved mill-owner. "When will you come down to Bournmill?"

"You can look for me tomorrow—and, by the way," added Blake, as Todd rose to go, "you might have a few samples of that rotten cotton for me. It will be interesting to see an example of such rapid deterioration."

"Very well, I will, although I can't see how it will help you in this case."

Blake only smiled, and the smile remained even after the door closed on his visitor.

"I wonder!" he muttered softly. "I wonder why you lied about those papers, Mr. Todd?"

Swinging round, he sank into his big chair and filled the old black pipe.

"What do you think of it, guv'nor?" asked Tinker. "Quite a coincidence, isn't it—his coming so soon after the young woman?"

"Yes, my lad, it is. As for what I think of it, it is a jumble of rotten cotton, and purple at that, my lad, broken machines, and a remarkable break; stolen money, stolen and re-stolen papers, a mysterious disappearance, and behind all a colossal brain, my lad. And now," added Blake, as he puffed out thick clouds of smoke, "leave me, Tinker. This case will need all our wits, and I'm not so sure but all our nerve as well."

Tinker withdrew softly, and only Pedro remained, his great body stretched immovably between the detective's feet.

The day was still young when Blake began to concentrate that brilliant analytical mind, but not till the shadows had lengthened and night had fallen did he stir himself. When he did, the room was full of heavy, stale smoke, burnt matches littered the floor, but even through the gloom came the dry glitter which still rested in his eyes.

The Fourth Chapter
Blake, Tinker and Pedro at Work—Tinker Returns to London

SEXTON Blake threw in the clutch, Tinker settled down beside him, Pedro flopped to the bottom of the tonneau, the big grey car gathered headway, and the famous Baker Street trio tore along at a fast pace on the long drive to Bournmill.

"Tell me, guv'nor," said Tinker, as London was left behind, and patches of open country appeared; "what do you make of this case?"

"I haven't formed any theory yet, my lad," responded Blake. "The first thing to do in every case is to find the motive. Once that is found, natural and logical deduction will lead to the solution. In some points this case presents many similar phases to the French arsenal scandal, which you will remember. But, on the other hand, the present case has some most peculiar features, and, unlike the other, bears the mark of a master brain.

"The first theory that is suggested is whether this fellow Fenwick is guilty or not. True, he may have been incensed at what seems to be Todd's theft of his discovery, and in revenge wrecked the factory. But if the young woman's story is true—and my common sense inclines to that view—he is evidently incapable of such an action.

"But, supposing Todd's statement were true, and he himself really discovered the dye process, to my reasoning that would give even less motive for suspecting Fenwick of such a wholesale outrage. No; the young woman's story bears the ear-marks of truth, for it is a natural conclusion that a man spending every day in a dye-room should cast about, if he be of an industrious and inventive turn, to endeavour to improve on present conditions. On the whole, I think we may assume that Jack Fenwick is innocent.

"The next theory that strikes me is—did Mortimer Todd commit the outrage himself? I think not, but before deciding definitely on that point I will make further investigations in Bournmill. As yet I can see no motive for his so doing, and if ever a man was in a genuine state of fear and collapse Mortimer Todd was.

"The next question is who would have sufficient motive to ruin him—for without doubt that was the end sought. Has he enemies, and, if so, who are they?

"That the whole affair was carefully arranged and planned there is no question. The broken steel part which Todd brought with him makes this a positive fact. It was not filed off, for it bears no marks, which it otherwise would. Besides, it would take an army to file through bits of every machine in the mill in one night.

"Again, it was not broken off, for the severed end is as clean and shiny as the rest of the piece. No, it was cut through scientifically, and again that says 'master brain.'

"Going on the hypothesis that it has been carefully planned, we naturally go back for a period of time—perhaps a month, perhaps six months, for the perpetrators would watch their chance, and an opportunity might be months in coming.

"Again—has the ruined cotton any connection with the outrage, or is it a pure coincidence? That is a very puzzling point. The first inclination is to cast out the possibility; but following out the theory that it was carefully planned, and that the starting point jumps back for a period of time, we see that the rotten cotton then comes within the radius of possible connection. In any event, it certainly capped Todd's ruin, and my deductions say, if that is the case, more than ever have we to search for a master brain.

"That is the case at present, my lad. I am certainly working along several points in addition, which at present I will not explain; but I have given you the rough facts."

The big, silent car bounded on, leaving London rapidly behind, and made hay of the run to Manchester.

Blake only stopped long enough for refreshments in the busy city, and half an hour after arriving was again on the road.

They arrived at Bournmill an hour later, and the detective directed the car to a quiet inn near the mills. He drove the car into a nearby garage, and with Tinker and Pedro entered the inn, and secured a quiet suite of rooms.

They were plainly, but comfortably furnished, and the location was just what Blake desired.

Disguising himself in a clerical garb, and with a flat, round hat on his head, Blake issued forth from the inn, leaving Tinker and Pedro behind to be ready for any messages or instructions.

The quietly-dressed cleric turned to his right on leaving the inn, and bent his steps in the direction of the mills.

Down the smoke-laden, din-filled, narrow streets he went past the cottages of the mill-workers, and along the high wall enclosing a mill-yard. From over the top came the roar and clatter of the belts and machines, and from further along heavy smoke poured forth, sweeping up the narrow lane, and filling the streets with a perpetual cloud. On he went past two more buzzing, busy mills until he came to a huge bulk, which he knew from its dark and silent condition to be the Todd Mill.

Blake opened a small gate set in the larger one, and walked with dignified stride across the yard to the mill door. The cleric's eyes were apparently bent on the ground in devout meditation, but in reality they were sweeping every inch of the great, red building.

A man admitted him who he knew afterwards was Allen, the foreman, and a moment later he stood in Mortimer Todd's private office.

Blake had sent a telegram to Todd saying he would arrive during the afternoon; but no look of recognition rested in the mill-owner's eyes.

He turned to the reverend gentleman who stood before him, and spoke impatiently.

"If you desire to see me about any charities or such matters, it will have to wait until another time. I am expecting a gentleman on very important business, and haven't the time to give to anything else at present."

Blake smiled.

"I suppose I ought to apologise to the order of clergymen for borrowing their dress, but, under the circumstances, I think it is necessary. It is evidently a success."

"Good heavens!" gasped Todd. "You, Mr. Blake! I would never have believed it!"

Again Blake laughed as he sat down.

"Now, Mr. Todd, as you say things are so urgent, perhaps we had better lose no time in getting to work. By the way, have the police found Fenwick yet?"

"No; not a sign. He seems to have left absolutely no trace."

"H'm, that looks bad! Is that the safe that was rifled?"

"Yes. Do you wish to examine it?"

"I'll run over it," said Blake, rising, and crossing to it.

Pulling out a small, powerful microscope, Blake dropped to his knees, and examined the lock with extreme care. Turning the handle he swung the door open, and went through the same performance on the inside. He made no comment as he rose, and Todd seeing the intense look of concentration in the detective's eyes, asked no questions.

"How did the intruder enter?" asked Blake, at length.

"Through the window in the outer office. Will you examine it?"

Blake nodded, and followed the mill-owner out.

The window had been left untouched since the discovery of the outrage, and Blake glanced keenly at the circular hole in the glass near the top of the lower sash. Again the microscope was brought into play, the detective going over every inch of the circle's edge, both inside and out. As he finished his examination he turned to Todd.

"Did you discover the piece of glass which was cut out?"

"No; the intruder evidently took it with him. Allen searched everywhere, but found no trace of it."

Blake made no reply, and, throwing up the sash, hopped over the sill. The high wall enclosing the mill-yard hid him from observation, and, after a sharp look round, he dropped flat to the ground, and went over every foot between the window and the gate.

The ground had been trampled over during the last few days, and any marks had been obliterated with the exception of a peculiar impression immediately under the window. Blake bent again to examine this, and, before he rose, drew a small mould from his pocket. Quickly making a cast of the impression, he thrust the mould back and straightened up.

"Now, Mr. Todd, I would like to examine the machines, and, after that, I would like several samples of the ruined cloths."

The mill-owner led the way to the weaving-room, and from there through every room in the mill.

Slowly and methodically Blake stopped at every machine, his eyes searching every spot for any sign which would enable him to reconstruct the crime.

Once or twice he stopped and examined the broken part of the machines with the microscope; but when he returned to the office, if he had gained anything by the examination, his face betrayed no sign. He seated himself, and lit a cigar.

"I suppose you still desire me to go ahead on this matter?" he remarked, crossing his knees.

"My heavens, yes!" answered Todd agitatedly. "Don't tell me you can't! If I don't get those papers back in ten days I will be ruined!"

"Very well, Mr. Todd," said Blake quietly, "I will do my best to solve the problem, and apportion the guilt where it belongs. But if I am to work intelligently, you must be perfectly frank with me."

"I will be. I assure you."

"Very well. Have you any enemies who would plan to ruin you? Put Fenwick outside of the question for the moment, and think well."

"No; I know of no one, Mr. Blake. I've had quarrels in my day, but nothing serious enough to cause such a revenge as this. No, I'm sure it's young Fenwick. He's the one to find."

"Do you mind telling me where you were before you arrived in Bournmill?"

"Er—well, I came here from America."

"And before that?"

"Oh, I was in different places—the East and Africa," replied Todd evasively.

"Ever in China?"

"No, never."

"H'm! Well, Mr. Todd, I will take the cotton samples now, and go to work on the matter. As soon as I know anything definite, I will communicate with you."

Five minutes later Blake, with several pieces of rotten purple cotton in his pocket, was walking briskly through the town. He stopped once to ask his way, and kept on until he came to a small cottage at the edge of the town.

He walked up the gravel walk and tapped at the door, which was opened by Phyllis Cameron. She stood back respectfully for the clerical gentleman to enter, and inquired if he wished to see her mother.

Blake waited until the door was closed, and then smiled as he revealed his identity to the astonished young woman.

Phyllis led him into the tiny sitting-room where Mrs. Cameron sat sewing, and, after a few trivial words, Blake went to the point.

"I have already made an examination at the mill, Miss Cameron, and I can tell you that I consider Jack Fenwick innocent. That is all I can say at the present moment, but I trust we will find him safe and sound. There are many difficult problems to solve, and it is just possible you may be able to assist me if you will."

"Oh, I will do everything I can, Mr. Blake!" cried Phyllis.

"I'm sure you are more than good, Mr. Blake, to help us in our trouble," said Mrs. Cameron. "My daughter and I feel positive that Jack Fenwick is incapable of such a terrible crime, and we fear some terrible thing may have happened to him."

"I trust we will find him safe," smiled Blake. "What I want you to do is not very difficult, Miss Cameron," he went on, turning to Phyllis. "I suppose you know pretty nearly everything that goes on in Bournmill?"

"Oh, yes! Everyone knows everyone else's business here. Besides, mother and I sew for several people, and hear everything."

"That is fortunate. Now think carefully. Do you know if Mr. Todd has any enemies in Bournmill?"

Phyllis knit her brows, and thought hard.

"No, sir, I don't. On the contrary, he has been popular."

"Is he—has he had much to do with the fair sex?" asked Blake.

"No; that is not until recently. He has been rather reserved socially."

"You say not until recently," repeated Blake, raising his brows. "Just how do you mean?"

"Well, they say he has been paying a great deal of attention to Miss Harmon, the daughter of the American millionaire."

"Ah, and does Miss Harmon live here?"

"She and her uncle came here three months ago, and took Sir George Waltham's place—Waltham Hall."

"And what does this American lady look like? Can you describe her?"

"I'll try," answered Phyllis. "She is of medium height, and slim and very beautiful. She dresses magnificently, and has the most lovely, gold-bronze hair."

"A typical woman's description," laughed Blake. "And her uncle? What does he look like?"

"I have only seen him once, and then only for a moment. He is a clean-shaven man of middle-age."

"I see. Thank you!" remarked Blake, rising. "And now, Miss Cameron, don't forget to keep my presence here a secret. I hope to have news of some kind soon."

Blake hastened back to the inn, and took off his clerical garb.

"Did you find out anything, guv'nor?" asked Tinker, as Blake came into the sitting-room in his usual garb.

"I have picked up a few loose threads, my lad, but they are still badly tangled. Get the books and chemicals which I brought, Tinker, and lay them out here on the table. Then I will want you to help me in some tests."

Tinker jumped to obey; and while he laid out the chemicals, Blake took off his coat and rolled up his sleeves. He then spread out the pieces of purple cotton, and made a careful examination with the microscope.

He next began his chemical tests, tossing down one piece as he finished, and picking up another, for each test failed to produce any reaction which would tell him anything.

Finally, he picked up the last piece. Spreading it out, he applied a strong acid test to one end. Nothing occurred, and he turned to the other end. He picked a small phial full of a thick fluid, the last remaining test possible for him to make.

He poured a small quantity over the purple cotton, and then held it near the light. As the heat made itself felt, the purple dye gradually grew paler and paler until it faded to a large grey spot covering the part where the fluid had been applied. But it did not completely change to grey, for as Blake withdrew it from the heat and laid it on the table, there still remained a multitude of small purple spots.

Blake in search of Tinker.

Blake's eyes were glittering intensely as he picked up the microscope and examined them; and Tinker, knowing a great discovery had been made, leaned over in excitement to watch.

Blake laid the microscope down and straightened up.

"Tinker, I have carefully taught you my methods of observation, and a chance has arrived for you to prove what you have learnt."

"What is it, guv'nor?" asked Tinker eagerly.

"Cast your mind back, my lad, to a little over three months ago. Do you remember the night we went to the Royal?"

"Yes, guv'nor, of course. Our cab broke down when we tried to follow Mademoiselle Yvonne."

"Quite right; but not so fast, my lad. Do you remember a Chinese gentleman, in evening dress, standing at the kerb as we came out?"

"Yes, guv'nor. He gave up his cab to us."

"Good! Can you describe him to me?"

"I think so," answered Tinker, wrinkling his brows. "He was tall, about your height, guv'nor, clean shaven, and had very high cheekbones. I noticed particularly that his eyes were very deep-set."

"Good, my lad, you are certainly coming along! Do you think you could pick him out again, even if he were disguised?"

"I think so, guv'nor."

"Very well," went on Blake, drawing a letter from his pocket and unfolding it. "This letter is the one which I got from Mortimer Todd in Baker Street. It is the one from a Chinese commission agent in London refusing the rotten cotton. I want you to return at once to London and disguise yourself. Go to this address and hang about carelessly. Watch everything, and see if you can get the track of the Chinese man you saw that night at the Royal. As soon as you do, follow him, find out where he lives, and wire me here. In the meantime, get a man to help you, if necessary, and don't lose track of him."

"Right, guv'nor," replied Tinker. "Has he anything to do with this affair down here?" he added, in a surprised tone.

"I don't know; but I have a feeling that I will shortly have a desire to meet that Celestial gentleman, and I depend on you to help me."

"I will do my best, guv'nor," promised Tinker. "When do I leave?"

"You can catch the evening train to Manchester. Wire me, in code, on your arrival, and again as to progress. I will keep Pedro with me."

The Fifth Chapter
Yvonne in Disguise—The Attack on Blake

AFTER locking Jack Fenwick in the cellar on her return from the mill, where she had captured him, Yvonne ascended to the library.

"This fellow changes my plans somewhat," she said, turning to her uncle. "If the yacht were near, I would bundle him into the motor and go through to her at once, but she will be tied up at Cherbourg for a week yet before the repairs are finished. The fellow works at the mill, and it is just possible suspicion may fall on him. If so, it will give us a chance to get away in a week when the yacht comes over, and we will have to take him with us and decide later what to do with him.

"Again, Todd's idiotic falling in love with me, has changed my plans somewhat, as well. I had intended our going away at once, because he is sure to come here and propose to me—it is his only hope.

"It would have been the final stroke to find us gone, but—wait, I have it! I will disguise Anna, my maid, as myself, and I in turn will disguise as Anna. Get ready at once to leave for London. I will stay here as the maid, and you take Anna to London with you.

"I will give out that Harmon and his niece have gone away for some weeks, and at the same time I will look after the boy with the help of the other servants, and as they are all members of the circle no one will know anything.

"Wire to Captain Vaughan to have the *Fleur-de-Lys* ready as quickly as possible, and to bring her over at once. As soon as he arrives, wire me, and I will motor on immediately with our prisoner."

These plans had been carried out, and just as dawn was breaking, Graves, with the small motor, had started for London, accompanied by Anna, the maid, disguised as Yvonne.

Yvonne, thorough as always, lost no time in assuming her new character. She ruthlessly changed her heavy, gleaming bronze hair to the same shade of black as the maid's, but found consolation in the fact that it was only a temporary dye, and could be quickly washed out. So thorough was her transformation, that she followed every line of the maid's features, even to applying a tiny artificial mole on her left cheek, and dressing throughout in the maid's clothes.

She even removed to the maid's room, and the car had been less than an hour on its way to London when Yvonne looked in the mirror with satisfaction, for she was a perfect reproduction of the maid.

In this character she answered the door when Mortimer Todd called on the morning after the happenings at the mill, and even Yvonne's deep-seated desire to revenge the ruin of her mother and herself was satisfied as she watched the broken, haggard mill-owner stumble down the steps and stagger to the motor.

Yvonne took her prisoner his breakfast a few minutes later, and skilfully extracted the boy's story.

Her eyes narrowed as she drew him out about the discovery of the new dye process, and found he had entrusted the papers to Mortimer Todd.

"Did you get a receipt for them?" she asked.

"No, I didn't think it was necessary."

"Do you trust him, then?"

"Well, I did, until lately, and—but I don't see why I should tell you all this. Who are you, and where is the young fellow that captured me last night."

Yvonne laughed.

"You needn't worry, I won't tell Mr. Todd. You suspect him of trying to steal your plans."

"I didn't say that," protested Jack. "And I'd like to know what that fellow was doing in the mill last night, and why I am held a prisoner here."

"You will know in good time, my friend," smiled Yvonne, "and let me advise you not to attempt to escape. It wouldn't be wise. You might receive a more convincing argument than you did at the mill."

She rose as she finished her warning, and went out, closing and locking the door, and once more Jack was left in total darkness.

He rose and made a careful examination in an effort to discover some loophole of escape, but none presented itself, and he sank back on his hard bench, a prey to worry and misery.

Two days passed without incident. After Todd had left, Yvonne had sent a telegram to London, saying he had called and that, her revenge completed, she was ready to leave as soon as the yacht was ready.

Since then she had waited quietly, sending one of the servants, who were also members of the "circle," into the town, to report what developments were taking place. She visited her prisoner regularly with his meals, but talked no more with him, and the mystified Jack still sat in his dark prison, wondering what Phyllis was doing, and what was to be his fate. That he was a victim of some plot, either accidentally or otherwise, he hadn't the faintest doubt, but all his efforts at a solution carried him back every time to where he started.

That afternoon Yvonne, in her prim maid's costume, entered the famous car that had once baffled Sexton Blake by its changing colours, and with the exact air of a maid going on a message for her mistress, had the chauffeur drive her into the town.

She desired to see the Todd Mill with her own eyes, and to discover, if possible, if any definite move had been made by the mill-owner.

She drove past the huge building, over which silence reigned with a particular intensity in the midst of the clattering, buzzing mills surrounding it.

As the car turned away from the mills and headed up a narrow, smoky street, Yvonne settled back, her inspection so far a disappointment, for the silent mill had told her nothing. Her eyes carelessly swept the varied architectural efforts which lined the street on both sides, but as her glance rested on an old-fashioned window above the street entrance of an inn, her whole body stiffened, and she drew a sharp breath.

Framed by the window and looking forth, his front feet resting on the sill, was a great hound, his lion-like head turned sideways in an endeavour to look up the unfamiliar street.

Yvonne took in every detail of the animal's head and shoulders, and as the car rolled on, she relaxed, her eyes bright and her lips compressed.

She signalled the chauffeur to drive on at once to Waltham Hall, her thoughts racing madly on the way.

"I'm positive that was Sexton Blake's hound," she muttered, as the car sped on. "I'd know his head anywhere. If he is here, his master or assistant must be here as well. What could bring Sexton Blake to Bournmill but a very important case, and what important case would Bournmill have at the present time but the mystery at Todd's Mill? None. Oh, my friend—my friend," she smiled, "forewarned is forearmed. We seem fated to meet, and each time you have written victory after our meeting, but this time I am ready."

Yvonne hastened into the house and wrote a telegram, advising Graves and Dr. San Lo of her suspicions, and despatched the chauffeur with it at once.

At the moment the warning message was being ticked over the wires to London, Sexton Blake was returning to the inn from his first interview with Mrs. Cameron and Phyllis. As he settled down to the experiments which ended in Tinker being despatched for London that evening, little did he dream that a message had already arrived there, telling of his suspected presence in Bournmill, and that the faithful Pedro had been the unwitting cause.

Shortly after Tinker had left that evening, an elderly man, of benevolent appearance, issued forth from the inn and wended his way, with a stately and dignified tread, in the direction of Waltham Hall.

His shoulders were slightly stooped, and a white, well-trimmed moustache and beard decorated his face. He carried a heavy stick, and walked with a military swing, and his whole attitude betokened the retired military man.

He rang the bell at the Hall, and bowed with the old-time courtesy to the trim maid who answered.

"Is Sir George Waltham at home?" inquired the benevolent old gentleman.

"No, sir," answered the maid, in a high-pitched tone, "'e 'as gone to Hafrica, sir, and 'as leased the 'All for a year."

"Ah, I am disappointed. I just arrived from Vienna, and wished to see him rather importantly. I was not aware that he had left England. Is your master at home?"

"No, sir; they 'ave gone away."

"Ah, that is unfortunate. They might have known Sir George's address. I will inquire elsewhere. Thank you."

The old gentleman turned and descended the steps, walking slowly down the drive. A puzzled look followed him, but he was unconscious of it, and kept calmly on his way.

"He looks genuine enough," muttered the maid, as she closed the door, "but since seeing the bloodhound I'm suspicious of everybody. I'll just send Alec to shadow him and make sure."

With this thought Yvonne hastened to the rear of the house, and a moment later through the shadows of the drive a dark figure hurried in the wake of the old gentleman, who was now nearing the gates.

Blake, for it was he, was disappointed in the result of his call. He had hoped to find the Harmons at home, and by getting into conversation with either of them discover if either was Graves or Yvonne. It was a setback which he had not anticipated, and he dared not ask when they had left or how long they would be gone. The check had caused him to sink into deep thought as he walked along, and so absorbed was he that he was unaware of the dodging figure which followed.

"This is certainly a check," he muttered to himself, "but indications seem to point positively to Mademoiselle Yvonne. Every thread goes back to that night at the Opera; a clear connection exists, and then my discovery outside the window at the mill. Is it possible that I am mistaken, and that she may be thousands of miles away?

"No, I can't believe it. A woman it certainly was that committed the outrage at the mill, and what woman could conceive of such a gigantic operation and carry it out? None that I know of but Mademoiselle Yvonne.

"And what has become of Jack Fenwick? Has he acted as an accomplice? No, the whole operation spells a single brain, and that—— I wonder, I wonder, mademoiselle! I would give a great deal to have a look at the beautiful Miss Harmon. The description certainly interests me."

He had seen the beautiful Miss Harmon only a few moments ago, in the garb of the maid, but so skilful was the disguise that even Blake's trained eyes had failed to pierce it. Yvonne, likewise, had failed to see anything suspicious in Blake's appearance, and only her suspicions which had been aroused by seeing Pedro had caused her to send a man after him.

Both were straining every nerve to definitely locate and successfully combat the other, and neither knew that they had so recently addressed one another.

Blake entered the inn and ascended to his room, where Pedro leaped gladly to greet him, for the great beast was lonely in his strange surroundings.

Although completely worn out with the great mental strain through which he had passed, Blake lit his pipe and stretched out to once more marshal all the facts before him and search for any possible flaw before going to bed.

"If Todd were only completely honest with me!" he muttered, as he rose an hour later to retire. "It's impossible to tell definitely what his game is, if he has one, and the consequence is I have to work in the dark. At the present it points to Yvonne, but the motive, the motive I can't see, unless——"

"Great Scott! I wonder if that is possible? I will investigate that point in the morning!"

Undressing, Blake threw up the window, in order to get some fresh air, and got into bed, Pedro dropping on the rug beside it.

Dog and master were soon fast asleep, blissfully unaware of the danger which was creeping on them through the dark night.

***

The man whom Yvonne had sent to follow Blake had kept the detective in sight until he had seen him enter the inn.

He sped back to the Hall with the information, and when Yvonne discovered it was the inn where Pedro had appeared at the window she knew her suspicions had been well founded, and Sexton Blake was really in Bournmill.

She brought her teeth together with a click as the man finished his report.

"What a chance I missed! Here he was at the very door, and I let him get away. You, Alec, take Taylor and go back. Find out where he sleeps, and if possible get into his room. Don't injure him unless it is absolutely necessary, but, of course, don't risk being caught. I will give you a powerful drug which will keep him quiet, and be careful of the hound. Take a revolver with a silencer attached, and shoot him if he makes any fuss. Bring Sexton Blake back here, and I will reward you both handsomely. Do you think you can do this?"

"I'll try, mademoiselle," asserted the man confidently. "I wasn't a second-storey man for ten years without knowing the ropes, and you know from past experience whether I have the nerve or not."

"Good, Alec! Lose no time. Take the motor, and bring him back unharmed for the present. Later I will deal with him."

"I'd like to do for him, mademoiselle, while I have the chance. I owe him one or two."

"No, you mustn't harm him unless it is necessary. If he puts up a fight, that is different, but I have as yet been unable to return the hospitality he showed me when I was his prisoner before, and I very much wish to do so."

Her eyes hardened slightly as she spoke, and the man nodded his understanding, hastening away to get Taylor, another member of Yvonne's circle, to go with him on his errand.

The motor stole silently along until it reached the street where stood the inn. It was just past midnight, and in that district the streets had been silent for hours. A dark, narrow lane ran behind the buildings, and parallel with the street, and down this Alec turned the motor, pulling up softly in the rear of the silent inn.

A single light gleamed forth from a window on the second floor, and as they peered up across the blind went a clean-cut shadow. They sat silently, watching the shadow appearing and re-appearing, its movements telling plainly that the occupant of the room was preparing for bed. A few moments later it again approached, and stood close to

the window. The blind was thrown up, and framed against the light behind was a figure familiar in outline to Alec—Sexton Blake. The light disappeared almost immediately after, but a full hour went by before the silent watchers moved.

Taking a small electric torch, Alec descended, followed by Taylor. A high wall ran along, shutting in the inn-yard, but Alec, assisted by his companion, soon gained the top, and drew Taylor up after him.

From here, cautiously using the torch, Alec stepped across to the roof of a low, sloping shed, which he crossed until he came to a wall.

Here he used the light again cautiously, and was forced once more to depend on his companion's shoulders. As he assisted Taylor up he cast the light about, and they discovered they were on the roof of what was apparently an outhouse. It sloped down sharply from the middle, but ran over until it butted against the main wall of the inn, and there, straight ahead, was the window in which they had seen Sexton Blake.

Alec shuffled along the sharp angle as quietly as possible, Taylor keeping close behind, until they reached the end. Six inches in front was the blackness of Sexton Blake's room through the open window, and in that room, asleep and unsuspicious, was Sexton Blake, the dreaded foe of every criminal.

Alec placed his hand on the sill, and began to lift his leg stealthily, when a slight sound from the room caused him to pause. It was not repeated, and, being urged by the impatient Taylor, he went on and disappeared inside the room.

He stood up and turned to see if his companion was coming, when a rushing noise caught his ear. He swung round in alarm, but was too late, and a crushing weight hit him with a terrific force and he shot forward through the window with a startled cry.

Taylor was in the act of climbing over the sill, but Alec's head caught him with a severe blow in the chest, and with a yell of fright both men rolled, clutching madly, down the sloping roof, and fell with a thud.

Pedro had retrieved himself, for the faithful fellow had been awakened by the scraping noise of their footsteps on the roof, and, with the sagacity for which he was famed, had bided his time.

Blake started up as Alec cried out, and was just in time to see the two dark figures disappear through the window. As he heard the noise of their fall he opened the door and dashed down the stairs, Pedro at his heels.

Hastening along the corridor, he unlocked the back door and rushed out, but the throb of a motor told him he was too late.

It they had been hurt, it had not been serious enough to prevent their getting away, and an examination later showed that a large pile of rubbish and old papers had broken their fall.

Blake explained as much as he thought wise to the astonished landlord, who had been aroused, and, just as a heavy rain began to fall, returned to his room, but not to sleep.

The Sixth Chapter
Tinker's Awful Peril

WHILE Blake was in such danger, Tinker was speeding on his way to London. He arrived at Baker Street early the next day, and lost no time in changing his appearance.

A very ragged suit, with a dilapidated cap and even more dilapidated boots, with a smudge here and there on the visible portion of his face, soon changed him into a typical street lad of the true gutter class.

He hastened out, and from a ragged urchin secured a supply of newspapers. With these under his arm, Tinker betook himself to the business address of Han Wo, commission agent, which was in a side street off Soho Square.

On the way he sent a code telegram to Blake, saying he had arrived, and was now on the scent. He then took up his stand on the opposite side of the street to Han Wo's, calling out his papers and at the same time keeping a sharp eye on the premises opposite.

It did not take Tinker long to discover that Han Wo's place of business was thoroughly genuine, and if, as he shrewdly imagined Blake thought, the rotten cotton had any connection with the outrage at the mill, Han Wo had doubtless been a tool in other hands.

His long association with the great detective, and his close study of the latter's methods, showed in that deduction, for therein he was right.

Many people went in and out of the commission agent's office, but none who looked in the least like the tall Chinese man, with the deep eyes, for whom Tinker was watching. The afternoon wore on without any success, and, as closing-time drew near, Tinker gave up hopes of getting any track of his man that day. It was at the best a forlorn hope; but Sexton Blake had thought the connection worth following up, and no doubt he had lots of reasons for thinking so, which Tinker did not know.

With this thought the lad again raised his voice to call "speshul 'dition, and sauntered along for a few yards, determined to wait until the last occupant of Han Wo's place had gone.

As the office blinds were drawn, and several employees hastened out, Tinker scanned each face closely, but they told him nothing. A last laggard came hurrying down the steps, and Tinker was giving up hope when a short, squat Chinese man appeared, and closed the door after him. Turning, he locked it, and, as he descended the steps and walked along with a waddling gait, Tinker strolled after him, keeping him in sight, for the locking of the door told the lad that the stout man was either Han Wo himself, or one in a responsible position.

Considering the corpulence of the Celestial, and the shortness of his legs, he might almost be said to be hurrying; but certainly Tinker found no difficulty in keeping up with him.

The chase, if chase it could be called, led along Tottenham Court Road, where, some distance along, the man turned down a narrow street. The ragged Tinker followed, and was just in time to see his quarry turn again into an even narrower street—a street filled with a medley of smells, and which had a sinister suggestiveness even at that hour.

The stout man stopped before a fried-fish shop, and disappeared inside. When Tinker arrived at the shop his man was nowhere to be seen, and the lad withdrew into a dark doorway to watch. He was puzzled at the Celestial's object in entering such a place, for his dress, which was European, indicated prosperity, and it was obvious he had not entered to purchase anything, for he had not stopped at the counter.

Tinker puzzled his brains over the object of his man's visit to the shop. What would bring him there? It must be to meet somebody, and if that were so, it would explain his disappearance probably into some adjoining room.

The fish shop was surrounded by dark, evil-looking tenements; but on one side of it ran a very narrow alley leading into a dark court which looked as though it might be the lair of half the cut-throats in London. The shop had a half-storey on the ground-floor, and from the narrow depths of the front part, Tinker judged there was a room in the rear, although from where he stood he could see no door. At any rate, it would have to be investigated, for he must not run the risk of losing his quarry through a back exit from the shop.

He strolled across the road, and, entering, walked to the counter. As he laid down three-halfpence, and demanded a "pennorth and 'aporth" from the surly woman in charge, he swept his eyes with lightning-like rapidity over the partition in the rear.

It was papered with a cheap, be-flowered paper, and in one corner was a small door. The reason Tinker had been unable to distinguish it from across the street, being for the reason that it was papered like the wall.

Picking up his fish and chips Tinker sauntered out, and, once in the shadow, stuffed his purchase in his pocket. With a sharp look up and down the narrow, dirty street he dodged into the alley beside the shop, and tiptoed stealthily along, keeping close to the wall. He had got over half-way when a low murmur of voices caused him to stop, and bend his head to listen.

It was impossible to tell what was being said, and even more so to tell from whence the voices came. When he stood up they seemed to come from above him. When he bent down they seemed to come through the wall, and when he stood a few inches away from the wall they seemed to come from beneath him.

Tinker dropped to his knees, in order to press his ear against the wall and endeavour to distinguish what was being said, when his head came into contact with cold iron. A quick examination showed it to be the manhole of a sewer, which evidently led from the dark court beyond.

In the darkness of the alley he had not seen the grating, and, as he made a closer examination he held his breath, for through the grating the voices sounded more plainly.

Rapidly pushing his fingers between the bars he braced his knees and lifted; the round grating tipped up, and, with another cautious look around, Tinker dropped into the black hole.

It was not as deep as he expected, and he found that when his feet rested on the bottom, his head projected through the hole. The stench of the sewer was awful; but the lad overcoming his repugnance, drew his head down and lowered the grating. As he crouched down and peered around the black tunnel, a faint chink of light caught his eye.

Lighting a match, Tinker looked carefully about in order to guide his footsteps, and, stepping with infinite caution, crept over to the crack from whence the light shone. His hands came into contact with a stone, cemented wall which appeared to serve the double purpose of a side wall for the sewer, and a cellar wall for the fish shop.

He looked up, and saw the thin thread of light just over his head, and, carefully clinging to the rough, projecting stone of the wall he drew himself up, and applied his eye to the chink.

As he did so the voices became very distinct, and Tinker wished fervently that Blake was there, for he could not understand what was being said; the tones were those of guttural Chinese.

The room into which he peered was a rough, stone-walled compartment, without doubt the cellar of the fish shop. All he could see was a rough, deal table, on which stood a bottle, in the neck of which a half-candle spluttered.

Sitting in a rickety chair was a man; but only his back was visible through the tiny crack. Tinker knew that many such places as the one he saw before him existed throughout that district, serving as meeting places for criminals, Anarchists, and their ilk.

He did not doubt for a moment that it was that type of place, and the fact that the conversation was being carried on in Chinese caused him to listen with all his ears in the hope of catching a stray word, which, from his long association with Blake, he might recognise. That hope was to be fulfilled, but it was to be a word in English, and not Chinese which he heard.

That word was "Blake," and, as it was uttered in a guttural tone. Tinker drew a sharp breath, for he knew that once again the great detective's mind was speeding on the right scent.

He was debating whether to climb out of the sewer, and again take up his post opposite the fish shop when a terrible thing happened.

As has been said the side of the sewer formed also part of the cellar wall, and the tiny crack through which Tinker peered was caused by the gradual crumbling of the cement between the rough stones. It was so small as to be unnoticeable; but in the process of decay the mortar had fallen to dust, some of which had fallen away causing the crack, but some still remaining in the crevice.

As Blake's name had caught Tinker's ears he had leaned closer, and drew a sharp breath. This was the lad's undoing, for in the indrawing of his breath several particles of the fine dust were drawn in at the same time, causing an irritation in his nose.

Tinker drew back and swallowed hard, grasping his nose and holding it hard; but his efforts were useless, and he sneezed with terrific force.

The voices in the cellar stopped, and dead silence reigned, broken almost at once by another loud sneeze from Tinker, and still another.

A scraping noise, followed by the hasty movement of feet came from the cellar, and Tinker, knowing he was in a tight corner, made a jump for the man-hole.

He pushed it up and sprang through, bracing his hands on the edge to draw his legs out. As he did so hurried footsteps came around the corner of the fish shop, and before the lad could get clear of the hole, two pairs of heavy hands descended on him.

"Here, you boy, what you do down there?" came a guttural voice, in almost perfect English.

And, Tinker, dangerous as was his position, thrilled, as through the darkness he recognised the same voice which he had heard over three months before on the kerb in front of the Royal.

"Garn," he replied, in newsboy slang, "wot's ther matter with yer? Carn't a chap look fer a penny wot 'e's dropped down this 'ere soor?"

It was a flimsy bluff, but none other was possible on the spur of the moment, and Tinker trusted in it to gain him a breathing space where he might probably get a chance to make a dash for safety.

It apparently satisfied his captors, for again the same voice spoke.

"If you go poking about in this manner, you'll be getting into trouble."

Tinker refrained from answering, and his muscles stiffened for a dash as he felt the heavy grip loosening; but at that moment fresh footsteps sounded, and a voice which Tinker knew only too well broke through the darkness of the alley.

"Is that you, doctor?" it inquired; and Tinker knew it was Graves.

"Yes," answered Tinker's captor. "Come here a moment!"

Graves came up, and was soon in possession of the facts of Tinker's capture.

"Don't let him go!" he replied. "Bring him inside to the lights, and let's have a look at him! There are fresh developments, and we have got to be very careful!"

Tinker knew those words spelled his fate, for an examination under the light would soon lead to recognition by Graves.

Risking all, he dropped suddenly, and made a dive for freedom, but the man who held him was too quick, and Tinker doubled up with a moan of pain as his arm was twisted with a sudden wrench.

They dragged him into the fish shop, and down to the dingy cellar. There he was placed in the chair so that the light from the candle fell on his features. As he looked up he knew he had made no mistake in his recognition of the Chinese gentleman's voice, nor in that of Graves, for both men stood before him as well as the stout Celestial he had followed.

But if that moment in the light of the candle had given Tinker recognition of his captors, it also gave his captors recognition of the lad, for, as Graves dragged Tinker's cap from his head and peered closely at him, he gave a harsh laugh of satisfaction.

"I was just in time," he drawled, "which is fortunate. Another five seconds and you would have been off to report to your master. This lad," he added, turning to Dr. San Lo and Han Wo, "is Sexton Blake's assistant, and you were lucky to catch him. How did it happen?"

Rapidly Dr. San Lo explained how he and Han Wo had been discussing the telegram from Mademoiselle Yvonne, advising that she had discovered Sexton Blake's presence in Bournmill, and how she was intending to capture him.

"Yes," growled Graves, "I had one, too, but I have also had a later one, which I will disclose anon when we dispose of the boy."

Tinker had kept his ears open, and was surprised at their discovery of Blake's presence in Bournmill, and endeavoured to gather whether they had succeeded in capturing Blake or not. But Graves was too cautious, and the lad knew nothing further would be repeated in his presence.

"But we must settle this lad now," went on Graves coolly. "He has slipped through our fingers several times, but this time we must see that he doesn't."

It remained for the cunning Chinese brain to devise a supremely appropriate and certain way without much trouble attached. It was the fat Celestial who made the suggestion, and Graves received it as eminently satisfactory.

"As he seems so fond of the sewer, why not return him to it?" said the stout fellow, whose name was Han Wo. "Bind him, and gag him—I know a good way—and leave him at the bottom. The rats will make things interesting for him, and he will just live long enough to repent of his naughty ways."

"A rippin' idea, Han Wo!" exclaimed Graves. "I believe in quick work myself, but he has slipped through my hands so often, a little reflection will do him good. Let us hasten, for things are urgent, and we have a lot to do. No one will go down that manhole for months probably, and there won't be much of him left by then."

Dr. San Lo and Han Wo made short work of binding and gagging Tinker. They used fine silk as his bonds, procured from heaven knows where.

Tinker had been gagged more than once, but never had he experienced such a disagreeable gag as the soft, yielding ball of silk which they thrust in his mouth. It seemed to expand and fill every part of his mouth, even to the throat, and he could not even make a sound, if he wished.

Graves went ahead—to see if the coast was clear, and the two Celestials followed with Tinker's bound body.

They carried him to the manhole and dropped him through to the bottom of the filthy, evil-smelling, rat-infested sewer, dropping him without any attempt at breaking his fall. And as the lad rolled over, every bone in his body aching from the fall, he heard the grating being dropped, and then silence!

Their punishment had been well chosen, and Tinker realised his position was of the utmost danger. He could hear the scurrying of the rats which infested the loathsome hole, and his blood went cold as he thought of all the terrible stories he had read of the dreadful sewer rats, and remembered other similar experiences.

At that moment a clammy body dropped on him, and cold feet went flying over his face. His nerves gave way in a repulsion of fear, and he tried to call, forgetful of his gag. His eyes had now grown accustomed to the darkness, and in every corner he seemed to see a multitude of glaring eyes, awed for the moment by his living presence, but soon to overcome their fear, and led by one bolder than the rest, fall upon him with ravenous teeth.

Tinker's only hope was to endeavour to keep them off until daylight should filter in through the manhole, but he doubted if he could stand the strain for so long, and as the glaring eyes seemed to be increasing every moment, he looked forward with fear and horror to the terrible hours of the night.

He breathed a prayer for strength, but at that moment several of the huge rats ventured close, and finding nothing happened, others followed, and Tinker's awful fight for life began sooner than he expected.

The Seventh Chapter
Blake Resumes the Chase—Baffled

IT will be recalled that Blake had returned to his room after the escape of Alec and Taylor from their unsuccessful attack on the detective.

The heavy rain which had begun ceased after a bit, and settled in for a steady, mild, all-night pour. It took little deduction on Blake's part to know from whence the attack had come. In some way, he calculated, his presence in Bournmill had been discovered, and the boldness of the attack convinced him more and more that his deductions had been correct.

He did not hesitate now as to where to credit the outrage of the mill, and the certainty of his knowledge only made him realise more than ever how desperate would be the chase. However, he would be prepared, and they would not again find him napping.

He bent down and took the hound's head between his hands, looking with affection into the great, faithful eyes.

"Pedro, old chap," he said, with an odd note of tenderness in his voice, "you certainly saved my life tonight! Not once, but many times have you done so, my faithful fellow. If you were human I could reward you, old chap; but I think you must almost feel my gratitude."

Pedro pressed his muzzle deeper between his master's hands, and his heavy tail lashed to and fro. Instinct told him the meaning of the strange note in his master's voice, and as far as his nature permitted, he showed his happiness.

Blake straightened up, his eyes full of the sombre look which only appeared when he was deeply affected. His deductive faculties were probably more perfectly developed than those of any living being, and his record spoke with sufficiency of his success in analysing the motives of his fellow men.

But lately he had failed strangely to analyse his own feelings. His work was, if possible, more brilliant than ever, but for the first time in his long career he found an unpleasant element in his duty—an element which he had to vigorously exclude from his thoughts.

It had only come since his first encounter with Mademoiselle Yvonne; and at times the thought that he was on one side of the fence and she on the other, that he must in performance of his duty, foil her plans and bring her to justice, had tightened his heart-strings in an odd manner.

He was not in love with her; no, he was positive of that. But he knew she was in love with him, and therein, perhaps, lay the reason of his tenderness for her; for a great tenderness he certainly had for the young woman, so misguided by her own bitterness of heart, and yet so lovable and honourable in her own peculiar way.

But the outrage at the mill was one that must be punished. Twice opportunity had permitted Blake to offer Yvonne freedom, which she had once accepted and once declined. But this time, hard as was his duty, he must bring the perpetrators of the outrage to justice; and, hard as it was, he knew he would put all personal feelings from him and keep on the trail until his duty was accomplished.

Blake turned with a heavy sigh, and slipped out of his pyjamas, which he still wore. He dressed rapidly; and, after packing his bags, sat down with his pipe, and Pedro, to wait for dawn.

As the first grey streaks appeared, he rose and walked to the window. It was still raining, although more lightly, and Blake's eyes quickly scanned the inn-yard and lane beyond.

He turned and slipped into a heavy coat, putting a soft hat on in place of the stiff one which he had worn the previous evening.

Quickly descending to the office, he sent the yawning boots boy up for his bags, and, in the meantime, crossed the street to the garage opposite and knocked up the night watchman.

Five minutes later, with Pedro beside him, Blake drove the big, grey car slowly up the street and turned around to the lane which ran past the back of the inn. He pulled up in the same spot where the other car had stopped in the night, and after a careful examination of his surroundings, turned the car, and followed the tracks of the other car, which were plainly visible in the soft, wet mud.

He had started early, for he knew the tracks would be visible after the rain, and he desired to follow them before the early-morning traffic had obliterated them.

A double line stretched plainly before him, broken here and there by the early-morning carters bringing in mill workers from outlying farms. But it was a plain trail, showing the car had returned the way it had come, and Blake was not surprised when he found it was leading in the direction of Waltham Hall. A third line, which now joined the others, caused him to stop for a moment, and follow with his eyes the direction which they took.

"They've lost no time in making for London," he muttered; "but it may be only a blind, and I'll investigate at the Hall first."

Putting on speed he sent the car racing towards the Hall, and turned recklessly in through the open gates. But dead silence reigned about the house and stables, and all efforts of the detective failed to raise any answer.

"Must have all cleared out after they failed to get me. I'd give a lot to know where the yacht is at present. Well, there's nothing for it but to take up the chase and endeavour to overtake them."

Blake turned the car, and without farther comment, started on the long run to London. He tore through Bournmill at a terrific pace, the shriek of the hooters roaring in his ears as he dashed past the mill workers, who were just pouring through the gates to begin another day's toil before the insatiable machines.

Out of the town he swept, the soft mud flying in a great whirling shower in all directions, covering Blake and the car, not to mention Pedro. But faster still he pounded on, reckless of skidding and regardless of the fountain of mud.

The car, under his delicate tuning, settled down to a steady, purring pace, taking hills with a whirr and a rush, and dashing down with even greater velocity. For some distance Blake had easily followed the tracks of the other car, but as he flashed through several good-sized towns, he found the traffic had obliterated them, and, without paying further attention to them, confined all his energies towards making record time for London.

He had covered over two-thirds of the distance, and had just gone whirring through a small village, when, far ahead at the end of a level stretch of road, he caught a momentary glimpse of a large car with several occupants, and through the spattered mud, which nearly covered it, could just distinguish a gleam of red.

It disappeared over the brow of a hill, but Blake smiled grimly.

"I'll be closer than this, my friends, before we get to London," he muttered; but for once he was mistaken.

Hardly had the words passed his lips when a loud, hissing noise came from one of the front tyres, followed in a moment by the same noise from the corresponding back one.

With a lightning-like movement, Blake threw out the clutch and clamped on the brakes, but quick as he was he was not quick enough. The tyres flattened, the car lurched wildly, and skidded dangerously, fetching up, with an ominous crack, against a bank at the side of the road.

Blake endeavoured to retain his seat when the crash came, but his efforts were fruitless, and he sailed over the side into a ditch, with Pedro after him.

Fortunately, the worst that happened was a sore shoulder and a fresh coat of mud, but the car had not fared so well. As Blake picked himself up and examined it, he discovered the front wheel buckled, and both front and back tyres utterly ruined. He peered closely at the covers, and his eyes narrowed as he saw they were covered with a multitude of purple spots, which were rapidly breaking into holes.

"If there had been any doubt before," he muttered, rubbing his aching shoulder, "this settles it. But how was it done? Ah, by Jove, I wonder—I wonder!"

He turned suddenly and limped back along the road for nearly a quarter of a mile. There he bent down and picked up a small length of wire which had been pressed into the mud by the wheels on the right-hand side of the car—the side which had gone down flat.

"Magnesium wire—eh?—and the stuff attached to it—what a clever idea! Really, mademoiselle, my admiration for you grows every day. I take off my hat to you. However, it was my own fault—I forgot for the moment that those keen eyes of yours would be searching behind for signs of pursuit."

Returning to the car, Blake started the engine, which was still intact, and, climbing into the seat, gingerly began to back the car out of the ditch. The front wheel creaked ominously, but held, and, reversing the gears, Blake started along the road expecting it to give way every moment.

During the trip from London to Manchester he had been compelled to use the spare wheel which he always carried, and for that reason had none with him now, when he so sorely needed one. All he could do was to put the car to the strain and creep on slowly until he reached the garage in the village ahead. It was over an hour later when Blake, with many skids and ominous creaks, pulled up in front of the garage. He limped in and inquired how long it would take them to make the necessary repairs.

The wheel on Blake's car was of a special make, after his own design, but he had been in hopes of getting it patched up sufficiently to carry him on to London. An examination soon showed this to be hopeless, and he impatiently inquired what time the next train to London would leave.

His eyes roamed about while he awaited an answer, and as his eyes lighted on an object over in the corner he turned to the man.

"How long has that car been in?" he asked sharply.

"Oh, 'bout an hour, I s'pose. Why?"

"Do you know which way the occupants went?"

"Yes, they said as how they was goin' to the railway station."

"Can you manage in any way to get my car into London tonight?" went on Blake, drawing a couple of sovereigns from his pocket.

"Well, sir, I guess I can patch it up to creep along slow-like. It'll take a long time, though."

"All right, make it as soon as you can. Bring it to Baker Street." And Blake added his name to the astonished man. "Here is a sovereign now. You will get the other on your arrival, in addition to your regular charges. Can I depend on you?"

"Yes, sir, positive. I'm proud to do it for you, Mr. Blake."

Without waiting further, Blake hastened out and crossed to the railway-station.

Inquiry here disclosed the fact that a lady dressed as a maid and three men had left on a train half an hour earlier. They had purchased second-class tickets, and had all entered the same compartment.

Blake sent a wire on to London to have the arrival of the train watched and to detain any passengers answering the description which he forwarded.

He paced up and down impatiently, and it was over an hour later before another train came through bound for London. Blake sank into a corner seat, and closed his eyes. Pedro crouched at his feet, also pretty well worn out, and the tired pair got what rest they could, in anticipation of a renewal of the chase in London.

But a keen disappointment was in store for Blake on his arrival in London. No passengers even remotely resembling the description he wired had descended from the train.

Had they got out at a junction and changed their route, or had they disguised themselves before arriving in London, and in this way escaped unnoticed?

All he could do Blake did. He wired to the junction, and, leaving instructions to have any answer forwarded on to Baker Street, called a taxi, and, utterly worn out, started for his apartments.

He, on his arrival, expected to find either Tinker there or some information which would tell him how the lad was faring.

But no Tinker appeared. The clothes the lad had worn in Manchester were hanging in the wardrobe, and Blake noticed that the ragged suit which Tinker often used as a disguise was gone.

"Must have gone as a newsboy," he muttered. "I wonder where he is? If I could find him I would know whether he had discovered our man or not."

He glanced at his watch, and finding it was past seven, rang for Mrs. Bardell, and had that good soul bring him a hasty meal, for food had not passed his lips since the previous evening.

Mrs. Bardell confirmed his conjectures regarding Tinker. The lad, she said, had arrived earlier in the afternoon, and after hastily changing had rushed out again, and had not returned since.

And even at that moment, as Blake consumed his hurried meal, feeding Pedro at intervals and listening to the worthy landlady's conversation, Tinker lay bound and gagged at the bottom of the loathsome sewer, gathering his remaining strength together to repel the awful attack which was just beginning.

The Eighth Chapter
Pedro Rescues Tinker—The Fight at Han Wo's—Captured

AFTER his hasty meal, Blake made a radical change in his appearance. The muddy but well-cut clothes which he wore were replaced by a seedy suit and villainous-looking slouch hat. Old, heavy boots replaced the neat ones, and a soiled neckerchief was knotted loosely about his throat, and a short clay-pipe in his mouth. An automatic pistol finished the alterations, and in this distinctly tough garb, and with Pedro at his heels, Blake once more took up the trail.

His first destination was the address in Soho Square where Han Wo did business. There he hoped to get track of Tinker, and learn what the lad had been able to discover—if anything. He was too conspicuous in his rough attire to hail a taxi in Baker Street, so, keeping in the shadow and at a brisk pace, he bent his steps to Oxford Street and Tottenham Court Road, intending there to get a cab.

Blake was a good walker, and with his long stride soon covered the distance. He knew every inch of London, his trails taking him at times into almost unknown and certainly uncharted alleys and courts, hidden far from the world in the heart of its teeming centre. On many occasions his deep knowledge of these districts had served him well, for more than once he had been enabled to make a short cut, unknown to his quarry, and head the latter off unexpectedly.

He used one of these little-known thoroughfares this night, in order to make rapid progress to Tottenham Court Road, little dreaming what its unknown and rarely beaten track would bring him.

As he swung down a dark street and again turned into a narrow, evil-smelling lane, sinister and dark, he settled his hand around the butt of his revolver, and quickened his steps.

Far ahead a single light shone forth into the darkness, and the unsavoury odour which floated down on the evening air told Blake it was a fried-fish shop long before he got to it.

Pedro seemed to feel an antipathy toward his surroundings, for he kept close to Blake and trotted along silently, without his usual inquiring side journey. The fishy smell was growing stronger, and the shop lay less than thirty yards ahead, when three men emerged from it. One was short and stout, and in the flare of the light Blake saw his features were distinctly Chinese. But it was the other two individuals which attracted his attention.

He stopped dead and drew into the shadow as he recognised the Chinese gentleman whom he had seen in front of the Royal, and a grim smile played over his face when the third man turned, revealing the languid countenance of Graves.

"By Jove, the fates are kind to me tonight!" muttered Blake, laying a cautious hand on Pedro, and drawing him into the shadow. "I expected a longer hunt than this before I caught you together. But I wonder where Tinker is? Has he failed to get on their track, or has some accident befallen him?"

BLAKE GLANCED KEENLY AT THE CIRCULAR HOLE
WITH A YELL OF FRIGHT, BOTH MEN ROLLED, CLUTCHING MADLY, DOWN THE ROOF.
BLAKE MAKES A MOVE
"HERE, YOU BOY, WHAT YOU DO DOWN THERE?"

The trio in front of the fish-shop turned at this moment and started in the opposite direction, Blake softly crossing the narrow alley and following at a discreet distance.

As he drew opposite the shop, Pedro, who until now had remained close at heel, suddenly dashed away and disappeared in the gloom. Blake turned, irritated. It was not like Pedro to go off after anything like that, and at the moment he needed him. What on earth had become of him?

The three men ahead were now rapidly drawing away from him, and through the gloom Blake could just distinguish their dark forms swing around a corner. He gave a soft whistle which never failed to recall Pedro, but no answering scurry of footsteps sounded, and he whistled louder. At that moment Pedro came tearing back, and, with a word of admonition, Blake started on quickly to overtake his quarry.

But Pedro, instead of accompanying him, acted very strangely. He got in front of the detective, and gently but firmly blocked his way.

Blake, realising that Graves and his companions were liable to escape him, spoke sharply to the dog and endeavoured to pass, but though his tail went down at his master's tone, Pedro refused to budge. On the contrary, he took hold of the leg of Blake's trouser and endeavoured to pull him back.

Blake brought his mind back from the subject of Graves and the two Chinese men, and glanced down at Pedro.

"What is the matter, Pedro? Something has upset you to make you act in this matter. We will lose our men, I'm afraid, but if it worries you so much, old chap, lead on, and we will investigate."

He turned as he spoke, and Pedro, with many anxious backward glances, trotted quickly across the lane and disappeared in a black alley.

Blake, with a puzzled frown, followed, and he grew even more puzzled as he almost stumbled over the dog, who stood in the centre of the alley, his muzzle on the ground. Blake, thinking the dog had scented something on the ground which his canine intelligence had failed to explain, bent down and ran his hand under the dog's muzzle. He felt the cold iron of a sewer grating, but as he attempted to straighten up again Pedro caught his sleeve and gently worried it, holding his arm down.

"All right, old chap," said Blake softly. "Since it means so much to you, we'll have a look. Stand away until I lift the grating, if it will lift."

He caught hold of the bars as he spoke, and heaved upwards, a black hole appearing before him. Before he could throw it back or investigate further, Pedro, with a soft, excited bark, dived headlong into the hole.

Blake's blood ran cold as he heard a rattling, scampering, squealing noise below, accompanied by the angry growling of the hound as he battled with the repulsive sewer rats.

Blake, now seriously wondering what was wrong—for he knew the rats alone would not cause Pedro to act as he did—drew his revolver and dropped through the hole.

As the awful odour of the sewer assailed him, and the cold clammy bodies of the scurrying rats dashed over his feet, their eyes gleaming like angry points of light, he was sickened with loathing, but was determined to fully investigate.

Hastily striking a match, he peered around the sewer, the sudden light sending hundreds of the vile rodents scurrying. Pedro tore back from routing one mob, and sank down before some object in the darkness at one side, whining excitedly as he did so.

Blake struck another match and bent over.

Before him lay a bound figure, with staring eyes in which the horror of a terrible nightmare still reigned, and as Blake saw the white, drawn features of Tinker he gave a gasp of pain and anger.

"My heavens, lad!" he cried, dashing forward and feverishly feeling the lad's face, "if I get my hands on the scoundrels who have done this thing I will deal with them without mercy. They will feel the hand of Sexton Blake, and it will be the heaviest hand they have ever felt!"

Picking up the bound body, he hoisted it through the manhole. He then bent down, and Pedro, using his back as a support, climbed through next, followed by the detective!

In his anger, reckless for once of all consequences, he again picked up the lad and carried him into the fried-fish shop.

"'Ere, wot the dickens do yer think this is—a 'orspital?" cried the surly-looking woman behind the counter.

Blake laid the lad down on a rude bench, and walked over to the counter.

"Look here," he said in a low tone from which the icicles almost dropped, "you keep your tongue between your teeth. Whether you were an accessory in this affair I don't know, but a single move on your part and you will find yourself in trouble. Come here, Pedro!" he called. "Watch her, boy! If she moves, go for her!"

The woman, thoroughly cowed by the look in Blake's eyes, shrank back, and so plainly had she understood the deadly reality of every word that Pedro's watchful attention was not necessary.

And it was not surprising that she had felt the power of his anger, for seldom had Sexton Blake blazed with such rage.

In his risky and dangerous calling he had looked for treachery, and even the knife of the assassin, and, at times, he realised Tinker must run the same risk. But the cold-blooded cruelty of the lad's assailants was past the limit, and he vowed vengeance on the authors.

Rapidly he unbound the lad, and released the puffy, silk ball from his mouth.

Tinker's eyes were now closed in a dead faint; but Blake, thrusting his pocket-flask between the lad's teeth, heaved a sigh of relief as the lids trembled and opened.

"It's you, is it, guv'nor?" whispered the lad weakly. "You were just in time."

"It wasn't I, my poor lad," answered Blake, with tears in his eyes, "it was Pedro. And, if he hadn't insisted on me going with him, I shudder to think of your fate."

"Dear old Pedro!" whispered Tinker. "Oh, guv'nor——" He broke off, the horror returning to his eyes. "It was awful! I was just about gone, and couldn't have held them off much longer."

"Never mind, my lad," returned Blake. "Take a little more of this spirit; it will revive you."

Tinker did so, and, as the unaccustomed stimulant flowed through him, he sat up.

"I feel much better now, guv'nor," he said, in a more natural tone.

"That's right. And now I will send you home, where you must go to bed and get a good rest."

"But how about Graves and those two Chinese?" asked the lad. "I tracked them here this afternoon."

Rapidly he told Blake his experiences up to the detective's arrival.

"If they have gone," he added, as he finished, "they may have gone back to Han Wo's in Soho Square."

"Probably, my lad. And I am going after them, but you must return home."

Tinker pleaded long and earnestly to be permitted to go along, arguing that he deserved a chance at them.

"Well, Tinker, I feel it's wrong to permit you to tax yourself further; but, however, if you feel that way about it, you can come."

With a last piercing look at the woman, Blake called off Pedro, and the three hastened along the dark lane. The detective put the hound on the scent, which was still fresh, and neither he nor Tinker were surprised when it led them to Han Wo's office.

The building was in darkness; but that told them nothing, for, if the men were in a rear office, the light would be invisible from the street.

Blake softly ascended the steps and tried the door, which yielded.

"They must feel pretty safe," he whispered to Tinker. "They didn't even trouble to lock the door."

"I was the only one of whom they were suspicious, and they think I am safe at the bottom of the sewer," whispered back Tinker.

Blake led the way into the dark interior, and the trio stealthily crept along the passage. Half-way down a narrow chink of light appeared from under a door, and they pulled up before making a rush.

"You haven't a revolver, have you?" breathed Blake.

"Yes, guv'nor. They felt so sure of me that they didn't trouble to remove it."

"Good! We will probably have a fight before we get them. Now, are you ready? Come on!"

Blake grasped the handle of the office door, and he dashed in with levelled revolver.

The three men were sitting at a long table, and looked up in amazement as the door opened.

"Hands up! Quick!" snapped Blake. "You, Graves, don't feel for your gun! I'll let daylight into you at once if you do!"

Up went three pairs of hands, for each realised it was suicide to attempt resistance with two levelled automatics pointing at them.

"You, Graves, I am disgusted with!" went on Blake, in an undertone. "You once laid claims to being an English gentleman. But your action in tossing this lad down that awful sewer tonight has made you surrender all such claim. And your friends here are no better. I arrest all three of you for conspiracy, and as being implicated in the outrage at the Todd Mill in Bournmill."

Graves went white at the detective's words; but the countenances of the two Chinese did not change.

"Tinker, my lad, there is some cord in the corner. Bind them at once. I think our Celestial friends are planning mischief."

Tinker turned to obey; but as his revolver was lowered, Dr. San Lo, knowing Blake could not shoot them all, ducked suddenly, and upset the long table. Blake fired as he did so, but the bullet hit the table, glancing off. Graves and Han Wo lost no time in taking advantage of their companion's move.

Graves ducked, and pulled out his gun, but Blake swung round and fired. Graves's arm dropped, shattered, and he reeled back, falling with a crash. Tinker had turned as the table crashed over, and had levelled his revolver at Han Wo; but the stout Celestial had leaped forward with surprising activity, a long knife gleaming in his hand.

He struck as Tinker fired, but both bullet and blade went wide, and they grappled. Dr. San Lo, with another knife, was making for Blake, and the latter, after disabling Graves, turned just in time to meet the attack. His left hand caught the Celestial's wrist; but Dr. San Lo was equally as quick, and the two powerful men struggled silently for the mastery.

Only a few seconds had elapsed since the beginning of the struggle, and Pedro as yet had not taken a hand; but as Tinker and the stout Han Wo met in a crash he sprang to the lad's assistance, landing with crushing force on the Celestial's back.

In that moment Tinker had got his arm free, and, turning his revolver around, he brought the heavy butt down between Han Wo's eyes. His adversary dropped without a sound, and Tinker turned to assist Blake. He had learnt a trick in the East during the famous chase after the abductors of President Pearson, and this trick he put into force on San Lo.

Springing forward, he landed on the doctor's back, his left arm pressed under San Lo's chin, and his right fist pressing with all his force into the soft, vital spot in his side. The combination forced the doctor to stagger back, his hands releasing their grasp on Blake's wrists.

As San Lo sought to lessen Tinker's pressure, the lad, with a sudden movement, caught his right arm, and brought it around with a jerk, twisting it high up on the doctor's back until the hand rested against his neck—a position of excruciating pain.

Blake lost no time in getting a piece of cord from the corner, and securely binding San Lo. At that moment an astonished policeman, attracted by the shots, poked his head in the door, and demanded gruffly what was the trouble.

His eyes opened wide when Blake revealed his identity and explained matters. He quickly handcuffed the prostrate Han Wo and the bleeding Graves, promising to take them in charge, and keep them safe until Blake could make the charge.

Blake, Tinker, and Pedro, tired and exhausted, returned in a taxi to Baker Street, hoping to at last get some rest, but they were doomed once more to disappointment.

The man from the village garage had arrived, and the big, grey car was standing at the kerb when they reached home. The man himself was sitting in the consulting-room awaiting Blake's return, and while he was there Blake had him attach an extra wheel in place of the patched front one.

He kept a couple of these extra wheels in his rooms in case of emergency, and, being made from his own designs, the man had no trouble in quickly putting it on. Blake turned to his desk as the man left, and on the top was a telegram.

He tore it open and discovered it to be a reply to his inquiry from the agent at the junction.

"Woman and three men, but not answering your description left train here, and bought tickets back to Manchester."

"Ah," he remarked, as he finished reading, "I said they might disguise themselves on the train, and slip unnoticed through the crowd at Euston, or double back over the line! And that is what they have done.

"Ring up Inspector Thomas at Scotland Yard, my lad," he continued, "and tell him to come around on an urgent matter. There is one arrest in this case which I prefer him to make. And now I'm afraid sleep is out of the question. It is back to Manchester as soon as the inspector comes. But, never mind, you can sleep in the tonneau on the way."

The Ninth Chapter
How Yvonne Baffled Blake—Off to Bournmill Again—
Blake Makes Still Another Capture

WHEN Alec and Taylor had returned to Waltham Hall after the ignominious result of their attack on Blake at the inn, Yvonne, with her usual clear perception and prompt decision, had at once laid plans for a speedy flight, knowing Sexton Blake would now be in a position of certitude regarding her presence in the neighbourhood, where, before, he was, in doubt.

She knew, in addition, that the detective would be after them as soon as it was light enough to follow the trail, and, consequently, while it was still dark, she had closed and barricaded the Hall, and started for London.

Jack Fenwick, still a prisoner in the cellar, and still being sought for by the police, was a complication. It was impossible to risk discovery by taking him with her; but the difficulty she overcame by leaving a member of the circle behind in the closed house, and this Alec was glad to perform, in order to retrieve himself for his failure at the inn.

No time had been lost; but these arrangements naturally consumed a fair amount of valuable time, and, consequently, although still dark, it was not far in advance of the pursuing Blake that they had finally got started.

It was at the top of a high hill that the ever-watchful Yvonne had caught sight of Blake's car. She had acted at once, and the success of her efforts was complete.

The appearance of the village and garage and the whistle of an engine had suggested to her the idea of leaving the car and doubling back. This she and her companions did, and when Blake and his car bumped into the village an hour later, the fugitives were half-way to London.

On the train Mademoiselle Yvonne exercised her brilliant faculty for disguise, and at the junction there descended a very different party from the party which had boarded the train an hour back.

Taylor, who was one of her companions, purchased tickets to Manchester for the party, and Blake, in the London-bound train, passed them on the way back.

On her arrival in Manchester, Yvonne sent an urgent telegram to Captain Vaughan of her yacht, the *Fleur-de-Lys*, at Cherbourg to bring the yacht over at once, without waiting for the completion of repairs. She also sent another telegram to Graves and Dr. San Lo, addressed in care of Han Wo's office, advising of her move, and little did she dream into whose hands this telegram would fall.

As soon as these details were attended to Yvonne procured a motor, and, with her companions, proceeded at once to Bournmill. She calculated that her safest move was to spend the two days before the yacht could possibly get ready at Waltham Hall, thinking Blake would be searching for her in London.

This plan, as far as it went, was wise, but naturally Yvonne was not aware that Sexton Blake knew of her connection with Dr. San Lo, and that while she was speeding in the motor to Bournmill the detective had captured her three accomplices.

The party made a quiet arrival at Waltham Hall, and for safety's sake Yvonne tabooed lights, except behind closely-drawn blinds. Fatigued from her exertions, but cautious as usual, she divided her companions up into alternate watches and sought her room.

In the meantime, Sexton Blake and Tinker were waiting at Baker Street for the arrival of Inspector Thomas, of Scotland Yard. He came at once on receipt of Blake's message, and the latter rapidly outlined matters to him.

"Splendid—splendid, Mr. Blake!" exclaimed the inspector, as Blake finished. "I'll not forget this favour. It will be the biggest haul I've made for a long time to catch the elusive mademoiselle. But are you sure she would go back to Bournmill? She might buy tickets for Manchester at the Junction, but leave the train and double back again to London. What do you think?"

"Very logical reasoning, inspector," smiled Blake, "and a chance I have already considered. If Mademoiselle Yvonne knew of the fate of her friends, doubtless she would do just that, but I think she is ignorant of my knowledge regarding her connection with the Chinese, and, that being so, will return to Bournmill, hoping I will search for her in London."

At that moment a knock came at the door, and a policeman entered. He saluted the inspector, and turned to Blake.

"I was left on duty at Han Wo's place, sir," he said, "and while I was there this urgent telegram was delivered. I thought it might be of use, and brought it along."

"Good; that was quite right," replied Blake, stretching out his hand. A grim smile played over his tired features as he read the contents and passed the telegram over to the inspector.

It was the one which Yvonne had sent to Graves and Dr. San Lo advising them of her movements and warning them that Blake was in London.

"Ah, your deductions were correct," remarked the inspector.

"So it seems," answered Blake. "And now we will leave. It is a long run, and will be a dark one, but we dare not risk waiting for daylight."

Tinker had fallen asleep in his chair, but Blake's movements as he rose woke the lad, and he started up.

"I think you had better stay and get some rest, my lad," remarked Blake. "You have been through enough this evening."

"Oh, no, guv'nor; please let me go with you. I can sleep on the way, and will be thoroughly rested by the time we get there."

"All right, my lad," smiled Blake. "After your performance tonight, I can't very well refuse you."

Ten minutes later the big car, once more sound, was picking its way through the dreary night, its powerful lights illuminating the road ahead with a brilliant, dancing path, the trees and fences fading away into ghostly forms beyond.

Tinker and Pedro lay curled up in the tonneau, the inspector dozed in front, but Blake, though utterly weary, peered ahead into the night with unblinking eyes, his thoughts racing on to the accompaniment of the engine's whirr, his mind preparing for every contingency while his hands mechanically directed the vibrating, tearing machine which dashed on into the night like relentless fate.

They pounded through Manchester without stopping, and the mills were still silent, the hooters had not yet shrieked forth their first warning, the tired workers still slept when the grey flying shape swept through Bournmill and took the direction to Waltham Hall.

Without lessening speed, Blake jabbed the inspector into wakefulness and told him to wake Tinker. The lad was still rubbing his eyes when the car entered the gates, taking the turn almost on two wheels, and with a sudden jolt pulled up at the front entrance.

At the moment the grey dawn spread upwards in the East a hooter sounded in the village, followed by another and another and yet another. The house stood a shadowy bulk behind them, silent as the grave. The shutters were all closed, and the stables looked deserted, but once more a smile flickered across the detective's features as he saw the tracks of a motor which had not been there when he left for London, and which gave a different imprint from the others.

To him Yvonne's movements lay revealed as though written in blazing letters of fire. He could read her movements from the time she had doubled back from the junction, and felt positive she was at that moment behind the closed shutters of the silent house, and might be even now watching their movements. The next few minutes would decide that.

Springing out, and followed by the others, he strode up the steps, expecting every moment to hear a bullet sing past him. But nothing occurred, and the whole party reached the door without any sign being given that their presence was known.

Nor was it, for Yvonne all unconscious of the approach of danger, lay sleeping, and the man on guard, weary from the stranger's chase, dozed in his chair.

Blake carefully examined the front door, and turned to Tinker.

"Slip back to the car, Tinker, and bring me the bag of tools under the back seat. You, inspector, be ready with your revolver. They may be asleep, but it is not like mademoiselle to be so careless, and we may be walking into a trap. This door doesn't look too difficult to force, and I see no other way of getting in."

Tinker returned with the tools, and Blake set to work. He had made a thorough study of locks, and no criminal could spring one with more neatness and despatch than could he.

No sooner did a new lock or combination appear on the market than Blake studied it point by point. Only in this way could he keep abreast, and had he taken to a criminal life his record would have been as brilliant as it was as a detective. Consequently the lock, being an old one, soon slipped back, and a moment later they stood in the dark, silent hall of the house.

"Follow me, and step softly," whispered Blake, leading the way. Down the hall and through the dining-room they went without discovering anything, but as Blake opened the door of the huge kitchen, where a lamp still burned, he brought up his revolver with a jerk, and spoke in a low, sharp tone.

"Hands up! Keep your distance, and don't move!"

The man on guard had come out of his doze with a start, and sat staring with open mouth and protruding eyes at the detective. A large service revolver lay on the table beside him, but he saw it was useless to reach for it, for Blake had him covered, and there was business in the detective's eyes.

Tinker and the inspector hastened over to the astonished man, and the inspector clapped the bracelets on him. Tinker took off his belt and tied the man's feet, and they left him on the floor while they searched for the others.

Alec and Taylor they found fast asleep in one of the servants' rooms, and before these astonished individuals could protest they lay bound with strips torn from the sheets of their own beds, glaring with a murderous look at their captors.

"Do you know if there are any more?" whispered the inspector, as they returned to the kitchen.

"I can't tell," answered Blake. "There may be several, but we'll have to risk their escape in order to find Mademoiselle Yvonne. She may have heard us already, and for all we know may have slipped away while we were attending to the others. However, come on, and we will have a look upstairs in the main part."

The party stole softly back to the front hall, and went stealthily up the stairs. A long passage ran off to the right and another to the left. Tinker and the inspector took the left, while Blake and Pedro took the right, and in this fashion the little party began their search for the elusive mademoiselle.

Blake passed several open doors, and a quick glance into the rooms showed them to be untenanted. Pedro had trotted on ahead, his feet making no noise in the soft carpet, and as Blake turned a corner of the passage he saw the hound snuffing at the bottom of a closed door.

Approaching it softly, Blake drew his revolver and knocked loudly.

"Yes?" came a sleepy voice from within. "What is it? I told you not to disturb me."

Blake's eyes filled with the old sombre look as he recognised the soft tones of Mademoiselle Yvonne, and even his emotionless nature thrilled a bit under the influence of her nearness. But he put such thoughts from him, and his tone was very level when he spoke.

"I am very sorry if I have disturbed your sleep, mademoiselle," he called through the locked door, "but I wished to see you urgently, and did not wait until a more formal hour."

His mouth twitched as dead silence inside the room followed the words, and he knew that, as he intended she should, Yvonne had recognised his voice.

For a full minute the silence reigned, and Blake was about to repeat his words when a silvery laugh came from the room.

"Really, Mr. Blake, it is too droll! I must confess I did not expect you, but I will join you in five minutes."

"Can I depend on that, mademoiselle?" asked Blake.

"Certainly!" came back the laughing voice. "There is no way of escape from this room, even if I wished to."

Blake retired up the passage to await her appearance, knowing full well she would keep her word. Tinker and the inspector returned at that moment from a fruitless search, and the inspector, on hearing Blake's news, was in a nervous sweat for fear the daring Yvonne would once more escape.

"She may attempt it afterwards," said Blake, "but she will keep her word, don't fear. After she makes her appearance it will be necessary to watch her, but until then there is no need for worry."

And Blake's reading of the young woman's nature was correct, for sharp to the minute the key of her door turned, and she appeared, looking bright and fresh, in a neat-fitting costume.

The inspector began at once to finger his handcuffs, but Yvonne caught sight of his action, and, smiling, waved her hand.

"Don't bother yet, inspector. Besides, I'm sure they're much too large for me."

"Well, Mr. Blake," she said, turning to the detective and holding out her hand, "can I guess the reason of your visit?"

"I'm afraid you can, mademoiselle," returned Blake, taking her hand and unconsciously holding it, "and this time I cannot offer you freedom. I regret to say that the inspector must arrest you for breaking and entering Mortimer Todd's mill, and also for damaging the machinery and robbing the safe."

"Quite a string of charges," answered Yvonne coolly. "But why do you say the inspector must arrest me, Mr. Blake?" she added in a low tone. "Why don't you make the arrest yourself?"

Blake dropped her hand, and looked away.

"I—er—I prefer him to do it, mademoiselle, that is all."

"You are good. It would have hurt to have you do it," she said simply.

Their voices had been too low to be heard by the inspector and Tinker; but at that moment the inspector approached, and laid his hand on Yvonne's arm to make the arrest.

Blake turned his head away as the officer spoke the formal words, his pompous voice sounding strangely harsh after Blake's clear tone. Yvonne went white, but did not falter, and not for a moment did her eyes leave Blake's averted face. Tinker stood behind the inspector, and the lad's eyes grew sober as he saw Blake's avoidance of the scene.

"Jiminy," he muttered to himself, "if she wants to be a criminal, why can't she be nasty at the same time? But she's so jolly decent with it all that I don't wonder the guv'nor finds it hard."

And in these words, all unknowingly, he expressed Blake's thoughts.

As the inspector finished the formal charge, with the customary caution that anything she said might be used against her, Yvonne withdrew her eyes from Blake's face, and all at once they filled with a great weariness.

"Very well, inspector," she said, in a toneless voice; "but I beg of you not to put those horrid steel things on my wrists. I give you my word. I will not try to escape while Mr. Blake's here."

"Well, I think we had better be getting along," said the inspector, placing his hand on Yvonne's arm.

"One moment, inspector, before we go," replied Yvonne. "I wish to have a word in private with Mr. Blake. May I?"

The inspector glanced inquiringly at Blake. He did not like being left out of anything, and he failed to understand the detective's attitude toward Yvonne. But he remembered that it was owing to Blake's generosity that he was being credited with the capture, and for the moment he felt compelled to follow Blake's wishes.

As Blake nodded he dropped his hand, and with Tinker withdrew up the passage.

"What is it, mademoiselle?" asked Blake.

Yvonne came close, and laid her hand on his arm.

"It is this, Mr. Blake," she said, in a low tone. "I am not making any excuse—but do you know why I ruined Mortimer Todd?"

"I can guess," answered Blake. "I presume he is one of the men who ruined you and your mother in Australia at the time of the Jig Saw Mine swindle."

"Yes, yes, you are right. But listen, that is not all."

Yvonne gave a brief explanation to which Blake listened silently.

"There is a young man named Fenwick," she added, "who has been accused by Todd. He has been a prisoner in the cellar ever since the night I was at the mill. He accidentally discovered me there, and there was nothing else to do but to take him prisoner, and keep him out of the way. He told me his story, and I find Mortimer Todd has not improved any with the years, for he robbed the boy of a valuable invention."

"I know," said Blake quietly. "It relates to a new dye process."

"How on earth did you know?" asked Yvonne, her eyes opening.

"I can't tell you the secret of my methods," smiled Blake. "But have you the papers?"

"Yes. They, with all the money and everything else I took, are in the safe down in the library. I haven't touched a thing yet; but I have had my revenge, Mr. Blake, for Mortimer Todd is a ruined man today. Will you return the papers to the boy, and release him? I do not wish to injure him, but for my own protection, was compelled to keep him out of sight."

"I will do so, mademoiselle. Is there anything else?"

"No; only to tell you that I will escape, if I can; but"—and her eyes grew strangely soft—"I want you to know that your consideration is appreciated. And now good-bye!"

"Good-bye, mademoiselle!" said Blake, taking her hand.

Tinker accompanied the inspector in order to drive the car to the village, and bring back some officers to look after the other prisoners.

In the meantime, Blake descended to the library and opened the safe, which was unlocked. He drew out the contents, and saw that they tallied with the list which Todd had given him. On top was the envelope containing Jack Fenwick's papers, and, thrusting this in his pocket, he replaced everything else in the safe, and hastened to the cellar.

A few moments sufficed to release the mystified prisoner, and Blake soon had his story.

Ascending to the library he told the lad as much as necessary, and then turning, he passed a sheet of paper to him.

"Write to my dictation," said Blake; and Jack, wonderingly took up a pen and obeyed.

Blake glanced at the finished sheet as Jack finished, and, to the latter's amazement, drew out the papers relating to the dye process and passed them over.

"Here, my lad," he said kindly, "I am satisfied these are yours, as the writing corresponds exactly with what you have just written. But take my advice, and, in future, don't trust them to anyone without getting a proper receipt. If you need some backing to proceed with it, I will advance you sufficient to do so."

Jack tried to thank him; but Blake laughed.

"It will be a good investment, from what I can see. And now hurry up, and go to Miss Cameron. She is a loyal young woman, and deserves the best you can give her."

The Tenth Chapter
Blake Performs a Disagreeable Duty—Jack's Reward— Yvonne's Fate

BLAKE had a disagreeable interview with Mortimer Todd.

He first told that gentleman of the arrest of Mademoiselle Yvonne for the outrage, and of her certain guilt, and of Jack Fenwick's innocence. He also explained how he had returned the papers to the lad. "For," he said, "you will remember, Mr. Todd, that I said in Baker Street I would return the papers to the owner, and I knew then that you were not the owner."

Blake then proceeded to give Mr. Mortimer Todd a candid opinion of him, and the mill-owner, seeing his last hope gone, was for once shamed by the detective's scathing words.

"If you will take my advice, you will leave England," finished Blake. "Mademoiselle Yvonne is in prison, and will doubtless get a long term for the damage to the machines in the mill. You told me the money taken from your safe was to meet the wages of the mill-workers on pay-day. Well, I have recovered it, and it's going to be used for that purpose. I want you to sign an authorisation to that effect."

And the thoroughly cowed Todd did so. He also took Blake's advice, and that same night departed silently for a more congenial climate.

The gratitude of Mrs. Cameron and Phyllis almost overwhelmed the modest Blake, and the grateful pair insisted on placing a big basket of homemade cakes in the tonneau of the car.

And once more his duty done—a duty that held an element of sorrow in it for the beautiful, misguided young woman, now sitting alone in her cell, but an element which was relieved by the happiness of Phyllis and her mother—Blake, with Tinker and Pedro, once more swung along the narrow streets of Bournmill on the long journey to Baker Street.

***

"I've been puzzling my head, guv'nor," said Tinker, as they left Bournmill behind, and gained the main road to London, "and I can't imagine how you knew the outrage at the mill had anything to do with the bales of rotten cotton."

"I don't wonder, my lad," answered Blake; "but if you will give me your close attention, I will give you a full explanation of my deductions in this case."

"I'll be awfully glad, guv'nor!" replied Tinker, settling back to listen.

"In the first place," went on Blake, "you remember the theories I told you were possible?"

"Yes, guv'nor, of course."

"Well, the more I thought of it, the more I was convinced that the whole thing was carefully arranged. To go back. On the night we went to the Royal, you will remember the accident to the tyre. I was immediately interested in the peculiar nature and colour of the holes, and, as you know, made an exhaustive chemical test of the tyre-cover later in the evening.

"I had tried almost everything, when, as a last resort, I gave it the radium test, and you can imagine my surprise when it answered. It showed great ingenuity, for it had been caused by a shower of radium molecules, and only an extremely clever person could have done it.

"Besides, it is not a usual thing for people to go about with such a valuable element on them as radium. I naturally connected it with Mademoiselle Yvonne; but reason showed me she could not have done it in her haste. Who then could have done it?

"I thought of the tall Chinese gentleman, and could only conclude he had been the cause of it. But for what reason, I could not guess, unless he also had been at the Royal, and acting in conjunction with mademoiselle had stopped our pursuit in that way. That I now know was the correct explanation. However, I lost all track of them, but expected at any moment to hear of some big feat being brought off, for I knew she was not in England without a purpose.

"When Phyllis Cameron came up to London and sought my assistance, I did not consider the case would be so important, but when Mortimer Todd turned up and described the outrage, which, to say the least, was colossal, and could only be the result of a very clever brain, I placed mademoiselle in the list of possible suspects.

"I did not for a moment consider Jack Fenwick guilty. The rotten cotton puzzled me, and although it might only be a coincidence, the fact that the purchasers had been Chinese threw my mind back to the Chinese gentleman at the Royal. Was it possible that there was a huge scheme to ruin Todd? If so, what was the motive? That was the puzzle.

"Well, on my arrival at Bournmill I questioned Todd. He had lied to me about Jack Fenwick's papers, and also lied to me about his past. I wondered if he could have committed the whole affair himself, but I threw out that theory on discovering the insurance on the machinery had lapsed only a month before, and besides, his suffering was too genuine.

"That he was a rogue I did not doubt, but of this he was innocent. I afterwards made a thorough examination of the mill, and outside the window which had been used as an entrance on the night of the outrage I discovered the imprint left by the toe of a shoe.

"It was of a peculiar shape, and could only belong to a woman, and I knew from its position that it had been made by someone hopping over the sill from inside. I next examined the machinery, and from its appearance and the fact that the whole damage had been accomplished in one night, knew it had been ruined by a very powerful acid.

"That again spelled brains. The footprint had strengthened my suspicions against mademoiselle, but as yet I could not tell positively. Phyllis Cameron made me more certain when she told me of a certain Cyrus Harmon, who, with his niece, had taken up their residence at Waltham Hall some three months previously, and I was not surprised when her description of Miss Harmon tallied roughly with that of Mademoiselle Yvonne.

"But the final link was forged when I made a test of the rotten cotton and discovered its condition had been caused by the application of radium molecules, and if I needed any further confirmation I got it from the fact that the cotton was purple, for on any other colour the spots would have shown.

"I then knew the whole thing had been carefully planned, and that Mademoiselle Yvonne was behind it. I also knew the two Chinese were accomplices, but did not know the reason until she told me at the Hall, when she spoke privately. I immediately sent you off to London to find out what you could, and you know the rest of my moves in drawing the net closer."

"She's clever, isn't she, guv'nor?" remarked Tinker after a long silence.

"Yes, my lad, she is more than clever, she is a genius, and the whole case bears out my theory that criminals today keep up with the latest discoveries of science, and in some cases—Mademoiselle Yvonne's, for instance—they make many discoveries themselves.

"For that reason the criminologist, to be successful, must keep abreast of them, otherwise a reign of terror would ensue and we would be helpless in their hands. But what a pity!" he muttered, half to himself. "Wonderful brain, a wonderful woman. She could rise to almost any height in the world of science, and instead she is now behind the prison walls."

***

The trial of Mademoiselle Yvonne created tremendous interest. The beauty of the prisoner, as well as the almost uncanny cleverness of her methods, found an untiring topic for the Press. Blake's evidence, except a mere formal statement, was unnecessary.

Yvonne made a sworn confession, taking all the blame on herself, and she was sentenced to five years. Graves and Han Wo both got off on a technicality, and Dr. San Lo only got six months, as the evidence against him was purely circumstantial. Alec, Taylor and the others received only six months each, owing to Yvonne shouldering the blame, and Blake made no statement regarding the attack at the inn.

True to his promise, Blake financed Jack Fenwick, and a new company is now being formed to take over the Todd Mill, the head of the dye-room being Jack, who is now a family man, for his marriage to Phyllis took place quietly soon after his release.

Mademoiselle Yvonne went smiling to her fate, but before the prison doors closed on her for the long years she sent a short note to Blake. He read it with his head in his hand, and gazed long at the fire when he had finished. It was very short, and read as follows:

"I bear you no ill-will. Once again, though to you it may seem far off, I say: To our next meeting!—Y."

"I wonder!" muttered Blake. "I wonder where we will both be in five years."

The UNION JACK. 1d
SETTLING DAY
Or;
The MONEY KING
YVONNE v. BLAKE.
NO. 495. NEW SERIES.]
April 5th, 1913.
[EVERY THURSDAY.

THE GREAT LADIES OF CRIME

"Well-behaved women seldom make history."
~Laurel Thatcher Ulrich

Female Master Criminals from the 1890s to the 1920s!

Now on Sale.

ROH PRESS

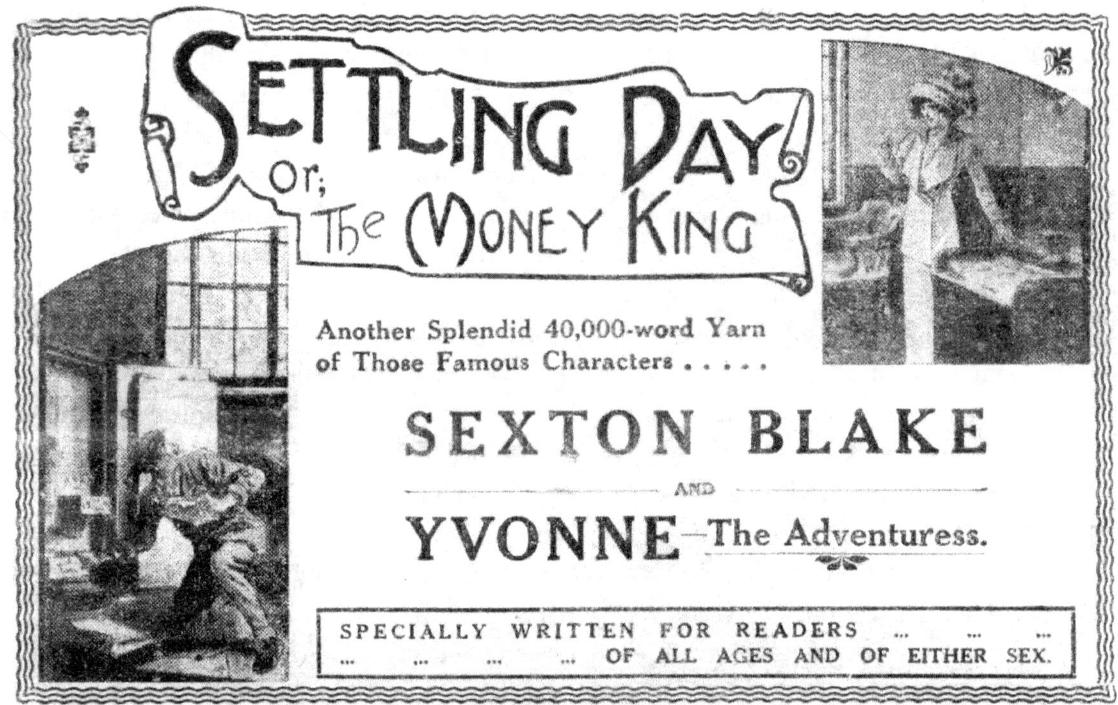

Prologue

THE sharp, biting sleet of a wild February night howled like the seven demons of legend about the black, obtrusive mass of Dalemoor Prison. The dreary, surrounding moor was obscured by the heavy, whirling rain and snow, and even the mighty prison itself was, at times, obliterated.

Inside the mighty prison, ordered existence beat on its way unmindful, and unaffected, by the anger of the elements. Nerves numbed by the monotonous life—hope either dead, or, in the case of short term prisoners, sleeping until the last lap of the sentence should be reached, they lay unheeding the storm—some sleeping with the calmness of a deadened or easy conscience—some tossing feverishly and muttering fitfully—some staring into the darkness of the cell with wide, open eyes.

In a small, whitewashed cell, the slim form of a young woman lay outlined on the rough prison-cot. Six months of prison-life had failed to alter the refinement and beauty of her features, and the coarse covering hardly concealed the youthful suppleness of her body.

She lay motionless, and as the measured beat of the guard approached the door, her eyes closed in feigned sleep. But inside the seemingly slumbering head was a keen, wakeful brain racing on heedless of the hours, seeking and weighing the pros and cons of a mighty question.

As Mademoiselle Yvonne, the adventuress, she had, in the outer world, found little trouble in meeting each difficulty, and deciding quickly. But here, behind the prison walls—a cipher in the numbered cogs of the prison machine, she had for months brought her every brilliant faculty to bear on one thought only—escape. And though she now had the means to accomplish her purpose, she had not yet been able to decide the torturing question.

Many plans had been weighed and cast out, and only the present one which filled her mind had been retained, promising success, but dangerous, in that it promised too much success. But something must be done, and done this wild, tempestuous night!

Graves, her uncle, with Captain Vaughan, and several other members of the "circle," which had been broken up by Sexton Blake, had been working incessantly from outside to devise means for her escape. And this very day she had received the result of their final efforts, which promised more chance, providing Yvonne could handle her end of it, than any other of which they had thought.

With her usual thoroughness for detail, and in providing for the future, Yvonne had months before made arrangements which were to be used in communicating with any member of the "circle" who was unfortunate enough to be caught and convicted. Little did she think that she herself would be the first one to benefit by the plan, but, during her sojourn at the expense of the Government, she had congratulated herself many times on her forethought.

The plan was simply this:

Any members of the circle who were free, were sworn to use every endeavour to assist to freedom any who were imprisoned. Realising that years of experience had taught prison officials to rigidly examine any incoming or outgoing articles of prisoners, Yvonne had thought it wise to devise a plan of communication which would defy detection.

Permission was to be sought to send in an occasional book to the member imprisoned, and knowing full well that the covers of the book would be minutely examined for any concealed writing or finely fashioned tools, Yvonne had improved on that idea. The pages themselves were to be used for communications, and it would be a shrewd prison official, indeed, who guessed that the thin, harmless-looking pages of a book could conceal anything which it ought not to conceal.

Any book was to be chosen, and for safety sake, the pages were to be picked at random. These pages were to be carefully removed, and new pages almost exactly similar, were to be printed. But they were different in one point. Only one side of the paper was to be printed upon, and, consequently, it would take two separate sheets of a thinner texture instead of one which had been removed.

The blank sides were to be placed against each other, but before carefully pasting them together, the note, or communication, written in the circle's code on the thinnest of cigarette paper, was to be placed between. The pages were then to be carefully rebound by an expert, and when completed, would defy detection by the closest observer. A carelessly turned down corner of one of the pages was to indicate that the next one was the one containing the message.

This plan had been followed after Yvonne's imprisonment. Permission had been sought and gained to send an occasional book to her, and each coverless volume had safely carried its little message of hope and cheer to her.

But today's book, the tenth in six months, had contained a note of urgent importance, and, if it was to be acted upon, that very night must see its adoption.

Every word of the message burned vividly in Yvonne's brain. Seeking any opportunity which offered, she had laboriously translated the tiny characters of the coded message from Graves, and this was his message of urgency:

"Just discovered, free pardon been granted Bertha Harris, Convict 1120, Dalemoor. She is innocent, and guilty person confessed. Pardon will be delivered evening of seventh, and her release follow immediately. Can suggest nothing for you to do, but in case you are able to do anything, will be waiting in car at Daleville, four miles from prison to make dash to coast. If you have opportunity at all, am sending ten bulbs drug. Don't hesitate if chance offers, for nothing can happen to pardoned prisoner through you, as she is innocent. Try hard. Best love.

"Bulbs concealed in pages 20, 26, 31, 37, 48, 63, 90, 101, 123, 160.—G."

This was the message promising freedom, and which seemed to hold out fingers of hope, for in her months in Dalemoor, Yvonne had been a model prisoner. She had been able to secure an occasional word with Bertha Harris, the convict mentioned by Graves, and Yvonne's kindly words cheered that delicate, innocent woman who had been convicted of a crime by the miscarriage of justice.

After reading Graves' note, Yvonne, during exercise, had been able to snatch a word with her fellow-convict. She had said nothing about the pardon, preferring that no one should know that she was in communication with friends outside. But the keen mind of the young woman had cleverly led the conversation around to the question of pardon, and she had made the wondering Bertha Harris promise, if she were ever pardoned, that she would ask permission to say goodbye to Yvonne. Then Yvonne would have to trust to chance and her own cleverness to devise some way of utilising Bertha's pardon for her own escape.

She knew Graves' information must be correct, and knew that even now, as she lay in her narrow cell, that Bertha Harris was probably listening to the joyous news of her pardon. Yvonne knew the frail prisoner well enough to know that with her promise still fresh in her mind, she would ask permission to bid good-bye to Yvonne, and in view of the fact that she had been wrongfully imprisoned, the prison officials were likely to be lenient.

Escape—freedom—the words beat with a sweet insistence in Yvonne's ears.

Only she—born to love freedom, knew how hard had been the weary, dreary, monotonous months of her imprisonment.

Her thoughts strayed back to sunny, blue-skied Australia, to the green-covered slopes of Binabong Station, where thousands of sheep had grazed in the shade of the giant pine and box, and where she had been so happy, riding recklessly through the paddocks, a stock-whip in her hands, and a long-haired sheep-dog at her heels.

Then sorrow had come with her father's death; but youth had healed the wound, and once again she had revelled in the joyous freedom of the paddocks.

A lump rose in her throat as the vision passed before her—the ewes nibbling at the bottom of the dried up Binabong, searching for green shoots which would make the milk for the little white lambs that hopped stiffly about in a ridiculous manner, with their still uncut tails waggling with joy in the very "living" of it all.

The vivid and picturesque language of the bullock-drivers, the hum of the shearing machines and the clean camaraderie of the men. Then had come the men who had directed the Jig Saw Mine, in which her father had held a large number of shares.

Swindled out of that, and then out of the great station, followed by her mother's death, and Yvonne went out into the world, her heart raging with a rioting inferno of black hatred and burning desire for revenge against the cowardly curs who had robbed and ruined them.

In the intensity of her desire for revenge, she had lost the clear perception of right and wrong, and what the law failed to punish she deemed right to punish herself. She had ruined Vineburg first, then Pearson, and finally, Todd; but she had broken the protective laws of society in so doing, and Sexton Blake, the guardian of those laws, had brought her career to an end.

As her life passed in quick review before her, and her thoughts reached the culmination in the narrow cell, Yvonne lifted her hands in an agony of mental suffering, and dropped them again in despair. In that moment she made her decision, and once the line was crossed she did not turn back.

With a suppressed sigh, she rose and stepped softly across the cold floor to a rude bench against the further wall. Picking up a coverless book, she sped back as the footsteps of the guard sounded, and a moment later was in her cot with the book beneath the blankets.

Once more free to move, she withdrew the book and opened it at the first of the pages she had marked earlier in the day—page 20—running her long, delicate fingers slowly down it. Half-way down her fingers stopped, and with great care she tore it straight across from the outer edge to the back.

The tear of its own accord followed a straight line, and the reason was obvious, for the page was one of the double ones containing the bulb. Between the printed sheets was concealed the finest of fine wires, and so fine was it that it yielded to every bending of the page, and unless its presence were known beforehand, not even Yvonne herself could have located it.

The tiny bulb, no larger than the head of a good-sized pin, was safely concealed where the pages were bound at the back, and Yvonne, working with extreme care, withdrew it carefully by the attached wire, and laid it on the coverlet. She repeated the operation at each page which she had marked and when the last had been finished there lay before her on the coverlet of the prison cot ten delicate, almost invisible wires, each with a tiny bulb at one end.

Drawing forth from under the pillow a small handkerchief, Yvonne, with a steady hand, lifted up the flimsy wires one by one, and with infinite care drew out the end from the tiny bulb. As each wire was withdrawn she laid the tiny bulb in the handkerchief. Dropping the last one in with its fellows, she rolled them up in the handkerchief, and worked the cloth about in her hands until a darkening stain on the white cambric told her the movement was working the fluid out from the bulbs through the tiny aperture which had been filled by the wire end.

Hardly had this been accomplished, when double footsteps sounded in the corridor outside, and Yvonne just had time to push the drug-soaked handkerchief back under the pillow, and sink back in the cot before a wardress peered through the grating.

"Are you awake, No. 1111?" she asked abruptly.

"Yes," answered Yvonne sleepily.

The rattle of keys sounded, and a moment later the cell door swung back to admit the wardress and a woman garbed in a long coat and dark hat, her features covered by a heavy veil.

"What is it?" asked Yvonne, sitting up, and apparently surprised, although her heart was beating wildly, knowing that the great moment had arrived.

"She'll tell you," jerked the wardress, nodding at the veiled visitor. "And don't be long," she added.

With this ungracious permission, the visitor threw up her veil, and, with a sob, dropped to the floor, and put her arms around Yvonne.

"Oh, my friend, my friend, I am so happy!" she sobbed. "They have discovered my innocence, and tonight my pardon came. Oh, think of it—to leave these cruel, grey walls where only you have shown me kindness!"

"I am so glad," answered Yvonne, with a soothing pat. "Of course, you were innocent, and now you will go back and take up your life just where you left off."

Yvonne hardly knew what she was saying. The wardress seemed determined to stay during the whole of the short interview, and Yvonne's head was whirling with a plan to get her out, if only for a minute.

When Bertha had fallen on the floor beside her and broke out sobbing, Yvonne's heart almost failed her, but her thoughts of the waiting motor firmed her resolve, and she comforted herself with the thought that it would only mean an extra night in the prison for Bertha at the most.

But her happy visitor was rattling on, and Yvonne brought her thoughts back with a jerk.

"Oh, I was so happy when they told me!" she was saying. "I refused to believe it, but when they took me to the office and gave me these clothes, I knew then I was free. They told me I could leave tonight if I wished, as I had never been guilty, and that a trap was waiting to take me to Daleville if I wished to go.

"They advised me as it was so stormy to wait until morning, but, oh, my friend, I must leave these horrid walls tonight! I asked permission to see you and say good-bye, for you have been kind to me."

"Can't we have five minutes alone to say good-bye?" interrupted Yvonne, turning to the wardress.

"Against orders!" snapped the wardress.

"But perhaps we won't see each other again," continued Yvonne.

And perhaps because the rough wardress had memories of her own, the plea found a hearing.

"Well," she snapped, "I'll give you three minutes, and no more! I'll stand right outside the door, so be quick."

She turned as she spoke, and passed out, almost but not quite closing the door after her.

Yvonne knew her plan had only one chance in a thousand of succeeding. The slightest noise would bring the wardress, and, besides, the end of the allotted time would bring her in any case.

But she was desperate, and even as the door closed she had grasped the startled Bertha by the throat, all the time keeping up a low, audible murmur in order to make the wardress think they were talking with each other.

She released one hand from Bertha's throat, and snatched the drug-soaked handkerchief from under the pillow. Pressing it tight against the choking woman's mouth, she held it for a few seconds until she felt the muscles relax and the body sink down.

And then Yvonne did perhaps the most risky and daring thing of her adventurous career, for be it remembered that all the time she was compelled to keep up the low murmur as though she were talking.

She worked with noiseless speed. Swiftly she removed the unconscious woman's hat and cloak, and then using all her strength, lifted her up and laid her on the cot, turning the face to the wall, and drawing the clothes up to the chin. Then, with fast-beating heart, and many nervous glances at the door, from outside of which came the noise of impatiently-dangled keys, Yvonne slipped on the coat, which came down to her feet, concealing her prison costume, and clamped on the hat, drawing the heavy veil well down over her features.

She just got the coat buttoned when she heard the wardress pushing open the door. Her heart almost stood still, for now came the awful test, and if she were discovered it would mean a further term inside the gloomy walls. But she kept her nerve, and as the wardress entered bent over the unconscious Bertha, and kissed her in order that the wardress might think it was Bertha kissing Yvonne good-bye.

With a choking sob, in order to disguise her voice, Yvonne said good-bye, and turned to follow her conductress. She put her hand to her face, and sobbed with apparent feeling as the wardress banged the cell door and turned the key.

"You must have thought a lot of her," grunted the wardress, leading the way.

Yvonne made a choking, inarticulate reply, and followed the rest of the way in silence.

She was passed along down the stairs to another wardress, and then along to the guard at the door. She breathed easier as she gained the stormy shelter of the prison courtyard, and it was hard indeed to keep from shouting aloud as the last barrier clanged behind her, and she climbed into the waiting trap.

The driver had evidently received his orders beforehand, and imagined his fare would prefer the company of her own thoughts, for beyond a cheery remark about the weather, the long, stormy drive through the blinding sleet was made in silence.

But every fresh gust of the gale was as the sweetest zephyr to Yvonne. So far, her daring plan had gone well, and it was probably on account of its very daring that it had, so far, succeeded. But she was by no means free yet. She realised that the imposture might be discovered at any moment and the chase be taken up.

"Poor Bertha!" she muttered. "How surprised she will be when she comes to in the morning. The drug will keep her unconscious for several hour's, but beyond that it will do no harm, and her freedom will only be a night longer in coming."

Every mile of the stormy way had to be fought through, and every plodding step of the powerful moor pony seemed to take an eternity to the anxious Yvonne; but at last a feeble light showed ahead, and the driver grunted "Daleville."

A quarter of an hour later, the storm-soaked outfit pulled up at the inn, and Yvonne was not surprised to see the black, shadowy bulk of a motor in the inn yard, and she noticed that it was headed toward the entrance.

With muttered thanks she slipped from the trap and made as though for the inn entrance as the driver continued on toward the stable. But her arrival had been watched for, and she stopped in the dark as two figures opened the inn door and stumbled out.

Yvonne stepped over noiselessly to where they stood peering about in the darkness.

"Is it you?" she asked in a low tone, and taking care not to mention names.

"Good heavens, Yvonne, you have succeeded!" came Graves' relieved voice. "We began to fear the night would spoil it, even if you managed to overcome the difficulties."

"It was risky, and I only just managed it. Who is with you—Captain Vaughan, or Hendricks?"

"It is I—Hendricks, came the voice of Graves' companion, the mate of Yvonne's yacht, the *Fleur-de-Lys.*

"Oh, thank you, Hendricks!" returned Yvonne. "But come, we have no time to waste; the trick may be discovered at any moment."

The three figures silently entered the waiting car, and turning the button of the self-starting attachment, and switching on the powerful road-lamps, the car crept out of the gate and turned down the moor road, being swallowed up a moment later in the blinding storm.

A hundred yards down the road the dark, bent figure of a man appeared from the side of the road and peered up at Graves.

"Are you going to try the short cut, mister, as you said?" he asked in harsh tones.

"Yes, I have decided to do so," replied Graves. "Are you sure you can conduct us through safely?"

"If I can't, no one can," growled the misshapen figure in the road. "I've lived on this moor for forty years, and I can find my way about blindfold. But come on, mister, if you're coming." And, so saying, he turned and sped on ahead, Graves driving carefully in his tracks.

"Who is that, uncle?" asked Yvonne.

"It is a moor shepherd I hired to guide us across the moor in case of pursuit. He knows every foot, and it will cut off sixteen miles. No one would dream you would risk crossing the moor on a night like this, and we want to make the yacht by daybreak."

The dark, bent figure turned off as Graves finished speaking and took to the moor, and from then on silence reigned, for it needed every faculty to keep the car from plunging into some of the abounding morasses.

If Nature had raged about Dalemoor Prison earlier in the evening, it redoubled its efforts now, after an apparent rest to recoup its strength and bring up reinforcements. Battalions seemed to come from every point of the compass, combining with all their strength to beat down the creeping resistance of the powerful motor.

Regiments of driving rain and howling gusts of wind joined forces in the attack, beating down with a blinding, whirling force, but without success.

YVONNE'S ESCAPE.
On crept the lurching car, following the hopping, misshapen figure in front.

The moor was a sodden black stretch, without mark and without direction; but on crept the lurching car, following the hopping, misshapen guide, the heavy, splashing rain obscuring their tracks almost as soon as they were made.

Two hours later the guide stopped at the edge of the moor, beside a rain-washed road, and the car pulled up, its occupants relieved at the sight of a highway.

Graves bent down and lifted a small bag, which chinked as he passed it over to the drenched misshapen man.

"Twenty sovereigns—all gold!" he jerked. "Don't forget your promise."

"Don't worry, mister," answered the guide, grasping the bag eagerly. "I don't git twenty sovereigns every day, I'll say nothing."

"All right. I depend on you not to," replied Graves. And as the misshapen figure hopped away, and was swallowed up in the storm and blackness of the moor, Graves again started the car.

***

Four hours later, when the storm seemed to have drawn off in angry defeat, the powerful mud-coated car, which had pounded its way for many miles in the teeth of the gale, pulled up at the top of a hill, and coasted slowly down under the cautious pressure of the brakes, stopping at the bottom on a thin stretch of gravelly beach, on which the rain-conquered waves rolled in white-fringed monotony.

Out from the beach, riding out the gale under double cables, was a small ship, the lines visible under her many lights proving her to be a yacht.

Hendricks sprang out, and, drawing an electric-torch, waved it back and forth. An answering light came from the yacht, followed a few minutes later by the sound of oars. A wide, shallow, raft-like boat, propelled by six sailors, grounded gently on the beach.

Two broad gangways were swung out on to the beach, up which Graves drove the car, stopping carefully in the centre of the deck, and clamping on the emergency brake in order to lock the wheels.

The gangways were swung back, the oars thrust out, and the boat headed for the yacht. There, boat, car, and occupants were swung to the deck by a silent electric derrick, and preparations were made at once to weigh anchor and depart.

After changing to dry garments Yvonne returned to the luxurious saloon, where jubilant but subdued cheers were given for the success of her daring escape.

Every man aboard, from the captain to the cook's boy, was filled with a deep regard for their mistress, and her fairness and loyalty at all times had gone deep in their hearts.

Consequently the ship's crew were joyously excited at the return of their daring leader, and it was a jubilant company which headed south as a stormy dawn broke over the now choppy seas.

The papers contained vivid accounts of the daring escape of Mademoiselle Yvonne. Some tried to hint that Bertha Harris, the pardoned prisoner, was an accessory, but the poor woman's innocence was obvious, and her release duly followed the following day.

And up in his rooms in Baker Street, Sexton Blake read and pondered, a grim smile playing about his mouth.

End of the prologue

The First Chapter
Beneath the Pyramids

ON a December day, some ten months after, the momentary flutter caused by the escape from prison of the famous adventuress, Mademoiselle Yvonne, when Egypt was invaded by sun-seeking tourists and England lay wrapped in fog, the streets of Cairo presented a vivid, bustling picture of rioting dirt and colour, squalid natives and opulent visitors, for the steamer had just come in, bringing its medley of tourists returning from the Third Cataract and the Assouan Dam, and officials from Khartoum, weary from the initial railway journey across the dust-driven desert.

Here and there a bearded sheikh, with sombre eyes, shouldered his disdainful way with a barely-veiled look of contempt for the chattering tourists.

Down the gangway poured a Cook's party, in the wake of which strutted a dignified dragoman, his capacious body clothed in vivid purple and scarlet. A few more seasoned travellers lounged in satiated indolence against the rail of the steamer, waiting until the crush should thin. From the shore came the nasal accent of Chicago the dominating cockney of London, the expressive gesticulations of Paris, and the guttural snort of Berlin.

Jammed together in a shrieking pandemonium of lying insistence were the donkey-boys, each and all calling upon Allah to witness that no such beast ever existed as the scraggy, listless donkey which was his. Persevering peddlers pressed on the already lumbered tourists handfuls of scarabs of wondrous age, but in reality manufactured in Manchester.

As the jumbled mass finally settled into its component parts, and betook themselves to the celebrated Shepheard's Hotel[11] or the Pyramids; as the Arab sheikhs faded away into the desert; as the deepening blue changed to the purple of night, and the day-whitened moon turned to gold, throwing back against the darkening west the clear-cut silhouette of the slender minarets and bulky circle of the mosque domes, a momentary hush fell as across the heavy Eastern-scented air came the deep tones of the muezzin calling the faithful to prayer.

As the last deep tones echoed away into the deepening night, a man and woman leisurely descended from the steamer and took their way through the narrow streets with the certainty of familiarity.

Direct to Shepheard's Hotel they went, and evidently they were expected, for even as they drank refreshing tea at a small table in the garden an obsequious Arab approached and handed a letter to the man.

Opening it, he read the contents, and passed it to the woman.

"Akbad has wasted no time," he remarked. "Do you feel well enough, Yvonne, to meet him this evening, or shall I send a messenger postponing it?"

"Oh, no, uncle!" replied Yvonne, in a slightly tired tone. "I feel a bit fagged after the steamer, but we must lose no time."

Graves nodded as he lit a cigarette.

"I'll go and arrange about horses. They will be more comfortable than donkeys. Will you wait here?"

"Yes! Don't be too long."

With another nod Graves sauntered away, while Yvonne leaned back and closed her eyes, breathing in with slow enjoyment the sweet-scented air.

Ever since her remarkable escape from Dalemoor Prison, Yvonne, under the care of her luxury-loving uncle, had sauntered by slow stages up and down Egypt.

A perfect student of Arabic language and customs, and a keen authority on Egyptology, she had loitered with a rare enjoyment among the ancient ruins, and in a simple hide tent had lived the desert life of untrammelled freedom and vast expanse.

But aside from this, she had loitered through Egypt and the desert for a twofold reason—viz., to get back her health and to make a radical change in her appearance.

Such a change would be very necessary if she were to anticipate the future with any degree of safety, and that change, with her usual thoroughness, had been accomplished in the lonely desert.

---

[11] Shepheard's Hotel was the leading hotel in Cairo and one of the most celebrated hotels in the world from the middle of the 19th century until its destruction in 1952 during the Cairo Fire.

There the heavy hair of burnished bronze had been changed to black, the deep eyes dyed to a morning blue, a slight change made in the contour of the face—a change which had taken months to produce—and heavy, black-arched brows.

Nature and art had been combined by her inimitable powers, and the result was a still beautiful, but radically different appearing woman. Graves had grown a beard of pointed silver, and the loitering, wealthy Justin Grantley and his beautiful niece seemed far removed indeed from the once famous Graves and Yvonne.

But Yvonne's change in appearance had not changed her nature, and during her desert sojourn her brilliant brain had been busy with plans for the future—plans which included the unswerving carrying-out of her sworn revenge.

She had been in constant communication with her agents. Captain Vaughan, and the crew of her yacht the *Fleur-de-Lys*, had steamed back and forth many times between Egypt and England on her commissions.

A thorough campaign of inquiry had discovered the whereabouts of Kelly—one of the men who had ruined Yvonne and her mother in Australia, and whose name was next on the list for revenge.

For some months her information had told her he was now a prosperous City man—in five years risen from a commission pigmy to a financial giant. Ever since she had discovered him her agents had watched his every move, and even the clerk who footed up his ledger was an agent of Yvonne's.

A month ago she had got wind of an important deal which was to come off soon, and, one of her Arab agents informing her further in the matter, she had decided to make a first more.

Some two years previously, after a sweeping victory on the Stock Exchange, from which he had emerged dripping with quickly-filched profits, Kelly had made a short time loan of exactly two hundred thousand pounds[12] in cash to a Cairo banking firm who were financing extensive operations near Khartoum.

Yvonne had become aware of this, and also that repayment would shortly be made to Kelly's agents, who were coming secretly to Egypt to receive it, and personally guard it on its journey to England. For gold was "tight" on the London money-market, and Kelly, shrewd as always, had taken advantage of a clause in the loan contract and stipulated repayment in gold.

Akbad, an Arab clerk in the Cairo banking firm, had yielded either to the charm of her persuasion or the love of her gold, and had become a valuable agent. It was his note which had been handed to Graves, and which had appointed a meeting on the edge of the desert.

It was these thoughts of the past months that drifted through Yvonne's mind as she drank in the languorous Eastern night, and so absorbed was she that Graves' returning steps failed to rouse her from her reverie.

"Everything is ready. I have secured two horses, and if you will change your costume we can get away immediately."

---

[12] £200,000 in 1913 is worth about £23,300,000 in 2020

Yvonne opened her eyes as his words roused her, and with a nod of acquiescence rose and departed for her apartments.

Graves met her on her return a few minutes later garbed in a neat, divided skirt, and, springing up with the ease of the born rider who had spent years in the saddle, she cantered on ahead, leading the way, every foot of which was familiar to her.

Through the narrow streets they went, the whitened houses looking ghostly beautiful in the play of light and shadow under the sailing silver moon. Out past the towering Pyramids and the crouching Sphinx they rode, setting the horses into a flying gallop as they gained the moon-splashed desert. They covered several miles before a motionless horse and rider appeared silhouetted against the line where sky and desert met.

They drew up beside the flowing-robed rider, who bowed silently and awaited for Yvonne to speak, which she did with her usual directness, using pure Arabic which brought a gleam of appreciation to the deep-set eyes of the dusky horseman.

"Your note says you have important news, Akbad. I trust it is good!"

"Whether it is good or bad only Allah can tell," replied the Arab, in deep, vibrant tones. "It is news which will please; but Akbad sees difficulty and danger."

"That is to be expected and to be risked," returned Yvonne, her eyes sweeping the desert as she spoke. "Failure or success, Akbad, follows everything, and either way one can only say Kismet—it is Fate! But tell me just what you have discovered."

"I have discovered that the information you have is correct. My people repay the loan in pure gold. The English *effendi* sends his agents in twelve days' time to receive it—all packed and sealed with the seal of my people."

"Ah!" breathed Yvonne, her eyes gleaming. "What else, Akbad?"

"It will be packed in boxes of wood," went on the deep tones of the Arab. "Five thousand[13] of the English pounds in each box—forty boxes in all. The weight I have estimated, and find it will be almost a hundred of your commercial pounds to each box. The exact sizes of the boxes I have not yet discovered, but tomorrow will do so."

"Good, Akbad! You have indeed done well, and your reward will be large. Can you at the same time secure an exact impression of the seal which will be used? Time is precious!"

"Yes, my lady, Akbad will do so, and at the same time discover the other details."

"That will be well, Akbad," replied Yvonne. "And now we will return—moon-mad tourists may wander past. Tomorrow night here at the same time," she added, turning her horse, followed by Graves, who, ignorant of Arabic, had been a silent spectator.

"*Inshallah!*"[14] replied Akbad, turning in the opposite direction, and the three horses were soon flying away, over the silent, shimmering desert.

---

[13] £5,000 in 1913 is worth about £580,800.00 in 2020

[14] Inshallah: Allah willing

The Second Chapter
"All is Not Gold That Glitters!"

UP in a dim sitting-room of Shepheard's Hotel, the shutters closed to keep at bay the early afternoon sun under which Cairo was broiling, sat Yvonne, Graves, and Captain Vaughan—the latter evidently just arrived, from his heat-flushed countenance and travel-stained linen garments. All three were puffing the eternal Egyptian cigarette, Yvonne's being a tiny, scented variety of her own special choosing.

She looked immaculately dainty and supremely cool as she lounged negligently in a low wicker-chair, a perfect foil of slim white to the shrouded green of the room. Graves, in thin tropical grey, was the picture of content, his languid gaze following the slow twistings of the smoke from his cigarette, and his whole attitude contrasting in a marked manner with the more vigorous pose of the energetic captain.

Yvonne was speaking in low, decisive tones, and the care with which her two hearers followed her every word showed the value past experiences had attached to her decisions.

"I think," she said, "that things will go through without a hitch. Of course, there is a big element of danger in making the transfer of the gold, but that is a risk which must be taken. Now let us go carefully over every point so that we all clearly understand the situation in order that no mistakes may arise.

"If present arrangements are carried out, the forty boxes of gold, containing five thousand sovereigns each, will be despatched under the seal of the Khartoum and River Nile Banking Co. to England. Forty duplicate boxes, bound and sealed but filled with lead, will leave under the rather ostentatious guard of the English agents for Alexandria; but the real gold will be quietly despatched under the guard of four trusted Arab police by rail for Port Said.

"There it will be transferred to a truck and taken to the docks, where it will be again transferred to a large felucca, which has already been secured to take it out to the P. & O. mailboat, which will leave at once for England as soon as the gold is aboard. You understand this clearly?"

Both men nodded silently; and Yvonne, lighting a fresh cigarette, continued:

"I will now go over my part, and then you can repeat yours. Firstly, the forty exact duplicate boxes which I have had made from the designs and measurements furnished by Akbad, and which are now aboard the yacht, will be transferred tomorrow to the felucca or lighter; and you, captain, be sure to have them piled carefully along one side under the deck, and cover them with a heavy tarpaulin. The Arab boatman will remain aboard the felucca, according to the arrangements you made with him when you bribed him, until I, disguised as an Arab boatman, shall arrive.

"I will then take charge of the felucca with four of the yacht's sailors disguised as Arabs, and await the arrival of the gold.

"The train will arrive about midnight, but it will be near one by the time the gold arrives at the dock. When it is transferred to the boat, the four disguised sailors will stow it under the deck on the opposite side from the duplicate boxes.

"There will lie the only danger of discovery, for if the Arab guards should descend below the deck to watch the stowing, they would discover the ruse; but it is hardly likely that will happen.

"I and the sailors, with the guards, scull the felucca out to the P. & O. boat and deliver it over to the purser. It will be risky work delivering over the lead-filled boxes, but if they lower a net, which I hope they will, the purser will not board us. I then return with the guards to the shore, and after dropping them off and waiting until they get away, scull out to the yacht, which will be anchored near at hand.

"We then transfer the real gold to the yacht, and scuttle the felucca, after which we will get under weigh, and drop the Arab boatman off at Alexandria on our way to England. I think that takes in every detail, but if there is any point which you do not understand, mention it now."

"It's all clear, Yvonne," remarked Graves, while the captain nodded. "Captain Vaughan and I are to remain aboard the yacht, and keep an eye out in case of trouble. If anything occurs we are to lower a boat, and make for the lighter. But it seems to me you are taking a big risk by yourself."

Captain Vaughan endorsed Graves' remark with a blunt rumble, but Yvonne waved her hand with decision:

"It is the only way. I speak Arabic like a native; and, besides, if I am there, accidents won't be so likely to happen. If the guards discover the ruse—well, I'll have the four sailors, and we'll knock their dusky heads together. Now, captain, you look dusty and tired, and I think a nap would refresh you. You, uncle, take yourself off! I know you're dying to show off that beard to some of the charming tourists."

"By George," grinned Graves, "I'd have grown one ages ago if I had known how handsome I would look! I heard that sweet-voiced Chicago woman with the glasses and the retroussé nose whisper to her daughter in an aside which could be heard for half a mile that she 'just loved those handsome aristocratic-looking Britishers', meaning me!"

"You ought to be flattered," laughed Yvonne. "From what I remember of the lady, she weighed about fifteen stone, and her retroussé nose seemed to point with chronic perseverance towards the sky. She was the one, I believe, who asked the dragoman if he thought Caesar was jealous of Antony, and didn't he think Cleopatra was fickle?"

"Yes; I heard her," laughed Graves. "The dragoman said he couldn't tell her, as, unfortunately, he wasn't alive then."

The captain chuckled as he rose, with a seaman's appreciation of the joke, and, with Graves, departed, leaving Yvonne to complete her arrangements.

The average individual would have picked the two men and the charming Yvonne as the last people to take to a criminal life, and had they been informed that the slim slip of a woman directed one of the most daring criminal organisations in Europe, they would have scoffed incredulously.

But, mistaken as was her point of view, Yvonne felt justified in her revenge, on society in general and the men who had swindled her mother and herself in particular, for the blackness of her life.

Sexton Blake, long ago, had pointed out her misconception of things, for he had seen then that such a life, while perhaps giving her momentary revenge, would make it impossible for her to enjoy the things really worthwhile and which a young woman of her beauty and talents should have.

Had he been able to return the love which the young woman had for him, perhaps her life might have been different. But, though he had a deep admiration for the native goodness in her, and of which she undoubtedly had a large element, he could not care for her in any deeper fashion, and it was one of the strange rulings of Fate that he, the one man she cared for, should be the one whose mission it was to track her down and thwart her plans, and through whose instrumentality she had been sent to Dalemoor Prison for five years.

Captain Vaughan, wrongfully cast out of the passenger service, was filled with somewhat similar feelings of bitterness towards the world; and Graves, luxury-loving, ease-seeking, and always impecunious, drifted along, care-free and happy, dominated by Yvonne's personality.

Such made up the leading spirits of Yvonne's famous circle which the British and Continental police flattered themselves had been buried in the limbo of the past, but which, phoenix-like, had risen from the ashes of Yvonne's escape.

On the following night a party of four Britishers, dressed in rather exaggerated tourist costume, pulled up a large motor in a narrow lane at the back of the offices of the Khartoum and River Nile Banking Co.

A series of mysterious precautions, almost too elaborate for a secret mission, followed their stoppage. The back door of the bank swung open, and from the blackness of the interior a dusky Arab face peered out. Sign and countersign, and from the bank was thrust a small, heavy box, which found its way to the bottom of the capacious tonneau. Another followed, and another, until forty in all had been piled in the car.

The door closed, the four tourist-clad figures scrambled in, and the car slowly glided off on its journey to Alexandria with its supposed burden of gold, which in reality was common unromantic lead.

Two hours later a rough-looking mule-drawn dray, driven by a ragged *fellah* (native), entered the narrow lane, and pulled up in the identical spot where the car had rested so recently. A soft knock caused the door to swing open once more, but this time no sign and countersign were given.

Four shadowy figures in the uniform of Arab police slipped out and took their places on the dray. Two more rapidly carried out and carefully piled on it forty more of the small, heavy iron-hooped boxes, exactly similar to the first lot. A rough tarpaulin was throw over them, the *fellah* clambered up, and the door softly closed.

Down narrow streets lined with shuttered houses, through silent plazas, from which could be seen the sails of the *dahabeeahs* hanging slack in the motionless night air which hung heavy over the ancient Nile, winding through and back again until the railway was reached, went the dray.

Here it backed up against a small baggage carriage, the date of whose origin was lost in the dim past, and as silently as they had been loaded, the forty little boxes full of precious golden tiers were unloaded and piled up in the carriage. A soft call, the appearance of a railway official, swinging a lantern, the shuffling footsteps of the four Arab police, as, with trailing rifles, they took their places on the boxes of gold, and the small, puffing, spluttering engine pulled out with its precious freight for the short run to Port Said.

Port Said lay almost silent under the dimming light of the sinking moon. Light-filled palaces of music and gambling—beautiful on the surface, but barren of good as Dead Sea fruit—still kept open. Further down, in the native quarter, where all the scoundrels and riffraff of the Mediterranean foregathered, silent darkness and sinister shadow reigned, no visible token showing of the teeming, skulking life which, night-born and night-bred, sought the shadows and the burrows.

Out in the roadstead, looking abnormally large in the slanting rays of the moon, rode a huge P. & O. liner homeward bound. Further along, riding with dainty grace, was a rakish white yacht, her awninged decks silent.

Just swinging out for the canal was a luxurious Orient liner resuming her long voyage to Australia, while here and there, with slow-moving oars and an occasional "*Allah, haly 'm, alla-haly!*"—sing-song of native boatmen and rivermen—were small craft of every size and shape, the felucca predominating.

Over in the shadow of the shore rested other craft—some empty, some with crew stretched out under the silver sky, but all were devoid of movement. All? No; not all, for in one, fairly large, with lowered sail and hatch opened deck, sat five dark figures in the garb of Arab boatmen. Four lounged amidships and the fifth, lithe and slim, smoked silently in the stern The silence was suddenly broken by the faint creak of wheels, followed by the padding footsteps of animals' feet and the soft, cursing voice of a native driver.

Louder grew the noise, coming straight to the water's edge. From the building-shadowed road appeared a loaded dray covered with a tarpaulin, on top of which lounged four Arab police with carelessly tossed rifles. It pulled up beside the moorings of the large felucca containing the lounging figures, and a guttural Arab voice descended.

A clear, low answer in water-front Arabic went up from the figure in the stern, and as it did so two of the men amidships dropped through the hatch, while the other pair reached up for the small boxes which comprised the dray's load.

Short work was made of the loading, and as the last box was passed through the dark hatch the four Arab police dropped to the deck and squatted down with a sigh of relief. The two men below the deck emerged, and, getting out oars, the four boatmen pushed off and headed over the placid, star-spattered water for the imposing bulk of the homeward-bound P. & O.

The nose of the felucca struck softly against the side. A hail in English came from above followed by the clanking of the winch. Out from the deck swung a large net which dropped slowly to the deck of the felucca. Once again the two boatmen disappeared through the hatch, and passed up to their two companions forty small iron-bound boxes, apparently the same which had been loaded a few moments before.

Into the net they were piled, and not one of the Arab police noticed that the two men below were working on a different side of the boat. The winch creaked again, and the "precious" load soared up and disappeared over the rail. A rope ladder was then dropped over, and one of the police scrambled up to get his receipt.

Even as he returned the huge liner began to churn up the water, and she was getting slowly under way as the little felucca was propelled slowly shorewards.

With a muttered "Allah be with you!" the police swung up from the boat to the waiting dray, and the four boatmen and silent figure in the stern lit cigarettes and lounged, without speaking, until the creaking of the dray had passed away and the lights of the moving steamer blended with the low-hanging stars.

Then, and not till then, did the figure in the stern sit up and rap out a command in English, the low tones being those of Yvonne—her identity a perfect concealment in her ragged clothes and darkened skin.

Once more the felucca headed out over the water, this time stopping on the further side of the rakish yacht. A soft hail brought an answer, followed by the almost noiseless hum of an electric winch. A net swung over the side, into which were piled forty boxes exactly similar to those just delivered to the P. & O. boat. A rope-ladder was lowered, but before ascending, one of the Arab-clothed sailors dropped through the hatch. A soft knocking sound came from below, followed by the rushing intake of water as the plugs were drawn. Up the ladder scrambled Yvonne, followed by the four disguised sailors, and barely had they gained the deck when the felucca began to settle down.

Yvonne dropped to the deck with a soft laugh.

"Well, uncle, there wasn't a hitch," she laughed. "The Arabs never suspected a thing, and everyone is quite certain that the P. & O. is taking to England a most valuable consignment of gold."

"By Jove! There will be an awful rumpus over this," grinned Graves admiringly. "Two hundred thousand in beautiful sovereigns! Yvonne, you are a wonder!"

"It wasn't done badly," she confessed. "As you say, Mr. Kelly will raise Europe over it. But what good will it do?" she said, with an expressive shrug of her shoulders. "In five minutes the felucca will be at the bottom, and her owner will be dropped by us in Alexandria, where he will soon be lost among his kind.

"Kelly will think a mistake has occurred, and that the gold has gone to Alexandria instead. It will be at least two weeks before they discover the Alexandria boxes contain lead also, and another two weeks before the police can have completed an examination. Every movement of the gold can be accounted for from the time it left Cairo until the boxes were delivered aboard the steamer. Who will ever discover forty other boxes waited in the felucca? No one. Voila, and there you are! And now I must change. Tell Captain Vaughan to get under way for Alexandria. Good-night!"

With another laugh Yvonne slipped away to her cosy cabin, while Graves ascended to the bridge where Captain Vaughan lounged, smoking.

A few minutes later the yacht slowly glided over the darkening waters, the moon having dropped away, the stars blazing out in low-hung clusters as their conquering rival dipped below the horizon.

Over the tropic waters into the hot, desert-scented night went the *Fleur-de-Lys*, with her cheerful, lawless company, and two hundred thousand pounds in illicit gold.

The Third Chapter
Sexton Blake Receives an Urgent Call—Puzzled

I MUST confess it is a most mysterious disappearance, Mr. Kelly."

Sexton Blake leaned back in his chair, and pressed the tips of his fingers together, the while his brow wrinkled in puzzled thought.

In answer to an urgent message from Gorgon Kelly, commonly dubbed the "Money King," he had cancelled an appointment of no great importance.

The wealthy and influential financier had lost no time in following the message, and had plunged at once, on his arrival at Baker Street, into the details of a story which had caused Blake's remark.

"Now let me run over the points I have gathered from your remarks," went on Blake; "and if there is any discrepancy, let me know. Briefly, I gather from what you say that these are the facts:

"The Khartoum and River Nile Banking Co. of Cairo, borrowed two hundred thousand pounds from you some few months ago, for the purpose of financing certain operations near Khartoum."

"Yes," answered the magnate. "They were going to advertise the loan for public subscription, but I had the ready amount at the time, and as Egyptian credit is exceptionally good, at present, I offered to take the whole thing myself—which offer they accepted."

"I see," said Blake. "Then, I understand that the loan contract contained a clause saying that when the loan was repaid it must, should you so specify, be paid in gold."

Kelly nodded.

"Owing to the fact that gold was in great demand, you took advantage of this clause, and arranged to send your own men to Egypt to bring the gold back to England."

"Quite right!"

"Then on account of the recent operations of certain Continental criminals, you deemed it advisable to have two lots of boxes made, forty in each lot, and each box an exact duplicate of the other. Into one lot the gold was to be packed, and the other lot was to contain lead. The lot containing lead were to be shipped as a bluff to Alexandria from Cairo, so that if any criminals intended to make an attempt to rescue the gold they would naturally think the lead-filled boxes contained the metal, and if they succeeded in getting them would get nothing for their pains. Then the forty boxes containing the actual gold were to be quietly shipped to Port Said, and transferred there to a P. & O. liner to be brought to England.

"These plans you followed out, but when the forty boxes which the P. & O. boat brought were opened, and which should have contained the gold, you discovered they contained only lead. Then, thinking there had been a mistake in Cairo, and that the gold-filled boxes had been sent to Alexandria, you cabled there and had them opened. They also contained nothing but lead. Am I quite right?"

"Quite, Mr. Blake," growled the Money King. "What on earth has happened, I don't know! I've sent reams of cables to the Khartoum and River Nile Banking Co., in Cairo, and they can prove that everything was all right when it left their offices, for the manager himself checked the gold into the boxes, and was there when the dummy boxes were sent to Alexandria, and the real boxes were sent to Port Said."

"H'm! It is quite evident," remarked Blake, "that the repayment was known about, and watched for, and that some time was spent in making forty more boxes exactly similar in every respect to the originals. That presupposes access to the affairs of the Khartoum and River Nile Banking Co., but it is at present difficult to see where the transfer took place. However, I will take up the case, Mr. Kelly, and begin investigations at once. I will take a run out to Cairo, and start there, my ostensible character being that of an English tourist. If you will give me a confidential letter to the manager of the Khartoum and River Nile Banking Co., I might find it of use."

"Very well, Mr. Blake," answered Kelly, a look of relief spreading over his features, "I will send my clerk right along with one when I get back to the office. I needn't say that this loss in hard cash is heavy even to me at the moment. We financiers can make and lose large fortunes on paper without any appreciable effect on our business, but when good, hard sovereigns are lost it is a different tale. I might add that I wish your investigations to be unknown; business reasons, you know!" He laughed.

"Very well, Mr. Kelly," replied Blake, rising. "That will suit me also. I prefer to work without publicity."

The letter promised by the magnate came an hour later, and Blake rang for Mrs. Bardell to pack his bags.

Tinker, who had been out on an investigation for Blake, came in during the afternoon, with Pedro at his heels, and looked questioningly at Blake's evident arrangements for a journey.

"Something new on, guv'nor?" he asked.

Blake, who was writing, swung round.

"Yes, Tinker. It's rather a mysterious case, originating in Egypt."

"Somebody's mummy been stolen?" grinned the lad.

"Worse than that," smiled Blake. He then gave Tinker an inkling of the facts, and the lad's eyes opened.

"Two hundred thousand! That's a great haul, guv'nor. Have you any suspicions?"

"Not yet, my lad," replied Blake. "I can tell better when I get to Cairo. At present, although the affair was undoubtedly planned for and arranged in Egypt, I rather incline to the theory that the actual exchange was made either on board the steamer or in London.

"But, of course, that is merely a tentative theory, and the journey from Cairo to Port

Said, where the gold was loaded, has to be accounted for. But I will go deeper into the theory on my return. While I am away I want you to look after things here and make quiet investigations in London. Find out who were passengers on the P. & O. boat.

"Have a talk with the purser. Get him to give you an account of every movement of the gold after he received it aboard, and have your report ready for me when I return."

"Right, guv'nor; I will. How long will you be?"

"Oh, not over two weeks, I expect! I will travel overland to Naples, and catch the boat there for Alexandria. That will save time and will get me back in London soon again."

Blake caught the Continental express that night at Charing Cross, and travelled by quick stages, arriving in Cairo a few days later. He sent a code message to Tinker announcing his arrival, and then, in his character of an English tourist, betook himself to the offices of the Khartoum and River Nile Banking Company.

Blake's first desire was to get a look at all the employees of the banking firm, for, without doubt, one of them had supplied particulars of the boxes to the authors of the theft.

Kalin Pasha, the head of the firm, expressed the customary Oriental desire to afford any and all assistance to the detective. He regretted exceedingly the loss sustained by Gorgon Kelly: but of one thing he was positive—the gold was all correct when it left Cairo. But when Blake suggested that designs of the boxes must have been furnished by some of his clerks, Kahin Pasha threw up his hands.

"I won't say they did, and I won't say they didn't," he said suavely, "But it would be as easy to locate the guilty one among a staff of Arabs, Mr. Blake, as to locate the famous needle, which you English say was lost in the—what do you say—ah, yes, the haystack. Find the people who got the gold, Mr. Blake, then you can work down to the Arab clerk who supplied the designs. But if you remain here until you find the clerk first, you will spend many months, perhaps years."

Blake doggedly persisted, however, in his Egyptian investigations.

Sitting in his room of Shepheard's Hotel smoking furiously, he made attempts after attempt to reconstruct the theft.

And the coincidence was that, in that very same room Yvonne had a short time previously explained, the details of the theft to Graves and Captain Vaughan. But that fact did Blake no good at the present juncture, and he confessed to himself, as he pondered, that the case was one of the most baffling nature.

He journeyed to Port Said, going over every step of the gold's journey from Cairo to the steamer. His searching investigations among the boatmen along the waterfront yielded him nothing, and as he returned to Cairo, absolutely barren of any clue, he confessed that Kalin Pasha's advice bore an element of truth.

If the gold was transferred before it left Port Said, he argued that the only point at which an opportunity would occur was either when unloaded from the train or transferred at the dock. But of any information to strengthen that theory Blake had got none, and he packed his bags in keen disappointment for the return trip to London.

He was in an irritable mood on his arrival, and Tinker's failure to discover anything during his absence did not lighten it any.

He spent long hours pondering over the matter and marshalling up the facts, but for once he could find no thread which would connect up a theory.

"It's one of those cases similar to the Vienna diamond robbery five years ago," he muttered; "carefully planned and faultlessly executed. Not the ghost of a clue to work on, and if it follows the same parallel, there won't be for some time. But it will come. It may be weeks, it may be months; but eventually a clue will turn up. It may be picked up through the execution of another crime—probably will be; and for the present all I can do is to sit tight and watch every ripple, no matter how insignificant."

Blake was right in his theory. It was to be some time before anything turned up to give him a clue, and the length of time would mean immunity from detection in most cases.

But whether a week, a month, or years, Sexton Blake would still have every fact in his mind, ready to seize on the slightest sign and build up his case.

That faculty of the great detective's was the reason of the fear he inspired, for a criminal who had once experienced the consequences of Sexton Blake's investigations, knew to his cost the deductive and constructive faculty of that brilliant mind.

The Fourth Chapter
Detective Grieg Makes a Discovery—The "Money King" Proposes

YOU'RE so mysterious, Arthur, I'm really quite curious."

Marian Powers, the young woman who spoke the words, leaned back in her chair as she drew off her gloves, her blue eyes and delicately-chiselled lips smiling at the young man seated opposite, with the frankness of perfect understanding.

They sat at a small corner table in a well-known little restaurant not a hundred miles from the Bank, and, from the smiling greeting of the neat waitress, were evidently well-known and well-liked customers.

From all around came the subdued rattle of dishes and silver, interspersing the strains of a popular waltz from an orchestra in a nearby alcove.

For several months had Marian Powers and Arthur Bentwood, the frank-faced young man opposite her, been lunching regularly at the same table.

Marian, after the death of her father and the resultant barrenness of his estate, had been forced to take up secretarial work, and, through the influence of friends and her own ability, at present held the position of private secretary to Gorgon Kelly, the City magnate.

Arthur Bentwood, chief clerk of Wallingford & Co., the well-known members of the Stock Exchange, had met Marian several months previously at some amateur theatricals, and, following up with laudable perseverance an instantaneous admiration, had contrived to arrange a daily lunch together.

Marian had started and kept their friendship on the basis of pure camaraderie, and the luncheon arrangement had been consented to only on the understanding that at the end of each week Arthur accepted from her the exact amount of her weekly lunches. Her threat otherwise to lunch alone had perforce caused his surrender to her conditions, and from that time not a day had been missed.

For some time Arthur had been hopelessly and completely in love with his fair comrade; but if she felt anything more than friendship on her part, she certainly contrived to conceal it admirably.

Never before had she seen him lacking in perfect sangfroid; but on the day in question, his nervous and mysterious actions, his changing colour, his starting of a remark and abrupt breaking off, his avoidance of her eyes—all these unusual signs had puzzled her and elicited her bantering remark.

Arthur went a sudden deep crimson as he met her smiling eyes, and again he looked away in a panic.

"I—er—I—er—I—er," he spluttered—"er—Marian, I—er——"

"The waitress is waiting for your order, Arthur," she said hastily, laughing outright at his fresh confusion as he looked up and saw the waiting young woman.

What he ordered he couldn't have told a moment after, and as the young woman hurried away he turned again to Marian.

"I—er—I—er——"

"You have told me fully half a dozen times, Arthur, that you 'er.' But is that supposed to be unique?" laughed Marian. "We all err, don't we?"

"Oh, hang it all, Marian! You're tormenting me purposely. I—er——"

But he was forced to join in her laugh of soft merriment as he again stuttered out the idiotic words.

But he was getting desperate. Time was passing quickly, and sharp on the three-quarters Marian would hasten back to her work, and his chance would be gone, for he was leaving for Liverpool that evening on business for Wallingford & Co. Taking the bit in his teeth, Arthur leaned over and spoke with the desperation of a man who had only a few moments to live.

As the young woman heard the tense words and looked into his face, the bantering smile left her face and the blue eyes dropped, the while she pulled nervously at her gloves.

"Tell me, Marian," he said, as he finished—"tell me—is there any hope for me? Can you return my love, Marian?"

"I—I'm afraid I can't, Arthur," she murmured softly, her eyes still down.

"Oh, Marian!" he almost groaned. "I—I'm sorry if I have hurt you. Forgive me, but can you tell me why you can't return my love?"

"It—it is because I want it for myself, Arthur," she answered, her eyes glancing up shyly at him.

His hands clenched with the exquisite pain of the reaction, and his voice came in an unsteady whisper.

"Oh, Marian!" he breathed, with a whole world of relief and tumultuous joy in the words.

And over the rest of the short luncheon hour which remained to the happy couple, no one else existed for them but each other, and when the clock pointed to the three-quarters, Marian dutifully rose, but with flushed cheeks and shining eyes, for is anything sweeter to a woman's soul than the adoring, whispered phrases of the one man in all the world?

Arthur told her, with joyous words, how for months he had loved her, but had refrained from speaking because his salary would not permit marriage. But now things were different. His firm had made immense profits lately on Argentines, American Rails, and several other speculative issues, and Mr. Wallingford himself had told Arthur to buy.

He had done so in a moderate way, and his profits had piled up into a tidy little sum. On top of this, Mr. Wallingford had told him he was to be admitted as junior partner on the first of the following month, and the bright future was only possible with Marian to share it.

"How strange, Arthur, that you should have made your money in those stocks."

"Why strange, dear?" he asked, in surprise. "Why those more than any others?"

"Oh, nothing!" she replied, "But it is all right to speak of it now that the movement is all over. Those stocks were the same ones Mr. Kelly was 'bulling' some time ago."

"I know," grinned Arthur. "We got in first every time, and your sweet-tempered employer was hopping with rage. I'm blest if I know how Mr. Wallingford got the tip, but get it he did, and acted on it before Kelly did."

"It's curious," remarked Marian; "but let us not talk of business, Arthur; you know we have both tabooed any mention of it from our conversation."

"Right-ho!" he smiled. "Hang business today, I say. I'd much rather have you tell me something else once more. Tell me now," he added, in mock severity, "do you?"

"Do I—do I what, Arthur?" inquired Marian innocently; but he had his answer in the pressure of her little hand on his arm.

The happy, self-engrossed pair, talked along until they reached the imposing entrance of the Equidential Building, where Gorgon Kelly had his luxurious offices. Here, with a quick pressure of the hand, and a soft look as she told him to hurry back from Liverpool, and that the three days of his trip would be lonely ones to her, Marian tripped through the door, and entered the lift.

Neither of them saw the little, shabby, rat-faced man, who shuffled along in the wake of Arthur Bentwood, keeping him in sight until he ran up the steps leading to the offices of Wallingford & Co.

Not until then did the shabby man turn, and when he did it was to pass through the swing door of a nearby saloon. He greeted the man behind the bar familiarly, and that individual nodded as the rat-faced man slightly raised his brows. He continued on through the bar until he came to a small door, which he pushed open and closed carefully behind him.

There, in a small, bare room, he effected a rapid change in his appearance. The shabby suit was rapidly removed, revealing a neat business-suit of blue underneath. The dirty soft hat was turned inside out, and when carefully creased and placed on the back of his head, would have passed anywhere as an almost new piece of headgear. The large, shabby boots were ripped off, disclosing a neat pair of black boots underneath, and looking nothing else than a prosperous City man—Nicholas Grieg, private detective, emerged from the little room, passed through the bar, and was soon swinging along towards the Equidential Building.

A lift shot him up to the offices of Gorgon Kelly, the "Money King," and sending in his card, a few moments later saw him closeted in private conversation with the magnate.

"Well," jerked Gorgon Kelly impatiently, "anything definite to report?"

"Yes, Mr. Kelly," replied the detective obsequiously. "I've got my finger on the leakage, and, when you wish, can put my hand on the cause of it."

"Are you positive?" snapped the financier.

"Perfectly!" replied Grieg confidently. "And, if you can spare a few moments, I will run over the steps, sir, and show you how I know."

"Well, go ahead, but be quick!" answered Kelly, drawing out a cigar and lighting it.

"Well, sir," went on the detective, "when I took this case, you told me that there was a leakage of information from your office. You said that every recent deal you had arranged had been anticipated in spite of the greatest secrecy on your part, and that purchases of the very stock you intended booming were made in large blocks before your own brokers began.

"Yes—yes," broke in Kelly testily, "Go on!"

"Well, sir," continued Grieg, "when you found the greatest secrecy failed to stop it, you adopted the precaution of having no writing of any kind, and arranged the deal in Tin Mines, in order to endeavour to trace the leakage. As you know, I traced the opposition buying orders to Wallingford & Co., and it was evident that in some way they had got information about the deal."

"Well!"

"Well, today, sir, I have found the key of the mystery. Your private secretary, Miss Powers, has been lunching daily for months with Arthur Bentwood, the chief clerk, and soon-to-be junior partner of Wallingford & Co., it is plain why he is getting a partnership," added the detective, with a leering smile. "His services have been greatly appreciated."

"Impossible!" snapped the magnate angrily, sitting up, and pounding the desk. "You must be mistaken!"

The detective spread out his hands.

"Ask her! Ask her, Mr. Kelly."

But the magnate's attitude had altered. The angry look had left his face, and was succeeded by an impassive expression, excepting for a hard glitter in his eyes.

"I will look into this, Grieg," he said in an even voice, "In the meantime, do nothing further. Here"—and he hastily scribbled a few words on a pad—take this to the cashier, he will give you a cheque for a hundred, and you will hear further from me."

"Thank you, sir!" remarked Grieg. "I will come at once, sir, whenever you send for me!"

"Very well," nodded the magnate shortly, and the scraping Grieg took himself off.

As the door closed behind him, Gorgon Kelly leaned over his massive mahogany desk, and pressed one of the several buttons which were set in an ebony-backed line in the centre.

Another door opened and Marian Powers, her wraps removed, showing a neat blouse and businesslike blue serge skirt, entered with a notebook and pencil, and advanced across the thick yielding carpet to the desk.

She drew up a chair opposite the financier, blushing slightly under his steady gaze as she opened her book and held her pencil ready for dictation.

"Miss Powers!"

The young woman started and looked up, startled, as the magnate snapped out her name in a sharp tone.

"Yes, sir!" she replied nervously, her thoughts racing back over the correspondence she had turned out during the morning, and wondering if she had made any mistakes.

"Did you lunch today with young Bentwood, of Wallingford's?"

"Yes," replied Marian coldly, for assuredly it was no affair of her employer's.

"And have you lunched daily with the same young man for some months?" he went on, in the same level tone.

"Yes," she answered, growing nervous under the questions.

"Ah!" The magnate stood up and began restlessly pacing up and down as he gave vent to the expressive monosyllable. Finally, he came to a stop in front of Marian, and, thrusting his hands into his pockets, looked down at her.

Gorgon Kelly was a man still in the prime of life. A healthy outdoor life in his younger days had added to an already well-knit frame. He was not ill-looking; brows of exceptional heaviness detracting, perhaps, from the line of his features. His chin was smooth-shaven, and not till one stood very close to him could one see that the greying moustache hid a hard, cruel mouth. His hair was still black, and, all-in-all, he looked ten years less than his acknowledged fifty years.

He had looked no different when he had dropped into the financial arena five years previously, and the burden of keeping up his reputation of the "Money King" did not seem to age him. He was wifeless and childless, and many a budding debutante, as well as faded spinster and blooming widow, had ogled and sighed in vain, for Gorgon Kelly was deemed the catch of the matrimonial market, and his hazy past was eclipsed by the blazing sun of his present and rosy glow of his future.

Such was the man who stood looking down on Marian Powers, his private secretary, who sat awaiting she knew not what. How on earth had her lunching with Arthur annoyed her employer, and anyway, how did it concern him? But her thoughts were cut short as Kelly spoke in the same level tone:

"Miss Powers, I am going to make a few remarks, and although I suspect it is all ancient history to you, I want you to listen."

Marian bowed her head in assent.

"In the first place," went on the financier, "several months ago I secretly organised a 'bull' movement in Argentines, but when my brokers began buying they discovered that they had been anticipated, and the firm who anticipated them was Wallingford & Co." He paused a moment, but as Marian gave no sign he went on. "That ended in a loss to me, and again I organised a movement—this time in American Rails. Once more my orders were anticipated, and again it was Wallingford & Co.

"After that I went to Mexicans—Wallingford & Co. again. A deal in Rubber gave the same result, and in order to make absolutely certain, I let it drop casually that there would be an upward movement in Tin Mines, but really intended to sell instead of buy. Miss Powers, every other brokerage house except Wallingford & Co. took the bait. They sold. And besides myself, you were the only human being that had access to my private order code. What have you to say?"

His jaws came together with a click as Marian, wide-eyed and white-lipped, stared up at him.

"Do you mean to intimate that I am suspected of passing on this information to Wallingford & Co. through Mr. Bentwood?" she asked in a horrified whisper.

"Just that," he replied.

Marian rose unsteadily and grasped the edge of the desk, a hot wave suffusing her face and neck.

"Mr. Kelly, you insult me grossly! I am incapable of such an action! Besides, I am engaged to Mr. Bentwood. Do you think for a minute he would marry a woman who sold her employer's secrets?"

"Oh," sneered Kelly, suddenly losing the hold he had kept on himself, "so that was the pay, was it? Marriage! And you believe he will marry you—eh?"

"Mr. Kelly, I refuse to listen to any further such insults."

She turned to retire, but the financier caught her in a grasp of steel and drew her back.

"Listen to me!" he panted, throwing all reserve to the winds. "You may as well drop that attitude of righteous indignation, for I have all necessary proof of your guilt. You have filched and sold the secret information of my business, and for two weeks a detective has had you and your lover under close surveillance. He is prepared to make an arrest and prove his charges. What have you to say to that?"

But Marian only stared in speechless horror.

"But there is one way in which you can save yourself, and one only. If you take it I will forget what has happened, otherwise, not only you, but Arthur Bentwood, will be arrested and convicted."

"You—you can't?" gasped Marian. "You daren't! We are both innocent, and have nothing to fear."

"Oh!" replied Kelly, raising his brows. "Then what view do you think a court of law would take of this?" As he spoke the financier drew from his pocket a folded cheque for five pounds, made out by Wallingford & Co. to Arthur Bentwood, and endorsed by him to Marian Powers.

And in a flash Marian remembered that, when she paid Arthur her share of the previous week's lunches, she had only had a ten-pound note—her wages for two weeks—and in her pride, insisting on the payment then and there, he had given her the cheque and some gold and silver in change.

She remembered missing it in the morning, but thought she must have left it at home. Now she knew Gorgon Kelly had abstracted it from her desk, and she realised just how strong it would be as evidence in the already strong circumstantial case against her.

Kelly had long suspected her, but had not desired Grieg to know his real feelings, and when that individual had pointed to Marian as the guilty person, Kelly was then sure his suspicions were correct, and for his own reasons had shut the detective off. The financier thrust the cheque back in his pocket again, and spoke to the now terrified Marian.

"Perhaps that will cause you to listen to me now," he remarked coldly, his feelings once again under perfect control.

"What is it you wish?" asked the young woman.

"You have been with me for several months, and in that time I have grown to care for you. To put it bluntly, I want you to marry me. Perhaps you have not thought of me in that way, but you will find I can make you happy. Come, what do you say? Is it 'yes,' and let bygones be bygones?"

If Marian had been horror-stricken before, she was doubly so now, and as his hand dropped to hers, where Arthur's had rested such a short time before, she almost screamed:

"You cad!" she blazed. "I—I hate you! Do what you wish! I would rather die than marry you!"

Kelly drew back suddenly, and his whole attitude changed like lightning.

Adopting a gentle, soothing tone, he said, in an obvious effort to be genial:

"There, Miss Powers, accept my apology. I was testing you, and, believe me, a perfectly honourable love, such as I have for you, does not necessarily make me a cad. I will confess that the strength of my desire led me to make an injudicious bargain, but I humbly ask your forgiveness. I will accept your statement that you have not passed the information on to Wallingford & Co. Come," he said, smiling, "shake hands, and let us revert to our old footing of secretary and employer. You must confess I had reason to suspect you."

And Marian, thinking perhaps she had been hasty, and that really because she loved Arthur was no reason for calling a man a cad for proposing to her, and glad to be free of the unjust suspicion, slowly put out her hand, and suppressed a shiver of repulsion as Kelly took it in his.

"Now, Miss Powers," he said briskly, returning to his old sharp tones, "take this letter, please, and then type it at once."

And Marian, in her reaction, forgot for the moment about the cheque, and here may be mentioned that the next day, when it did recur to her, and she asked for it, she was told that he had accidentally torn it up, Kelly giving her one of his own instead.

When she had finished taking down the letter, which sealed the truce and tacitly formed the return to the old relations, Marian returned to the outer room to type it out.

As the door closed, the repressed expression on Gorgon Kelly's face relaxed, giving place to one of hard cunning.

"The little minx!" he muttered. "She is as clever as they make 'em. It's a certainty that she's guilty, for it is an absolute impossibility for anyone else to pass on the information. But I went too fast, and scared her off. Besides, this cheque doesn't put her altogether in my hands. A little more, and then we'll see—we'll see, my clever young lady. Curse Arthur Bentwood! I'll settle him. She'll marry me, or marry no one."

And he meant it, for his hard, cruel nature had never been touched by love, and consequently when he had fallen in love with Marian Powers it had gone deep. But he made a mistake in thinking that he only had to reach out and take her, or bully her into accepting him, as he reached out and took a business or bullied men into doing his will.

"What I need is more proof against her," he muttered, "and I'll cook up a little plot that will catch her."

And forthwith Gorgon Kelly, the "Money King," proceeded to work up his little plot that would send the stock market into a maze of uncertainty, driving some firms to the wall and crushing others. But that mattered not to Gorgon Kelly. It would gain him his ends, which this time happened to be a throttling hold over an unknown, unimportant, and hapless young woman.

The Fifth Chapter
The Young Woman with the Opera-Glasses—The Battle on the Stock Exchange

MR. Justin Grantley—known to his intimate friends under the name of Graves—opened the door on which was the name of "Justin Grantley," over the rather vague description "General Agent," and entered his suite of smartly furnished offices in the imposing Equidential Building. As he passed through the reception room and entered an office marked Mr. Grantley "Private," he was met by peal upon peal of girlish laughter.

His face relaxed into a laugh of sympathy, although ignorant of the cause, for, a rare laugher when she did laugh, Yvonne, the guilty one at the moment, infected all within hearing with a feeling that something awfully funny must be happening.

She was leaning back in a chair, holding a pair of opera-glasses in one hand, and using the other to wipe the laughter tears from her eyes with a small lace-bordered handkerchief.

"Something seems to have struck you as being amusing," smiled her uncle with his usual drawl.

"Oh, you have missed the richest thing yet!" gasped Yvonne, sitting up. "Never did pantomime or play have such a funny situation as I have just witnessed."

"Well, don't keep it to yourself," answered Graves, or Grantley, as the world know him then.

"I have just been watching our dear friend Gorgon Kelly," remarked Yvonne, the laughter again threatening. "And what do you think has happened?"

"I can't guess," said Graves, lighting a cigarette and walking to the window.

The window looked out on a light well from which the Equidential offices received their light. Directly across, and one floor lower than the window from which Graves looked, were the offices of Gorgon Kelly, the "Money King," and in a straight, slanting line was the financier's own private sanctum. He could be seen writing at his massive mahogany desk, and as he lifted his head Graves drew back into the shadow.

"What was it you saw, Yvonne?" he repeated.

"He thinks his secretary has been giving Wallingford & Co. the information on his stock deals, and accused her of it this afternoon. Then he turned and asked her to marry him, and—oh!—it was too funny," gasped Yvonne, again laughing. "She refused him unceremoniously, and then he changed in that crafty way of his, and passed it off with a laugh. After she left him, he began to cook up another stock deal, and, incidentally, it is to be a trap for her. He has telephoned his brokers to begin buying American Copper shares on the opening of the market tomorrow, and then to suddenly turn and throw all they can back on the market after the price has been forced up.

"He also told them to keep it as mum as the grave, and threatened if it got out he would break them, one and all. He also told them to watch carefully and see if Wallingford & Co. took the bait and bought.

"I have just phoned Wallingford to sell American Coppers as soon as the market opens—thousands of them—and when Kelly's brokers begin to buy they will be buying my shares. Then when Kelly's brokers begin to sell, I have ordered Wallingford's to buy back every share as the market drops, when Kelly's brokers unload, and I think when I get through, Mr. Gorgon Kelly will be in a worse maze than ever, besides being half a million or so poorer, and, incidentally, I will be that much richer.

"Oh, if the wonderful "Money King" only knew that by my knowledge of lip reading I almost know his very thoughts and every word he utters in his office, whether in an interview or over the phone on his desk, he wouldn't be so puzzled as to how Wallingford & Co., my brokers, have been able to anticipate his every move on the market and cause him to lose so much!"

"By thunder, Yvonne," grinned Graves, "my admiration for you grows every day! When you told me the funds of the 'circle' needed replenishing, and refused to replenish them by touching any of that two hundred thousand we got in Egypt until Kelly was completely ruined, I thought we were in for a slow time. But I never dreamed legitimate money-getting could be so exciting as it has been since we tackled stocks. Gad, we must have cleared up over a million[15] already!"

"Yes," smiled Yvonne, "I make it a little over that. But of course, you must remember

---

[15] £1,000,000 in 1913 is worth about £116,000,000 in 2020

Gorgon Kelly has been the toughest nut of all to crack. The millions he cleaned up and his big interests have kept him going. The two hundred thousand cracked him hard, and he dared not let it get out. He muzzled the banking firm in Egypt; and has had Sexton Blake on the case for months, but our old arch-enemy hasn't the faintest notion yet what became of it.

"Then the coups I made in Argentines, American Rails, Mexicans, and Tin shook him a bit, but he has reserves yet. Tomorrow he will get another shock, and if we catch him heavy enough, it may put him down. But I told Wallingford's I would send around a code confirmation of my orders, and you had better drop in there with it on your way to the club."

"Right-ho!" drawled Graves. "I was going to toddle along, anyway, and have a rubber at bridge before dinner."

"Are you losing much?" asked Yvonne absently, as she wrote the confirmation.

"Not much," replied Graves. "Made a cool hundred last night. That's one thing I can do, anyway, I always win at bridge."

"I'm glad you excel at something," replied Yvonne, tempering her sarcasm with an affectionate smile.

But Graves was proof against such shafts, and only grinned good-naturedly in reply. His association with Yvonne gave him plenty of money and the life of luxury which he loved, and he really had a deep regard for the young woman, who, in return, had strong affection for him, principally for the reason that he was the greatly loved brother of her frail, dearly loved mother, who had fared so hard at the hands of the cowardly swindlers, of whom Gorgon Kelly had been one.

As Graves picked up the confirmation note and departed, Yvonne took up the opera-glasses again, and, with a little pad on her knee, turned to the window to train the glasses on Gorgon Kelly, and as she read every word uttered by him, to jot it down on the pad.

***

The day following the proposal of Gorgon Kelly, the Money King, to Marian Powers, and the plan of Mademoiselle Yvonne to baulk him after she had gathered his plans by her knowledge of lip reading, was a memorable one on the London Stock Exchange.

Marian had hurried away from business the previous evening to meet Arthur Bentwood before his departure for Liverpool, and tell him the strange happenings of the day.

She had, however, been met with the information that urgent matters had made it advisable for him to leave on the afternoon train.

Marian had returned to her lodgings, disappointed and lonely, and confessed freely to herself that she was the most miserable young woman in London.

But the stress of business next morning had needed her every faculty to cope with the work Gorgon Kelly threw at her.

He was in one of his cold, silent rages, and every clerk from the chief down to the stamp boy bowed his head in silent application to his work.

As soon as the Exchange opened the Money King's brokers began to quietly buy American Coppers. They had no trouble in being supplied, for block after block appeared on the market from some mysterious source, being snapped up at once by Kelly's men.

The price began to climb, and other speculators, guessing the source of the buying movement, joined the "bull" crowd, sending the prices again higher at a jump. Still the unlimited supply poured in to meet the demand from a source which contrived to remain unknown, and then things began to happen.

Not a suspicion had Kelly's brokers been able to get that Wallingford's had bought a share, and so carefully had Yvonne's plans been laid that Kelly did not know Wallingford's was the source from which came the mysterious supply of Coppers.

The shrewd Money King began to grow suspicious that something was wrong. To him the Stock Market was a delicately-tuned instrument on which he played with all the technique of a born pianist on his instrument.

He could feel any discord, no matter how faint, and this morning he felt but could not locate. Something somewhere was in opposition to him, and the more his baffled methods failed to locate it, the colder his rage grew.

He knew now that no information Marian Powers could give was behind this mysterious, hostile movement. A master brain, keen and subtle, was pulling the strings, and it angered him the more that he had not the faintest notion from whence it came.

For the first time since taking control of the great money machine, and earning the title of Money King, Gorgon Kelly made his moves with a faint stirring of apprehension and fear.

In addition to the mysterious opposition, he was now beginning to feel serious misgivings as to the ultimate outcome of the day, for if this coup failed it would hit him far deeper than the general public dreamed, and it would need careful manoeuvring to keep the wound from proving fatal.

With a savage gleam in his eye, he reached for the desk phone. If they wanted a fight, whoever they were, they would get it. He had followed the pulse of the market, and felt now was the moment to begin throwing back his shares on the market. The price was still rising, and the public were greedy for more.

This was that he had counted on. His known brokers would gradually ease off buying, just taking enough to keep the public thinking the Money King was still a buyer. His unknown brokers would then begin to sell quietly, getting rid at the high prices of the thousands of shares he had bought at lower prices.

He could see no hitch, and there seemed to be a certain clean million pounds of profit ahead.

He lifted the receiver, and gave the number. Quickly he passed word over the line to one of his lieutenants, who would see that his plans were put into execution at once. But across the light well, with a telephone beside her, and a pair of powerful glasses trained on him, sat Mademoiselle Yvonne, reading his orders from the movements of his lips as he sent them out.

She dropped the glasses, and turned to her desk, writing madly for a few moments. Ringing for a boy, she sealed the note and sent the boy racing with it for Wallingford's. Almost before Kelly's secret brokers had begun to get rid of the Money King's shares, a disturbing rumour swept around like wildfire that the American Congress had put a prohibitive tax on every copper mine in the United States.

And it was then that things began to happen. Copper shares didn't drop, they exploded, the price, hurtling down like a spent rocket. Kelly's agents who had hoped to sell their purchased shares at the high prices, found that before they could take a breath the price was already ten points lower than when they had bought, and still dropping.

They worked madly and with feverish haste, getting an official denial of the report, and disseminating it about as rapidly as possible. But the mischief had been done. Gorgon Kelly, the Money King, was a certain loser of hundreds of thousands, and thousands more had been lost by his followers.

For a wonder the general public came out with good profit on the day, and Wallingford's, who had jumped in openly and bought everything that offered when the bottom fell out of the market, were reputed to have cleaned up a cool million.

And no one dreamed that the whole subtle deal had been engineered, financed, and carried out by a mere 'slip of a woman' in the Equidential Building, and that Wallingford's huge profits went to her.

But Gorgon Kelly's mind was clear of all doubt as to a hostile undercurrent in the market, but rack his brains as he would he could not put his finger on the source. He was hit terribly hard by the calamity of the day. And when settling day came round, "Well," he thought grimly, "he could settle his full liabilities about as easily as his head clerk could."

Everything for months had been going dead against him, but how had his plans been anticipated every time by this mysterious force? Was he going mad? He certainly would if this kept on. He knew from Wallingford's exact moves at the critical moments that they had received no tips from Marian Powers, for if they had acted on any information available to her, they would have bought as Kelly's brokers bought, and sold as they sold. No, there was something far more deep than Marian Powers behind the matter, and if he was to keep from going under he would have to find out pretty quick what it was.

But he had taken care in this last disastrous deal that a few slips of memorandums should lie about his desk, showing his intention to buy American Coppers, but containing no hint of his intention to sell. Marian Powers had goods to these and he could at least bluff her about the matter, and say he thought she had given this information to Wallingford's.

But he must go very, very slowly, or she would take alarm and escape him after all, for Gorgon Kelly had a very cogent reason for desiring to make Marian Powers his wife.

As has been said, her dead father's estate had yielded nothing, and no one knew that two hundred thousand pounds'[16] worth of securities which had been tricked out of Marian's trusting father lay at that moment in the Money King's safe. And, moreover, no one knew that the urgent need for funds had hastened his declaration of love to the young woman, from whom, as his wife, he could soon get control of the securities, and throw them into the ocean of his liabilities, which were threatening to rise up and submerge him in their depths.

Was it possible there could be any connection between the theft of the two hundred thousand in Egypt and the steady anticipations of his moves on the Stock Exchange? It looked that way, and if that were so he must get Sexton Blake off the case at once, for if there was a connection, and the detective succeeded in ferreting it out, he might drop on the truth of those securities which he had secured from Marian Powers' father, and that wouldn't do. No, decidedly not, for if that young lady did not meet his desires in the proper spirit, either forcibly or otherwise, she would have to be got out of the way in some manner, and he would be compelled to bring into play his ability to imitate signatures.

For those securities must go to prop up the tottering foundations of his position even if he had to forge a transfer, and he could not risk either Marian Powers or Sexton Blake finding out anything about their existence.

"Curse those people, anyway, who got away with that haul in Egypt! Who on earth could it be?"

Gorgon Kelly shivered slightly, with a sudden, undefined fear of the mysterious Nemesis which seemed to be pursuing him so persistently, but he threw off the feeling of chill foreboding and turned back to his desk to construct in detail his plans for the future.

The Sixth Chapter
Blake Grows Suspicious—Arthur Bertwood's Call—On the Track

"YOU mean then, Mr. Kelly, that you wish me to drop the case entirely?"

Sexton Blake leaned back in his chair before the Money King's desk, and wrinkled his brows in puzzlement.

It was the morning after the memorable flurry in American Coppers, and Blake, in answer to a telegram from Gorgon Kelly, had motored down to the Equidential Building, thinking the magnate, perhaps had further news of the forty boxes of gold which had disappeared so mysteriously. Consequently he was greatly surprised when he discovered Kelly had sent for him to request him to drop the case.

"Yes, I wish nothing more done in the matter, Mr. Blake. If you will present the account for your services, I will have a cheque forwarded to you."

---

[16] £200,000 in 1913 is worth about £23,300,000 in 2020

"Thank you, Mr. Kelly," remarked Blake coldly. "Since I have so far failed to discover the author of the theft, there is no charge for my services. But your decision, if I may say so, seems peculiar. One doesn't lose two hundred thousand pounds every day, Mr. Kelly. One would almost think you had recovered it."

Blake carelessly drew out a cigar as he made the shot, for, although his face was impassive, he was greatly surprised at Kelly's request, and wondered as to the reason.

The detective did not take the defeat lightly, and his failure to discover who had so cleverly stolen the forty boxes of gold had caused him great chagrin. And although he seemed careless in manner and preoccupied with his cigar, he was keenly watching every expression on Kelly's face.

"Er—yes, Mr. Blake," came the magnate's answer shortly. "That is exactly the reason. The gold was returned as mysteriously as it was taken—the whole forty boxes of it."

Had Kelly been less absorbed in the hasty manufacture of this sudden lie he would have seen a lightning-like gleam spring into Blake's eyes, and as quickly fade out again. But it had already gone when he glanced up, and Blake was looking calmly at the ash on his cigar.

"Very well, Mr. Kelly," he remarked shortly. "Of course, you———" But he stopped for just the fraction of a second, his gaze riveted on something out of the window. "As I was saying," he went on quickly, "you, perhaps, have your own reasons for concealing any further details about the gold, but you are to be congratulated on its return. However," concluded Blake, rising, "I am rather pleased than otherwise, for I have another matter on hand at present, and really could not do justice to your case."

He walked towards the office door as he spoke, and with a careless nod departed.

But Blake's attitude changed with marvellous rapidity as he walked along the corridor towards the lift. The careless nonchalance departed, and he stepped briskly with sudden decision written on his face.

Entering the lift, he was soon dropping downwards, but instead of leaving the lift at the ground floor, he continued on to the basement. There he got out, and walked along slowly through the twisting corridors until he came to an angle in the passage, where stood a hand-basin and mirror. Blake glanced sharply about and listened carefully, but no one was in sight, and no footstep sounded on the stone floor of the passage.

He turned, and began hurriedly to make a change in his appearance. It was lucky his suit was blue, for that would pass under any disguise. Drawing out a wig and beard, he adjusted them carefully; the wig being of pure silver, and the beard black, slightly tinged with grey. From a capacious pocket in his coat he drew out a silk hat, which had been made collapsible after the fashion of opera hats. He next slipped off his light grey overcoat, and turned it inside-out, revealing a neat black coat with silk lapels. He then thrust the soft hat he had been wearing into the pocket from which he had taken the silk hat, and buttoning up his coat, turned back along the corridor just as footsteps approached.

Blake entered the lift again, and was shot up to the floor on which Kelly had his offices. Leaving the lift, he walked down the corridor, continuing on past the Money King's door until he came to a staircase. He walked up with a dignity befitting his aged appearance, and on reaching the next floor walked past door after door until he came to a small alcove in which a window was set looking out on the light well. Here he stopped and took his bearings, continuing on almost at once until another turning brought him face to face with a heavy ground glass door, on which was the name, "Justin Grantley, General Agent."

Blake glanced sharply at the name as he passed, and walked a trifle more slowly, but just as he reached the next door on which was the same name, it opened suddenly, and a young woman hastened out, almost colliding with the elderly gentleman in the corridor.

"Oh, I beg your pardon!" apologised the young lady hastily.

"It is I who must apologise," replied the elderly gentleman, in the measured accents of age. "I am looking for the offices of Carfax & Co., and seem to be fated not to find them."

"They are on the next floor above, I believe," answered the young lady, with a smile, waving her hand as she spoke.

And as the courteous old gentleman bowed and thanked her, he kept his eyes on her slim, graceful hand. But it was not the beauty of the member which had drawn his attention, it was a large ring which formed the only ornament on her hand, and in that ring was set a huge Egyptian scarab.

The polite old man turned, and sought his way to the floor above, where he had luckily remembered Carfax & Co. had their offices, but he did not favour that firm with a call. Instead he entered the lift, and descended again to the ground floor, where he walked slowly to the street, and climbed into a large grey car which stood at the kerb.

"Here, I say!" exclaimed the lad who was lounging at the wheel. "You've made a mistake in the car, sir!"

"Do you think so?" said Blake, in his natural voice, as he sat down; and Tinker gasped in amazement. "Start the car," he went on curtly, "and drive quickly to Baker Street."

Tinker, seeing that Sexton Blake was in one of his rare tempers, said no more, but threw in the clutch, and certainly his master had no fault to find if he wished to make rapid time to Baker Street, for Tinker, with a suppressed grin, twisted through the traffic rapidly, taking most of the corners on two wheels.

Blake's face relaxed a trifle as the car skidded into Baker Street, almost colliding against the farther kerb before it straightened around, but he still spoke curtly as Tinker pulled up.

"Leave the car here and come in," he ordered; and Tinker followed, wondering what had occurred to upset his guv'nor.

"Get out the 'Index,' and look up every item which has been entered referring to Gorgon Kelly since I first took on the case relating to the theft of the forty boxes of gold," ordered Blake, as they entered the consulting-room. And Tinker hastened to obey, while his master went into his dressing-room in order to remove his disguise.

Tinker had the cuttings all ready when Blake returned, and the detective ran over them quickly, muttering aloud as he did so.

"Gorgon Kelly," he muttered, "commonly called the Money King! Theft of two hundred thousand; some place between Cairo and London."

Then followed a maze of pencilled notes and figures relating to Blake's unsuccessful investigations. The next slip was a newspaper cutting, headed "Money King and his Followers Beaten!" Then followed a report of the attempted boom in Argentine shares, in which Gorgon Kelly and his associates had dropped thousands. The next clipping gave an account of his losses in American Rails, the next an account of his losses in Mexicans, and so on, each clipping being a record of Gorgon Kelly's market operations since Blake had taken on the case of the stolen gold.

"H'm!" muttered Blake, as he finished reading. "Just jot these figures down, Tinker."

The lad jumped to obey, and wrote rapidly as Blake snapped out sum after sum.

"Add those up and tell me the total," he ordered.

"One million exactly, guv'nor," answered Tinker.

Blake picked up the slip and verified it, afterwards tearing it into shreds and tossing the pieces in the fire.

Closing the index, and pushing it away, he turned to Tinker.

"I want you to get into some disguise and go at once to the Equidential Building. Watch there until Gorgon Kelly comes out, and follow him wherever he goes. Find out all you can about what he does. Come back here some time tonight and report his movements."

"Is there something new about his case, guv'nor?" asked Tinker, turning towards his room.

"I don't know yet," answered Blake shortly and Tinker, seeing the detective's mood, wisely refrained from further questions.

As the lad changed and departed on his errand, garbed in his ragged newsboy disguise, Blake was already wrapped in complete absorption, hunched up in his usual manner in the big armchair, puffing furiously at his pipe. Pedro, the only privileged person at such a time, lay stretched out in silence at Blake's feet.

The room was a mass of stale smoke, and the day had grown into night before Blake roused himself.

Mrs. Bardell had knocked to inquire if he desired food, but had scuttled away in haste as she took in the situation, for she knew to her cost the result of disturbing Blake at such a time.

Neither man nor dog had changed their position for hours, but as the room grew dark Blake roused himself and sat up, the dry, hard foreboding glitter in his eyes.

"Pedro," he said, stroking the huge beast's ears, "I am the most colossal idiot in London! To think that all the time I have been working on the theory that the gold was secured by the thieves either on the P. & O. boat or after its arrival. We have several points to clear up, old chap," he continued—"one of which is why did Gorgon Kelly lie today when I suggested the gold had been returned? For certainly that reason for turning me off had not occurred to him until I suggested it. If it had been true he would have stated at once how it had come back, and in his haste he forgot that two lots of lead-filled boxes had been found. I wonder if my first theory of another lot of duplicate boxes is to prove correct after all? And since then by actual figures he has lost a million on the Exchange, and, that being so, the return of the two hundred thousand would be a decided windfall.

"I wonder—I wonder just what your little game is, Mr. Gorgon Kelly? It will be interesting to discover if you have deposited the two hundred thousand you claim has been returned.

"And another point, Pedro my boy, is to discover just why that young lady sits at the window across the road with a pair of opera glasses trained on the window of the Money King's private office. Rather injudicious of her to sit in such plain view this morning!

"And another thing Pedro—did she get that scarab which she wears in Egypt, and what is her great interest in Gorgon Kelly? I was none too soon this morning, and as it happened I just reached the office from which she emerged in time.

"Who is Mr. Justin Grantley, and who is the interested young woman with the thick black hair? There is something strangely familiar about her, Pedro." And Blake's eyes grew momentarily sad. "She has an elusive something which reminds me of Mademoiselle Yvonne, and yet her appearance is too genuine to be merely disguised.

"Is there a new female criminal rising into the criminal constellation, or is that charming young woman merely the tool of Justin Grantley, if any such person exists? Yes, there are many points to be cleared up, and if you think, Mr. Gorgon Kelly, I intend to accept my congé about the gold robbery you are mistaken, for I am going to stick on that trail until I know just what became of the bullion, and incidentally discover just what your little game is."

The words Blake had just muttered to Pedro aptly summed up the result of his day of detective thought. He had been positive Kelly's statement that the gold had been returned was a hastily-trumped-up lie, and the detective wondered why, for it wasn't natural a man would waive such an amount aside without a strong motive.

What was the motive? Had something occurred which made it undesirable that Blake should discover the truth about its disappearance?

At any rate, his desire to get rid of Blake had been obvious, and it indicated either a desire to hide past events or future intentions which he did not wish to be discovered.

What was that motive, and just what was the whole truth regarding Mr. Gorgon Kelly? And again, who was the young woman he had caught a vision of in the morning while talking with Kelly, who sat in the office across the well with a pair of opera-glasses trained on the Money King's office?

Had she anything to do with Kelly's losses on the market? Had those losses anything to do with the gold robbery? And what was she doing with an Egyptian scarab on her finger?

Yes, it would be interesting to know if she had ever been in Egypt, and to get a peep at Mr. Justin Grantley, and also to know just when Mr. Justin Grantley took those offices in the Equidential Building.

Before he had marshalled together the facts of the morning, which seemed at first view barely possible of connection, Blake had made a first step of shadowing Kelly, although at the moment he was only vaguely suspicious. But as his keen mind turned and twisted the facts, laying them out in every possible combination, mathematical deduction had shown the possible and logical connection of several trifling points which apparently bore no possible relation towards each other.

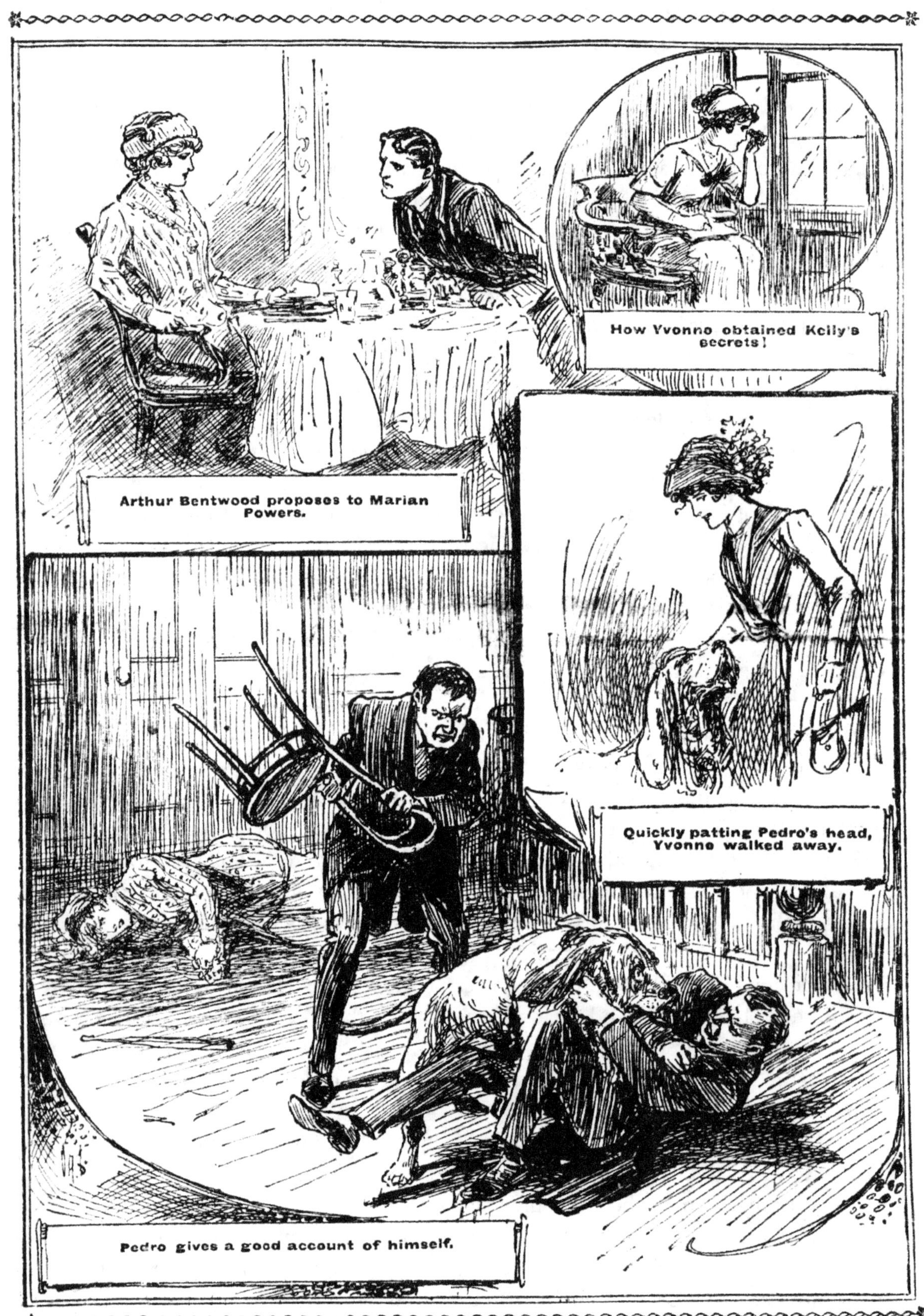

Arthur Bentwood proposes to Marian Powers.

Quickly patting Pedro's head, Yvonne walked away.

Pedro gives a good account of himself.

All day the impression had been growing on him that Kelly's persistent run of bad luck was more than just the successful operations of other plungers on the market, and a strong link was forged in his suspicions when he saw that they all dated since the gold robbery.

Blake got up and turned on the lights, looking in surprise at the clock, which he found pointed to nine. Tinker ought to have been back long before this. Where was he, and what was keeping him? He had been told most emphatically to return and report.

At that moment the bell rang, followed shortly by Mrs. Bardell's voice in the hall saying she would see if Mr. Blake would see anyone, but she didn't think he would.

She knocked at the door, and started back in surprise as she saw Blake standing before the desk. She started to speak, but Blake cut her short, telling her to return and send in the caller.

He came a moment later, and Blake looked up to see a tall, clean-shaven young man with frank eyes which at the moment were clouded with suffering.

"Are you Mr. Blake?" he inquired, as he entered.

Blake bowed.

"My name is Arthur Bentwood," cried the visitor. "I am with Wallingford & Co., the Stock Exchange house, and I wish to see you on a personal matter."

"Ah, yes! Be seated, Mr. Bentwood," remarked Blake, drawing up his own chair. "Let me see—Wallingford & Co. That is the firm which has been the leading power lately against the Kelly crowd, isn't it?"

"Er—yes!" answered Arthur, in a surprised tone, as he sank into a chair. "It's curious you should mention that, for it is about Gorgon Kelly I came to see you."

"Ah!" exclaimed Blake. "You interest me, Mr. Bentwood. Proceed, please!"

"Well, firstly, Mr. Blake," replied Arthur, "I will give you all the facts I know myself, and will be as brief as possible. Gorgon Kelly has a secretary," he went on; "a Miss Powers—Marian Powers. I have—er—admired Miss Powers for some time back, but said nothing to her until three days ago. I have made quite a little money lately on the Exchange, following the advice of Mr. Wallingford, and three days ago, when he told me I was to be admitted as a partner on the first of next month, I felt I was in a position to marry Miss Powers. She and I have lunched together for months past, and when we met at noon three days ago I proposed to her.

"You may think a crowded restaurant an odd place for the purpose," he remarked, his face rather red, "but I had to leave later in the day for Liverpool, and wanted to know my fate before leaving."

"She accepted you, of course," remarked Blake.

"Yes, she did; and I went away practically walking on air. But yesterday I got a letter from her which I fail absolutely to understand. You will see when you read it why it worried me, and after sending her a telegram this morning I cut my business short and came on at once. It was after business hours when I arrived, and so I went at once to her lodgings. Well, Mr. Blake, she left for business as usual this morning, but has not been home since, and my telegram was still waiting there for her unopened."

Blake made no comment as he reached over and took the letter which Arthur had withdrawn from the envelope and opened.

"I—er—there are a few remarks there which don't refer to the matter," he said, blushing with embarrassment.

"It's all right," smiled Blake; "I'll skip that part. Just point out where the part begins which you say worried you."

Arthur placed his finger at a point near the bottom of the first page, and Blake read on, his eyes gleaming as he took in its purport.

"'And now, dear,' he read, 'I want to tell you the strangest thing about Mr. Kelly.'"

Then followed a detailed description of Gorgon Kelly's accusation that she had passed on his secrets to Arthur Bentwood, of Kelly's proposal of marriage and his sudden change of attitude when Marian refused him.

"'And you know, dear, we always made it a point never to discuss business matters when we were together, and the only time in all those months was the day you went away when you told me you had made money on the particular stocks on which Mr. Kelly lost, and I remarked that it was strange. But don't be a jealous boy over this, because there is no cause to be. I feel both a physical and mental repulsion, towards Mr. Kelly, but thought you ought to know of his strange accusation. I was really awfully frightened, but you can see how foolish it was, for we were both innocent, and had no cause for fear. However, he is quite like his old self now, dear, and I will stay on until we are married, for I don't want any trouble; and, besides, there are ever so many things I want to get before I am Mrs. Bentwood.

"'There, sir, how does that sound? Hurry home to me!'"

But Blake laid the letter down, and looked up as it went off again into personalities.

"Rather a remarkable occurrence, Mr. Bentwood," he remarked "What do you make of it yourself?"

"I don't know, Mr. Blake. I was so astounded when I read it. I am afraid I paid more attention to what she wrote about his proposal than to any other part. But when I discovered she hadn't come home after business, I went down to the Equidential Building, thinking she was working late, but it was closed and dark."

"It is needless to ask if there is any truth in Gorgon Kelly's accusation?" remarked Blake drily.

"Certainly!" remarked Arthur indignantly. "Miss Powers is a young woman of the highest sense of honour, and I never discussed Kelly with her in any way whatsoever."

"All right; I'm satisfied you are both innocent," smiled Blake. "But tell me, how does it happen that your firm were the leaders against Kelly in every deal?"

"I can't tell you, Mr. Blake," replied Arthur, and Blake saw by his earnestness that the young man was telling the truth. "Only Mr. Wallingford knows, and he keeps the information strictly to himself."

"Hm! I see. You are as much in the dark as everyone else?"

Arthur nodded.

"Have you any suspicions?" went on Blake.

"Well—er—I don't think it would be right for me to say yes or no," answered Arthur.

"You can answer me this," said Blake, "without betraying any of your firm's private affairs. Do you know if there is a woman connected with the matter at all?"

"Well, I have thought so, Mr. Blake, as I have answered the phone several times when a woman's voice asked for Mr. Wallingford, and each time we have made heavy deals on the Stock Exchange the following day."

"I see," nodded Blake. "That is all I wish to know. Oh, I don't suspect Miss Powers of being that woman!" he laughed, as he saw the thought cross the young man's face. "And now, Mr. Bentwood, I wonder if you can put your own personal feelings in your pocket for a few days. Of course, we may discover in the morning that Miss Powers has gone to spend the night with friends, not expecting you back until the morning; but, on the other hand, to be frank, I think not. Her disappearance happens to bear on another matter which I have in hand, and, although it will be hard, I want you to go to business for the next few days and act as though nothing had happened whether Miss Powers returns tomorrow or not. Will you trust me, and do this? Believe me, it will help matters in a way which at present I can't tell you. All I can say is that if you go around investigating it will create suspicion, and that I wish to avoid. Above all, do not breathe to a soul that you have been to see me. Can you do this?"

"It will be hard, Mr. Blake, but I trust to you, and will do as you say."

"That's right," replied Blake, putting out his hand as Arthur rose.

The next moment he was gone.

"I wonder if this is your motive in getting rid of me, Mr. Gorgon Kelly?" muttered Blake, reaching for his pipe. "And I wonder how, in the name of all that is wonderful, does the charming young woman with the scarab on her finger anticipate every move of Mr. Kelly's. Truly, my mysterious friends, the case grows exciting."

The Seventh Chapter
Marian Powers Tricked—The "Money King" Makes a Mistake—Tinker's Misfortune

GORGON Kelly had sat far into the night at his desk on the night of his disastrous deal in American Coppers, and when he finally rose and took his way out of the silent building, his mind was made up.

He had gone over his private ledger, and although he knew his recent losses had made his position precarious, he did not know he stood so close to the brink of ruin as the ledger showed. It would need all his iron nerve and delicate tuning of the present discordant market, coupled with a more than ordinarily successful coup, to even momentarily save the situation, which every moment loomed more menacingly before him.

To accomplish that, he would need further large supplies of funds. He already had every penny the banks would advance him, and he, better than anyone else, knew the value of the almost imperceptible coldness which had grown in that quarter with his recent disasters.

Did a whisper get abroad regarding his present financial condition, every avenue of relief would be closed to him. And then how the vultures would laugh at his ruin. He—Gorgon Kelly—the "Money King," to go down under the system of his own creation amid the sneers and laughter of the "Street."

The thought seized him with an agony of fear and dread, and his face worked with passion as he thought of Marian Powers' refusal. That he loved her, in so far as his nature could love any being, there was no doubt, but he realised even the great desire must wait in the urgency of other things. Money—plenty of it—he must have and quickly, and that money would have to come from the two hundred thousand pounds' worth of securities in his safe which, until now, he had not risked disposing of.

If Marian Powers would marry him, he could easily word a transfer which she would sign not realising what it was, and as the securities really belonged to her; he could then realise on them safely.

But if she wouldn't? Well, she must be dealt with summarily.

They were his only hope, and no time was to be lost if he was to weather the storm. He would ask her again in the morning to marry him, and if she refused, he would threaten. If she still refused she would have to be got out of the way for the time being, and he would have to forge a transfer in her father's name.

She would have to be kept out of the way until they were disposed of, and in the meantime he would force her to marry him by hook or by crook. But he would have to get Sexton Blake out of the way. It would be awkward if he stumbled on any information about the securities, or should suspect anything about Marian Powers' disappearance—if that were found necessary.

But pshaw! his reverses were making him nervous. No one suspected his real condition, and if any questions were asked about her, he would simply say she had left his employ, and who would dare to question the Money King more closely?

Kelly braced up a bit as this thought came to him, and when he finally retired, after a confidential conversation with the butler of his big, lonely luxurious house, he felt in a better frame of mind.

Early next morning Kelly sent the butler in the closed motor to the offices in the Equidential Building with a note to Marian Powers to return in the motor in order to take dictation at the Money King's residence, as he was indisposed and would not go down until later.

The butler, provided with Kelly's keys, had entered the private office from the corridor, and rung the bell on the desk which was labelled "Secretary." Marian, who had just arrived and was taking off her jacket in the room which had been set aside for her, entered at once. Forbes, the butler, handed her the note, and stood waiting while she read it.

"Have you the motor waiting?" she asked, glancing up at him.

"Yes, miss; and the master says would you please come at once, as he has some urgent letters to be written."

"Certainly!" replied Marian. "I will join you in a moment."

"Thank you, miss!" answered Forbes. "I will be in the car."

He turned and went out the way he had come, and Marian, all unsuspicious, returned to her room for her jacket, and hurried out through the main office, saying nothing to the clerks of her errand. And not until afterwards did she remember the significance of the butler's entry and exit through the private door on the corridor, for there were none to see him enter or leave, and all that was known was that Marian had come at the usual time, and had left before Mr. Kelly's arrival, without saying where she was going.

Kelly received her in the library with a smile.

"I'm sorry to have bothered you, Miss Powers," he said, closing the door, "but I have some urgent matters to get through. By the way, did you tell the chief clerk where you were going?" he asked casually, walking back to the desk.

"No," answered Marian, looking up in surprise. "I didn't think it was necessary, I just came right on when I got your note."

"Ah," breathed Kelly, turning quickly, with a sudden change in his bearing; and Marian shrank back in sudden fear, realising, all too late, of the trap she had walked into.

"Now, listen to me," went on Kelly, seizing her hand, and drawing her to him forcibly. "I asked you the other day to marry me, and you refused. This time I inform you that you are going to marry me, and the sooner you make up your mind the better."

"Let me go! You must be mad!" panted Marian. "I'll call for help!"

"Call—call," he sneered, "for all the good it will do you. Here you are, and here you stay until you are married to me."

"That will be never," answered Marian. "I hate you! Why do you persecute me and torture me so? What have I ever done but my duty?"

"You wouldn't believe me if I told you it was my love for you," replied Kelly. "But come. I give you one more chance. My time is precious. Will you marry me?"

"No! A thousand times, no!"

"Very well," he went on, "so be it. No one knows you came here, and I'll take good care no one ever does. Until you make up your mind to marry me, you stay here."

"You can torture me, you can keep me a prisoner, but I'll never marry you, I'll die first!" answered Marian. But her voice broke in an involuntary sob as she thought of Arthur Bentwood.

Kelly turned without speaking and rang, the door opening a moment later to admit the butler.

"Is everything ready, Forbes?" asked Kelly.

"Yes, sir. The room is all fixed up."

"Very well. Give me a hand with my fair guest. She seems unwilling to accept my hospitality."

Marian opened her mouth to scream in desperation for help, but Kelly clapped his hand over it, and, assisted by Forbes, carried her out and up the stairs, depositing her on a couch in a large richly-furnished sitting-room, from which a door opened into a bed-room.

"There, you can think things over here," remarked Kelly as he straightened up. "A maid will attend your wants, and that bell will bring the butler to phone me, if you change your mind. I will come and see you this evening myself, and trust to find you in a more amicable frame of mind. Until then, *au revoir*!"

Marian made no answer as Kelly and the butler withdrew, and she lay for some minutes after their departure in a fit of reproach for being caught so easily. She got up after the first shock had passed and made an examination of her gilded prison. A look at the windows showed her the folly of endeavouring to escape in that way, and a glance at the doors proved them to be equally hopeless. She turned back in despair to the couch and cast herself down, a flood of hot tears coming to her relief.

In the meantime, Kelly had betaken himself to his office, taking care to enter through the main office, bidding a curt good-morning to the busy clerks.

Two minutes later he had elaborately rung for Miss Powers, repeating the ring at intervals. Finally he rang for the chief clerk, and inquired shortly where Miss Powers was.

"Why, I don't know, sir!" stammered that individual. "She came as usual, and went out again almost at once."

"Ask outside if she left word where she was going!" snapped Kelly, and waited with a grim smile while the clerk left to do so.

As he anticipated, the clerk's errand was barren of information, and the Money King frowned in anger.

"Most extraordinary!" he snapped. "phone up some agency, and get the smartest girl they have at once. If Miss Powers comes in, pay her a fortnight's salary and dismiss her. I can't put up with this kind of thing."

The clerk retired hastily to do so, and a few minutes later Sexton Blake, in answer to a telegram from Kelly, entered. It was then that Kelly had told Blake not to go any further with the investigation of the gold robbery. It has been seen how Blake accepted the request and his movements after leaving the magnate.

Barely had Blake departed, and even while he was traversing the corridors in the garb of a benevolent-looking elderly gentleman, Kelly had rung again for the chief clerk, and had issued orders that on no account whatsoever was he to be disturbed until he rang.

As the door closed he stepped softly across the thick carpet and softly turned the key in the well-oiled lock, then drew down the blind and turned on the electric light, for what Mr. Gorgon Kelly proposed to do must evidently be free from curious eyes.

Stepping softly to the safe, he set the lettered combination and swung open the door.

A brief search amongst the bundles of documents, and he drew forth a bundle of folded securities, clasped together by a heavy rubber band.

The Money King then did a curious thing. He took off his coat and tossed it aside, after which he rolled up his shirt-sleeves. A curious onlooker would have thought then that the great financier was going through a series of physical exercises, for he twisted and turned his left arm in all directions, working steadily, until every muscle of arm and hand had been brought into play. Then, opening a drawer in his desk, he drew out a bottle containing a thick white liquid, which he applied, rubbing it in thoroughly.

"There," he grunted, as he recorked the bottle and returned it to the desk, "that will take the stiffness out, and now we'll see if I've forgotten my old accomplishment."

He seated himself at his desk, undid the bundle of securities, and spread one out on the desk before him. He studied the signature on it closely, and then drew forward a blank piece of paper. The signature looked very plain and very simple, just John Powers, in round letters. Kelly's first imitation looked like an exact duplicate, but he filled many blank sheets before he was satisfied with his imitation. Then, carefully cleaning the nib, he turned over the certificate, and with his right hand wrote in his ordinary style a transfer of the certificate to Gorgon Kelly, dating it two years previously. Then with a steady hand he transferred the pen and wrote in exact imitation of the signature, "John Powers." Slowly and methodically he filled in every certificate, fully two hours passing before the last was completed.

He heaved a sigh of relief as he sat back and surveyed the result of his labours.

"That would fool John Powers himself!" he muttered with satisfaction. "That specially quick-drying ink will be totally dry in an hour, and then I defy the sharpest man in London to question it."

He carefully folded up the securities and returned them to the safe, after which he turned off the lights and threw up the blind. Then, softly unlocking the door, he returned to his desk and rang, demanding shortly of the chief clerk, who answered the summons, if the new secretary had arrived and if Miss Powers had returned. The clerk answered the first in the affirmative and the second in the negative, and hastened out again as Kelly told him to send in the new girl.

Gorgon Kelly dismissed the new secretary to her room, and, rising, took out the bundle of securities from the safe and put on his hat. Five minutes later he was walking with dignified step to the bank, replying shortly here and there to the obsequious bows of less powerful men flattered at being acknowledged by the great Money King.

He did not notice—nor, in fact, did anyone notice—the ragged newsboy who dogged the footsteps of the great man; but Tinker, who had been waiting for some time outside the Equidential Building, lost no time in following his quarry.

He was close behind when Kelly entered the bank, and he was at the door when half an hour later the magnate emerged with a look of satisfaction on his face. For the manager had been very pleased to grant the great man a heavy loan on the securities, which were gilt-edged, and a cursory examination of the transfer proving satisfactory—"just a formality in your case, Mr. Kelly," as the manager had hastened to state—the loan had at once been made, and the amount—nearly the two hundred thousand pounds face value of the securities—credited at once to the Money King's account.

Then Mr. Gorgon Kelly had returned to his office to plan out a coup which would shake the market from top to bottom, and get back for him some of his losses, and this time, he muttered grimly, no living soul, would know his intentions until the Exchange opened for the day's business.

Tinker had a long and weary wait during the afternoon, and his voice was tired calling out his papers before Gorgon Kelly again emerged from the Equidential and entered his waiting motor.

Tinker was close at hand, and heard Kelly's order "Home," and as the powerful monster glided smoothly away, Tinker threaded his way through the home-going crowds and sought a directory. He hailed a taxi on his return to the street, and after convincing the sarcastic driver that he really wished to hire it, and, despite his rags, he could pay for it, he got in. For safety's sake, he dropped out at the corner of Piccadilly and Park Lane and the chauffeur gasped in speechless amazement at the faultlessly-clad youth who descended.

"Here, old ginger face," grinned Tinker, tossing the man a half-crown; "take the clothes you'll find inside, and wear them to church next Sunday! You look as though a gentleman's clothes would make a man of you. And take my advice," he added, "and keep that mouth shut. You are no beauty with it open." And before the spluttering driver could reply, Tinker was away, his neat garb passing without comment in the aristocratic neighbourhood.

He walked slowly up Park Lane, and turned down a narrow, quiet street, lined with towering, imposing houses. He glanced keenly at one in particular as he passed slowly by, but the front was in darkness, only the shadowy, outlines of the windows being visible in the gloom of deepening night.

"Can't see much there," muttered the lad as he got past. "I suppose I ought to go back and report progress to the guv'nor; but I'll have a look at the back and see if I can find out anything worthwhile. It seems silly to go back and report that he was in his office all day, with the exception of a trip to the bank."

But that trip to the bank which seemed so insignificant to Tinker would have been considered important news by the waiting Blake, and much trouble and anxiety would have been avoided if the lad had strictly followed instructions.

But, in his zeal, Tinker was anxious to discover what appeared to him as something tangible, and, consequently, instead of returning, he turned down another street until he came to a narrow lane steeped in darkness, which ran past the back of the imposing houses he had just passed.

Tinker turned down the dark lane, and walked softly along until he came to the rear of Gorgon Kelly's house. A high-spiked wall separated the grounds from the lane, and a moment's examination proved the gate which gave on to the lane to be locked.

By backing across to the further side of the lane, Tinker could see the yellow oblong of lighted upstairs rooms against drawn blinds.

It certainly looked like degenerating into a wild-goose chase, and the lad was seriously debating whether perhaps it wouldn't be better to return to Baker Street, when his thoughts broke off sharply, and he strained forward tensely.

Against the drawn curtain of one of the upstairs rooms two shadows had appeared, and from the outlines the lad could see one was the figure of a woman. But what had caused him to lean forward and watch breathlessly was the gesticulations of the woman's shadow—gesticulations which clearly and undoubtedly were those of anger and refusal.

"Jiminy, that's funny," muttered Tinker, "It's common knowledge that old Kelly isn't married and has no children, so who can that woman be? From the shadows of the man's arms against the blind, he is certainly laying down the law to the woman. Wonder if it's Kelly himself, or only a couple of the servants? Here goes, anyway, to try and find out. I'll gain nothing standing out here, and something may turn up inside."

As he came to this decision, Tinker stole back across the lane until he reached the door in the wall. He felt around until he found a small iron handle, and then clutching as best he could at the protruding corners of the wall, he sprang upwards.

His hands came into contact with the sharp spikes at the top, and he fell back before his fingers could slip down between them and get a grip. A second trial proved equally unsuccessful; but the third time he managed to hang on, and by dint of careful manipulation, he pulled himself up and dropped over, landing on the soft turf, but at the cost of a torn pair of trousers, where the bottoms had caught in the spikes.

Picking himself up, Tinker stole across to the big, shadowy bulk of the house, but was brought up sharp as his face went full tilt into something.

He pulled back and listened for a full minute to discover if the noise had been heard; but silence still reigned, and he cautiously felt for the object he had run into.

"Great Scott," he chuckled softly, "the glass wall of a conservatory! I wasn't expecting this."

He followed it around until he got its outlines.

"By thunder, it butts up against the wall right under that window!" he muttered. "I wonder if I could climb up over it. The glass seems pretty thick, but it's hard to say whether it will hold me or not."

Tinker stepped back to gaze upwards and judge where would be the best place to make the attempt, when his eyes again caught sight of the gesticulating hands against the blind, and he was decided.

He again approached the conservatory, and slowly and with infinite care worked himself up by the assistance of the steel framework until he drew himself over the edge to the top.

Here he felt about until his hands encountered a broad, steel division running straight across in an upward, slanting direction to the wall of the house. He drew himself over to it, and began to creep slowly along, keeping as much of his weight as possible on its three inches of surface.

With great care he had safely toiled over half the distance and was beginning to breathe easier as the window grew steadily nearer, when his hand in reaching out for the support of the glass roof encountered emptiness where a pane had been opened for ventilation purposes. Tinker caught himself, and swung his weight wildly to offset his fall and save himself; but he had leaned forward too far, and his arm dropping through the black opening, he fell over heavily, and, with a deafening crash of broken, flying glass, he dropped helplessly through the roof into a mass of pot plants below.

Although blood was streaming from him in half a dozen places, Tinker picked himself up and made blindly for the glass wall at the rear of the conservatory, intending, if no other way offered, to kick a pane out and crawl through. But before he could put this plan into execution, a door opened, and the conservatory was flooded with light.

A growl of surprise followed, and Tinker turned to see the figure of a burly butler hastening across the conservatory.

Escape was now out of the question, and Tinker was rapidly forming some bluffing explanation of his presence there when, without questions of any kind, Forbes, the butler, reached out and gripped the lad in a grip of iron. Dragging him across the conservatory, he switched out the lights, and disappeared into the house, dragging his prisoner with him.

The Eighth Chapter
Tinker and Marian Attempt to Escape—The Butler's Triumph

WHEN Gorgon Kelly had left Marian a prisoner, and had locked the door on her, it will be remembered that, all at sea regarding her fate and Kelly's purpose, and thinking desperately of Arthur Bentwood, she had examined her prison, and then thrown herself down on the couch in a passion of weeping.

Once, a grim, silent woman, evidently the maid of whom Kelly had spoken, brought her food, and although Marian tried to force herself to eat, the food sickened her, and she thrust it away. All the long afternoon she lay unhappily thinking on the couch, but as the shadows lengthened into dusk, she rose and bathed her face, determined at least to show an unaffected front to Kelly, if he should put in an appearance.

And true to his statement of the morning he came, a smile of triumph on his face, as he closed the door and switched on the lights.

"I trust you have been made comfortable," he said, with mock politeness.

"How long do you propose to keep me here?" demanded Marian, disregarding his remark.

"My dear young lady," smiled Kelly, raising his hands in protest, "you are really too impatient! It reflects on me, as a host, that my guest should show a desire to leave so soon."

"Oh, stop this trifling!" blazed Marian. "What do you want of me, and why am I kept here against my will? I demand to be released at once. Don't you think Arthur Bentwood will turn London upside down to find me?" she asked passionately.

"You ask what I want of you and why I keep you here!" snapped Kelly, his manner changing suddenly. "I have already told you, I give you your chance

to accept my conditions gracefully, and marry me of your own free will. If not—well, I know a way of making you do so, and then Arthur Bentwood, with the whole of London at his heels, is welcome to know of your whereabouts, for you will be my wife, and as such it will be none of their business."

"Never—never! I will die first!" cried Marian. "You brute, I hate you! You won't dare do such a thing!"

"No!" replied Kelly, coldly raising his brows. "You will discover tomorrow, my dear young lady, that Gorgon Kelly dares do anything. And now———"

But he broke off suddenly as a deafening crash of glass sounded from outside, for it was at that moment that Tinker had fallen through the roof of the conservatory in his endeavour to hear what was being said by the figures whose gesticulating shadows he could see against the blind.

Kelly rushed to the window, and throwing it up, peered out; but beyond a scuffling sound from below in the conservatory he could discern nothing. He closed the window with a snap and hastened to the door without vouchsafing any remarks to Marian. Switching out the light, and locking the door, he hastened down the stairs, and was just in time to meet Forbes the butler dragging in his prisoner from the conservatory.

"Who is it? What is it, Forbes?" he asked sharply.

"I don't know yet, sir! Seems to be a lad playing burglar. He fell through the roof of the conservatory. I just managed to catch him before he got away."

"Good! Bring him out into the hall under the light, and we'll have a look at him!" jerked Kelly, leading the way.

The unfortunate Tinker knew the game was up if Kelly got a look at him, and he gave a sudden wrench in a desperate endeavour to make a break for freedom back through the conservatory. But Forbes was not to be caught napping, and all Tinker succeeded in accomplishing was an extra painful twist of his arm as his powerful captor dragged him along and jerked him to his feet under the hall light.

Kelly glanced at him curiously, evidently of the opinion that he was just some youthful burglar, and Tinker hoped and prayed he might continue to do so, for arrest would be the quickest road to freedom. The lad being so well known to the police as Sexton Blake's assistant, his release would follow as a matter of course on reaching the station. But as the Money King scrutinised the lad his brows puckered in puzzlement, to finally clear and give way to a glint of anger.

"Ah, ah, ah!" he muttered, rocking back and fro on his heels. "I remember you, my lad. I saw you once with your master—Sexton Blake. And what, might I ask, were you doing on top of my conservatory?"

Tinker remained dumb, hoping that at the best they would not attempt to force an answer from him.

"He seems dumb," went on Kelly. "Twist his arm a trifle, Forbes—slowly. It is much more effective as a tongue loosener. That's it! Now, my lad, perhaps you will answer my question."

The excruciating pain in his arm made Tinker gasp in agony, and the tears forced themselves into his eyes, but he gritted his teeth, vowing that as his indiscretion had led him into such a mess he would at least not acknowledge that he was shadowing Kelly by Blake's orders, no matter what his captors might suspect.

Had matters of moment not been pressing on the Money King, it is doubtful if Tinker's resolution would have survived the torture which the gentleman was capable of devising, but since his successful interview at the bank in the afternoon he had formed the embryo of a plan for a hurricane attack on the stock market, and it would need many hours of careful thought and calculation to mature the details.

Consequently, for the moment Tinker's obstinacy succeeded in its purpose, and Kelly waved his hand to the butler.

"Take him away, Forbes, and lock him up. That room upstairs with the barred windows will do. I will make him talk tomorrow by more forcible means."

He turned and strode along to his library as he finished speaking, and once more Tinker was dragged along at the heels of the butler.

Up the stairs they went, and along a short corridor, where Tinker was thrust unceremoniously into a small room, and the door locked on him.

What the room had originally been used for it was difficult to say, but as he struck a match and peered around Tinker found its present use to be for storing trunks, with which it was half filled. There was no electric light as in other rooms, and by the light of a second match he discovered there was neither gas-jet nor candle.

He would have to husband his matches, of which an examination showed him there were only three left. So in darkness he stumbled across the floor and felt for the window-catch. Throwing it back, he lifted the sash, his hand coming into contact with several iron bars set a few inches apart and forming an effectual barrier to his escape in that direction.

He lit one of his three remaining matches, and by its light took careful stock of the walls, which were without break except for a small ventilator set high up and evidently giving into another room.

As the flame grew hot against his fingers Tinker blew out the match, and softly climbed up on a pile of trunks which had been placed against the wall under the ventilator.

He managed to reach the top without any apparent noise, and felt along the wall for the ventilator. As his fingers touched it he lifted himself up and applied his eyes to the grating, but only impenetrable blackness met him.

Turning his head Tinker applied his ear and listened, for he was determined to try every avenue to effect an escape, and he desired to know if the adjoining room was occupied by any of the household.

At first only silence greeted his silent listening, and he was about to clamber down again and make a more thorough examination of the window-bars when he held his breath as the sound of a stifled sob floated through the grating from the blackness of the other room.

He again bent his head and listened tensely. Yes, there was no doubt about it. Someone was quietly sobbing in the next room, and it sounded like a woman. Could it be the woman whose shadow he had seen against the blind? And, if so, was the adjoining room the one over the conservatory? If it was the same woman, that must be so.

It seemed a reasonable supposition, for the shadows he had seen had certainly had an antagonistic appearance, and the sobs he had heard might well follow a scene of that description. But who was the woman?

Was she friend or foe of Kelly's, and dare he risk attracting her attention? He couldn't be very much worse off than he already was, and as the sobs grew louder Tinker decided to risk it.

He pressed his mouth to the ventilator, and gave a soft hiss. No answer came, so he gave a louder one, and then again pressed his ear to the grating.

Dead silence again reigned in the dark room. The sobs had stopped, indicating that the noise had been heard—which was the case; for Marian caught the sound from where she lay on the sofa, and was sitting up staring into the darkness, her eyes wide with terror at the fear of some unknown fate.

Tinker again broke the silence with another soft hiss, adding in a whisper:

"Who are you? Come to the ventilator in the wall. I am on the other side."

The soft rustle of skirts and slow approaching steps told the lad that the person was following his instructions, and a moment later he heard her shaking whisper float up to him.

"Who are you? What do you want? Have you been placed to spy on me?"

"Not much, miss," whispered back Tinker cheerfully. "I was placed here very much against my will, after falling through the roof of the conservatory. But tell me, who are you?"

"Oh, I heard the crash," she whispered back. "I am Marian Powers, and am being held here by Gorgon Kelly against my will."

"Jiminy—I mean, great Scott!" whispered back Tinker. "This is luck, Miss Powers. I am Tinker, Sexton Blake's assistant, and was crawling up the roof of the conservatory when I fell through."

Tinker quickly explained how he had come to be in the rear of the house, and how the shadows had started him on his unfortunate climb.

"But tell me, Miss Powers—are your windows barred?"

"No; they are not even locked," whispered Marian, who had grown more cheerful at the fact of a friendly voice to talk to. "Why do you ask?"

"Because I've got a strong knife, and I'm going to try and get this ventilator grating out. If I can do that, I can cut away enough of the wall to get through, and we'll both try and escape through your window."

"Oh, do try, please!" whispered Marian. "I am so frightened here. He threatens me with all kinds of things if I don't marry him."

"Huh! Don't you worry! That old codger will never marry you, Miss Powers!" said Tinker cheerfully. "I have no light here," he went on. "Have you any there?"

"Yes; electric."

"Good! If you switch it on it will throw enough light through the grating for me to see to work, and I'll have this ventilator out in no time."

Marian did so, and returned to talk in whispers with Tinker, who had lost no time in getting to work.

Tinker's plucky fight to help Marian Powers to escape from the clutches of Gorgon Kelly.

Tinker falls through the glass roof of Gorgon Kelly's conservatory.

Strange sounds from time to time caused them to stop and stare in apprehensive silence, but the work went steadily ahead. They shook hands in silent delight through the hole when Tinker finally succeeded in removing it, and, feeling encouraged by his success, he went ahead valiantly on the plaster and bricks.

It was no sinecure, and hours of racking work had been put in before Tinker had a hole large enough to permit his body, to squeeze through.

He had noticed a large pile of trunk straps in one corner of his prison and before clambering through the hole he passed them through to Marian. Then, slowly and carefully, in order not to knock out a loose brick, he crept through and stood a moment later, safe and sound, in Marian's sitting-room.

Tinker switched the light out, and threw up the window. Below him he could see the glass roof of the conservatory which had been his Waterloo a few hours earlier. He looked in surprise at the paling sky, realising his work had taken him until dawn, and that they must make haste.

Quickly buckling the straps together, and fastening one end around the handle of the door, he lowered the other end from the window, and smiled as he heard it tap on the glass below. He turned to whisper to Marian that everything was ready, when the words froze on his tongue, as she grasped his arm in a grip of fear.

From outside in the corridor came the sound of stealthy footsteps. The two prisoners scarcely breathed as a handle turned and a door opened. The warning light from a lamp came suddenly through the newly-made hole in the wall and Tinker realising their attempt had been discovered, wasted no more time in further caution.

"Quick" he rapped. "Over the sill, Miss Powers! Never mind about me, I'll get out all right! Hang on to the strap, and watch the glass roof when you get down!"

He disregarded Marian's protestations, and by the sheer urgency of his tone, got her to the window, and began to help her over the sill. But while she still poised on the edge, gripping the strap before launching herself out, the door was burst open, and Forbes, the butler, rushed in.

Tinker grasped a chair, and made for the butler, while he shouted to Marian to make haste and get out. But Forbes was taking no risks, and acted with decision. Catching up a heavy brass ornament from the table, he hurled it with unerring aim at Tinker, and before the lad could ward it off with the chair, it caught him fair on the forehead, and sent him down with a crash.

Keeping straight on, the butler reached out, and grasped Marian just as she was disappearing over the sill, dragging her back without regard to the gentleness of his hold.

Forbes proved himself worthy of better things in his following actions, for he wasted no time in recriminations.

Instead he drew up the buckled straps, and used the would-be means of escape to bind up his captives. Marian he placed in a chair, to which he strapped her firmly while Tinker was bound where he lay, and left to come round as he could. Then, with a sardonic smile at the despairing Marian, he picked up the lamp and left.

The Ninth Chapter
Blake Makes an Important Discovery—Pedro Recognises an Old Friend—Blake Turns the Tables

JUST about the time Tinker crashed through the glass conservatory roof at the back of Gorgon Kelly's house, Sexton Blake was opening the door to admit Arthur Bentwood, the purpose of whose visit has already been related. After Arthur departed Blake returned to his big chair before the fire, in order to await Tinker's return, and go over the new elements in the matters which Arthur Bentwood's tale had introduced.

Certainly, Kelly's movements looked suspicious, and did he wish to marry Marian Powers simply out of love, or was there a deeper purpose behind it all? Why his threatening her in order to make her submit, and had she really disappeared?

It certainly looked that way. But why? As yet the detective could see no motive, and until he had that, although his deductions would mathematically block out the problem in its component parts, the two sides of "question" and "solution" would not balance until he had the motive and its following effect.

And then, again, who was the woman with the scarab? What was her object in keeping the opera-glass trained on Gorgon Kelly's window, and had she any identity with the woman's voice which spoke over the phone to Mr. Wallingford before every market operation of that firm?

Did the Egyptian scarab indicate a knowledge of Egypt, and was there any possibility of its being a first faint clue to the mysterious robbery of Kelly's gold, which had baffled him for so long? She certainly had some strong interest in the Money King, but just where and how she came in was as yet wrapped in mystery.

Over and over the points of the case went Blake, endeavouring to piece together the scattered fragments of the puzzle.

Midnight was long past when he finally rose and knocked the ashes from his pipe.

"Why on earth hasn't Tinker returned to report, as I told him to?" he muttered. "With the new points introduced by Bentwood's story, it is essential that I know every move of Kelly's during the day."

But no Tinker returned, and when morning revealed no sign of the missing lad, Blake's irritation turned to worry.

Rarely had a case baffled Blake so persistently as had the robbery of the gold payment of Kelly's Egyptian loan, and now that all other cases had been shelved in order that he might devote his every effort to its elucidation, Blake needed Tinker at any and every moment. Consequently, his continued absence made him slightly uneasy on top of Marian Powers' supposed disappearance.

Leaving a note for the lad, in case he should return during the morning, and with the reflection that he ought to be able to look after himself by now, Blake, with Pedro at his heels, started for the City, to begin the first move of what was to prove one of the busiest days in his long career.

The detective's first stop was at the Equidential Building, where a little judicious questioning of the lift-boy elicited the fact that Mr. Gorgon Kelly had arrived at his office at the usual time.

From there Blake took himself to the offices of Wallingford & Co., where he got from Arthur Bentwood the name of Kelly's bankers, and also discovered that the young man was in a state of collapse, for the morning had as yet showed no signs of Marian.

With a final word of caution not to do anything rash, Blake hurried along to "Kendrick's," the big bankers with whom Kelly banked. Blake felt positive Kelly had lied about the return of the forty boxes of gold; but, to be on the safe side, he would inquire at the bank. If it had been returned, it was a safe conjecture that Kelly would deposit it, particularly as the fattest of bank accounts would need bolstering up after the heavy losses which the Money King had experienced.

As Blake and Pedro ascended the broad steps which led up to the pillared portals of the bank, a fashionably-gowned woman descended.

As Blake drew aside to permit her to pass, he glanced up to see the young woman of the Equidential Building, whose use of the opera-glasses had excited his curiosity.

As his eyes met hers—Blake was not in disguise—he could have sworn that he caught a fleeting look of recognition in her eyes. It passed so quickly he began to think he had been mistaken, but his momentary wonder changed to amazement when Pedro, the most reserved and formal of dogs, showed unmistakable signs of pleased recognition.

He submitted his head quite gravely to the hurried pat of a tiny gloved hand, and, with a fleeting roguish smile, the vision in blue serge was gone.

"Well, I'm hanged!" muttered Blake, stroking his chin in puzzled wonder. "I only know of one woman who dabbled in mysteries and against whom I was arrayed to whom Pedro ever held any regard, and that is Mademoiselle Yvonne.

"There is something elusively familiar about you, young woman, that makes me begin to think. Is it possible—— No; pshaw, of course not! But who is she? Pedro, you rascal, why can't you speak and tell me the name of your mysterious acquaintance?

But the only answer he got from the hound was a wise look from the great eyes and a slow pounding of the heavy tail.

But a strange sense of elation ran through Blake as he continued on through the door of the bank. Yvonne had been the only opponent whom Pedro, although loyal to Blake, had entertained a good-natured canine regard for, and the dog's friendship for their fair enemy had been only a confirmation of Blake's judgment of her clean, wholesome nature, which lay submerged under her mistaken and quixotic ideas of law and order.

Mr. Cameron, the manager of Kendrick's had been a personal friend of Blake's ever since the latter had saved the bank a matter of thirty thousand pounds[17] some twelve months previously, by anticipating and frustrating a clever swindle on it. Consequently,

---

[17] £30,000 in 1913 is worth about £3,500,000 in 2020

he was pleased to see the detective, and, although not strictly in order, stretched a point, and answered Blake's questions regarding the condition of Gorgon Kelly's account.

Blake's eyes glittered when the manager told him that instead of depositing two hundred thousand pounds, the amount contained in the forty stolen boxes, he had borrowed almost that amount on securities, the face value of which was exactly two hundred thousand.

The thought came to Blake that the gold might have been returned, and in turn invested in the securities, which happened to run into the same amount. With a desire to settle this point, he asked the favour of examining one of the securities.

The manager laughed.

"You don't suspect anything wrong with Kelly's securities, do you, Blake?"

"Oh, no," smiled Blake; "but I have a curiosity to see one of them, if you can strain the point that far!"

"Well," laughed Cameron, rising, "it is out of the strict rule of the bank, but I guess in view of your standing, and what you did for us a year ago, I can risk it."

He called a clerk as he spoke, and a few moments later was handed the rubber-clasped bundle of securities on which the Money King had borrowed so heavily the previous day.

The manager took off the clasp and handed one of the securities to Blake, but he did not see the quick flash in the detective's eyes and the sudden set of the jaw as Blake read the transfer from John Powers to Gorgon Kelly. He was right, the gold had not been returned and then invested in these securities, for John Powers was long dead, and the transfer was dated two years previously.

So that was why Kelly entertained such a deep admiration for Marian Powers, was it? But if John Powers had transferred the securities in the regular course of business, where was Marian Powers necessary? This matter would certainly bear further investigation.

Blake needed his strongest powers of persuasion to gain the manager's assent to his taking one of the securities along with him, but in the end he triumphed, and a moment later was tearing along in a taxi to Baker Street, with Pedro at his feet and the security in his pocket.

On his arrival there Blake went at once to his laboratory, where he spread out the security on the glass-topped table. He then applied several chemical tests to both the original signature of John Powers and to the writing of the transfer to Gorgon Kelly, and he gave a muttered exclamation as the ink of the transfer yielded at once to the test, but the old original signature failed to do so.

"Forged, by thunder!" he snapped. "The pigment must be less than a week old to yield to the yellow test! Gorgon Kelly, my clever friend, you made a mistake when you tried to turn me off. It was a bad day's work for you. And now to business, for there are many loose strings yet."

Blake straightened up and refolded the security grimly, stuffing it back in his pocket. Leaving Pedro in charge of the rooms, and writing another message to the still absent

Tinker, he entered his dressing-room. When he emerged he was disguised as a casual labourer, and in this guise hastened out and hailed a taxi.

Blake left the taxi at a convenient corner, and walked to the entrance of the Equidential Building. He now felt certain of Kelly's duplicity, and smiled grimly as he thought of the eruption the exposure of the Money King would cause.

But many points, as he had said, were still obscure. Had Kelly, after all, stolen his own gold, and for some hidden purpose claimed it was stolen by some mysterious criminals? It didn't seem reasonable in the light of what Blake knew.

But what puzzled the detective more than any other point was the young woman with the scarab on her finger. He must solve her identity and connection with Kelly before making any other move, for she might, in a roundabout way be an accomplice of Kelly.

Blake had a long interview with the caretaker of the Equidential Building, who gaped in astonishment when the detective revealed his identity. The upshot was that the caretaker, an autocrat in his own realm, informed the office-boy, who happened to be the sole occupant of Justin Grantley's offices, that a man was coming up to clean the windows.

Five minutes later Blake, in his garb of casual labourer, entered with mop and pail, and, to the accompaniment of the office-boy's cheeky repartee, worked valiantly at the windows in the outer office. His objective was the private office, but it would not do to arouse the boy's curiosity, and although the tenants might enter at any moment, Blake suppressed his impatience and completed the windows in the outer office before entering the inner.

He entered leisurely and approached the windows which looked across into Gorgon Kelly's private sanctum. The Money King was in the act of speaking over the phone, and Blake, mechanically watching him, was surprised at the ease with which he distinguished from the movements of Kelly's lips most of what he was saying. And in that moment of his absorption it flashed across his mind, with lightning-like rapidity, the reason of the opera-glasses.

As the solution occurred to him, he lifted his head and laughed softly at the simplicity and yet the cleverness of it. "No wonder Kelly's operations were anticipated!" he said to himself. "What a scheme and how infallible the source of information! My dear young lady, who makes a certainty of your lip-reading by using opera-glasses, and who wears a large Egyptian scarab on your finger, I long to meet you! Are you a new jewel in the cluster of criminal gems, or an old solitaire in a new setting? And yet there is nothing criminal in reading what Gorgon Kelly says and following the information gained. But the scarab—I am still curious to know its history."

Blake turned and cast his eyes rapidly around the small, richly-furnished office.

The desk was littered with unimportant papers, mostly referring to stocks and bonds. Over in the corner reposed a small steel safe, and this Blake cautiously approached.

"It would be a great assistance if I knew the word of that," he mused, as he listened for any movement in the outer office. "I wonder if I have time to try? I'll risk it, at any rate."

Dropping on one knee Blake thought for a moment, and then set the letters until they spelled out "scarab," but the door did not yield. Rapidly he tried Huntley, Cairo, Kelly, and Gorgon, but all failed to release the combination.

"I wonder if it's any use?" he muttered. "I'll try it on a chance." Quickly he again began, spelling out Yvonne, and his lips twitched in a smile as the handle turned softly and the door swung open.

Inside was a mass of papers and securities, through which Blake went with feverish haste. His eye lighted as his search revealed a small packet marked "Plans and specifications," which, on being, opened, proved to be carefully-drawn plans for a small wooden box, with specifications for a particular kind of wood and nails, and at one side specifications for iron bands to bind it. Another sheet disclosed a minute sketch of a seal, bearing the name of the Khartoum and River Nile Banking Co.

But Blake clutched the papers tight and stiffened as a voice broke the silence of the office.

"You deserve credit, my window-cleaning friend," came in slow, icy accents. "The fact that you have discovered the combination of that safe reveals your identity, for I know of no one else who could do so. Get up, Mr. Blake, and please keep your hands away from your pockets, for my finger is on the trigger, and it pulls very easily."

Blake turned slowly, to find himself looking into the barrel of a small automatic revolver, over which the young woman of the scarab looked with a satirical smile.

"I bow for the present to your obviously superior argument, Mademoiselle Yvonne," he smiled, covering his chagrin as he rose; "but my inferior position is tempered by the pleasure of meeting you again."

Yvonne broke into a laugh.

"So you suspected, did you?" she asked merrily.

"I must say I did not," smiled back Blake, "at least, not until Pedro recognised in you an old acquaintance."

"Ah, yes, at the bank this morning! It was injudicious of me to pat him; but he is such a dear old chap, I couldn't resist it. But I'll trouble you to pass over those artistic efforts, Mr. Blake; they are not exactly the kind of documents I wish you to have."

"Certainly, mademoiselle," smiled Blake, holding them out.

Yvonne approached, and reached for them, but as she did so, Blake ducked quickly, and brought his hand up suddenly. His fingers closed in a vice-like grip around Yvonne's wrist, and his other arm shot around her waist as, with an exclamation of surprise, she struggled in his arms.

But her physical strength was hopeless in his barely exerted grasp, and if Yvonne prolonged the futile struggle longer than necessary for the secret pleasure of being near him, who can criticise her.

With a little choking gasp, her fingers loosened, and the revolver dropped harmlessly to the soft carpet as Blake bent quickly for it and released her.

"Now, mademoiselle," he smiled, "we can talk more comfortably. I always dislike to carry on a conversation with a revolver pointing at me."

"I—I wouldn't shoot you that way," panted Yvonne; "but why—why do you always step in and thwart my plans, Mr. Blake? I felt in my new identity I was safe to go my way, since you don't approve of it?"

"It is because my duty is to uphold law and order, mademoiselle," replied Blake gravely. "But, come, I am anxious for knowledge, and before arresting you would like to know if my theory is correct. I presume you did it for the sake of revenge?"

Yvonne nodded wearily as she sank into a chair.

"Yes—revenge. Gorgon Kelly was one of the men who swindled us in Australia, and left us without a penny."

"I imagined so as soon as I suspected you in the matter," remarked Blake. "And the lip-reading through the opera-glasses, and the subsequent forestalling of Kelly on the Exchange was part of the plan to ruin him?"

Yvonne nodded in amazed admiration.

"How on earth did you know that?" she asked.

Blake smiled.

"It wouldn't do to tell you all my methods, mademoiselle. You know enough about them now. But your plan to ruin Gorgon Kelly has gone through better than you thought. Do you know that he is on the brink of ruin?"

"Yes," answered Yvonne, "and when he gets through today he will be worse off than ever."

"How do you mean?" asked Blake sharply.

"Oh, he is plunging heavily on the Exchange," she returned, "and through my brokers I am fighting him! Wallingford & Co.'s success lately has sent the public after them like sheep, and Kelly is playing a lone hand today."

"Ah," breathed Blake, "I am glad to know that! It means I must move soon. But to return to the forty boxes of gold, mademoiselle, which the plans I found tell me I am right."

Rapidly Blake sketched his recently-formed theory of their mysterious disappearance, and Yvonne's eyes lit up with admiration as she listened.

"All correct, but in two points," she laughed. "You are right about a second set of duplicate boxes, but the exchange took place at Port Said, and although you are correct in imagining we bribed an Arab boatman, the plan was carried even further, and I myself acted the part."

"I see," nodded Blake. "I might have imagined you would carry out your plans thoroughly. But, mademoiselle, I want the gold back. If you have used it, I want its equivalent."

"You speak confidently, Mr. Blake," she laughed. "What will you give if I return you the forty boxes unopened?"

Hardened as he was, Blake's eyes gleamed for a moment at the undoubted triumph of such a return.

"I am in a position, mademoiselle, where I have to give nothing; but providing that is the only crime which you have committed against the law since your escape, and for certain reasons considering the man from whom you stole it, I will, if you observe the condition I lay down, give you twenty-four hours' start before notifying the authorities at Dalemoor Prison of your whereabouts. Perhaps that is too lenient, but——" And Blake waved his hand comprehensively.

"I agree, Mr. Blake," smiled Yvonne. "It is the only crime I have committed, so tell me your conditions, please!"

"Since you know what has gone on in Gorgon Kelly's office," said Blake, with apparent irrelevancy, "perhaps you know the name of his secretary?"

"Yes," nodded Yvonne, "Marian Powers. Kelly has been plotting to make her marry him."

And then Sexton Blake, the famous criminologist, and Mademoiselle Yvonne, the famous adventuress put their heads together in a temporary partnership that would secure for Yvonne a short start, and would dramatically cap one of the greatest exposures of the famous detective's career.

The Tenth Chapter
Another Shattering Day on the Exchange—Kelly Plays Another Card Blake Takes the Trick

GORGON Kelly went to his office in the morning after Tinker's capture and attempted escape with an uneasy quiver of fear in his heart.

Not until he brought up the magnate's breakfast had Forbes told him how he foiled the plans of Tinker and Marian. He had become suspicious in a very simple way. The long, burning light in Marian's sitting-room had shone out, and been reflected from the roof of the conservatory.

He could see it from where he slept, but though he watched it, felt no suspicion until he saw and heard the soft raising of the window. Then he had started to see if the prisoners were all right, with the result already related.

Tinker's attempt to rescue Marian Powers told Kelly, without his forcing the lad to speak, that in some way Sexton Blake had become suspicious, and the knowledge sent the quiver of fear into his heart.

But he did not dream that Blake was as hot on the track as really was the case, nor did he know that while he had spent the evening planning out his big market coup for the following day, which he would finance with the arranged loan on the forged securities, that Sexton Blake had been listening to Arthur Bentwood's agitated tale of Marian's disappearance.

Had he known that, and that the morning was to bring to Blake the discovery of the forgery, he would have realised on what he could and started at once for abroad.

But he did not know these things, and though he experienced a vague, undefined fear, he felt that a profitable day on the Exchange would yet make things right, and give him an opportunity to put into operation his plans to marry Marian Powers. With her as his wife, he could snap his fingers at the discovery of the forgery, for the securities were legally hers, and his wife would not prosecute.

Not even Blake suspected yet that Gorgon Kelly had of late made secret use of funds belonging to companies for which he was trustee, and for which he would soon have to give an accounting.

That worried the Money King far more than the forgery and was the chief spur in the planning of the day's coup, which, he muttered grimly, would shake the market as it had never been shaken.

He was right there—it was to shake the market, but in a way for which he didn't bargain.

However, he put away his nervousness regarding Blake, and arrived exceptionally early at his office. He immediately began to put into operation the many forces over which he still held control, for none as yet suspected the real condition of the great magnate.

The moment the Exchange opened he had an army of brokers buying any and all quantities of American Coppers which had proved so disastrous to him two days previously.

All morning the buying went on, until he had accumulated heavy obligations, but still heavy blocks of shares kept being thrown to his hungry brokers, and it was no secret that Wallingford & Co. were the sellers.

At any previous time the general public would have followed the least move of the Money King with feverish haste. But his persistent losses of late, and Wallingford & Co.'s success had changed the fickle public, and where Kelly had counted on their bolstering purchases, he found that they had one and all joined the selling ranks, and that he was playing a lone hand against the whole street.

He grew desperate as the price of Copper shares went lower in spite of his constant purchases, and fresh brokers were sent to boom it up.

But Wallingford's still kept throwing unlimited blocks on the market, and for the second time that day Kelly, who sat in his office watching the pulse of the market, felt a thrill of fear.

A cold sweat broke out on his forehead as he thought of that grim visitor, and the awful fall of the Money King if he lost all. The thought maddened him again to phone to send more brokers on the market in a last desperate effort to stop the downward course of Coppers.

And while he sent his feverish orders over the phone, Sexton Blake sat in the office of Kelly's bankers, making a tentative examination of one of the forged securities, an examination he was to elaborate a little later in Baker Street.

Kelly did not go out for lunch. The news he was receiving was too serious, and he dreaded to walk down the street, for every broker would know that once again the impregnable Money King was being beaten, and Kelly knew he could not keep the awful fear he felt from showing.

Blake, it will be remembered, did not tell Cameron, the bank manager, his exact reason for desiring the loan of the forged security, and his purpose was to keep all suspicion of discovery from Kelly's ears until he was ready to act, for then he had not unmasked Yvonne.

But the manager had pondered the matter on Blake's departure, and the more he thought of it, the more serious he became. When he went out to lunch he heard of the heavy movement on the Exchange against the Money King, and that decided him. He bolted his lunch, and hastened back to his office, where he called up Kelly on the phone.

In cold, formal words, he informed the magnate that his bank would be obliged if Mr. Kelly would make repayment of the last loan before the bank opened in the morning.

Kelly froze in his chair as he heard the bank manager's words. He jerked out a reply in the affirmative and hung up the receiver, but he knew he could not repay a thousand pounds by the morning, let alone nearly two hundred thousand! What had caused the sudden recall of the loan? Was the bank getting nervous over his losses on the market, or—good heavens, could they be in any way suspicious of the securities?

And then Gorgon Kelly, white and shaking, did something he had not found necessary for years. He reached down and opened a drawer in his desk, from which he took a flask, unscrewed the cap, and put it to his lips, drinking long and deep of the brandy it contained.

The phone rang, and he mechanically lifted the receiver to listen, with a strange, detached, apathetic interest, to the latest news of the market. He hung it up, and sat in absorption, his mind clouded by the realisation that not only poverty, but disgrace, was marching on him with rapid footsteps.

Across the light well Sexton Blake, in guise of a window-cleaner, sat talking with Mademoiselle Yvonne, who, strange to say, had yielded to the detective's conditions, and for the nonce was working with him.

But Kelly was deaf and blind to everything but the awful menace which stared him in the face, and as the brandy coursed through his blood his mind cleared a little, and he began to scheme in a last desperate effort to escape the net.

He thought rapidly. All hope in the market was gone. Every minute there was only making things worse. He could not meet his obligations and repay the loan to the bank, and that would mean exposure. On top of that would follow a demand for an account of his several trusteeships, and he knew what that meant. There was no way out but one—flight.

But how could he go? He was penniless; and he drew from his pocket, with a bitter smile, a few pieces of silver. But wait; Gorgon Kelly was still the powerful Money King to the City. His cheque would be cashed with alacrity in a thousand different offices. But if he was to do that he must act quickly.

Yes, he would. There was nothing else. He would write out a sheaf, and send the chief clerk about the City. He would make them small, in order not to create wonder or inquiry, and as he made the decision, the man who such a short time before had controlled every heartbeat of the money-market actually gloated in childish glee at the cleverness of his plan.

Blake, after the acceptance of his conditions by Yvonne, had detailed rapidly to her his plan. She, in conformance with her promise, was to return the forty boxes of gold, without Blake arresting her. Blake and Yvonne would motor out to Maida Vale, where Yvonne had her house, and get the gold, after which they would return to the City and go at once to Kelly's bankers.

Yvonne's motor was waiting below, and they lost no time in carrying out that part of their plan, for Blake had been angry at Kelly's lie about the return of the gold, and he had determined to make the exposure of the magnate complete and dramatic.

Had he known that, as they drove away in the direction of Maida Vale, Kelly was writing sheafs of cheques, which he hoped to cash, Blake would not have risked leaving; but he did not know this, and so it was that he and Yvonne—friends and allies for the moment—chatted in friendly fashion as Yvonne's big, luxurious car sped over the ground.

Graves nearly collapsed in an apoplectic fit of fright as Yvonne entered with the dreaded enemy, but he soon regained his drawling nonchalance on learning the truth, although he lost no time in making his exit to prepare for the twenty-four hours' start which Blake was granting Yvonne on condition that the gold was returned.

Blake's eyes gleamed slightly as he watched the forty famous boxes, still intact, being carried down and stowed in the capacious car, but he smiled carelessly as Yvonne looked at him roguishly and said:

"There, Mr. Blake, are you satisfied? Am I never to be free of you and your ruining of my plans?"

"I thought we were allies for today?" he smiled.

"We are, and I wish——" But what it was she wished Yvonne bit off, though her colour deepened a trifle.

They entered the car as the last box was stowed away, and, room being scarce, dispensed with the chauffeur, Blake himself taking the wheel.

He sent the car along, stopping at Baker Street for Pedro, at a sound pace, and frowned when he found on reaching the bank that it was after banking hours and the door was closed. He mounted the steps, however, and his brow relaxed as Cameron himself responded to the detective's knock.

"I suppose you have brought back the security you borrowed," remarked Cameron, ushering him into the office. "By the way, what is the matter with them, Blake? You got me nervous this morning, and this afternoon I called in the loan from Kelly."

"You what?" almost shouted Blake. "Good heavens, man, why did you do that? My whole plan will be ruined, and perhaps the bird has already escaped! Why couldn't you have waited until you heard from me?"

"Well, you see," answered Cameron apologetically, "I don't dare take risks, for the bank's sake, and to be on the safe side called it in."

"Do you think I wasn't considering the bank?" snapped Blake shortly, for the news had sent him into one of his rare fits of anger. "But come, there is no time to be lost! You'll never get that loan in, but I've got enough of his funds to settle it. But I may be too late to catch my man. Get the whole bundle of securities, put this with them— here," and Blake dug out the one in his pocket. "Then get your hat and come with me. I haven't time to explain now."

And the agitated and wondering Cameron hastened to obey, not attempting to ask questions while Blake was in his present mood.

A few moments later, wondering still more, Cameron scrambled into the car, which held one of his new but largest customers in the form of Yvonne, and his jaw opened with a gasp as his practised eye recognised the nature of the piles of iron-clamped boxes.

Blake sent the car at a reckless pace to the office of Wallingford & Co., when the wondering Arthur Bentwood was hauled forth unceremoniously to join the bank manager; and Yvonne's delicious laugh of appreciation caused the detective's frown to relax as he smiled back at her.

"I see now the reason of your success," she softly said. "Really, Mr. Blake, to work with you is quite as exciting as—as———"

"Revenge," he finished gravely.

And Yvonne's eyes filled for a moment with the old weary look as she realised all that one word stood for.

Blake pulled up with a jerk in front of the Equidential Building, and, leaving the others in the car, hastened in to the offices of the Money King.

But what he feared had occurred. Mr. Kelly had left in his motor half an hour before, and Blake muttered savagely as he dashed out again.

"Just as I thought!" he jerked out to Yvonne, as he threw in the clutch and sent the car bounding ahead. "Cameron's message made him suspicious, and he has flown."

"His day on the Exchange was about enough to do that," replied Yvonne.

But Blake was too absorbed in threading his way through the traffic to reply.

Twenty minutes later they pulled up in front of Kelly's imposing residence.

"Follow me!" snapped Blake to the others, as he leaped out and dashed up the steps.

He pressed the bell and waited impatiently, hardly daring to hope that his summons would be answered.

"Stand aside," he ordered, as he heard footsteps approaching. "You, mademoiselle, watch the car. If I catch him I will keep my promise that you say to him what you have to say."

Yvonne obediently descended the steps, and Blake turned as the door was opened by a grim-faced woman.

At that moment an angry voice floated through the hall, ordering the woman to admit no one. She tried to close the door, but Blake thrust his foot inside and pushed it open. The woman gave way, and the detective rushed inside, followed by Pedro, Cameron, and Arthur Bentwood.

"We'll try the library first!" called Blake, drawing his revolver and keeping on. He reached the door and flung it open, to find no occupant there, although the littered condition of the desk told of a hurried departure.

He dashed out again, but pulled up as he heard Pedro's heavy bay from the floor above.

"Pedro has tracked them!" he panted. "Come on!" And up the stairs raced the trio.

Blake called loudly on reaching the top, and Pedro's answering bark came faintly, followed by the report of a revolver.

With a muttered growl Blake dashed on, opening each door, until the noise of a scuffle reached them. They discovered its nature a moment later, as they turned another corner and came out into a small square hall, at the head of which was evidently a rear staircase.

There a strange sight met them.

On the floor, bound and gagged, lay Marian Powers with wide-open eyes of terror. Crouched on his knees was Gorgon Kelly, his right arm held in a grip of iron by Pedro's jaws, while his left vainly endeavoured to choke the dog into releasing him. His revolver lay on the floor, where it had evidently fallen after he had fired at Pedro.

Over and over rolled the man and the dog, while Forbes the butler was dancing about with a chair endeavouring to brain the dog, but withheld from doing so by the danger of hitting Kelly.

Blake dashed forward with levelled revolver, but Forbes swung and hurled the chair at him. Blake, instead of dodging, dropped like a shot, and the chair sailed past his head to catch Cameron on the chest, but fortunately only with enough force to send him down with nothing worse than the breath knocked out of him.

Blake fired from the floor, the bullet injuring the butler's wrist, and Arthur, although Marian's frightened eyes were calling him to her, withstood the temptation and grappled with the now disabled Forbes. Thanks to Pedro's prompt action and bravery, Kelly was made an easy prisoner.

They trussed up master and servant, and then released Marian, who was suffering from shock more than anything else. She at once began to tell them where Tinker lay bound, but Pedro's distant bark told Blake that the energetic hound had already found the lad.

Blake had determined to speak forcibly to Tinker about his folly, but on hearing of the lad's plucky attempt to rescue Marian he refrained, thinking truly that the experience was lesson enough.

Ten minutes later the whole party, with the two prisoners, were stowed into the motor, and, Yvonne at the wheel, were heading for the City again.

In view of Marian's condition Arthur descended with her at Piccadilly in order to take her home.

The rest continued on to the Equidential Building, where the amazed caretaker admitted them.

Willing hands carried the forty boxes of gold into Kelly's office, and then, after placing the fallen Money King in a chair, with Pedro, Tinker, Yvonne, and the still puzzled Cameron seated near, Blake began to speak.

Slowly, and with painful distinctness, the very air chilled by his tone, he denounced the Money King. Beginning at his engagement for the recovery of the gold, he followed the events of the months past, dwelling on Kelly's double-dealing regarding the gold, and his dishonourable intention to force the helpless Marian to be his wife.

"And then," he added, "I have kept until the last the most important thing, Gorgon Kelly, for I realised that your other deeds would not recoil on you in a court of law. I know your history, and the swindle in which you participated in Australia when you beggared two helpless women—killing one with the shock, and driving the other into the world, her whole life spoiled by bitterness you and your associates instilled in her.

"But I thought you too clever a man, Kelly, to stoop to forgery, and it is for the forged transfer of two hundred thousand pounds' worth of securities that I arrest you!"

If Blake had anticipated his remark to reach home his anticipations were realised, for without a sound Kelly, utterly broken, dropped forward on the floor insensible to everything; and Yvonne, quite satisfied with the completeness of her revenge, refrained from speaking further.

She held out her hand to Blake, and, though her lips smiled, her eyes clouded with weariness.

"Thank you, Mr. Blake, for your splendid action to me. Believe me, it was good of you, and my arrest would have served no good purpose at present."

"I am in doubt about that," smiled Blake, taking her hand; "but if it will make you change your ideas I will feel I did right."

"You know the only thing that will do that," she retorted, looking at him. "I am sorry, mademoiselle, believe me! If I could———"

"Don't—please don't!" she interrupted. "My life is bleak and lonely enough without hearing that again."

And before Blake could reply she had turned hastily, and with a nod to Tinker and a quick pat on Pedro's head she was gone, the throb of the motor reaching them from the street as once more she went out of Blake's life to reappear—how and when?

***

The trial and conviction of Gorgon Kelly, the Money King, stirred the City to its depth. It caused more than the usual nine days wonder, and for a time it looked as though a panic would ensue on the Exchange. But Wallingford & Co., grown rich through Yvonne's operations, and backed up by Cameron's Bank, jumped into the breach. The public, still remembering the recent successes of Wallingford & Co., felt confidence when that firm took hold of things, and in two days the crisis had passed.

Gorgon Kelly got fifteen years' penal servitude, for on top of the forgery his use of trustee funds was discovered.

Wallingford & Co took over the different companies and reorganised them—Arthur Bentwood, the new partner, being put in charge of that department. The shareholders got pound for pound back, and the contents of the famous forty boxes went to repay Cameron's Bank for the loan on the forged securities. These, after a long process of red tape, were returned to Marian Bentwood, for Arthur insisted on an immediate marriage, and, as he was backed up by Sexton Blake, she capitulated with a shy, happy blush.

Yvonne made good use of her twenty-four hours' start, and while Gorgon Kelly was being tried the *Fleur-de-Lys*, with Yvonne and Graves and the rest of the "circle" on board, was steaming at a steady pace for Yvonne's island retreat in the South Pacific.

Blake, in accordance with his decision, informed the authorities at Dalemoor of Yvonne's presence in England. But by the time his report had been questioned and passed through a maze of red tape the bird had flown, and considering this Tinker was rather astounded when on the receipt of the news Blake rose and walked to the window whistling softly.

The UNION JACK. 1d
YVONNE DRUGS SEXTON BLAKE'S COFFEE.
A MINISTER OF THE CROWN
Her Intended Cry Dropped Into A Gurgle
YVONNE
NO. 498 NEW SERIES.]
April 26th, 1913.
[EVERY THURSDAY.

SUITS

Send us your word of honour to pay 6s. on receipt of suit and 2s. per week, and we will despatch Gent.'s 30s. Stylish Tweed or Navy-Blue Serge Suit to any approved address.

SEND NO MONEY

Just send your measure and promise to pay or return Suit. Three Shillings discount for Cash on receipt.

ORDER FORM.

Height..

Chest over Vest......................................

Trousers Leg..

Trousers Waist......................................

Pattern ....

The BRAUNT COY., 164, Howard Street, GLASGOW.

IF YOU WANT Good Cheap Photographic Material or Cameras, send postcard for **Samples** and Catalogue FREE.—Works: JULY ROAD, LIVERPOOL.

SPLENDID VALUE
Gents & Ladies' Packed Free. Carriage Paid
ROYAL AJAX CYCLES
Accessories Free   Fully Guaranteed.
EASY TERMS from 7'6 per month.
with immediate delivery of Cycle
LOW PRICES from 50' upwards
Write for FREE PRICE LIST
BRITISH CYCLE Cº Lᵗᴰ Dept J.B.
THE OLD FIRM. 1 & 3 Berry Street, LIVERPOOL

MOUSTACHE!

A Smart Manly Moustache grows **very quickly** at any age by using "Mousta," the guaranteed Moustache Forcer. Boys become Men. Acts like Magic! Box sent in plain cover for 7d. Send now to—

J. A. DIXON & Co., 42, Junction Rd., London, N.

STARTLING REDUCTIONS

MARVELLOUS BARGAINS.
OPPORTUNITIES FOR KEEN CYCLE BUYERS.

DIRECT FROM FACTORY THE

ART LISTS FREE

You will save the shopkeepers' profit by sending your order **direct** to our Factory and buying 1913 Gold Medal Quadrants at **Wholesale Trade Price.** Here's cycle value. **We only charge £3 12s.** for our Popular Model, listed at £6 15s. and sold in shops at full list price. Our superb Standard Model (List Price and Shop Price £9 15s.), supplied **direct** for £6 9s. 3d. cash, or 7/10 deposit and 18 monthly payments of 7/10. We fit **DUNLOP TYRES, 3-SPEED GEARS, BROOKS' SADDLES**, etc., etc. We grant **10** days' approval, give a **10 years'** warranty, and guarantee perfect satisfaction or return your money in full. Write **at once** for Art Lists.

THOUSANDS OF TESTIMONIALS.

from 5/- A MONTH

QUADRANT CYCLE CO., Lᵀᴰ., (DEPT 3), COVENTRY.

WORLD'S RECORD
166,000 MILES

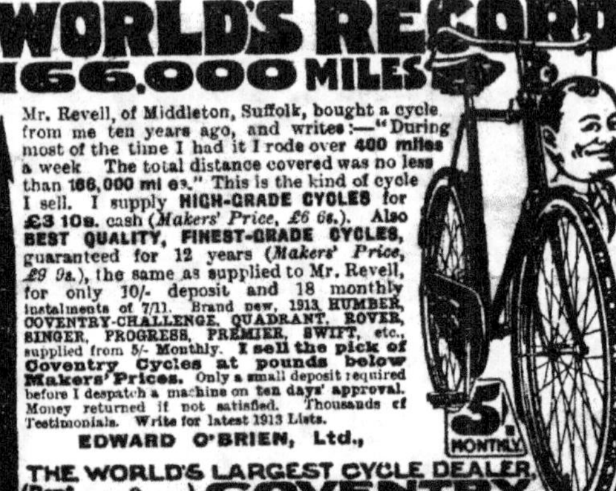

Mr. Revell, of Middleton, Suffolk, bought a cycle from me ten years ago, and writes:—"During most of the time I had it I rode over **400 miles** a week The total distance covered was no less than **166,000 mi es.**" This is the kind of cycle I sell. I supply **HIGH-GRADE CYCLES** for **£3 10s.** cash (*Makers' Price, £6 6s.*). Also **BEST QUALITY, FINEST-GRADE CYCLES**, guaranteed for 12 years (*Makers' Price, £9 9s.*), the same as supplied to Mr. Revell, for only 10/- deposit and 18 monthly instalments of 7/11. Brand new, 1913 **HUMBER, COVENTRY-CHALLENGE, QUADRANT, ROVER, SINGER, PROGRESS, PREMIER, SWIFT**, etc., supplied from 5/- Monthly. **I sell the pick of Coventry Cycles at pounds below Makers' Prices.** Only a small deposit required before I despatch a machine on ten days' approval. Money returned if not satisfied. Thousands of Testimonials. Write for latest 1913 Lists.

EDWARD O'BRIEN, Ltd.,

THE WORLD'S LARGEST CYCLE DEALER, (Dept 2), **COVENTRY.**

LOOK ! Fun, Magic, &c., 250 Jokes and Riddles, 16 Feats in Parlour Magic, 15 Tricks with Cards, 52 Money-Making Secrets, 51 Verses of Comic Poetry, 40 Amusing Experiments, 12 Gay Love Letters, 12 Flirtation Cards, and 100 more Splendid Amusements. 7d. lot. Catalogue and Love Letter Free.—BRITISH SUPPLY CO., ILKESTON.

ACCORDIONS

These beautifully finished organ-toned instruments, made of the finest selected materials, are unsurpassed for power and richness of tone, for which these instruments are famous. All the latest improvements. Exceptionally low prices.

Sent on Approval. Easy Instalments. Catalogue Free.

Douglas, 83, King's Chambers, South St., London, E.C.

TEN DAYS' FREE TRIAL.
Packed Free. Carriage Paid. No deposit required.
MEAD Coventry Flyers.
Warranted 15 Years. Puncture-Resisting or Dunlop Tyres, Brooks' Saddles, Coasters, Speed-Gears, &c.
£2. 15s. to £6. 19s. 6d.
Won *Cycling's* Century Competition Gold Medal. Shop-soiled and Second-hand Cycles, from 15/- Write for **Free Art Catalogue**, *Motor Cycle List*, an-l *Special Offer.*

MEAD CYCLE CO., Dept. 44D 11 Paradise St., Liverpool.

VENTRILOQUISM made easier. Our new complete enlarged book of easy instructions and ten amusing dialogues enables anyone to learn this Wonderful Laughable Art. Only 7d.; post free. 'Thousands Delighted.' (Dolls supplied.) Thought-Reading, 8d.; Mesmerism, 1s. 2d.—G. WILKES & CO., Stockton, Rugby, Eng

FUN for SIXPENCE.

VENTRILOQUIST'S Double Throat ; fits roof of mouth ; astonishes and mystifies ; sing like a canary, whine like a puppy, and imitate birds and beasts. Ventriloquism Treatise free. Sixpence each, four for 1s.— BENSON (Dept. 6), 239, Pentonville Road, London, N.

6/6 each

The "LORD ROBERTS" TARGET PISTOL.

Beautifully plated and finished. May be carried in the pocket. Will kill birds and rabbits up to 50 yards. Noiseless Ball Cartridges, 9d. per 100. Shot, 1/6 per 100. 100 birds or rabbits may be killed at a cost of 9d. only. Send for list, **CROWN GUN WORKS, 6, Whittall Street, BIRMINGHAM.**

FREE, ABSOLUTELY FREE. This beautiful 12-ct. Gold-filled Signet Ring. We make this extraordinary offer to introduce our new catalogue. All we ask of you is to send your name and address, with P.O. for 10¼. to cover the cost of engraving your initial and postage. Two-Initial Intertwined Monograms, 1s.1d.—SIMS & MAYER (Dept 15), Walker House, 418 to 422, Strand, London, W.C.

THE CHINESE PERIL.

BIRTH of a MYSTERIOUS BROTHERHOOD.

RUMOURS OF A WONDERFUL YELLOW BEETLE

WILL SEXTON BLAKE PROBE THE MYSTERY ?

INTRODUCING PRINCE WU LING

ONE OF SEXTON BLAKE'S MOST FORMIDABLE FOES!

THE TEED FILES VOLUMES 2, 3 & 4

The First Chapter
The Bait is Taken

MR. Carfax Morton, cabinet minister, paced up and down the lofty, richly hung apartment which he called his study.

He usually carried all the expansive dignity incumbent on one who held one of the most honoured positions in the gift of the nation, but this evening, in the silence and seclusion of his own apartment, the impressive carriage had drooped to a slack slouch on the withdrawal of the superficiality which sustained it in public.

Not for many years had Mr. Carfax Morton relaxed, even in private, to that slouch, for in the era of better things which had followed his arrival in England a few years previously, he had relegated it to the now distant and to be forgotten past.

What strange, almost indefinable changes, wealth and prosperity makes in the strangely-evolved biped called man!

In early life, Carfax Morton, then known to his intimates as "Tin Dish Charlie," had wandered into an embryo Australian mining town, which at the time of his arrival consisted of a small cluster of hastily erected shacks. Tin Dish Charlie had joined the eager and always hopeful crew which spread out over the gravelly gullies in an endeavour to discover some of the "colours" for which he was always peering in the battered pan, and from whence came his cognomen.

For Tin Dish Charlie and his pan were inseparable, and if perseverance counted for anything, the quantity of gravel which he washed—it must have been tons in the long run—should have revealed the glittering particles which would spell wealth and the subsequent opportunities for the indulgence of Charlie's desires, which at that remote period of his life consisted of having the wherewithal to live a life of ease in the cities of the world.

But bad luck seemed to dog Charlie's footsteps with relentless vigour, the climax coming when a little shooting affray smashed Charlie's trigger finger, which had served a more useful purpose in its ability to do wonderful things with a pack of cards.

With this source of income now gone, which he derived from gambling, for the loss of his finger compelled Charlie to play straight, he surveyed his future with gloomy foreboding.

But Fate's wheel was to swing again, and in its revolution bring into the sphere of its influence Tin Dish Charlie.

As though in reward for his forced virtue in giving up gambling, Charlie's luck turned. The battered tin dish showed a glittering string of colours one day, and Charlie soon graduated from a slovenly fossicker to the possessor of a claim.

Then had come Ike Vineburg and Jim Pearson, with whom Charlie had joined forces, the result being a rapid inflow of wealth to the new firm.

From that on, Charlie—now Carfax Morton—had prospered.

He had seen the crazy shacks of the miners give way to more substantial houses—had seen a semblance of law and order evolve from the chaos of lawlessness—had seen the railway come, and, finally, the disappearance of the individual miner, and the rise of the mining company. Then did Charlie and his partners blossom forth as real magnates.

Charlie, who had a facile pen, wrote reams of glowing prospectuses, which commanded attention in the first paragraph, got the reader excited half-way through, and on reaching the end fairly dripped with the gold which Charlie had portrayed to the reader.

With Vineburg's glib tongue, and Pearson's technical knowledge, facts, figures, and glowing prophesies had been sent broadcast, bringing in return a golden stream for which the guileless investors expected fabulous returns, and they got them—on paper.

This had formed a rich field for Charlie and his friends, and the company had later been expanded to admit Mortimer Todd, Gorgon Kelly, and one or two others.

John Cartier, not aware of their true calibre, had admitted them to a share in the Jig Saw Mine, a genuine producer, and the cream of the district. The new directors, so long accustomed to dealing in worthless mud holes, had gasped in fascinated amazement as the Jig Saw turned out to be enormously productive.

Then, with their true instinct, they had begun to plot for the ousting of John Cartier, who held the major portion of the Jig Saw shares; but his unexpected death had made the way easy for them.

It had been an easy matter to swindle John Cartier's widow out of the mine, and, not content with this, even out of the rich sheep station which was her home. For Mrs. Cartier was delicate and frail, and knew about as much of the ways of such sharks as the sheep on her station knew about escaping the shears.

The shock had sent her to her grave, leaving her daughter Yvonne penniless, friendless, and homeless.

The slimy pair of scoundrels who had brought the false news of the Jig Saw's failure to Mrs. Cartier had quailed at the time under Yvonne's blazing denunciation and threat of vengeance, but had laughed it off five minutes later, and, on her disappearance shortly after, had assumed control of the mine and station, and had fattened on the result.

But, as is the way with such partnerships, the canker of distrust had started among them. Each and all plotted to gain a richer share of that peer of mines, the Jig Saw. The inevitable had occurred, and in the general storm of recrimination, the organisation had been wrecked. Some, more shrewd than their fellows, had scrambled out with a fortune, others had betaken themselves to other climes with changed fortunes and changed names.

But each and all had forgotten the vow of the grief-stricken Yvonne to hound them down to ruin, as she and her mother had been ruined, and not until her vow had actually been accomplished did her victims remember.

Tin Dish Charlie had been one of those who emerged from the maelstrom with a fortune in his belt, and, throwing off all his Australian associations, he had journeyed by roundabout stages to Paris, where he blossomed forth as Carfax Morton, Esq., author, patron of art, and last, but not least, bachelor millionaire.

In this guise he had adopted the regulation trip to the Riviera, where he had met Lady Barlow, widow of the late Lord Barlow, the poor, but famous statesman.

Lady Barlow was entranced with the charming wit and repartee of the coming writer, and his witticisms lost none of their effect by being set to the background of his reputed wealth, although the visible token in the form of the gold in his teeth grated somewhat on her ladyship's fastidious ideas.

But Lady Barlow was sick of poverty and its hardships. She had reached that stage when even the newest of the new American millionaires would have found favour in her eyes as a husband, and having prepared her sensitive nostrils in anticipation of one from whom the odour of the pork factory or cattle yards still emanated, she found the superficial culture of Carfax Morton, a sugar-coated pill in comparison, and consoled herself with the fact that his "lovely black moustache hid his gold teeth, except when he laughed."

Consequently, she had been graciously pleased to favour his suit, and Lady Barlow's seal of approval had "made" Carfax Morton.

Lady Barlow, always passive, and with a horror of poverty instilled in her since childhood, had accepted his attention in the manner in which one accepts a doubtful pleasure. To be sure, his occasional lapses into mining camp English grated on her ears at times, but he would get over that.

He had been honoured in having Lady Barlow accept the loan of his motor at different times, and, had he known, it was really the soft embrace of its luxurious cushions which sealed his fate. For the prospect of giving up the golden future, of which the motor was the first taste, was most repugnant to Lady Barlow, and while she spun along the hot dusty road between Nice and Monte Carlo, she decided that the luxury of a motor must form a constant adjunct to her future.

"He says nothing of his past," she mused, "but he can be made quite presentable, and, if I am any judge, has the ability to go higher. Once married to him, I can die in peace, knowing that Alice will have a home and a father to look after her."

That drive had been followed by Lady Barlow's ingenious arrangement of affairs, and Carfax Morton found his subsequent proposal received with her passive smile and a murmured "Yes."

And he did go higher. Lady Barlow did not misjudge his ability, and patronage did much for him.

Morton had established himself in an imposing place, and their entertainments became a byword for sumptuous perfection under the guiding hand of Lady Barlow.

Then had followed his entry into Parliament, and his rapid advancement by the same lady's assistance.

She had lived long enough to see him a member of the Cabinet, when she had gone where it mattered not whether she was rich or poor. Alice, Lady Barlow's twenty-year-old daughter, took her late mother's place, and carried on, to the best of her ability, the entertainments which Carfax Morton now deemed a necessity.

His tall, slouching figure had straightened and grown expansive with his advance. His heavy black hair had turned to thin silver, and his black moustache now formed a white veil to the gold teeth which he still retained.

His jaw, although spoiled in outline by the thickening of his neck, still showed determination, and the black, piercing eyes still glowed with the fire of ambition under the bulging brow.

An important political dinner had brought him face to face with Gorgon Kelly, one of his old partners in Australia, then at the heyday of his position as the "Money King."

A mutual desire to keep the past buried had made a pact of silence and sympathy between the two, and in exchange for many little tips on what the Government proposed to do, the Money King had given Carfax Morton tips of equal value on the Stock Exchange.

After Lady Barlow's restraining hand had been withdrawn by death, Morton had begun to yield to his old weakness of gambling. Not the half-sovereign rises of the poker table, but the more expensive lure of the market. At first his following of his old partner had brought him in easy profits, but when the Money King's star began to wane, Morton had been compelled to make deep draughts on his principal.

Stronger and stronger grew the hold of his old enemy, until the ruin of Kelly by Mademoiselle Yvonne had left Morton's finances in a precarious condition.

The six months following Lady Barlow's death, and Gorgon Kelly's conviction, had been months of steady loss on the Exchange. And to make matters worse, the Prime Minister had intimated that he felt disposed to suggest Morton's name for participation in the coming New Year's honours, and with proper management and deeds of sufficient worth, Carfax Morton knew that was only a stepping stone to the revival of the peerage which had ended with Lord Barlow.

But for a campaign of this kind he would need money, and plenty of it. The Prime

Minister, wrapped up in his country and his office, never dreamed that his trusted Minister, Carfax Morton, was next door to bankruptcy, and imagined in the depths of his kindly soul, that the honour which would be given to Morton would cause the latter to make a large donation to charity from the depths of his, as the Prime Minister thought, inexhaustible purse.

These things and their attendant kind were the thoughts which formed such unpalatable food for thought as Carfax Norton paced up and down his luxurious room on the night this story opens.

Although his rise to wealth and position had only taken a few years—in fact, six years from the time of the Jig Saw Mine Swindle—his hair was silvering, and his face beginning to age perceptibly.

He was evidently expecting someone, for he glanced from time to time at a small clock on the desk—a magnificent sixteenth century example of the silversmith's triumph— the gargoyle which formed the subject of the supporting stand seeming to grin up at him this night with particularly unholy glee. As its tiny silver chimes struck eight, he paused before the desk, and, unclasping his hands from behind him, thrust the fingers of his right into a capacious waistcoat pocket.

He drew forth a small piece of folded paper and spread it out, reading once again the few words he already knew by heart from repeated readings of it, since it had been thrust into his hand by a ragged urchin earlier in the day. He had turned in astonishment as the boy scuttled away, and was half tempted to toss the note away, deeming it one of the many threats he received when the policy of his department displeased certain elements of the people.

But a native caution had impelled him to glance at its contents, and ever since the few words had danced in his mind with tantalising persistency.

He read them over once again without gaining any further light on the mystery which they might cloak. It read simply:

"One who knows can tell you how the position can yet be retrieved. Be at home at eight tonight, when it will be demonstrated to you. Secrecy must be observed."

True, the cryptic words might only be a hoax, or the wanderings of an unbalanced mind, but the opening sentence had arrested his mind and gave colour to its genuineness. For someone, somewhere, must know of his critical financial position and the embarrassing offer of the New Year's honour.

As he finished reading the note he turned to the desk and pressed the smooth surface on a part which appeared no different to the rest of the rich, dull top. His pressure was followed by the appearance of a small opening, into which he dropped the note. Then the panel closed, presenting once more the smooth, unbroken surface.

Barely had this been accomplished when a soft knock came on the door, followed by the turning of the handle.

Carfax Morton had given orders to his butler to admit without announcement any caller who came at eight, and he looked expectantly at the door which stood in a shadowy corner. It opened and closed softly, and the Minister gazed into the shadow with expressionless eyes and immovable features as a soft, swishing noise followed the closing of the door. From the shadow came the dark figure of a heavily-veiled woman, stopping at the edge of light where the rays from the desk lamp were conquered by the shadow of the lofty room.

Carfax Morton was aware that his visitor was richly if plainly garbed, and an intangible something told him the heavy veil concealed the features of youth, not age—a fact which the throwing up of the veil proved in the next moment.

He stiffened slightly as he saw the beauty of the features which it had covered, and although all his life woman's beauty had been a powerful road to his favour, he restrained his natural inclination, and spoke in cold, measured tones.

"You are the writer of the note, I presume?" he inquired.

The fair vision nodded, but did not speak.

"Why do you wish to see me?" he went on still coldly.

"Aren't you going to ask me to sit down?" came the voice of his visitor, in silvery tones.

"You will pardon me, but until I know the object of your visit, I fear I must be rude enough not to do so."

"Very well," replied the young woman, "that being so, I suppose, I must tell you standing, and I dislike speaking in that position."

She shrugged slightly as she spoke, but continued after a moment, looking straight into Carfax Morton's black, expressionless eyes with steady gaze.

"I know of your heavy losses on the Exchange, Mr. Morton. I know of the blow Gorgon Kelly's failure was to you. I know of the honours which will be offered to you by the Government,

CARFAX MORTON—
Minister of the Crown.

and I know of your inability to accept them. Knowing all this, I can show you the way to wealth without risk and without exertion. Now, will you invite me to sit down?"

"Who are you to know all this?" whispered Morton hoarsely.

"Who am I!" came back the silvery voice. "That you cannot know—yet. Sufficient that these things are known to me and me only. Do you wish to listen to the proposal which will throw open the door of wealth?"

"Be seated," answered Morton briefly, drawing up a chair, and Mademoiselle Yvonne, his mysterious visitor, sat down and faced him, knowing the first move had been victorious.

"Now, madam——" began Morton.

"Mademoiselle, please!" interrupted Yvonne.

"I beg your pardon!" smiled Morton, for the first time relaxing his impassive expression. "Will you be good enough to inform me, mademoiselle, what is the proposal which you say you have to make?"

Yvonne threw open her jacket and drew from some mysterious source a tiny silver cigarette-case. Withdrawing a cigarette and lighting it, and nodding permission for Morton to do likewise, she leaned back and puffed slowly for a few moments before answering.

Morton studied her every feature, but could not stir the slightest chord of memory of ever having seen her before.

He noticed that her costume was the perfection of good taste, its quiet harmony indicating the mind of the artist—the appropriateness of it for the present occasion indicating a capacity for details, and the general air indicating prosperity. So far, so good, he thought.

But the deep-blue eyes were as inscrutable as his own, and the heavy black hair told him nothing. But then Morton did not know that it had once been a glorious heavy bronze, and that stress of circumstances had forced his fair visitor to change its colour.

The little straight nose, though a triumph of nature, was practical, and the red lips which puffed slowly at the tiny cigarette surmounted a daintily-determined chin. Beyond a large ancient-looking scarab on one finger, she wore no jewellery, but he imagined, from the general atmosphere which she breathed, that it was not because she did not have any—and he hit the truth nearer than he thought.

She had been apparently gazing into space, and her words, as she brought her eyes down, startled him.

"Well, Mr. Morton, now that you have inspected me thoroughly, do you still wish to hear what I have to say?"

Morton flushed slightly, and sought refuge in silence, merely bowing. He realised that she had been quite aware of his gaze, and further realised that he had to deal with a personality for which he would require all his brains if he were to read her purpose.

"My proposal," went on Yvonne slowly, "is one which, as I said, will spell wealth. You will wonder many times—in fact, you are wondering now, who I am and whom I represent. But I tell you it is useless for you to attempt to find out. Sufficient is it for the purpose that you know I am able to do what I say.

"Now please don't interrupt what I am going to say," she went on, settling herself in the chair. "Of course, Mr. Morton, it is general knowledge that the British Government is considering a radical change in policy in Southern Persia. It is also generally known that Russia is contemplating a similar change of policy in the northern half of that country. But it is not generally known that Russia and Britain are negotiating secretly with regard to the matter and that France is included in the negotiations. It follows, as a matter of course, Mr. Morton, that certain powerful quarters would give a good deal to know the contents of the despatches which leave London for the French and Russian Foreign Offices."

"Well," broke in Morton, with slow laboured accents, "what has that to do with me?"

Yvonne's attitude was carelessness personified, but behind her assumed attitude her brain was working rapidly.

"Will he succumb?" she was asking herself. "Dare I go on or not? Political life has taught him to veil his thoughts, and I may spoil everything by risking it."

But she showed none of this uncertainty in her manner, and when she again spoke, it was in the same level tones, the while she unobtrusively drew from beneath her jacket a neat packet of banknotes.

"You ask what it has to do with you?" she asked. "Well, nothing personally. But the same powerful quarters which I mentioned are anxious to know just when the messengers leave with the despatches, and by what route they travel. Nothing much, you must acknowledge. A mere limit which could never be traced, and they do the rest. They are disposed to be generous," she added, and, with a careless gesture, threw the bundle of banknotes on the desk in front of him.

Carfax Morton, in all his chequered life, had never been a traitor, and had Yvonne been a man, she would undoubtedly have been thrown out before halfway through her proposal. But she was a woman, and a more than ordinarily beautiful one, and that fact enabled her to get to the end of her statement.

Morton, in the first flush of his patriotic indignation, had started to rise and coldly order her from the room, but Yvonne, past-master in the art of reading human nature, had seized the psychological moment for tossing the banknotes under his nose.

Morton sank back again and stared at the notes, which brought back to him with redoubled force the critical state of his position.

That crisp, neat bundle spelled release, and would open the road which led to the peerage.

He tore his gaze away, and fought hard to conquer their lure, but they drew his eyes like a magnet. He wavered, hesitated, and was lost.

"You—you say nothing risky is required?" he asked hoarsely, the shreds of his shame forcing his eyes to the floor.

"None, I assure you!" replied Yvonne. Her own eyes dropped, not to hide shame, but triumph. "If you agree to my proposal, that bundle on the desk—ten thousand[18]—is the first payment. What I want in return is simply that you give me full advice regarding the movements of the messengers who carry the despatches to the French and Russian capitals."

"But it will be discovered soon!" muttered Morton. "Suppose—suppose I were suspected?"

---

[18] £10,000 in 1913 is worth about £1,160,000.00 in 2020

"You won't be," replied Yvonne crisply. "Your standing is too strong. Almost everyone would be suspected before you were."

"Just—what—do you want!" whispered Morton.

"How soon are messengers leaving?" she asked.

"The first leaves on Friday."

"That is four days yet. Very well, I will come again Thursday night, when you can give me full particulars. Will you agree to that?"

Morton nodded.

"Then there is no reason to prolong the interview. There is plenty more of those notes from whence they came, Mr. Morton—don't forget that. Thursday night, then, at eight," she added, rising.

Morton stumbled to his feet, and held out his hand with a forced smile; but Yvonne had turned, and was moving towards the door, murmuring:

"Don't bother to show me out. I can find my way."

She disappeared in the shadow, and a moment later the door closed, leaving Carfax Morton to his money and his thoughts.

The Second Chapter
Off to Paris—The Stolen Despatch

"MY dear Dick, you will ruin everything in the room!" said Lady Robins, in a tone of mild reproof, as Dick Robins, her only son, sent a small table crashing to the floor.

"Sorry, mother!" laughed Dick, picking it up again. "But I'm in an awful hurry."

Lady Robins forgave him with a smile, for Dick represented her every interest in life, and would have stood a good chance of being forgiven had his offence been far more serious.

"You ought not be permitted in a drawing-room!" she laughed, "but I'll forgive you this time. Come and have your tea!"

"Right-ho!" grinned Dick, as he shifted a nicked leg of the table so that his mother couldn't see it. "I'll just have time before I pack. I must get the night Continental from Charing Cross, and have to return to the office first."

"Where away this time, Dick?" asked Lady Robins, as she dropped two lumps of sugar in his cup.

"Oh, the same old trip—the Continent!" replied Dick, "I would like to have seen Alice before I left, but you'll have to say good-bye to her for me, mother."

"You may see her before you go, Dick. She said she would come round after tea!"

"Oh, I hope so!" mumbled Dick, giving his undivided attention to a tea-cake.

"How long do you expect to be gone?" asked his mother.

"I'll be back by Monday at the latest. It's rather a special trip this time, and I won't be long. But I'll toddle along, mater, and pack a bag. If Alice comes, tell her to wait till I come down."

"All right, Dick!" nodded his mother; and with an endeavour to get out of the room without another accident, Dick hurried out as fast as such a resolve would permit.

Dick Robins had been for some time under-secretary to Mr. Carfax Morton, the eminent Cabinet Minister. Sir George Robins, Dick's father, had been a very old friend of Lord Barlow's, and this connection had provided Dick with the necessary opening for a diplomatic career when he left Oxford.

Lord Barlow, irrespective of his intimacy with Sir George, had demurred somewhat at the time over appointing Dick without the customary examination, but that young man had settled the difficulty by taking the exams on his own initiation, and his highly successful passing had opened the door without further trouble.

He was not an extraordinary young man by any means, but he was a worker, and above all had unbounded honesty of purpose, and a conscience. These attributes had by their own pushed him along where other more brilliant but less steady men travelled more slowly. Dick had acted more than once as King's Messenger and being known now by that enviable description, "a thoroughly safe man," he had of late been entrusted as messenger with the safe custody of the most secret papers of the diplomatic department.

Little did Lady Robins dream that his careless, hastily-decided trips to the Continent were trips as custodians of such priceless papers, for although Dick knew his secrets would be safe with her, he followed the rule of his department to the letter, and did not even permit himself to think about his missions, in case he might talk in his sleep.

He whistled cheerily as he tossed a few necessary things into his bag. He was not the drawling type of man to have a valet for his every need. As he put it himself, "he only got salary enough to buy cigars and clothes for himself, and couldn't afford to supply a valet as well; and besides he didn't know what a valet johnnie would find to do, as his wardrobe was more serviceable than extensive."

Dick grabbed up his bag and rushed down the stairs. At the bottom he almost bowled over a tall, dark, young woman who was just about to enter the drawing-room, and as he caught that startled young lady, he startled her more by giving her a lightning-like kiss just as a servant appeared.

"Heavens, Dick, you startled me!" she gasped, trying to look unconcerned before the maid. "I didn't know who it was!"

Dick grinned, and opened the door.

"Sorry, dear, but I simply couldn't resist it. It's been such ages since I saw you, and surely your future husband can take that privilege after being parted from you for so long."

She looked at him with what was intended to be a look of annihilation, but her eyes refused to do their duty, and she burst out laughing.

"You ridiculous boy!" she said. "Parted from me for a long time, indeed! And I almost had to drive you home last night at eleven. And you speak of being my future husband as though it wasn't only since last night that you have been that. As for kisses—well, you are incorrigible. No, no—not again. Your mother——— Oh!"

The last exclamation was one of helpless, muffled protest as Dick took the law into his own hands as he calmly proceeded to take another, and the knowing twinkle in his mother's eyes as the blushing Alice stumbled into the room, indicated that the lady had a shrewd idea as to what had occurred.

Alice Morton, daughter of Lady Barlow, had been one of the previous season's debutantes, and it was at her first dance that she and Dick had met. A friendly chat had left them both desirous of more, and at further meetings, Dick had not been slow to offer, nor Alice slow to accept, the many talks and dances together.

The passivity of Lady Barlow had been reproduced in her daughter only in sufficient force to give her a calm and composed demeanour under most circumstances.

To give Carfax Morton his due, he really loved his stepdaughter passionately, with all the love of a father, and he now had a terrible horror of her ever being poor, without the luxuries she was used to, to fight the world with the rest.

And it was really for her sake that he was ready to listen to Yvonne's proposal—a fact which Yvonne knew.

Had Carfax Morton consulted frankly with his daughter, her clear conception and honesty would have found a way out, and even if she had failed, his retirement from public life would have been an honourable one.

The friendship between her and Dick had grown into regard and from regard into an unspoken understanding which the night previous Dick had put into words. Had Alice been the daughter of anyone else but his chief, Dick would have spoken just the same, for his love contained no element of self-interest, and, be it said, neither did hers.

Lady Robins, a lady of the old school, had raised her eyes a trifle, for she was one of the few who had not forgotten Carfax Morton's lack of a past; but her honest liking for Alice had triumphed, and that morning she had driven around to the Morton's, and there had taken the motherless young woman and soon to be daughter, straight into her arms and her heart.

Of all the three who laughed and chatted over the cups, it was Alice who reminded Dick of the passage of time.

"Heigh-ho," he grumbled regretfully, getting to his feet, "between you and mother I can see little peace ahead for the poor, downtrodden breadwinner."

"You are terribly overworked, poor boy," replied Alice, with mock sympathy. "I'll go to the door with you in case the prospect of the hard work you'll do in Paris, driving down the boulevards and lounging around the Embassy, should decide you to give up the trip."

But in the friendly shadow of the hall she dropped the bantering tone. "Hurry back, boy," she whispered, "I'll be lonely."

And Dick ran down the steps with a smile of happy recollection.

He hailed a taxi, and, on looking at his watch, told the chauffeur to drive like "ballyhack," for he had loitered in the attractive atmosphere in his home longer than he ought.

On his arrival at the departmental offices, he found Carfax Morton pacing up and down with an irritable frown on his face. What would have been his answer to the tempting offer of Mademoiselle Yvonne had he known Dick and Alice were engaged, it is hard to say. But Dick had no time to speak to his chief, and that gentleman was not aware as yet that Dick was to be his future son-in-law.

"You're late, Robins!" he snapped. "You'll have to hurry to catch the train."

"I know; I'm sorry, sir," replied Dick, setting his bag on a nearby chair. "But I'll make it all right. Have you the despatches ready, Mr. Morton?"

"Yes," answered Morton, turning to his desk, and picking up a long heavy blue envelope sealed with many seals. "Here they are. I needn't tell you, Robins, that these are exceptionally important, and must be delivered at the Paris Embassy at once on your arrival. Inside is a duplicate lot for St. Petersburg, but they will be taken by another man from Paris. You quite understand, do you—immediate delivery?"

"Oh, yes, quite, sir," answered Dick, taking the envelope. "I'll drive direct from the station to the Embassy, and deliver them at once."

He turned as he spoke, and, pressing an innocent-looking brass tack near the bottom of his bag which was apparently there for the purpose of reinforcing the edges, like its several fellows, he lifted the bag up, and a cleverly concealed aperture appeared in the bottom. It was barely deep enough to accommodate the thick envelope, and had the bag's depth been measured from without, and within, it is doubtful if its presence would even then have been discovered. Thrusting in the envelope, he closed the opening, and turned to Carfax Morton.

"Well, good-bye, sir; I'll be back by Monday, and will send you cipher advices as usual on my arrival in Paris."

"Yes, do!" replied Morton, holding out his hand; and Dick would have been puzzled at the odd look which followed him.

He had kept his taxi waiting for him, and the promise of extra fare acted as a stimulant to their speed in the short journey to Charing Cross. Dick tossed the man a sovereign on his arrival there, and dashed through, barely having sufficient time to get his ticket and reach the train.

He was too absorbed to notice the slim, heavily-veiled figure of a smartly-dressed woman which paced up and down the platform, the veil hiding a look of anxiety. But the look cleared as Dick hastened past, and she stopped her pacing to reach for a small bag on a nearby seat and follow.

"He told the truth," she murmured, as she walked along, keeping Dick in view. "I was afraid he'd fail at the last moment, when he had time to realise; but he must want those New Year honours more even than I thought. And now, my friend, Mr. Robins, I'll just follow you into that compartment. Between here and Paris I ought to get possession of the despatches you think are so cleverly concealed in the bottom of that bag; but you don't know yet that your chief is a traitor."

Mademoiselle Yvonne smiled in the security of her heavy veil as she opened the door of a compartment and met Dick's frowning gaze on finding his solitude invaded. At that moment the train began moving slowly, and the guard slammed the door on Yvonne, who had made a pretence of backing out.

"I am so sorry," she apologised; "I really did not know——"

"Oh, it is quite all right, I assure you!" replied Dick, jumping up. "I won't deny I was rude enough to frown," he laughed, "but I thought it might be a party of undesirable travelling companions."

"And am I then to consider myself outside that category?" laughed Yvonne, her soft, liquid laugh creating a curiosity on her companion's part to see the face of its owner.

"Most assuredly," he smiled, gallantly trying, but without success, to pierce the thick veil.

Yvonne sank into a corner and nodded to him to do likewise.

"I'll try and live up to the idea you have of me," she said, and as she spoke, carelessly threw back her veil, causing Dick to stare in amazement at the beauty of the face opposite him.

He was not a susceptible man, by any means, but on a long, lonely trip to Paris, he was hardly to be blamed if he felt himself lucky in having such a charming companion for the journey where it might have been a garlic-scented German. Had he known that, at the very moment he sat in Carfax Morton's cosy drawing-room the previous evening telling Alice of his love, the beautiful young woman opposite had been making a secret visit to Carfax Morton in the library, and that during her visit, she had received full particulars of Dick's projected journey to Paris and information as to the hiding-place of the despatches he was to carry, he would have grabbed his bag unceremoniously, and sought another compartment. But he didn't know this, and his first feeling of polite interest changed to a protective elder brother air as Yvonne, with true insight into his nature, led the conversation into pathetic channels.

"You go to Paris?" she asked.

"Er—yes. Just a little week-end trip," he replied. "And you?"

"Oh, yes!" she smiled. "I am going over to meet my uncle. And do you know," she said, looking at him with wide, innocent eyes, "I feel so nervous. They say Paris is so large, and so wicked, and suppose my uncle should miss me at the station?"

"Oh, there's nothing to feel nervous about!" laughed Dick cheerily. "Paris isn't half as terrible as it is painted. Besides, I'll set you right when we get there if you miss your uncle."

He thought of how he would feel if Alice were travelling alone and unprotected, and a wave of protective sympathy swept over him at the thought. "Poor little thing," he thought to himself. "She's scared half to death at the prospect. I'll just look after her on the way, and see that she meets her uncle. She ought not to be travelling alone like this."

With this conclusion he laid himself out to be agreeable. "Would she like a book? Was she quite warm enough? Was she too warm? Could he do anything to make her more comfortable?"

Yvonne met each solicitous question with one of her sweetest smiles, and intimated that there was nothing he could do.

By the time they arrived at Dover they were quite like old friends. Dick took personal charge of her at the pier, and selected a cosy nook on the steamer. Spreading out their rugs, they settled down for the choppy night trip. Dick smoked and talked, not realising that Yvonne's occasional questions and remarks controlled the current of the whole conversation.

At Calais they joined the rush for the restaurant, and although she refused food, Yvonne played the tyrant, and forced him to eat, compromising with his entreaties by taking coffee.

It was then that she, in her turn, took up the conversation, and kept her companion in a state of suppressed amusement by her naive remarks.

It was very easy in her apparent innocence to ask questions, and from inanimate things to come down to the people about them. As Dick turned his head to look at someone behind, about whom his fair companion made a remark, Yvonne, seizing the opportunity she had so carefully created, glanced sharply around, and reached across the table. Her hand hovered for the barest fraction of a second over his cup, and something dropped into the coffee, the tiny ripples dying away almost at once. With this tiny pause her hand continued on over the cup, and grasped the sugar basin, and as Dick turned back, with a laughing remark, his fair companion, with dainty fingers, was putting a lump of sugar in her cup.

Ignorant of the small but potent capsule she had introduced into his coffee, he lifted the cup and drank.

A moment later a uniformed guard put his head inside the door and shouted a warning.

They rose hastily, and emerged into the open air, and walked past the waiting carriages in an endeavour to secure a compartment to themselves.

Fortune favoured them, and barely had they entered when the train started.

"Just in time," laughed Dick, as he settled into the seat.

"Yes, just in time," replied Yvonne, but not in the way Dick meant.

The cold chill of early morning was creeping through the carriages. Tired from the journey, and drowsy from the hot coffee, it would have been an effort in any case to keep awake, and Yvonne, wrapping her rug about her, leaned back with closed eyes.

"Poor little thing," he thought. "I've talked her to death, and she's dead-fagged. I'll let her drop off to sleep. Wish I could myself, but I'll have to wait. She's safe enough, but someone might get in, and orders are orders."

He leaned back, and gazed at the beautiful face opposite him, wondering if he dared smoke, or would it disturb her.

As though in answer to his thought, her eyes opened, and she murmured drowsily that he might smoke if he wished, closing her eyes again and sinking back.

Dick lit a cigarette, and while his companion apparently slept, his thoughts travelled back to Alice.

"She's fast asleep by now," he thought, his eyes softening, "and just about the time I arrive in Paris she'll be having her breakfast. Gad, I'm a lucky dog! What the dickens she sees in me, I don't know! I wonder what the chief will say when I tell him I'm going to be his son-in-law? He was a bit wild because I was late. Seemed mighty keen on the despatches, too. I wonder if they're about the Persian matter? Probably!

"Gad, I'm sleepy, must brace up! I'll toss this cigarette away, and—here, here, my boy, wake up, don't go to sleep! What on earth's the matter? My eyes feel, as heavy as lead. This compartment is hot, too. Dash it! I just can't keep my eyes open. I'll h-a-v-e-to——" But his thoughts trailed off as his heavy lids dropped and he rolled off into oblivion, the powerful capsule having done its work.

Deep silence reigned for a full five minutes, broken only by the heavy breathing of the sleepers. But at the end of that time Yvonne's eyes opened, and she sat up.

All the drowsiness had gone, and she moved briskly. She rose and bent over the sleeping Dick, taking his hand, and placing her finger on his pulse.

"A bit weak," she muttered, "but it wasn't too strong. He'll sleep for six hours, and a cannon won't wake him before. Now, my young friend, I'll have a look for those despatches."

She reached down, and lifted up his bag, running her fingers over the brass tacks which reinforced the bottom corners.

"Morton didn't know which one worked it," she muttered, "but said I'd have to find that out myself, and—oh, that's it!"

She had pressed the one which released the false bottom, and as it dropped open, she thrust her hand in, and drew out the heavy blue envelope, which contained the despatches.

"Trick No. 1, Mr. Carfax Morton," she murmured with a smile, as she transferred the envelope to her own bag. "It is a good lead, and I think I hold the winning hand. It's a pity to leave that nice place of concealment empty. I'll just leave a little memento for our young friend."

With a soft laugh, she again opened her bag, and drew forth a small pad and pencil. Placing it on her knee, she wrote busily for a few moments, and then, tearing off the sheet, with a soft laugh of amusement, thrust it in the secret receptacle of Dick's bag and closed it.

When the train pulled into the Gare du Nord station in Paris, Yvonne picked up her bag and was one of the first to descend.

"Poor boy, I hope you won't get into trouble!" she said, with a last look at her victim. "You were so nice and kind, but in the time of war the innocent must suffer."

She joined the hurrying crowds, and tripped along to the street, where she was met by a middle-aged man, who greeted her affectionately.

"Well, Yvonne, what luck?"

"Oh, splendid, uncle!" she laughed. "It seemed a pity it was so easy. Have you brought the car?"

"Yes. Are you tired?"

"Horribly fagged. Let's go along and get breakfast, and then I'll get some rest. I'll have to return to England in a day or two, and this campaign is going to require all my brains."

"Don't you think it's a bit too risky meddling with despatches of the British Government?" asked Graves, her uncle, as they entered the big car.

"Of course, it's risky," she replied; but it can't be helped."

She greeted the chauffeur in friendly fashion as she sank back, for in this, the latest of her exploits, she had domiciled most of the "circle" in Paris, only keeping the necessary number of agents in London.

Back in the station the officials were having a strenuous time with the passenger, whom they found calmly sleeping in his compartment, while the other passengers had hastened to depart.

His clothes indicated a man of position, and where they would have dealt summarily with him had his garments been poor, instead, they carried him into the stationmaster's office, and endeavoured to revive him,

"These English seem to sleep as thoroughly as they do everything else," grunted one.

"Poof, it's more than sleep. He's had too much of their bad beer," replied the other.

"Here, what's this?" jerked out the dapper little stationmaster, hurrying into the office.

"An Englishman who sleeps and sleeps, and won't waken," replied the guard.

"Is he drunk?" began the stationmaster. "Why, good heavens!—here you, Jules, go to the buffet and get some brandy, quick! I know him. He comes to Paris often."

The guard hastened away, while the other assisted the stationmaster to lift Dick into a chair.

The stationmaster took the brandy from the guard the returned at that moment, and forced a stiff draught between the unconscious man's lips.

Whether it was because Dick had only drunk half his coffee, or whether the capsule hadn't had time to thoroughly dissolve, the effects were not as lasting as Yvonne had intended, for the fiery spirit revived Dick somewhat, and a strenuous half-hour of walking him up and down the office floor enabled his healthy system to throw off the remaining effects of the drug.

"Where am I? What has happened?" he asked in French, looking in amazement at the guards and the station-master.

The latter rapidly explained how they had found him, and Dick's eyes grew grave as he listened.

"My bag!" he jerked. "Where is my bag?"

"Here, monsieur," replied one of the guards, handing it to him.

Dick grasped it feverishly.

"Ask them to step outside a moment," he said, turning to the station-master.

At his nod, the guards retired and closed the office door. Dick reached down and pressed the tack which released the false bottom. As it opened he thrust his hand in, and a momentary look of relief overspread his countenance as his fingers touched the paper, but it returned with redoubled force as he felt, not the heavy envelope, but a thin sheet of paper. He jerked it out and looked at it.

"Thank you so much for your care on the journey. It really broke the monotony wonderfully. I hated to do what I have done, but it couldn't be helped. In future, take my advice and don't be so solicitous of poor little unprotected travellers. I trust you feel refreshed after your sleep."

That was all. As his brain took in the ironical words Dick's hand went to his head, and he staggered back, his face growing white. Surely he must be going crazy. That young woman had never got the despatches from him. No, no, they must be still there. He would feel again.

But his hand came back empty and only the note remained—a mocking answer to his frenzied search.

"My heavens, what shall I do? What can I do? Fooled, played with, like a baby! This will ruin me. How can I explain to the chief? Oh, I can't! Let me think. She must be still in Paris, and if she is I'll find her! And when I——"

Snapping his bag to, he thrust the note in his pocket, and with eyes full of dread, tore out of the office.

The dapper little stationmaster, who had been a silent and wondering spectator of Dick's tragic discovery, threw up his hands as the door slammed.

"These mad English!" he exclaimed. "They get worse and worse. Not a word of thanks, and he rushes out with murder in his eye."

He dismissed the incident with a shrug and returned to his duties, little dreaming how serious was the discovery which had caused the "mad Englishman" to dash out so precipitately.

The Third Chapter
Sexton Blake Puts Two and Two Together

IT was Sunday morning, and London was just turning out to worship at the pealing insistence of the bells.

The well-dressed crowds which hurried along or loitered slowly, glanced up in cheerful envy, at the windows of that popularly-considered favoured of mortals—the Prime Minister.

Behind those heavy-curtained windows their minds pictured a luxurious interior with the Prime Minister lounging in a comfortable chair taking his ease.

But in reality what a different picture!

Up and down the room paced the tall, gaunt, slightly-bent figure of the first Parliamentarian.

His face was drawn and haggard, his eyes, which had not known sleep for many hours, were clouded with worry, his thin, nervous hands were clasped behind him. From time to time he glanced at the tall clock in the corner, and then at the door, only to continue his feverish walk.

The first note of eleven was striking when the door opened and the old butler announced "Mr. Blake."

Sexton Blake entered, and stood inside until the door closed and the butler's footsteps receded.

"You were able to come, thank Heaven!" said the Prime Minister, unclasping his hands and holding one out.

"The demands of the country come first, Lord Fanbury," replied Sexton Blake, seating himself. "I judged from your note that the matter was serious."

Lord Fanbury nodded.

"Serious isn't the word for it," he answered, sinking into a chair opposite his visitor and nervously tapping his knee. "It's calamitous, Blake."

"I'm sorry to hear that," replied Blake. "What is it—some new move of our friends across the North Sea?"

"I don't know. I can't tell yet. That is why I sent for you. You must strain every nerve, Blake, to clear the matter up. Things are in a most critical position at present."

"You know I will do what I can," remarked Blake quietly. "Tell me all you can, and I will ask questions after."

"Very well," replied Lord Fanbury, pushing over the cigars; "firstly, as you know, things are in a ticklish condition in Persia. We have worked honestly in conjunction with Russia in an endeavour to let the country straighten itself out, but it can't be done internally. Their Government and finances are in a hopeless muddle, and getting worse. Consequently, we have been negotiating recently with Russia and France in an endeavour to come to some arrangement whereby order may be restored and foreign interests protected. The preliminaries were completed a fortnight ago, and we had arrived at the actual proposals.

"They were drafted out in detail last Monday, and two copies made—one to be presented to our Embassy in Paris for the consideration of the French Foreign Office, and the other for St. Petersburg.

"These were placed together in a large blue envelope and sealed on Friday morning. Friday afternoon the envelope was given to an under-secretary who has been acting as King's Messenger lately on important matters. He left for Paris on Friday night with the despatches, intending to deliver them at the Embassy there on the arrival of the train.

"We had advised the Embassy in cipher to expect him, and when he did not appear, they telegraphed us in code asking us if he had left. We wired back that he had, and although against orders, must have gone for breakfast before delivering the despatches. It was noon before we got an answer. They waited for some time longer, and as he did not return, sent to the Gare du Nord to investigate.

"There the station-master recognised by their description a young man who had been found asleep in his compartment. They had great difficulty in waking him, and when they did he opened a secret compartment in his bag. From there he drew out a piece of paper, and, after reading what was on it, acted in a very agitated manner, winding up by closing his bag and dashing out. Since then, despite the fact that a thorough look-out has been kept, he has disappeared entirely, and worse than that the despatches as well. That is all, Blake. If you have any questions, I will endeavour to answer them."

"What was the messenger's name?" asked Blake, slowly puffing his cigar.

"Robins—Dick Robins."

"A son of Sir George?"

"Yes."

"Do you suspect him in the matter?"

"I didn't at first, but now I am inclined to do so."

"On what grounds?"

"Well, Morton and I have thrashed the matter out, and have come to this conclusion. If someone had succeeded in getting the despatches away from him by strategy, his first move would have been to inform us at once of the fact. Again, supposing they were stolen, and in a panic he tried to recover them himself, he would have informed us after the first day. Instead, he has completely disappeared, and it points very strongly to his guilt. But guilty or not guilty, the despatches are gone, and he has disappeared."

"How many as yet know of their loss?" inquired Blake.

"Myself, Carfax Morton, and the ambassador in Paris. Of course, one or two secretaries know some despatches are missing, but they have no idea as to which ones."

"How many people here knew they were leaving on Friday night?"

"Myself, my secretary, Carfax Morton, who assisted in the framing of the proposals, the Foreign Minister, his secretary, and of course, Robins, the messenger."

"H'm! And you haven't informed the Foreign Minister yet of the loss?"

"No; he is in Scotland, and as he has been terribly overworked lately, I kept the news until he returns."

"Think well, Lord Fanbury. Do you know of the very remotest grounds for suspicion against any of those who knew the despatches were leaving Friday night?"

"No; I have gone over every one carefully. They are all out of the question, as far as I know. Of course, I suspect Robins, but I didn't think him capable of it until his disappearance."

"Who knows you sent for me?" asked Blake.

"Nobody. I wanted to see you first."

"Well, naturally I will put everything else aside for the time, Lord Fanbury, and take up the matter at once. But you know my methods of old, and I must be given a free hand."

"I know, Blake—I know," replied the worried Prime Minister. "Take your own course. Everything here is at your service, but I needn't tell you that. Whatever you suggest I will follow out. Only find those despatches; you know what rests on them."

"If they are to be recovered before our friends' get them we will have to move quickly," answered Blake. "At present, however, I can form no theory. As yet I can't put my finger on the motive. But one thing, Lord Fanbury, tell no one—not even the Foreign Minister or Morton—that I am investigating the matter. At least, not until I give you permission. I want to think the matter over first, and can't tell you what my plan of action will be. I will return here tonight at ten under the name of Wilkins. You had better give your butler orders to admit me at once. Then I will tell you what I propose to do."

"Very well, Blake; I will arrange matters tonight, then, at ten."

***

The tall, grave-faced man with the deep, piercing eyes who sauntered along Whitehall a few moments later looked the typical clubman out to enjoy the fresh morning air.

From the top of his shining silk hat to his quietly immaculate shoes, the delicately-toned waistcoat, and the small flower in his frock-coat, all spoke the prosperous particular man of affairs pondering calmly. None realised that every fibre of that athletic figure was perfectly tuned to create just such an impression while the most brilliantly-deductive mind of the century whirled in mathematical concentration.

But such was the case, for although he didn't doubt his almost infallible system of deduction would eventually reconstruct the disappearance of the despatches, and trace them to their destination, Blake knew if their recovery was to be accomplished in time, it would have to be made very soon, or the contents would be known.

He turned mechanically until he reached Baker Street and entered the consulting-room, where Tinker sat reading, and Pedro lay stretched out in the path of the warm morning sun which came through the window.

"You're back early, guv'nor," remarked Tinker, looking up, while Pedro lazily pounded his tail and opened one great eye.

"Stir yourself, my lad!" rapped out Blake, "Get down the index and look up that last Government case I had—the one that took me to Berlin. Get together all the notes, and in addition dig up all the notes I have relating to Lord Fanbury and the Prime Minister, his secretary, the Foreign Minister, Carfax Morton, and the secretaries of the last two."

"What! Is it something new?" asked Tinker, rising to obey.

"No questions now!" snapped Blake, proceeding to the dressing-room: "but I can tell you this much. There is a month's long investigation to be made and solved in about three days, so make haste."

Tinker stared after his retreating master, and with a soft whistle, turned to the index.

"He is in a sweat!" he muttered to himself, as he rapidly noted down the information Blake required. "Must be something pretty stiff, and his mind must be working sixty to the second to make him so sharp."

But Tinker knew Blake's moods, and his long association with the great detective had enabled him to read clearly when that great mental machine was in full action.

He endeavoured to connect the individuals of whom he was making notes with some of the recent happenings in the papers, but failed; and as he laid the finished memorandums in a neat pile on the detective's desk, Blake entered, his former attire having been exchanged for his long smoking-gown.

He dragged a jar of strong smoking mixture across the desk and picked up the old pipe. Then, with a grunt of acknowledgment, as Tinker indicated the pile of clippings, he lit his pipe and settled down.

Tinker stole to the door and quietly disappeared in the direction of the laboratory, informing Mrs. Bardell on the way that if she valued her life she'd better not disturb the guv'nor, and if any callers came to send them into the laboratory.

In the consulting-room, Blake, after a rapid review of the cuttings, settled down to endeavour to ferret out the weak spot which would wind through the mystery until he could place his finger on the motive.

First he drew his mental circle, inside which he placed every person who had the slightest knowledge of the missing despatches. Not even the Prime Minister escaped inclusion, for, although Blake knew him to be absolutely beyond suspicion, his method, to be successful, must be thorough.

Slowly, one by one, starting with Lord Fanbury, he began to go over every detail of the knowledge he possessed. Which one would have sufficient motive to turn traitor to his country and sell such important information, for it was a certainty that the information had come from the inside.

Lord Fanbury was eliminated, and then he came to the Foreign Minister, and so on.

Was there any hidden point in the past life of any of them which would account for the present mystery? What was the life of the several secretaries outside the office? Would Carfax Morton have any motive? Had any of them any reasons, or were they intimate with foreigners?

And so his mental questions went on, examining and advancing, testing and accepting or rejecting each point.

Hours passed, and still the detective sat in the same bunched-up position, his eyes two pinpoints of concentration, his ears deaf to the occasional passing of vehicles on the street, the smoke-cloud from the old black pipe growing denser and denser.

The afternoon waned, and the shadows grew as the sun dropped, and the day melted into the peaceful calmness of Sunday evening.

Still he did not move, nor did the frown on his face relax. Over and over each man he had gone, but no breath of suspicion seemed to rest on any except one—the missing messenger, Dick Robins. But what madness, the detective's mind reasoned! If he had intended allowing the despatches to be stolen he had certainly planned it clumsily, for when he had come out of the drug at the Gare du Nord Station in Paris, why hadn't he telephoned, or gone at once to the Embassy?

The very strength of the suspicions which condemned the missing Robins even in the Prime Minister's eyes meant nothing to Blake. Often had he seen circumstantial evidence so strong that it sent a man to the gallows, but it was the hidden clue and the frail chance that lent a zest to the chase, and made him love it for itself. But reason as he would, he could not at present reconstruct the disappearance, and as nine o'clock drew round he rose, and with quick decision entered the dressing-room.

He returned to the consulting-room a few minutes later, and Tinker, who had heard his movements, entered at the same time. He put his hand to his face to hide a grin, for instead of the usual keen-looking Blake, he saw a tall, drawling individual with a monocle screwed in one eye, and a drooping, sandy moustache.

Blake saw the grin, and his frown relaxed.

"Well, what's the joke?" he drawled, in a perfect imitation of the type he represented in his disguise.

"I couldn't help it, guv'nor!" grinned Tinker. "Every time I see you in the outfit I can't help it.'

Blake smiled.

"I've got an important appointment, Tinker, and up to now I don't think I will need

Sexton Blake disguised as "Major Wilkins."

you tonight, but you had better wait up until I return, developments may take place."

"All right, guv'nor. I can't go with you?" asked the lad.

"No," replied Blake. "I'll tell you something about matters when I return."

He strode to the door as he spoke, and two minutes later he was bowling down Baker Street in a taxi. The cab drew up in front of the Prime Minister's, and Blake, telling the man to wait, walked up the steps, tugging at his sandy moustache.

He was admitted at once by the butler, who turned in the hall and asked him his name.

"Aw—er—you might say Majaw Wilkins!" drawled Blake.

"Oh! I was to admit you at once, sir," replied the old butler. "Kindly step this way!"

"Aw—very good!" replied Blake.

"Aw—how d'y do, Lord Fanbury!" said Blake, still in his drawling tone as he entered; but as the door closed, and the butler's footsteps died away, he returned to his natural tone.

"By Jove, Blake," said the Prime Minister, unable to repress a smile, "you are a wonder! You told me you would come under the name of Wilkins, but I really thought another man of the same name had called!"

Blake laughed.

"It is one of the best disguises which can be adopted," he said, as he seated himself, "but the average man who adopts it overdoes it. Nothing new, I suppose?"

"No—nothing, Blake. And you—have you decided on a course of action yet?"

"Yes," replied Blake. "Frankly, Lord Fanbury, the matter is pretty mysterious, and it is going to be very difficult to unravel it in the time at my disposal. I won't deny that circumstantial evidence points strongly to the missing messenger, but I can't conceive of any man doing the thing in what seems to be such a clumsy manner. But in view of the limited time, a test will have to be made quickly to decide that point, and I think I have hit on the necessary test."

"Ah, what is it?" asked Lord Fanbury eagerly.

"It is this. I want you to prepare some despatches—duplicates of the missing ones will do. Tomorrow night, disguised as a King's Messenger, I will leave for Paris with them. I want you to let it be known to exactly the same persons who knew of Robins' departure, only no one but yourself is to know my identity."

"I see—I see," replied the worried Lord Fanbury. "Then if the leak should happen to be here you will know it?"

"Naturally. If Robins is guilty, no attempt will be made to get the despatches from me. On the other hand, if the leak is here, it is very probable that another attempt will be made in order to keep the despatches from reaching the French and Russian Governments until the first lot reach their destination."

"Good. I quite agree with you, Blake. I will have the despatches prepared tomorrow, and I think it will make a certainty of your test if I let it be known that they contain new proposals regarding Persia."

"I was going to suggest that," said Blake, "and if it will not complicate matters with France and Russia, it would be better."

"I'll manage that it doesn't. If you recover that missing lot, Blake, before their contents become known to outside parties, I needn't tell you that it will not only be a big relief to me as Prime Minister but to me personally. I want the traitor, Blake. More than I can say depends on it, for you yourself know the feverish condition of Europe at present."

"I quite understand, Lord Fanbury, and will do all in my power. The time is woefully short, but——" And he shrugged his shoulders. "However, I will attend here tomorrow at four in order to receive the despatches, and again let me impress upon you, Lord Fanbury, the necessity for concealing my identity."

"It shall be done, Blake," agreed the Prime Minister, and once more adopting the drawl of his disguise, Blake rose to go.

The Fourth Chapter
Yvonne and Blake Again in Grips—The Smash

IT was the following afternoon when Blake, after a busy morning in the City, hastened into the consulting-room.

He had spent ever since early morning following up several points which had suggested themselves to him, but each road had led into a mental cul-de-sac. More and more he had to confess that things looked black against Dick Robins, and yet his every reasoning said no.

However, he argued, his test, although it would take him out of London for a couple of days, was the quickest way in which to prove whether Robins was guilty, or whether the information had originated from some other source.

He had told Tinker nothing as yet, beyond the fact that he was leaving for Paris on the evening train, and the lad, under long training, asked no questions, although his mind was working actively in an endeavour to read beneath Blake's mood. But he possessed his soul in patience, knowing Blake would tell him as much as he could when the time was ripe, and as yet he had never been disappointed, nor was he this time.

Blake called Tinker into the dressing-room, and as the detective tossed a few things in his bag, gave the lad an inkling of the case.

"Disappearance of important despatches, my lad," he jerked between trips from the wardrobe to the bag. "Messenger gone as well. It looks as though he were the traitor, but I can't tell yet. I'm going over to Paris tonight as a messenger in order to make a test reconstruction. Developments may take place here while I am gone, or I may need you to come to Paris at a moment's notice. Be ready, in any event. If I wire, it will be the usual code. Keep your eyes open here, and see if you can discover any further details of the persons you looked up in the Index. Do you understand thoroughly?"

"Yes, guv'nor. I'll dig up all the facts I can, and if you wire I'll come at once. It's a pretty serious affair, isn't it?

"Very serious," replied Blake grimly, "and the worst of it is, there is a very short time in which to recover the despatches. Europe at present is like an open keg of gunpowder, and if those despatches reach certain European Powers they will be the flame which causes the explosion. So, open eyes and ears, and your tongue between your teeth, is the watchword, my lad."

"Right, guvnor," answered Tinker, picking up the bag and following Blake to the consulting-room.

There the detective made a few hasty notes, and once more returned to the dressing-room, emerging five minutes later in the guise of a typical lounger of the Paris boulevards. He had taken particular pains with his disguise, for he knew if an attempt were made to steal the despatches from him he would need all his wits to frustrate the attempt.

Consequently, from the shape of his silk-hat to the pointed toes of his shoes, he was correct in the latest detail of French fashion. His moustache and imperial, slightly tinged with grey, were masterpieces of the hairdresser's art, and so perfectly were they attached that it would have taken a microscope even in daylight to discover where the false, flesh-coloured backing blended with his own skin.

His hair was done in the approved French fashion, and his clothes had the perfect air and cut of the café *habitué*. But what lent the finishing touch, and stamped him as the real genuine article, was his inimitable accent and expressive gesticulations, accompanied by the flourish of the monocle, which had already done duty the previous evening.

Such was Sexton Blake in one of his most successful, as well as most difficult, disguises, and had the grinning Tinker been told nothing, the adoption of the disguise in question would have been sufficient to inform him that something more than usually important was on the tapis.

Blake relaxed into a very English smile as he saw the lad's grin, but he had no time to lose, and with a last injunction to Tinker to hold himself and Pedro in readiness for action, he picked up his bag and hastened out, his face once more assuming the proper squint which from that moment he would have while he wore the disguise.

Hailing a taxi, he was soon speeding along to keep his appointment with the Prime Minister.

That harassed man looked up from his desk with an impatient frown as he saw the fashionable Frenchman shown in, and his lips pursed in order to state that he could spare the visitor but a moment, when Blake advanced and spoke in a low tone.

"Well, by thunder, Blake," gasped Lord Fanbury, "you are almost uncanny! I swear I can hardly believe yet that you are really you."

"I'm not—at present, and you can't do better than to keep that in mind, Lord Fanbury," smiled Blake. "Just remember that I am Monsieur Fournet, attached to the British Embassy in Paris, and but arrived from there to return at once with important despatches."

"Good. No one will ever dream that you are other than you seem. And now I will ring and have the despatches brought in."

"Have you taken pains to let the same people know that despatches will leave today?"

"Yes. I passed the word that important despatches were going, but that if any department had anything of moderate urgency to send it could be included."

"Ah, that is splendid!" remarked Blake, as Lord Fanbury pressed a button on the desk.

They sat in silence for the following few moments until a knock came at the door, which opened as Lord Fanbury cried "Enter!"

Blake looked up as he caught a momentary look of surprise in the Prime Minister's eyes. Instead of the expected under-secretary, he saw Carfax Morton himself bringing the despatches to his chief.

"Ah, Morton, thanks!" remarked Lord Fanbury. "You needn't have bothered to bring these yourself, a secretary could have done so."

"I just finished making them up," replied Carfax Morton, his deep eyes sweeping over the figure of the Frenchman who sat beside the Prime Minister. "I thought it just as well to turn them over to you myself."

"Ah, yes, very well!" returned Lord Fanbury. "By the way, I don't think you have met Monsieur Fournet from the Embassy in Paris. He is acting as messenger this trip."

Blake rose and clicked his heels in true military fashion, and then bowed with extravagant Latin courtesy to Carfax Morton.

"Monsieur, I am honoured," he said in French.

The Cabinet Minister bowed, and mumbled an acknowledgment of the introduction. Then, turning back to Lord Fanbury, he said:

"I have placed all of importance in, and left the envelope open in case you wished to add anything."

"No, I have nothing else," replied the Prime Minister. "I will seal it up now."

He reached over as he spoke, and drew toward him the heavy official seal and a thick stick of violet sealing-wax. With methodical care he sealed the valuable envelope, and in the presence of Carfax Morton handed them to Blake.

The detective, with another elaborate bow, took them, and, picking up his wide silk-hat, pressed gently on a portion of the brim. The solid-looking brim came away, revealing a narrow space between the crown and the lining. Into this he thrust the envelope, and then snapped back the brim turning to the amused Prime Minister with a smile.

"Voila! Zere Lord Fanbury," he said, in strongly accented English, "zat will fool any—vat you call zem?—ah, yes, interested parties! I think ze little place will keep zem safe."

"It ought to, monsieur," replied Lord Fanbury, unable to resist a smile at Blake's accent.

"A very good place," remarked Carfax Morton. "I will be going now, Lord Fanbury, unless you have any matters you wish to talk over?"

"No, there is nothing else, thank you, Morton. I have a few more instructions to give Monsieur Fournet. You will be at the meeting at five, I suppose?"

"Oh, yes, indeed!"

And with a brief nod to the Prime Minister and Monsieur Fournet, Carfax Morton departed.

The disguised Blake would have given a good deal, not to mention the trouble he would have saved, could he have heard certain remarks of Carfax Morton's half an hour later, for that gentleman lost no time in donning his coat and hat, and hastening down to his motor.

Fifteen minutes later, in a low, hurried tone, he was giving a detailed description of Monsieur Fournet, King's Messenger, to a slim, heavily-veiled woman who sat in the big library at his private residence, nodding at each word.

"Good—very good," she replied. "You have fulfilled the bargain, Mr. Morton, and I have here the balance of the money."

Yvonne—for it was she—drew out a bundle of crisp notes, and tossed them across to him.

"You will find them all correct," she murmured; "and now I must make haste in order not to miss the train."

"For Heaven's sake be careful, won't you, mademoiselle?" whispered Morton hoarsely. "If the slightest whisper of suspicion over this arose against me, I would be ruined at once."

"No one will know of your complicity except through me," she murmured, "and you may rest assured I won't tell—yet," she breathed to herself.

That conversation would have made everything plain to Sexton Blake; but while it was in progress, he was on his way to Charing Cross, ignorant of the fact that Mademoiselle Yvonne, the most brilliant adventuress in Europe, was in possession of his full description, and even knew the location of the despatches, thanks to the information of a Cabinet Minister himself.

He was also ignorant of the fact that the same elusive young woman, by hook or by crook, intended travelling through to Paris in the company of the same Monsieur Fournet, trusting to her own charms and reckless audacity to again secure the precious despatches of the British Government.

But what neither she nor Carfax Morton knew was that the fashionable Monsieur Fournet covered the personality of Sexton Blake, and had they known—well, Mademoiselle Yvonne perhaps would not have been dismayed at the coming duel of wits; but Carfax Morton, who knew only too well the power of that brilliant mind, would have withdrawn his hand from Yvonne's tempting bribes with the same alacrity as he would from a white-hot brick.

However, with his bundle of notes tucked safely away, he returned to the meeting of the Cabinet, and, be it said, that he had nothing but remorse for his inexcusable yielding to the tempting offer, which he fondly hoped would banish that grim spectre—ruin.

Monsieur Fournet strolled up and down in front of the train, apparently engrossed in studying the hurrying figures of his English cousins, but in reality keeping a watchful eye open for the slightest ripple on the surface of suspicion.

From the moment he had left the Prime Minister, he had begun his watch for any move on the part of the unknown thieves, for were information of his journey and an attempt made to secure the despatches, he knew it must be made between Charing Cross and Paris. On the other hand, if no developments took place, it would point strongly to the innocence of everyone in Downing Street, and the guilt of Dick Robins.

Not even after he boarded the train did he relax his inspection of the platform; but nothing of a suspicious nature occurred, and he sank back and gave his individual attention to any possible developments aboard the train as the wheels slowly revolved, and amidst the shouting of guards, and the banging of doors, they started on the run to Dover.

But ere the train gathered speed and left the station behind, a porter rushed across the platform and grasped the handle of a compartment, pulling it open, and lifting up with a sweep the slim young lady who had raced along beside him. Thrusting her in, he slammed the door, and turned back, the tightly clutched sovereign in his hand having formed the force which caused his successful dash for the train.

Blake looked up sharply as the door of his carriage was thrown open and a heavily-veiled young woman stumbled in.

"Oh, pardon, pardon!" he exclaimed, jumping up and steadying her, "Madame had ze close shave!"

Yvonne, who had barely caught the train owing to a long block in the traffic, and was breathing in gasps from her rapid entry, sank into a seat and broke out into silvery laughter at the Frenchman's comical mixture of French and English.

"*Merci* (thanks) monsieur," she said, still laughing and speaking in pure Parisian. "I beg your pardon for my unceremonious entry into your compartment, but I was compelled to take this train, if possible."

"Ah, madame!" cried the gallant Frenchman. "It gives me ze greatest pleasure to be able to offer one of my countrywomen ze use of my compartment. Madame, then, is going through to Paris?" he asked.

"Oh, yes, monsieur!"

Blake thought for a moment that he had caught the barest hint of a familiar ring in certain tones of that silvery voice, and asked the question in order to compel an answer. But if Yvonne had made an involuntary return to her usual tones in her breathless state, she soon recovered, and before he could be quite sure whether the tones were familiar or not, she was rattling along in effusive conversation, and he began to think his ears had played him a trick.

"I'd give a good bit to see her face," he thought to himself. "Her veil is so thick, I can't make out her features at all, except to guess at her youthfulness. I wonder who she is, and if I ever have heard that voice before? It seems familiar, and yet I must be mistaken. However, I'll meet her lead, and if my charming companion opposite should have anything to do with the missing despatches, she won't catch me napping."

But if Blake expected to catch his fair companion making any suspicious move, or asking any suspicious questions, he was disappointed. She showed not the slightest interest in his name, his business, or his destination, and on arriving at Dover, he had to confess to himself that certainly she had as yet given no signs of being implicated.

"I'd better keep my eyes open for others," he remarked to himself as he assisted Yvonne to alight at the pier. "I have been so suspicious of her that someone else may get at me while I'm watching her."

With this cautious reflection he escorted his companion aboard the boat, and secured a couple of sheltered seats aft.

His instinct, had he known it, was only too true; but in the suave, agreeable Frenchman, Yvonne had instinctively scented a more formidable man than Dick Robins. Under any guise Blake breathed power, and the cautious Yvonne was clever enough to know that she must play her cards very carefully if she were to outwit the present messenger.

Everything seemed normal and open on the trip across the Channel, and on the arrival at Calais, Blake was beginning to wonder if, after all, circumstantial evidence was right, and Dick Robins really guilty of the theft of the despatches.

If he could only get a glimpse of the face beneath that veil! If it were known to him, no disguise would hide the truth from him if he could get a proper look at it; and as they walked up and down the platform at Calais, he racked his brains for some plan which would cause her to throw it up.

"Good heavens," he muttered to himself, as a plan occurred, "why on earth didn't I think of it before? I won't have any more than sufficient time, but I'll chance it."

Turning to Yvonne, he smiled and said:

"Will madame honour me by taking refreshment? We have yet sufficient time."

Now that was exactly what Yvonne had been in her turn working to get him to ask, and the heavy veil hid her smile as she graciously thanked monsieur and accepted with pleasure.

They entered the crowded restaurant, and monsieur managed to secure a table for two in the corner. There his fair companion followed exactly the same course which she had a few nights previously, when Dick Robins had been her companion and she had posed as a friendless, frightened young woman.

Blake chatted carelessly, but his eyes missed nothing as she slowly pushed up her veil, disclosing a distracting mouth and chin and the tip of a dainty nose, but no more, for the cautious Yvonne was not again going to risk disclosing her complete features, and particularly not to the gaze of the man opposite, whose power she could feel.

Blake had to be satisfied with half a loaf, but he surreptitiously examined those smiling red lips and the curve of that velvety cheek.

"Curious," he thought; "it is familiar, and yet not familiar. If I could only see her eyes, I could tell."

But she was talking rapidly, and it needed his attention to answer her remarks.

"Would she have coffee?"

"With pleasure, and was monsieur joining her in a cup?"

"Yes, monsieur would do so."

Then Yvonne rattled on in the same strain about the surrounding people as she had with Dick Robins, and, regardless of his puzzlement, Blake had perforce to smile at her remarks.

"That old couple behind you, monsieur," she said, with a smile. "See, they are from the country, and oh, so nervous at all the noise, and so frightened lest the train leave them behind. See how anxiously the old man watches the door."

Screwing in his monocle, Blake turned to look at the old couple. As he did so, Yvonne's hand stole carelessly across the table, and into his coffee dropped a tiny capsule, with all the dexterity which she had used with Dick Robins. But it was ever so much safer with this tall Frenchman, for he seemed quite interested in the old couple, to judge from the length of time he kept his head turned.

Little did she realise that it was something far different from the old couple which interested her companion so much. From the position in which he held his head he could not see the table or Yvonne, but mirrored in the monocle which he had screwed in, was a full view of the table, and as his fair companion had so cleverly doctored his coffee, Blake, with a grim humour had watched every movement of the dainty arm.

"So—so," he breathed softly. "I was after all not mistaken. Really, mademoiselle, you are not growing less clever. What madness on my part not to guess before whose features that heavy veil covered, and whose lovely lips were smiling at me. But not just yet, mademoiselle. I will give you a little more rope, and see if you won't hang yourself. I would give a great deal to know how you discovered the fact about my leaving with despatches, and if you also know where they are concealed. You don't know my identity yet, for if you did, you would not have risked lifting that veil as much as you did. But one thing is certain. Dick Robins is not guilty, but has been the victim of your charming self, mademoiselle. But who—who has played traitor, and would you really sell British despatches to a foreign Government? I didn't believe it of you, Mademoiselle Yvonne."

These thoughts flashed through Blake's mind far more rapidly than it takes to put them down, and his complete summary had been ended, and he was turning back to Yvonne with a polite smile just as that audacious young woman was calmly dropping a lump of sugar in her cup.

"They are very amusing, the old couple, mademoiselle," smiled Blake, as he turned round, "and I think— Oh mademoiselle, a thousand pardons!" he exclaimed, with effusive regret, as his arm accidentally struck his cup of coffee, sending it crashing to the floor. "What clumsiness! What stupidity!" he went on. "I deserve your eternal contempt, mademoiselle, for startling you so!"

Madame smiled sweetly as she graciously pardoned his clumsiness, but her mind was whirling behind that protecting veil.

"Now, I wonder, monsieur, if that was really an accident, or, do you suspect? The game grows exciting, but those papers inside your hat, monsieur, must be mine before we reach Paris, if I have to take them at the point of the revolver."

At that moment a guard put his head inside the door and shouted to make haste; and Blake, who had ordered another cup of coffee, rose with a mental chuckle and assisted his companion to do likewise.

He was quite as anxious as was Yvonne to secure a compartment to themselves, and with both bent on the same purpose, they had no trouble in doing so.

He assisted her in, and sprang in, slamming the door after him. A guard ran along rapidly, seeing that the doors were secure, and they had started on the run to Paris—the detective and the brilliant adventuress bracing themselves for the coming move.

Blake, after making Yvonne comfortable, sank back in his corner and beneath those lowered lids, watched her as her talk trailed off, and her eyes closed in apparent slumber.

"Very well done, mademoiselle," he chuckled, "quite natural. I'll just see if I can do it as well."

Suiting the action to the thought, he settled lower, and closed his eyes tight, although he knew he risked a lot by taking them off Yvonne for even a minute. His breathing grew more regular, and silence reigned in the compartment for a full twenty minutes while the express thundered on its way to Paris. Then a faint rustle broke the silence, subsiding almost at once. Again it came as Yvonne moved cautiously and opened her eyes.

Apparently satisfied with her scrutiny of the sleeping man, she opened her handbag and drew forth a small vial full of a dark, heavy liquid. Pouring a few drops on her handkerchief, she closed the bag and leaned softly across to her sleeping companion, moving ever so gently. Carefully, and with a steady hand, she slowly raised the handkerchief, which was stained with the powerful drug, from the vial.

Permitting the faintest whiff to be breathed in in order not to cause him to cough and waken, and holding her own head aside to escape the effects, she raised her hand nearer until it almost brushed his lips.

Then the sleeping man turned into a galvanic battery fully charged, and Yvonne gave an involuntary startled cry as his hand shot up with a lightning-like jerk and grasped her wrist in a grip of steel. His eyes opened as his body stiffened, and he laughed softly into her surprised face as he wrenched the drugged handkerchief from her hand and tossed it through the half-open window.

"I am sorry if I have startled you, mademoiselle," smiled Blake, and behind her veil Yvonne's eyes began to sparkle with a glimmer of the truth. But her position was a most compromising one, and she realised she must act quickly if she were to recoup herself.

"Really, monsieur, I—I———"

"Don't, please, Mademoiselle Yvonne," smiled Blake, with a significant pause between the words. "Why were you trying to drug me, and why were you———"

But Blake never finished that question. The words ended abruptly as a crashing, tearing, grinding pandemonium broke upon their ears, throwing Yvonne with terrific force into Blake's lap. The opposite wall seemed to rush to meet him, the floor shot up, the windows crumpled up, and as the heavy carriage telescoped with the one ahead, Blake's head struck something with crushing force; he remembered no more, while Yvonne, cushioned from the shock by Blake's body, but locked in his protecting hold, rolled down with him, her mind following his into oblivion.

The Fifth Chapter
Dick Robins in Disgrace

SO upset was Dick Robins by the discovery of his loss in the Gare du Nord Station in Paris, that he knew, as vaguely as did the astonished stationmaster, where he intended to go or what he intended to do. Only one thing kept ringing in his head, and his dry lips kept repeating it over and over as he rushed along, recklessly dashing between hurrying cabs and lumbering drays.

"I must find her—I must find her, and get the despatches back!"

How he intended doing so, his stunned brain as yet failed to imagine; but, as the first shock passed, and the waves of reason flowed back and overcame the dull, pounding agony of his legs, he pulled up and gazed in surprise as he saw his aimless course had taken him outside the city into the first touches of the country.

Wearily he stumbled to the side of the road, and cast himself down with his bag beside him. Then he got himself in hand, for now that the panic had passed, he realised he had wasted valuable time, and, if the despatches were to be recovered, matters must be faced and at once.

"Who on earth would have believed that beautiful young woman could do such a thing?" he muttered. "But it could be no one else. She must have drugged me; but how she managed to do it so cleverly, I can't imagine. And then the irony of her note! Oh, if I get my hands on you, I'll make you suffer!" he growled savagely. "But that doesn't get the despatches back, and if I am to find them, I'll have to think up some plan. If I go to the Embassy, and tell them they were stolen, it's ten to one they won't believe me, and if I cable the chief, it'll be the same.

"Good heavens, what will Alice say? She'll think I'm more fit to join a kindergarten than to get married. I'm ruined if I don't find that woman. But I'll risk staying away from the Embassy today, and see if I can pick up any trace of her in the Montmartre district."

With his jaw set, and a look of resolution on his face, Dick rose and made his way back into the city. He had only gone a short distance through a neighbourhood of tumble-down cottages when a dilapidated fiacre rattled past, and he hailed it.

In fair French he managed to make the cold-eyed cabby understand where he wished to go, and while the cab lurched and rattled over the narrow, roughly-paved streets, he tried to formulate a definite plan.

At that moment the wires were being kept hot between London and Paris by messages regarding his disappearance, and an exhaustive search was being organised by the Embassy in Paris. But all unconscious of this, and engrossed with plans for the recovery of the despatches, Dick rode boldly past the very men who were looking for him, but not until later did he know why it was they failed to recognise him.

The cab pulled up at a street leading into the Latin Quarter, and there Dick dismounted. Paying the cabman's exorbitant charge without a murmur, causing that individual to mourn deeply that he hadn't asked even more, Dick picked up the bag from the seat, and betook himself to a café which he had visited on many happier occasions.

He greeted the waiter familiarly, and, although the latter replied readily, Dick, who knew the fellow well, wondered momentarily why the man didn't seem to really remember him. Taking off his hat, he sat down at a small table, and ordered brandy, for he badly felt the need of a stimulant. He glanced casually about, and as he gazed straight ahead, wondered why he hadn't before noticed the white-haired man who sat right opposite him.

"He looks kind of familiar," he mused, as he slightly wrinkled his brows, "and he seems to be looking in a puzzled way at me. Wonder if I know him? I'll—— Good heavens!" he gasped, half rising and sinking back into his chair. "That's a mirror, and it isn't another man—it's myself! My hair has turned white with the shock!"

It was only too true. While Dick had strode on madly during the morning, his heavy hair had turned snow white as the full force of the shock made itself felt on his overwrought system, and was a very cogent reason why the searchers had not recognised the white-haired, haggard-looking man who had driven past them.

Not waiting for his drink, and stumbling to his feet, Dick grasped his bag, and staggered out, his reason dulled completely for the moment by the second shock which caught him during the reaction of the first.

Once again his footsteps turned aimlessly, and headed towards the open country.

With clouded eyes and dragging steps, he wandered along all through that sunny afternoon.

Dusk found him still plodding on, but as the darkness descended, and the sweet-scented air from the fields and hedges soothed his fevered brow, he turned mechanically in at the gate of a small cottage, up the narrow path he went, inhaling the sweet breath of the honeysuckle which bordered it.

The farmer and his wife glanced up in amazement at the strange-looking figure which stumbled forward, and the worthy peasant was just in time to catch the swooning figure which as overwrought nature rebelled, crumpled up in a heap at their feet.

The motherly soul prepared a big snowy bed redolent with the smell of sweet hay, and into this the worn-out stranger was tucked. He woke once in the night, but his tortured brain still lay steeped in the fever of delirium; but as Sunday morning dawned, the demon of unreason fled with the night, and though weak, he awoke to the smiling sun with a cleared vision and a new resolve.

Where he was, Dick hadn't the remotest idea; but that he had fallen into kindly hands was evident. How long he had been there, or how he had come he neither knew nor, for the moment, cared. It was very pleasant to lie there and listen to the happy chirping of the birds outside as they flitted through the honeysuckle, which forced its scented caress into the room in soothing rivalry with the fleeting, elusive scent of the sweet hay which seemed to be everywhere and yet nowhere.

But his drowsiness left him suddenly as his trouble again sought him out.

"I was a fool," he muttered. "Here I've gone and lost my head, and who knows what the chief will be thinking by now? What I should have done was to make a clean breast of it at the start, and instead, I've fiddled about on my own until that siren who got them has probably managed to get across the border. I'll get up and make tracks at once for Paris."

He crawled out of bed as he made his decision, but found, to his amazement, that his legs refused to support him, and with a groan of irritation he crept back under the snowy sheets just as a knock came at the door and the peasant entered.

His round, good-natured face lost its anxious look as he saw returned reason in his unknown guest's eyes, and he smiled cheerily.

"Well, my friend, it gives me joy to see you better. It speaks well for my good wife's care last evening."

"I am more than indebted to you," replied Dick, with a weak smile. "I fell into the hands of good Samaritans, but I had a great shock, and knew not what I did. What is your name?"

"Bertot—Jean Bertot," replied the peasant. "But you are Anglais—no?"

"Yes, you are right," nodded Dick, whose accent had betrayed his nationality. "But I have many questions to ask you, Jean," he went on. "What day is it? When did I arrive here? How far is it from Paris? When——"

"Oh, oh, oh!" laughed the farmer. "One at a time, my friend! Sit you back in the bed, and I will tell you all. Last evening, when the meal was over and the milk in the pans, the good wife and myself sat down in front to rest from the day's labour. Up the path you came, and just managed to reach me when you went—flop." And he turned his hands over with an expressive gesture. "The good wife prepared the room, and I put you to bed. You talked all the night in your own tongue, but now you are better. It is six leagues to Paris, monsieur, but you can't go today—tomorrow, yes."

Dick stared in astonishment as the farmer spoke. He must, indeed, have gone crazy for the moment to wander so far without knowing it. But now that he had made up his mind to return and explain everything to Carfax Morton, his chief, he was all impatience to be getting along.

But the old farmer, wise in his generation, saw the inevitable result would be another break-down, and resolutely shook his head.

"No, no, monsieur, you could not do it. After you got there you would be unable to do your business after all. Rest here today. It is quiet, and the good wife will put new strength into you with her wine, made with her own hands. Then sleep tonight, and I will harness up tomorrow morning. By noon the old van will get us into Paris. Voila!"

Dick was forced to see the soundness of the old man's argument, and settled down as best he could to follow it.

"But why do you show me so much kindness?" he exclaimed. "I am a total stranger to you."

"I will tell you," replied the old man quietly. "Many years ago when I was a young man just married, I followed the sea for a living. One night off the Brittany coast, I was out in my boat, when a boat from my village went past and told me my wife was suddenly ill. I put about, but it was getting choppy, and before I got far it grew so bad, I was compelled to lower the sail and put about."

He paused, and his eyes grew thoughtful, but, clearing his throat, he continued:

"I battled with the gale for hours, but it was too much for me, and when the little boat finally capsized, I was just able to hang on to the upturned bottom. When morning broke, I saw land near, and shortly after the boat and I were cast on the rocks. But we had been seen, and two men braved the slippery, wave-swept rocks to save me. They succeeded, and when I revived I discovered I had been swept across to the English coast in the night, and that my rescuers were English fishermen. I told them my tale, and what do you think they did, monsieur?"

"What?" asked Dick.

"They manned a boat, monsieur, and in the very teeth of the gale put to sea. We battled across, and monsieur, I arrived home in time to bring hope to my wife, and welcome the little stranger which had come in the night while I battled with the waves in the channel. That is what they did, monsieur, and that is why no Englishman, be he king or be he peasant, is a stranger in this poor cottage," finished the old man quietly.

His eyes were wet as he rose, and Dick held out his hand.

"Thank you, I understand!" he said, as the old man withdrew. Dick sank into a restful slumber, his rebellion against Fate conquered by the farmer's simple story of never-ending thanks to the power which had used a few brave English fishermen that wild day many years ago as the instrument of Jean Bertot's happiness.

Dick's day of rest and the nourishing food of the farmer's wife did wonders for him, and the next morning, when the farmer harnessed up the old grey mare, and they clattered along in the old farm waggon towards Paris, he felt almost optimistic. His optimism was still with him as he descended at the Embassy and thanked the old farmer for his kindness. But he was to receive a cold douche very soon. At first, in his changed appearance he was not recognised, but when he explained matters to the Ambassador his explanation was met with an incredulous smile.

"Really, Robins, your story is not for me to discuss. I have no instructions regarding you, except to send you back to London."

"You needn't send me back!" replied Dick hotly. "I'll go only too willingly myself. I admit I made a mistake in losing my head, but I'm anxious to make amends, and both the chief and the Prime Minister knows I'm incapable of such a thing as selling information."

"I trust they may look at it as you imagine they will," replied the Ambassador coldly.

"But look at my hair," cried Dick. "Isn't that proof enough of what I've been through since Saturday morning?"

"If it is genuine, I must admit it is a strong argument in your favour. However, as I told you, I have no power to deal with the matter, and I would advise you to return to London at once."

"Indeed I will!" answered Dick shortly; and before the Ambassador could speak again he strode out of the Embassy.

The Ambassador turned and wrote out a cipher message to be sent on to London. It arrived there after the Prime Minister had departed for an important reception, and the secretary, not having a copy of the cipher, it lay unread until the next morning.

Dick caught the night train out of Paris, and little did he know, as he flashed past a train rushing on to Paris, that it contained the young woman, for the finding of whom he would idly sacrifice ten years of his life; nor did he know that she was at that very moment creeping softly over to a sleeping men opposite her, slowly raising a drugged handkerchief to his face, and that barely had the sleeping Blake frustrated her plans, when their train went crashing off the line, its fine, painted carriage being converted with marvellous rapidity into a tangled, twisted wreck, from which came the hissing of steam and the moans of the wounded.

Dick sat moodily smoking until Calais was reached, and there heard news of the wrecked train; but in his desire to get to London as quickly as possible gave the news only a passing thought. Indicative of the lesson he had received was his almost abrupt avoidance of a young woman who asked him if he knew any of the names of the passengers in the wrecked train, and this time she happened to be a perfectly genuine young woman who feared a friend had travelled by the ill-fated train.

"Not for me!" growled Dick, eyeing her askance. "No more kindness to lone females for me. They'll have to show me their written endorsed pedigree before I'll ever tell 'em the time."

Bar that innocent question, nothing more happened to cause him to worry until he reached London in the early morning. Buying a paper, he betook himself into the hotel to wash and brush up. He felt refreshed after, and a moderate breakfast caused him to hope for a better reception from his chief, Carfax Morton, and Lord Fanbury, than he had received from the Ambassador in Paris. He read the latest about the train wreck between Calais and Paris, and as the hour crept round with leaden steps when he knew Morton and the Prime Minister would be at the offices, he braced himself, and with a firm step strode along to meet his fate.

***

Many things had happened at Downing Street since Dick Robins had left, and what took place up to the time of Sexton Blake's departure has been related.

Carfax Morton had neither stopped nor helped on the growing suspicion against Dick Robins. But when his daughter Alice had come to see him on Monday night, with an inquiry as to Dick's return, he had glanced up sharply.

"Why do you wish to know?"

Then Alice, with many shy blushes, told her secret, and for once Carfax Morton was dumb with the full realisation of his dastardly action. But that news had set his back to the wall. It spelled danger on every hand, and at any moment complications might arise. Robins was young, and could live the matter down under a new name abroad. But he—Carfax Morton—who had striven to reach a permanent position of honoured and affluent old age—no, no; it was impossible!

He truly loved Alice, and it hurt him to shatter her happiness, but better that than she should turn in loathing and contempt from the stepfather she had always honoured.

No, then there was no other way out of it. Robins must shoulder the guilt and take the consequences. Had he known the things before he would have acted differently, but his hand was at the plough, and he dared not turn back, he must go to the bitter end, suffer who must.

And so he spoke harshly to the nervous young woman, who stood with shyly-drooped eyes after the disclosure of her secret.

"You must put this fellow out of your mind, Alice!" snapped Morton, his eyes on his boots. "He is not the man for you. I have every reason to think he has just done a most traitorous and dishonourable thing, and instead of marrying you he stands a good chance of either being court-martialled or banished in disgrace!"

"Dick Robins—traitorous—dishonourable!" she whispered, with wide eyes of sudden horror. "Oh, father, you can't mean that Dick—my Dick—impossible!" And she drew herself up in blanched, but brave pride.

In a few, harsh, biting words, Carfax Morton told her of the loss of the despatches, and, with all the force of a father who is loved and respected by his daughter, he drove home the final nail which stunned her with its force.

"Dick—oh, Dick!" she whispered, stumbling from the room. And Morton Carfax collapsed into a chair, for he had just done the hardest thing of his whole life.

"Gad, I'm worse even than I thought!" he muttered, loosening his collar with a shaking hand. "But there was nothing else. She'll get over it, and when I get the peerage I'll make it up to her!"

His accumulated worries forbade him any sleep, and so it was that he heard the first cry of the early-morning news boys as dawn was breaking, crying out the train wreck which had taken place between Calais and Paris.

He read the brief wires with ravenous eyes, but it told him nothing. What a miracle it would be if that mysterious woman whose money he had taken had met her death in the wreck! He would have the money, and nothing could be traced to him. She and the messenger would both be on the ill-fated train, and he felt a sudden relief as he read the paragraph which told of the many deaths.

He was at his office in Downing Street sharp to the minute, anxious to miss no detail of further particulars as they came in. He looked up in surprise as an old young man walked in, his silver hair looking incongruous over the young, vigorous face.

"Aren't you aware that I receive no one without an appointment?" asked Morton coldly.

"Good heavens, have I changed so that even you don't know me, Mr. Morton?" said Dick, with a smile, holding out his hand.

"You!" almost shouted Morton, his jaw dropping in amazement. "What have you done to yourself?"

Rapidly Dick related every detail he himself knew of his disastrous trip from the time he left London for Paris on the previous Friday evening.

"Do you expect us to believe such a fairy tale as that?" asked Morton harshly.

"Why—why, sir, it's true—every word!" gasped Dick, beginning to feel an awful grip of fear in his heart. "Here, sir—here is the note she left in my bag!"

Carfax Morton endeavoured to keep his hand steady as he reached out and took the note. He knew every word Dick said was the truth. No man knew better, considering the crisp notes which had been his price, but he was playing for time against the complication of Dick's return.

At that moment, as luck would have it, Lord Fanbury entered with the cipher regarding Dick, which the Ambassador in Paris had sent the previous evening, but which until now had remained unread.

"Ah, you're engaged Morton!" he said," not recognising Dick. "I've something rather important to show you when you finish"

"Don't go, Lord Fanbury, please!" exclaimed Morton, rising. "This is the missing messenger, and he has a very entertaining tale to tell of his experiences."

"You, Robins," said the Prime Minister, wheeling and regarding Dick in stern surprise. "Why are you masquerading in white hairs," he snapped, "and where are the despatches with which you were entrusted?"

With bowed head and hoarse voice, Dick repeated the story which he had told to Carfax Morton.

"What is your opinion, Morton?" asked Lord Fanbury, turning to the minister.

"It might pass in a novel, Lord Fanbury," replied Morton slowly, "but I must confess that I find it hard to apply to the very real disappearance of those despatches."

And in that slow spoken remark, he branded Dick Robins as a traitor, and killed any hope Dick may have had before the kindly justice of Lord Fanbury.

"Robins," said the Prime Minister sternly, although his eyes grew blurred as Dick's heels came together, and he looked the Prime Minister in the eye. "Your father and I were very dear friends," went on Lord Fanbury, "and I had hoped great things for his son. This message which I received this morning from Paris notifies me that you were coming. It also intimates that you told an unbelievable tale at the Embassy there. But that would not weigh with me in dealing out justice. Your own chief, however, under whom you have worked for some time, disbelieves you, and by his decision I temper mine. For the sake of your father"—and his voice broke—"I say no more except—go!

If you are innocent, and by any chance we are doing you a wrong, bring back those despatches, and I will listen to you. Take your belongings and—go!"

With brimming eyes, the Prime Minister turned, his head bent in sorrow at the sentence he had just delivered on the son of his old friend.

Dick stood frozen to the floor, unable to comprehend the full meaning of the blow he had received. He came to himself as the cold voice of Carfax Morton broke on his ears.

"My daughter Alice told me last night that you had asked her to become your wife," he said. "I told her why such a thing was impossible. You understand that she never desires to see you or hear from you again."

"You told—Alice—that—I—was—a traitor!" breathed Dick, every word reeking with his agony of mind.

Carfax Morton bowed his head.

"And—she—believed—it?" went on Dick.

For the barest fraction of a second the better part of Morton's nature caused him to hesitate, then he again bowed.

Dick spoke not another word. Turning, he put his hands before him in the manner of a blind man seeking his way, and, with the deep sigh of a crushed soul, he stumbled from the room and out into the street.

The Sixth Chapter
Tinker is Anxious

AFTER Blake's departure for paris, Tinker took down the Index once more, and spent a long evening in going over every detail he could dig up relating to the ministers and the secretaries of the Government. It was midnight when he retired, and, fagged from his labours, he was not long in getting to sleep.

He expected a cipher message from Blake the next morning, as the detective had promised to send one announcing his arrival; but he had eaten his solitary breakfast, and still it did not appear.

"That's funny," he remarked to Pedro, as they entered the consulting-room. "The guv'nor promised to send one, and it should have arrived before now. Maybe it's been delayed, and I'll just run through the papers while I wait."

He settled down, with Pedro at his feet, and picked up the pile of papers which lay on the table. Tinker had a way of his own in reading the papers, and although it wasn't exactly like the haphazard reading of the average person, it gave him a quick grasp of the news, as well as a complete knowledge of everything in the paper.

He invariably started at the first column on the outside page, and after a close scrutiny of that went on to the next, and so on, to the next page. Consequently, it was some minutes before his eyes lit on the headlines announcing the wreck of the boat-train between Calais and Paris, but when they did he sat up with a startled cry, causing Pedro to open his eyes and leap to his feet.

"Good heavens, the guv'nor was bound to be on that train! I wonder if he is hurt? This article came through at once after the accident, and gives no details, but there must be later particulars. I'll ring up the office of the paper and ask if they know anything further."

With anxious eyes, Tinker turned to the desk and lifted the receiver. The newspaper office felt little inclined to answer his question, but when Tinker told him who was speaking they condescended to tell him what they themselves knew. But that was woefully little, and Tinker hung up the receiver more worried than ever.

"If I only knew what the guv'nor's address was in Paris," he muttered, "I'd send through an urgent wire; but I don't, and there's nothing for it but to wait. He may be all right himself, but may have been delayed in assisting someone else, and as he said particularly I was to stay here today, I'll have to do it."

He began pacing up and down in a state of nervous apprehension, lifting the receiver every hour in order to ask the newspaper office if any names had been sent through yet. Had he known what took place after the wreck he would have known the message he expected would never arrive, for the grey, cold hours of dawn saw a pitiful sight at the scene of the wreck.

When Blake had felt the shock he had involuntarily made a buffer of his body for Yvonne, and though this undoubtedly saved her life, it did so at the cost of an extra shock to Blake, for it will be remembered that she was hurled into his lap with terrible force as the carriages telescoped.

They lay where they had fallen, still unconscious, while all around them rose the cries of the injured and the dying. To make matters worse and complicate the rescue, one of the carriages near the wrecked engine took fire, adding that horror to the terrible scene.

The engine had left the rails, and rolled down a bank on the outskirts of a small village, and it was only a few moments before the villagers were doing what they could to rescue the injured and unconscious from the wreck.

Fortunately, the compartment containing Blake and Yvonne was near the rear of the train, and the flames had not succeeded in spreading so far before two burly peasants squirmed through the tangled, twisted wreck of the carriage, and dragged them out, Yvonne still grasped in Blake's protecting arms.

First aid, as understood by the villagers, consisted of cold water outside and brandy inside, and, primitive as was the method, it succeeded in bringing Yvonne to a conscious knowledge of her surroundings; but Blake still lay as one dead, his mind not responding to the efforts to revive him.

Yvonne took in the situation at a glance, and as she gently disengaged herself from Blake's tight grasp, her eyes grew suddenly anxious as she looked at the detective's white face.

"Oh, is he dead?" she cried, dropping to her knees and feverishly pressing her ear to his chest. "Try, try, again!" she said, turning to one of the men, who had stood back. "He saved my life by holding me as the crash came, and I am unhurt, while he is so white and still."

"We've tried, mademoiselle," said the man gently, "but he must be hurt internally. A doctor will be here soon, though, and perhaps he can do more."

The man started to move away in order to help some other injured passenger, but Yvonne called him back.

"Wait!" she called, darting again into the wreck, and dragging out her handbag.

Opening it, she drew out a little writing-pad and pencil, and rapidly scribbled a telegram to Graves in Paris, telling him to motor at once to the scene of the wreck. She gave the man a louis and the message, with instructions to send it off at once from the village, and then turned back to the unconscious Blake.

Gently lifting his head, she rested it in her lap, and then she sat in motionless, brooding silence, everything forgotten in the great fact that Blake, the man whom she continued to love, regardless of the fact that they were on different sides of the law, was injured, probably very badly. Men passed her, and though they did not disturb her, glanced curiously at her; but the brooding pain in the eyes told its own story, and they left her undisturbed.

The little doctor who arrived shortly after, bustled up and tried to revive the unconscious man; but his efforts were in vain, and he shook her head.

"He's not dead, but the shock has been terrible, and he needs more thorough attention then I can give here."

"All right, doctor," answered Yvonne, with white lips, "look after the others. I have wired for a motor from Paris, and it will be here soon. I will take him into the city and have him attended to there."

Almost as she spoke the big car came into view, tearing along recklessly, and bringing up with a jerk beside the wreck.

"Good heavens, Yvonne, are you hurt?" cried Graves, her uncle, leaping out and running forward.

"No, uncle, I'm all right, thanks to Sexton Blake. He saved my life."

"Sexton Blake—where is he?" asked Graves nervously.

"It's all right, uncle," smiled Yvonne wanly. "He can't arrest you now. This is he, and we must get him into Paris at once.'

"That—why that can't be Blake!" exclaimed Graves, looking at the unconscious Frenchman on the ground.

"It doesn't look much like him, but it is he. But, come, let us hurry; he needs attention at once."

With the assistance of the chauffeur, they gently carried Blake to the car and deposited him in the tonneau. Before climbing in, Yvonne ran back to the wreck. The flames were creeping closer and closer, but risking a collapse of the carriage, she crawled back into the wrecked compartment and secured Blake's hat and bag. With these she returned to the car, and climbed in, taking the wheel herself.

"You, uncle, take the chauffeur, and support Mr. Blake, so he won't be jolted too much. I'm going to drive hard."

And she did drive hard, the great monster bounding along the road at a terrific pace.

When they arrived at Yvonne's house, which was set back from the street in a quiet, beautiful garden, they carried Blake in, and while Graves superintended his removal to a big, sunny room, Yvonne sent the car off to fetch the best doctor in the district.

On its return she ushered the doctor into the room where Blake lay on the big couch, and while every effort was being made to restore his master to consciousness, Tinker was pacing up and down the consulting-room in Baker Street, waiting anxiously for the telegram which never came.

Nor was he to receive any word which would lessen his anxiety, and that night the loyal lad fell asleep in the big chair—still waiting and hoping, not knowing of the rapid march of events.

***

The events which were to lead up to sudden action on Tinker's part developed from Dick Robins' actions after stumbling out of Carfax Morton's office, broken and crushed.

Morton's lying insinuation that Alice believed him guilty was the last straw. He realised in that moment all the raw torment of a soul in agony, and, with his brain drumming over the almost unbelievable words, he bent his steps to a quiet hotel in the Strand.

"It's no use," he muttered, as he entered the lounge and cast himself into a low chair. "If I had been a traitor, and cooked up some feasible cock-and-bull story, I would have been believed; but because I told the actual truth I'm thrown out, disgraced as a traitor. To think that Alice believes it, too! I can't face mother with this hanging over me, and I am completely ruined unless I can produce those despatches. That seems impossible now; but, by heavens, I'm not going under without another effort! I'll go to Paris, and work from there, and I swear I'll never rest until I ferret out the young woman who took those despatches!"

His jaw set, and a new look of resolution rested on his face as he made the vow.

He rose and entered the writing-room, where after several attempts he managed to frame the following note:

Dear Alice,

Needless to say, I am dumbfounded to know you have condemned me without a hearing. However, there is nothing for me to say now except to protest my innocence. I was foolish—yes; but I am not the type of man who sells his country. I leave London to-night, and will never rest until I find the only person who can prove the truth of this assertion.

But you can hardly be interested in my movements now, so I will not bore you further.

Dick Robins

Sealing this, with a grim set of the lips, he went out and dropped it in a pillar-box, after which he drew all the money he had in the bank, and completed his arrangements for leaving London that night.

He caught the Continental train from Charing Cross, and his heart was sore and his thoughts bitter as he watched the last of London.

She placed her cool hand on his forehead - for a moment their eyes meet.
'That - why that can't be Blake,' exclaimed Graves
"I am sorry if I have startled you, mam'selle"

His note reached its destination that night. Her father's denunciation of Dick had amazed Alice and stunned her, but Morton was mistaken in saying, and Dick in believing, that she believed in Dick's guilt. She had suffered in the silence of her room, waiting and hoping for some message from Dick, when she could see him personally and tell him that she did not believe a word of the terrible things she had heard.

That he would communicate with her she did not doubt for a moment, but the possibility of what happened in her father's office never occurred to her. Consequently, when his bitter letter was delivered late that night, her silent sorrow turned to the blazing rage of the lioness whose cub has been stolen in her absence.

She descended to the library to demand an explanation from her father. But Carfax Morton was not in, and she returned to her room to pass a night of misery. Her heart cried out across the dark waste to Dick that she did not believe him a traitor, and, if he would only come back, they would fight the battle out together. But only the mocking wind answered, and when dawn came, it found her drawn and haggard, but determined.

Before any of the servants were astir, Alice packed a small bag, and slipped the bolt in the front door.

"I'll find him," she muttered, "if I have to search Europe! To think you could believe, Dick, that I thought you a traitor! I'll go to Sexton Blake and ask his help. Dick can't have got far yet, and perhaps he can reach him in some way."

An early-morning taxi was passing, and twenty minutes later it set her down at the door of Sexton Blake's apartments in Baker Street.

"It's an atrocious hour," she thought, walking up the steps; "but things are too urgent to waste any time."

Tinker, who had fallen asleep in the big chair, was awakened by the ringing of the bell and Pedro's following bark.

Stiff from his cramped position, he stumbled to his feet, rubbing the sleep from his eyes; but as his anxiety regarding Blake returned he grew suddenly wide-awake.

"Just daylight," he muttered. "I wonder who it is? Maybe a messenger from the guv'nor."

He hastened along the passage and threw open the door, to stare in astonishment at the tall young woman, who was in such evident distress.

"Is Mr. Blake in?" she asked quickly.

"No, miss, he's not at present," returned Tinker cautiously. "Did you wish to see him importantly?"

"Oh, yes! It is very urgent."

"Won't you come in? Perhaps I can do something. I am Tinker, his assistant."

"Oh, I don't know! I was so hoping to catch Mr. Blake! But I will come in for a moment, if you don't mind. His absence will make a change in my plans."

Tinker ushered her into the consulting-room, and placed a chair for her.

"There, miss," he said. "If you care to tell me your trouble, I may be of use to you. Mr. Blake confides in me, and I assure you your story will be quite safe."

"Oh, thank you! I will tell you, if you don't mind. It will be a relief to unburden it. But I haven't introduced myself. My name is Morton—Alice Morton."

Tinker acknowledged the introduction, and seated himself, ignorant as yet that Carfax Morton was her stepfather.

Briefly Alice related the details of Dick's return and his departure in disgrace.

"But he is innocent, Mr. Tinker!" she cried, her beautiful eyes filling. "I am sure of that. I so hoped Mr. Blake would be here! It may not be too late yet to find him; and I know Mr. Blake could find the real traitor."

Tinker, who was naturally astounded at the coincidence of her coming to Blake, managed to conceal his astonishment, but his mind worked rapidly.

Dick Robins, the suspected man, had returned, and had been dismissed as the guilty man. Blake must be ignorant of this latest development, and, unless something serious had happened, he would have kept his promise to advise Tinker of his arrival.

The lad was puzzled as to what to do. Clearly Blake ought to know of the latest development. There might be more beneath the surface, which the detective's shrewd reasoning would ferret out. This young woman believed in Robins' innocence. It might be only the blindness of love, but Blake ought to know.

If Tinker had had Blake's Paris address he would have wired the details at once. No, there was only one thing to be done, and that was, to go to Paris at once. There he would try to find Blake, and he might run in to Robins at the same time. How much could he safely tell the young woman in order to get the necessary information from her, without disclosing the fact that Sexton Blake was already working on the case. He would have to sound her.

Naturally, he said as he made his decision:

"I am very sorry to hear of your trouble. But Mr. Blake is away, and I don't know just when he will be back. I myself, however, am going to the Continent today, and if you will give me a description of the missing man, I will endeavour to find him."

"Oh, you are going to the Continent!" cried Alice. "Then I will come, too. I simply can't rest now until I find him, and if you can help me in any way I shall be so grateful!"

Tinker smiled at the unexpected development.

"I wonder if I tell you something if you can treat it as a secret?" he smiled.

"Of course. I am the daughter of a diplomat," she said simply.

Then Tinker told her as much of the truth as he thought necessary, and five minutes later they were laying their plans to leave for Paris, Alice with a brighter look in her eyes on knowing that Sexton Blake was there.

The early morning train found them on hand, with Pedro in attendance; but before leaving, Alice sent a telegram to Morton explaining the reason for her trip.

Tinker did not know of this until they had been on their way some time, and he spoke firmly against her faking any such action again. For in matters of this kind the slightest thing might spoil every plan.

Alice apologised contritely, and promised not to act on her own initiative again, assuring him that nothing untoward would happen from it.

But she was mistaken. Tinker's intuition had been correct, and before they had covered two-thirds of the journey a message was being ticked over the wires from London to Paris which was to cause them to be met on their arrival.

The Seventh Chapter
Yvonne's Love—Morton's Terror—A Way Out

THE efforts to revive Sexton Blake proved successful after a long hour of uncertainty. He opened his eyes with a puzzled look, but the indomitable will forced the flicker of a smile as he saw Mademoiselle Yvonne's anxious face.

"You took that trick, mademoiselle," he whispered weakly.

"Don't—oh, don't, my friend!" she said softly, dropping to her knees. "You saved my life, and that I can never forget. Rest! You are quite safe. The doctor says no bones are broken, and that you will be all right with rest and quiet. As for the other matter, it is the fortune of war. You have lost this time, and, believe me, were it possible, out of consideration for a brave foe, I would call a truce; but matters have gone too far, and I must finish them. There is no disgrace in your position, and this time it will be my victory without your defeat."

"It is impossible for me to look at matters in that light," replied Blake. "True, the fortune of war has beaten me for the present, but you know I will never rest until I ferret out just what your connection is with those despatches, and recover them, mademoiselle, for this I know—the missing messenger is innocent."

"True," she smiled. "He fell a victim to my charms."

Blake, weak as he was, had to smile.

"Then he is not to be blamed too much," he said. "But watch me well, mademoiselle. I haven't cried off yet. I will get free and finish this case, I give you fair warning."

Yvonne smiled with her lips, but her eyes were grave.

"Give me your promise not to do anything so rash, please," she pleaded. "I must keep you here, and at present you are too ill to leave, even if I permitted it. But after what you did, I don't want to be your gaoler, and yet believe me, it must be."

"I can't promise that," said Blake. "I told you if I could escape, I would."

"I am sorry," said Yvonne simply. "It will be necessary to have you watched, and I didn't wish to do so."

She placed her cool hand on his forehead for a bare moment, and their eyes met. As Blake's closed under the soothing pressure of her hand, Yvonne heaved a deep sigh, and rose wearily. With a long, last look at the man who held her heart and yet could return her so little, she stole softly across the room and opened the door.

Graves was in the library, and thither Yvonne bent her steps.

"He won't give me his promise not to attempt to escape, and so you'll have to watch him," she answered. "I've got to return to London to bring things to a finish, so keep your eyes open. But, don't forget," she said steadily, the colour mounting, "everything possible is to be done for him. No tricks. If a hair of his head is harmed, I promise you it will be the worst day's work ever done by the one who harms him."

"Thanks," drawled Graves. "I will look after him all right. I don't want to see you again as I saw you when you thought we had killed him after the abduction of President Pearson. Personally, I fail to understand why you think so much of the man who has continually thwarted your plans, and was even instrumental in sending you to prison for five years, where you would be yet if you hadn't managed to escape. But I give it up. A woman's nature is too baffling for me."

Yvonne smiled.

"I'm sorry for speaking as I did, uncle, and now that you know how I feel regarding Sexton Blake, I know you will respect my wishes. I know we are fated to be pitted against each other, but I cannot help my feeling for him just the same. And as that is all it will ever amount to, I don't think you can begrudge me that. But keep your eye on him. When he seems most harmless, and you think you have got him safely, is just the time to watch him the closest."

Graves nodded and Yvonne left the room, as fresh outwardly as though she had not begun the day with a terrible train wreck, and completed her arrangements for returning to London.

On the way across she went carefully over the points of her campaign.

"This train wreck has helped matters in one way, but it has complicated them in another," she mused. "It has helped them in that it has placed Sexton Blake in my hands, but complicated them by forming a very good reason for the non-delivery of the second lot. I don't think I have got Carfax Morton just where I want him yet, but I can tell better when I get to London. When I discover what has developed regarding the first messenger, I can tell better what to do. Morton may be slippery enough to get out of things yet, and I'll have to play my cards carefully to catch him. True, Sexton Blake knows Robins is not guilty, but if I freed him, he would only get the papers back, for there is no other proof against Morton. I have the numbers of the notes, but if I am any judge of Carfax Morton, he is clever enough to dispose of those through channels which will cover up their origin. No; I'll have to go and see him, and lay another trap for him."

Carfax Morton was feeling the strain of events, and had sat in his office until dawn, going over every detail in order to leave no track uncovered.

He had left for his residence in order to bathe and get breakfast, and was pacing up and down his library, not knowing that his daughter Alice had left the house just before his arrival.

Ever since the news of the train wreck had come the previous morning, they had been waiting for news from the Paris Embassy regarding the fate of the second lot of papers.

The previous evening a laconic message had come saying the papers had not been delivered, and that all attempts to get tracks of the second messenger had failed. He seemed to have vanished into thin air, and the Prime Minister was on the verge of a collapse. He had rushed in to Morton's office with a message, and, under the stress of his emotion, had blurted out the fact that the second messenger was really Sexton Blake.

Morton had gone cold on hearing Lord Fanbury's confession, but he had managed to collect his scattered wits.

"I have some work to do, Lord Fanbury, which will keep me here late," he said. "I will watch out for any further news, and if anything comes, will let you know at once."

"All right, Morton, I will be obliged. I feel that I will break down if I don't get some rest."

With the chill grip of fear on him, Carfax Morton had spent the night, as has been said, in going over every detail to prepare against discovery by Blake.

He felt vicious at Lord Fanbury's suppression of the messenger's identity, and had he known who it was, he would never have given the description to the mysterious veiled woman. But perhaps fate was with him, and they had both been killed in the wreck. He sincerely hoped so, at any rate, for it would do away with many complications.

Leaving instructions to call on him on the 'phone if anything came, he hurried home and was feeling in a slightly better mood as he paced up and down the library. In this case no news was decidedly good news, for it meant the probable death of Sexton Blake and the mysterious woman.

He sat down and forced himself to eat, and after breakfast, returned to the library. The sudden stopping of a motor outside took him to the window in a hurry, but he was too late to see the occupant, who had already ascended the steps.

He waited in a fever of suspense until he heard footsteps coming down the hall. Supposing Blake had not been killed, and had discovered all, and supposing it were he coming to denounce Carfax Morton? The cold sweat broke out on his forehead as the steps paused at the door, and a moment later the handle turned to admit, not Blake, but the mysterious veiled woman whom Morton hoped was dead.

She advanced quickly as the door closed, and spoke in a low, clear tone.

"You look startled, Mr. Morton," she said.

"I—I—er—you did startle me a bit," stammered Morton, sinking into a chair. "What do you want? Did you get the despatches?"

"Yes, I got them, Mr. Morton, and I got the messenger as well," she said slowly. "Why didn't you tell me it was Sexton Blake, the detective?"

Morton stared at her speechlessly.

"You have got him, and he knows it was you who got the papers?" he gasped. "I didn't know myself that he was the messenger until last evening. He will discover everything, and I will be ruined—ruined. I had covered my tracks so well, too—Robins blamed, and I hoped Blake had been killed!"

"Ah! So Robins came back, did he?" asked Yvonne quickly.

Morton nodded.

"Yesterday morning. He has disappeared again. The Prime Minister believes he sold the first despatches."

This was news to Yvonne, and she thought rapidly. Although he was in a panic of fear, Morton would recover, and when he did, would begin at once to form plans to slip out of the net. And things were in such a state that he had a big chance of succeeding.

In his panic he would refuse utterly to sell any more information, and would endeavour to break his connection with her. No; she must contrive in some way to entice him into a trap which would catch him firmly, and suddenly a daring plan flashed across her mind.

She opened her mouth to speak when an interruption occurred.

A knock came at the door, and the butler entered with an urgent telegram for Morton.

With a muttered apology he tore it open, and read the words. As their meaning entered his mind he half-rose, and then sank back, his eyes filled with terror. He signed weakly to Yvonne to read it, and she picked it up. It was Alice's telegram, sent just before she and Tinker left for Paris, and was as follows:

"AM LEAVING FOR PARIS WITH SEXTON BLAKE'S ASSISTANT TO SEARCH FOR DICK ROBINS. HE IS INNOCENT, I KNOW. SEXTON BLAKE IS IN PARIS, AND I WILL SEEK HIS ASSISTANCE.—ALICE."

"This is from your daughter, is it?" queried Yvonne.

"Yes—yes," answered Morton. "And can't you see what it means? She will find Dick Robins, and persuade him to fight the thing out. If she gets in touch with Sexton Blake, they will combine, and everything will come out."

"Certainly, I cannot keep Sexton Blake a prisoner for very long," said Yvonne, watching him closely as she spoke. "I must release him soon, and if he meets your daughter, I am afraid it will be bad for you."

"I wish I had never seen you!" cried Morton, sitting up, his eyes drawn with fear.

"Don't lose your head, my friend," said Yvonne. "I can yet suggest a way out, if you have the nerve to take it."

"What is it?" asked Morton eagerly.

"Well, it seems to me that you are ruined unless Sexton Blake is put out of the way. He is safe now, and I can keep him a few days. If you have the nerve to save yourself, he is at your disposal."

"What do you mean?" asked Morton sharply.

"Just what I say."

"You mean that I ought to kill him?" he whispered.

"That is a disagreeable word," said Yvonne, with a shrug. "He is there if you want him, that is all I care to say!"

"It is too dangerous!" he muttered.

"Of course, it is," she said quietly. "But so is his freedom. Those New Year's Honours will disappear forever if he discovers that you are the guilty one. Besides, if you came to Paris, you could bring your daughter back. There are plenty of Apaches there who would put a man out of the way for a louis," she added, with a yawn.

Morton dropped his head in his hands, and silence reigned for some minutes. Finally he looked up with a dry, feverish glitter in his eyes.

"I'll come," he said slowly. "I will have to spend the day at the office, but tonight I will leave. Will you travel by the same train?"

Yvonne nodded.

"From Charing Cross," she said, rising. "I will meet you there. Take my advice, and put on a false beard. It would be dangerous if you were recognised."

Morton nodded—he was too upset to say anything; and Yvonne, seeing he had taken the bait, departed.

On her way back to the City she stopped at a telegraph-office in order to send a telegram to Paris, telling Graves to meet Alice Morton and Tinker at the station, and then she took a room at a quiet hotel, where she retired, and calmly slept until late afternoon.

The Eighth Chapter
Sexton Blake Escapes

AFTER Yvonne's departure for London, Blake lay for hours, apparently asleep, but in reality scheming desperately to devise some plan of escape. If he were to do so, he knew it must be by strategy, not force, for, in his weak state, he was far from equal to a struggle of any great degree, and any further strain on his already overtaxed system might prove serious.

An occasional cough in the adjoining room told him Graves was on watch, and he knew Yvonne had kept her word.

"What a woman!" he thought. "With all her misguided actions, as precise in matters as he was himself. How anxious she had been about him, for her eyes had certainly held a very keen anxiety in them when he regained consciousness. What an awful pity she should perish in her wayward course, but what a gist there was in thwarting her."

Blake smiled as he thought of the farcical journey they had taken together, and of his seeing in the monocle the action which had told him who his fair companion could only be. Then, how Fate had taken hand, and just as he was going to push matters to a finish, she had been snatched free, and, instead, he occupied the under position.

But she had stated her intention of finishing her campaign, whatever it was, and, before further mischief could be done, he must in some way get free and make his way back to London. This much was certain. Dick Robins was not guilty, and one among those in London who knew of the journey, was the traitor. Who it was he could not as yet tell, but once in London he would soon put his finger on the guilty man.

Graves entered at that moment with a servant, who bore a tray of food, and Blake, although he had no appetite, forced himself to eat, in order to regain his strength as rapidly as possible.

No chance of escape presented itself during the night, and by morning he had almost worried himself into a fever in his fruitless attempt to devise some plan. If he could only get a word to Tinker, the lad might be able to do something; but Graves had been relieved in his guard by a burly manservant, who declined to even answer the most innocent questions, and Blake knew bribery was out of the question.

Graves made his appearance early in the afternoon, and informed Blake he was going out, and would be glad to get him anything he felt a fancy for.

"No, thanks!" replied Blake. "What I want you would refuse to do, and, besides, I hope to get what I want myself soon."

"I wouldn't build much on escaping," drawled Graves, "it is hopeless!"

"Perhaps," said Blake, with a yawn.

But he noticed with pleasure that Graves called the big manservant to accompany him, leaving a strong, harsh-featured woman in charge of the patient.

With a parting injunction not to worry, and that there were several menservants downstairs, who would attend to him did he endeavour to escape, Graves took his departure for the station to meet Alice and Tinker, for Yvonne's telegram of instruction had just arrived.

Blake lay in despair. He had gone over every plan of escape that suggested itself to him, but all seemed hopeless. As his eyes swept aimlessly about the room they came to rest on a small table in the opposite corner, on which were several bottles of drugs and medicines. He looked at it for some moments before it occurred to him that amongst that lot there might be something which would help his head, which was beginning to ache with a dull, heavy pain.

The woman had gone downstairs with the tray, so he slipped out of bed, and stepped shakily across the floor. Rapidly running over the labels, he looked to see if there was anything which would serve his purpose, when his eyes lit up as he saw a small bottle with a torn label on which was written "Chloroform."

"Might come in useful!" he muttered, picking it up.

And as he heard the returning steps of the woman he staggered across to the bed, with the bottle clutched in his hand.

The woman glanced at him suspiciously as she entered, but Blake lay with closed eyes.

She moved to enter the adjoining room, when Blake's long groping mind found a plan. He realised there was no time to be lost, and promptly put it into execution. Groaning heavily, he opened his eyes, and asked weakly for water, while under the clothes his hand was jerking out the stopper of the bottle of chloroform, and emptying the contents on his handkerchief.

The woman filled a glass and approached the bed, hanging over to hold his head while he drank. Suddenly his left hand shot up, and pressed the handkerchief against her mouth, while his right grasped her neck with what strength he had. She opened her mouth to yell, but only succeeded in drawing a deep breath loaded with chloroform.

Her eyes started from her head in fear, but she was a strong peasant woman, and didn't intend to succumb without a struggle.

She worked her hands up until they gripped Blake's throat with a choking pressure, and the two strained silently.

To struggle was out of the question for Blake. All he could do was to hang on and hope the chloroform would have its effect before her hold on his throat forced him to give in. He had managed to get the handkerchief fairly over her mouth and under her nose, and this fact was his salvation, for as the drug overcame her resistance, her grasp on his throat relaxed, and she collapsed on the floor in a heap.

Blake drew in a deep breath, and lay for a moment recovering his strength. On the table was a decanter of brandy which had been used in bringing him back to consciousness earlier in the day. He took several swallows, and, under the stimulating effect of the spirit, crept out of bed and entered the adjoining room. There were his clothes laid out neatly, and as rapidly as his weak state would allow he got into them.

After he was dressed he made a rapid survey of the room, and smiled grimly as he came across some old garments which evidently belonged to the unconscious woman in the other room. With many twistings and turnings, he managed to squirm into them, and then, under their partially protecting appearance, he opened the door into the corridor, and stole along the hall.

The first room he came to proved to be a small, daintily-furnished dressing-room, and he was not surprised to find it opened into a large luxurious bed-room, the quiet, sumptuous furnishings typical of Yvonne. A small inlaid, rosewood desk decorated one corner, and Blake, after listening for a moment, stole across and again smiled as he found it unlocked.

"Really, mademoiselle, you are getting quite careless, I must caution you about this," he said softly.

His search in the pigeon-holes revealed nothing, but as his fingers searched rapidly for the secret compartment, which he felt positive it must contain, he gave a gasp of satisfaction as a small panel dropped, and there, under his hand, lay two large, official-looking blue envelopes, sealed in many places with the seal of the British Foreign Office.

Blake's eyes gleamed as he thrust his hand in and drew them out. With difficulty he managed to stow them away in the pocket of his coat, under the woman's jacket which he was wearing.

"It's a good thing she was a big woman!" he muttered, as he straightened it again. "Now for a revolver. If I can get one, I'll get out of here, even if Yvonne and every member of the 'circle' try to stop me."

His search, however, was fruitless, and he turned to depart, when his eyes caught sight of a long rapier hanging on the wall.

"That's better than nothing," he said. "I'll just take it, and if they try to stop me— well, I don't think I've quite forgotten how to use one."

With the rapier held ready, he crept along the hall and down the stairs, but dead silence reigned on every side. He reached the lower floor in safety, and smiled as he suddenly realised that Graves' remark about the menservants was pure bluff. He tossed the rapier aside, and rapidly divested himself of the woman-servant's old garments.

Then, pulling out a cigar and coolly appropriating one of Graves' hats, he scribbled a note, and placed it in a prominent position on the hall table.

"Many, many thanks for your kindness and hospitality," he wrote. "When we meet again, which will be soon, I will have great pleasure in thanking you personally.
Sexton Blake."

Then, lighting his cigar, he opened the front door and boldly strode down the path to the street, chuckling to himself as he thought of Graves' chagrin when he read the note.

It was late in the afternoon when Blake made his escape. He hailed the first cab he saw, and ordered the cabby to drive direct to the Gare du Nord Station. There he purchased a ticket for London, but before entering the train for Calais sent a telegram to Tinker at Baker Street, all unconscious that Tinker, Pedro, and Alice had arrived in Paris barely ten minutes before, and had just entered a taxi previous to his arrival at the station.

The detective managed to get a compartment to himself, and sank back with a sigh, for the reaction was beginning to make itself felt, and the strain, in his weak condition, had been severe.

"I've got the despatches, anyway," he sighed. "And now for the man who sold the information, and I know now who that was. Yvonne never discovered those papers so quickly in the hat, without knowing beforehand that they were there: and although several persons knew a messenger was leaving for Paris with despatches, only two knew where the despatches were hidden—Lord Fanbury and Carfax Morton—and I'll stake my life that the traitor is not Lord Fanbury."

The Ninth Chapter
The Capture of Tinker, Alice and Pedro—Pedro Escapes

TINKER, Pedro, and Alice Morton had much to say and much to plan on their way across from England to Paris. Alice poured into Tinker's sympathetic ear all her hopes and fears; and that young man, wise in his generation, nodded his head sagely. Then he, in his turn, made a few cautious references regarding Blake's mission in Paris, and led up to a discussion of their plans after they arrived there.

"I think, Miss Morton," he said, rubbing his chin, "I think our best plan will be to go direct to the Embassy. There I will be able to discover if the guv'nor has called, and, incidentally we may get track of Mr. Robins, for it is just possible he would call there again if he came to Paris."

"Oh, yes, Mr. Tinker! Whatever you think is wisest to do we will do!" she cried.

Tinker did not tell her his real reason for desiring to go at once to the Embassy, deeming it unnecessary that she should know. But there he hoped to discover if the second messenger, in the person of Monsieur Fournet, had arrived, and if not, what had been found out about him. Was he in the wreck, and, if so, was he killed or injured? Tinker argued, and soundly, that on the non-appearance of the second messenger with the despatches, the officials at the Embassy would institute rigid inquiries at once.

He paced the platform at Calais, proud in being the escort of the beautiful Miss Morton; and well he might be, for many a fastidious man would have been quite content to take Tinker's place beside the dark, stately young woman with the sorrowful eyes. Many a curious glance was thrown at them, but Pedro, bringing up the rear, caused the eyes of the curious to pop open as the big, slow-pacing hound came into view.

Their anxiety to reach Paris impelled them to enter the train a full ten minutes before it started, although Pedro had to be left in the guard's carriage. From the expression on that individual's face, he would evidently have been very glad to have Tinker take the dog with him, but a generous tip on the part of the lad received a half-hearted consent to look after the dog.

Alice lay back and closed her eyes, and her heavy breathing a few minutes later told Tinker tired nature had asserted itself, and compelled her to sleep. He was just as well pleased, for he desired to devote some time to the planning of his future movements.

In the middle of the afternoon they swept past the scene of the wreck, and the lad leaned eagerly out at the tangled, twisted, scorched mass which had been cleared from the rails.

As it disappeared around a curve he sat back, and the worried look returned to his eyes. Had Blake been in the wreck, and perhaps mangled, or even killed? The scene brought a vivid picture to the lad's mind of what the suffering must have been, and the full realisation of what the loss of Blake would mean to him.

He tried to comfort himself by the reflection that perhaps, after all, the guv'nor had escaped injury, and that other matters had prevented his keeping his promise to wire.

In this mood he looked impatiently out of the window as they entered the suburbs of Paris, and, leaning over, he gently touched Alice on the shoulder.

"We're here, Miss Morton," he said, as she sat up, looking delightfully embarrassed with the warm flush of sleep still on her cheeks.

"Oh!" she exclaimed. "Have I slept the whole way? How terrible! I really owe you an apology."

"Not at all," laughed Tinker. "I was glad you could sleep, for you may have many wakeful hours ahead, and you needed rest badly. But here we are. We'll get Pedro, and then take a taxi down to the Embassy."

They gathered up their things, and joined the hurrying crowd, stopping only long enough to get Pedro. Then they pressed through the street, not noticing in their absorption that several men, also with bags and rugs, walked along beside them. When they reached the line of taxis they still did not notice that the same men crowded over, sending Tinker and Alice to one side directly in front of a yellow taxi in their endeavour to escape the crush.

"Heavens! They seem in an awful hurry to get out of the station," remarked Alice. "They don't mind crowding over people."

"They are typical travelling hogs," replied Tinker. "It's the same that litter the racks over everybody's head with their bags and bundles, evidently under the impression that because they've paid for a ticket they are entitled to the whole compartment. But we might as well take this taxi, Miss Morton; it's the nearest, and looks comparatively clean."

"All right," she laughed. "Since they drove us right into it we may as well."

The chauffeur was remarkably courteous for one of his calling, and solicitously saw that they were comfortably seated, not even forgetting Pedro, who, on his part, glared at the man with a forbidding, bloodshot eye. However, he obeyed Tinker's command and entered the cab, where he stretched out on the floor.

The chauffeur closed the door, and so dexterously that his passengers did not see him, as he emptied on the bottom of the cab the contents of a small dark phial which he held concealed in the palm of his gloved hand. For the crowding, hustling travellers who had pushed Tinker and Alice down against the taxi were not the travelling hogs Tinker took them for, but members of Yvonne's circle and confederates of Graves in his meeting of Tinker and Alice, according to Yvonne's instructions.

They had succeeded in forcing their victims down against the yellow taxi, and there the obliging chauffeur—who was Graves, disguised—took up the game. He knew it was risky dropping the drug inside the cab while Tinker was there, but had he done so earlier it would have lost most of its potency; and the risk had to be taken. His eyes gleamed with satisfaction as he saw he had succeeded in doing so unnoticed, and, slipping the phial into the pocket of his coat, he sprang into the driver's seat.

Tinker had told him to drive at once to the British Embassy, and as the taxi started he leaned back, glancing casually out of the window as they drove along.

Several streets were passed, and Tinker was looking for the turning which would take them to the Embassy, when he turned, as Alice remarked:

"Don't you find it frightfully close? I can hardly breathe. Would you mind dropping the window, Mr. Tinker?"

"With pleasure, Miss Morton! I was just going to remark myself how close it was. I'll drop both of them, and we can get a current right through then."

He rose as he spoke and endeavoured to drop the window in the door beside him; but it resisted all his efforts, and, with a faint laugh, he turned to the other.

"They're evidently not very fond of fresh air in Paris," he grunted, as the second also refused to budge. "But we certainly must have some air. It seems to be getting closer and closer. Don't you think so?"

He turned in surprise on receiving no reply, but gave an exclamation of consternation as he saw Alice lying back in the corner with closed eyes, her face deathly pale.

"Great Scott, she's fainted!" he gasped. "I'll get air, if I have to smash the window! Here, you!" he called, rapping on the front window in an endeavour to attract the driver's attention. But that individual seemed to be utterly deaf.

Tinker turned, and stumbled over Pedro on his way to kick the window out, when he happened to glance down, and his look of amazement gave place to one of sudden apprehension as he saw Pedro was lying with his great jaws apart, obviously affected in a similar manner to Alice.

A sudden wave of dizziness which swept over him settled Tinker's doubts, and, summoning all his power to keep his reeling senses, he again made for the window. He reached it, but his knees collapsed, and he dropped. Still he persevered, and managed to raise his hand and pound feebly against the glass. But his power to resist snapped, and, gasping "Drugged!" he dropped unconscious to the floor of the taxi.

Whether Graves, the disguised chauffeur, knew of the success of his plan or not, he gave no sign, but he evidently counted strongly on its efficacy, for not once did he turn his head to glance back into the cab. He drove on steadily until he reached Yvonne's house, where Blake had been taken after the wreck the previous day. Driving around to the back, he drove the yellow taxi through a gate and up a short drive into a sort of stable and garage combined. It was an annexe to the rear part of the house, and communicated with it by means of a covered passage.

As he stopped the cab and jumped down he looked around expectantly, as though somebody ought to have been there to meet him.

"Why on earth isn't Jules here?" he muttered, looking around with a frown. "These innocents must be carried in at once and received, and——"

He broke off as the door opening from the passage into the stable flew open, and Jules, the burly manservant, dashed into the stable.

"You are late!" began Graves, but stopped as he saw the expression on the man's face.

"Sexton Blake has escaped while we were at the station!" he gasped, his eyes rolling.

"What!" almost screamed Graves, startled for once out of his drawling manner. "Escaped? Impossible! He was too weak to overpower a kitten, let alone Jeannette!"

"I didn't stop to see how he had done it, but Jeannette is lying on the floor unconscious. And I found this on the hall table."

Graves snatched the note which the man held out, and tore it open.

As he read Blake's ironical message his jaw came together, and he looked savage.

"When will Yvonne get over her silly infatuation for this man?" he growled. "If she had listened to reason, I could have put him out of the way a dozen different times! But, no. She must let him live on account of her feeling for him. And every time he plays ducks-and-drakes with our plans! Even after she was landed in prison by him, she hasn't altered! Her romantic nonsense will land the whole lot of us back there again the first thing I know; and the next time it won't be so easy to escape. And the worst of it is, when she comes back from London, she'll blame me for letting him escape.

"Here, Jules," he snapped, turning to the man who stood apprehensively watching the angry Graves, "give me a hand with these innocents! We'll carry them upstairs, and tie them safely. You go on guard, and, by heavens, if you let them escape, I'll skin you alive!"

Jules moved with alacrity, and promised fervently he would not let them escape, as he had no desire to meet such a fate.

After lifting out the insensible bodies of Tinker and Alice, they carried them one at a time to a large room next to the one where Blake had been. Jules bound them with thoroughness, while Graves went to revive the woman-servant, and hear her story. She came-to after a strenuous half-hour's work, and gave her story, with many vindictive adjectives for the departed Blake.

Graves had rapidly gathered what had happened, and was turning, with a feeling of dread, to see if Blake had gone away empty-handed or not, when Jules entered.

"What will we do with the dog?" he asked. "The lad has come-to, and asked as a favour that we don't hurt the dog."

"Take your revolver—the one with the silencer—and go down to the stable. Take the dog and shoot him. By thunder! If I can't have my way about Sexton Blake and his confounded assistant, I'll get rid of the big, ugly beast that has tracked us so often!"

Jules departed quickly to obey, and Graves hurried through to the desk in Yvonne's room. Pressing the panel, he bent over the secret compartment, but as his eyes told him what had happened, he looked up with startled eyes, white to the lips.

"Gone! That Blake is a fiend! By thunder, I'll get rid of him the next time I have the chance, and risk her ladyship's temper! With those despatches, he may land us all in for life!"

He closed the panel, and strode moodily from the room, to encounter Jules returning up the stairs.

"Well," snapped Graves, "did you shoot the brute?"

"No," responded the man slowly. "I just got down in time to see him vanishing over the back fence. We left the door of the cab open, and while we were upstairs he had revived."

Graves turned, with a muttered curse, and descended to the library, where he drafted an urgent cipher message to Yvonne in London, informing her of Blake's escape, and the capture of Tinker and Alice. But Yvonne never got that message, for she was already on her way for Paris with Carfax Morton, whom it will be remembered she had successfully enticed into coming to Paris in disguise, where she meant to drop the mask and confound him.

The Tenth Chapter
The Prime Minister is Undecided—The End

SEXTON Blake found on his arrival at Calais that a cross-Channel steamer was just about to start. The regular passenger steamer was not to leave for some hours, but he knew how anxious Lord Fanbury was about the missing despatches, and, after sending an explanatory telegram to the Prime Minister, he persuaded the captain of the little steamer to take him across.

The captain, a crusty old salt, demurred at first, but on Blake revealing his identity, and hinting vaguely that it was on business for the nation, the old fellow turned and moved swiftly.

"If that's the case, Mr. Blake, I'll certainly run you over in double-quick time!"

He signalled the engine-room as he spoke, and Blake, who was fighting with all his will against his returning weakness, lay down in the captain's cabin, to try and get a little rest. The captain kept his word, and Blake felt as though he had barely got to sleep when the captain shook him into wakefulness.

"Here we are, Mr. Blake; the quickest time the old *Polly* ever did it in. But you look ill, sir. If I were in your place, I'd get home and get to bed."

"I do feel a bit offish," smiled Blake, wondering what the captain would say if he told him why, "and I intend doing just what you advise. But I've got one or two things of importance to do first."

He stumbled to his feet as he spoke, and was surprised at how weak his legs felt. But, gathering himself together, he went out on deck, and, after thanking the captain, walked slowly down the gangway.

Blake's idea was to get the first train he could for London, and after an interview with the Prime Minister, in which he would inform him of his certainty regarding the guilt of Carfax Morton, go at once to Baker Street and get into bed.

He was walking slowly up the dock, not desiring to overtax his strength, when an engine with only one carriage behind pulled up at the head of the dock.

"Must be a special," muttered Blake. "I've a good mind to engage it to take me back to London. By Jove, I will!"

He hurried somewhat to put his plan into execution, when a man stepped from the solitary carriage, and Blake gave an exclamation of surprise as he saw who it was.

"Lord Fanbury," he said. "What has he come down in a special for? He can't be on the way to the Continent. Ah, I have it! He is so anxious about the despatches he has come himself to meet me. It's mighty decent of him!"

He was rapidly drawing near the Prime Minister, and, as the latter turned to walk away from the special, Blake called to him.

Lord Fanbury turned, and a look of pleasure appeared on his haggard countenance as he saw who it was.

"Hallo, Blake!" he exclaimed, approaching quickly. "Good heavens, man, you look ill enough to drop! What is the matter?"

"I'll tell you later, Lord Fanbury," smiled Blake. "I've got a lot to tell you, and some of it will startle you considerably. Where can we talk without being disturbed?"

"Come! We will go back into the carriage of my special," answered Lord Fanbury. "There are some easy-chairs there, and I'll have something mixed to revive you."

He turned and led the way into the luxurious interior of the special carriage, and Blake sank, with a sigh of relief, into a luxurious lounge-chair.

Lord Fanbury hastened to a cupboard, and, with his own hands, mixed a reviver for Blake, who sipped it gratefully, feeling much better as the strong spirit coursed through him.

"Firstly," he said, when he had finished and set the glass down, "I'll ease your mind of what worries you the most. I succeeded in getting the despatches, and I am glad to say they have not been opened."

"What!" cried the delighted Lord Fanbury. "Not even the first lot?"

"No," smiled Blake. "But you can see for yourself."

He drew them from his pocket, and passed them over.

"Yes, yes; you are right!" cried Lord Fanbury, rapidly examining them. "They are just exactly as they were when they were sealed, Blake"—and his voice grew husky with emotion—"I won't try to tell you what you have done, not only for me, but for the country. It is beyond value. It seems to me you ought to reconsider your decision not to accept a baronetcy. You have extinguished the flame just as it was about to drop into the magazine, and the explosion of which would have set Europe ablaze. That scoundrel Robins——"

"Wait, Lord Fanbury," said Blake quietly, holding up his hand. "You are mistaken. Young Robins is neither scoundrel nor traitor. He was foolish—yes; but no harm has occurred, and the lesson will do him good. The man who sold the information relating to the despatches is far higher up in the councils of the nation than Dick Robins. Robins was the victim."

"Far higher up!" gasped the Prime Minister, dropping the despatches in his agitation. "Far higher up! What do you mean, Blake? What do you mean, Blake?" he added, in a hoarse whisper.

"Before answering that I want to ask you a question first, Lord Fanbury. Do you remember when you gave me the second lot of despatches in your office?"

"Yes."

"You and Mr. Carfax Morton were there?"

"Yes."

"Do you also remember where I concealed the despatches?"

"Yes; in your hat."

"Quite right. Well, listen!"

Blake then related in detail his adventures from the time he left London, and met the veiled woman on the train, until he reached Calais. Then he related how the mysterious woman had tried to drug him, and how he had seen the reflection of her movements in his monocle. How he had just been about to seize her when the wreck occurred and accidentally turned the table, throwing him into her hands. Then how he had escaped, and finally recovered the papers.

"Now, Lord Fanbury," he concluded, "there is the story. With her own lips she has exonerated Dick Robins. But what I proved when I recovered both lots of despatches was that she had been fully aware, before the wreck, that they were concealed in my hat. And you and Carfax Morton were the only persons who knew where they were hidden."

"Then you mean," whispered the Prime Minister, in tones of horror.

"That Carfax Morton is the traitor!" finished Blake quietly, as he leaned back.

"My heavens, Blake, I can't believe it! It seems utterly incredible. A trusted Minister of the Crown! Why, he was to get high honours at the New Year! I can't believe it, Blake!"

"Order this special to run back to London at once, and I'll prove it!" said Blake, slightly nettled.

"Yes, yes; but we'll have to wait a day or two to confront him," answered the Prime Minister. "He asked yesterday for two or three days' leave. He said he was feeling run down, and wanted a rest in the country."

It was Blake's turn to gasp.

"What!" he snapped, sitting up suddenly. "He has left London?"

Lord Fanbury nodded.

"More likely he has gone to the Continent," answered Blake. "Will you send for all the officials who were on duty here yesterday, Lord Fanbury? I'd like to have a talk with them."

Lord Fanbury signalled a porter, and gave him the order, and both men sat smoking in silence until the stationmaster and a guard hurried up and saluted respectfully.

"We want some information," said Lord Fanbury, "and I want you to answer fully any questions my friend asks you."

"Yes, sir; certainly, sir!" they both answered, and Blake faced them.

"Do either of you remember seeing, yesterday, at any time, a tall, grey-haired man with very dark eyes, descend from the London train on his way to Calais? He would be about my height, but stouter, dressed in frock-coat and silk hat, and had a moustache, but no beard."

Both men shook their heads.

"No, sir; I can't say that I remember seeing anyone of that description, sir," said the stationmaster, shaking his head.

"Nor I, sir," replied the guard. "I came down from London on the late train, too. I did notice one elderly gentleman, sir, with a lady—his daughter, I imagine. He would about fit your description, but he wore a beard, sir."

"Ah, a lady with him! Would this description fit her?"

Rapidly Blake gave a detailed description of the costume in which he had seen Yvonne before she had come to tell him she was leaving for London.

"Why, sir," cried the guard in surprise, "you've described her exactly! But the man wore a beard, I'll swear to that sir!"

"No doubt," smiled Blake "But, tell me, did they leave at once for Calais?"

"Yes, sir; they took the first steamer."

"Very good. That will do," replied Blake.

And, saluting again, the two men departed.

"Lord Fanbury, I was right. Carfax Morton, disguised by a beard, has gone to Paris in the company of the woman who got the despatches. What may be his errand I can't imagine, unless it is to sell more of his country's secrets."

"Who is this mysterious woman, who seems to have the power to almost reach the very heart of the Government?" asked Lord Fanbury, his jaw setting in a way that many old Etonians would have recognised, for they had seen the same expression on the face of the future Prime Minister when a particularly difficult situation occurred during a footer match.

"The mysterious woman," replied Blake, with a smile, "is the cleverest woman I have ever met. Her name is Mademoiselle Yvonne."

"Good heavens! The young woman who escaped from Dalemoor Prison?"

"The same," nodded Blake. "But this news regarding Carfax Morton means I must return at once to Paris. He will hardly have reached there yet. And I think I know where Mademoiselle Yvonne would take him first. Perhaps I can catch him red-handed, and convince you that I am right."

"Gad, Blake!" thundered Lord Fanbury, "I'll go with you. I'll ferret this thing out with you now. If Carfarx Morton has betrayed his high position, I'll be tempted to shoot him with my own hand!"

"Good, Lord Fanbury!" exclaimed Blake. "I'll be delighted to have you with me! Let us make haste. I came over in a tug—the *Polly*—and if the captain hasn't left the dock, we can get him to set us across at once."

Lord Fanbury sprang up, and a few minutes later the captain of the *Polly* was eagerly consenting to take them across, proud of such distinguished passengers, and flattered by being informed that Lord Fanbury trusted in him to preserve his trip as a secret.

On the way across Blake heard how Dick Robins had returned, and how, at Carfax Morton's suggestion, Lord Fanbury had dismissed him in disgrace.

"Ah, Blake," he said heavily, "I see it all now! Morton was vile enough to allow Dick Robins to shoulder the blame. I see that he really told the truth that his hair had turned white from the shock. But we will find him, and I will endeavour to atone for the wrong I have done him."

Blake was dubious about finding Dick Robins so easily, for he imagined that the last blow would about finish him, but he saw how cut up Lord Fanbury was, and so he held his peace.

Captain Dickson laid himself out to make a record, and succeeded in making slightly better time than when Blake had crossed shortly before.

At Calais no train was leaving; but Lord Fanbury sent a cipher message to the French President, which must have astonished that gentleman, but which was the means of having a special train at their disposal in a very few minutes.

Then they were thundering along on the way to Paris, orders having been flashed on ahead to give them a clear run. On the way Blake pointed out the wreck, and as it flashed from view Lord Fanbury held out his hand.

"I realise more and more, Blake, what we owe you." And in the sincerity of that grip Blake felt he was amply rewarded.

They descended quickly at the Gare du Nord, and were hurrying out to the line of taxis, when Blake stopped, with an exclamation of amazement.

Just disappearing down the street was a big hound, with nose to the ground. It looked like Pedro. And yet Pedro and Tinker ought to be in Baker Street. Could it be possible they had come to Paris to search for him?

He gave a peculiar whistle, which, although not piercing, carried clearly through the noise of the street. The hound stopped, lifted his head, and looked back. It was Pedro and Blake's eyes grew wet as he realised the faithful fellow was doubtless trying to find one of his masters in a strange city. But where could Tinker be?

Again he whistled, and Pedro, who had been standing at attention, saw him. Along the street he came bounding, with jaws open in delight, and as he threw himself at his master the surrounding people gasped with horror, for they thought the dog had gone mad and was attacking the man. But a moment showed them their mistake, and they turned away, smiling.

Blake hailed a taxi, and ordered the chauffeur to drive to a street near where Yvonne's house stood. It was only a short drive, and on the way Blake stopped and bought two automatic revolvers—one for himself, and one for Lord Fanbury. Then they proceeded, and, on descending, began walking, when a startling incident occurred.

Lord Fanbury, who had been moodily silent, suddenly stopped, and pointed in speechless horror at a ragged, unkempt figure, with wild, haggard eyes and white hair. The man was walking toward them, and seemed oblivious of his surroundings.

"My heavens!" finally gasped the Prime Minister. "Look, Blake—look! That is Dick Robins!"

"What?" cried Blake. "Are you sure?"

"Yes, yes! He looked just that way when I dismissed him!"

"Leave him to me," said Blake quickly. "Turn your back, so as he won't recognise you. He is in a critical condition, and another shock would be dangerous."

Lord Fanbury turned, and Blake advanced alone to meet the approaching Robins.

The haggard man barely glanced at Blake, but was forced to come to a stop as the latter stood fairly in his path.

"Can I trouble you for a match?" asked Blake quietly.

Robins seemed to come with a jerk to the present.

"Oh—er—yes, certainly," he said, feeling in his pocket.

That was what Blake wanted, for, with his mind back to the present, the good news would not be so liable to prove too much of a shock.

"Thanks, Robins!" said Blake quietly.

Dick looked up quickly.

"Robins," he said, "do you know me?"

"Yes," replied Blake. "And I've got something to say to you. Can you stand some good news?"

"Good news! What good news can you have for a man branded as a traitor?" said Dick bitterly.

"Suppose I were to tell you it is now known you are not a traitor?" said Blake, watching him closely for signs of collapse.

Dick sprang forward and gripped him by the arm.

"What? What?" he shouted. "Don't play with me, man! Who are you? Are you playing a cruel joke on me?"

"Did you ever hear of Sexton Blake playing a cruel joke on anyone?" asked Blake.

"No. Are you Sexton Blake?"

"Yes. And I have got the proof of your innocence."

"Oh, thank Heaven!" cried Dick. And, strong man though he was, the tears of happiness coursed down his cheeks.

"Pull yourself together," went on Blake, "and come with me. I can give you quick proof of the truth of my words."

He took Dick's arm as he spoke and led him along to where Lord Fanbury stood.

The Prime Minister turned slowly round and looked at the astounded Dick.

"I wish to ask your pardon for my unjust belief in your guilt, Robins," he said, holding out his hand. "Can you forgive me?"

"Oh, sir!" cried Dick. But there his voice failed, and Blake turned away as he gripped the hand of his chief.

"We'd better get along now," said Blake, turning, and rapidly explaining matters to Dick. "Do you feel well enough to come along, Robins?" he asked.

"Oh, yes, I could face anything now!" answered Dick, with shining eyes.

They turned, and started again. But Pedro seemed to have different ideas, for he worried at Blake's feet until the latter pulled up, and looked down with a smile.

"What is it, old chap? Why don't you want us to go?"

Pedro pointed his tail, and turned in the opposite direction.

"We'll follow," said Blake. "It's hard to tell what he has on his mind, but it must be something. He never acts this way without reason."

Pedro went on quickly, looking back from time to time to see if they were following. Finally Blake turned to Lord Fanbury, with a chuckle.

"By Jove! The dog is taking us to the same house, but by the back way. Now, what is the meaning of that?" Suddenly his face grew sober. "I wonder if it is possible that Tinker has fallen into their hands?"

He quickened his steps, and a moment later Sexton Blake, the famous detective, the Prime Minister of England, and Dick Robins, were following Pedro over the fence which bounded the garden at the rear of a house in Paris.

Pedro led them at once to the stable, and Blake whistled softly as he saw the yellow taxi.

"Ah, I begin to see light! Tinker must be here, and that is how they captured him."

Pedro was snuffling at the door which led from the stable into the passage, and Blake, as he saw him, turned to Lord Fanbury and Dick.

"If we can open that door we can probably get into the house from there. We will try, anyway. Get your revolver ready, Lord Fanbury, and you Robins—have you a revolver?"

"No," answered Dick. "But this will do." And he picked up a heavy bar of iron which lay on the stable floor.

Blake crossed and tried the door, and chuckled silently as the latch yielded and it opened.

Signing to his companions to follow silently, he held Pedro back, and the quartet began to creep softly along.

They passed several outer rooms, finally coming to the kitchen.

Blake smiled grimly as he recognised the harsh-featured woman-servant from whom he had escaped. She was ironing at a table with her back toward them, and Blake signed to Pedro to stand back, and stole softly forward.

The woman heard him just as he reached her, and turned, with terror-stricken eyes, to scream, but Blake caught her suddenly, and her intended cry dropped into a gurgle.

They lost no time in binding and gagging her with some of the linen she had been ironing, and then the quartet again started forward.

Through the dining-room they went, but as they softly opened the door leading into the hall the sound of voices in the adjoining library came to them, and Blake stopped with his fingers on his lips.

Had Lord Fanbury any doubts of the guilt of Carfax Morton it was settled by the words they overheard while standing in the dim corner of that hall, and as for Dick Robins, he was too astounded to move.

Cold and clear came the voice, and Blake recognised it. It was Yvonne's.

"And now, Carfax Morton," she was saying; and the listeners bent forward, "I have told you who I really am, and why I tempted you with money to betray your country.

"I had no intention of disposing of those despatches to a foreign Government. I may wage war on certain members of society, but I would scorn to be a traitor. And if I, who am outside the pale of the law, should scorn to be a traitor, how much more contemptible is your fall—you who were a trusted minister of the Crown.

"When I swore, in Australia, to be revenged on the men who swindled my mother and myself out of the Jig Saw Mine and our home, you all thought it was the idle raving of a grief-stricken girl. But Vineburg, Pearson, Todd, and Kelly, have all met with their deserts, and you, Carfax Morton, are the next on the list, and you are going to meet with yours.

"When I told you Sexton Blake was a big element of danger, and that your only way to escape discovery was to kill him, you fell into my trap. Like a babe in swaddling clothes you took the bait. You see, you would even stoop to murder. Do you think I would permit you to kill Sexton Blake—enemy though he is?

"Faugh, you baby! He is a man—a man—do you hear? And you—you know yourself what you are. I intended to lure you here by telling you I would turn Blake over to you, but it was only to confront you with him, and tell him what you were.

"Then, my revenge completed, I intended making my escape. But once again he was too clever for me, and not only has escaped, but has succeeded in taking the despatches. But here you are, and here you stay until I complete your ruin."

"Oh, my heavens, you fiend!" cried the hoarse, broken accents of Carfax Morton. "Have mercy on me! Think of my position. I am honoured and respected, and I swear I would not have fallen had you not tempted me."

"Mercy! You are a fine advocate of mercy," laughed Yvonne. "Did you or your friends have mercy on my mother or myself? No, Carfax Morton; here you stay until I finish with you!"

Lord Fanbury moved forward, and Blake, who had put out this hand to detain him, pulled it back on seeing the expression on his face, and followed.

Turning the handle of the library door, the Prime Minister entered, and never before did England's first man radiate forth more impressive dignity than he did at that moment.

Inside, Yvonne stood leaning against a desk facing Carfax Morton, who sat, huddled and broken, in a big chair. He looked up with deadly fear written on his face as he saw the Prime Minister.

"It will not be necessary to keep Mr. Carfax Morton here any longer in order to accomplish your purpose," said the Prime Minister; and even Yvonne was at a loss for words under the spell of that dignity.

As for Carfax Morton, who had thought the vision of the Prime Minister must be a ghost, he dropped forward insensible on hearing the voice of his chief; and Dick Robins, forgiving and forgetting the great wrong which had been done him, sprang forward and supported the inert figure in his arms.

Lord Fanbury turned back to Yvonne.

"Can I trouble you for a match?"
Pedro threw himself at his Master.
"It will not be necessary to keep Mr. Carfax here any longer."

"I have heard much of you," he said slowly; "and am sorry to see a woman of your attainments so misguided. It is a serious matter to interfere with the business of the British Government, but I am glad to hear that you would not stoop to sell our secrets to a foreign country.

"But you might have caused a great deal of mischief by meddling, and for that you deserve to be punished. But it is probably obvious to you that this chapter in the history of our Government must not be revealed, and for that reason there must be no publicity."

"My lord, I pledge you my word of honour I will never make public any part of this affair."

"Your word of honour," said Lord Fanbury contemptuously.

"Mademoiselle Yvonne will keep her promise!" interrupted Sexton Blake.

"Will you guarantee that?" asked the Prime Minister, turning to Blake.

"I will."

Yvonne flashed a look of tenderness at Blake as he spoke, and her vision blurred with tears of gratitude.

"Your word of honour is accepted," went on Lord Fanbury. "Never, while you live, are you to mention this. Is that understood?"

"Yes, my lord," replied Yvonne, in a low tone.

"Then go!" commanded Lord Fanbury; and though it was her own house Yvonne, awed by that majestic dignity, bowed her head and obeyed.

With a word of explanation, Blake turned and followed, catching up Yvonne in the hall.

"Where is my lad, mademoiselle?" he asked, looking at her quizzically.

"Don't look at me!" she burst out. "He—he is so fine, and I feel like a beast!" And she burst into tears.

Blake was embarrassed at her show of emotion, and put his hand on her heaving shoulders.

"Don't," he said quietly. "Try to profit by the lesson, Yvonne."

"I wish I could, to please you, but I can't. Don't make it harder. Tinker is a prisoner upstairs, and with him is Carfax Morton's daughter, but they are unharmed."

"Where is Graves?" asked Blake.

"I sent them all away but the woman-servant, when I heard of your escape. I was afraid you'd track me down."

Blake turned, and ran lightly up the stairs, and burst open the door of the room, where Tinker and Alice lay bound and gagged. He quickly undid their bonds, and while they chafed their stiff limbs, hurried explanations followed.

"You must prepare yourself for a great shock, Miss Morton," said Blake gravely, turning to Alice; "but be thankful that it is tempered by good news."

Pedro had followed up, and was showing his joy at finding Tinker again, and Blake signed to the lad to take the dog and leave the room.

Then, with all that great gentleness of which he is capable, Sexton Blake led the frightened young woman by degrees from one bit of news to another, tempering as much as possible her step-father's guilt.

Barely had he finished when a knock came at the door, and Dick Robins entered.

Tinker had told him of Alice's presence in the house, and the reason of her trip to Paris. The last drop of bitterness had gone from Dick's heart as he heard of her loyalty through all, and he dashed upstairs at once.

And Blake, when he saw the look which passed between the lovers who had suffered so much, stole softly to the door, leaving them to find the way, on the wings of love, into calm waters of peace, and later on happiness.

He went slowly downstairs, and passed from one room to another in search of Yvonne, but on reaching the kitchen he found the woman-servant had disappeared, and he sighed wearily, for he realised Yvonne had gone.

***

Carfax Morton had to be removed to a private hospital for treatment, the shock having shattered his nerves, and Alice stayed on in Paris for the time being to look after him.

Lord Fanbury, Blake, Dick, Tinker, and Pedro took the special back to Calais, and crossed at once, reaching London early the next morning.

***

It was given out that Carfax Morton had broken down in health, and beyond this slight ripple, the public never dreamed of the dangerous moments through which the country had just passed.

Dick Robins was reinstated, and is on a fair way now to get the former position of his old chief, Carfax Morton. He and Alice were married quietly, only Lord Fanbury, Blake, and Tinker being present.

They have a charming little home down in the country and there they took Carfax Morton, who never recovered from the shock. He has lost all remembrance of the past, and spends his days in childish amusements in the tangled garden. Alice, looking at him with great, pitying eyes, suffers when she remembers, but then comes the thought that Dick, whom she lost, has been found, and she turns to the gate to wait for him with a warm glow in her eyes.

NEXT WEEK'S SPECIAL AERIAL ADVENTURE YARN:
"THE DETECTIVE AIRMAN,"

In announcing this special attraction for next week, my chums, I do so with a certain knowledge that it will be received with universal pleasure, for I have been repeatedly requested to give a stirring aerial yarn, depicting Sexton Blake as a daring airman.

For a long time I have not been in a position to publish just such a yarn, although I would like to do immediately all that my chums ask me, in reason, yet, of course, it must be obvious to all that I cannot always do so.

But now at last it is coming—the best aerial yarn the *Union Jack* has ever given! The general excellence of the Yvonne v. Blake yarns is now a continued topic for wonderment in the publishing trade, and it is an admitted fact that no novel, whatever the price charged, can go one better than the *Union Jack* published at the modest figure of ONE PENNY.

The knowledge that next week's aerial yarn will be an Yvonne v. Sexton Blake episode will cause an immense increase in orders from newsagents, for they are experiencing what it means to order too few copies of the *Union Jack*.

Now a few words about next week's story. I can safely state that it is certainly the best of the series so far, for the author is thoroughly at home on the subject of aviation. Being an enthusiast himself, he fairly makes the yarn "rip" and carries the lucky reader off into a world of delight and happiness. There is one thing I want to impress upon all chums, and that is **Everything in the Yarn is Absolutely Possible** and feasible. Nothing is far-fetched, nothing is improbable, nothing strikes one as being "tall." Read the aviation accounts in the daily papers, and you will readily admit the truth of this when you have finished the yarn.

The chapter devoted to a great aerial race to Paris and back, between Yvonne and Sexton Blake, is worthy of special mention. The fine excitement of it, depicting an airman's true feeling when travelling at a great pace at a great height, is most exhilarating.

Another splendid thrill is the chapter where **Sexton Blake Makes a Daring Flight Through a Thunderstorm** with the rain and hail beating down with all its fury. His terrible peril, and his true bravery is vividly set forth, as only the author of these yarns can set it.

Altogether, my chums, "The Detective Airman" will be one of the finest yarns ever offered to the reading public. This is a bold statement, but I will stand by it, feeling secure in the knowledge that it is what I say.

Sexton Blake—Airman!

The First Chapter
Mr. Cornelius Patterson Plays a Double Game—Mlle. Yvonne Takes a Hand

THE *Mastodonic*, the latest achievement in the feverish race for the passenger supremacy of the Atlantic, was forging down the English Channel. Her gigantic, powerful engines were whirling unceasingly as she ploughed on through the night, her teeming army of stokers and oilers looking like a horde of modern Ulysses at the feet of a mammoth steel Cyclops.

Up on deck, where only the distant throb of the steel monsters was heard, and the quivering, all-pervading, yet impalpable jar was felt, the passengers lolled in dreamy enjoyment of the heavy summer night.

Some were dancing on the windward side, while the plaintive, distant sounds of a violin indicated the occupation of the saloon by the musical enthusiasts. Bridge and poker devotees lounged in the smoking-room and the divan, alternating their play with frequent sippings from ice clinking glasses.

A few laggards strolled out from the up-to-date restaurant, for the most part pacing slowly up and down the broad promenade, or joining the greatly-preponderating number of white-garbed loungers who lay in shadowy rows, victims of the night's loveliness.

Curving upwards and outwards from the merciless bow, the water rose like twin pillars of sapphire and ivory, opal and pearl, falling into rolling masses of boiling phosphorescence, to conquer with silver wings the giant sinister patches of deadly black.

Further out the silver wings were in their turn conquered and absorbed by the all-pervading black—intense, limitless and terrible in its might. Mirrored in its tossing bowl was the blurred reflection of the night sky which hung like a motionless purple veil studded and splashed with spangles of gold. A faint breeze blended with the steady ship-born wind as the mammoth forged on, stealing with warm embrace into the most shadowy nooks of the deck.

Truly a night for thoughts—a night for dreams and, from the close-drawn chairs in the shadows, a night for the whispers of love.

As the energetic dancers grew tired and strolled around to join in the enjoyment of the languorous night—as the desultory conversation died away, and youthful hands met in the friendly shadow, the slim, white-garbed figure of a young woman detached itself from a dark corner of the deck, and strolled slowly to the rail, where she stood leaning over and drinking in the soft air.

A slight stir went through the silent, lounging passengers as her graceful figure was silhouetted against the purple sky, and once again the whispering started, but this time it was confined to the feminine element, and, had a light suddenly been thrown over them, it would have been seen that the whisperers were mostly old or plain.

Like all beautiful women, the young woman who leaned over the rail was the target for many feminine shafts born of envy, and their points were not dulled by the fact that her conduct was as reproachless as that of a nun.

As the ship rolled in gentle caress to meet the black, silver-edged lips of the water, the light from the golden spangles in the sky caught her features in a thousand facets, bathing her in seductive lambent hues.

She lifted her face, a triumph of delicate beauty, until all unconsciously her gleaming coils of heavy bronze hair blended with the lighter bronze of the golden light. She was clad in soft, clinging white, with the daintiest of white shoes on two deliciously-tiny feet. A solitary antique Egyptian scarab decorated her hand, and the green depths of a gigantic emerald rested in perfect harmony against her white throat.

To those whispering envious women—to the admiring, yet baffled men, who, with all their experience and their millions had failed to pierce the armour of her reserve, she was Miss Ford, travelling to New York in the captain's care. But to a tall, stern-faced man in Baker Street, London—Sexton Blake—she was the elusive, charming, and altogether delightful Mademoiselle Yvonne, whose every fibre responded in futile vibration to the touch of his hands, the look in his eyes, the sound of his voice.

She sighed deeply, and rested her chin on her hand. Her thoughts travelled back to the last time she had seen Blake—to his continuous crossing of her path and his domination of every situation. Like puppets on the human stage, she could dominate and move to her bidding every man but one, and that one, not only reversed the situation and dominated her, but, strange to say, she could not bring herself to hate him. On the contrary——

Her thoughts broke off as from the corner of her eye she saw the elaborate carelessness of a strolling man in white, and knew from the blatant innocence of his attitude that he intended to speak to her. Her eyes had been heavy with weariness as she thought of the man who held her heart shackled by his power, but whose own heart-strings failed to respond. They cleared, however, as she watched the approaching man, and an imp of mischief filled them as she watched her victim approach, for victim she intended to make him.

Closer and closer he got, and still she did not turn. Finally, with a painfully-sudden interest in the sky, he approached the rail, and leaned over near her. Apparently utterly unconscious of his presence, Yvonne turned carelessly in the opposite direction, and as a titter of amusement went through the interested spectators of the little drama, Yvonne tripped daintily along the deck, not permitting herself to laugh until she reached a shadowy spot. Her discomfited victim glared viciously at the grinning spectators, and betook himself to the smoking-saloon and poker.

Leaving the alluring deck, and passing through the divan, Yvonne approached the lift with which the newest of the ocean monsters are being equipped.

She smiled in a friendly fashion at the lift boy, and that delighted young man closed the door and sent the lift downwards, to stop with unaccustomed gentleness at her deck. Through several white-walled, heavily-carpeted passages went Yvonne, until she came to a small branch passage.

She opened a door, and entered a richly-furnished suite—sitting-room and sleeping-cabin. They were more contracted in area than her apartments on her own yacht—the *Fleur-de-Lys*; but even the most blatant of the new millionaires would have found them pleasant for a journey.

Yvonne locked the door, and entered the sleeping-cabin, from which she emerged a few moments later clad in a dark-coloured costume.

Then from a small black bag she drew forth a small square, mahogany box, which looked as though it might be the receptacle of a good-sized traveller's inkstand. At first glance it would have been difficult to distinguish which of its polished sides was the cover; but the puzzle presented no difficulties to Yvonne.

Running her fingers along one edge, she pressed gently half-way down, the result being a tiny click, and the flying open of one side. Inside was revealed a tangle of thin coiled wires, with a gleaming needle of steel in the centre, looking for all the world like a coppery snake with fang out-thrust.

Yvonne gently lifted the needle, pulling slowly until fully a yard of the delicate wire had uncoiled. The bottom, which was visible when the needle and wire had been drawn out, was evidently only half-way down the box, for the space was far more shallow than would have been the case had it extended the full depth. One end of the wire passed through this black partition into what was evidently another compartment, and this fact Yvonne speedily made certain by her next movement.

Leaving the needle and wire to dangle, she turned the box over and once more pressed on an edge.

The opposite side flew open, and at first the contents appeared to be almost similar to those of the other compartment. But as she thrust in her fingers and drew them out again it could be seen that there was a slight difference. Instead of the long, gleaming steel needle, she drew out a tiny miniature receiver in form like those of the ordinary telephone. Like the needle, however, it was attached to a length of copper wire, which in turn was attached to a small battery.

To this also was screwed the end of the other wire, which ran through the division from the needle. Then, with her box in her hand, Yvonne walked over to the large couch which had been placed under the yawning porthole of her sitting-cabin. If her movements before had been curious, they were even more so now. She picked up the needle, and resting one knee on the couch, leaned over against the wall at the head of it. The tiny hole into which she thrust the needle's point would have defied discovery except under the closest scrutiny, but the ease with which she located it proved its position had been made familiar by repeated use.

She thrust the needle through until fully half of it had disappeared into the wall, and then, laying the box and receiver on the couch, she stepped noiselessly across to the switch and turned out the light. Returning to the couch, she placed the box against the wall and lay down, picking up the receiver as she did so. With this against her ear, she lay in motionless silence, her eyes narrowed and her lips slightly parted as she breathed silently.

It had taken Yvonne several weeks of the most careful investigation, and the use of much money, to discover the facts which had started her out on the *Mastodonic's* maiden trip, and had caused her to pay a big fee in order to secure the particular cabin which she desired.

Naturally, the maiden trip of the newest, biggest, and fastest ocean leviathan had created intense interest, not only in the shipping world, but amongst all classes. This fact, however, was only of passing interest to Yvonne, compared with the fact that it would have as a passenger one Cornelius Patterson.

To the world at large, Cornelius Patterson was simply a shrewd Canadian millionaire— to his own intimate acquaintances, a cold, self-centred man whose heel was heavy, and whose weight had been felt by many since his sudden access to wealth and power after the remarkable rise in Canadian lands.

To Yvonne, however, he was simply one of the men who, years ago in Australia, had denuded herself and her mother of everything in the world, and whose name was the next on her list of revenge. Slowly had she drawn a line through the names preceding it—Vineburg, Pearson, Todd, Kelly, and Morton. It had cost her much money and more skill in order to reach them, but she had succeeded, and although the Todd affair had sent her to Dalemoor Prison from which she had escaped, the fact that Scotland Yard were wanting her did not deter her from going ahead on her plan of revenge.

It was a well-known fact in Europe that Turkey was struggling with a last effort to secure funds for its impoverished treasury with which to continue its ill-fated war with the Balkan allies. It was also a fact, but not so well known, that in her last desperate endeavours, the great gleaming central jewel of the gem-studded throne which had been captured from Persia centuries ago had been removed and taken secretly to Berlin, and on which it was hoped to raise an initial loan.

A huge glass imitation had been set in the throne, and rumour had it, that certain German interests had advanced the Turkish emissary half a million on the famous jewel. Yvonne's agents had discovered, however, that this was incorrect. The jewel called the "Sun's Eye" had, it is true, been taken to Berlin, but an American and Canadian Syndicate, represented by Cornelius Patterson, had advanced the loan on it.

Patterson, who was in Europe at the time, had formed his syndicate by cable, and had himself taken charge of the stone on his return to America by the *Mastodonic*.

Yvonne, after a careful consideration of the details, had decided to get possession of the great jewel if possible, and once her decision was made she acted swiftly. An examination of the passenger-sheet at the shipping-office had disclosed the cabin which Cornelius Patterson had reserved. It seemed a foregone conclusion that he would place the jewel in the care of the purser, but Yvonne, with her usual tenacity of purpose, had resolved to risk no chance to secure it. If no opportunity occurred during the trip, she would have to make the attempt after landing. But even so, she had followed her usual thoroughness. From the moment she had come aboard she had carefully studied the millionaire's movements, and knew by now his every habit.

The tiny hole in the partition between the two cabins through which she had thrust the steel needle came out on the other side underneath the bunk where Patterson slept, and from its position ran no risk of discovery.

The thin needle was hollow, and the black partition through which it passed was a sounding-board—the whole outfit of box, wires, battery, and receiver, being a most compact and complete instrument which collected every sound in Patterson's cabin, and transmitted them through the needle and along the wire, to be magnified to clarity and distinctness, and thence to the receiver against Yvonne's ear.

And it was because she knew the millionaire would retire early that Yvonne had deserted the charms of the deck, and began the usual listening to her neighbour's movements and mutterings.

For fully half an hour no sound travelled along the thin wires of her delicate instrument, but her patience was at length rewarded. She heard her neighbour's cabin door open, and then along the faithful recorder came the sound of a turning key. The movements after that were muffled and shuffling like the noise of a trunk being dragged out from under a bunk, but as she heard her neighbour muttering brokenly, Yvonne held her breath, and strained to listen.

"There's no better time than right now," came the voice of the millionaire, muttering to himself as he worked with the straps of the trunk. "The captain and purser have both seen it, and can swear I had it with me; then, when the purser comes to get it tomorrow and take charge of it for me, I'll discover it's gone. No one dreams that this trunk contains a little form of transportation which will escape the sharpest eye. Ah, you beauty—steady, steady! You can go free in a minute, but there is a little package to be attached to your leg first."

Each word of her neighbour's monologue had been heard by Yvonne in puzzled surprise. She could gather no meaning from the strange remarks. That he was speaking of the great jewel she felt certain, but what did he mean by "transportation which would escape the sharpest eye"?

At that moment a peculiar sound came to her ears, and as she heard it she laid the instrument down and leaped softly to her feet, breathing quickly.

"Good heavens!" she breathed, everything made clear in a flash. "Is it possible?"

She hastily picked up the instrument again and listened, her lips parting in a smile as she heard the words which the tiny needle collected and sent along.

"There, my beauty, stop your flapping!" Patterson was saying. "You'll be free in a minute, and can fly back home. But you must carry cargo with you and it must be secured, for after all my elaborate plans, I don't want to risk having it drop into the Channel."

Yvonne again dropped the receiver, and began working feverishly. First she sped to the corner of her cabin and unstrapped a bundle of parasols and umbrellas. Selecting a black umbrella with a long handle, she then drew a golf-club from a bag which also stood in the corner. Stepping swiftly across to the couch again, she laid them down, and from her black bag drew a small coil of wire. She then placed the handle of the golf-club against the handle of the umbrella, and with the hand of an expert bound them firmly together with the wire.

When she had finished she had a remarkable-looking umbrella, for by the addition of the golf-club she had lengthened its handle some three feet. Still moving noiselessly, she thrust it partly through the open porthole, and followed it with her head and shoulders. Patterson's port was lit up, but the shadow which crossed it from time to time indicated that its occupant was moving about. A moment later it grew still more obscured, and a hand appeared holding something which was struggling and fluttering.

As her eyes perceived it, and she saw her suspicions were correct, Yvonne released the catch on the umbrella, and firmly clutching the business end of the golf-club, thrust it outwards and upwards as far as she could. The wind caught it and opened it completely, just as the hand in the next porthole released its struggling prisoner.

For a moment the fluttering object poised, and then rose to freedom; but, carried along by the ship, the umbrella came directly over, and, as it rose, Yvonne drew in sharply until her free hand reached the release of the umbrella. Too late the bird saw the dark object descending. Its impetus carried it upwards within the clutch of the black descending cloud, and as its wings fluttered against the ribs of the umbrella, the top closed. Once more a prisoner, the bird struggled to get free; but the trap was strong, and a moment later Yvonne had drawn the umbrella back through the porthole, and stepped from the couch to the floor.

Laying down her hastily-devised trap, with its prisoner inside, she turned back to close the port, listening for a moment as a scraping noise sounded from the next porthole, followed by a splash.

"That's the cage which he had concealed in his trunk, I suppose," she murmured softly, brushing the flying spray from her forehead. She closed the port, and turned again to the umbrella, whose soft folds were heaving and bulging as her prisoner struggled.

"And now, Mr. Cornelius Patterson,"—she smiled softly—"we'll just see what cargo your aerial messenger was carrying."

She cautiously opened the umbrella, and thrust in her hand, drawing it out a moment later with a firm hold on her captive.

"So, so," she nodded, as she looked on the soft feathers and graceful lines of a powerfully-built homing-pigeon. "Very clever, Mr. Patterson, and it is a pity your aerial post was interrupted. Steady, you darling; I wouldn't hurt you for worlds. But I must see what that little package is which my neighbour has tied to your leg."

For a moment she held the soft, feathery bundle against her cheek, petting it and soothing it until it grew quiet under her touch. Then, holding it firmly with one hand, she began unfastening the tiny package from its leg. After five minutes' work it dropped into her lap, and she began rapidly unwrapping the paper which covered it. As the last covering fell off she drew in a quick breath. There, scintillating in a thousand flashes of gleaming fire, lay the great "Sun's Eye," which had provided the Turks with funds to continue the war, and which, as she had discovered only this night, was temptation enough to cause Cornelius Patterson to lay elaborate plans in order to possess it himself and bluff the world it had been stolen.

For Yvonne had read in a flash his purpose. The fact that he was secretly sending the jewel to England by a homing-pigeon told her enough to make her suspicious; but the words she had heard had added light to the matter, and again she smiled as she thought of her successful frustration of his plans.

She laid the jewel down on her lap, and was preparing to release the bird when her eyes caught sight of some written words on the last paper wrapping which she had taken off. Sinking back, she picked it up and read:

"On receipt, leave at once and meet me as arranged. Advise arrival by wireless code. Be careful."

That was all. It contained neither address nor signature, but Yvonne laughed softly as she studied the metal band around the pigeon's leg.

"No. 1873 S," she murmured. "I suppose that is your registered number. I'll just jot it down, at any rate, and as soon as I have written another message you can start on your long journey."

She tucked the pigeon under her arm, and going to the black bag pulled out a small pad and pencil. She wrote only a few words, and, after folding up the note, carefully attached it to the pigeon's leg.

Then, after once more petting and caressing it, she opened the port and released it. For a moment it poised on outspread wings, and then, driven sideways by the wind, rose in ever-widening circles until it became a mere speck against the night sky, and disappeared a moment later as the great leviathan pounded on its way.

Then Yvonne went through a very strange procedure. Picking up the instrument which had served her so well, she dropped it through the open porthole into the sea. After that she drew out her trunk from under the couch and opened it. A hasty examination revealed several instruments—appliances of steel and silver which she ruthlessly sent after the instrument.

A scrutiny of the umbrella-handle showed that the wire had cut into its dull surface, and, careful as always, the umbrella and golf-stick followed the other things. From the trunk she next drew a long, narrow cork affair which might have been a giant yard of French bread except for the material of which it was made. Laying this on the couch,

Yvonne again reached into the trunk, and drew forth three small steel globes the size of a cricket ball. From the surface of each projected a tiny key, and on the opposite side from the key a small square knob.

Next, she lifted out three small wooden floats in each of which was a small square hole into which fitted the knobs of the globes.

Yvonne next proceeded to turn the key of each one, after the manner of winding a clock, and then, laying them on the couch beside the long cork float, she locked the trunk and thrust it back.

After a final look around, Yvonne crossed and entered the sleeping-cabin, and when she returned her costume had been replaced by a short tweed golf-skirt and light canvas shoes. Her heavy bronze hair was enclosed in a tight-fitting bathing-cap, and a bathing-jersey took the place of a blouse.

Thus equipped, she drew a roll of notes from the black bag, and picking up the three floats, to which she had attached the steel globes, hooked them to her jersey by tiny hooks which had been placed in the end of each.

Then crossing to the switch she plunged the cabin in darkness and returned to the couch. Climbing up, she put her head through the porthole and listened intently for some moments.

The star-studded sky was now obscured by scudding clouds, and the silver-and-black of the sea had turned to a leaden grey. No sound floated down from the decks above, and as eight bells struck on the fo'c's'le she knew the passengers had sought their berths. Only the officer on the bridge and the watch would be about, and Yvonne gave a sigh of relief as the scudding clouds grew thicker.

She drew back and picked up the cork float, which she thrust through the porthole. Pulling herself up, she squirmed through after it, and twisted around in order to hang by one hand from the rim of the open port. It was fortunate for her purpose that her cabin was near the water, for had it been high up, unless the ship was rolling considerably, a splash would have been inevitable. But the sea was still, gently moving in long, rolling lines, and as the great ship slowly sank downwards Yvonne waited until it paused a moment before returning, and then, clutching her float, dropped silently into the black water beneath.

She lost no time in pushing her float in front of her and striking out with all her strength as soon as she came to the surface, for she had no desire to be drawn near those mammoth whirling propellers by the leviathan's suction. At the same time she had to swim noiselessly in order to avoid the eagle eyes of the watch on deck; but the smoothness of the sea assisted her, and as the stern of the great, lighted, floating castle swept past she rested on her cork float and gazed after it.

"Perhaps I'll wish I was back," she murmured. "But if uncle has followed instructions there will be no risk. If not, I'm afraid no ingenuity will get me out of this; but there's time enough for that. I'll start the signals going."

Still resting on the float which was buoyantly riding the long, rolling swell, Yvonne detached the three globes from her jersey and set them on the surface beside the float.

By this time the *Mastodonic* was a blurred tangle of lights, and before releasing the three globes Yvonne waited until the vessel grew even more indistinct.

Then she gave the key on each steel globe a rapid turn backwards, a buzzing sound followed, and as she pulled the keys out and threw them away a tiny wire appeared in the aperture left.

With a strong heave she sent them out one after the other to ride the waves at a safe distance, and then covered her eyes with her hands. It was well she did so, for barely had the floats settled in their new resting-place than the tiny wires blazed out a blinding flash of vivid blue. They died down as the delicate machines inside each globe cut off the power.

Again they blazed out with a blinding flash, to die down once more for their momentary extinction before flashing for the third time. Then they went out for a longer spell, and as they lit up with a less blinding flare to burn steadily, Yvonne removed her hand from her eyes and began anxiously gazing upwards into the cloud-hung night.

For fully five minutes she gazed before her features relaxed, and then far distant in the black sky, in the direction of the now invisible *Mastodonic,* there appeared three blue lights, which went out almost immediately.

But Yvonne knew her signal had been seen, and that the three steadily burning wires would guide her uncle to her.

Barely three minutes later a long, narrow, graceful shape appeared above her, flying at a low elevation, and as it settled down noiselessly the shape of a slim waterplane could be made out. A soft hail floated down to Yvonne, and a moment later, like a giant bird, the waterplane settled on the waves close behind the floating young woman.

It was a radical advance on the more cumbersome form of machine. Built of a light alloy of metal, with wings outspread, it could rise by a central lifting propeller without any preliminary run. Built on gigantic lines, as compared with other machines, it was capable of tremendous lifting-power, in addition to a heavy cargo allowance. Every exposed inch was finished in silver-blue, which in daylight blended with the sky, making the machine totally invisible from the ground when only a few hundred yards up.

The engine was of a hundred horsepower, and one of the most reliable she had been able to purchase.

With a light but very effective type of float attached to the chassis, it could be used as a waterplane, and, with floats lifted, rise gracefully from the water, to disappear rapidly in the upper strata.

When leaving on the *Mastodonic,* Yvonne had instructed Graves, her uncle, and Captain Vaughan, to follow with the yacht, and watch for her signal in case she were unsuccessful in her purpose during the trip.

Even in mid-ocean she would have risked putting her daring plan into operation; but luck was with her, and well was it that the men on the yacht had watched closely for her signal from the very start.

As the long shape floated gracefully beside her, she pushed the float around to the side.

"Are you all right, Yvonne?" asked Graves anxiously, reaching down his hand to her and helping her aboard.

"Yes, thanks!" laughed Yvonne. "Wet to the skin, but successful."

"Do you mean to say that you got it?" exclaimed Graves and the captain together.

"You don't imagine I would take this midnight swim unless I had, do you?" replied Yvonne. "It was lucky you followed my instructions to the letter. If you hadn't, I would have been in a nice position riding around on that float all night, with inquisitive fishes nibbling at my toes."

Graves laughed.

"You are bewildering, Yvonne. But here, put this heavy coat around you, or you will catch cold. I've got a Thermos flask full of hot lemon for you. Drink it! It will keep off a chill."

Yvonne got into the heavy coat and drank the hot liquid, while Captain Vaughan steered the waterplane around, in order that Graves could pick up the cork float and globes, which were still burning with the steady blue light.

Then the captain turned.

"Shall I drive her back to land, mademoiselle?" he asked.

Yvonne nodded.

"Yes. Not too high, though. It will be cold. Take this seat, uncle, and let me sit there. The wind won't catch me so much."

"Tell me, Yvonne," said Graves as he changed, "how did you succeed? I'm keen to know."

Yvonne lit a cigarette before replying, and then watched the black waves as the great wings spread out and they rose silently in the air.

"Well," began Yvonne, turning back to Graves, "in the first place, our friend, Mr. Cornelius Patterson, hasn't improved since the old days in Australia. I don't know the details of his plan, but this I do know. He intended getting rid of the Sun's Eye himself, and then giving the alarm that he had been robbed."

"Did he have an accomplice aboard?"

Yvonne laughed gaily.

"I hardly think one could call 'it' an accomplice."

Then she related to the chuckling Graves how the millionaire had taken a homing-pigeon, concealed in his trunk, and had tied the great jewel to it, and sent it back to England to some unknown accomplice there. How she had caught the bird, and secured the jewel and note, and had sent it on its interrupted journey with another note tied to its leg.

Graves laughed in delighted appreciation, while the captain smiled appreciatively as he guided the machine through the night.

"By Jove, Yvonne," drawled Graves, "that was about as rich as I've ever heard! But, I say, what did you write in the note you sent?"

Yvonne laughed gaily.

"I simply wrote, 'What price the Sun's Eye?' and I would give something to read the wireless our friend Mr. Cornelius Patterson will get when the note reaches its destination."

Tossing her cigarette away, Yvonne drew the folds of the heavy coat about her and leaned back. Her eyes closed, and in five minutes she was asleep, her hair was falling in distracting waves about her forehead as the wind caught it, and her lips parted with a soft tender smile as she floated away into pleasant dreams.

Little did she look like a world-famous adventuress, and Graves, cynic though he was, sighed heavily as he watched the unconscious appeal of his young niece. He turned to see the hardened captain looking at her with the affectionate look of a father.

"She's just like a tired child!" said the captain gruffly as he turned back to the steering-wheel.

Graves nodded, but said nothing, and silence reigned as the long, slim shape tore on through the night, the black sky above and the water beneath.

The Second Chapter
The Great Circuit Race—A Message from the Night Sky

NEVER did Hendon Flying Grounds present a more gala appearance than on the day which would see the end of the great circuit race for fame and a fortune. Several days previously the great meeting had been inaugurated with the start of the race.

Starting from Hendon, the 'planes were to fly to Land's End, and from there circuit east over the Channel, thence up to John o' Groats. From there they were to make Belfast, return over the Channel, circle Eddystone, and return to Hendon. In itself the race presented difficulties of the most trying description.

A great portion of the course lay over water, and, to add to the difficulties, each pilot must carry a passenger, and a hundred pounds weight in addition. With air conditions ideal it was a gruelling test, but with the rapid strides of other nations in aerial navigation, England was forced into keen competition, and the great circuit test had been devised in order to choose a standard machine on which to concentrate.

Five all-British machines had started on the race, and ever since they had risen and disappeared with a whirr and a roar, Hendon had been packed each day to watch the minor flights and tests of lesser machines.

Little word had been heard from any of the five starters since they had left, and little hope was felt that all of them would finish. All had been reported at Land's End; then one at a time they had been heard of as they flew up the eastern coast.

Then came a long silence, until word came through from Belfast that two had landed in the teeth of a gale. No word had been heard of the other three, and opinions were freely expressed that the gale had probably sent them into the sea.

After replenishing their fuel and lubricating tanks, the two machines had braved the gale, and started once more on the last lap around Eddystone. Not a word of any kind had been heard since, but if schedule time was kept to, this day would see the finish, providing there were still any left in the race. No one had eyes for the evolutions being performed overhead. Every head was turned southwards to catch the first glimpse of the expected machines.

Now and then an aviator flew southwards to scout about for the expected racers, but each time he returned with no news, and the excitement of the crowd grew intense as the afternoon waned.

Four o'clock came, and still no sign. Five would see the end of the time limit, and if they arrived after that hour, all their long, dangerous flight would go for nothing.

Half-past four drew round, but barely had the fatal half begun, when, far away in the south, a tiny speck, no bigger than a swallow, appeared.

Was it only another bird like those which many times that afternoon had raised false hopes? If so, it was certainly of a larger species, and as it grew nearer, heading straight up for Hendon, a terrific cheer went up. It must be the first of the returning circuit racers. All the scouts had come to earth, and no other machines were known to be out.

On and on it came, ever growing larger until the first faint throb of its engines was heard. Then the more experienced eyes recognised the outlines of the machine, and powerful glasses read the big, white number painted on the underpart of the wings. There was no need for the excited crowd to ask who drove it. As the first user of the glasses shouted:

"It's No. 4!" the cry was taken up, and repeated from end to end.

"Who's driving No. 4?"

"Sexton Blake, on his own machine!"

A deafening cheer arose.

Blake's name was shouted wildly, programmes were waved madly, and the slim, grey shape of Sexton Blake's machine grew ever nearer. As the throb of the engine stopped, and it volplaned gracefully to earth, the enthusiasm broke all bounds. Shouting and cheering, the crowd surged forward, endangering themselves and the aviator as he came to earth.

Almost in their centre he landed, and only the ceaseless work of the officials kept them from swarming completely over machine, aviator, and passenger in their excitement.

Blake, black with grease and oil, was helped from the machine by willing hands. He staggered with weariness, and answered their questions hoarsely.

"I don't know where the others are. Haven't seen a machine since I left Belfast in the teeth of a seventy-mile gale. But see to my passenger. I think he's asleep."

It was true!

Tinker, who had gone as Blake's passenger, lay crouched in his seat, sound asleep, worn out with the strain of the long journey and racking fight with the elements. They lifted him out, and followed the staggering Blake into the hangar, while the crowd cheered itself hoarse over the man who, by his great flight, had won a fortune.

Fame was his already.

Regardless of the crowd or his greasy state, Blake signed to his mechanic to look after the machine, and, stumbling to a pile of canvas in the corner of the hangar, he dropped down, his eyes closing in the deep sleep of utter weariness almost before his head had touched the rough couch. They laid the sleeping Tinker beside him, and while every paper in the country came out with a special edition over the great race, the man who had won it and his passenger lay unconscious of everything.

***

Early the next morning Blake and Tinker were awake, and on their way to Baker Street in the big grey car.

After a bath and change, they felt better, and Blake, setting Tinker to work opening letters, ran through his mail rapidly. Noon saw them again on their way to Hendon, for a vigorous speed test was to come off, and Blake was determined to give his machine a full test of every description.

"I say, guv'nor," remarked Tinker, as they wound their way through the crowded vehicles which circled the ground, "it's going to be a bully day for the flight. The *Grey Panther* will be getting all it wants."

"It can stand it, my lad," laughed Blake. "As far as a test of strength goes, the circuit we finished yesterday proves the worth of the system of wing attachment which I am trying out; but the flight today will require speed and sharp work to locate the battleship. The last race which comes off in two days' time will be purely a speed race from Hendon to the Eiffel Tower, in Paris, and return. We'll go in for that, too, if the *Grey Panther* hangs together."

"We are having a week from work, guv'nor, but this flying is as much strain as following up a case."

It should be explained that the race on which the intrepid Blake was entering this day after his magnificent win of the great circuit, was a flight from Hendon to a super-Dreadnought which was stationed off Land's End.

A large platform had been arranged over the after part of the battleship, and the test was to carry despatches from Hendon, the arrival of the aeroplane to be notified by wireless. There was no specified time for returning, but after a rest, the aviator could choose his own time, providing his leaving on the return journey was notified by wireless.

Only a general idea of the whereabouts of the battleship was given, and, in addition to great speed being required, the aviator would have to scout about in the air and pick up the ship. The test appealed to Blake, and after his success in the grand circuit, he decided to enter it, and if the machine hung out, go in for the final event, a speed race to Paris and back.

Consequently he was on the ground early, and, stopping his car beside the hangar which sheltered his monoplane—the *Grey Panther*—he and Tinker got into overalls, and with the mechanic, began going over every inch of the machine.

"What time will you start, sir?" asked the mechanic, as Blake twanged a wing stay with the finger of an expert.

"Oh, I don't know, Barrow!" replied Blake. "I saw Gordon landing in his Bleriot as I drove in, and he tells me the air is full of pockets, and choppy. If we finish with the machine by sunset, I may start then. In any event, I'll make a preliminary flight and test the air currents. By the way, how many others entered?"

"Only one besides yourself, sir. They thought it would be a lone hand until they heard you had decided to try it."

Blake laughed.

"Who is the other man, Barrow?"

"Whitcomb, sir. He's driving a biplane, and says he'll try and start at three. He's taking his mechanic as passenger, sir."

"Ah, if that's the case, I won't leave before evening, in any event. Any news heard of the other machines in the circuit race, Barrow?"

"Gardener returned to Belfast sir, and Cartwright came to earth on the west coast of Scotland. They haven't heard anything from the other two, sir."

"I'm sorry to hear that," said Blake gravely. "I'm afraid the gale in the North Sea has caught them. Tinker and I had our work cut out to get through. Just give me a hand here, Barrow, and we'll tighten up this joint."

Two hours later word came that Whitcomb, in his Farman, had made a preliminary flight, and was starting on his long run for the battleship at four. Blake and Tinker dropped their tools and went outside where the aviator was running over the machine preliminary to starting.

"Well, Blake," he smiled through his goggles, as Blake approached, "I thought I was the only one until I heard you were going. Are you after all the glory?"

"Oh, no!" laughed Blake, shaking hands. "But, you see, you are driving a machine which has been tested for speed, strength, and endurance, while mine has only had the test of the circuit race. I want to put her through the whole thing, and then I can tell just what I've got."

"They say she's a wonder, Blake," remarked Whitcomb enviously. "I'm blest if I see how you find time to fool with flying when you seem to be working on cases night and day!"

"Oh, Tinker and I get through quite a few experiments in the lab., and beyond a preliminary flight, I hadn't the faintest notion what my machine could do. You're leaving at four, are you?"

"Yes, and you?"

"I intended leaving about sunset, but I haven't quite decided; I may wait until midnight."

At that moment Blake's mechanic beckoned to him, and, shaking hands with his solitary competitor, and wishing him luck, Blake hurried away, followed by Tinker after he had compared a few notes on air currents with Whitcomb.

Tinker had developed into a most enthusiastic airman. Under Blake's tutelage, he was rapidly picking up a thorough knowledge of aerial navigation, and the lad had watched the growth of the *Grey Panther* from the plans born of Blake's brain to its present graceful, speedy lines.

He knew every bolt and nut and stay, and on necessity could have under-studied Blake in driving it. He lost no opportunity of comparing notes with other aviators, and the lad's frank, sunny ways had won him a host of friends on the flying ground. After shaking hands with Whitcomb, he hurried into the hangar, where he found Blake fuming over a snapped stay.

The mechanic had thought to improve on Blake's tinkering, with the result that he had overstrained. It meant a long two hours to replace it, and then a fairly long flight to test it before risking the journey out over the Atlantic.

Round after round of cheers told them Whitcomb was starting, and Tinker lifted the flap of the hangar to see the biplane wheeling in ever-widening circles like a great bird, until finally, Whitcomb, reaching the thousand-foot level, threw out a flag, on which was written "Good-bye," and, heading his machine west, was soon a tiny speck in the blue.

It was after seven before Blake was satisfied with the condition of the *Grey Panther*, but late as it was in the day, the crowd was as numerous as it had been when Whitcomb got away.

Word had gone round that Sexton Blake, winner of the grand circuit race, was also in for the test, and that had been sufficient to keep them.

Cheers and questions greeted Blake, as he and Tinker wheeled the 'plane out. Blake good-naturedly held up his hand, and, picking up a megaphone from one of the officials, turned to the crowd.

"Thank you, my friends!" he shouted. "I was too fagged yesterday, to say anything. I heard several asking what time I intended getting away. We are going to make a preliminary flight now, and if everything seems satisfactory, we will start in about two hours, after we have had something to eat."

Renewed cheers broke out as Blake finished and returned the megaphone. Then, assisted up by the mechanic, he took his seat before the driving-wheel, and took the waterproof covering off the chart and compass. Tinker followed him in, and as the mechanic started the powerful engine, the long, slim *Grey Panther* ran ahead easily for a short distance.

Then, as Blake slightly canted the wings, the 'plane rose gracefully, in gradually-widening spirals, until they were up a thousand feet. Blake banked slightly, and started sweeping around in a great circle, until he was heading east. Then headed straight, and, like a great winged arrow, shot away into the growing dusk. The brilliant arc-lamps were blazing when they returned and volplaned back to earth, satisfied with the flight.

It was now full night, and overhead the stars blazed brilliantly.

A hurried meal was consumed while they sat in the machine, and after replenishing the fuel and oil-tanks, the engine was once more started. The crowd had hung on to watch the start, and not until the grey shape with her two muffled occupants was lost in the starry realms above did the cheers die away.

"What's the general direction, guv'nor?" asked Tinker, turning up his collar and gazing at the swiftly-passing lights far below.

"We will drive dead south for a bit, and then change to a westerly direction. That ought to put us in the neighbourhood of the warship by daylight."

Almost as Blake spoke they rushed towards a revolving light beneath the last outpost of the land. Far away a few glowing spots indicated the presence of other lights, but though flying at a moderate pace, the land dropped away behind with almost uncanny suddenness, and they were left with that indefinable feeling of being the only beings in a vast limitless expanse of great hanging stars above, and tossing, black water beneath, broken only by the steady drone of the Gnome, and the business-like whir of the propeller.

On clearing the land, they hit a down-Channel breeze, and Blake canted the planes, sending the machine up to the two-thousand-foot level. They found, however, that the lower current, though strong, was steady and more reliable than the "pockety" higher level.

Suddenly below them appeared a brilliantly-lighted steamer ploughing on her way, and in a spirit of reckless test in manoeuvring, Blake sent the *Grey Panther* volplaning down, and circled within a few yards of her excited passengers.

Then, turning, he continued on, and finding the lower level steady flying, stuck to it as he again shot westwards. For two hours they hummed on through the night without speaking, and Blake smiled as he saw Tinker dozing. The pilot's seat and the passenger's seat of the *Grey Panther*, were built to face each other—the glass-framed chart being in front of Tinker, but on account of its pivoted hinges easily accessible to Blake.

The steering-wheel and levers occupied a very small space immediately in front of him; the result being a much more workable arrangement than the ordinary method of having the passenger facing the same way. He was just starting to rise again to the thousand foot, when through the night came a small, whitish object, which struck him with some force in the chest, and dropped fluttering at their feet. Blake grunted from the impact, and started to call Tinker's attention to the fact by tramping on the lad's toe. The fluttering object at his feet, however, awoke the lad, and he stared down in amazement.

"Crumbs, guv'nor! What is it—a seagull? How did it get in here?"

"We ran into it!" shouted Blake. "Pick it up, and if it isn't injured, throw it over again!"

Tinker bent and picked up the bird, which was flapping about in a crippled manner. As he did so his eyes opened wide with amazement, and, holding it firmly, he held it up for Blake to see.

"Look, guv'nor!" he called. "It's a pigeon, and a homer, too!"

Blake leaned forward quickly.

"See if it is carrying any message, Tinker!" he said. "It's strange for it to be about here, but someone may be sending it from a passenger steamer with a farewell message. Did Whitcomb carry any with him?"

Tinker shook his head, and held the bird while he began searching for any message. As Blake expected, he found one tied securely to the bird's leg, and steadied the struggling pigeon between his knees while he undid it.

Blake divided his attention between the machine and watching Tinker, but, as he saw the lad open the note to read it with puzzled brow by the light of the chart-lamp, he released one hand and held it out for the paper.

"I can't make anything of it!" shouted Tinker. "Seems to refer to a horse-race."

Blake signed to him to swing the chart-lamp around to him, and by the light he read:

"What price Sun's Eye?"

For a long moment he gazed at the words, and then, releasing the map-holder, dropped the note inside.

"Has the pigeon got a band on its leg?" he asked.

Tinker nodded and swung the chart-lamp back.

"Yes, 1873 S."

"Is it hurt?" went on Blake.

"Its wing seems to be injured," replied the lad.

Blake nodded.

"Put it in the grub-locker, Tinker, until morning. We'll go into matters then. Turn on the searchlight. I think we'll get it pretty dark, and from those scudding clouds it looks like a stiff blow coming on. Get out some sandwiches and a bottle of tea. We will eat while we can!"

It was well they did, for Blake's prognostications were correct, and barely had Tinker put the bottle back with their imprisoned bird, and turned on the powerful searchlight, than the blow came and Blake shot up to a higher level.

For a bare moment he seemed to see far, far away on the black, watery stretch, three blue lights blaze up three times, and then go down to burn less brightly. He had half an idea of changing his course and investigating, but at that moment the *Grey Panther* veered dangerously in the air-pocket, and it needed all his attention to keep her head into the wind.

By the time he had discovered the wind was only on the higher levels, and that by flying low, he escaped it, the blue lights had disappeared.

A vague, shadowy shape seemed to shoot past them a moment later, but if it was a 'plane, the noise of its engines were drowned by their own. So quickly did it disappear, that Blake thought he must be mistaken. Half an hour later, as dawn was breaking, they passed the brilliantly lighted *Mastodonic*, and Blake, making a rapid mental calculation which he verified by his distance-register, knew he must be near the battleship.

He changed his course, and, as the sun came up like a great golden orange out of the waves, he began sweeping in ever-widening circles in a comprehensive all-seeing course which must eventually pick up the battleship.

The Third Chapter
Breakfast on the *Thor*—Another Message from the Air— Blake Makes a Move

THERE she is! There she is, guv'nor!"

Tinker was leaning over the side with a pair of glasses glued to his eyes, and one hand pointing southwards, while he shouted excitedly.

Blake turned his head, and with his sleeve rubbed the mist from his goggles. It was some time after sun-up, and since the great disc had changed the black waters to leaping silver-edged platinum, Blake had been flying in great circles in an endeavour to pick up the battleship which would mean the end of their flight.

Tinker was right, it was the super-Dreadnought *Thor*, and as Blake's eyes made out the landing platform over the stem, he swung the *Grey Panther* around, banking slightly, and then, straight as an arrow, shot southwards. As they drew nearer they could make out Whitcomb's Farman, which had already landed, and from the efforts being made to push it aside, and give Blake a clear landing, he knew they had been sighted. Judging his distance to a fraction, Blake shut off the engine, and volplaned down in a great curve, ever drawing nearer and nearer the platform, which looked more like a tiny plaster on a grey rock than a landing platform.

Suddenly it seemed to jump to meet them, and Blake, again banking, swung once more before putting the *Grey Panther*'s nose to it.

But he hadn't won the grand circuit race without knowing his machine's every move, and, as it swung about on the last volplane, they dropped gently, and, with a jar which would barely have broken an egg, they landed and ran forward into the stopping net. It was a pretty piece of work which on land would have brought its reward of admiration, but on the landing platform of a battleship in mid-ocean, it was a masterpiece of judgment and handling, and Whitcomb showed his good sportsmanship by leading the cheering which rolled from aft, forward, and back again.

Blake and Tinker tumbled out, and beginning with Commander Villiers, had to shake hands all round.

"Blake—Blake," laughed the commander, shaking an admonitory finger at the greasy, goggled detective, "what next will you be taking on? But when Britain needs a cool hand for despatches, I'll see that you are raked out of your den in Baker Street and put into service."

"That's exactly why I am spending so much time on the matter," smiled Blake. "It is my country first and always," he added, more soberly.

"I say, Blake," remarked Whitcomb, who had been trying to make himself heard for several minutes, "what was your time?"

"Exactly what time was it when I struck the ship?" asked Blake.

"Five forty-three to the second!" replied Lieutenant Bruce, whose duty it had been to act as timekeeper.

"Well, we left Hendon about midnight. But hasn't the wireless come through yet? It would give the exact moment."

"Yes, I have it," remarked Lieutenant Bruce. "I didn't announce the time of your leaving until you should arrive. You left Hendon at twelve-twenty exactly, and that makes your trip consume just five hours and twenty-three minutes."

"What was your time, Whitcomb?" asked Blake.

"You have beaten me outwards by six minutes," laughed Whitcomb good naturedly. "But I'll beat you going back. I've got the hang of this biplane now, and I'll drive like sixty devils!"

"You'll have to do better than that," replied Blake. "I intend driving like seventy or even eighty!"

Laughing and joking they turned, Blake under the guidance of a steward to get a hot bath before breakfasting with the commander and officers in the mess-room, and Tinker into the charge of several admiring middies, who insisted on every detail of the trip being gone over and over, and when they discovered he had also made the trip with Blake around the grand circuit—well, the flood of excited questions can be imagined.

Blake, thorough as always, had not forgotten their feathered captive, and the strange manner in which they had collided with it during the night.

Stopping, he spoke to one of the engine-room assistants, who was looking after the machines, and warned him about the injured pigeon in the grub locker. The man promised to look after it, and after breakfast Blake intended examining it in order to see if its injured wing could be mended, or if it would be more merciful to put it out of its pain.

The strange, almost frivolous words of the note, had caused him much thought during the long, silent night journey; but although the reference to the Sun's Eye brought to his mind the jewel which had been the recent talk of Europe, he could not see where there was any connection, and was almost inclined to agree with Tinker that it must refer to a horse-race.

But running into a homing pigeon far out at sea was too remarkable an occurrence to be dismissed without investigation, and after he had satisfied the conditions of the race, Blake intended to look more closely into the strange message which had come to them through the night.

Little did he know how that modern wonder, the wireless system, was to start him on the investigation far sooner than he dreamed.

After a hot bath and a change, a steward conducted him past the middies' mess, where Tinker was guest of honour, into the officers' mess, where Blake was shown to a seat on the commander's right.

Whitcomb sat on his left, and down each side of the table ranged the bronzed, energetic officers of the *Thor*. Their very faces, clean-cut and vivid with the stamp of the sailor, spoke well for England, and Blake knew every man of them would dash into the teeth of death with the same intrepid nonchalance with which they broke their eggs.

It was a merry breakfast; Blake was famous as a conversationalist, and while seeming to dominate the situation, he was, in reality, keeping the ball rolling up and down the table. Like Tinker with, the middies, he had to recount the details of that gruelling race around the grand circuit, and when he finished, Whitcomb related an experience which he had had over the English Channel, when, by colliding with another machine, both men and 'planes had gone tumbling into the water far below.

Breakfast was over—at least, in the officers' mess—and pipes and cigars were going around the table, when the wireless operator entered, and saluting, passed a long message to Commander Villiers.

"What's this?" asked the commander.

"It's a news item through to the Press from the *Mastodonic*. I picked it up, and thought you might wish to see it. It's rather remarkable."

"Very well," replied the commander. "Pardon, gentlemen, I'll just see what it says."

The conversation began again, but as the commander uttered a cry they broke off, and looked inquiringly at him.

"Just listen to this!" he exclaimed. "If it's true—and it must be—it is certainly a remarkable occurrence.

"'*S.S. Mastodonic.*

"'Mid-ocean.

"'A remarkable occurrence has taken place on board the *Mastodonic* during the night. Mr. Cornelius Patterson, the Canadian millionaire, who is a passenger, is, by his own statement, head of the syndicate which advanced the Turkish emissaries in Berlin half a million pounds on the jewel known as the "Sun's Eye." Last evening he made arrangements with the purser to have it taken care of on the journey, but put off getting it until this morning.

"'When he opened his trunk and looked in the cashbox in which he carried it, the jewel had disappeared, and it is feared that it was stolen during the night. Mr. Patterson is positive that he placed it in the cashbox on retiring, and had it out only a few hours previously to show to the captain. A thorough search has failed to reveal it, and Captain Brown has put the ship's detectives on the matter.

"'On top of this, a lady passenger has been discovered missing. Miss Ford, who was travelling to New York, and, who evoked the admiration of the whole ship by her remarkable beauty, cannot be found. On knocking at her cabin this morning, the stewardess got no reply, and on entering she discovered everything in order. But the bunk had not been slept in, and the lady was missing. Miss Ford was very reserved, and had no intimate acquaintance on board, although nominally under the captain's care. Owing to this, it is not known whether she had any trouble which would cause her to throw herself overboard. She was last seen on deck early in the evening, and went below a little after nine. A remarkable coincidence is that her cabin adjoined that of Mr. Cornelius Patterson, from which the jewel was stolen; but whether there is any connection between the two is not known.'"

"There, gentlemen, what do you think of that?" asked the commander, laying down the wireless and looking down the table. "Come, Blake, this is in your line. What do you think of it?"

But Sexton Blake did not answer. He was sitting with furrowed brow, in deep thought. It had flashed across him while the commander was reading that the jewel which had been stolen during the night on the *Mastodonic* was called the "Sun's Eye." From that his mind leaped to the frivolous message carried by the homing pigeon.

Where had it come from? What was the meaning of that message? That it had some connection with the theft he had now no doubt, and so strangely had it been drawn into the mystery, that he had more than an ordinary interest in the matter.

Above all, did the missing Miss Ford have any connection with the theft? It did not seem reasonable. If anyone disappeared from a ship in mid-ocean, with no other craft about, it seemed a certainty that they could only go to the bottom. No. It was probably pure coincidence. And Lieutenant Bruce was voicing almost that very thought in replying to the commander's remark.

"I don't see, sir, how the missing young woman could have any connection with the theft. If she is not on board the *Mastodonic*, she must be in the sea. And surely, even if she were insane, she wouldn't steal the jewel, only to jump overboard with it."

The commander smiled.

"Always the ladies' champion, lieutenant. But, come, Blake! You seem wrapped in mystery. Does your deductive mind see further than ours?"

Blake looked up.

"I don't know, commander," he said slowly. "In a certain way, this has come as a bit of a shock to me, for it just happens to come on top of a most remarkable thing which happened during the night on our way out."

All eyes turned to Blake, intense interest written in them.

"Is it something which you can tell us, Blake?" asked the commander.

"Certainly!" answered Blake. "But before doing so, I will ask you all to please consider it confidential. I have a half-formed plan in my mind, and if I put it into execution I would not care for any publicity."

Commander Villiers turned to a steward who stood near the door.

"Retire, Smith, and close the door. Now, Blake, I can answer for the discretion of myself and my officers."

"And for mine," put in Whitcomb.

Blake lit a fresh cigar, and leaned back.

"Well, commander, and gentlemen, if I begin by telling you that during the night I ran into a homing pigeon bound landwards, you will see that what I speak of is rather remarkable."

Then, with that vivid detail which seemed a part of him, Blake recounted the story of the pigeon and the note it carried. A breathless interest followed him until he reached the point where he had read the note.

"As you know," he said, "the name of the jewel which was stolen from the *Mastodonic* was the 'Sun's Eye.' This is what was in the note: 'What price Sun's Eye?' Nothing more. I have the note in my map-holder, and the wounded pigeon in the grub-locker."

A gasp of astonishment went around the table.

"By Jove, Blake, that is one of the most remarkable coincidences I ever heard!" exclaimed the commander.

"For whom do you suppose the note was really intended?"

"I haven't the remotest idea. If we knew, I imagine it would throw some light on this extraordinary occurrence."

"It almost seems as though you ought to follow it up, Mr. Blake," remarked Lieutenant Bruce.

"That was just what I was thinking," replied Blake. "It certainly presents some interesting points."

"But how would you go ahead?" asked the commander.

"How far away is the *Mastodonic* from here?" countered Blake.

"Between eighty and a hundred miles. You surely don't intend——"

"Exactly," interrupted Blake, smiling. "Since we have been talking I have decided. The *Grey Panther* is able to make that in a short time, and I can overtake the *Mastodonic*. If you will send a private wireless to the captain, and, tell him I am coming, he will have time to rig up a landing-float of some kind. But I would tell him to keep it secret. Then I can look into matters without being bothered. I'm afraid, Whitcomb, you will have to start homewards alone."

"By Jove, I'll wait here until we get a wireless from you!" laughed Whitcomb. "The interest in this thing has swamped my interest in the race."

"I'll do everything I can for you, Blake," remarked the commander. "I'll fix up a wireless to Captain Brown, and get him to rig up a landing-platform for you. I'm in the same position as Whitcomb. If you really overtake the *Mastodonic*, send us a wireless, or, better still, stop off here on your way back. We'll be at fever-pitch to hear what you discover."

"Thanks, commander!" laughed Blake. "I will stop off here on my way back. I really intend going, and the sooner I start the better."

Commander Villiers rose, and a minute later they were all congregated on the landing-platform. The engineer's assistant lifted out the wounded homing pigeon, which was passed round, and then Blake showed them the note which had been attached to its leg.

"It's simply marvellous!" remarked the commander again and again.

Blake, at the commander's suggestion, turned the pigeon over to the care of the ship's surgeon, until his return, and, sending a sailor for Tinker, began getting into his flying-togs. Tinker, with the middies surrounding him, came up, with a look of wonder on his face.

"What is it, guv'nor? Are we returning already?"

"No. We are going to make a test flight from here to the *Mastodonic*," jerked Blake briefly.

Tinker was devoured with curiosity; but he had been trained to instant obedience as well as the midshipmen about him, and, without further remark, reached for his flying-togs.

They wheeled out the *Grey Panther*, and headed her towards the side. Then Blake climbed in. But Tinker turned to shake hands with his new friends.

"We're coming back here," said Blake. "Come my lad!"

Tinker dropped his hand and climbed in, and while two sailors held the graceful grey shape Whitcomb started the engine. He signed to them to release her, and she shot towards the side. For a bare moment she hovered over the water after leaving the platform, but as Blake canted the wings she soared upwards in a wide turn.

Tinker waved his hand to the tiny dots already far below, and settled down as Blake, hunched over the wheel in deep thought, with his eyes on the compass, headed for the track of the *Mastodonic*.

The Fourth Chapter
Captain Brown Receives a Shock—On Board the
Mastodonic—Blake Suspicious

CAPTAIN Brown, commander of the *Mastodonic*, and commodore of the Northern Star Line, sat in his chart-room chewing the end of a cold cigar and frowning over a brief wireless message which had just been handed to him.

It was, to say the least, rather startling to be informed that an aeroplane would board him at sea, and that fact, together with the wireless advice, was certainly a radical advance over the old windjammer days when he had received his first initiation into the mysteries and hardships of navigation.

But Captain Brown was not in command of the most luxurious floating palace without having earned his position, and no man living could have fulfilled the responsibility and duty with more suavity blended with decision. If he accepted the words of the wireless message as fact, it meant that Sexton Blake in an aeroplane would make his appearance out of the sky in something under two hours, and there would not be more than enough time to erect a landing-platform.

On the other hand, it meant the *Mastodonic* must be slowed down to half speed, and Captain Brown saw his hoped-for maiden record going by the boards. Had it been the robbery of the "Sun's Eye" alone he would have kept straight on and left the discovery of it to the ship's detectives, but a missing passenger was no light matter.

If Sexton Blake could throw any light on the matter it would be a great relief. Besides, Cornelius Patterson was making no bones about connecting the disappearance of the great jewel with the missing Miss Ford, and that was bad for the ship.

No; the record must be given up this trip, and everything possible done to clear the matter up. As he made his decision Captain Brown stuffed the wireless message into his pocket and betook himself to the bridge. He sent a man for the purser and the wireless operator, and then retired again to the chart-room, where he wrote busily for a few moments.

The purser was the first to appear, and as he stood and saluted the captain looked up.

"You might copy this notice out and post if about on all the notice-boards, Mr. Baily," he said briefly. "Also have it inserted in the ship's papers."

"Very good, sir," replied the purser. His brows went up in astonishment as he read what the captain had written, but he made no remark as he hurried himself away to post up several copies.

Half an hour later every notice-board on the ship carried the following notice:

"NOTICE.

"The captain of the *Mastodonic* has been informed by wireless that an aeroplane will land on the ship during the day. A landing-platform will be put up over the stern, but no passengers will be admitted to the deck for the present. Later, before the departure of the aviator, a full opportunity will be given to inspect the machine.

"BY ORDER."

The wireless operator was the next to put in an appearance, and after writing out an answer to Commander Villiers of the *Thor*, Captain Brown warned him to keep the coming aviator's identity a secret, and then sent for the fourth officer.

That individual was soon busy with a gang of sailors erecting the landing-platform.

Several iron stanchions were put up, and with the true ingenuity of the sailor a large stretch of canvas was dragged to the scene of operations. Stretching and pulling, with many lusty yells, they soon had a sound if yielding platform fixed up, and stretching clear across the stern.

Another hour of anticipation went by before the look-out sighted a black speck on the horizon, which rapidly grew until it achieved the proportions of a bird. On and on it came, and when the glasses showed it to be the expected 'plane a wild rush was made on every deck to witness the approach.

Under the fourth officer the gang of sailors on the hastily-improvised landing-deck stood by to receive the 'plane. Every eye was glued to the long, graceful lines of the speeding grey shape, and as the hum of the Gnome reached their ears, and then stopped for the volplane, Captain Brown signalled the engine-room the "full stop."

The great mammoth liner forged slowly ahead under the force of her former impetus, but Blake, high up, was judging her speed with careful eye.

Slowly he swung round until he was astern, but planing in the same direction. Then, slightly dipping the nose of the *Grey Panther*, he volplaned straight for the stern. Every breath was drawn in sharply as he disappeared from the view of those on the lower deck, but up above the wheels of the chassis had bit the yielding surface of the stretched canvas, and had run forward to stop in the centre in a magnificent landing.

Captain Brown received Blake, who climbed stiffly out, and, signing to Tinker to follow, still goggled, he followed the captain to the chart-room.

"Well, Mr. Blake," remarked the captain, as he closed the door and waved Tinker into a chair, while Blake divested himself of his goggles and cap, "I must confess Commander Villiers message gave me a great surprise. It is odd that you should have been on the *Thor*. But let me give you and your young companion some refreshment."

"The wireless operator of the *Thor* picked up your message, and as the matter is of more than ordinary interest to me I came on in the machine," replied Blake, as the captain rang for a steward. "I'd like to investigate the loss of the jewel and the disappearance of your lady passenger."

"Certainly you are welcome to do so, Mr. Blake! The matter is in the hands of the ship's detectives, but when I heard you were coming I was glad, for it is an easy matter to conceal a small jewel on a ship like this with so many passengers, and of course it is impossible to make an individual search. I wouldn't mind that so much, for it is liable to happen on any ship, but in forty years I have never lost a passenger, and I am more than puzzled over the sudden disappearance of Miss Ford."

"Ah! Well, the first thing to do, captain, is to keep my identity a secret. Then if you can supply me with an officer's uniform as a disguise, and come with me, I would like to make a thorough examination of Cornelius Patterson's cabin and also that of the missing lady. Then I can ask any questions that occur, and get away again without causing you too much delay. There will be no objection to the examination, I suppose?"

"Oh, no; I guess not. The ship's detectives have already made one, but I will send for Mr. Patterson, and he can accompany us."

Captain Brown rang, and sent for the Canadian millionaire.

"Oh, Mr. Patterson," he said, as the millionaire entered, "have you any objection to one of my officers making another examination of your cabin?"

"None at all," replied Patterson. "All I want to do is to recover my jewel; but my opinion is it won't be found until the missing woman is found."

This was pure bluff on Patterson's part, for he thought the "Sun's Eye" safe by now in the hands of his accomplice in England.

The disappearance of the lady who occupied the adjoining cabin had been seized upon by him as a remarkably lucky coincidence, and he had lost no time in hinting that she could probably inform them as to the whereabouts of his property. It is not hard to imagine his chagrin had he known that all unknowingly he had hit on the truth, and instead of the "Sun's Eye" travelling gaily by pigeon post to England it was even then in the possession of his fair neighbour who had so mysteriously disappeared.

Blake, while waiting for Patterson's arrival in the chart-room, had himself got into an officer's uniform and procured a middy's uniform for Tinker.

Consequently, Patterson never dreamed that the officer and midshipman who accompanied Captain Brown to his cabin were the two who had just landed in the aeroplane, and that their identity was that of the greatest detective living and his assistant.

But even had he known he would not have objected to another examination, so sure of himself did he feel.

Blake closed the door on entering the cabin, and turned at once to the millionaire.

"Do you mind showing me the trunk or box from which your jewel was stolen, Mr. Patterson?"

"Not at all," he replied.

Leaning down, he pulled out a black steamer trunk from under the bunk, and unlocked it.

"There it is. That cashbox in the corner was where I put the jewel before retiring, and you can see for yourself, neither its lock nor that of the trunk bear the slightest marks of violence."

Blake picked up the cashbox, and made a close examination of the lock of the trunk, but what Patterson had said was true. They bore not the slightest sign of having been forced.

As Blake bent down to replace the cashbox in the corner of the trunk, his eye caught something which seemed to cause him some interest, for he bent closer and pretended to again examine the cashbox.

"Do you always have a couple of holes in the back of your trunk, Mr. Patterson?" he asked, casually straightening up.

For a bare moment Patterson hesitated, but so brief was it that Blake was the only one to notice it.

"Oh—er—no, not always," he said, in as careless a tone as Blake's. "That trunk has holes owing to the fact that I brought it home from the West Indies, filled with cigars, and desired to prevent them from getting too dry."

Which was a very reasonable explanation, and one which Blake seemed to accept, for he nodded, and said no more. But something else had caught Blake's eye in the bottom of the cabin trunk, and of this he made no mention. But it told him that Cornelius Patterson was lying.

What he saw was two small bits of grain such as is used for bird food, and more than anything else that told him he had found the originating source of the homing pigeon's strange journey. But what of the seemingly frivolous note which it had carried? He could see absolutely no meaning in it, and with wrinkled brow he turned and said shortly:

"I'd like to look at the cabin of the missing passenger, captain. That will be all here, thank you, Mr. Patterson."

They were just turning to go out, when the wireless operator entered with a message for Cornelius Patterson. With an apology, he tore it open, and, accustomed as he was to control his features, the closely-watching Blake saw his face pale and his hand shake ever so slightly as his eyes remained glued on the words.

"No bad news, I hope, Mr. Patterson," remarked Blake suavely.

Patterson came to himself with a jerk.

"Er—no—no!" he said hastily. "But if you will excuse me, gentlemen, I will go up and send a reply. It's a matter of business which must be attended to at once."

He departed hastily, and Captain Brown led the way into the cabin of the missing Miss Ford.

Blake first made an examination of the sleeping cabin. Beyond a trunk and a bag, however, there was no luggage, and his closest scrutiny of their contents failed to reveal the slightest thing beyond some very fine and very dainty, feminine garments.

He then led the way to the outer cabin, and examined the trunk under the couch and the black bag. They, like the luggage inside, revealed nothing, and, signing to the captain to lock the door, he pulled out his glass and dropped to his knees.

First tackling the partition between the cabin they were in and that of Cornelius Patterson, Blake began a minute examination. Up and down over and across he went, covering the area in dozens of tiny imaginary squares, which took in every tiny speck on the white wall. For half an hour he worked in silence, while Tinker followed him with his eyes, and Captain Brown stood looking on in wonderment. But at the end of that time Blake paused in his survey, and concentrated his attention on the line where two of the panels joined.

"Go into the next cabin, Tinker," he said, "and come close to the wall on the other side of where I am."

Tinker hurried out, and a moment later his voice came from Patterson's cabin.

"Is this right, guv'nor?"

"No—a little more to your left."

"How's this?"

"That's right. Now watch carefully where the panels join."

Blake reached in his pocket as he spoke, and drew out a tiny, slim, steel instrument. He thrust the point in the small hole he had discovered, and pushed it through until he judged the point to be on the other side.

"Can you see anything where they join?" he called.

"No, guv'nor; but there's a bunk here, you know."

"Look underneath it then!" snapped Blake. "If it's dark, run your finger up and down the wall."

For a moment there was silence, then——

"Oh! I should say there was something! I've run something sharp into my finger!"

Blake smiled grimly.

"Just wait a moment, captain. I want to see where this goes through."

He hastened into Patterson's cabin, and looked underneath the bunk where the steel point came through.

Then with Tinker following, he returned to the other cabin and proceeded to go through a mysterious course of actions. First he rang for a steward and requested the man to bring a long piece of rope. While he waited, he took off his shoes and stood up on the couch. When the man returned, he tied the rope under his arms, and squeezed with difficulty through the porthole, and Tinker and the captain lowered him slowly. When his eyes were about three feet below the porthole, he called to them to stop, and, pulling himself in close, began examining a mark which he saw on the white paint. From his pocket he drew a delicate mould, and took an impression of the mark; then, signalling to the captain and Tinker, he worked his way up and back through the port.

"What on earth did you go out there for?" asked Captain Brown, in amazement.

Blake laughed.

"I'll explain later. A certain theory has been forming in my head; it suggested an examination of the outside under the porthole. And now, captain, let us return to the chart-room. I wish to ask some questions."

On their arrival Blake went straight to the point.

"Firstly, captain, can you give me a detailed description of the missing Miss Ford?"

"I certainly can," replied the captain energetically. "She wasn't aboard long, but, by James, sir, there never was a better conducted young lady in the world. She was one of the most beautiful women I ever saw. Medium height, slim and perfect features. One of those women that made a man feel sort of protective towards her at once."

"Your description is enthusiastic enough," smiled Blake drily, "but I'm afraid hardly of much use for my purpose. Perhaps I had better ask you a few questions. You say she was of medium height?"

"Yes, about five feet five."

"What colour was her hair?"

"The most beautiful shade of bronze you can imagine. Tons of it, too."

"Ah!" said Blake sharply. "And her eyes?"

"Blue—blue as the bluest sea."

"I don't need to ask about her dress," went on Blake. "I can judge that from the luggage in her cabin. How about jewellery? Did she wear much? Anything distinctive?"

"No; on the contrary, she wore hardly any. Usually just a big Egyptian scarab on her left hand."

Blake leaned forward.

"Are you positive of that fact?" he asked.

Captain Brown nodded.

"Certainly. I noticed it when she came up on the bridge before sailing, and again when chatting with her in the restaurant. In fact, I remarked on it, and she told me she got it in Egypt."

"Can you arrange that I see a copy of the wireless message which Mr. Patterson received in the cabin, and a copy of his reply?"

"It's against the regulations, but I'll arrange it. Will you wait here, and I will myself bring a copy of each?"

"What do you make of it, guv'nor?" asked Tinker, as the captain left.

"I don't yet know, my lad," replied Blake. "It's baffling, but I am going to try to make arrangements to leave you here, and I'll navigate the 'plane alone. I want you to follow Cornelius Patterson wherever he goes. I think that gentleman knows more about the disappearance of the Sun's Eye than he appears to. So does Yvonne!"

"What, guv'nor! You don't mean to say——"

At that moment the captain returned with the copies of the wireless messages, and Blake spread them out on the table. The one which Patterson had received was very brief, and would convey no meaning to the uninitiated. It originated from a place in Surrey, and read simply:

"GROUNDLESS NOT RECEIVED YET. WAS IT SENT?"

But Blake read "groundless" as referring to nothing more likely than something not dependent upon the ground, and what more logical in view of what he already knew than the homing-pigeon? The next was a trifle longer, and was addressed to:

"BROWN, HORTON, SURREY.—GROUNDLESS ARRANGED. SENT POSITIVELY. INVESTIGATE THOROUGHLY. ADVISE."

For several minutes Blake studied the two messages, and then he turned to Captain Brown.

"Captain," he said, "I think I can state that your missing passenger, Miss Ford, is not at the bottom of the sea; also, that the jewel missing from Mr. Patterson's trunk is not on the ship. These two messages clear up the points which were missing in my theory, but I am very sorry that I cannot tell you more now. Will you leave the matter in my hands, and trust to me to clear it up? I am afraid I can tell you nothing definite until you return to England on your homeward trip."

"I am very anxious to clear matters up, Mr. Blake; but if you are quite positive Miss Ford is not drowned, and that there is a chance of recovering Mr. Patterson's property, of course I'll wait. But I can't imagine how she could have disappeared."

"How did I arrive, captain?" asked Blake quietly.

"Good heavens, do you mean to say——"

"Steady, captain; you must have patience!" smiled Blake. "What I want to do is to leave my assistant on board to follow up a clue. Will that be satisfactory to you?"

"Yes; if you wish."

"Very well; he can keep on that uniform, and pose as a midshipman. He may possibly return with you, and I wouldn't be surprised if you had another passenger returning with you—Mr. Patterson."

Disregarding the captain's astonished look, Blake rose.

"If the passengers want to have a look at the machine, they had better go up now," he remarked. "I'll go into the restaurant and get something to eat, and then get away. Come, Tinker, I will give you your instructions while we lunch."

Tinker followed Blake to the restaurant while the captain permitted the passengers a hurried view of the aeroplane.

Then as he saw Blake approaching, his features concealed in cap and goggles, he waved the last curious one below, and ordered the sailors to wheel out the *Grey Panther*. Blake climbed in, and five minutes later shot over the side, and, to the accompaniment of the passengers' cheers and a long, deep blast of the *Mastodonic's* siren, he circled and rose, putting the 'plane ahead on its journey, of which the super-Dreadnought was to be a landing-stage.

The Fifth Chapter
The Race with the Hurricane—Blake Deduces

BLAKE had a battling journey from the *Thor* to Hendon. He had landed on the super-Dreadnought after a clinking trip from the *Mastodonic*, and found his good-natured rival Whitcomb smoking and kicking his heels in patience until Blake's return.

Blake told the interested officers of the *Thor* as much as he thought wise of his discoveries, and, after watching Whitcomb get away with a good start for Hendon, he began preparing for his own return journey.

The ship's surgeon had discovered the homing-pigeon to be not badly injured, prophesying that it would fly with its former vigour in a day or two.

In compliance with the passenger condition of the test flight, Blake borrowed a delighted midshipman from Commander Villiers, the only difficulty being to decide which one.

Every middy on the *Thor* applied, and so pressing were their each and every argument to be taken, that Blake settled the matter by drawing lots.

The youngster to whom the choice fell was a bright lad about Tinker's size, and, after packing the pigeon in the grub locker, Blake made hurried farewells and got away. Whitcomb was already long out of sight, putting the reliable Farman to her pace in his endeavour to win the test.

In the light of the blue flares Yvonne waited.
Blake volplaned straight for the stern.
A vivid flash of lightning revealed the land close at hand

On the first part of the journey back, after the middy had got over his first taste of being high up and driving along at over eighty miles an hour, Blake explained, the details of aeroplaning.

The grey hulk of the *Thor* had dropped behind, and but for the presence of a brig under full sail far below, sea and sky were empty of life besides themselves.

For a full two hours they drove along, but failed to sight the Farman.

A lowering of the sky in the west caused Blake to look at the barometer. He was amazed at its sudden drop, and, swinging round the storm-mirror, gazed frowningly at the reflection therein of the western sky.

"We're in for a bad blow, my lad!" he shouted. "It's following us up, but unless it's going a hundred miles an hour we'll beat it yet!"

The middy nodded. Young as he was, a season on the China station had inured him to sudden storms, and the elements had no terrors for him. He swung the barometer around, and squinted at it in a comical imitation of Commander Villiers.

"We'll get it all right, sir!" he shouted. "It's coming after us pretty sharp!"

Blake nodded, and tightened the storm stays. Carter, the middy, true to his sea-training, dug around and found the waterproof which covered the chart-stand. To the accompaniment of Blake's approving smile, he fastened it on, and then turned on the searchlight.

As far as possible, the frail little aeroplane was now storm-ready, and Blake settled into his seat.

Even through the noise of the engine and the whir of the propeller they could feel a deadness in the air.

Although it rushed past them at a tremendous pace, its life seemed gone like the stirring of dust in a giant vacuum.

Blake watched the west in the mirror before him. The ever-growing blackness was climbing behind them to the zenith like a black, sinister hand ready to pounce down on the ships on the tossing waves far below and the bold grey shape which raced through the air.

The brig, a mere dot on the horizon, had stripped to bare poles. Carter picked up the glasses, and watched her as the hurricane struck and heeled her over.

"It's got the brig!" he shouted. "It will hit us in a few minutes! Must be travelling at a quick rate!"

Blake nodded, but before he could reply, and even through the noise of the machine, came a faint moaning sound, which grew and grew until it dominated and swallowed everything else.

Driving as they were at over eighty miles, it overtook them with its fury, and, had they been flying in its teeth, the *Grey Panther* would not have lived a second. Darkness spread with marvellous rapidity as the giant black cloud leaped over the sky.

Below, the waves were being whipped to a frenzy of white, and then came the first blinding flash of lightning, accompanied by a terrific crack of thunder.

The gale was upon them in its full fury!

The *Grey Panther* was doing her very best. Did she falter now, it would be a hopeless race. Spurred on by the hurricane, Blake sent her on with every ounce of speed the whirling Gnome could muster. But still the flame of lightning in the rear seemed to grow and grow until it threatened to engulf the little aeroplane and her two intrepid occupants in its scorching maw.

Whether it had overtaken Whitcomb, Blake did not know; but that ever-approaching lightning cloud behind was spur enough to make fast time without thinking of the race itself.

In the light of a particularly brilliant flash Blake sighted land, and, throwing the chart-lamp on the compass, set his course for Hendon. A driving rain overtook them then, threatening in its fury to beat them to earth.

Carter twisted around, and swept the searchlight ahead, but it was really the lightning which eventually showed them Hendon.

Shutting off the engine, Blake volplaned to the enclosure, and was met by the news that Whitcomb had not yet arrived. It transpired later that the storm had forced him to ground a bare hour out of Hendon, and once again the papers rang with the triumph of Blake and the *Grey Panther*. It seemed a foregone conclusion that the staunch little machine should tackle the final test of the meeting—the race from Hendon to Paris and back.

Blake didn't look for any further developments of any importance in the mystery which he had so oddly become mixed up in until Tinker reported from New York. He decided to take Carter as passenger on the Hendon-Paris race, and with that end in view installed the delighted youngster in Tinker's room at Baker Street.

He then set out for the City, where he spent a profitable morning around the insurance offices, for he discovered there that Cornelius Patterson had insured the Sun's Eye against theft for half a million,[19] paying a substantial premium for the cover. Part of the mystery Blake could now reconstruct, and as he sat hunched up in his chair in the consulting-room that night, he went over the points one by one.

"It is Yvonne! I am sure of it!" he muttered. "It bears her stamp in every point. But Patterson himself is a crook. I wonder if she knew that when she succeeded in getting possession of the jewel? But how on earth did she manage it? A homing-pigeon collides with the aeroplane at night over mid ocean. We find a most frivolous note attached to it which refers to the Sun's Eye. Then the next morning we hear that the Sun's Eye has been stolen from its owner in mid ocean, and on the top of that comes the news of the mysterious disappearance of a lady passenger. Patterson lied when he said those two holes in his trunk were for permitting air to circulate when bringing cigars in it from the West Indies.

"I'll stake anything it was the first time the trunk had ever been used. Then those two grains of bird food. That proves the homing-pigeon was kept secretly in the trunk, and the holes were to provide it with air when the trunk was closed.

---

[19] £500,000 in 1913 is worth about £58,000,000.00 in 2020

"Then I discover the Sun's Eye was insured for half a million against theft. From that, if mathematical deduction be correct, it would seem a certainty that Patterson robbed himself, and sent the jewel by the homing-pigeon to a confederate in England. I must find that confederate, and I think when Master Pigeon is well enough to fly, I can use him for the purpose.

"Then there is that tiny hole between the cabin of the missing lady and Patterson's. In view of the possible identity of that passenger, I think it quite likely that mademoiselle kept herself informed of her neighbour's movements by a sound magnifier. The *Mastodonic* is on her maiden trip, and mademoiselle was the first occupant of that cabin. Consequently, it was safe to assume that the hole was made by her own charming self.

"Next, how did she get hold of the pigeon? Patterson would release it probably at night, and the chances are through the porthole. If she was aware of this and acted sharp, she might be able to intercept it; but if your ingenuity really has accomplished that, mademoiselle, I bow to you.

"At any rate, I'm certain Patterson didn't write the note which I found on the pigeon. Proof that the bird passed through someone else's hands after leaving him. Then there was his agitation on receiving that wireless from Surrey and his reply. If 'groundless' didn't refer to the pigeon, I'll be very much astonished. No wonder his accomplice is worrying about the bird's non-appearance. At any rate, I'll take the bird to Horton in Surrey, and follow it home. Patterson's accomplice will wire him to New York, that the bird hasn't arrived, and I'll wager Patterson comes back to Europe hot-foot to investigate. They will look sick when the pigeon turns up a fortnight late.

"But by the terms of the insurance contract, the company will have to pay up the half million if the stone is not recovered. Patterson deserved to lose it to mademoiselle's superior cleverness, but since the company has authorised me today to go ahead on it, I'm afraid, mademoiselle, it will be an interesting chase to outgeneral you and regain it. I'll attend to Patterson's case, too. I really must caution you, mademoiselle, to leave off wearing that scarab, although I really believe Captain Brown's fervent description of your hair and eyes would have told me who the missing lady passenger was. It will be interesting to hear from your own lips the story of how you managed to leave the *Mastodonic* at sea.

"But if I'm going to tackle that race tomorrow I'd better get some sleep. Plucky little chap, Carter, but I wish it had been possible to have had Tinker."

Blake went to bed that night with a strange elation filling him, but he would not admit even to himself that it was caused by the thought that the coming days might bring him once more face to face with that perverse yet altogether lovable young woman, who held such an unrealised place in his life, and who through all her wanderings and exploits wore next her heart a tiny miniature of the man who for her loomed head and shoulders over all others—Sexton Blake.

The Sixth Chapter
The Hendon-Paris Race—Sexton Blake Sees an Old Friend

ARE you really determined on taking part in the Hendon-Paris race, Yvonne?"

It was Graves speaking, and he stood under a big spreading elm on the lawn of a beautiful old Tudor country house in Surrey. Centuries had elapsed since the stately stone pile had been reared to form a fitting home for the son and heir of a hard-fighting baron. The trees and soft yielding turf reflected the dignity and beauty of the mansion which they set off, and not least fitting and harmonious was the charming, bronze-haired young woman, who lay back gracefully in a long, low chair on the lawn, the sun dancing distractingly through her hair as it shot its ardent spears between the tangled branches and leaves of the giant elm.

By her side was a small wicker table, heaped with magazines and, let me whisper it, sweets. The solemn old butler, who had passed to Yvonne with the mansion, gazed with cold eye on his young mistress's weakness, and little did he dream that the dainty, charming young woman who ruled so imperiously yet kindly, was that much famed and much sought after—by Scotland Yard—Mademoiselle Yvonne.

After her daring escapade on the *Mastodonic*, Yvonne, always whimsical, had gone down to Surrey to the old mansion which she had bought, there to revel in the things which really appealed to her. Over and over again had she pictured herself walking back and forth under that shady, dignified elm walk for which the place was famous; and over and over again she had pictured as her companion Sexton Blake.

She feared it could never be, but love always hopes, and though Yvonne was renowned as a fearless adventuress, at heart she was still a bit of a romantic. That he was using the power of his brilliant mind to discover the whereabouts of the Sun's Eye, Yvonne hadn't the remotest suspicion. She thought the thing still a complete mystery, and laughed with delicious enjoyment as she thought of Cornelius Patterson's discomfiture and Captain Brown's mystification.

Her agents in America would advise her when Patterson reached home, and then she would send him a brief communication informing him that the loss of the Sun's Eye was his share of the debt contracted long ago in sunny Australia. The birds and the grass, the fields and the trees, in all their summer softness and splendour, appealed to her, and she would for the present put everything else aside. Her life was not too happy, and the old Surrey place formed a charming retreat.

She glanced up lazily as her uncle asked the question.

"Why, yes, uncle, I think so. Any objection?"

"Little good it would do if I had," drawled Graves, who was lounging about in keen enjoyment in a well-fitting flannel suit. "You know it's dangerous, Yvonne. Suppose you were recognised? Scotland Yard would have the drag-net out for you in an hour."

Yvonne laughed.

"Don't worry, uncle. They won't recognise me. I have a particular reason for taking part in the race. Have you read this morning's paper?"

"Yes, why?"

"Well, then, you must have seen that Sexton Blake is in the race. The papers have been full of nothing else but his exploits with that monoplane of his. I've an idea that my own *Silverwings* can beat his, and I can imagine nothing better than racing Blake to Paris and back."

"But the entry," protested Graves. "They will investigate each participator, and you know the risk."

"Oh, I am not going to enter!" smiled Yvonne, lighting the tiny cigarette. "I'll fly about on a higher level over Hendon until the race starts, and then I'll join in. On the return I'll finish over Hendon, and keep right on to here.

"*Silverwings* is absolutely invisible five hundred feet from the ground. Only the competitors can see me, and then only when they are in the air. They will be surprised, of course; but during the race they will be too busy, and after they finish they won't know where I've gone to. I'll put on goggles so they won't recognise me. By the way, uncle, what time is it?"

"Just gone eleven."

"You might give orders to have the machine got ready. I will leave here at twelve, in order to be over Hendon in plenty of time."

***

Sexton Blake wheeled the *Grey Panther* out of the hangar at Hendon, and made a last examination of wings, stays, and engine before leaving on the Hendon-Paris race, which was to be more than anything else, a speed test.

Lennox, in a Bleriot, had got away at one o'clock, while Whitcomb had limped into Hendon with his Farman that morning, disappointed, but determined to make another try for a record. He was just leaving as Blake walked across the ground, and the great detective joined the crowd in a hearty send off.

Then he climbed into his own machine, and, with young Carter in Tinker's seat, started the engine. Making a preliminary low flight, he came back to the ground, in order to give Whitcomb half an hour's start. Then, once more sending the Gnome engine whirling, the *Grey Panther* shot in the air, and headed for Paris.

During the first few minutes Blake was too occupied in getting the engine warmed up, and watching how the *Grey Panther* shaped, to notice anything else. On rising he had, as is usual with the pilot, cast his glance around the horizon, but Whitcomb had already disappeared, and, of course, Lennox was well on his way. As he finished his inspection, however, and swung the mirror around facing him, he glanced up, and was puzzled at the look on Carter's face.

"What is it?" shouted Blake.

"I—I don't know exactly," replied Carter. "I thought for a moment that I had seen another aeroplane behind us, but it shot up so quickly I'm not sure."

"I hardly think it possible," shouted Blake. "We are the last to start, and there are no other competitors."

"But it didn't look like any machine I have ever seen," persisted the lad. "It was silver-blue, and seemed to melt into the atmosphere."

"I am afraid you are getting airman's false eye," called Blake, smiling, but the smile quickly passed as his eyes fell on the mirror before him.

There the blue sky had been mirrored with only the reflection of delicate sky to spoil its azure depths. But now, as he looked, from the very centre of the blue seemed to appear a vague silver line, which grew until it took the form of a giant bird, and then that of an aeroplane. But what, an aeroplane! Gigantic as compared to the slim lines of the *Grey Panther*, its great wings stretching out in lines of silver.

It was indeed well-named by Yvonne—*Silverwings*.

Blake looked up and spoke.

"You were right, after all, my lad, but I can't imagine whose it can be. I know they claim to have machines in France, and also in Germany, which are invisible a short distance from the ground, and I wouldn't be surprised if this is one of them. I'm going to send the *Grey Panther* for all she is worth. Watch our friends behind, and see if they follow. It may be a foreign machine, surreptitiously watching our tests."

Carter nodded excitedly, and kept his eyes glued on the great machine which was coming on above and behind at a pace which threatened to overhaul them before they got over the Channel. From time to time he shouted out its progress to Blake, who, hunched over the steering-gear, was sending the *Grey Panther* along at a pace equal to that which they had achieved in their thrilling race with the gale.

At last a sparkling sunlit streak appeared. It grew and grew in width until the land dropped suddenly behind, and they were over the Channel. Up to now the mysterious machine following them had kept at a uniform distance, but as the *Grey Panther* ate up the miles between England and France, the great silver body shot past them, and the *Grey Panther* tipped and rocked ominously in her back draught.

"Whoever is driving it is a good sport, anyway," shouted the lad, as the other machine, seeing the danger its back draught had caused, shot up to a higher level.

Then the *Grey Panther* leaped forward again, and neck and neck the two 'planes shot forward over French soil, leaving the Channel a rapidly-diminishing streak behind them.

At that moment Lennox, in his Blériot, raced past on the return journey, but the driver of the strange machine had evidently spotted him in the distance. By the time he had passed Blake, the detective's mysterious competitor had disappeared far above, and not until Lennox had dwindled to a dark speck did it descend again.

Rapidly the country unfolded beneath them like a mammoth map, and soon after passing Lennox, they sighted Whitcomb in his Farman. Again the strange machine shot up out of sight, but when Paris appeared like a tumbled mass of soiled chalk beneath them, it once more dropped, and, still racing neck and neck, they headed for the towering, graceful lace-like lines of the Eiffel Tower.

"Whoever it is, they didn't want Lennox or Whitcomb to see them," muttered Blake. "I wonder what their object is? Is it possible they know I am driving this machine, and are making a personal race with me? If that is what they want, by thunder, they will get it! With the wind behind us going back, I think the *Grey Panther* will do herself justice."

Blake turned the wheel, and the right-hand wing shot up as the *Grey Panther* banked in a short, dangerous, but second-saving circle round the Eiffel Tower, where the judge dropped a flag to signify that the condition had been satisfactorily complied with. By wireless from Hendon he had been advised that only three machines were in the race, and he must have rubbed his eyes with astonishment as the giant silver-blue shape of Blake's competitor flashed past after the *Grey Panther*.

In this fashion they tore back on their return trip—Blake grim and determined, and his unknown competitor evidently no less so. There was very little to choose between them. Over the Channel, the big machine held the lead, but as the water shot behind, the *Grey Panther* gained once more, pulling up steadily. As they drew nearer Hendon, Blake knit his brows in puzzlement as he saw his mysterious competitor drop to the thousand-foot level on which the *Grey Panther* was flying, and draw steadily nearer and nearer.

"Now, what does he want?" muttered Blake. "If he keeps on that course, we'll be crashing into each other."

What the other wanted, however, was not long in doubt. Barely two hundred yards now separated them, and, as far as he dared, Blake was giving his attention to the powerful lines of the other machine. Up in the cockpit, he could just see the head and shoulders of the other driver. He riveted his gaze there as he saw one hand reach up and tear off cap and goggles.

Then Blake gazed in stupefaction at what he saw, and so surprised was he that the *Grey Panther* swerved dangerously as his hand relaxed. Over the edge of the other machine he could see the sun glancing off the heavy bronze coils of a woman's hair. He needed no more to tell him the identity of his mysterious competitor, but he smiled a grim smile as Yvonne turned around and laughed at him, waving her free hand as she did so.

Blake waved his hand in reply, and for a moment he was tempted to keep straight on after the other machine. Hendon swept in view at that moment, and before Blake had time to decide, Yvonne with another laugh and wave, sent her machine high up, to be lost a moment later in the deep blue above.

"That settles it," muttered Blake. "I might search the sky all day, and never pick her up again. What a machine, though! Its colour is ideal for the purpose, blending, as it does, with the colour of the sky. But wait, mademoiselle; I'll locate you yet."

He had no more time then for anything but the machine, for Hendon was below, and, with a last glance into the unfathomable blue sky, where Yvonne had disappeared, Blake volplaned down to the ground, to be greeted with thunderous applause. He had beaten Lennox and Whitcomb in the great race, and through every test the *Grey Panther* had passed supreme.

"But not supreme," muttered Blake, as he walked wearily into his rooms that night. "Yvonne has as much speed, and I think I will change the colour of the *Grey Panther* to silver blue. And now that the flying is over, mademoiselle, I will have time to look more thoroughly into the matter of the Sun's Eye, and perhaps—perhaps we will meet again."

The Seventh Chapter
Tinker on a Long Chase—A Suspicious Quarry

TINKER'S instincts rebelled at being left on the *Mastodonic*, on a seemingly tame mission, while Blake departed in the *Grey Panther* without him; but he realised with a sigh that duty was duty, and since he had to stay he might as well find out as much about Mr. Cornelius Patterson as possible. At his suggestion, Captain Brown installed him in the cabin which had been occupied by the missing Miss Ford, and Tinker grinned to himself as he found himself in the atmosphere created by Yvonne's remaining belongings.

"I can't see through as much as the guv'nor evidently does," he mused, as he sat on the couch his first evening; "but from what the guv'nor said, it's a certainty that Mademoiselle Yvonne listened to Patterson's movements through that hole by a sound-magnifier. If she contrived to do that I guess I can, I'll go down now and get some materials from the electrician. I can make one after the pattern of the guv'nor's which ought to do the trick."

Tinker suited the action to the words, and ten minutes later was wheedling a small battery, wire, and other things necessary for his purpose from the gruff electrician. He stole back to the cabin with his materials, and set to work to make a rough, but serviceable, sound reproducer.

Into a small battery-box he fashioned a sounding-board, and then attached his battery. After that he snipped off a couple of lengths of wire which he attached to the battery, letting one end fall free, while the other he coiled and passed through the partition. While the electrician had been searching for a battery Tinker had commandeered an old telephone-receiver, which he connected up to the loose hanging wire. The reproducer had been the most difficult to get, but with a small piece of mica and a hollow steel wire guard he had made a passable substitute.

Tinker scouted about on the deck until he saw Patterson safely ensconced at a game of cards in the smoking-room, and then he slipped down to his cabin again to fix his reproducer. He found the hole left by Yvonne was a trifle small for his steel tube, and had to cautiously enlarge it before he could go ahead. Then thrusting it through he squatted on the couch and pressed the receiver to his ear.

Although the sounds which his hastily constructed instrument carried so plainly to his ears, told Tinker his reproducer was a success, he heard nothing beyond a few grunts and muttered curses until they had docked in New York. Then, while all the ship was a bustle of departing passengers and visitors who had come to meet friends or inspect the newest ocean leviathan, Tinker turned the key in his cabin, and, with the receiver to his ear, listened to his neighbour's movements. The sound of scraping and banging indicated that Patterson was packing. Tinker was just about to roll up the reproducer, and get ready to follow the millionaire, when he heard a knock and Patterson's voice calling "Come in!"

"I thought you were the steward," he continued ungraciously. "What do you want?"

"Are you Mr. Cornelius Patterson?" Tinker heard the newcomer ask.

"Yes. What is it you wish?" replied Patterson testily, "Can't you see I'm busy getting my luggage out?"

"I am representing the *New York Echo*, Mr. Patterson. We got the wireless news about the theft of the jewel which you were bringing over with you, and I thought you might be willing to give me the story with your own lips."

"Oh, you did, did you?" snapped the millionaire. "The wireless contained all I know myself, so clear out!"

"But, sir," persisted the reporter, "have you any suspicions? Such a jewel as that would tempt the cleverest thief."

"Listen to me, young man," snapped Patterson. "You read the wireless message, did you?"

"Of course."

"Well, did you read that during the evening I showed the jewel to the captain and the purser?"

"Yes, sir."

"And did you read that next morning, when I opened my trunk to get it, I found it gone?"

"Yes, sir."

"You also read, I presume, that a young lady occupying the cabin next to mine disappeared the same night."

"The impression is that in some way she fell overboard!"

"Oh, she fell overboard, did she?" mimicked the millionaire. "Well, I think differently. I think she is still concealed aboard this ship, and I'm going to have every person examined by the police as they leave, or know the reason why. If that fails, I'm going back to Europe on the return trip of the *Mastodonic*. Further, the jewel was insured against theft in England for half a million—its value—so the syndicate of which I am the head will lose nothing. Now you know all I propose telling you or anyone else, so clear out!"

And the reporter cleared. The fact that the jewel was insured was news to him, and Tinker, while the reporter tore off to his paper, ruminated on the fact.

"The guv'nor must have imagined some such thing!" he muttered, as he rolled up his reproducer and stuffed it in Yvonne's bag which she had left behind. "I begin to see now why it was important to follow Cornelius Patterson. It was hard to give up that race to Paris, but the guv'nor knew best, as usual. I wish I had old Pedro here to help me keep track of Patterson, but I haven't, and as I hear him going out I'd better hook it after him."

He waited until he heard Patterson's footsteps echoing down the corridor; then, opening his door, he hurried after.

The millionaire paused to speak to Captain Brown, who was being harassed on all sides, and while Patterson waited his chance Tinker sidled near in order to hear the conversation.

"Ah, Mr. Patterson!" said Captain Brown, turning to him. "I am very sorry we haven't got any trace yet of your property, but the ship's detectives are co-operating with the dock police, and if any passenger tries to get through the Customs with it they will be nabbed, sure."

"I'm glad to hear that," replied Patterson. "The thing is insured, but I and the syndicate I represent would prefer the jewel; and, besides, I don't know just what attitude Turkey may adopt, and if we can't produce it, I'm blest if I can see how they can be forced to repay the money!"

"Ah!" remarked the captain, thoughtfully, stroking his chin. "I hadn't thought of that. If it's not recovered the insurance company then stand to be the losers."

"Naturally," snapped Patterson. "But what I wished to speak to you about, captain, is a return passage in case the jewel is not discovered here. I still persist in my theory that my missing neighbour has it, and in a ship of this size there must be some spot where she could lie concealed, particularly if there are any accomplices to cover it up."

"The ship's detectives have searched thoroughly," answered the captain coldly. "But if you wish to return to Europe you can occupy the same cabin you had."

"Very well. I'm not sure yet that I will go back. When do you sail?"

"The day after tomorrow."

"All right. I'll go along now, and see how the dock-police are making out."

Tinker flashed a look of understanding at the captain as he carelessly followed the millionaire down the gangway. The captain stood looking after them with thoughtful eyes.

"I don't know just what Blake suspects," he muttered; "but I'm beginning to think the leaving of his assistant wasn't so pointless as it seemed to be. I am inclined to agree with the detective that you will occupy a cabin on the return trip of the *Mastodonic* after all, Mr. Patterson. But I'd give something to know where Miss Ford has gone. What I'll say to the directors I don't know. Forty years at sea, and to have this happen on the maiden trip of the *Mastodonic*!"

Blake's prophesy proved correct. Patterson was a passenger for England two days later, and Tinker, tired with the two days' continuous shadowing, once more occupied Yvonne's old cabin.

In New York, he had sent a cable to Blake advising him of Patterson's movements and intentions, and later, on leaving, had cabled again. Blake's answer was transmitted by wireless, and read simply:

"GOOD! DON'T LOSE SIGHT!"

"Not much chance now that we are such close neighbours again," grinned Tinker, as he tore Blake's message into tiny shreds, and let the wind carry them away.

The *Mastodonic* was going for the record which had been spoiled on her outward trip, and a trifle over two days out from New York, saw half the distance left behind. It was on the third night that Captain Brown sent for Tinker to come to the chart-room. On the lad's entry, he pointed to several slips of paper lying on the chart-table, and said:

"I don't know what your master suspects, or what his plans are, but he seemed keen on having a look at Patterson's messages when he was on board, and after some thought I have decided to let you copy these. One of them was sent by Patterson just before leaving, and the other three have come one each day since we left. They are all the same, but Mr. Blake may see something in them which I can't."

"Oh, thank you, Captain Brown!" answered Tinker, flushing with pleasure. "It will please the guv'nor immensely that I have been able to get copies of them."

"All right, my lad—go ahead. I wouldn't do this, only I feel sure you will be discreet."

"Indeed I will!" cried Tinker, as he bent over the table, the one which Patterson had sent was as follows:

"SAILING TODAY. FEAR COMPLICATIONS. ADVISE IF GROUNDLESS ARRIVES."

Tinker copied it out, mentally noting the fact that the word 'groundless' had been in the other message which Blake had seen. Then he picked up the others, which were each sent a day apart.

"NO GROUNDLESS. WILL ADVISE DAILY."

They were all the same, and he merely made one copy.

"Seems a funny sort of daily message to get, sir, doesn't it?" he remarked to the captain.

"Yes, my lad; and it was that fact which impelled me to show them to you. This theft and the disappearance of a passenger worries me greatly, and it will be a tremendous relief if Mr. Blake can clear it up."

"If he can't, no one can!" said Tinker loyally.

Once after that the captain told him a similar daily message had come for Patterson, and then once more all was bustle and hurry to land. They had made Liverpool early in the morning, after smashing every transatlantic record.

Tinker dumped his rough sound-producer into the Mersey, and, donning a bulky American suit, which he had thought wise to purchase in New York, he followed Cornelius Patterson ashore, looking for all the world like an American tourist. He had been in New York often enough to pick up the American accent and expressions, and to test his disguise, he deliberately walked over and stood in front of the millionaire. Patterson never dreamed the lad was the same who had occasionally passed him on deck and in the passages, and, turning to hide a grin, Tinker followed his quarry to the train.

Patterson bought a ticket for London.

So did Tinker.

Patterson went into the telegraph office.

So did Tinker.

Patterson sent a telegram.

So did Tinker.

Tinker looked over Patterson's shoulder, but Patterson didn't look over Tinker's. Consequently Tinker knew what Patterson's contained. It had read:

> "BROWN, HORTON, SURREY. LANDED. WILL LEAVE LONDON BY EVENING TRAIN."

Tinker's was to Blake, and simply advised his arrival, and a code word had been added, which told Blake he was still on the chase, and would keep him posted. But Blake was not to receive the telegram, as will be seen in the next chapter. Consequently Tinker was left to follow up the chase alone.

The Eighth Chapter
The Trail of the Pigeon—Blake Takes Afternoon Tea

WE left blake on the night after the great Hendon-Paris race, planning his next move to locate Mademoiselle Yvonne, and recover from her the Sun's Eye.

His first move was to send Carter to Portsmouth to meet the *Thor*, which was returning with the official record of the ocean test. Then Blake had another conversation with the president of the insurance company which had ensured the Sun's Eye against theft.

The balance of that afternoon he spent smoking and thinking, bringing his mind to bear on every point which would give him a clue as to Yvonne's whereabouts.

That she was in England, he felt sure. He argued that, had she been on the Continent, and come to England merely to take part in her audacious race to Paris, that she would have been satisfied with simply racing him from Hendon to Paris, and then would have dropped out. But, instead, she had returned to Hendon with him, which seemed to point to the fact that she was lying low somewhere in this country.

"I'll send out an inquiry to every source I have," muttered Blake. "It is just possible that some of my agents have heard something about this peculiar aeroplane, although the Press has contained nothing. Tomorrow I'll have a scout around in the *Grey Panther*, and see if I can find out anything myself. Then, if the pigeon is well enough to fly, I'll take it down in the machine to Horton in Surrey, and start it for home. The *Grey Panther* ought to be able to follow it and see where it goes."

With this reflection Blake went to bed. Early the next morning he sent out a sheaf of telegrams to his agents, and was preparing to leave for Hendon, when Mrs. Bardell entered with a letter.

"This just came," she announced, passing it over.

Blake merely nodded and glanced at it. It was printed, not written, and bore neither stamp nor postmark.

Ripping it open, he read the words on the single enclosed sheet, and a grim smile played around his lips as he did so. The audacity of the thing struck him forcibly, and once again he read slowly:

"Mademoiselle Yvonne's compliments, and she would be delighted if her competitor in the Hendon-Paris race would take tea with her next Thursday afternoon at three. Mademoiselle Yvonne also thanks Mr. Blake for the interesting race he provided, and looks forward to discussing the merits of his own machine and hers. For obvious reasons she regrets that it is impossible to append her address, or even give Mr. Blake the clue of a postmark, but no doubt he is clever enough to find her and keep the appointment. She would remind him that he has a clear week in which to do so."

That was all, and as he read it, Blake could see in his mind the delightful bronze head of Yvonne and her silvery laugh as she wrote the mocking note. He examined the paper and envelope closely, but it could have been purchased in any stationer's in Great Britain, so conventional was it. A thorough interrogation of Mrs. Bardell failed to reveal anything further. She had simply found it thrust under the door, and wanted to know, with some asperity, "if he expected her to sit behind the front door waiting for people who stuck things underneath, and pounce out at them before they got away."

Blake dismissed her when she reached this stage, and completed his arrangements for going to Hendon. All that afternoon, until late in the evening, Blake was in the *Grey Panther*. He had mapped out a regular campaign of flying, allowing a certain area for each day, and that night he reflected grimly, as he wheeled the aeroplane into the hangar after a fruitless journey, that if he was unsuccessful, the *Grey Panther* would at least get test enough to suit any Government.

Had the search been on the ground, Pedro would have been invaluable; but even his keen scent could not pick up the trail of an invisible aeroplane. Instead, he had to be left at Baker Street, pacing the floor restlessly, probably worrying his great head over the unaccountable absence of Tinker and Blake without him.

The next day was the same. Blake got away early in the morning, and flew in a northerly direction, but beyond passing Whitcomb, who was trying out his biplane, he saw not another soul. From the thousand foot level he worked up by stages until he was nearly ten thousand feet high. He had lost sight of the earth below; no birds were about—he seemed the only living being in a vast, empty expanse, and for all visible purposes the earth might have been nonexistent.

Only the drumming of the faithful engine and the whir of the propellers invaded the emptiness, but it was an ideal place for threshing out a problem which he was facing.

Over and over the points he went, while the slim *Grey Panther* soared upwards and onwards, but although his deductions told him Yvonne had the jewel, and Patterson was playing a double game, they did not tell him where Yvonne was, and for a moment he almost regretted that he hadn't followed her instead of landing at Hendon.

Only his desire to give the *Grey Panther* a fair test had prevented him, but the mockery of Yvonne's note had spurred him to action.

"I'll work day and night," he muttered savagely. "If it's within my power to keep that invitation, mademoiselle, rest assured I shall do so, and I might take more than tea from your charming, audacious hands. If I can find you, I'll get that jewel before I leave."

That night Blake received Tinker's cable, saying that the *Mastodonic* was sailing for England, and that he was aboard with Patterson. It was then he cabled Tinker and put off going down to Surrey with the pigeon until Tinker should arrive.

His persistent non-success in locating Yvonne irritated him. Not one of the agents had heard of the silver-blue waterplane, nor had their far-reaching inquiries disclosed anybody who had.

"It's a lone hand," muttered Blake savagely, "and I suppose she is spending her time chuckling at my failure. She'll send me a nice note if I fail."

The days passed, however, and still Blake got no clue. Wednesday night saw him savage and irritable. He had covered every direction from Hendon except one—Surrey. This he had left, intending to combine the pigeon test with it, and make one flight serve.

He realised that up to the present Yvonne had cleverly hidden herself, and with an irritable remark, he made his plans to leave for Surrey in the morning. He knew the morning would see the arrival of the *Mastodonic*, and he also smiled grimly at the fact that it was Thursday, and Yvonne seemed very likely to triumph over him. But there was nothing else to be done, and he was up at daybreak, prepared for a hard day.

"Tinker will probably follow his man straight on, and if Patterson goes on to Surrey, the chances are Tinker will keep right on there. He may, however, get a chance to come here, and in case he should, I'll leave a note for him telling him it is likely I will be in Surrey as well."

He did so, and patting the disappointed Pedro's head, betook himself in the motor to Hendon with the homing-pigeon in his bag. The bird was now thoroughly strong again, and Blake had given it a fly around the room in order to see if it was strong enough for the test. He spent some time with the mechanic in going over the *Grey Panther*, and stuffing some sandwiches in the grub-locker, he wheeled the machine out, and once more shot away on his quest.

It was barely noon when Blake, from his chart, saw he was over the Horton Barracks. The fact that Patterson had received a message from Horton made it evident that the accomplice must live in the neighbourhood; but he shrewdly guessed the name Brown to be assumed. Moreover, the many pigeon-cotes which he knew were in the district would baffle a ground search, and he had hit on the plan of making the pigeon show the way as a test which would be irrefutable proof.

He wheeled, and flew beyond the village, and then, dropping to the five hundred foot level, he reached in the grub-locker, and drew out the pigeon. For a moment it struggled in his hand, but the time it had been with Blake told it he meant no harm, and it rested quietly until he let it get its bearings. Then, with a wide fling, Blake tossed it out into the air, watching keenly as he did so to see what direction it took.

The pigeon spread out its wings, hovering and circling for a few moments, and then, dropping a little, it headed due east at a rapid pace. Blake swung the aeroplane around, banking dangerously as he did so, but if he lost sight of the pigeon, his test would be useless. Swiftly the *Grey Panther* raced full speed after the dwindling bird. It was soon evident to Blake that he could keep it in sight, unless it dropped into a belt of woods which he could see in the distance. The pigeon was making straight for them, and Blake rose a trifle in order to look down upon it from a more perpendicular position.

He saw the bird clear the belt, and then a large farm appeared basking in the noonday sun. On one side of its ample barn appeared the entrance to a dovecote, and as Blake watched, he saw the pigeon fly straight as an arrow towards it, and disappear. At that moment a man appeared at the stable door, his back toward the detective. Blake, not desiring to be seen at the moment, and realising if he flew nearer, that the noise of the engine would draw attention to himself, seized the opportunity of landing on a small clearing which he saw in the wood below.

Volplaning down, he had reached the highest tree-tops, when over a slight hill not half a mile away, he saw a giant silver-blue waterplane slowly rise, her bulk outlined against the heavy green of some giant elms beyond.

She slowly turned and made off in the opposite direction, but before she had blended with the blue above, Blake smiled grimly, and leaped to the ground.

"I'm not sure," he muttered, "but I rather fancy I will be able to accept your invitation after all, mademoiselle. This has been a very profitable morning, and if Tinker only succeeds in keeping track of his man, I think tonight will show more light on matters than there has previously been. But in case curious eyes should spy the *Grey Panther*, I'll just wheel it in under cover of the trees."

Blake suited the action to the word. When he had finished, the slim grey shape, with wings folded, was standing in a shady, mossy hollow secure from prying eyes. Then taking off his goggles and flying togs, Sexton Blake made a radical change in his appearance. A cool spring nearby supplied the means of washing the grease from his hands. Then from the locker in the aeroplane he took a small bag, and began his work. A pointed black beard and black moustache turned up à la Kaiser Wilhelm, gave him a distinguished foreign appearance. A fashionably-cut frock-coat and silk hat completed the change, and made him look for all the world a foreign diplomat, and nothing else.

The friendly little spring provided a cooling beverage while he munched his sandwiches, and after clearing away the last signs that the mossy hollow was occupied, he strode boldly through the wood to the dusty road.

***

Mademoiselle Yvonne watched the departure of her 'plane *Silverwings* on a message to Captain Vaughan on the *Fleur-de-Lys*, which was cruising in the North Sea while waiting.

Graves was at the wheel, and neither he nor Yvonne had emerged from the hangar in time to see the slim grey shape which dropped into the belt of woods not a mile away.

After the big machine had disappeared above, Yvonne returned to the shady lawn and stretched out in the long low chair which was her favourite. Lazily she watched a fat, overfed robin struggling with a huge worm in the middle of the lawn, while pleasant dreams chased each other through her head. Up above in the giant elms the birds twittered in drowsy content, and blended with the seductive heat came the pure odour of honeysuckle.

The multitude of cushions at her back, and the magazine-piled table at her side, made it evident that Yvonne intended putting in a lazy afternoon. A dreamy smile flickered across her face as she thought of the note she had sent to Sexton Blake a week earlier.

"Oh, he will be angry," she murmured drowsily; "but I couldn't resist it. He always wrecks my plans, but this time I have managed without him suspecting a thing. I must keep up the farce, and order tea for two to be served at three sharp. Then what a regretful note I can send him."

The staid, old butler was passing on the terrace just then, and Yvonne called him and gave the order. Then she went back to her daydreams, indicative of the nature of which was the pulling out of Blake's miniature and gazing long and steadily at it. Even as she gazed at it her eyes grew heavy with the heat of the afternoon, the miniature dropped from her hand, lying against her white, softly-pulsating throat face up, and she slept.

Yvonne's dreams were of the same tenor as her thoughts with the exception that while waking Blake was at a distance, and while she slept, he seemed to be with her walking up and down beneath the shady elms, as she had often imagined. Still she slept on, and ever so slowly the hands of the great clock in the old mansion crept around towards the hour of three.

At precisely one minute to three a tall, well-dressed gentleman, with his silk hat in his hands, turned down from the terrace and walked across the soft, yielding turf of the lawn until his shadow fell across the sleeping young woman.

He stood gazing down at her for a moment until his eyes caught sight of the open miniature lying face up against her throat. He withdrew his eyes at once, but not before they had seen whose face it was, and as the fact was borne in on him his eyes softened wonderfully and the stern lips relaxed. Far up the terrace the butler could be seen with a loaded tray, and the man standing before the sleeping young woman coughed slightly.

Yvonne opened her eyes suddenly, and started up quickly as she saw the tall man with the black beard and moustache standing before her.

"Who are you?" she gasped. "What brings you here?"

The man smiled.

"I was rather uncertain whether I could accept your kind invitation, mademoiselle, but fortunately I was able to do so, and, as you see by the clock, I am in time."

Yvonne's hand flew up to her neck, and her face and throat were dyed a deep scarlet, for she knew he must have seen the miniature.

"You—you!" she gasped, in a futile endeavour to collect her scattered wits. "I—I——Oh, it is too ridiculous!" And she laughed in silvery tones to cover her embarrassment. "You are too uncanny, Mr. Blake."

Blake smiled.

"Now that I am here, may I sit down, mademoiselle?"

"Oh, I beg your pardon!" she cried, trying surreptitiously to tuck the miniature back into her dress. "Sweep those books on to the grass. Ah, here comes tea! As you say, you are just in time, Mr. Blake."

She was once more the cool, self-possessed Yvonne; but neither she nor Blake could forget the incident of the miniature.

They carried on a desultory conversation while the solemn old servant placed the tray and departed.

"Do you take one lump or two?" laughed Yvonne, reckless of the consequences of his finding her, and yielding herself entirely to the fulfilment of her dreams.

"Have you forgotten?" replied Blake, smiling, while an odd feeling tugged at his heart as he watched her slim hands hovering amongst the tea-things.

"Oh, yes; of course I do! Two, isn't it? But tell me, please, Mr. Blake, how did you find me?" she added, as she passed the cup over.

"Later, perhaps," replied Blake. "That's a fine machine you've got, mademoiselle."

"Isn't it! I think it is a trifle faster than yours, Mr. Blake."

"I don't know, mademoiselle. You see, the day of the Hendon-Paris race I had a passenger, whereas you were alone."

"True!" she nodded. "I hadn't thought of that. Mine is a splendid machine, though. The trouble with yours is that like all aeroplanes the engine makes such a noise."

"It won't soon. I'm working on an electric adaption which will do away with that."

"Ah, mine is already so equipped," said Yvonne. "But tell me, please, how did you find me?"

"I must refuse for the present," smiled Blake. "To tell you the truth, mademoiselle, I have been anxious to see you for some few days. In fact, I was looking for you when I saw you at Hendon."

"Ah! For what?" inquired Yvonne.

Blake looked her in the eye and smiled.

"I thought I might persuade you to give up the "Sun's Eye," which you managed to secure so cleverly from the homing-pigeon which Cornelius Patterson was sending with it to England."

If a bombshell had dropped from the sky amongst the tea-things it would not have caused Yvonne more consternation than Blake's remark. For a moment she was speechless. She had no idea that he was on the track of the "Sun's Eye," and much less did she imagine he had connected her with the missing Miss Ford who had disappeared from the *Mastodonic.*

"How do you know I have it?" she asked tersely.

Blake laid his teacup down and lit a cigarette.

"It wasn't hard to imagine," he said coolly. "When a valuable jewel disappears in mid-ocean, and a passenger with it, it is natural to look for a connection between the two. Of course, it is always possible on a floating city like the *Mastodonic* to dodge about and escape detection, especially if one has accomplices."

Then, beginning at the discovery of the tiny hole through which Yvonne had thrust the needle of her sound reproducer, Blake went over her movements as he had mentally reconstructed them.

"I think I am not far wrong," he wound up, "except that I am not quite clear as to your movements after dropping through the porthole. Were some blue signal-lights on the water yours by any chance?"

Yvonne nodded, too astonished to speak.

"I thought that possible," continued Blake. "Then my theory that you dropped into the sea and were picked up by your aeroplane was correct."

"Yes," said Yvonne, in a low tone, "But how do you know all this when the *Mastodonic* was on her way to America and you were in England?"

"I didn't happen to be in England, I was quite close to the *Mastodonic*, on board the super-Dreadnought *Thor*, whose wireless operator caught the Press message of the occurrence."

"Ah! I see," nodded Yvonne slowly. "I'll remember to attend to the wireless next time. It was careless of me. But what do you propose to do, Mr. Blake?"

"Well, by all rights, I ought to arrest you," smiled Blake; "but since Cornelius Patterson was playing a double game, and your intercepting of the pigeon and leaving the *Mastodonic* was really the cause of my ferreting the thing out, I'm inclined to stretch a point providing you give up the jewel."

"Ah!" breathed Yvonne. "You know, then, what Patterson's game was?"

Blake nodded.

"Yes! Why were you on his track? Was he one of the men for whom you are risking your freedom to be revenged upon?"

"Yes; he was one of the crowd in Australia who ruined us."

"I see. Well, Tinker is on his trail, and I think my evidence will put Mr. Cornelius Patterson out of the way for a little time. He was endeavouring to get the jewel for himself, and make the insurance company pay for it, in order that the syndicate wouldn't lose. Of course, if you refuse to give it up, I will have to adopt means to get it."

Yvonne's eyes dropped to the ground, and a slow flush spread over her face as she plucked nervously at her dress.

"I'll give it up, Mr. Blake, since Patterson will be prosecuted by the insurance company, but on one condition."

"What is it?" asked Blake.

"That you come and walk with me for half an hour under the elms."

"I will be delighted to do so!" replied Blake quietly, reading her thoughts.

Yvonne's hand trembled slightly as she placed it on Blake's sleeve, but she was happier than she had been for many a long day.

While they paced under the elms Blake told her of the proximity of Patterson's accomplice, and how he expected Patterson to reach Horton that night with Tinker at his heels.

"I never dreamed of such a thing," replied Yvonne, "but if that is the case, let me come with you, please, when you go over. Stay here to dinner, Mr. Blake. The train from London doesn't reach Horton until nine, and we will have plenty of time."

"Thank you; I will!"

"Ah, that will be nice!" said Yvonne simply, her hand tightening on his arm. "And, Mr. Blake, at your place at dinner you will find the Sun's Eye."

And Blake did.

The Ninth Chapter
Tinker Loses His Quarry—A Long Chase—Found Again

AFTER sending off his telegram to Blake, Tinker hastened out after his quarry, who was pacing up and down the platform, waiting for the London train to start.

He appeared thoroughly unconscious of the presence of the lad in American clothes who passed and repassed him, and as Tinker strolled by for at least the twentieth time, he chuckled under his breath.

"Tracked him to New York and back again," he muttered, "and he hasn't twigged yet!"

But Tinker was shouting before his horse passed the judges' stand, speaking metaphorically. If the lad had been satisfied to watch his man from a safe distance, all might have been well; but Patterson was no fool, as his business associates might have proved. The persistency with which he met the lad finally caused him to take unconscious notice of his features. From that his mind jumped to the fact that there was a vague familiarity about them. To a man who was capable of conceiving the plan of using a homing-pigeon for his purposes, it was not much of a jump to the point where he began to wonder where he had seen the lad before.

Slowly his mind worked back to the *Mastodonic*, and he remembered him as a fellow-passenger from New York. The memory of the features seemed to go back past that, however, and as he sent his mind over every detail of his movements in New York, he suddenly remembered that a lad had been lounging near him in the cable office when he had cabled to England to his accomplice.

As he passed Tinker the next time, he mentally stripped him of his disguise, and drew a quick, whistling breath as he realised, not only had he seen the lad in New York, but he had also seen him in his own cabin, where the strange officer of the *Mastodonic* had asked such pertinent questions, regarding his trunk, and the two ventilation holes at the back of it.

"Is it possible," he growled, as again Tinker passed, "is it possible that officer was a ship's detective, and that he can have suspected anything? I'll swear that is the same lad who was there at the time. My heavens, if they have suspected me all along! I'd better play warily. But, surely if they did, they would send an older man on the trail than that boy. By heavens, if I had suspected anything on board, the *Mastodonic* would have had another missing passenger! I can't take the time now to double about. I can't imagine what has become of the pigeon, unless Brown is playing me double, and I don't think he dare do that. But if he is, I'll settle him quick. I'd give something to know what became of that missing woman who had the next cabin to me.

"I wonder if she by any chance really did have any suspicion of the jewel. She might have seen me send the pigeon off, and put up a bluff that she had disappeared, in order to catch the first steamer from New York back to England, and try to get some trace of it. Anyway, her disappearance was fortunate for me. It enabled me to throw suspicion on to her. But what can be the trouble? It was a long trip for the pigeon, it is true; but it was possible. I can't imagine—— Thunder, there is that boy again! I must give him the slip in London."

He wheeled and entered a first-class compartment, and Tinker, all unsuspicious that his quarry was on his guard, entered the same carriage, and sank into a corner.

Patterson took no notice of Tinker's presence on the journey. Had they been alone, it is most probable that it would have gone hard with the lad. A buxom, elderly woman, however, also occupied a seat, and little did she realise that her presence was the means of averting what would undoubtedly have been a struggle till death.

At London both Tinker and his quarry arose, and donned their coats with simulated carelessness, but the lad proved to be sharper than Patterson deemed him, and quite worthy of his master's long training. As they crushed out of the narrow door Tinker spied the corner of a handkerchief sticking out of Patterson's pocket.

Little dreaming it would later be his only clue to his quarry's whereabouts, and only taking it in conformance with Blake's persistent poundings never to neglect details, no matter how small, Tinker stuffed it in his pocket, and kept on after his man. Up the platform they went until they reached the line of taxis.

Here Patterson entered one, and Tinker tumbled into another, not knowing Patterson was keeping a wary eye on him through the glass at the back of the taxi. When quite convinced that his suspicions were correct, and that Tinker was really following him, Patterson picked up the speaking-tube and spoke to the driver.

"A sovereign over your fare if you lose that yellow taxi behind," he snapped.

And the sudden increase of speed, together with the driver's nod, told him the man would do his best. If he failed—well, there were other ways; and Patterson leaned back, and lit a cigar, peering back through the window from time to time, to see how the chase was going.

Tinker's driver merely had orders to keep the head taxi in sight, and, not thinking the other driver knew he was being followed, had let some distance stretch between them, trusting to his eyes to follow the vivid red of the front machine.

That carelessness was his undoing. Tinker, also watching his quarry through the front window, saw him suddenly quicken his speed, and the lad at once grew suspicious that

Patterson was aware he was being shadowed. He jerked down the tube, and yelled through it to the driver.

The intervening space, however, was fatal, and as a big policeman held up his hand for the traffic to stop, Tinker saw the other taxi shoot on, the last vehicle through.

With an exclamation, he ordered the driver to go on to Baker Street, as soon as the traffic was released.

"Anyway," he muttered, as they drove along Oxford Street, "I've got his handkerchief, and if he takes the evening train for Horton, I can pick his trail up with Pedro, and follow him, even if he is disguised. I wonder how the dickens he twigged I was following? I am certain he didn't know it on board. It's a good thing I did as the guv'nor has always maintained a detective should. If I hadn't pinched his handkerchief, I couldn't even put Pedro on the trail now."

The cab pulled up at Baker Street, and Tinker hurried in, after paying the man, hoping to find Blake at home. He was doomed to disappointment, however, and found instead Blake's note, written early that morning, saying he was going to Surrey to try the pigeon test. Underneath was Tinker's wire from Liverpool, still unopened.

"Well, if Patterson does as he said he would in the telegram I read over his shoulder, he will go on to Surrey, and the guv'nor's presence there will be fortunate, providing I can locate him, or he hasn't left on his return. I'll get these rags off, and get into a disguise that will fool Mr. Cornelius Patterson, and then I'll make for the train with Pedro."

Pedro had exhibited unusual signs of joy when Tinker dashed in, for it had been a lonely week for the big hound. Ever since the lad had sat down at the desk, he had been sitting with his head on Tinker's knee, begging, with as much intelligence as his great eyes would convey, that he be allowed to go along. As Tinker laid Blake's note on the desk, he looked down and read the look.

"It's all right, old chap," he said, pulling Pedro's ears. "You can come with me tonight, and I guess you'll have your work cut out for you."

Pedro's tail pounded on the floor, and he followed Tinker to his room, where the lad got into the disguise of a young farm lad.

"This will create no suspicion," he mused, as he tugged at the heavy boots. "I might be some farm-hand up to London for the day, and as I'll travel third, and trust to picking up his trail after the train reaches Horton, Patterson won't even lay eyes on me."

Five minutes later, with Pedro on the leash, he was at Victoria, standing in the shelter of a big baggage truck, watching every man who approached the Horton train. His watch was fruitless, however; and when it wanted only two minutes to the time for the train to leave, he began to fear his man had again given him the slip.

Drawing out Patterson's handkerchief, which he had carefully wrapped in paper, he held it to Pedro's muzzle, and then sent the bloodhound up and down the full length of the train. A minute passed, and still Pedro got no trail. Another half-minute passed, and Tinker risked letting Pedro poke his nose in the open doors of the carriages, but the dog only worried hopelessly. As the guards closed the doors and shouted, "Stand clear, please!" Tinker drew back in dismay, and watched the train pull out.

"Well, by thunder, that beats me!" he muttered. "That is the train he said in his telegram he would take, and there isn't another one stopping at Horton tonight. But I'm certain he couldn't have been aboard. Pedro would have picked up his trail somewhere. Now where can he be? Great guns! Why didn't that occur to me? If he got suspicious of the taxi following, he might drop all idea of going by train, and motor down instead. I'll bet dollars to doughnuts that is what he has done! All right, Mr. Patterson; I may be going on a wild-goose chase, but the guv'nor's got the aeroplane, and the car is in the garage. I'll take it, and go to Horton, and try to pick up the trail there."

It happened that Tinker had hit on exactly that which Patterson had done. On thinking things over, he remembered seeing Tinker in the telegraph-office at Liverpool, and, in case the lad had seen any part of his message, he decided it would be safer to motor down. Had it been possible to give up the trip altogether, he would have done so, but he was suspicious of his accomplice; and could not rest until he had solved the mystery of the homing pigeon's non-appearance. Consequently, while Tinker was pursuing his fruitless search at the railway-station, Patterson was speeding along in a motor bound for Horton.

Tinker lost no time in getting a taxi, and dashing back to the garage. The big, well-known grey car was always kept ready for any emergency, so he was not compelled to waste time in getting it ready for the trip.

Turning on the lights, and pressing the button which released the compressed air and started the powerful engine, he threw in the clutch and backed out. Pedro lay at his feet while they bounded along through the outer fringe of London, and from time to time he rose and poked his nose over the edge of the car, as though he realised they were endeavouring to pick up the scent which had baffled him at the train.

Tinker did not stop to make any inquiries, however, until he had covered a good twenty miles, and then he pulled up at a small inn, which was the main centre of a village through which he was passing. A car had passed through not an hour before, and—yes, he was on the right road for Horton, in Surrey. With hurried thanks, Tinker leaped into the car, and again they dashed on. Only once more did he stop to hear almost a repetition of his first information.

"I'll bet it's Patterson, old chap!" he said to Pedro, as he leaned over the wheel, and gradually increased his speed. "We'll keep after the car ahead, anyway, until we make sure."

Pedro pounded his tail in reply, as though to signify his thorough accord with his master's intentions.

Horton, named after a prominent family whose estate had once embraced the whole district, was almost barren of lights as Tinker swept up its main and only street, for the inhabitants were early risers, and consequently retired while the evening was yet young.

A constable, however, informed Tinker that a car had barely passed up the street ahead, to the garage at the inn, and Tinker, disregarding the officer's suspicious look, drove cautiously on. Up the street a few hundred yards he saw the light which shone out from the inn, and a dark blotch on the side towards him indicated the presence of the yard entrance.

He risked arousing the suspicions of his quarry, and turned in. There, sure enough, was the car standing to one side, her lights out. Tinker drove in behind it, and stopped his engine. Then, turning out the lamps, and throwing on the emergency brake, he slipped out, and stole along to the car ahead. Quickly he passed his hand along the bonnet, and smiled in satisfaction.

"Engine still warm," he muttered. "This is the car all right. And now for the man who drove it."

Once more he put the handkerchief against Pedro's muzzle, and then, with the dog on the leash, gave him his head. Pedro went direct to the front seat of the motor Tinker had followed. Then he climbed up and across, leaping to the ground at the other side, with Tinker after him, muttering triumphantly:

"By thunder, I was right! Pedro has got the trail this time."

From there Pedro went quickly along, head down, until he came to a pause at the inn door. As he started to enter, Tinker pulled him back, and just then the hound caught the scent again, a little distance away.

"Ah! He's been in, and out again," muttered Tinker, as Pedro turned and trotted confidently down the dark road.

Once more they passed the policeman, who looked curiously at them, and cast his lantern in their direction, but Tinker ducked and hurried on.

Pedro travelled without fault along, through the village and past its outskirts, until they entered a belt of woods. At that moment, just emerging from the woods, and silhouetted against the sky, Tinker saw a man whose walk told him it was his quarry.

"Crikey! I do wish I could find the guv'nor!" he muttered. "But I suppose he went back to London before dark. All I can do is to follow my man, and wire the guv'nor in the morning."

He had just reached the further edge of the wood, and some distance ahead could see his man turning and entering a gate at the side of the road. The black bulk of the house and barns told Tinker it was a big farm, and, dragging Pedro off the scent, he also turned aside, intending to circle around and reach the buildings from the rear.

Pedro showed an indisposition to leave the scent, but Tinker persisted, and they turned into the woods.

At that moment a soft, peculiar whistle sounded ahead in the shadow of the trees, and before Tinker could prevent it, Pedro had jerked the leash from his hand and dashed ahead.

"Crikey! That was the guv'nor's whistle, or I'll eat my hat!" muttered the lad. "Pedro wouldn't have done that unless it were."

Softly Tinker whistled—a peculiar bar which only he and Blake used—and when the answer came back he knew he was right.

"What luck!" he muttered in delight, as he cautiously wound his way through the bushes. "Is that you, guv'nor?" he whispered, as loud as he dared.

He almost jumped when Blake's voice came from near at hand, and then Pedro's head touched his knee.

"Yes, Tinker. Drop down in here, my lad."

Blake stood gazing down at Yvonne.
"Hands Up!"
Discovery seemed inevitable

"How did you know Pedro and I were near?" asked Tinker, as he sank to his knees.

"I saw your silhouettes against the sky," replied Blake. "Was that Patterson you were following?"

"Yes, guv'nor. He gave me the slip in London, but I picked him up again all right."

"Good boy! I looked for you and your man this evening."

"But, I say, guv'nor," said Tinker, leaning forward, "Is that a shadow, or someone behind you?"

Blake laughed.

"No, it is someone, my lad. Perhaps she will tell you herself."

"Can you recognise my voice?" came a soft, laughing voice over Blake's shoulder.

"Merciful Caesar! I beg your pardon, but is it Mademoiselle Yvonne?"

"Right first time," she said softly. "Pedro recognised me more quickly than you."

"Well, you were the last person I expected to see!" answered Tinker. "Is she—is she———" he began, turning to Blake, and hesitating on the words.

"You mean, is she friend or foe?" asked Blake, in an amused tone. "She is a friend tonight, my lad. But no more talk at present. Our man has entered the house, and after a few minutes we must go forward. It is lucky I saw you, Tinker. I want to get both of them. But there may be more.

"Now this is my plan. I will go ahead, and you, Mademoiselle Yvonne and Pedro follow quietly. Keep out of sight, but near, and on no account rush up unless you hear me either call or fire. Do you understand?"

"Yes, guv'nor. But suppose they get you from behind?"

"If you hear nothing by what you consider ten minutes, then go ahead, but not unless. Now I will be going on. Wait until I get across the first fence, then follow, and stick to the shadow."

The Tenth Chapter
Blake Moves—Pedro's Disaster—The Great Fight in Mid-Air—The End

WITH a final word of caution to his companions, Blake slipped out of the bushes and stole over the fence, the barely perceptible noise of his movements blending with the soft rustle of the leaves and branches as they fell back into place.

There were two small paddocks and three fences to be crossed before he could gain the shadow of the buildings. But Blake was a past master in the art of scouting. Dropping to the ground, and taking advantage of every mound and shadow, he crept along until he reached the second fence. A dilapidated farm waggon, which had been left standing in the paddock against the fence formed a convenient bulk for covering his movements in climbing over. Without its background, his silhouette could have been seen by any suspicious eye, but so carefully did he work that not even Tinker and Yvonne were aware of his exact position.

It was when the last and riskiest fence had been crossed that Blake needed to use his greatest caution, and half-way across to the barn he thought discovery was certain. The kitchen door flew open, sending a flare of light into the yard, and as Blake sank close to the ground he perceived two dark figures outlined against the light. Then the door slammed, and the crunch of heavy footsteps sounded coming across the yard in the direction of the barn.

Blake, looking like a log against the ground, slipped his hand into his pocket and gripped his revolver.

Discovery seemed inevitable, but he breathed easier as the footsteps passed on without pause and entered the black opening of the barn door. For the moment he had forgotten that their eyes, coming from the lighted kitchen into the dark yard, had not got sufficiently accustomed to the change to notice him.

He wriggled forward over the turf until he reached the side of the barn, but stopped again as the sound of voices came to him.

"Do you take me for a fool?" demanded one voice angrily, and Blake recognised it as Patterson's.

"Well, you can believe it or not, just as you wish!" snapped the other—evidently the farmer.

"But it is all rot, and you know it!" blazed Patterson. "Nearly two weeks ago I sent the pigeon on the wing with the jewel strapped to it. I get a wireless from you saying it hasn't arrived. I get to New York, and received further cables saying it still hasn't arrived. I leave at once for England again, and each day you advise me by wireless that it hasn't arrived. I land in England this morning, and come down at once. Then what do you say—that the pigeon arrived this afternoon, and without the jewel." He laughed with angry sarcasm. "You'd like me to think the pigeon was taking a holiday until I returned. But come, Lewis, don't try to bluff me! I have offered you a good rake-off. You thought you could play me double, and make me swallow a yarn like that. But I'll overlook it. Pass over the jewel, and you get your rake-off just the same."

"I tell you I'd pass it over quick if I had it!" cried the man called Lewis. "But I'm telling you the truth. The pigeon landed here today. I saw it in the dovecote this afternoon when I went up to feed them, and I tell you it had no jewel. I searched every inch of the place. But if you despatched it when you say you did, where has it been all this time? How do I know you haven't had the pigeon with you all the time, and only sent it from Liverpool today?"

Blake smiled grimly as he heard the two cheerful rascals quarrelling. He could have explained to the mystified millionaire that the farmer was for once telling the truth, and vice versa, he could have set the farmer's mind at rest regarding the strange length of time it took the pigeon to reach home.

But he decided to lie low for a bit. The more they quarrelled between themselves the easier their eventual capture would be. He knew now without the shadow of a doubt that Patterson was guilty, for he had convicted himself by his own lips.

What the eventual outcome of the quarrel would have been it is hard to say. Patterson was positive the farmer had received the jewel, and had played him double; while the farmer felt himself in the mystifying toils of the millionaire's cunning brain. He felt that Patterson, for some deep purpose of his own, was using him and bluffing him, and in his blind fear he spoke wildly in an effort to see light.

He was beginning an angry tirade against Patterson when Blake heard a soft rustle behind him, and remembered that Tinker and Yvonne were to follow him. He wished devoutly that he had said twenty minutes instead of ten; but there was no help for it now, and he would have to act at once.

He rose softly, and stepped around the corner of the barn. From his left pocket he drew an electric torch, and from his right a revolver. Then, switching on the torch, and levelling the revolver, he strode boldly into the shadowy doorway of the barn. As the white circle of light fell on the angry, arguing men, the farmer stopped in his tirade, and gave an exclamation of fear and amazement. Patterson gaped speechlessly, first at the light, and then at his companion. What mysterious man or men was behind that blinding light neither of them knew, and, as before, they suspected a trap set by the other.

They swung round, and would have volleyed forth recriminations and curses at each other, but stopped as a cold voice came from behind the light.

"Don't move, either of you. You, Mr. Patterson, keep your hands out of your pockets, and you, Mr. Farmer Lewis, don't look so longingly at that hayfork. I hate to see two worthy individuals like you doubting one another; but, really, I think I ought to inform you, Mr. Lewis, that Mr. Patterson has for once told the truth.

"According to schedule he despatched the homing-pigeon from the English Channel with the jewel attached. And I don't mind informing you, Mr. Patterson, that Mr. Lewis also spoke the truth when he said the pigeon had only arrived today without the jewel.

"So you see, my friends, you are both truthful men. At present, however, the jewel is reposing in my inside pocket."

Then Blake's voice turned to a steely snap.

"Cornelius Patterson, I arrest you, in the name of the King, for attempting to swindle the Central Insurance Co. out of half a million pounds. And you, Lewis, will have to come along as his accomplice."

Both men stared stupefied at the light which hid the owner of that icy, mysterious voice in its shadow.

Patterson was the first to recover his wits, and spoke in a husky whisper:

"Who are you?" he gasped.

"Sexton Blake—at your service!" came the voice. "I had the pleasure of meeting you before, Mr. Patterson, when I made an examination of your trunk, which had holes pierced in it to provide ventilation for cigars."

"Ah!"

The cry came from Patterson, who had gone livid with rage. Risking all in one mad leap, he dashed forward, calling to his companion. His voice and movement brought the farmer out of his trance with a jerk, and he jumped for the hayfork.

Blake didn't wish to fire unless it was absolutely necessary, consequently, when Patterson leaped forward, the detective whistled shrilly for Tinker, and shouted sharply:

"Back, back, Patterson! I'll fire if you don't. There are more with me, and you are only making your case worse. Back, you——"

He broke off and dodged, as Patterson jerked out a revolver and took a flying shot. Blake refrained no longer as he heard the bullet whistle past his ear. Levelling his automatic, he fired, but at that moment something long hurtled through the air and knocked his aim aside, the revolver going off harmlessly into the air as it dropped from his hand.

It was the hayfork which the farmer had thrown in a frenzy, and, with his revolver lying on the floor, Blake stood helpless before the levelled aim of Patterson, who was preparing to fire again.

The pointing of his revolver made it obvious that he intended wasting no time in putting the detective out of business, and, in a last effort to save himself, Blake dashed the torch full in Patterson's face. It was not before Patterson had pulled the trigger, however, and things would have gone very hard with Blake, but for an unexpected occurrence behind him.

Tinker and Yvonne, with Pedro on the leash, had crept across after Blake, and held themselves in readiness to dash forward to his assistance. As arranged they were only to follow him sooner than arranged if they heard a shot, but when Blake whistled, Tinker leaped to his feet and led the way.

As they dashed in through the open door they took in the situation at a glance. The farmer was in the very act of hurling the hayfork at Blake, and Tinker, levelling his revolver, fired at the very moment Blake had done so. Pedro, unfortunately, pulled slightly on the leash at the moment, and Tinker's bullet flew wide.

Before he could turn to his master's assistance, Blake's revolver had dropped from his hand, and Patterson was preparing to fire. It was when his revolver spoke, and Blake, in a last effort to save himself, dashed the torch into his adversary's face that the unexpected happened. Yvonne had drawn her revolver, and an infinitesimal fraction of a second before Patterson fired she fired also. Her bullet struck the gleaming barrel of his revolver, and, glancing along, tore a livid furrow in his hand. His finger barely had time to pull the trigger when the bullet struck him, but the shock against the barrel was sufficient to spoil his aim, and Blake was saved.

Lewis, who had regained his nerve, and realised just how desperate their situation was, turned to Patterson with a cry, and shouted: "Follow me!"

He kicked the fallen torch as he spoke, and broke the current, plunging the stable in darkness, but not before his companion had seen which way he was going.

Blake, in fear that Yvonne or Tinker might fire, called sharply:

"Don't fire yet. Come on!"

But it was easier to say "come on" than to do so. A hurried scraping in the darkness told them that the farmer and Patterson were moving, but in what direction they could not tell. Blake dashed forward blindly with the others at his heels, but Tinker was busy with his pocket and to good purpose.

Drawing out a small torch, he fumbled with the button. A moment later he was sending a wavering patch of light around the barn. No sign of their adversaries was to be seen, but as he threw the light at a rough set of steps in the corner, he saw a pair of heels disappearing through a trapdoor above. Blake and Yvonne saw them at the same moment, and Blake made fresh plans with lightning-like rapidity.

"Give the torch to mademoiselle, Tinker," he called. Then he turned to Yvonne. "Watch the stairway, mademoiselle!" he jerked. "The torch will keep things lighted so they can't attack you in the dark, and you have your revolver. Come, Tinker, they will endeavour to leave from a top window. We must head them off."

Yvonne nodded, and grasped the torch from Tinker's hand as he tore out after Blake. Outside all was still, and against the starlit sky Tinker saw Blake hold up his hand for caution. He pulled up close behind his master.

"Which way do you think they would go, guv'nor?" he whispered.

"I don't know yet," breathed Blake. "There may be a back window opening on to that low shed at the rear. On the other hand, you can see from here the barn joins the back of the house by a passage. Take Pedro, and work quietly around the house, Tinker. If you see them, call or fire. I will work around the back of the barn, and signal in the same way. I think mademoiselle has nerve enough to hold the stairs."

Tinker stole one way with Pedro, and Blake another. Outside and inside dead silence still reigned, and but for the creeping forms of Blake and Tinker, one would never have imagined that there were five human beings playing a tense waiting game of hide and seek about those silent farm buildings. Blake found no sign of the fugitives at the rear.

The low shed was a lean-to of the bigger one, and from the moving and heavy breathing inside, Blake knew it to be a cow-shed. As he thought might be the case, a window in the loft opened on to it, but it showed no signs of having been raised by the fugitives.

He began working slowly around to meet Tinker, when he heard a shout from the lad, and the crashing of bushes ahead. Dashing recklessly around, he gained the road just in time to see two shadowy figures tearing away at top speed, and then disappear into the woods. For a bare second he caught the silhouettes of Tinker and Pedro as they dashed in after, and, with another shout to Yvonne, Blake tore after.

The strategy employed by the farmer and Patterson was suddenly plain to him. They had crept softly through the passage connecting with the house, and while the three watchers were trying to watch every point of house and stables, they had dashed out of the front door of the house which was in Tinker's area.

That the lad and Pedro had lost no time in tearing after them was evident, and as Blake thought of the desperate condition of Patterson's mind and the shot which would have been his end but for Yvonne's marksmanship, he redoubled his speed.

As he tumbled over a fence, and headed into the woods, he caught a glimpse of Yvonne coming behind, and then he was in the shadow of the trees trying to follow the chase by the noise of crashing branches ahead.

Into trees and bushes he went crashing blindly, getting many a scratch from their branches, but he knew he was at least holding his own.

Suddenly the noise ahead stopped, and he knew the quarry, with Tinker at their heels, must have hit open ground again.

It was so, for a moment later Blake himself stumbled out into the open to see Tinker and Pedro just vanishing over the brow of a hill.

At that moment a gigantic black screen seemed to be thrust between Blake and the starry sky. In the act of jumping a fence, he paused and looked up. It was Yvonne's plane returning from the yacht, and it was gracefully volplaning down to earth. Blake could see that it would land just over the hill, and knew they must be on the outskirts of Yvonne's place. Not waiting longer, however, he dashed on, but as he reached the brow of the hill he stopped for a second in dismay at what he saw.

The fugitives also had seen the aeroplane, and with the desperation of drowning men, had seized the opportunity presented. Blake saw the two black forms leap to the side of the machine, and grasp it. A moment later Tinker and Pedro were there, too. Pedro, with a leap, gained the interior, but Tinker fared not so well, and with a growl of rage, Blake raised his revolver and began emptying every chamber at the dark figures. What he had seen was a crushing blow delivered at Tinker just as the lad raised his revolver to fire, and a moment later he saw three figures in the aeroplane, their shapes clear cut against the sky as the great bird-like machine again left the earth.

Tinker had dropped to the ground unconscious from the blow he had received, for the butt-end of a revolver had caught him fair between the eyes; but Pedro was still in the machine.

One of the three figures was holding a revolver to the head of the man who drove the machine, while the struggles of the other proved Pedro was putting up a great struggle.

Again and again Blake saw an arm descend on the dog's head, and then he gave another cry. Pedro was lifted up and thrown out, his body hurtling down a full thirty feet to land with a heavy, sickening thud beside the unconscious Tinker.

At that moment Yvonne came up panting heavily, and Blake, who had emptied his revolver, grasped hers without ceremony, and began firing rapidly at the rising aeroplane. The calibre was too small, however, to do any damage at that range, and he finally desisted to listen to Yvonne's excited words.

"Where is your machine, Mr. Blake? We might overtake them yet. They are forcing my uncle to drive them, but if we can get near enough, I can signal him what to do."

Blake thought rapidly for a moment.

"See how Tinker and Pedro are," he jerked. "If they are injured badly, I won't follow; but in case they are not, I will be getting my machine ready. It is only a short distance in the woods. Meet me where we were in hiding tonight, and if Tinker and Pedro are not too badly hurt, we will follow the other machine."

Yvonne nodded, and dashed ahead, while Blake tore off to the spot where he had left his machine. Not caring to risk a delay by losing his way in the woods, he made for the road first, and then made his way into the little mossy valley where the *Grey Panther* lay concealed.

It was only a minute's work to pull the slim, light machine out and rebrace the wings. Then he leaped in and laid his hand on the engine, waiting impatiently for Yvonne's reappearance.

Every second was of the utmost value, and he was almost tempted to rise and follow the other machine alone. But he could not bring himself to do so until he knew in what condition Tinker was. His plucky chase had at least served to show the way taken by the fugitives, even if his rash attack, single-handed, had ended so disastrously, for even from the distance separating them, Blake had heard the impact of the blow, and he knew the result must have been severe on the lad, if not perhaps fatal.

At that moment the bushes clashed in the darkness ahead, and he called out:

"This way—more to your right!"

Barely had he spoken, when Yvonne came stumbling into the open space, panting heavily from her run, her dress torn by the bushes, and her hands bleeding from a multitude of scratches.

"They're all right," she gasped, as she scrambled in opposite Blake. "Go ahead! I'll tell you the rest on the way."

Blake nodded, greatly relieved, and lost no time in starting the engine. As the propeller whirred with terrific speed, the *Grey Panther* leaped ahead over the soft sward, as though propelled by a giant's boot; then, as Blake canted the wings, it rose at a sharp angle, clearing the tree-tops by a dangerous proximity. As soon as she was clear of the woods, Blake sent her ahead on the level, and then, when she had gathered speed, he rose again.

At first they could see no signs of the other aeroplane, but suddenly Yvonne pointed wildly, and shouted.

"There she is! See her outline against those bright stars to the south?"

Blake looked southwards, and saw she was right. At first it looked but a huge night bird wheeling in the sky, but he knew it was only one thing, their quarry. He slightly altered the course, and settled himself in the seat to drive the *Grey Panther* for all she was worth.

Well it was for Blake that night that his search for Yvonne had necessitated so many long, hard flights. In those every part of engine and aeroplane had received a thorough test. Each bolt had been gone over countless times, each nut had been renewed, each brace had been tried, and the engine tuned to perfection. Consequently he knew what he had to depend on, and knowing that, did not spare it.

As the engine drummed at top speed, and they tore after the other black patch ahead, he nodded across to Yvonne.

"Tell me!" he shouted.

"They were both unconscious," she replied, "but I think not seriously injured. I whistled for one of my men, and told him to get others from the house. They will carry both of them there, and attend to them."

Blake nodded his thanks, and said nothing. He knew he owed Yvonne his life that night, by her prompt action in shooting back in the barn, and that fact made no easier the problem which was troubling him.

True, the present occasion was not a case to put into the hands of Scotland Yard. Had she refused to return him the jewel, he would have been compelled to arrest her on the lawn that afternoon. But she had not refused, and, although technically she had stolen it, still it was from Patterson, who himself intended stealing it and defrauding the insurance company of its value.

Her return of it had enabled him to prevent the swindle without causing her arrest, and now he only desired to get his hands on Patterson's shoulders, and a pair of steel bracelets on that individual's wrists.

But he could not forget that Yvonne was still wanted by the authorities. True, at the time she had tampered with despatches of the British, the Prime Minister had technically pardoned her, providing she left England; but that pardon had never been put in black-and-white, nor had it been endorsed by the Home Secretary.

He had once before warned Scotland Yard of her approximate whereabouts, but the information had been received in an ungracious spirit, and if he warned them again, he imagined he would receive the same curt treatment.

Absorbed in his thoughts, his eyes glued on the black patch ahead, and his ears listening mechanically for the slightest alteration in the perfect rhythm of the engine, he did not see Yvonne's thoughtful gaze riveted on his face.

Womanlike, her intuition told her she was the subject of his thoughts, and she knew her act in saving his life had placed him in an embarrassing position. But just as his mind was working on the matter, so was hers, and while Blake was still pondering the ethics of the matter, she had already reached her decision.

Far ahead the other machine was growing to look more like what it really was, and less like a bird.

Blake dragged himself out of his thoughts as he saw this, and looked across at Yvonne, whose back was towards it.

"We are gaining!" shouted Blake, through the racket. "They are heading to cross the Channel, but if we keep on, we will overtake them."

Yvonne laughed.

"She has more weight than we have," she replied. "But, even so, if I had had a passenger, I think you would have beaten me after all in the Hendon-Paris Race.

Blake smiled and nodded.

It was true. They were steadily overhauling the other machine. The weight of the three heavy men in her was telling, and if all went well with the *Grey Panther*, it would be only a matter of time before they were abreast. But that moment must be before they reached French soil.

Blake sat tense and silent, watching every move of the machine ahead. Below them lay the shadowy earth with an occasional patch of lights to show where a village nestled. A long string of coloured lights told them they were following the railway.

Then, suddenly, far ahead, Blake saw a mass of lights reflected from the blackness surrounding them, and he knew it was Dover. To right and left he could see the powerful gleam of lighthouses, and moving lights beyond, danced and tossed from steamers in the Channel. A bare dozen lengths now separated the two planes.

The extra weight was decidedly a big disadvantage to the leading machine, and Blake didn't doubt for a moment that the threat-driven Graves would have been tossed out long before had Patterson or the farmer had the faintest notion of driving.

On and on they went, ever creeping closer and closer, until the nose of the *Grey Panther* was level with the tail of the other. Dover swept beneath them at that moment, and almost neck and neck they tore along over the tossing waters of the English Channel.

Then, as she had promised to do, Yvonne signalled to Graves, who could now be seen leaning stiffly over the driving-wheel, with Patterson holding a revolver at his head. Lewis, the farmer, crouched behind them, a revolver resting on the side of the car, and pointing in the direction of the *Grey Panther*.

Less than a dozen yards now separated them, and Blake could see Patterson urging Graves to do something.

Yvonne leaned out, and Graves turned his head slightly, regardless of the revolver so close to his head, and probably realising Patterson would not risk his own life by shooting the only man who could drive the machine, unless things were extremely critical.

Yvonne pointed downwards, and then tapped her revolver. Graves shook his head in despair, but she made an imperative gesture, and then fired. Blake, watching closely, saw that her gestures had dominated her uncle even more than his fear of Patterson, and as the great machine began to volplane toward the water, Blake sent the *Grey Panther* down also.

Patterson stood irresolutely for a moment, and none but he knew exactly how close to death Graves was in that moment. His eyes caught sight of the water beneath, however, and with a movement of anger he swung and began firing at Blake and Yvonne.

Blake was too much taken up with the machine to reply, but as the farmer also opened fire on them, Yvonne began firing also, Blake pressed the lever which lowered the water-floats, and still neck and neck the two machines took the water together.

Skimming the surface of the water, Blake put the *Grey Panther* straight for the course being followed by the other then he shut off the engine, and by their own impetus they were carried along until with her engine also stopped, the other machine crashed into them.

Patterson, in his rage, had emptied every chamber in his revolver, and though Lewis had one shot left and viciously pressed the trigger, it hit the side of Blake's goggles, and glanced harmlessly off into the water. Then, while the two machines tossed side by side, Blake unceremoniously grasped Yvonne's revolver, and leaped.

Lewis met him with his empty revolver reversed, and struck with all his strength at the detective's face.

Blake took the blow on his arm, and kept on, bringing down the end of the barrel between the farmer's eyes. He then wheeled and raised his arm to strike at Patterson, but he was too late. The other was upon him, and they fell to the bottom in a fierce grapple. Blake's right hand with the revolver in it was still free, but his left arm was numb from the blow he had received.

Unless Graves acted quickly, and came to his assistance, Patterson, with the strength of desperation, would overcome him. A lurch of the machine sent them rolling, and as Blake came on top, he dropped the revolver from his hand and struck with his bare fist. It took Patterson on the point of the chin, and his arms dropped as he lost his senses.

Blake scrambled to his feet, and found Graves sitting in gaping surprise, while Yvonne was keeping the *Grey Panther*'s head to the waves. If Graves had been slow to join in the fray, he showed alacrity enough in assisting Blake to bind the two prisoners. Then he sat back and waited, for he was still in the dark and puzzled to know why Yvonne was apparently working in with her archenemy.

Blake wasted no time in explanations, however, and Yvonne had her hands full with the machine. Climbing across into the *Grey Panther*, Blake leaned over to Yvonne.

"Can your uncle take them back to Horton in your machine?" he asked. "If so, I can transfer them to the motor Tinker came down in, and take them to London from there."

Yvonne nodded.

"Of course, Mr. Blake. I'm only sorry I couldn't have given you more assistance, for you know how I feel toward Patterson."

"You have helped me considerably tonight already," smiled Blake, "and when we get to Horton, I'll try and thank you properly for saving my life."

"Please don't," pleaded Yvonne, and Blake turned away, silently reading in her eyes the hopelessness of it all. For a bare moment he had entertained an idea of having a long talk with Yvonne, and endeavouring to get her to give up her course; but in her eyes he read the price he would have to pay in order to induce her to do so, and he felt he couldn't pay it.

Five minutes later as a steamer left her course to investigate the strange-looking objects dancing on the water, Graves rose in the air, followed by Blake, and in dead silence they headed for Horton.

***

Blake hurried into Yvonne's cosy sitting-room, where both Tinker and Pedro had been taken. Tinker had a bad bruise on his forehead, but had recovered, and beyond a terrific headache, was all right. Pedro, however, had received a terrific shaking from his fall, and was still too weak to move. In fact, it may be stated here that Blake and Tinker spent an anxious two days before the faithful fellow was quite himself again.

Yvonne had left Blake alone with Tinker and Pedro, but after satisfying himself about them, he turned to leave and look after his prisoners, Tinker insisting on coming with him. A servant met them on the way, however, and handed Blake a note. Rapidly tearing it open, he read the pencilled words:

"Dear Mr. Blake,—Realising the mental struggle you are having between duty and gratitude, I am forestalling your decision. Even while you read this, I shall be on my way for Paris in my waterplane, carrying with me the memory of our eventful, and, to me, happy days together. When you reach London, I will be out of the jurisdiction of Scotland Yard. My uncle goes with me. I hope your assistant and the dear old dog will be all right soon. Good-bye. I wonder when and how we shall meet again?

YVONNE.

"P. S.—Your machine is a better one than mine.

"P. P. S.—The servant who will give you this has instructions to prepare supper for you before you leave for London. Y."

Blake folded the little note up, and put it in his pocket. He smiled with a strange tenderness as he thought of her very feminine postscripts, and then, with a sigh, he turned to Tinker.

"Come, my lad, we will have supper before leaving for London. I will drive the *Grey Panther*, and you can take the prisoners in the motor."

They turned and followed the servant to the dining room, where a dainty supper had been laid out, and while they ate, Blake detailed the incidents of the chase and capture to Tinker.

"But, I say, guv'nor," remarked the lad tenderly feeling his forehead, "there is one point which has puzzled me for ever so long."

"Yes?" inquired Blake. "What is it?"

"Do you remember when Captain Brown and I lowered you out of the porthole in Mademoiselle Yvonne's cabin on the *Mastodonic*?"

"Yes."

"Well, what did you discover out there? I crawled out after you left, but I couldn't see anything."

"I found the faint print of a woman's rubber-soled shoe, my lad," smiled Blake, "and from that fact, I knew the missing woman passenger had left the *Mastodonic* voluntarily.

"If she had been leaning out, and had fallen, there would have been no footprint. It showed that she had climbed down in order to drop into the water noiselessly. But come Tinker, let us get Pedro, and then start. It is late, and the journey will take some time."

***

Cornelius Patterson used all his resources to fight Blake's evidence, and had he not convicted himself by his conversation in the barn with his accomplice, he would undoubtedly have got off. Blake's testimony was too convincing, however, and the jury returned a unanimous verdict of guilty. The judge gave him the minimum—three years—but extended his privilege to Lewis, the farmer, and bound him over to come up for sentence if called upon.

The insurance company presented Sexton Blake with a very handsome cheque in token of his brilliant capture, but the satisfaction he felt over the case was as nothing to Blake compared to his sorrow when he thought of the whimsical young woman with the wistful eyes who had been both his friend and his foe in the case, and whose note breathed the heartache of a woman.

The UNION JACK. 1d.
The MISSING GUESTS.
INTRODUCING
YVONNE AND SEXTON BLAKE
505 NEW SERIES.]
June 14th, 1913.
[EVERY THURSDAY.

THIS IS A PORTRAIT OF NELSON LEE
THE FAMOUS DETECTIVE

READ ABOUT HIS
GREATEST FEMALE FOE IN:

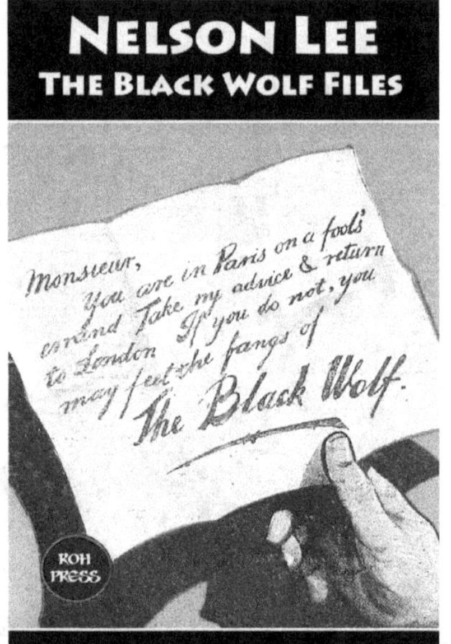

The First Chapter
Yvonne Prepares Her Plans

THE yacht *Fleur-de-Lys*, sailing from the South Pacific and bound for England, was forging ahead on the last stage of her long trip.

The early morning sun was throwing up the green and grey of Cape Finisterre into a blend of purple and brown, and the Bay of Biscay, into which the yacht was just entering, was in one of its rare moods of quiet and calm.

Early as was the hour, the deck of the yacht contained many white-clad figures, indicating that her passengers were early risers.

Standing apart from the others, and leaning over the rail was the owner of the yacht, Mademoiselle Yvonne Cartier, who, after a long absence from Europe, was looking tanned and healthy after her free and open life on the island in the South Pacific which formed at one and the same time her home, and a safe retreat from the arms of justice.

Graves, her uncle, was standing forward, talking to Captain Vaughan, while Hendricks, the mate, was on the bridge. Clad in Yvonne's uniform of white, with a gold fleur-de-lys on the sleeve, the sailors worked industriously, painting, scrubbing, polishing, and cleaning generally for the arrival in English waters.

As Yvonne turned back from her contemplation of the quickly-passing, white-flecked water, she gazed with a fleeting smile at the contented members of her "circle," and then, drawing out a tiny cigarette-case, she lit a cigarette, and walked forward to where Graves and Captain Vaughan were standing.

Both men gazed in undisguised admiration at the picture she made as she walked up the deck. Like the rest, clad in white, with the gold fleur-de-lys on the sleeve of her blouse, she looked very young and very fair.

The salt-laden air was blowing her bronze hair about in distracting little wisps, and the sun fell back in laughing little glints from its assault on her eyes.

Though it was some years since she had left the cattle-station back in Australia, she still walked with the free-limbed, dainty swing of the bush, swaying gently from side to side as the dainty yacht swung to the waves.

"I trust you slept well, mademoiselle!" remarked the captain, touching his cap. "You looked a bit tired last evening."

"Thanks, yes!" smiled Yvonne. "I was a bit weary, but I feel much refreshed this morning. And you, uncle?"

"Splendidly, thanks!" drawled Graves. "It has been an ideal trip this time. But a few hours will see us in the English Channel, Yvonne, and you promised you would disclose your plans before we reached there."

"I know—I know!" she nodded. "That is what I am going to do now. If you and Captain Vaughan will come down to the saloon, I will unfold them."

Tossing away their cigars, they followed her down the deck to the companionway, and as she waved them into chairs they glanced at her expectantly.

Yvonne walked over to a rack which contained several newspapers, and, after selecting a file, she returned and spread them out on the table.

"Now," she said, seating herself, "as you know, I have been endeavouring for the best part of three years to locate Travers Bentley, who was, as you will remember, uncle, one of the eight men who financially ruined father, mother, and myself in Australia. He has evidently been moving constantly about, or living under another name, for all my efforts to find him have as yet been fruitless, or, I should say, were fruitless until a few days ago.

"I started on this trip primarily in order to find either him or Henry Forsythe, the only two of that coterie on whom I have not yet taken revenge. Fate, however, seems to have relented, for after my long search I suddenly drop on two things which place them within my reach. One was a message from one of our London agents, saying that he had finally located both Bentley and Forsythe, who are now partners; and the other thing was a newspaper which came aboard with the bundle we got at Gibraltar. The agents' cable may be disregarded for the moment, as it contains the bare cipher statement, but if you will give me your attention, I will read you the paragraph in the paper which caught my eye."

Graves and Captain Vaughan settled themselves to listen, while Yvonne unfolded the papers and glanced up and down until she found the paragraph she wanted.

"Here it is," she said, as the heading caught her eye. Now listen! It is headed:

"'FURTHER DEVELOPMENT OF ENGLISH WATERING PLACES.

"'It is acknowledged by all that England contains many healthy and charming retreats on her coasts which only await development to spring into popular favour and rival the much-advertised resorts on the Continent. For our part, we believe in advancing home enterprise, and, as far as possible, keeping in England some of the money which goes to swell the coffers, of Continental hotel-keepers.

"'Consequently, it gives us great pleasure to state that Mr. Travers Bentley and Mr. Henry Forsythe have enough confidence in English seaside attractions to invest large sums for the development of a charming spot on the coast of North Devon. The exact locality is called Traders' Bay, and already a huge, luxurious hotel has been erected. It will be open to the public in a fortnight, and from our own personal knowledge of the locality, we can say a trip to the Traders' Bay Hotel will well repay the cost.

"'Mr. Bentley and Mr. Forsythe are both wealthy Colonials, and we consider it commendable to see our children from beyond the seas spending their money for the development of the mother country. An advertisement of the opening will be found on page——'"

"They don't mind piling it on thick," grinned Graves, as Yvonne finished reading. "Our children from beyond the seas. That sounds well when applied to Bentley and Forsythe!"

Yvonne smiled.

"They are apparently as smooth and as shrewd as ever," she said. "But now listen to this. It is the advertisement of the opening, and occupies half a page:

"'GRAND OPENING OF TRADERS' BAY HOTEL.

"'The most glorious spot on the English coast. Restful for the Tired. Bracing for the Convalescent. Boating, Fishing, Golfing, Riding, Swimming, Motoring, and Walking.

"'This magnificent spot has lain hidden since prehistoric days, but now its beauty is available to all through the enterprise of Messrs. Bentley and Forsythe, who have erected an immense and luxurious hotel, and have spent enormous sums in developing the natural beauties of the place. Grand opening on June 1st. Bookings are being rapidly made, and early application is advised. For full particulars, address the proprietors Messrs. Bentley and Forsythe, The Traders' Bay Hotel, North Devon.'

"That is all," remarked Yvonne, laying down the paper; "but for my purpose I think it is enough."

"What do you propose doing?" queried Graves.

"I will tell you. As soon as we arrive at Plymouth I shall wire through for rooms at the Traders' Bay Hotel. Then, while I land and proceed on there by rail, you, Captain Vaughan, will take the *Fleur-de-Lys* around the coast and drop anchor in Traders' Bay. It will be as well to paint out her name and use another for the time being. Also remove all the fleur-de-lys escutcheons and replace them with something else."

"And then?" asked Captain Vaughan, who up to now had been silent.

"Then—then I shall tell you the rest, my dear captain!" smiled Yvonne. "I have the germ of an idea, but cannot tell yet whether it will be possible to put it into execution or not. Firstly, I must see the hotel and make a careful examination of the surrounding country. I know the north coast of Devon fairly well, but do not know this Traders' Bay, but if it is like the rest of the coast it ought to suit our purpose admirably."

"Where do I come in, Yvonne?" drawled Graves, lighting a cigar.

"You will have plenty to do, uncle. As soon as the yacht drops anchor I want you to come ashore to the hotel. On my arrival there I will book rooms for you, and for a time at least we will adopt the role of wealthy uncle and niece on a yachting cruise. If my plan develops into anything it will tax the yacht's capacity to her utmost, and I shall use every effort to bring things to a head as soon as possible. By the way, captain, have her well provisioned. It is just possible we may need to make a hasty departure and remain at sea for some time!"

Mr. Travers Bentley.

"I'm hanged if I can guess at what you are planning, Yvonne!" remarked Graves, puffing thoughtfully at his cigar. "You say we must go around and anchor in this outlandish bay on the north coast of Devon, while you go overland and book rooms at the new hotel being opened by Bentley and Forsythe. Then you say the carrying out of your plan depends on whether the country and sea coast thereabouts is similar to what you think. It looks like a dead end to me!"

"Wait, my dear uncle," smiled Yvonne, rising. "It is not like you to be impatient. On the contrary, I have found you only too willing to drift along in careless ease."

"Oh, I'm not impatient, my dear! I am only curious to know what you were scheming."

"You'll know in good time," replied Yvonne. "In the meantime, captain, I think you had better start preparing the yacht at once. It will take some time, and I don't want any hitch to occur."

Graves and Captain Vaughan returned to the deck as Yvonne made a gesture of dismissal, and when they had departed she made her way through the saloon and through several passages until she reached the laboratory which stretched from side to side across the stern of the yacht.

Unlocking the complicated dock with the tiny key which always hung around her neck, she stepped inside, and as carefully closed and locked the door after her.

The laboratory was Yvonne's sanctum sanctorum. Not even Graves, her uncle, was permitted to enter there. With its great glass-topped experimenting-table; its maze of insulated wires ranging in size from a delicate thread of silk to the thickness of a lead pencil; its rows of neatly-labelled jars; its bewildering array of crucibles, test-tubes, and phials; its shining instruments of steel and brass and ebony, all betokened the beloved tools of the scientist, and formed an array which would have been envied by the most learned savant.

After locking the door it was not to any of the instruments Yvonne went, but to a small black palm panel against the farther wall. Here she pressed gently on a hidden spring, and as the panel slid back, she thrust her hand in the small opening which appeared.

When she drew it out again, it contained a small brown-paper parcel, and leaving the panel open, she approached the experimenting table and seated herself in the solid glass laboratory chair.

Her nimble fingers soon slipped off the broad rubber band which encircled the package, and she heaved a deep sigh as the contents fell out on the table before her.

There were three photographs, a rough pencilled sketch, and a sheet of paper containing what looked like a list of names with lines drawn through them. Her eyes grew weary as she bent over and picked up the photographs.

One was of her father, John Cartier, the man who had achieved wealth and ease in Australia, and who had, as he thought, left his wife and child well guarded and well provided for; the second was of the frail mother who had gone down under the blow of ruin when she and Yvonne had been swindled out of first, the Jig Saw Mine, and finally out of the sheep and cattle station which was their only home and last possession; the third was of Yvonne herself.

It had been taken as she was riding through the paddocks with a couple of dogs racing beside her, and a stockwhip in her hand. Behind her rolled the paddocks, and her whole being breathed youth, health, and happiness.

It was hard to believe that the young woman in the picture was the same young woman who had set all Europe talking; but such was the case, and had it not been for the money-juggling schemes of the men who had brought ruin upon her and her mother, it is hard to tell to what heights her beauty and charm would have carried her.

Her eyes were sombre as she laid down the photograph of herself and picked up the rough sketch. Although the expression of her eyes did not change, her features relaxed, and a tender, wistful smile played around her lips as she gazed at the face portrayed.

It was a strong face—strong and quiet, with a hint of reserve strength, which sat well on the firm, square jaw. It was a head sketch of Sexton Blake, the great criminal investigator, and had been made by Yvonne many months previously.

Mr. Henry Forsythe.

She had fought hard and long to smother the love which she bore for Blake, but all her efforts had been fruitless. She had told herself over and over again that Blake was her enemy, that he always baulked her plans, and that it was he who had been the means of sending her to Dalemoor Prison on long sentence, and that it had only been owing to her own daring and ingenuity that she had escaped. But ever the reaction came, and she knew that no matter how she might try, she could never bring herself to hate him.

Many men had fallen victims to Yvonne's charm, but to all she had been indifferent, and her ears tingled as she thought of the time on board the *Fleur-de-Lys* when confidence in her own attraction and the call of her heart had impelled her to offer her love to Blake, only to have it refused. She had come nearer to hating him then than at any other time, for it is not an untrue saying that "hell hath no fury like a woman scorned."

But the very immovable, granite-like calm of the man had shown her how very feminine she was, and though one of the cleverest and most daring adventuresses the world had ever known, her calm exterior covered a wistful desire for the quiet and peace of a good man and a home.

She laid the sketch of Blake down with a sigh, and picked up the sheet of paper which contained the list of names. There were eight in all, the first six having lines drawn through them. Only the two at the bottom were without, and, picking up a pencil Yvonne made a tiny cross before each.

Then she cast her eyes down the list, and a smile of satisfaction passed over her face as she read them one by one. Vineburg, Pearson, Todd, Kelly, Morton, and Patterson.

Six of the eight men who had swindled them in Australia had been revenged upon, and now only two remained.

Fate had shown her their whereabouts, and, all being well, she would be revenged upon them also. Then her vow would have been fulfilled; but beyond that point, she did not permit herself to look.

As she wrapped the papers up again and returned them to the secret aperture in the wall, a slight hissing noise came from a crucible which was standing on an electric stove. Hastily closing the panel, Yvonne darted across, and with the aid of a pair of asbestos gloves, lifted the crucible on to the glass experimenting table. Then she quickly assumed an oxygen mask containing a glass front, and, replacing the asbestos gloves by thin rubber ones, went to work.

First, she lifted down a small phial from the shelf above, and into the crucible poured half its contents.

She leaped hastily back as a severe agitation occurred in the contents of the crucible, but as it subsided, she returned and emptied the rest of the phial's contents into the mixture.

This time no agitation occurred, but the contents, which before had been a dull green, now began to slowly change. They grew paler and paler until they faded to light green, and then to a sickly yellow. As the last tinge of green disappeared, Yvonne reached down another phial filled with a white liquid, and this also she emptied into the crucible.

The contents at once took on a rich amber hue, and as they did so, Yvonne hastily reached for a glass cover with a small, funnel-like hole in the top. Over this hole she fitted a rubber tube, and the other end she placed tightly in a long narrow bottle.

She was none too soon, for barely had she secured the tube and lifted the bottle, than the contents of the crucible were obscured by a heavy vapour which could be seen through the glass-topped cover.

Its lightness sent it up through the tube into the long glass bottle which could be seen filling, and in five minutes the rich amber liquid had entirely disappeared from the crucible, while the long phial was entirely full of the vapour.

With a deft movement Yvonne withdrew the tube and thrust in a stopper made of rubber, for the mixture she had prepared with such care would soon have eaten through one of cork. Then she carefully placed the glass tube-like bottle in a steel case, padded on the inside, which had been specially made for it, and, screwing on the cap firmly, laid it on the experimenting table.

She next brought into play a large bottle, with a bulb and spray fitted on it, and before removing her mask, she thoroughly sprayed the air of the laboratory. On removing the mask, her eyes dropped heavily, and she stumbled slightly as she made her way across and threw open the artificial ventilators.

"It's been a success all right," she muttered, as she recovered somewhat under the fresh current of air. "Barely a whiff could escape, and even after spraying with the preventative, it almost overcomes me. If I get the opportunity I devise, I think I can bring off my plan. If not—well"—and she shrugged—"I have to think of something else. But this much is certain, Mr. Travers Bentley and Mr. Henry Forsythe, now that I know your whereabouts, I will stay on your trail until I have fulfilled my vow to make each and every one of the men who ruined us suffer as I have suffered."

She turned as she spoke, and after carefully cleansing the crucible and phials, unlocked the door and passed out.

The Second Chapter
The Traders' Bay Hotel Opens, and the Guests Arrive

IT was the opening day of the Traders' Bay Hotel at the resort of the same name on the north coast of Devon.

Mr. Travers Bentley and Mr. Henry Forsythe sat in the luxurious private office of the hotel, discussing matters and preparing themselves generally for the first batch of guests who would appear in an hour's time.

Outside in the lobby, the pageboys and porters hung about in brand-new uniforms, waiting also, and from the proprietors down to the boots boy, all seemed imbued with a spirit of expectancy.

Mr. Bentley himself was a big man, and from the viewpoint of Mr. Bentley, a handsome one withal.

His head was massive, his nose big and fleshy, his mouth graduated down into three chins, each larger than the one above it. He invariably affected a spotless white waistcoat over his expansive chest, while his boots would have done credit to the most ambitious bootblack.

A rich brown moustache was his especial pride and joy, and when he smiled, which he did frequently, it turned up at the corners in a way which would have been termed by impressionable ladies "cute."

He looked a decidedly well-fed, comfortable, sleek animal, and that description was in reality not far wrong.

His imposing appearance had more than once been the means of carrying through to a successful issue many little deals which a less impressive personality, Mr. Forsythe, for instance, would have found impossible. With Mr. Bentley in the chair at a directors' meeting, even the most nervous investor felt disposed to trust the management of everything to his confidence-inspiring personality, and no man could smile with more suave regret when announcing "an unavoidable withholding of dividends for the year just ended" than could Mr. Bentley.

Mr. Forsythe, on the other hand, was a thin, cadaverous, melancholy-looking individual. He would, by his very appearance, chill the most sanguine speculator, but when Bentley would smile and playfully poke a prospective investor in the ribs the while he exclaimed: "And now, my dear sir, let me introduce you to my partner, Mr. Forsythe— my watchdog, I call him; he is a marvel for detail, I can tell you—no waste! Not a postage-stamp escapes his eagle eye?"—then one felt that Mr. Bentley had only once more shown his ability for putting the right man in the right place.

Such was the partnership of Bentley and Forsythe. For some years they had worked together, and in that time had contrived to corral a comfortable fortune from the promotion of companies of all descriptions, and many other ways known only to themselves.

On the morning in question they were, as has been said, discussing the outlook. Forsythe sat in an armchair before a magnificent mahogany desk, on which were piled many bundles of important-looking documents, while Bentley stood a-straddle before a fire which was crackling cheerfully in the big open grate.

His hands were tucked under his coat behind him, and his whole appearance simply shouted prosperity.

"My dear fellow," he was saying, "I think we have cause for congratulation. I'll warrant you there isn't another seaside resort in England with every room booked for its opening-day. Splendid, I call it, splendid! Eh—what?"

"Not bad—not bad!" admitted the gloomy-looking Forsythe, without a smile. "If we can keep it up for three months we'll be able to form the company and dispose of it at even more than we had figured on!"

"Just what I'm thinking," replied Bentley. "We have invested here pretty close to a quarter of a million[20]—on paper. If we can't form a company and make them turn over a cool million to us, well, my dear fellow, I will be disposed to go to work!"

---

[20] £250,000 in 1913 is worth about £29,000,000.00 in 2020

Forsythe permitted his gloomy face to break into a smile, which gave him a really startling appearance.

"We'll land it all right with you to do the talking," he said. "It's a good thing, I am thinking, that we have such an aristocratic crowd on the first day. That will go down strong with investors."

"Yes, decidedly! Let me see! Just what titled people are there?"

"I've jotted them down here to put in a booklet which I thought of calling *The Resort of the Aristocracy and Nobility!* There is Lord Cray, the Marquis of Rondel, the Duchess of Foreland, Lord Wells, Lord Carside, Sir Henry Brue, and half a dozen others. Not bad for a first day, considering that only Lord Cray was being booked free for the sake of his name."

"Splendid, my dear fellow!" smiled Bentley, rubbing his hands. "But wasn't there some titled woman wired from Plymouth for rooms?"

"Oh, yes! But I imagine hers is a Continental title. The Comtesse de Rastonet, it was signed. She specified rooms overlooking the sea, so I gave her that suite right over the cliff. She'll get sea enough there. It's a sheer drop of forty feet into the water!"

"And the price?"

"Oh! She said that was immaterial, so I'll make it enough. But it must be time for the train. Hadn't we better go out and receive the first arrivals?"

"By all means!" replied Bentley, and these two shrewd gentlemen departed for the lobby.

***

Bentley and Forsythe had good reason to feel a glow of satisfaction over the result of their extensive advertising campaign. All the resources of their finished art had been brought to bear on the matter, and the result was, as Bentley stated, that every room had been booked for the opening day.

On the first train, which arrived about noon, came the bulk of the guests, and Bentley was kept busy for some time giving a genial welcome to the newcomers. Almost one of the last to enter was a slim, graceful-looking young woman, who registered as the Comtesse de Rastonet, and who asked to be shown at once to her apartments. Forsythe, who was looking after the house-management, deputed a boy to take her up at once, and, after dismissing both the boy and the chambermaid, who had appeared, the young Comtesse softly locked the door, and proceeded to go through a remarkable pantomime for one of the aristocracy.

The apartments comprised three rooms, and a private bath, and the first thing the new arrival did, was to make a rapid tour of each room. Then she approached each window in turn, and surveyed the outlook.

Before her stretched the broad blue of Traders' Bay, which seemed to break against the very walls of the hotel, for, standing as she was, it was impossible to see the beach. On opening the window of the sitting-room, however, Yvonne, for the reader will have guessed her identity, leaned out and gazed down at the sheer drop from the windows, and which ended in the limpid depths of the sea itself.

A smile of satisfaction overspread her face as she saw from the colour of the water that it must be deep down below, and turning, she reached for a small black bag which stood on the floor near at hand. From this she took a spool of fine black wire, on the end of which was a small lead-sinker, such as is used by fishermen.

Again approaching the window, and holding the spool in one hand, she dropped the weighted end over the sill, and permitted it to run freely through her fingers.

As it slipped silently along over the sill, a series of red marks on the wire could be seen, and their very regularity made it evident that they were marks of measurement. This was the case, for as after a few moments the sinker struck the bottom, and the wire stopped running out, Yvonne began to pull it back rapidly, counting the red marks as she did so.

"Five—six—seven-and-a-half!" she murmured, as the wet sinker flopped over the sill on to the floor. "That makes forty-five feet to the bottom, or roughly forty feet to the surface. It is a good distance, but I think it could be managed. Heavens! Who would have dreamed of such ideal circumstances? With one or two exceptions, it couldn't have fitted my plans better if I myself had designed it. Now, if the yacht turns up this afternoon as arranged, I'll lose no time in beginning operations. But first, I must have lunch, and then get a list of the guests who are staying here, with the numbers of their rooms."

She turned as she spoke, and, unlocking the door, proceeded down to the dining-room, where most of the other guests were already assembled.

Yvonne noticed several whose faces she knew as those of well-known people in society, and the fact that the majority were lunching in golfing costume indicated that they intended trying the much-advertised Traders' Bay links without delay.

As her eyes swept over the tables, Yvonne saw a man whom she knew to be the wealthy Marquis of Rondel, and just beyond she noticed the equally wealthy Duchess of Foreland. Making a mental note that her recognition of these two would make it unnecessary to study the guest-list at once, and deciding that she must find out the numbers of their rooms without delay, Yvonne returned to her lunch with the faintest glint of amusement in her eyes.

But that glint of amusement faded with remarkable suddenness, and she drew in her breath with a quick whistling intake as her eyes saw at a nearby table, a man whose outline looked startlingly familiar.

His back was towards her, but the set of his shoulders, and the poise of his head, made her positive it was Sexton Blake and no other.

"What on earth can he be doing down here?" she asked herself, dropping her eyes to her plate, and wrinkling her brow in puzzlement. "Has he any suspicion that I am in England? Does he know who Bentley and Forsythe really are? No, no; impossible! He must be just taking a few days' rest and has come up here for the golfing.

"Heavens! How fortunate I have taken the precaution of disguising myself. I do hope Captain Vaughan has thoroughly changed the appearance of the *Fleur-de-Lys*! It will be extremely risky carrying out my plans under the very nose of Sexton Blake; but I am not going to change them now. In fact, it will add a zest to it with Blake, of all people, on the spot. I wonder if he is here under his own name.

"Not likely! He rarely travels under it, and if he is here for a rest he is probably trav-elling incognito. He's evidently going to golf. What fun it would be to play him a round! I must get this scarab ring off and keep it hidden. If he saw it he would be sure to recognise it."

Her thoughts broke off as the object of her attention pushed back his chair and rose.

It was indeed Blake, and as his eyes swept the surrounding tables on his way out, he looked full at Yvonne, who returned the glance coolly. Inwardly her heart was going like a trip-hammer, but as Blake passed on without any sign of recognition, she heaved a sigh of relief.

"So far, so good!" she muttered. "But I think I will follow you, Mr. Blake. I really must find out if you are staying here under your own name, and what is the number of your rooms. It should be interesting, if opportunity, permits, to make an examination of your luggage."

Yvonne rose and passed out after Blake. As she entered the lounge, she saw him ahead of her, and evidently bound in the direction of the lift. She hurried on in his wake, and as the door of the lift swung open, she heard him say:

"Number sixty!"

It was not part of her idea now that she had so fortunately heard the number of his room to enter the lift and ascend with him, but as the boy looked at her expectantly, she entered in order to avoid any cause for suspicion on Blake's part.

Blake was wrapped in thought, and beyond removing his hat, gave no indication that he was aware of her presence.

Yvonne gave her number, 63, which was on the same floor as Blake's room, and glanced surreptitiously at the detective as the lift shot up. She was wondering what he could be thinking of, but at that moment it was nothing more serious than golf, and she had no need to be cautious, for as yet Blake hadn't the faintest notion of her identity.

Blake stood aside as the lift stopped, and as she entered 63, Yvonne saw him enter a door a few yards down, and knew that No. 60 was, indeed, very close to her.

She stood just inside her door, and a few minutes later heard his door re-open and close, accompanied by the unmistakable rattle of golf-clubs.

"I was right," she muttered; "but I must be careful. However, I have the advantage, for I know him, and I'm positive he hasn't the faintest idea as to who I am!"

She approached the window and gave an exclamation, as, far out in the bay, just com-ing around the point, was a graceful white yacht.

Captain Vaughan had kept to the schedule she had prepared, but so far out was the yacht, that she could not see what means he had taken to hide her identity.

Yvonne turned hurriedly, and, reaching for the black bag which had come in useful before lunch, she dragged it over beside her. Opening it, she drew out a small compli-cated-looking instrument, which the initiated would have pronounced as being a very recent and very complete model of the wireless telephone.[21]

---

[21] "The wireless telephone is a tested possibility, and has a future, according to the experts. ~The Skipper.

Graves, as previously arranged, was seated on the bridge of the disguised *Fleur-de-Lys* with a similar instrument, and after attaching the wires to a series of dry batteries in the black bag Yvonne set to work.

First she opened the window and set the machine firmly on the sill. Then, after a few delicate manipulations, she lifted up a peculiarly-shaped receiver and waited.

For some minutes nothing occurred, but at the end of that time a faint, clicking buzz came to her ears. She at once pressed a black button several times in rapid succession, and a moment later the message began coming; first very faint, but finally growing in volume until the measured syllables were very distinct.

It was Graves sending his message, and as she jotted it down she heard:

"Hallo! Hallo! Are you there?"

Yvonne quickly answered:

"Yes; go ahead. The connection is good."

"We have finished everything," came back Graves. "The yacht is perfectly changed in appearance. You would never know her from the exterior, but of course her interior is unaltered."

"Good!" replied Yvonne, not daring to make too much noise. "Now listen carefully, uncle. I have secured rooms which are perfect for my purpose, but my first idea that you should come ashore and stay at the hotel has been changed. Firstly, the hotel is full; and secondly, who do you suppose is staying here?"

"I don't know. Who?"

"Sexton Blake."

Yvonne could not help laughing as an agitated clicking noise came over the expanse of water and registered on her machine. Finally, she made out Graves asking:

"Are you joking?"

"Certainly not."

"Then as far as I am concerned I'm quite prepared to remain on the yacht. But you won't go ahead while he is there, will you?"

"Of course! I won't let his presence scare me off."

"You're mad, I tell you," replied Graves.

"Perhaps; but now listen. I have measured the distance from my sitting-room window to the water below. It is forty-five feet from the sill to the bottom, and from the water-line on the wire I judge it to be forty feet to the surface. That gives you five feet at low tide, for it was low tide when I measured. That means there will be plenty of depth for my purpose, and as there are no rocks there we should experience no difficulty. Prepare about sixty feet of that silken rope you will find in the store-room next to the laboratory, and have a boat ready to come at any time. Send Hendricks with the boat, for as there is no window directly beneath me I will need him to climb up by the rope, as I am not strong enough to do the lowering. Have the oars muffled, and hold yourselves in readiness to act at once."

"Very well, but I still say you are mad to go ahead while Blake is there."

"Never mind that. Leave that part to me. Tell Anna, my maid, to prepare the cabin next to mine to receive a lady. And don't forget what I said. I will call you up at six o'clock tonight and would advise Captain Vaughan not to anchor in too close, for Blake might recognise some part of the yacht. He is so uncannily sharp, you know."

With this Yvonne ended the conversation, and, removing the machine from the sill, she replaced it in the black bag. Carefully locking this, she put it away, and then, picking up a bag of golf clubs, she made her way to the lift, humming gaily as though she were incapable of anything deep, and above all things of putting into operation one of the most daring plots which had ever been perpetrated on society.

The Third Chapter
A Game of Golf—Yvonne Acts

SEXTON Blake had come to the Traders' Bay Hotel for rest and quiet, and, as Yvonne had imagined, was travelling incognito. At present he gloried in the name of Mr. Barker, and was vaguely supposed to "do something in the City."

An old friend, Colonel Alliston, had promised to join him, and Blake was looking forward to a pleasant round of golf. At the last moment, however, the colonel had been compelled to give up the trip, and Blake, his arrangements all made, had left Tinker in charge of affairs at Baker Street and had come on alone.

He was looking forward to a solitary round during the afternoon, and was waiting until the foursomes had started when he saw another solitary player approaching the links.

Travers Bentley, in his anxiety to get things well started for his guests, had been hustling about arranging here, smoothing over there, and making himself generally agreeable. He noticed Blake sitting alone, and smilingly inquired if he were waiting for his partner.

"No," replied Blake. "I'm playing alone this afternoon."

"Ah! Quite so—quite so! And you, Comtesse de Rastonet," he said to Yvonne, who came up at that moment, "are you playing alone?"

Yvonne nodded.

"Yes," she replied briefly, and, turning, beckoned to a caddie.

"Permit me to introduce you, Mr. Barker," whispered Bentley. "You can then play together."

"All right!" drawled Blake lazily. "I don't mind." And a moment later the officious Bentley had effected the introduction.

The Comtesse de Rastonet was delighted to play with Mr. Barker, and after some good-natured argument regarding the handicap Yvonne drove off.

It is not essential to the story to give in detail that game of golf played so strangely between Yvonne and the unsuspecting Blake. Like everything else, Blake went at it in dead earnest, and he found he needed all his skill, for Yvonne played a very consistent game.

One conversation, however, should be recorded as having some slight bearing on the story. This conversation took place when they were walking from the third hole, and arose from a remark made by Yvonne.

"Do you do everything as seriously as you play golf, Mr. Barker?" she asked, with a smile.

"I suppose so," replied Blake, also smiling. "One must, nowadays, you know."

"True," she laughed; "but one would almost think being pitted against women was not unusual to you, Mr. Barker. You seem to respect their prowess, no matter how poorly they play."

"You are right, comtesse," replied Blake. "I have played the game very often against the opposite sex."

"And do you always win?" asked Yvonne archly.

"Is that a fair question?" smiled Blake.

"I was curious to know."

"I'm afraid I must decline to answer. Perhaps we had better leave it to the result of the game you and I are playing against each other."

"Ah, yes," she said gaily, "the game you and I are playing against each other now. And do you think you will win this game, Mr. Barker?"

"If I do it won't be for lack of a worthy opponent," said Blake gallantly. And with that they continued the game.

It may be stated here that Blake won the game by a very narrow margin, but he did not know that when speaking of the game his charming opponent was referring to a very different contest, of whose existence he was not yet aware.

It was almost six when Yvonne returned to the hotel, and it would have surprised her late partner had he seen her movements on reaching her rooms. She all at once brought the wireless telephone into use again, and as the hands pointed to six o'clock she got into communication with Graves on the yacht, which now lay at anchor in the bay a mile or more from the shore.

"Leave the yacht at midnight, and bring four men. Row right up to the cliff, as it will be very calm tonight. You will know under which window to stop as I will leave my light low and the window open the whole way. Against the light you will be able to see it. Don't fail."

She removed the instrument, and, after putting it away, began to dress for dinner. Then she descended to the lounge, stopping on the way to examine the guest-list. She discovered that the Duchess of Foreland occupied a room on the same floor as herself, and she smiled with satisfaction.

"That simplifies matters somewhat," she muttered, as she entered the lounge. "I don't imagine she stays up late, and if the boat arrives by one o'clock I should be ready for them. I must keep my eye on Sexton Blake, though. He didn't seem to suspect anything this afternoon, however."

She moved in to dinner with the others, and found that Blake had already taken his seat.

After dinner Yvonne ascended at once to her room, passing on the way the room occupied by the duchess.

For two hours she sat in the darkness peering out to sea, where the lights of the *Fleur-de-Lys* could be seen. At ten-thirty she rose and descended once more to the lounge.

Very few guests were there, and after a careful look about the balcony and the drawing-room Yvonne once more went up to her room. She had failed to see the duchess about, and was confident she had gone to bed.

For an hour and a half longer she waited, and then, slipping a dark cloak over her evening gown, she rose and opened the black bag. From it she took the steel tube into which she had packed the tube of vapour in the laboratory on the yacht. Unscrewing the car, she drew out the tube, and, holding it carefully, reached again into the bag.

This time she drew forth a tiny bulb and syringe with a thin, hollow-threaded screw on the bottom. This she slowly and carefully screwed through the centre of the rubber cork in the phial, and when this had been completed, she concealed the phial in the voluminous sleeve of her cloak. Then, turning the light lower, and opening the window wide, she softly turned the handle of the door leading into the corridor.

The lights had been lowered, and everything seemed still. Through the transom over the door of No. 60 she could see a light, and knew that Blake had not yet retired; but even as she looked the light went out. Closing her door behind her, Yvonne crept softly along the thickly-carpeted corridor, stopping from time to time to listen.

No sound broke the quiet, however, and she kept on until she reached the door of the room occupied by the duchess. Not more than five seconds did she stand before the door, but that five seconds was long enough for her to slip the phial out of her sleeve, insert the mouth of the syringe in the keyhole of the door, and to press gently on the bulb, the result being that one of the strongest and most effective narcotics known was injected into the room, and, in the form of a powerful vapour, was seeking every corner and crack of the apartment.

So strong was it that only an unforeseen accident would prevent its action; and, once under its influence, the strongest man living would sleep as one dead for several hours. Yvonne had made it particularly, though not dangerously, strong, as, being summer, she had taken into account the possibility of an open window through which some of the vapour was bound to pass.

As soon as she was satisfied the spray had done its work she sped softly back to her own apartments, and slipped through the door.

It was now just past midnight, and Yvonne, after returning the phial to its steel case, sat down at the open window, and began to wait patiently for the arrival of the boat from the yacht. Although the yacht was only a mile or so from the shore, Yvonne knew the trip would take some time, as even with muffled oars, they would be compelled to row slowly in order to avoid making a noise.

It was, in fact, nearly one before a very soft whistle came from below, and, peering through the window, she could just make out a dark patch on the water below.

She made no reply to the whistle, but drew out the thin wire which she had used earlier in the day, and dropped the leaden end over the sill.

Three sharp tugs, and she began pulling upwards, to reveal on its arrival a thick, strong, silken rope tied to the sinker. Untying this, she dropped the wire, and moved across to the door, which she had securely locked. Then, with the fingers of an expert, she knotted one end of the cord around the handle, and returned to the window.

She gave the cord three jerks, and a moment later it grew taut under a heavy weight. A few seconds later a dark figure appeared, and climbed softly over the sill, and dropped to the floor beside her.

"You did that very well, Hendricks!" whispered Yvonne. "Is uncle there?"

"Yes, mademoiselle," replied the mate. "There are three of the sailors as well."

"Good! Signal down for one of the sailors to follow you, and then we will go ahead!"

Hendricks did so, and, with as much silence as the mate, one of the sailors scrambled up the rope, and dropped inside.

"Now, wait here!" went on Yvonne, in low tones. "I will slip along, and spring back the lock. As soon as I have got her ready, I will return, and you can carry her out."

Hendricks and the sailor nodded; and Yvonne, reaching once more into the black bag for a small steel instrument, which looked not unlike a giant spider, opened the door softly, and sped along the silent corridor to the door where she had used the spray not long before.

The fact that the key was on the inside of the lock presented some difficulties, but under the persuasive powers of the steel instrument the bolt slipped back, and she stepped inside.

The room was in darkness, and Yvonne felt for the button of the electric light. Turning this on, she then lit the gas, after which she turned it low, as in her own room, and extinguished the electric.

It was a large, luxuriously-furnished bed-room, and in the big brass bed against the further wall could be seen the outline of a figure. Softly approaching it, Yvonne bent down, and boldly lifted one hand which lay on the coverlet. The pulse was faint but steady, and she knew the vapour had done its work well.

She worked rapidly then, and five minutes later the unconscious Duchess of Foreland lay fully dressed and wrapped in a heavy cloak. As she finished her work, Yvonne, after peering cautiously up and down the corridor, returned to her own apartments, and signed to Hendricks and the sailor, who crept after her until the three stood once more in the room of the duchess.

They evidently knew what they had to do, for, without waiting for instructions, they lifted up the heavily-cloaked figure, and, guided by Yvonne, carried it back to Yvonne's sitting room.

Hendricks then drew up the end of the silken rope, and, after tying it securely under the arms of the duchess, he and the sailor lowered her carefully into the waiting boat. Graves and the other sailors untied the rope, and took care of the burden in the boat, while Yvonne sped back to the duchess's room, followed by Hendricks.

There Yvonne went through every particle of the luggage, and when she had finished a sparkling heap of gold, silver, diamonds, emeralds, pearls, and other gems lay on the dresser before her.

These she unceremoniously piled into Hendricks' pocket, and signed to him to return to the sitting-room. This he did while Yvonne turned out the light and brought the steel instrument into play again in order to lock the door.

When she had finished, the Duchess of Foreland had disappeared from her bed-room, together with every belonging of value which she possessed; but otherwise the room showed nothing suspicious in any way.

Hendricks and the sailor followed the duchess into the boat, and untying the rope from the handle of the door, Yvonne dropped it after them. A soft splash told her the boat was getting underway; and, returning the wire and steel instrument to her bag, she closed the window, turned out the light, and entered the bed-room, where, ten minutes later, she lay asleep as though no mysterious midnight events had taken place.

The Fourth Chapter
Three Mysterious Disappearances—Sexton Blake at Work

MR. Travers Bentley was so delighted with the initial success of the opening of the Traders' Bay Hotel that on the morning of the second day he was already preparing a glowing prospectus which would make the readers of it anxious to invest their money under the guidance of such a successful financier as Mr. Bentley. He already had a rough draught of the estimated revenues and profits of the new hotel—based on the supposition that as at present every room would be occupied—and was putting down the alluring figures which would dazzle the would-be investor, when Forsythe entered the office, looking even gloomier than ever.

"Good heavens, Henry," Bentley exclaimed, "if I didn't know you so well, I'd say that your gloomy countenance accurately reflected the condition of your mind!"

"You'd make a pretty correct guess if you did," replied Forsythe, sinking into a chair. "I've had terrible news!"

"Terrible news!" exclaimed Bentley. "Why, what do you mean, man?"

"As I came down the stairs just now I saw one of the maids come tearing along with a face as white as the apron she wore. I caught her by the arm, and asked her what was the matter."

"Yes, yes; go on!" cried Bentley.

"She says that during the night the Duchess of Foreland has disappeared!"

"What!" cried Bentley agitatedly. "You're not joking?"

"Do I look like a humorous individual?" asked Forsythe drily. "But look here, Bentley, this is serious! If it gets noised about the hotel we are done for! All her friends and relatives would swoop down on us like a hurricane, and the hotel would be ruined almost before it got started."

"And things were going so beautifully, too!" groaned Bentley, looking regretfully at his interrupted calculations. "But what have you done? Surely there must be some mistake, Henry?"

"I'm afraid not," replied his partner. "I went to the duchess's apartments with the maid, and found the duchess's own maid in hysterics. I thought at first that the duchess had gone to the bath, or was out for a walk. But what do you think I found?"

"Well?"

"I found the door of her bed-room and sitting-room locked on the inside, with the keys in the locks!"

"But how did you gain admittance?"

"You know that all the bath-rooms in the building have doors opening into the corridors, which are kept locked, and no key of which is given to a guest. Well, I got into the apartments by the housekeeper's master-key. It seems that when the duchess's maid went to call her this morning she got no answer. This alarmed her, and when she found the door locked she hunted up the hotel maid for that floor. The hotel maid got a chair, and peeped in over the transom, but when she saw the bed empty she started for me. As I said, I went back, and, by the use of the housekeeper's key, got in through the bath-room. It's a mystery to me. There was everything apparently undisturbed, but the duchess, with the clothes she wore yesterday, was missing!"

"Was anything else touched?" asked Bentley hoarsely.

"Apparently not; but I don't know yet. Her maid is trying between hysterical spasms to make an inventory."

"My heavens! Henry, this is awful! Did you impress upon them the need for silence?"

"Certainly. I told them we should find the duchess had gone for an early walk; but you can't get away from the fact that the doors were locked and the keys on the inside."

"How about the window?" asked Bentley, pacing the floor in his agitation.

"I thought of that. It was down a few inches at the top, but if the duchess had had any idea of committing suicide by throwing herself out, we would have found it open. She is middle-aged, and stout, and it would take a very athletic woman to get out of the window and balance herself on the sill while she closed the window after her. However, I have sent Gregory, the head porter, to make a thorough examination of the rocks below; but I don't expect anything."

"We must get a detective at once," said Bentley decisively. "This is a terrible thing, and too deep for us. It we don't clear the matter up in a day or two it is bound to get out, and every paper will be full of it. We must keep the servants from talking, at all cost."

"I've seen to that; but——"

Forsythe broke off as the door flew open, and the duchess's maid dashed in with a terror-stricken face.

"Robbery, robbery, murder," she shrieked, wringing her hands helplessly.

"See here," said Bentley sternly. "Calm yourself, and tell me what is wrong."

"I have looked through her Grace's things, and everything—everything is gone," cried the maid, breaking into sobs. "Her diamonds, her pearls, her rings—everything is gone.

Oh, my poor mistress—my poor mistress! I know she has been murdered! What shall I do? What shall I do?"

"Collect yourself, my girl," said Bentley sternly, putting his hand on her shoulder. "Now, tell me, is this the truth?"

"Yes, yes," she wailed. "Everything is gone."

"Send for the housekeeper, Henry," said Bentley quickly. "Have her take this young woman and keep her out of the way until she gets quiet. If she goes on this way the whole hotel will know what has happened."

Forsythe did as his partner bade him, and a moment later the housekeeper appeared.

"Take this young woman," ordered Bentley, "and keep her in your quarters until she grows calm. In the meantime see that no talk is made by the servants about this affair. The duchess will return all right. Lock the door of her bathroom, and give me the key."

"Very well, sir, I'll see that no talk is made," replied the housekeeper, and forthwith led the weeping young woman away.

"This is more serious than I thought," remarked Bentley, carefully closing the door. "I felt positive at first that the duchess had only gone for an early walk, and that in some way, perhaps by the slamming of her door, the bolt had slipped forward. But if her jewellery is all gone, it means a plot of some kind. We must have a detective at once."

"Whom do you suggest?"

"I don't know. We don't want Scotland Yard meddling just yet. And then, again, it must be kept from the papers, at all cost. No, it must be a private detective, and a good one, who can clear matters up in a short time."

"How about the man Sexton Blake? He's high-priced, but they say he's a wizard."

"Good! We couldn't do better. I'll send a wire off to him at once, asking him to come down without delay, and to name his own figure."

He sat down as he spoke, and wrote an urgent message to Blake, and, calling a boy, despatched it immediately. He never dreamed that as he did so the tall man who sauntered out with a bag of golf clubs was the very man whom he most desired to see.

After the despatch of the telegram he and Forsythe ascended to the duchess's rooms, and made a minute examination of everything; but to their eyes nothing was revealed.

"I guess we can't do anything until Blake turns up," remarked Forsythe gloomily.

"No, I guess not. All we can do is to hope she'll return all right. We'd better leave the rooms just as they are, in case Sexton Blake desires to make an examination."

With this conclusion they passed through the bathroom and locked the door behind them.

It was very hard for even the optimistic Bentley to keep a smiling countenance before his guests that day. One or two old ladies with a desire to impress their fellows that they were on intimate terms with the Duchess of Foreland remarked rather audibly, that they "wondered if the dear duchess was feeling fatigued after the journey," but Bentley succeeded in staving off these occasional curious ones, and the day passed without the truth becoming known.

As night drew on the partners began to grow nervous. No reply had come as yet to their urgent telegram to Sexton Blake, and as Mr. Barker retired to rest at an early hour, he did not that night receive the telegram which came about ten o'clock.

Yvonne played a very consistent game

Tinker was just in time to see a white arm disappear over the sill.

"Robbery, robbery, murder!" she shrieked

If Forsythe had known, as he placed it in the rack, that "Mr. Barker" was Sexton Blake, and that the telegram was a copy of the one sent by Bentley to London, which had been repeated back to Blake by the astonished Tinker, it is safe to say that the detective would have had little sleep that night. But Fate rules at times with a baffling autocracy, and seemed determined to sport about at the expense of Messrs. Bentley and Forsythe for some little time. At least, that was the natural conclusion which those two harassed gentlemen came to on the following morning, when an even worse shock shook their equanimity than on the previous day.

It was very early, and Forsythe was about in the vague hopes of hearing something about the missing duchess, or, in any event, receiving a reply from Sexton Blake. He was doomed to disappointment, however, and was sitting gloomily at his desk awaiting Bentley's appearance, when the head porter rushed in with another agitated individual behind him.

"Please, sir," gasped the porter, "something terrible has happened during the night."

"What?" almost shrieked Forsythe, half-rising. "What is it? Quick, man!"

"Please, sir," gasped the terrified porter, "this is the Marquis of Rondel's valet, and he says his master has disappeared during the night."

Forsythe fell back speechless, and his jaw dropped. At that moment Bentley entered, and his partner flapped his hand feebly in the direction of the porter and the valet.

"What is it?" asked Bentley, coming to a stop.

Again Forsythe flapped his hand, while the valet broke in with the statement the porter had already made.

Bentley sank into the nearest chair and tried to speak calmly.

"You say the Marquis of Rondel has disappeared during the night?" he said, with an effort. "Are you sure of what you say?"

"Positively, sir," answered the valet. "When I went to call him this morning I got no answer, and, finding the door locked, I got the housekeeper. We entered through the door leading to his bath-room, and found he was gone. His clothes which he wore yesterday are missing also, sir, and I can't find any of his valuables."

"My heavens!" gasped Bentley, trying to collect his scattered wits. "Here, you, Gregory," he said finally, "take this valet and keep him in your rooms, until I send for him. Then return here!"

As the porter took the agitated valet by the arm and forcibly led him out, Bentley turned to Forsythe.

"Has nothing come from Sexton Blake yet?"

"Not a word. I got up early particularly to find out."

"Then we must send another urgent message," went on Bentley, "and if we don't get an answer in a couple of hours, we will have to wire somebody else. This is getting serious, and unless we take radical steps, we can't keep it from the papers for long. The Duchess of Foreland and the Marquis of Rondel are too prominent to disappear without causing comment. Come in!" This as a knock came at the door, and, in answer, it was pushed open to admit the tall man in golfing costume known at the hotel as "Mr. Barker." Carefully closing the door behind him, he approached the harassed partners.

"Good morning, gentlemen!" he said, smiling slightly.

"Good morning!" echoed Bentley. "What can we do for you, Mr. —er—Barker? I trust you are not contemplating leaving us so soon?"

"Oh, no, indeed!" laughed Blake.

Then he suddenly dropped his voice and said:

"What is the trouble, gentlemen? Why have you wired to London to Sexton Blake?"

"Trouble? Wired to Sexton Blake?" gasped both partners at once. "Why? What do you mean, Mr. Barker?"

For answer Blake thrust his hand in his pocket and drew out the telegram which Tinker had forwarded on to him.

"Listen, gentlemen," he said, "and tell me if you sent this. 'Sexton Blake, Baker Street, London. Come at once, if possible. Urgent. Prepared pay any figure. Bentley and Forsythe.'"

Bentley glanced up sharply as Blake finished and thrust the telegram back in his pocket.

"How did you get hold of that? Good heavens! You are not really——"

"Sexton Blake, at your service," smiled Blake, bowing. "But come, gentlemen, let me hear what is troubling you. This telegram was repeated back here to me by my assistant in London, and had not I gone to bed so early I would have received it last night. However, perhaps I can be of some assistance to you."

Both of the partners reflected the relief which they felt at having Blake so opportunely at hand, and Forsythe signed to Bentley to tell the detective the facts.

Rapidly he sketched the details of the strange disappearance of the Duchess of Foreland two nights previously, and of the equally mysterious disappearance of the Marquis of Rondel the preceding night. When he had finished, Blake looked grave.

"It is a most remarkable state of affairs," he remarked thoughtfully, "but let us take up the points one by one, and then I should like to make an examination of their apartments."

Bentley indicated his willingness to answer any questions, and after lighting a cigar, Blake leaned back and smoked in silence for a few moments.

"The first point to be considered," he said finally, "is this. Have you any reason to suspect any of the guests of the hotel?"

"No, I have thought of that," replied Bentley, "but they all seem to be perfectly genuine holiday-makers. Of course, you know fully half of them are well-known society people and beyond suspicion."

"Possibly—possibly," replied Blake. "However, we will leave that point for the moment, and go on to the next. Two nights ago you say the duchess disappeared?"

Bentley nodded.

"And last night the Marquis of Rondel disappeared?"

Bentley again nodded.

"In both cases we find a similar condition of affairs?" went on Blake, preparing to tick the points off on his fingers. "Firstly, we find all the doors locked and the keys in the locks on the inside. Secondly, the beds were upset, indicating that in both cases they had already retired for the night. Thirdly, the windows were closed, with the exception of the top sash being lowered a few inches. Fourthly, you say there are no signs of a struggle. Fifthly, in each case they seem to have worn the clothes they had on during the previous day. Sixthly practically all their valuables disappeared with them, and lastly, you have been able to find not the slightest trace."

"That is the case exactly," murmured Bentley.

"Have any guests left the hotel during the past two days?"

"None."

"Have any given notice to leave?"

"None that I know of. Do you know of any, Forsythe?"

That gloomy individual shook his head.

"No; there have been none."

"If any do so, let me know at once," remarked Blake. "In the meantime, I desire to send a telegram to London at once, and then I should like to make an examination of the rooms. I trust they have not been disturbed?"

"No; we left them just as they were in case you should desire to see them."

"Good!" exclaimed Blake.

A boy entered at the moment, and Blake hurriedly wrote a telegram to Tinker, instructing him to come down at once and bring Pedro with him. After the boy had departed with it, he turned to the partners.

"Now, gentlemen, I am ready; but first let me impress upon you one thing. I presume you desire to keep the state of affairs from reaching your other guests or getting into the press?"

"Rather!" cried Bentley. "It would knock us into a cocked hat at once!"

"Then let me impress upon you the fact that no one but yourselves must know my identity. It is essential that you should remember this."

"You can trust us to do that," replied Forsythe grimly. "Only solve this mystery, that is all we ask."

"We have seen the effect, and know that it must have a cause," returned Blake briefly, "and as the cause is never less than the effect, we must, judging from the importance of the effect, look for a fairly powerful cause. And now, gentlemen, let us move upstairs."

The two partners and Blake ascended by the stairs until they reached the rooms of the missing duchess. There they paused a moment until Forsythe had unlocked the door leading into the bath-room, where they passed in closing the door carefully behind them.

Bentley led the way into the sitting-room, and paused, looking inquiringly at Blake. The latter, however, kept right on to the bed-room, and after a cursory glance at the bed walked to the window. There he drew out his powerful pocket glass, and inch by inch, point by point, proceeded to examine every particle of the window-frame and sill, working in a series of imaginary squares. Finally he desisted, and, throwing up the sash, leaned out.

Directly below him appeared a tumbled mass of jagged rocks on which the water broke in white-rimmed regularity. Over to the right, however, the wall of the hotel rested on the edge of the cliff which dropped sheer into a quiet, miniature cove, and for some moments Blake contemplated this point.

"I presume you have examined the rocks below?" he asked, turning to the partners, who had stood just inside the door, while he worked.

They both nodded.

"Yes, Gregory, the head porter did so," replied Bentley.

"By the way," went on Blake, "does the window of the marquis's room give out on to the sea front?"

Bentley looked inquiringly at Forsythe.

"No," replied the latter. "It has the gardens in front."

"Ah! And whose rooms, might I ask, are those over that miniature cove to the right here?"

Forsythe walked to the window and looked out.

"Let me see," he muttered; "that would be sixty-three. I just forget. Oh, no, I remember now! A lady occupies them. The Comtesse de Rastonet."

"Ah! I remember her," replied Blake, nodding. "A charming woman. I played golf with her on the first day of my arrival. Now let us examine the door."

Blake moved across, and, turning the key in the door, swung it open a few inches.

"You had better keep guard out in the corridor," he said, turning to Bentley. "If any curious people are about, you can casually remark that I am fixing the door."

Bentley nodded, and hurried out, while Blake once more brought the powerful glass into use.

First he drew out the key and examined it minutely. As he finished, he gave a grunt, and dropped it in his pocket. Then he turned his attention to the bolt and keyhole, and after some ten minutes' careful scrutiny, he rose. Signing to Bentley to return, he closed the door, and turned his attention to the carpet. Both of the partners stared in surprise as Blake dropped to his knees, and began going over every inch of it in a series of imaginary squares such as he had used on the window.

For a full half-hour he worked without result, until he reached the part of the floor which was directly under the gas-jet. There he picked up the burnt end of a wax vesta, but nothing else rewarded his search, and with the remainder of the vesta in his hand, he rose and turned to the partners.

"What kind of matches do you provide in the hotel?" he asked.

"Why—er—just the ordinary wood safety matches, with our name on the box," replied Bentley. "Why do you ask?"

"Do you use any wax vestas at all?" asked Blake, disregarding his question.

Bentley shook his head and turned to Forsythe.

"Have we any of those?"

"No, none in the place that I know of," replied Forsythe.

Blake nodded.

"Very well, gentlemen. Let us go now to the rooms of the marquis. I have finished here, but for the present I think you had better leave these rooms just as they are."

Bentley nodded, and led the way to the rooms of the Marquis of Rondel, which were on the floor below, and there Blake went through practically the same performance which he had gone through in the duchess's rooms.

First he made a minute examination of the window, then the door, and finally the floor. As he had done in the other case, he saw something on the key which caused him to drop it in his pocket, and on the floor he found not one wax vesta, but two—one being barely burnt, indicating that it had gone out almost at once on being lighted, and the second burnt half-way down in a similar manner to the one he had found in the duchess's room. Putting these in his pocket, he walked to the window and gazed out at the gardens below. Nothing of interest rewarded his gaze, however, and he turned back to the partners.

"Well?" they asked eagerly. "Have you found any clue?"

"It is too early to say one thing or another yet," replied Blake, with a shrug. "One thing I can tell you is that in my opinion the perpetrator of the deed is residing in the hotel, but the fact that both victims have been removed indicates that there are powerful accomplices on the outside. However, I wish to think matters over for a bit, and will let you know as soon as I have hit on anything. After lunch I will start to work on the outside; but if anything occurs worth reporting before then, I will be in my room. Let me impress upon you the necessity for keeping my identity secret, and if any guest gives intimation of leaving, let me know at once. As I said, the effect is important, and I am more than ever convinced that there is a powerful cause behind it. That is what we must find, and only logical mathematical analysis and deduction will put us on the right road. Now, gentlemen, keep up your courage, and don't let anything get out."

With this sage remark, Blake left them, and made his way to his room. There he sank into a big chair, and, after filling his pipe, began to marshal mentally one by one the points which he had discovered.

First, he made a further examination of the two keys, and then of the three wax vestas, after which he placed the whole lot carefully in his portmanteau. For two hours he smoked in silence, hunched up in the familiar attitude, the while his keen mind searched and probed about like a surgeon's knife, discarding here, picking up there, until finally he should hit on something which would meet his deductions and coincide with the result. Although he had expressed to Bentley the opinion that the perpetrator was residing within the hotel, he did not confine himself to that one hypothesis in his analysis, but rather left his mind open to receive any and every hypothesis which the analysis should suggest.

His pipe had gone out, and he was feeling for a match when a hurried knock came at the door, and Bentley entered with blanched cheeks.

"What is it?" said Blake sharply, sitting up.

"By heavens!" gasped Bentley. "I can't imagine what fiendish power is working against us."

"Well, well," snapped Blake impatiently.

"Lord Cray, one of our most distinguished guests, went to play golf early this morning," jerked Bentley. "He promised to be back by eleven, but did not turn up. Inquiries were made, and a boy sent over to the links to see what had detained him. The caddie said he left at half-past ten, and walked back by way of the shore. That is two hours ago, and although a thorough search has been made, we can't find the slightest trace of him. Mr. Blake, can't you do something? It means ruin—ruin—ruin!"

Blake looked very grave when he heard Bentley's gasped out story of the sudden vanishing of Lord Cray. That was the third in as many days, and on top of the other two it certainly looked serious. He had realised a strong force must be behind matters, but only the most reckless and the most daring would kidnap a man in broad daylight.

All Bentley could tell him was that Lord Cray had apparently vanished into thin air; but Blake knew that was nonsense, and that a very material cause must be at the bottom of it all.

He went downstairs at once, and, after a hurried luncheon, and a warning word of caution to Bentley and Forsythe, he slipped a pair of powerful opera-glasses into his pocket, and left the hotel.

His first destination was the golf-links, and without one look aside, he strode on there with long paces. After a few minutes' search, he found the caddie, who had seen Lord Cray depart for the hotel, but that youth could only repeat the story he had already heard from Bentley. Lord Cray had left the links at ten-thirty, and had taken the path along the sea.

It was less than a mile from the links to the hotel, but the sea-path ran through thick, stunted woods, which ended only at the beach edge. Blake, after questioning the boy, walked slowly along the path supposed to have been taken by the missing peer, but as he reached a slight eminence he pulled up, and looked about him.

Behind him stretched the really fine links, with the clubhouse in the far distance; on his right were the woods with the hotel towering at the edge of the cliff, three-quarters of a mile away; to his left stretched the primitive woods with nothing to break their line, while in front rolled the deep blue bay, with a white, graceful yacht lying at anchor far out.

It truly was a delightful scene, but Blake had then no eyes for its beauty. His mind was concentrated with all its intensity on the mysterious problem which had been presented. As he stood there on the little hill, he marshalled up the facts and drew his mental circle, which enclosed all the possibilities so far as he could see them.

Firstly, what method had been used to remove Lord Cray as suddenly as had apparently happened? In the present day scheme of things, an aeroplane would be possible, but this notion he scouted at once. No flying-machine could soar so near the hotel without immediately being seen by dozens of people. Then there was the possibility of a motor, but the only way of approach to the sea-path was by way of the links. That seemed almost impossible without being seen; but, of course, it must be counted as a possibility until it should be proven otherwise.

Then, what remained? It would be possible to waylay a man in the shelter of the woods, and carry him off through the thick woods to the left, through which a way might run to the main road, or a better method than all would be by the sea, for right at that point the beach sloped gently, and was entirely hidden from view until one was right upon it.

The last two theories seemed to him the most tenable, and if either had been used, it seemed a foregone conclusion that they would proceed to the left—if the attack had been made on foot they would have carried their victim, or if a boat had been used, it could slip around the jutting point right ahead, and be safe from view.

But stay! How about that yacht out there in the bay? Whose was she? Did she belong to any of the guests in the hotel? If not, what was she doing there? Blake remembered that he had seen her there ever since the first day of his arrival, but he did not remember having seen any communication at all between the yacht and the shore.

That was not conclusive evidence to Blake, however, and as the thought occurred, he descended from his point of outlook, and made his way through the trees to the sandy beach.

On reaching it he sunk down in the shelter of some bushes, and, pulling out his field glasses, trained them on the yacht. Long and silently he looked at her, studying her thoroughly from bow to stern and from water-line to the tips of her two masts and funnel.

So well had Captain Vaughan disguised her, however, that net even Blake's sharp eyes could identify her as the *Fleur-de-Lys*, although the whole outline seemed vaguely familiar to him.

"I suppose she looks like some yacht I have seen," he muttered, "but I can't place her. I must make inquiries at the hotel and see what they know about her. I'll just make my way back to that eminence I left, and have a look at the hotel through the glasses. If I remember rightly, I can get a good view of that little cove under the windows of the comtesse and from here it looks as though it would be almost in a line with the yacht."

He rose quietly, and made his way back to the eminence where, dropping flat to the ground, he trained the glasses on the part of the hotel overlooking the sea. Slowly Blake swept the glasses over the little cove, and then gradually brought them to bear on the windows of the rooms lately occupied by the Duchess of Foreland.

From there he swept them from room to room, and from floor to floor, until finally they came to rest on the sitting-room window of the Comtesse de Rastonet.

He was just about to return to his scrutiny of the little cove, when he saw something which arrested his movement, and caused him to keep them on the comtesse's window. As he looked, he saw a woman approach the window and throw it up. Nothing extraordinary in that, to be sure; but it was her subsequent actions which engrossed Blake.

After lifting the window, she walked back, only to reappear a moment later with a peculiar-looking contrivance in her hands. This she calmly proceeded to settle firmly on the windowsill, and the puzzled frown on Blake's brow relaxed as he saw what it was.

"Good heavens!" he muttered excitedly. "What on earth does the Comtesse de Rastenet want with a wireless telephone, and with whom is she communicating? The only visible thing is the yacht. I wonder if it is possible that she is communicating with it, and why. Why? Why? It seems, my charming friend, that your actions are quite extraordinary enough to bear investigation. I wonder if you are, by any chance the member of the conspiracy who resides in the hotel. I must wire at once for my wireless telephone, and tonight I must contrive to dine with you."

He broke off as he saw the comtesse remove the machine and close the window, and then rising from his place of concealment, Blake made his way back to the hotel very thoughtfully.

His first act on arriving there was to wire to London for a wireless telephone to be shipped at once to Mr. Barker at the Traders' Bay Hotel. He knew it was useless sending word to Tinker, for the lad would already be on his way with Pedro.

After that, he despatched Forsythe himself to inquire at the railway station, and get full information regarding all the passengers who had departed that day. He hoped for little in that direction, but no stone must be left unturned. Meanwhile, he sought Bentley in the private office, and found that gentleman full of eager questions.

"Hold on, my friend," smiled Blake. "I think I know a little more than I did, but I am to be the questioner, not you. Firstly, tell me: Do you know anything about that yacht lying at anchor out in the bay?"

Bentley looked somewhat surprised.

"No; I haven't given her much thought. She's been there for three or four days, but as far as I know, no one has come ashore. I suppose she is just cruising about the coast."

"H'm! Then, as far as you know, there is nobody in the hotel who would have any connection with her?"

"Certainly not! As I told you, nobody has landed."

"I see. By the way," remarked Blake carelessly. "I was thinking of inviting the Comtesse de Rastonet to dine at my table with me tonight. A charming woman, but surely her title is Continental, not English?"

"Oh, yes; I suppose so!" replied Bentley absent-mindedly, wondering how Blake could think of such frivolous things when such serious business was afoot. Little did he dream that the detective was cleverly leading up to a certain point which he wished to reach without arousing Bentley's curiosity.

"She's been here ever since the opening-day, hasn't she?" went on Blake, seating himself and lighting a cigar.

"Yes."

"I don't seem to remember seeing her on the train. I suppose she came on from London?"

"No!" replied Bentley. "She wired from Plymouth for rooms, and came on from there as soon as we wired her we had reserved them."

"I see. She certainly has good judgment in picking rooms overlooking the sea, or perhaps they were the only ones you had left. You have been full up, haven't you?"

"Yes, we have!" agreed Bentley. "But things look black enough now! I'm afraid to pick up a newspaper for fear of seeing something in it about this terrible affair. But you were asking about the comtesse's rooms. If I remember rightly, she wired from Plymouth insisting on having rooms overlooking the bay. Why do you ask?"

"Oh, only curiosity!" yawned Blake, anxious now to turn the conversation since he had got the information he wanted. "Is this head porter of yours thoroughly trustworthy?" he continued.

"Oh, yes. He has been with me in different capacities for some years, and when we erected this hotel, I made him head porter."

"In that case I'd like to borrow him tonight for a little while. He looks strong, and as I am going on a little expedition his strength may come in usefully."

"Is it relating to your investigations?"

Blake nodded.

"Yes, I don't mind telling you, since you are so worried, that I am on a clue which may or may not lead to somewhere. In any event, I propose following it up."

"Very well. I will send for Gregory, and you can tell him what you want."

Bentley rang as he spoke, and a few moments later the head porter appeared.

After binding him to secrecy, Blake told him what he wanted, and the porter promised to be on hand during the evening. Then Blake sauntered out and wrote a note to the Comtesse de Rastonet, inviting her to dine at his table with him that evening, after which he ascended to his room and sank into the big chair to ponder on the different events of the afternoon.

It would have been well if he had sought the little eminence after despatching his note to the comtesse, for, after writing a charming acceptance, Yvonne, with a smile on her lips, threw up the window, and, once more placing the wireless telephone on the sill, got into communication with the yacht.

Her message was very brief and very emphatic, but when she had finished she murmured:

"There, Mr. Sexton Blake. I don't know how you have grown suspicious, but I can't explain your invitation on any other basis. If you are not, nothing will happen, but if you are, you are bound to go ahead in your investigations, and if you do tonight, I'm afraid you will get your fingers burnt!"

***

There was no more beautiful or more faultlessly-dressed woman in that critical and aristocratic assemblage at dinner that night than the Comtesse de Rastonet, who, contrary to her usual habit, dined at the table of Mr. Barker the London gentleman "who did something in the City." His handsome, dark, grave face formed a fitting foil to the radiant beauty of his fair guest.

Blake was a finished artist at ordering a dinner, and when he had completed his choice of dishes, his waiter looked at him with added respect. He was a no less finished conversationalist, and his companion proved equally sparkling.

The result was that the dinner proved a huge success, and even Blake, though he had studied his companion with extraordinary care, had seen nothing suspicious. He did not then even suspect her of being Yvonne, for she had spent many long weeks in a slow but perfect system of disguise, and so finished was it, that even to remove it would require many hours, as well as a large assortment of instruments, cosmetics, and lotions.

Bit by bit Yvonne had, by the use of paraffin injections, changed the contour of her whole face, even the brow being brought under the force of the instruments. This alone will cause such a radical change in one's appearance that it will deceive the greatest expert.

But she did not stop there. Knowing the searching power of Blake's eyes, she had

451

even changed the shape of her hands by the same method, and just before landing at Plymouth the heavy coils of bronze hair had been changed to gleaming black.

Following her change of features, she had practised for months speaking in a different tone of voice, and when she finished, the result had been perfect.

It was for these reasons that Blake was unaware of her identity, for clever as he was, he could not do the impossible, and penetration of her disguise was an impossibility.

He was still curious to know the reason of what he had seen during the afternoon, and the fact that the comtesse had insisted on rooms overlooking the sea had added to his curiosity.

Intent upon following up his investigations, he led the way to a quiet corner of the lounge, where a mass of palms partially shielded them from general view. After bowing the comtesse into a seat, he drew out his cigarette-case and offered her a cigarette. She refused with an apology.

"If you will excuse me, please," she said, smiling, "I will smoke, but can only smoke my own, if you will permit me!"

"With pleasure!" smiled Blake, selecting one himself and sinking down beside her.

Yvonne drew forth a tiny, gold-tipped cigarette-case from her chatelaine and looked inquiringly at Blake, who was feeling in his pockets.

"Pshaw!" he said irritably. "I have forgotten to put any matches in my pocket. Pardon me for a few moments, comtesse, and I will get some!"

"It is not necessary, so pray don't trouble!" she smiled. "See, I have some here!"

And forthwith she drew from the chatelaine a tiny gold matchbox, which was a companion to the cigarette-case. Pressing open the cover, she offered it to Blake, and when he looked at the vesta which he drew forth he saw it was a perfect duplicate to those he had found in the duchess's and the marquis's rooms!

He hurriedly dropped his eyes to hide the gleam of excitement in them, and, striking the vesta coolly, held it until the comtesse had got her cigarette alight. Then he lit his own, and, blowing out the vesta, dropped it carelessly on the floor at his feet. With an apology, he took two others from the box and returned it to the comtesse.

"Just in case of emergency until I get some," he smiled. "And now, comtesse, when am I to have the pleasure of another round with you on the links?"

The comtesse gave a silvery laugh as the conversation turned on golf, and for half an hour they chatted interestedly.

Then Blake's companion rose, and after thanking him for the pleasant evening he had given her, said good-night, and withdrew, apparently with the intention of going to bed.

Barely had she departed when Blake slipped back to the corner in the lounge and whipped up the burnt vesta, which he had dropped under the seat. Then he made his way out of the lounge and sought Gregory, the head porter, for more than ever did he desire to follow up his plans for the night.

While waiting for Gregory two telegrams were handed to him. One was from Tinker, saying he was on his way with Pedro in the motor, and the other was from Mrs. Bardell, and read:

"ACCORDING YOUR INSTRUCTIONS. HAVE SENT BLACK STEEL BOX LABELLED NUMBER FOUR ON THIRD SHELF TO LEFT OF DOOR IN LA-BORATORY."

Blake smiled as he read the repetition of his message to Mrs. Bardell, and then thrust the messages in his pocket as the porter came up.

"Well, sir, have you decided to do anything tonight?" queried Gregory.

"Yes," replied Blake. "I will slip up to my room, and get on a coat. You had better do likewise. Have you got such a thing as a revolver?"

"No, sir, I haven't!"

"Never mind; I will bring two. Meet me here in ten minutes."

"Very good, sir; I'll be ready!" And Gregory sped away to get a coat while Blake ascended to his rooms.

After confirming his suspicions regarding the vestas, he put them all but one carefully away, muttering: "I must contrive in some way to get you safely out of your rooms tomorrow morning, my dear comtesse. I have a consuming curiosity to examine your luggage and inspect that wireless telephone of yours. Who knows? I might even find other things of equal interest. I don't know yet whether I am going for a mare's nest or not, but if you haven't any connection with these mysterious disappearances your actions are certainly peculiar. And then those vestas. That is a very strong point against you, comtesse, but tonight, I hope, will tell us more."

With this conclusion Blake slipped on a heavy pair of boots, and, lifting a couple of automatic pistols from his bag, thrust them into his overcoat-pocket. Then he turned out the light, and, locking the door after him, descended, to find Gregory waiting below.

Telling the porter to wait a moment, Blake sought the partners in the office. Then he drew out the vesta he had kept, and, laying it on the desk in front of Forsythe, said:

"I want you, please, to thoroughly examine the remaining luggage of the duchess and the marquis and find out if it contains any vestas similar to this. Then interview the duchess's maid and the marquis's valet, and discover from them whether they ever saw any such vestas being used by either."

Forsythe wonderingly picked up the vesta.

"All right," he said; "but I don't see the point."

"That makes no difference!" jerked Blake sharply. "The point is important. What did you find out at the railway-station this afternoon?"

"Nobody has departed all day, with the exception of two local villagers whom the station-master knew well. You see the line was extended on here, for the hotel business, and outgoing passengers would not be numerous outside of the hotel guests."

"I see," nodded Blake. "Well"—and he turned to Bentley—"I am taking Gregory with me on the investigation I spoke of. I expect to be back about two or three in the morning."

With that he turned and passed out, joining Gregory on the way. But little did he know how many hours were to pass before he again entered the portals of the hotel.

The Fifth Chapter
Sexton Blake Disappears—Tinker and Pedro Arrive

IT was six o'clock in the morning. Bentley and Forsythe had not made any attempt to go to bed, but had sat in the private office awaiting the return of Blake and Gregory the porter. Blake had said he would be back very early in the morning, but when three came, and then four, and he did not turn up, the partners began to look more anxious than ever. As five pulled round, and then six, the morning light showed their faces to be drawn and haggard with anxiety and worry.

Fully twenty times had they travelled from the office to the front entrance to peer into the dark, mocking night for some sign of the expected ones. But each time they turned back with a heavy sign of growing anxiety. Early in the previous evening Forsythe had set guards in every corridor, in order to prevent any repetition of the strange series of disappearances, and so far nothing had happened to cause any apprehension of a fresh disaster.

But with the dawn came the early-morning train, and with the train came the London papers of the previous day, bearing a fresh shock to the partners. More with an idea of taking their minds off the subject of their troubles, both partners seized on the newssheet as soon as they arrived.

Forsythe was the first to see the fatal paragraph, and with an exclamation of rage he bounded to his feet, waving the paper excitedly.

"Listen—listen!" he gasped to the astounded and apprehensive Bentley.

"What is it, Henry?" he asked quickly.

Without further preamble Forsythe began to read in excited tones:

"'STRANGE HAPPENINGS ON THE NORTH DEVON COAST.
"'MYSTERY AT THE NEWLY OPENED TRADERS' BAY HOTEL.

"'It has come to our ears that two very prominent people have mysteriously disappeared from the Traders' Bay Hotel. We refrain from publishing their names, as the report may be a hoax; but so prominent are the names mentioned, that we have sent a special representative down to investigate fully. We sincerely hope the report has no truth in it, for such an unfortunate occurrence would mean a decided set-back to the new enterprise at Traders' Bay.'"

"My heavens," groaned Bentley, as his partner finished, "the cat is out of the bag. That means ruin to us. Who do you suppose has got wind of it, and sent the report to the paper?"

"Who but the mysterious person or persons who are engineering this campaign against us," muttered Forsythe savagely. "But see here, Bentley, we've got to do something quick. Unless we settle this affair quickly, and publish an unqualified denial of the whole report, we will stand a poor chance of floating the company in London. Everyone will fight shy of the place."

"I know—I know," replied the harassed Bentley. "But what can we do? We depended so much on Sexton Blake, and now he has not returned. Perhaps he has gone the way of the rest."

"Possibly; but in any event it means that we have powerful enemies working secretly against us. Now, the question is: Who are they? Can you think of anyone interested enough in our ruin to start this thing going?"

Bentley shook his head.

"No," he said gloomily. "I have thought over that point, and can't think of a soul."

Forsythe rose, and after walking to the door and peering out, closed it again and resumed his seat.

"Travers," he said, in a low voice, "has it ever occurred to you to follow the careers of our old associates in Australia?"

"No, not particularly," replied the surprised Bentley. "Why?"

"Well, I have done so, and it strikes me that there is something odd in the coincidence of it."

"I don't understand you, Henry. How do you mean?"

"Listen, and I will tell you. Take Vineburg, for instance. He left Melbourne and came to London, where, under the name of Bechstein he bought one of the biggest Bond Street jewellery establishments. After being ruined, he committed suicide."

"Well, that is liable to occur to anyone," remarked Bentley.

"Yes, but wait. Take Pearson. He went high, as you know, for he eventually got into the Presidency of Santa Rita, the South American Republic. You must remember reading in the papers of his end."

Bentley nodded.

"Yes, I do remember that," he muttered.

"Very well. Then take Todd—Todd whom we all considered second only to Kelly in shrewdness. What happened to him? Ruined in a mill town in the north, and had to flee. Next Kelly, who, you know, climbed as high in the financial world as a man could climb. What happened to the Money King? Ruined. Then Tin Dish Charlie, or, as he was known in later years, Carfax Morton. He climbed right up to the Cabinet, only to be ruined and broken. Lastly, Patterson, who was, as you know, as eleven as they make them. You must remember his little flutter when he tried to land the insurance people for half a million over the 'Sun's Eye.' Doesn't that strike you as a rather sinister sequence of events, Travers?"

"Heavens, yes," muttered Bentley, "if this is true! That means, Henry, that only you and I are left, and—and, Henry," he whispered, "there seems to be some force at work with the determination to ruin us."

Forsythe nodded.

"Yes, that has dawned on me during the night. But"—and he spoke savagely—"I'm not going to take it lying down. Sexton Blake said at least one of the perpetrators must be living in the hotel. On what he based his notion I don't know but if it is so, I'm going to find out who it is, and when I do, Heaven help them."

"Yes, yes," agreed Bentley quickly. "We must ferret this thing out. It may be only a series of coincidences, Henry; but it looks as you say, and, besides, if we don't find out what has become of the missing guests, we shall be ruined in a week."

Forsythe rose, his jaw set grimly.

"I'll go along and see if there are any signs of Blake and Gregory. Then we'll figure out what we are going to do."

At that moment a knock came at the door, and in answer to Forsythe's gruff summons the door was pushed open, and there entered a sturdy, keen-looking lad, clad in a capacious motoring coat, and following him was a gigantic bloodhound.

"Good-morning, gentlemen!" he said cheerfully, as he closed the door and removed his dusty cap.

"Good-morning!" returned Bentley. "Might I inquire——"

"Who I am?" finished the newcomer. "Certainly. But first, may I ask if you two gentlemen are Messrs. Bentley and Forsythe?"

Forsythe nodded, while Bentley jerked out:

"Yes, and if you are a newspaper representative——"

The newcomer held up his hand.

"No, gentlemen, I am not. I have the honour to be the assistant of a gentleman by the name of Barker. I understand he is a guest here, and perhaps you can tell me where I can find him."

"Is your name Tinker?" cried Bentley eagerly.

"The same," replied Tinker, with a low bow. "How you could possibly guess though I can't imagine."

Bentley, with all his worry, was forced to smile.

"Never mind that," he said. "You are just the person we want most to see."

"Oh!" said Tinker, growing suddenly grave. "What is it? Where is the guv—Mr. Barker?"

"Sit down, please," replied Bentley, "and I will tell you everything. You seem pretty young, but from what I have heard you know your master's methods, and perhaps can throw some light on matters."

Rapidly he sketched in detail the series of mysterious events which had occurred, beginning at the disappearance of the Duchess of Foreland and all her jewellery, and winding up with Blake's expedition of the night before, and his non-return.

Tinker had wondered exceedingly in London when he received the wire from Bentley and Forsythe asking Blake to come to the Traders' Bay Hotel at once. He had marvelled at the coincidence of Blake's presence in that identical spot, and ever since forwarding the telegram back to Mr. Barker he had been very curious to know what was going on. Things were fairly slack in London, and when he had received Blake's summons to bring Pedro and come down at once, he had wasted no time in getting the big touring-car ready for the long journey.

His idea had been that it was a case of hotel theft on a big scale, but his wildest imaginings did not soar to the actuality. Consequently, although he gave no sign, he was excited at the prospect of such a case. But when he heard of Blake's non-return, he grew very grave.

He was about to speak when another interruption came at the door. This time it was a deputation of guests who had read the paragraph in the paper, and the partners braced themselves to meet the shock. It took all Bentley's suavity, coupled with his most convincing "directors' meeting" smile to convince them that it was only the spiteful hoax of persons who were trying to injure the reputation of Traders' Bay as a resort, and after a strenuous half-hour of this the deputation retired, for the moment satisfied.

Again Tinker was about to speak, when once more a knock came at the door, and this time there entered an alert-looking young man, whose whole appearance shouted " reporter."

"Morning, gentlemen!" he said briskly. "Messrs. Bentley and Forsythe, I presume?"

The partners sourly acknowledged their identity and waited.

"I represent *The Daily Report* gentlemen," went on the brisk young man. "Possibly you have seen the par. in our paper. I have come down to investigate it. I trust, gentlemen, we will be able to publish a complete denial of the rumour."

"Certainly," replied Bentley suavely. "It is a pure concoction from start to finish. Nobody is missing from the hotel."

"Oh!" replied the reporter, bringing out a notebook and pencil. "Then I presume you have no objection to me interviewing the two people mentioned as missing—the Duchess of Foreland and the Marquis of Rondel?"

"That will be impossible," said Bentley, taken aback at this unexpected complication.

At that moment the reporter glanced about him, and his eyes fell on Tinker and Pedro.

"Why, hallo, Tinker!" he cried. "What on earth are you doing down here? Ah, ah, ah!" he said suddenly turning a shrewd eye on Bentley. "Just a little harmless joke of yours, Mr. Bentley, in saying there was nothing in the report. So it's serious enough to put Sexton Blake on it, is it? Gad, this is a scoop. Come, gentlemen, better let me have the details, and perhaps the publicity we shall give them will be the cause of clearing up matters."

"I tell you there is nothing in it!" persisted Bentley stubbornly.

The reporter, however, only wagged his head, and smiled.

"I know, gentlemen," he said soothingly. "I know you are anxious to avoid publicity until the matter is cleared up. But, really, you know, if you don't tell me the facts, I shall be compelled to ferret around myself, and then something might be published which you wouldn't care about!"

"By heavens," cried Forsythe, speaking for the first time, and stepping forward, with clenched hands, "if you do that I'll wring your neck!"

Tinker, seeing a serious altercation was imminent, rose and held up his hand.

"Wait a moment, gentlemen," he said; "I have an idea. I'll make a proposition to you, Roberts," he continued, turning to the reporter. "It is true that there has been a series of unfortunate happenings here, and it is true that the guv'nor is on the case, but truly, Roberts, publicity at present would do no good, and only injure Messrs. Bentley and Forsythe.

"Now, this is my proposition. Wire your paper that there is nothing to report at present, and stay on here. You can help in the investigation, and when it is cleared up, I'll guarantee that you have the whole story for yourself. It will be a bang-up scoop, and worth waiting for. You know, the guv'nor has given you some valuable items, and it is only fair to agree to this, for his sake."

"By James, Tinker," cried the reporter, "I'll do it! What do you say, gentlemen?" he said, turning to the partners. "Are you agreeable to Tinker's proposal?"

"Yes, yes!" said Bentley hastily, looking gratefully at Tinker for his timely solution. "Anything to avoid publicity at present. What do you propose doing first?" he added to Tinker.

"I want to make an examination of the guv'nor's room," replied the lad. "He may have left some notes on the case. Also, I shall occupy his room for the present, and I suppose there is no objection to my keeping Pedro up there?"

"Certainly not!" replied Bentley. "Wait here for a few moments, and I will get you the key of the room."

On his return Tinker took the key, and ascended to Blake's room, leaving Roberts, the reporter, in the office awaiting his return. As soon as he entered the room he closed and locked the door; and then, pulling out a duplicate key of Blake's bag, he opened it, and began making a rapid search. The only things which he brought to light, however, were three burnt wax vestas, and one unused one, together with two hotel bed-room keys bearing on their tags the numbers 69 and 54.

Tinker sat on the floor, and made a close examination of the articles he had found; but, beyond discovering the scratches on the ends of the keys, he could make nothing of them, and put them back, resolving to ask Bentley and Forsythe if Blake had mentioned to them anything about matches or keys. Then, slipping the leash on Pedro, and discarding his motoring-coat, he descended to the office with the intention of starting out to trace the missing Blake.

Forsythe had a vague idea, from what Blake had said, that the detective had gone in the direction of the golf links the previous afternoon, and judging the nocturnal expedition of his master had developed from the results of his afternoon trip, Tinker bent his steps in that direction, with Pedro pulling on ahead and Roberts, the reporter, beside him.

They walked on in silence for some time until they took the turning leading to the shore path, where Pedro suddenly showed signs of great excitement.

It did not take much deduction on Tinker's part to know that the bloodhound had found the scent of his master, and had there been any doubt on the subject, Pedro's anxiety to proceed settled it. Tinker gave him his head, and with Roberts following, hurried on after Pedro, who was going strong.

Down the tree-lined sloping path they went, until they came out suddenly on the little patch of beach. From there Pedro led the way towards the dense woods further on, and a moment later they were following a narrow, perilous path which wound around the jutting point which had caused Blake to ponder the previous afternoon.

Twenty minutes brought them on the downward slope again, and a few moments later they burst out on a tiny beach which was almost a perfect duplicate of the one they had just left. Pedro led the way straight on to the narrow strip of sand, and then he suddenly stopped, and seemed puzzled.

Around and around he worked, while Tinker encouraged him with his voice: but, try as he would, the dog could not seem to pick up the scent again. For all practical purposes it might have vanished in mid-air or—and Tinker turned suddenly as the thought occurred—in the blue water which was rolling in so gently at their feet.

He stood there in deep thought for some moments, and as his eyes travelled along the shores of the little cove, they finally came to rest on the white yacht riding at anchor.

Passing Pedro's leash to Roberts, Tinker dropped to his knees, and began making a close examination of the sand.

Two tides had washed over its soft, white surface since the previous afternoon, and the chances of finding any footprints, had there been any, were slim; but, true to his training to leave no suggestion of his mind uninvestigated, Tinker did not give up.

Working in ever-widening circles, which gradually brought him to the edge of the water, he searched minutely for some clue which would explain the sudden ending of Blake's trail on the narrow beach.

Nothing, however, was to be seen at the water's edge, and as a last resort he turned his attention to the bushes which lined the shore. Suddenly a broken branch caught his eye, and then another and another, until further investigation disclosed a tumbled, broken mass of bushes, the newness of whose breaks told him they must have been made recently.

Signing to Roberts to bring Pedro, he sent the dog into the bushes, and knew from Pedro's excited actions that Blake had been there. The hound, however, on leaving the bushes trailed along the scent to the shore path and back to the beach, only to bring up in the identical spot where he had stopped before.

Tinker scratched his head in puzzlement.

"Well, I'm jiggered!" he muttered. "No matter where the trail starts, it stops at the same point every time!"

Dropping to his knees, he began a minute examination of the ground at the foot of the bushes, and his eyes gleamed with excitement as he saw the ground was torn up and disturbed by a mass of footprints.

Drawing out a powerful pocket-glass similar to the one used by Blake, Tinker signed to Roberts to hold the bushes aside, in order to give him more light.

Then he went to work, and had Blake seen him at that moment he would have known his teaching had not been useless. Tinker blocked his piece of ground out in imaginary squares, and endeavoured to estimate how many different prints there were.

When he had half-covered the area, he saw a clean heel-print which caused his young, firm jaw to set grimly, for he had seen that print too often not to know it was Blake's. That endorsed Pedro's conclusions, and the more he searched the more positive the lad was that the confused prints had only been caused by a struggle, and that Blake's non-return to the hotel, as well as the mysterious ending of his trail at the water's edge, strongly indicated the fact that Blake had met with foul play.

He got to his feet, and once again swept the blue waters of the bay. Then, turning to Roberts, he said:

"I think we'll go back to the hotel. I want to make a few inquiries there."

"All right!" agreed the reporter. "But what do you think so far? Have your investigations told you anything?"

"They have and they haven't," replied Tinker enigmatically. "But this I do know," he exclaimed savagely—"the guv'nor has met with foul play, and I'm going to find out who is behind it!"

"Ah," exclaimed Roberts, hastening to draw out his notebook and make a note, "the plot thickens! Gee! I shall have a beautiful scoop when this thing is finished! If they don't make me at least a sub-editor after this—well, all I can say is they are permitting a brilliant journalist to shine unseen!"

"Oh, rot!" grinned Tinker.

And, setting the pace, he started at a dog-trot for the hotel.

On arrival there they found that no new developments had taken place, and Tinker went at once to the point.

"Tell me, Mr. Bentley," he said, "do you know anything about that yacht out in the bay?"

"Curious!" replied Bentley. "That's the very question Sexton Blake asked me!"

"Ah," exclaimed Tinker quickly, "he was interested in it, then, was he? Can you repeat to me just what you told him?"

"Oh, of course! I simply told him what I knew. She has been there ever since the opening day; but, as far as I know, nobody has come ashore nor has anybody gone out to her."

"I see," remarked Tinker, slightly disappointed, but determined to follow up that point, since he knew it had interested Blake. "By the way, Mr. Bentley, will you tell me what guests have rooms number sixty-nine and fifty-four?"

"Why, yes! The Duchess of Foreland had number sixty-nine, and the Marquis of Rondel had number fifty-four."

"Oh!" said Tinker. "'Then that is the reason the guv'nor had the keys of those rooms in his bag. I begin to see a little more light now. Tell me," he continued, "did he ask you any questions about any wax vestas?"

"Yes," broke in Forsythe, "he asked me to make inquiries of the duchess's maid and the marquis's valet as to whether they had seen their respective mistress and master use wax vestas. I made inquiries last night."

"And what did they say?" asked Tinker.

"They don't remember ever having seen any being used."

"Can you tell me if the guv'nor made any inquiries regarding anything or anybody else?" asked the lad. "I am on a clue and anything like that may be of assistance to me."

"Well," remarked Bentley, smiling slightly, "I don't imagine this has anything to do with the case, but Mr. Blake did show an interest in the Comtesse de Rastonet, whom he invited to dine with him last evening."

"Can you remember what he said?" inquired Tinker.

"Oh, we just discussed as to whether her title was Continental or not, and as he showed some interest as to where she had come from, I told him."

"And where did she come from?"

"From Plymouth."

Bentley had forgotten all about the fact that he had told Blake the comtesse had insisted on rooms overlooking the sea. He had never dreamed that Blake's whole conversation had led up to that one vital point, and had he only remembered it, it would have been of great assistance to Tinker.

Seeing there was no more to be gained from the partners, he signed to the reporter, who had been busily taking notes, and, followed by the anxious requests of the partners, "for goodness' sake, try and find out something soon," he had led the way back to the shore path.

As he reached the first strip of beach he turned off and headed for the golf links, where he had a conversation with the caddie regarding Lord Cray's disappearance.

Bentley and Forsythe had not told Roberts of the peer's disappearance, and as Tinker had refrained also until he found it necessary, the reporter's joy at this fresh plum was unbounded. As he had nothing to lose and all to gain, he was enjoying every moment of the investigation, and as he had been promised a monopoly of the story, he didn't mind how exciting and drawn out the chase was. The bare story which the caddie had to tell told Tinker nothing beyond what he already knew, with the exception that to his mind it formed part of the reason for Blake's nocturnal expedition along the shore path.

After hearing all the boy had to say, he led the way back towards the shore, coming to a pause on the same eminence where Blake had stopped the previous day. From where he stood Tinker could see the yacht and the little miniature cove at the base of the hotel sea wall, but unlike his master, he did not see any curious performance at any of the windows to attract his attention.

Slowly he descended, and thoughtfully led the way back to the hotel. When they were nearly there he pulled up, and, turning to Roberts, said:

"I say, are you game for a little quiet expedition tonight?"

"Rather!" replied that energetic young man.

"The whole thing may develop into a farce," answered Tinker, "but I want to have a closer look at that yacht out in the bay. My idea is that we get a small boat, muffle the oars, and row out there about ten o'clock. Are you game?"

"You can count me in on that, old son!" replied Roberts. "That will go great in the story, won't it, eh—what? Listen to this: 'Dangerous and Perilous Night Journey by Our Special Representative. Thrilling Episodes. Taking his Life in his Hands.'"

"Oh, forget it!" grinned Tinker. "More likely the truth will be, 'Our Special Representative Overslept Owing to an Asinine Boat Trip the Night Before.' But come along. I'll arrange about a boat, and will lie low until ten. It won't do to be too conspicuous."

They continued their way to the hotel, and as they started up the broad stone steps which led to the entrance they drew aside to permit several guests to emerge. Most of them had golf-bags over their shoulders, but Tinker had eyes for only one—a radiantly-beautiful young woman who tripped along with a free-limbed, graceful swing, and who carried her golf-bag as though it weighed nothing. As she passed them a whiff of delicate perfume swept across the summer air, and Tinker only withdrew his eyes when Pedro showed a strong disposition to make acquaintance with the charming stranger.

So occupied was Tinker in speaking to Pedro that he did not see the slim fingers of the stranger tighten on the strap of her golf-bag until the knuckles showed white against the rounding pink. A moment later she was gone, and Tinker drew a deep breath as he turned to Roberts, and said:

"Wasn't she a dream? I wouldn't mind turning caddie just to watch her!"

"She certainly had the rest of them looking like stray bits," replied Roberts flippantly, as they continued the way into the hotel.

Had Tinker known that it was the Comtesse de Rastonet, or in reality Yvonne, and that the sight of the lad with Pedro had caused her great agitation, he would have found many puzzling things suddenly grow clear. He had no suspicion of the fact, however, and, all unconscious of the truth, proceeded to make arrangements about the boat for that evening.

Yvonne, on the other hand, had tightened her hand around the strap of the golf-bag, for she had seen Pedro's recognition of her, regardless of her perfect disguise, and knowing the sharpness of Tinker's mind, she was alarmed lest he should grow suspicious of Pedro's anxiety to go to her.

Yvonne was one of the very few enemies of the law with whom Pedro was on friendly terms, but in the several times they had met he had shown a great liking for her, which, in his canine way, bore out Blake's opinion of the innate goodness of her nature. The dog had recognised her at once, and though she, in her turn, had a deep affection for the bloodhound, it did not suit her purposes that he should recognise her there.

Although she apparently had not seen Tinker and kept straight on for the links, her mind was working rapidly. She had not known that Blake had sent for Tinker and Pedro, and in taking a certain step regarding the detective, she thought she had disposed of all danger in that direction. But now she knew otherwise, and as she walked along she was planning how she could keep her eye on Tinker's movements and forestall any move he might make. For she knew from experience that with the dog's assistance he was very liable to stumble on some vital fact which might upset all her plans. They were going just as she intended, and a week longer, in her opinion, would see the completion of her revenge.

***

"Ssh! Don't make so much noise!"

It was Tinker speaking in a whisper to Roberts as they launched the little boat in the cove at the foot of the hotel sea wall. Up above them a light shone here and there, but many of the guests had retired, and they apparently ran no risk of being seen.

All unknown to them, however, a window some forty feet directly over their heads was open, and protected by the darkness of the room the beautiful young woman who had excited their admiration earlier in the afternoon was leaning on the windowsill watching their every movement.

As the little boat took the water Tinker whispered to Roberts to take the tiller-ropes. Then settling Pedro at his feet, he took up the oars which had been carefully muffled, and began to silently row out of the little cove.

It was a glorious summer night, and, even without the reason they had, would have been a perfect night for rowing. Though intent on his business, Tinker gazed up in rapt admiration at the heavy jewelled curtain of the sky, which seemed to fall in soft curves to the horizon. The water, so blue by day, was now a black mirror, reflecting the studded bowl overhead, and as the blades of the oars were lifted out of the water, the phosphorescence gleamed silver white against the black. He was facing the hotel as he rowed, but from the distance could see no sign of life. In one of those rooms, however, there were signs of great activity.

As soon as she had seen them depart, and had watched their course, Yvonne knew the yacht must be their destination. With a quick intake of her breath, she realised that in some way Tinker had grown suspicious of the yacht, and with his usual energy was losing no time in investigating, spurred on no doubt, she reflected, by the mysterious disappearance of his master.

As this thought occurred she turned quickly, and reached for the black bag which had proved so useful since her arrival at the hotel. Dragging it over to the window, she pressed it open, and drew out the wireless telephone which made possible the carrying out of her plan. Then after hastily connecting up the wires, she began quickly pressing the black button, sending out an urgent call across the starlit waters. From time to time she listened for a reply, but none came, and she grew agitated as she knew the tiny boat bearing Tinker and Pedro must be ever getting nearer to its destination.

She was working feverishly now, but signal as she would no reply came. With a muttered exclamation, she hurriedly placed the machine on the floor, and turning to a cabin-trunk against the wall, quickly unlocked it and threw up the cover. After a few moments' occupation with its contents, her hands emerged bearing a large machine with a curious drum-like attachment at one side. She staggered slightly under the weight as she carried it to the window, but there was no time to be lost. Rapidly she placed it in the position formerly occupied by the telephone, and after connecting up a medley of wires and batteries, she settled down with a sigh of relief.

Placing her finger on a black key, she began pressing it at regular intervals, which, to the initiated, would have at once proclaimed it to be the Morse code, and the instrument on which she was working a portable wireless telegraph instrument such as is now used on the aeroplanes in the French, American, and German services.

Even Yvonne's scientific application had not brought this machine much past the experimental stage; but it served very well up to a distance of five or six miles, and she had hopes that the signal would attract the attention which the wireless telephone had failed to get.

After tapping urgently for some moments, she put the bowed receiver to her ear, and ever so faintly heard a reply from the wireless operator on the yacht. Rapidly she tapped out a message, telling him to instruct Graves to prepare for a message on the wireless telephone, and, not waiting to hear the reply, removed the receiver from her ears. Then she dragged the wireless telegraph instrument to the floor, and once more set up the telephone. This time her first call was answered, and through the quiet night air she got into perfect communication.

"Tell Captain Vaughan to weigh anchor and sail at once," she ordered. "Tell him to cruise about all night and come back to anchor in the morning for further instructions."

"But we were going to send the landing party ashore tonight," came back the reply.

"I know; but Sexton Blake's assistant and the bloodhound are down here. They are rowing out to the yacht tonight, and are even now over half-way. There is no time to lose."

"But why not let them come, and detain them?" asked Graves.

"Because it is dangerous at this stage!" snapped Yvonne. "Do as I say, and make haste."

Down on the bosom of the bay Tinker had been rowing steadily. At first the lights of the yacht seemed to grow no larger, but as they got out further, Roberts could distinguish them more plainly, and kept encouraging Tinker by reporting their progress.

"You're doing fine," he said. "We are getting nearer at every stroke."

"Of course we are, fathead," grumbled Tinker. "Do you think I was rowing backwards?"

"No, indeed," replied Roberts, grinning. "I know I never could row half as well."

"Think not?" said Tinker. "You'll have an opportunity to try, going back, anyway. But how far do you judge we are now?"

"Less than a quarter of a mile I should say, though it's hard to judge at night."

"We'd better get our revolvers handy," remarked Tinker, stopping and shifting his into his outside coat pocket. "You never can tell what tonight——"

"Oh, I say!" cried Roberts, interrupting him. "Look quickly! I declare the thing is moving."

With an exclamation Tinker turned and gazed at the yacht.

What Roberts had said was only too true. Even as the lad gazed, the phosphorescence gleamed at her stern as the propeller churned up the water, and like a white phantom she stole off into the night.

The Sixth Chapter
Sexton Blake's Great Fight—A Bid For Liberty

BLAKE'S nocturnal expedition from which he had not returned had been based on the result of his reflections concerning his afternoon investigations along the shore. To begin with, it will be remembered that Blake's suspicions of the Comtesse de Rastonet had been aroused during the afternoon by seeing that aristocratic lady go through a very strange performance with a wireless telephone at her window.

Subsequent to that, the detective had formed his mental circle, which embraced all the possible ways in which the several disappearances could have taken place.

As will be recalled, he discarded the aeroplane theory as being too public and the motor theory as being too risky. From that he had gone to the possibility of the dense woods on his left having been utilised, and finally, there had remained the sea.

That the water formed an ideal method there was no doubt; but—and the thought caused him to once more turn his attention to the woods—Lord Cray had disappeared in broad daylight from the shore path, and not even the most daring would risk taking a kidnapped peer over the waters of the bay at midday with a crowded hotel close at hand.

He pondered over the position of the yacht, and then turned his attention to the jutting point on his left. From where he stood, he could see a rough, almost hidden track winding up through the trees and obviously going over the point to the other side.

Mentally fixing its position in his mind, he turned his attention back to his immediate surroundings. It was then that he had seen Yvonne at the window with her wireless telephone, and what he had seen caused him on his return to the hotel to wire for a wireless telephone instrument, and to invite the Comtesse de Rastonet to dine with him.

The discovery that the wax vestas which he had found in the rooms of the Duchess of Foreland and the Marquis of Rondel, had, almost for a certainty, emanated from his companion, had increased his suspicions of her; and in his mind he felt positive she knew a great deal about the mysterious happenings of the past few days.

True, he had no shred of proof, but a search of her effects might reveal that, and he promised himself he would do that on the following day.

Chief of all his deductions, however, was the conclusion he had come to regarding Lord Cray. He remembered that both the disappearance of the duchess and the marquis had taken place at night, when their removal from the immediate neighbourhood of the hotel would be comparatively easy.

But with Lord Cray it was different, and on that difference Blake hoped to gain an inkling of the truth. His idea, and, in fact, it seemed the only possible conclusion mathematically, was that, though Lord Cray had apparently vanished in thin air, he was still within a short distance of the hotel, and that his removal to a safe distance would not take place until nightfall.

The next step to consider was, this hypothesis being tenable, where would Lord Cray most likely be kept? Where but in the confines of the dense woods which fringed the shore to the left of the hotel, and which ran unbroken clear around the shore of Traders' Bay, until they ended in a mass of green at the far point which formed the left hook of the bay?

If that were so, it seemed that the next step should be the beating up of the woods without delay. But Blake thought differently. To begin with, a big force of men might beat up the woods until dark without finding any trace of those whom they sought; and, secondly, it was imperative the investigation should be kept as secret as possible, for the birds might take alarm, and fly before he could accomplish his purpose.

With this conclusion he decided to leave matters until nightfall, when, with Gregory, the head porter, he would make a quiet expedition through the woods and up the rough path which led over the jutting point to the other side, and there watch for any movement on the waters of the bay.

If Lord Cray were being kept concealed in the woods for removal at night, and if the yacht in the bay were the destination of the kidnapped prisoners, then the expedition promised well.

But, as yet, this was all theory, and, unknown to Blake at the time, there were two very strong elements working against him. One was the fact that he had no idea then of the identity of the Comtesse de Rastonet, and the other was that the comtesse knew the identity of the supposed "Mr. Barker," and acted accordingly.

When Blake left the hotel with Gregory, the porter, all unknown to him, Yvonne watched his departure, and then, hastening to her room, she got in touch, through the medium of the wireless telephone, with her uncle, Graves. Her instructions were very brief, but later events proved them to have been sufficient.

As soon as Blake left the hotel, he cautioned his companion to tread silently, and, leading the way, struck off in the direction of the shore path, which led towards the links, and which was to be trod so anxiously by Tinker and Pedro the following day.

For some time they walked on in silence, and then, on reaching the point where the path branched off to the golf links, Blake swung to the right and kept on until he reached the little strip of beach where he had stood earlier in the day.

From there he got his bearings, and, starting once more, led the way along the tough, narrow path which led over to the other side of the jutting point.

Realising that if his deductions were correct. Lord Cray might be even at that moment very close to them, Blake moved with the stealthy caution of an Abenaki,[22] and Gregory, to the best of his ability, followed the example of his leader.

Only when they had crossed the low ridge and had descended the other side to the second strip of beach did Blake pause.

By the faint light of the myriad of stars overhead he could see the shape of the little cove and choosing a thick mass of bushes at the edge of the beach, he signed to Gregory, and led the way into their concealment. He touched Gregory peremptorily as the latter cracked a branch beneath his foot, but with this one exception, their movements were made in silence.

As soon as he had got his companion settled, Blake dropped flat to the ground and, gently parting the bushes, drew out a pair of night glasses, and turned them on the shadowy form of the light-studded yacht far out in the bay.

Gregory made an attempt to whisper a question, but a warning thrust of Blake's foot caused him to desist, and silence reigned again.

Twenty minutes went by—half an hour, and then a full hour crept round, and still Blake lay like a carved figure in granite, motionless and silent, with the glasses pointing over the waters of the bay.

It must have been midnight before a soft sigh escaped him, but beyond that he gave no sign that anything had happened.

Something decidedly interesting was happening, however, and in a man of less iron

---

[22] The Abenaki are a Native American tribe and First Nation. Their original territory included parts of Quebec and the Maritimes of Canada and northern sections of the New England region of the United States. ~Editor

control the proving out of the truth of his deductions would have caused an exclamation at least.

Not so Blake, however, and beyond the soft sigh, he gave no indication that his whole being was tense with excitement.

Far out on the waters of the bay he had seen through the glasses the faint gleam of phosphorescence.

A single gleam or even many gleams might easily be caused by the jumping of fish, but from the very regularity of them, and from the fact that they finally developed into regular shining patches, which came and went methodically, as well as the narrow, unchanging space between them, he knew they were caused by nothing else but the regular dipping and withdrawal of oars in the water, and that the space between represented the width of a rowboat.

A quarter of an hour endorsed this, for, as the splashes grew nearer and nearer to the shore, Blake, through the glasses, could make out the shadowy form of a small boat, and above it a dark mass, which later resolved itself into six distinct black patches, and then into the forms of men, two of whom were rowing.

Gregory, unaided by glasses, and his view blocked by the bushes, had been unable to see anything, but now, as the boatload of men was visible to the naked eye, Blake lowered the glasses and signed to the porter to look.

"That is what we may run foul of!" whispered Blake softly. "On the other hand, we may be able to avoid a hand-to-hand fight. It all depends on where they land. In any event, have your revolver ready, and on your life don't make a noise!"

Gregory nodded, and peered out at the little boat.

Fate, however, took the arrangement of the matter out of Blake's hands, for, as they neared the shore, the men in the boat stopped rowing, and then, shifting the boat's head a trifle, they headed direct for the little beach where Blake and his companion lay concealed. Their muffled oars made no sound as they entered the little cove, and the very manner in which the bow of the boat grounded on the soft, white beach indicated the control of the finished sailor.

As silently as they had landed they tumbled out on to the beach, and as they stood together Blake had the whole party at his mercy had he cared to adopt the methods of men less punctilious.

His natural love of playing the game forbade anything of such a nature, however and, keeping them covered, he watched in silence. True, he had no actual proof that the men before him were guilty of anything, but since his deductions had proved without flaw so far, it was safe to assume that they would continue so as far as he had calculated.

Had he only known just who the Comtesse de Rastonet was, instead of bringing one man with him, he would have brought half a dozen, for knowing that, he would have known the identity and calibre of those six men on the beach who, without the slightest hesitation, would have gone to their death for their leader, Yvonne.

Imperative as Blake felt was the need for making some definite move before the numbers on the beach were augmented, still, reason told him that they were only two against six, and a move at that moment might only precipitate the situation he was endeavouring to avoid.

From the silent, waiting, expectant attitude of the figures not ten yards away, Blake knew the little cove was a rendezvous, and felt certain that the intended removal of Lord Cray from the depths of the woods was the cause of it.

His conclusions proved only too true, for, after another five minutes' silence, a soft whistle sounded in the woods behind them, followed by an answering signal from one of the men on the beach.

Then the soft swish of branches followed, and a black mass broke through the bushes on to the beach, to resolve itself a moment later into the figures of three men, one of whom was being led between them by the other two, and as they cleared the shadow of the bushes it could be seen that his hands were bound behind him, while a bandage was wound tightly around his mouth.

"Lord Cray, by all that's great!" breathed Blake. "Correct to the last detail. I'll swear that boat came from the yacht out yonder and no place else."

His conjectures broke off as the sound of low voices came from the little knot of men on the beach, and he bent his head to listen.

"That you, sir?" asked one of the new arrivals.

The low-voiced answer could not be heard by Blake at such a distance, but the first speaker was evidently satisfied, for the party moved on until their figures blended with those of the others. Then a hurried consultation took place, and Blake heard another remark, as the same voice which had first spoken said:

"No, sir; we haven't heard a sound nor seen a soul. If he is anywhere about, he can't have come in this direction."

Blake puzzled his mind as to whom they could be referring, nor did he dream that he himself was the subject of the remark consequent on Yvonne's message to the yacht after she had watched his departure from the hotel.

At this point the men on the beach started for the boat with their captive in the midst, when a perverse imp of Fate caused a calamitous and sudden crisis through the medium of the unfortunate porter.

Eager to hear what was being said, he had leaned forward as far as he dared; but, careful as he was, his action brought about the upheaval.

A tiny twig, which it was impossible for him to see, was immediately under his face, and as he bent lower it suddenly popped into his nose, causing an acute tickling sensation.

He tried nobly to allay the irritation and prevent an outburst by holding his nose and rubbing it, but the effect would not be denied; and, after several choking gasps, he broke forth with a terrific sneeze, to Blake's consternation.

It happened that even at ordinary times the husky porter was noted for the resounding force of his sneeze, but coming as it did after this frantic struggle to prevent it, and in the silence of the little bay, the effect can well be imagined.

The group of men paused in consternation as they were about to enter the boat, and

Blake, with a muttered remark, leaped to his feet just as Gregory gave a second and still louder display of the nasal art.

This, together with the crash of the bushes as he followed Blake and scrambled to his feet, broke the spell which had seemed to enfold the men on the beach; and, with a low murmur, they drew their revolvers, and dashed forward.

Blake, though savagely chagrined at this upsetting of his plans, and in spite of the enormous odds against them, saw there was nothing for it but to fight. If they must go down, it would not be without leaving their mark on their opponents; and, calling sharply to Gregory to follow, he spread the bushes apart and, with levelled revolver, stepped out on to the sand.

Coolly facing the oncoming men, he raised his hand.

Despite the fact that they had overwhelming odds on their side there was something in that stern, sphinxlike face, with its cleanly-chiselled features, which caused them to pull up at the silent command of that imperious gesture.

Only when they had paused, and he had an opportunity of sweeping their features with his glance, did Blake draw in a sharp breath of surprise, for there, in the very front rank, was the familiar face of Hendricks.

"So—so," said Blake, in slow tones, "it is you, Hendricks? It has been some time since we have met. I might have imagined that only the complex and brilliant mind of Mademoiselle Yvonne could be behind the occurrences of the past few days."

As Blake mentioned Yvonne's name, one of the sailors in the rear uttered an imprecation, but Hendricks quickly silenced him.

"That is as it may be," he replied gruffly; "but no matter who is behind the affair, it is going through this time without your interference, Sexton Blake! I have my orders regarding you, and I'm going to carry them out!"

"Ah, that was an unpardonable oversight on my part!" remarked Blake coolly. "It should have occurred to me that the Comtesse de Rastonet"—and he dropped the name out with slow emphasis—"would bring into use her form of communication with the yacht. However, Hendricks, since you say you have your orders regarding me, perhaps you will be good enough to enlighten me as to your intentions."

"My orders are to capture you if I catch you prowling around. How you managed to get here tonight without being seen or heard, I don't know. But you must come with us, and you must see that it is useless for you to resist. Better surrender, and save trouble!"

"You think so, do you?" remarked Blake pleasantly. "I must confess, Hendricks, that your argument regarding overwhelming odds seems a very forcible one, but at the same time, I don't propose joining Lord Cray without resistance. I realise that it will be an impossibility to shoot you all, and on that basis I will act. Out of the lot of you I have my eye on two men—two men, Hendricks. You don't know which two, but I do, and as surely as one of you moves towards us, I will disable those two. My companion will also pick out two, and do the same, and then, unless we have gone under the odds will be more equal, Hendricks!"

Blake, in the hopeless position in which he found himself, had hit on the shrewdest idea possible. As a body, and risking stray shots, most men would leap forward at once, but Blake had said that he would drop a certain two, and his companion would do likewise.

It was a tantalising remark, for each man in the crowd wondered if he was one of the two, and if a bullet from that so steadily-held automatic would find a resting-place in his body.

A nervous shifting of feet took place, and Blake set his jaw as he saw that his high-handed methods were holding out a chance of success, but at that moment one element obtruded itself into the situation which the detective had not expected.

It was launched by Hendricks with lightning-like rapidity, and it changed the vacillation of his men to a mood of reckless determination.

This element was a remark of just three words, "remember your mistress," but its tonic-like effect was magical. Spurred on by Hendricks' following command the whole body leaped forward as one man, and Blake, with a sharp command to Gregory, opened fire.

True to his word, Blake sent a bullet at first one man and then another, causing them to sink to the beach with a groan, and had Gregory been equally successful even then they might have won out. But the porter's aim was shaky, and his bullets flew wide, boring harmlessly into the tightly-packed sand.

The oncoming party were not slow at replying, and Blake, after pulling the trigger for the third time, shifted his revolver, butt outwards, and leaped forward at Hendricks as Gregory sank to the ground with a groan.

The attacking party held their fire at once as Gregory dropped, and Blake leaped forward with clubbed revolver, for it would not do to attract attention by the sound of too much firing.

Then Blake and Hendricks came together with a stunning crash, and, outlaws though they were, Yvonne's sailors stood back while those two physical giants, Blake, and Hendricks the mate, struggled for the mastery.

Blake knew that even if he won the sailors would attempt to close in and overpower him, but he might get a chance to make a dash for freedom.

Besides, he was in one of his rare cold rages at the failure of his plans, and not at all averse to the struggle as an outlet for his feelings.

Hendricks, on his part, was not backward either, and, being on his mettle before his men, he put forth every ounce of strength against the human whirlwind which had struck him.

Revolvers fell to the soft sand with a dull thud, and using only their bare hands the two men met and countered.

Hendricks, being on the defensive, guarded and knee-locked, and Blake, carried into close quarters by his rush, met the guard and started a long, slow, heart-breaking twist on his opponent which was almost as gruelling on himself as the other.

The sailor was hard and in good fettle, and in a weaker man than Blake the trick would have been futile against the bulwark of Hendricks' resistance; but the lithe, supple back of the detective bent freely to every turn, and Hendricks' efforts to crush him by pure force were without effect.

Like a giant pine suddenly endowed with life, Blake slowly insinuated his leg outward and around that of the panting Hendricks.

Knowing his opponent's aim, the sailor struggled to prevent it, and great beads of sweat stood out on his forehead with the effort.

The excruciating pain of his back, however, was maddening, and he knew if he for the slightest fraction of a second relaxed his defence the awful pressure of those steel-like arms would crumple him up as a dried leaf is crumpled by the hurricane.

Blake, with the unrelenting force of a resistless Nemesis, was keeping up without the faintest sign of relaxing his remorseless pressure, and the sailors, true to their nature, forgot for the time being their respective positions in their absorption in the struggle.

Just when Hendricks was giving the least trifle in a desperate endeavour to ease his breaking back, Blake seized the opening for all it was worth, and, with a movement so quick that the tensely-watching sailors could not follow its course, he sent his leg around in the position at which he had aimed.

Then, twisting like a lithe python, he ducked and heaved, and a gasp of unconscious admiration went up from the watching sailors as Hendricks, forced to yield or break, was sent flying over the detective's head in one of the prettiest cross-buttocks possible, and landed with a heavy groan on the sand, where he lay motionless.

Blake, though panting and breathless from his exertions, leaped back at once and stood on the defensive, for, with the fall of their leader, the spell which had seemed to hold the sailors in its grip broke, and with a savage growl they hurled themselves at Blake.

One—two—one—two went Blake's hard fists, as he drove right and left to jaw and face of the oncoming men.

One—two—one—two, and in the quiet of the summer night the blows resounded clearly.

One went down, but still the other two came on. Fighting desperately now, with all his skill and cunning coupled with the force of his cold rage, Blake backed slightly and blocked the rushing rain of blows which assailed him.

Had he had Tinker beside him at that moment he would have finally won out of what seemed an impossible position, but Gregory was useless, and even Blake's iron physique was feeling the strain of that last half-hour.

The sailors, on the other hand, were fresh, and spurred on by the fate of their comrades the remaining two made a determined rush at their solitary foe—a rush which even the whip-like hail of blows which met them could not withstand, and, like a monarch of the forest which bows to the sudden onslaught of the tornado, he sank to his knees, still fighting, and then dropped forward on his face.

Fallen though he was, his victors had little to rejoice over, and the way in which they rolled him over in order to gaze on the still face, showed the respect they felt for the man who had put up such a splendid fight against overwhelming odds.

Hendricks had come round from his forcible acquaintance with the ground, and sat up with a groan, spitting out a mouthful of sand as he did so.

"What in the name of thunder hit me?" he mumbled, getting stiffly to his feet. "I'm willing to tackle anything human, but when it comes to trying to stem a whirlwind, well, I prefer the China Sea."

He gazed around dazedly, but as his eyes fell on the two sailors bending over the prostrate Blake he remembered everything.

Walking over, he gazed down with deep respect at his fallen foe, and not a man there heard the soft rustle of bushes a few feet away as a dark-cloaked figure withdrew and stole back through the woods towards the hotel.

Nor did they know that the same figure had watched with tense eyes and heaving breast the whole course of the fight.

But so it was. Yvonne, restless and worried as to Blake's movements, had, after her orders to Graves, slipped on a coat, and by a back staircase had left the hotel. She had arrived at the beach just in time to see Blake's first hurricane rush at Hendricks and his following struggle against the four sailors.

Though her reason and loyalty were on the side of her own men, her heart was with the man who fought so bravely, and when he finally went down she gave an involuntary dry sob, which in the general excitement of the moment passed unheard.

It was easy enough for Yvonne to issue orders to her men to do this or to do that with Blake, but lately, in order that they might be carried out, she kept away; for in her great love for the man who was forced by circumstances to be her enemy she found she could not trust herself to enforce her own orders, and the sudden realisation of that knowledge frightened her.

As she made her way back to the hotel, leaving Blake to his captors, her heart contracted with the pain of her hopeless love, which, like a rushing torrent that could not be stemmed, seemed to be bearing her on and on with no port, no harbour in sight.

Hendricks seemed to recover his spirits at the sight of the prostrate Blake, for he straightened himself with more vigour and surveyed the scene before him. It was difficult to believe that one man had caused the disastrous spectacle which met his eyes, but it was painfully true, and merely showed the result of determined science coupled with coolness and perfect training.

Crumpled up in the sand lay Gregory just as he had fallen, a bullet through his thigh; further down lay the two disabled sailors whom Blake had sent to earth, while almost at his feet lay the sailor who had been dropped by a clean left hook to the vital point of the chin. Then he looked at the two remaining battered-looking sailors, and a grim smile spread over his weather-beaten face.

"I wish we had him with us," he grunted, with a nod at Blake. "He'd have made his mark as captain of a windjammer in the old days when the rows in the fo'c's'le had to be straightened out. However, there is no time to lose. It must be one o'clock, and we have a lot to do. Tie him up, and see that you do it well. If he comes to and gets loose in the boat he'll upset us and have the whole caboodle in the bay. Then carry him down to the boat and turn to the other two who are looking after Lord Cray, and then see what you can do with the wounded. I'll bring Bill round and look after Blake's companion."

The sailors hastened to do as he bade them, and the mate bent over the prostrate figure of Bill, the man who had gone down under Blake's blow.

A strong dose of whisky from a flask which the mate had served to open Bill's eyes, and he sat up asking what had happened.

Hendricks was unable to suppress a grin as he thought of his own sensations on coming round, but he made no comment as he helped the man to his feet. Directing him to lend a hand to the others in looking after his wounded companions, the mate then turned his attention to Gregory and roughly bound up the porter's wound.

Then, working rapidly, they got the wounded in the boat, and after the gagged Lord Cray had been helped in they pushed off. As silently as they had entered the little cove did they row out, leaving the rising tide to wash over the scene of the recent fight and sweep away on its restless bosom all traces of the conflict.

Not until they were some distance out in the bay did Blake stir and open his eyes. At first he gazed about him stupidly, seeing only the bottom of the boat, and what seemed like a forest of dark-trousered legs.

Then somebody put a flask to his lips, and the raw spirit which he gulped down, coupled with the fresh night air, revived him considerably. He still felt weak and sore from head to foot, but as no one tried to prevent him, he sat up and looked around.

"Feel better, sir?" inquired a voice from behind him, and turning, he saw the visage of Hendricks broken by a good-natured grin.

"Hallo!" grunted Blake. "You have revived, have you?"

"And no thanks to you, sir," grinned Hendricks, who was good sportsman enough not to hold hard feelings against his conqueror. "How do you feel—better?"

"Yes," replied Blake, "and no thanks to you," he added, with a grim smile, and imitating Hendricks' bantering tone.

"Come and sit here, sir; you'll find it more comfortable."

Blake rose and moved cautiously along until he reached a vacant seat, and found himself beside Lord Cray, who was now without his gag.

Turning his head, Blake could see now, far behind, the lights of the hotel, while dead ahead were the lights of the yacht.

Blake had never met Lord Cray, but having passed him in the corridor, and on the links several times during the earlier days of his stay at the hotel, he had no difficulty in recognising him. As the peer spoke, however, he turned.

"If my hands weren't tied behind me, Mr. Blake," he said, "I'd like to shake hands with you. I had no idea who you were until I heard them call you by the name on the beach, but you put up the prettiest fight I ever saw. I'd have given a thousand pounds to have been free to take a hand with you. Curse these fellows! What the deuce is their game, Mr. Blake?"

Blake smiled.

"I'm sorry you couldn't take a hand, Lord Cray," he said. "If I had had your assistance we would have won out. As to what they want of you I had no idea until an hour ago, but I begin to see more light on the matter now. As to what they want of me, however, I think I can guess. For the present they have the advantage, and a rash move to escape would only precipitate matters. We can only watch our chance and take the first opportunity which offers."

Hendricks was sent flying over the detective's head ——.
They lowered her carefully into the waiting boat.
Tinker dropped to his knees and closely examined the ground

"Not too much talking, there, please!" said Hendricks gruffly from where he sat in front; but Blake paid no attention and went on:

"Tell me, Lord Cray, how did they get you? I figured out that you were attacked on the short path and kept in the woods for removal by night. That was the reason of my being on the beach tonight, and results proved my deductions to have been correct. I am curious, however, to learn the details."

"There isn't much more to tell than you seem already to know," answered Lord Cray, in a low tone. "I left the links at ten-thirty and started back along the shore path, as I had promised to be at the hotel by eleven.

"Well, I hadn't gone very far when two fellows—that pair up in the bow—leaped out at me from the bushes and tackled me. I was handicapped by having my golf-bag over my shoulder, but put up what resistance I could. They were too much for me, however, and before I could do anything, they had me gagged and bound. Then they picked me up and carried me along a rough path through the woods until they came to a sort of grassy hollow. There they laid me down and there I was kept until tonight, when they untied my feet and led me down to the beach.

"What puzzles me is, what the dickens is their object? Do they intend to hold me for a ransom, or what? I've racked my brains over it, but can make nothing of it. And do you know, Mr. Blake, I'm wondering if the Duchess of Foreland and the Marquis of Rondel have fallen into the same hands. They weren't about yesterday, and as I know them both well, I naturally inquired for them, thinking perhaps they were ill. I thought at the time Bentley acted kind of queer over it."

"You are quite right, Lord Cray," remarked Blake. "They have fallen into the same hands, but as yet that is about all I can tell you. I do not know the motive of the affair, and until I do it would be futile to conjecture. I know the cause now, however, and I think after a night's analysis of the matter, will be able to make a shrewd guess at the motive. I think we will find that the duchess and the marquis will be fellow-prisoners, but we must scheme to escape quickly, or I am afraid we will find ourselves taking an enforced cruise."

"Who owns the yacht?" asked Lord Cray, as the boat drew in against the ladder which had been lowered. "Does it belong to our captors?"

"It belongs to one of the cleverest individuals living," replied Blake slowly, "and at the same time our hostess. After you, Lord Cray."

This, as Hendricks signed to them to ascend. The two wounded sailors, with Gregory, had been hoisted up, and there now remained only Hendricks and one other sailor, the rest having gone up with the wounded.

As Blake spoke Lord Cray moved forward, and for a bare moment Blake was hidden from view. With a lightning-like movement he drew out his knife, and, opening the blade, slashed the other's bonds. Then, with a "Now, Lord Cray, take the sailor, and I'll take the mate," he leaped forward and drove his right fist to the point of the astounded Hendricks' chin.

With a feeble grunt, Hendricks tumbled over the gunwale into the water, and Blake turned to see how his companion was faring.

Not slow to take advantage of his unexpected freedom, Lord Cray had leaped for the sailor, and, putting all the pent-up force of his smouldering rage into his blow, he literally knocked the sailor into the water without the man touching the gunwale in going.

"Good, good!" cried Blake, leaping for an oar. "Get an oar, Lord Cray, and row like mad! They will be after us hotfoot in a moment!"

The peer jumped to obey, but through the very force of his zeal misfortune overtook Blake for the second time that night. He himself settled his oar and began rowing, in order to put as much distance as possible between them and the yacht. Lord Cray, however, put all his strength into his first stroke, and Blake almost groaned as a splintering crash told him the thole pin had gone.

Then a sharp command rang out from above, and like a mad horde of angry bees, fully twenty sailors tumbled headlong down the ladder and swarmed over the boat. The two escaping prisoners wielded the oars with a will, and many a man went down with a cracked head; but it was a physical impossibility to stem that tide of angry humanity.

For the second time Blake was beaten to his knees, and five minutes later, bound hand and foot, he and his companion were being hustled up the ladder in no gentle fashion.

The Seventh Chapter
Tinker Uses the Wireless Telephone—The Last Disappearance

TO return to Tinker. When the lad saw the yacht stealing off in the night and eluding him after all his elaborate preparations, his face wrinkled up in comic despair.

"Well, I'm blest!" he muttered savagely to Roberts, the reporter. "After my pulling out here with all the caution of a cat, to see her slip away just as we were getting near. It's uncanny—that's what it is!"

"It's a bit queer," replied Roberts, unable to repress a smile at Tinker's chagrin. "One would almost think they knew of our coming, or had seen us approaching."

"It settles one thing in my mind, anyway!" muttered Tinker, more to himself than to his companion. "I'm certain that yacht has some connection with the disappearances which have taken place, but the main questions now are, where is she bound, and is the guv'nor aboard? If he is, it's hard to tell when he'll fetch up, and he may even be in danger."

"What's that you say?" asked Roberts.

"Oh, nothing!" replied Tinker. "I was talking to myself, and don't need any answer. However, let's get back. There's nothing to be gained floating around the bay tonight. You can do the rowing!" he added grimly.

"I'm positive I couldn't row half as well as you do!" protested Roberts, who had a chronic dislike for manual labour.

But Tinker was adamant, and routed him out of his comfortable position in the stern unceremoniously.

It was a silent pair which covered the distance back to the shore, and beyond a couple of "crabs," which Roberts caught in an endeavour to "feather" his oars, nothing happened to break the monotony.

Tinker was thinking, and thinking hard. He was growing more worried every moment over Blake's non-appearance, and to his mind the silent stealing off of the yacht seemed to bear an intangible, sinister suggestion.

Blake, he knew, was thoroughly capable of looking after himself, but the fact that he, as well as Gregory, the porter, had vanished during a secret midnight expedition, seemed to point to a disaster of some kind.

If he only knew on what grounds Blake had been working and the exact reason for his expedition, he would then perhaps be able to follow up his master's line of inquiry. But, not knowing this, he must perforce follow his own line, and he confessed to himself, as the boat grounded softly on the beach, that his theory was very vague indeed.

He had been with Blake too long, and had studied the latter's methods too closely, not to know that the sudden disappearance of three prominent society people indicated a powerful and daring cause behind it. And the later disappearance of Blake and the porter made it obvious that the same cause was fully aware that Blake was Mr. Barker, and that his investigation of the matter was no secret.

On entering the hotel he found Bentley and Forsythe in savagely irritable moods. Disquieting inquiries had come from the Duchess of Foreland's solicitors, on one hand, and the Marquis of Rondel's son, on the other.

To cap this, a steady impression had been growing among the hotel guests that all was not right. What was the matter they had no idea, but as is always the case in such instances, many wild rumours began flying about which even the suave diplomacy and tact of Bentley could not stem.

Fully half of the guests had indicated their intention of leaving by the morning train, and the partners knew that as soon as they arrived in London all kinds of stories would at once be sent broadcast.

Very few new arrivals had come to take their place. A sickly curate, a bombastic old gentleman and his wife, and a newly-married couple on their honeymoon had been the only arrivals by the evening train.

Altogether, the future of the hotel enterprise looked black; for, above everything else, give a hotel a bad name, and, like that of the proverbial dog, it sticks.

Tinker's report that his expedition in the bay had been a failure did not improve their tempers, and only the lad's powers of persuasion kept them from then and there throwing up the sponge and calling in the police.

The lad's reasons for this course were based on his loyalty to Blake, for he reasoned it was just a possibility Blake had seen something which required to be followed up, and, without hesitation, had gone after it.

If by any chance this should be the case, if the police were called in it meant the upsetting of all Blake's work, and until he knew something definitely, Tinker was resolved that such a step should not be taken if he could prevent it.

After gaining his point with the partners, he said good-night to Roberts, and, with Pedro at his heels, ascended to the room so recently occupied by Blake.

Disturbed and anxious as he was, it was some time before he dropped off to sleep; but finally he did so, and little did he dream of the next step in his investigations which he was to take on the morrow.

He was awakened at eight o'clock by a heavy pounding on his door, and, springing up, he threw it open, and admitted a boy bearing a heavy parcel.

"What is it?" asked Tinker sleepily.

"I dunno, sir," replied the boy. "It's addressed to Mr. Barker, but the boss said give it to you."

"Oh, all right!" replied Tinker. "Just set it on the floor!"

When the boy had departed, he bent to make an examination of the package, and whistled in surprise as he recognised in the address the handwriting of Mrs. Bardell.

"Looks like a machine," he muttered. "Ten to one it's one of those machines from the lab. Now, what the dickens was the reason of the guv'nor's sending for a machine, and just which one is it? I guess I'll risk it, and open the blessed thing!"

Suiting the action to the word, Tinker moved across to where his garments hung, and getting a knife from one of the pockets, cut the cord which bound the package.

As layer after layer of paper fell to the floor there suddenly stood revealed a large steel case, and, lifting off the cover, Tinker gave another whistle of surprise as he saw the polished surface of a wireless telephone.

"Now, what the dickens——" he muttered, scratching his head in deep thought as he surveyed the instrument. "The guv'nor must have wired for this immediately after I left in the car, and that means something's happened in his investigations which caused him to do so."

"I think I'll get dressed on the double-quick, and then, Mr. Machine, I'll give my attention to you. I'd give something to know on what lines the guv'nor was working. Then I'd know what to do with the blessed thing, but maybe I'll hit on something as it is. If the guv'nor would have found it useful, then I ought to."

Muttering to himself and pondering deeply, Tinker rose and mechanically dressed himself. Then calling Pedro, who was lazily stretching himself in the path of sunlight which fell through the window, the lad placed the steel cover back on the case, and descended to the dining room.

Instead of seating him at Blake's old table, the waiter led him to a table at the window and overlooking the bay.

As he took his seat and gazed out at the beautiful scene before him, Tinker half-started up and rubbed his eyes, for there, out in the bay, riding gracefully at anchor as though she had never left, was the rakish white yacht which had caused him such chagrin the previous night.

At that moment Roberts entered, and seeing the astonishment depicted on Tinker's face, he looked out of the window.

"Good heavens!" he cried. "Am I dreaming, or was our expedition last night a dream?"

But Tinker was too busy with his thoughts to answer. Slowly a conviction was forcing itself on his mind, that there was something deeper than he had thought in the yacht's departure the previous night. Her sudden return started him on a certain line of reasoning which led him to the conclusion that the yacht had left and returned for only one purpose—to avoid him and Roberts.

From that conclusion he took the next obvious step, which was that, supposing the first theory to be correct, then there must be some person or persons who were aware of his identity and purpose, and who were watching his every movement.

His smooth, young face set grimly as he reached that point, and then, by a more roundabout method, he reached the same conclusion which Blake had reached at one jump, after his examination of the rooms of the missing guests. That conclusion was that some person or persons connected with the mystery were residing in the hotel.

As soon as he had finished his breakfast, Tinker rose; but, on reaching the office, he paused in the shadow of the great staircase, and looked in amazement at the usually undemonstrative Pedro.

There, near the main entrance, and dressed in a charming close-fitting costume of white serge, with a big panama hat on her graceful head, was the same young woman who had aroused his admiration the previous day, and submitting to her dainty pats with every sign of delighted recognition was the staid, solemn Pedro.

Tinker gasped.

"Well, by jiminy!" he muttered. "If this isn't the queerest place I ever struck! For Pedro, of all people in the world, to take up like that with strangers! Not that he hasn't good taste!" he added hastily, as his eyes caught the delicious profile of the young woman in white.

Leaving his position by the staircase, he sauntered along towards the young woman and the dog, and Pedro, as he saw his master, left his fair friend and padded over to him, while the young woman looked up with a dazzling smile.

"I hope you don't mind my petting your dog?" she said, with the faintest trace of a foreign accent in her voice.

"Oh, no, indeed!" replied Tinker, bowing low. "It is rarely that he takes any notice of strangers. It would almost seem that he knew you."

As he made the remark, Tinker glanced straight into the eyes of the young woman; but hers were wide-opened wells of innocence. And, after a few more polite words, Tinker turned away, deciding there was nothing of a suspicious nature there.

Had he turned suddenly he would have surprised a tender little smile of amusement on the face of his fair friend, who was following him up the staircase with her eyes, and in it he would have read the riddle of much that was obscure.

Carefully closing the door of his room after him, Tinker sat down on the edge of the bed, and contemplated the steel case which lay on the floor in front of him.

Ponder as he would, he could not fathom Blake's idea in having the machine sent down; but he knew the need for it must have been imperative, otherwise Blake would not have sent for it. He decided, however, that as there seemed nothing else definite to do he would attempt to hit on the reason by chance. With this idea in view, he rang the bell and, on the boy answering it, said:

"You see that steel case there?"

"Yes, sir," replied the boy.

"Do you think you can manage to wrap it up, and take it along the shore path towards the links without anybody seeing you?"

"Oh, yes, sir! I can go by the back way."

"Very well. Wrap it up and take it, but bear in mind that not a soul must see you! Don't start for twenty minutes, and walk along the path until you hear a whistle. Then follow its direction, and you will find me waiting. If you think you can do this without being seen, there's half-a-sovereign for you!"

As he finished Tinker rose, and, calling Pedro, picked up Blake's bag of golf clubs, and started out.

He had no desire for the reporter's company that day, and, seeing Roberts in the distance, achieved an adroit manoeuvre which left that breezy young man wondering what had become of him. Then, with the bag over his shoulder, he sauntered along in the direction of the shore path, which he entered boldly.

Half-way along, however, he paused, and, after a careful look around, dodged into the trees which stretched to the shore.

After ten minutes' cautious search, he discovered a small clearing which proved ideal for his purpose.

In front of him stretched the bay with the yacht in the distance, while from where he stood he had a perfect view of the side of the hotel facing the sea, with the tiny cove at its foot.

Barely had he decided on the spot as suitable when a broken whistle sounded behind him, as the author of it endeavoured to get around the intricacies of the latest rag-time.

Tinker, recognising that it must be the boy with the case, whistled in reply, and a few moments later proved him to be correct, for a crashing of the trees followed, and his messenger broke through into the little clearing.

Tinker gave him the promised half-sovereign, and, after a final word of caution, dismissed him. Then, squatting on the ground, he set to work.

First he took off the cover, and, settling the steel case upside down on the soft turf, used it as a stand for the machine. After that he spent some time connecting up the complicated system of wires, batteries, etc., and in tuning up.

Then, cautioning Pedro not to wander about, Tinker settled down, and applied the receiver to his head. Once this was settled, he drew out a pair of powerful glasses, and trained them on first the yacht, and then the hotel.

In this position he was destined to pass many long, weary hours; but Blake had long ago inculcated in him the axiom that in their work impatience was to be avoided like poison, and the very patience and thoroughness of the lad's watch was proof as to how well he had learned his lesson.

It was past four in the afternoon before anything occurred to attract Tinker's attention.

He had eschewed lunch for fear of perhaps missing something, and the close application which he had given to the business in hand had wearied him considerably.

He was determined, however, to find out if possible for what reason Blake had desired the wireless telephone, for if he knew that, he felt he would be a long way ahead of his present position.

At last something happened which caused his flagging energies to revive, and he bent forward keenly with the glasses trained on a window in the hotel overlooking the tiny cove. A white-clad figure had approached the window and thrown it up, and through the glasses Tinker had no trouble in recognising Pedro's new acquaintance.

Watching closely, Tinker saw the figure disappear and return a moment later, and his heart bounded as he saw she bore a complicated-looking machine not unlike the one before him.

So excited was he that the hand holding the glasses trembled, but as he saw the machine put into place on the window-sill, and the shapely head of the Comtesse de Rastonet bend over it, he dropped the glasses and quickly ran his fingers over his own.

For a minute it was as dead as it had been all day, but at the end of that time a sudden change took place as it registered the call which was being sent out on the still air.

Hardly breathing for excitement, Tinker waited until he heard the reply, first faint and then clear, and his chest heaved as he caught the following:

"Yes, yes; is it you? How is everything on the yacht?"

"All right! We gave the boat the slip all right."

"Yes, I saw them returning, and they looked disappointed. Listen now. It is time to bring things to a head. Half the guests have left on account of the rumours, and the rest will be departing in a day or two. If I stay after the others leave it will attract suspicion to me. I have made up a full report, which I will send to the Press, but before doing so we will take one more to make the climax beyond doubt."

"Very well. But isn't it risky?"

"Of course, but that must be managed. Have the boat at the old spot at the same time tonight."

"All right! Is that all?"

"Yes! Oh, a moment. How is the last arrival?"

"You mean the enemy?"

"Yes."

"Oh, he's all right He has succeeded in nearly killing half a dozen of our men. I don't think there is any cause for worry on your part."

"Very well; that is all. Good-bye!"

Tinker heaved a long sigh of joy as the machine went dead again, and, picking up the glasses, he saw the white-garbed figure at the window lift the machine off the sill and close the sash. Then the lad removed the receiver from his head, and, clasping his hands behind him, lay back on the soft turf and gazed up at the flawless blue overhead.

Pedro approached and nestled his great muzzle on his master's chest, looking at him with great eyes which plainly said:

"Have you forgotten that there is such a thing as food, and that a big dog like I am needs plenty?"

But Tinker was absorbed in the contemplation of the startling conversation he had just heard. Slowly he mentally ticked off the points. Firstly, he now knew why Blake wanted the wireless telephone.

In some way he had discovered that the Comtesse de Rastonet was using one, and had been curious to know why.

Secondly, he knew that in her he had found the hotel guest who was mixed up in the mysterious disappearances which had occurred.

Thirdly, he knew that still another kidnapping was intended, and if he worked carefully he could forestall them and perhaps capture them red-handed.

Fourthly, he knew that the "last arrival" to whom the conversation referred was almost certain to refer to Blake, and he grinned in delight at the remark that he had nearly killed half a dozen of their men.

But the point to receive urgent attention was the third one—namely, the projected plan for making another capture that night. Who it would be he had no idea, but to be on the safe side he must keep careful watch. She had said the same place and time, and the question was, just what did that mean? Where would the place be but the small beach where his investigations led him to believe, and rightly, that Blake had been captured.

"And as for the time—well," he muttered, "he would not risk losing on that point." As soon as it was dark he would get Bentley and Forsythe to supply him with half a dozen able men from the hotel. Then they would conceal themselves in the bushes and watch developments if it took all night.

With this decision, Tinker rose, and, packing up the machine, concealed it in the bushes to await the boy whom he would send for it. Then, calling Pedro, he started back for the hotel to make the necessary arrangements for what he hoped would be a grand coup.

Bentley and Forsythe listened like two thirsty men to Tinker's proposal, and drank up greedily all the information which he thought wise to give them. They had reached such a stage that they clutched at the slightest straw of hope, and when Tinker had finished, Forsythe left at once to make arrangements for the necessary men.

Roberts entered the office at that moment, and forgave Tinker his desertion of him in the prospect of coming copy. Then the party broke up and adopted an elaborate carelessness of manner.

Tinker had told Bentley and Forsythe that the coming night's operations, as well as the previous disappearances, were the work of one of the hotel guests, but he decided not to tell them her identity yet, and to all their persuasive arguments he turned a deaf ear.

He would, if he could, spoil her game, and then lead a party to Blake's rescue; but he knew if the partners were aware of her identity now they would immediately place her under arrest and send the police to raid the yacht, a proceeding which in Tinker's mind would be abortive of result, and only cause the birds to fly.

After dinner, when darkness had fallen, and the soft fragrance of the summer's night was stealing across the water, had one been curiously inclined, one might have seen several stealthy figures creep out through the back entrance of the hotel and one by one take their way through the gloom in the direction of the shore path.

Along this they went until they reached the first small beach near the golf links. There the first arrival found Tinker and Roberts waiting, and when the last man had arrived there were, besides Tinker and the reporter, six of the most able-bodied of the hotel servants.

With a silent gesture Tinker, with Pedro, led the way, and in single file the little party wound silently along over the jutting point until they reached the second beach where Blake had put up his courageous battle against overwhelming odds.

There Tinker came to a pause, and choosing for purposes of concealment the self-same bush which Blake had chosen, he arranged his men behind it and cautioned them against noise.

Then, with Roberts and Pedro beside him, he sank down behind it himself, and, lying flat, as had his master before him, he trained his glasses over the waters of the bay.

Had Tinker known that his move that night was the very one above all others which Yvonne desired him to make, his chagrin would have been too deep for words. Knowing nothing whatever about the heavy silken cord which on certain occasions hung from the Comtesse de Rastonet's window, he had at once jumped to the conclusion that the "same place" was the beach to which he had led his men.

With the draft he had made on the hotel staff there were very few employees about its corridors, and all unconsciously Tinker had cleared the way for the intended operations of the comtesse.

However, he was in ignorance of that fact then, and as hour after hour went by without any sign on the waters of the bay, his interest or expectation did not abate a jot, for he felt he was in the one spot where it would be possible to forestall the plans of the other side.

Had he carried his deductions a little further, as had Blake, he would have remembered that the duchess and the marquis were kidnapped at night, and that being so it must have been an impossibility to convey them from the hotel to the beach during those hours.

But Tinker had his whole plan of campaign mapped out, and as far as he could see it offered every sign of success. Who was this night's intended victim he did not know, but his plan was to intercept the captors at the beach, capture the whole lot with the aid of the force he had brought, disguise his men in the garb of the prisoners he would take, and leave at once for the yacht, which he would raid and capture. Certainly it looked well and promised well.

It must have been midnight before two shimmering splashes of phosphorescence far out told him, as it had told Blake, that a boat was approaching the shore. Nearer and nearer it came, but not until it was only a few hundred yards from the shore did Tinker see with a gasp of surprise that instead of making for the beach where they lay concealed it was disappearing behind the jutting point, and seemed to be heading in the direction of the hotel.

Had his plans gone wrong? Was there, after all, another rendezvous than the one he had felt confident was the chosen spot? As the minutes sped by and the boat did not reappear it seemed so, and, realising that he might after all lose his quarry, he leaped to his feet.

"We've made a mistake," he said quickly. "Up, men, and lose no time. Follow me! Ready? Double-quick!"

With that, Tinker led off at a sharp dogtrot with the others trailing along in surprise behind him. Back up the rough path they went, and down again to the first beach. There were no signs of the boat there, and Tinker redoubled his pace towards the hotel.

A smothered groan behind him told him someone had gone down with a turned ankle, but he did not pause. Every moment was precious, and he knew it. Pedro was travelling easily, and seemed from his alert poise to know something critical was in the air.

Somebody close behind was breathing heavily, but whether it was Roberts or not Tinker couldn't tell, nor in the tensity of his excitement and the keenness of his disappointment at his mistake did he care.

It was no sinecure travelling along the densely-lined shore path at night, but, though treacherous, it was the shortest way, and the lad gave a panting gurgle of relief as he cleared the woods and broke out on to open ground.

Beyond him lay the hotel, with only an occasional light dotted here and there. Inside, he knew Bentley and Forsythe were anxiously awaiting the result of the expedition. Little did they dream that right over their heads the last act of the night's drama was even then being played.

As he drew nearer to the hotel, Tinker saw to his left a dark blotch, with several dark figures in it, and he shouted with a hoarse croak to his companions behind as he turned and headed towards it.

It was the boat, not fifty yards away, but whether it had just reached the little cove or was just leaving, Tinker could not tell. A warning shout behind him, however, brought him up just in time, and he paused with widened eyes and heaving chest as he saw he had been on the very point of going headlong over a twenty-foot cliff on to the jagged rocks below.

Turning quickly, he panted out:

"Isn't there a way down here?"

"No, sir!" gasped the man who had warned him. "The only way is through the hotel."

"All right, come on," jerked Tinker, and, turning, he tore back in the direction of the hotel entrance.

Running as he was he could see the dark figures of his men trailing along at varying distances, but of Roberts there was no sign. Unceremoniously pushing open the door, Tinker dashed in and almost collided with Bentley.

"Quick, quick!" gasped Tinker. "Which way can we get to the cove on the sea side of the hotel?"

"Why—what?" stuttered the amazed Bentley.

"Quick, man!" jerked Tinker. "Every moment is precious."

The man who had warned Tinker at the edge of the cliff, dashed in at this moment and panted:

"Come on, sir. I'll show you the way!"

Butting the stuttering Bentley to one side, Tinker dashed on, followed by Forsythe, who had come out to see what the noise was. The guide led the way up the staircase, and turned to a corridor leading to the left; but at that moment another racing figure coming towards them collided with him at the turn, and they both went down, Tinker and Pedro turning complete somersaults over them.

"Who is it?" gasped Tinker. "Grab him—hold him! He may be one of them!"

The man of whom he spoke, however, fought like a wild cat, and struggled to his feet, gasping:

"My wife, my wife! Where is she? I can't find her, and, by heavens, if anybody around here is playing a joke, I'll make him suffer for it!"

Suddenly Tinker recognised the face of the man who had arrived shortly before with his wife for a honeymoon, and it flashed over him that with true, diabolical cunning his wife had been chosen as the next victim of the kidnappers. Dashing forward, he seized the crazed man by the arm, and said sharply:

"Come with us, and perhaps you will find your wife. Hurry!"

Before the man had time to reply, Tinker was following the guide again, and the honeymooner had no choice but to follow. The man in the lead took several turnings until he finally brought up at the head of what was evidently a rear staircase of the hotel. Down this the whole party clattered pell-mell to bring up, panting, at a big door at the bottom.

"This door opens out on to the back," panted the guide, who happened to be one of the under porters.

"Good!" rapped out Tinker, as he caught hold of Pedro's collar and dragged him back. Then, in a louder tone, he shouted: "Revolvers ready, everybody! We'll have to make a dash and do the job quickly!"

A murmur of agreement met his words from the men behind, who, including Forsythe and the honeymooner, now numbered four. Neither of those two had revolvers, but from the expression on their faces it was very evident that they were quite prepared to tackle anything with their bare hands.

All this time the under porter had been struggling with the door. The key had turned readily, but pull as he would he could not drag it open.

Tinker dropped his hold on Pedro's collar, and endeavoured to help the other, but even their united efforts were of no avail; the door held fast.

"I have it," panted Tinker, "they have tied it from the outside. Is there no other way to the beach?"

The under porter shook his head.

"No," he jerked, "this is the only one."

Tinker drew back, and for a moment the boyish look faded from his face as his eyes swept over the men about him. Then he spoke, and his clear voice trembled ever so slightly as he did so.

"In that case," he jerked out, "there is only one course left. Follow me!"

"Where to?" asked Forsythe quickly.

"To the rooms of the Comtesse de Rastonet!" cried Tinker, and with that he tore back up the stairs, the whole crowd at his heels.

Up staircase after staircase they went, until Tinker reached the floor on which was his own room, or, to be more correct, Blake's. There he paused until Forsythe gained his side.

"Which is it?" he rapped out.

"Sixty-three," panted Forsythe, and Tinker started on.

Only a few steps sufficed to bring him up before the door of Yvonne's sitting-room, and without preamble of any description, Tinker began a vigorous tattoo on the door. Then he held up his hand to the others to be quiet, and listened with his ear against the door. Not the slightest sound rewarded his efforts, and he began pounding again.

"Mademoiselle, mademoiselle," he cried, "open. It is useless to resist."

"Mademoiselle," interrupted Forsythe, "it isn't. She is the Comtesse de Rastonet."

"A lot you know!" grunted Tinker, beginning another attack on the door. "Mademoiselle," he called. "I will count ten. If you do not open then, we will force the door!"

Still no answer came, and in a loud voice Tinker counted one—two—three—four—five—six—seven—eight—nine—ten. Then he turned to the others:

"Come on! Stand back, and rush it together! Look out when you get inside the room!"

"But," began Forsythe, "you can't force in the door of the comtesse's room that way. She has nothing to do with the matter."

"She has this much to do with it," blazed Tinker, "that she is responsible for all the disappearances!"

Then to the men he cried:

"Are you ready? Then come on!"

They gave a hoarse shout as they drew back for a run, and dashed forward.

The door yielded to their rush like a flimsy screen, and as it crashed down they tumbled in a tangled mass into the room. Tinker was the first on his feet, and as he stood up he was just in time to see a white arm disappear over the sill, and to hear a mocking laugh float in through the open window.

He dashed forward, and leaned out, grasping wildly at the figure just a few feet below him. As he peered down, the descending figure looked up, and by the faint light he saw, not the features of the Comtesse de Rastonet, but the old familiar features of Yvonne.

He had been certain ever since the afternoon that the comtesse and Yvonne were one and the same person, although, search the features of the comtesse as he would, he could not reconcile them in any one point with those of Yvonne, unless, perhaps, it might be the eyes.

How the radical change had taken place he could not guess, but there was no time for conjecture. Every moment she was slipping down, and as she laughed again that mocking laugh, it stung Tinker to action.

Drawing back, he raised one leg over the sill in order to follow Yvonne down the rope, but suddenly something happened, and so quickly, that at that time he did not know just what it was.

Forsythe had been unable to believe that Tinker was right in raiding the rooms of the comtesse, nor was be able to believe that she was, as Tinker said, responsible for the mysterious disappearances which were threatening to ruin him.

As he heard her first mocking laugh, however, he realised the truth with stunning force. The sight of the rope secured to a heavy bureau cleared his mind of any doubt whatever, and at the sound of the second mocking laugh he sprang forward with a savage growl of rage, determined to wreak his vengeance on the author of all his troubles.

Just how it happened it would be hard to say. Tinker was half out of the window, and Pedro was standing on his hind legs, his front feet on the sill. The men behind were crowding up to take their turn in going down the rope.

Then a knife flashed in Forsythe's hand, his eyes shone with the madness of suddenly snapped control, and, leaping forward, he bent recklessly out of the window, evidently intending to cut the rope below Tinker and above Yvonne in order to send her hurtling to the beach below.

Tinker vaguely divined his purpose and endeavoured to stop him, for though he and Yvonne were on opposite sides, such methods against the opposite sex were not in his curriculum.

At the sign of opposition, Forsythe went stark-staring mad.

He made another lunge, but this time he did not attempt to reach below Tinker to cut the rope. The sharp blade of the knife struck the rope where it bent taut over the edge of the sill, and he made a vicious cut.

In some canine way Pedro divined the madman's purpose, and realised the danger to his master. With red, open jaws, and great bared teeth, he sprang forward, but he was the barest fraction of a second too late, and with a soft, ripping sound the rope parted.

Tinker clutched madly for the sill, but he was too late, and the next moment Tinker, Yvonne, and Pedro went crashing down, with Forsythe following to the accompaniment of a mad, cackling laugh.

The Eighth Chapter
Blake's Escape—The Chase—Yvonne Gives In—The End

WHEN through the unfortunate breaking of the thole-pin by Lord Cray, Blake's plans for the second time that night were ruined, nothing remained but to swallow his chagrin and to submit to the far from gentle handling of his captors.

Once he had gained the deck, the immaculately-dressed and drawling Graves sauntered up and nodded cheerfully at him; but even without that, Blake would have recognised from the familiar deck surroundings that he was aboard the *Fleur-de-Lys*, which, as far as outside appearance went, was perfectly disguised.

"You must pardon the necessity for keeping you bound," drawled Graves, puffing nonchalantly at his cigarette. "Your latest exploit in the boat, however, has disabled several of our men, and until mademoiselle arrives, I can't take the responsibility of losing you. Of course, you won't give your word of honour not to attempt to escape?"

"Certainly not!" snapped Blake shortly.

"Ah," sighed Graves, "I thought not! That being so, much as I regret it, I must carry out orders, though, to tell you the truth, Mr. Blake, in my opinion, the safest thing to do with you is to tie a fifty-pound shot to your heels and drop you over the side."

"No doubt," replied Blake; "but if you have quite finished expounding your theory as to what should be done with me, I'd like to be taken to wherever you intend keeping me."

"By all means," grinned Graves, as he saw the irritation his remark had caused.

He turned and beckoned to a white-jacketed steward, who led the way, and, assisted along by a couple of sailors, Blake descended the main companionway.

While he had been talking with Graves, Lord Cray had been led away, and, scan the deck as he would, he saw no signs of the missing duchess and marquis.

Blake had made no attempt to analyse the new aspect which had presented itself since his discovery on the beach earlier in the evening that it was Mademoiselle Yvonne who was behind the events which had caused a reign of terror in the hotel during the past few days.

In the first place, his fight with Hendricks and the sailors had taken all his attention, and, since then, he had had no opportunity. But as the steward unlocked the door of a small cabin and stood aside, Blake entered, and without ceremony, cast himself down in the single bunk which it contained, tired, sore, and irritable, at what he considered the evening's fiasco.

Those who have seen the *Fleur-de-Lys*, or a picture of it, will remember that the whole stern from side to side was occupied by Yvonne's laboratory. Separating that from the cabins and saloons was a narrow passage, running also from side to side, and containing a porthole at each end. Then came the cabins, and, though he did not know it at the time, Blake was occupying the one on the port side next to that passage, and consequently, his cabin was the one containing the second large porthole from the stern, as the laboratory was lighted by portholes in the stern, and contained none on either the port or starboard side.

As Blake lay in the bunk and shifted over on one side to ease his aching arms, he began reflecting over his discovery that Yvonne was the Comtesse de Rastonet, and much that had been obscured by clouds suddenly became clear to him. He saw, as in a flash, the reason for the yacht being left at anchor in the bay. He saw, as though he had been present at each coup, just how the clever ingenuity of Yvonne would accomplish its purpose, and, knowing that, his thoughts went, as always, to the motive.

With Blake the solution of every case rested on this. Without discovering the motive, a crime might be submerged in impenetrable mystery for months, years, or perhaps forever; but his tireless investigations to discover that element had formed the keynote of his brilliant career.

It may be said that any and every detective goes for the motive, and to that may be answered—yes. But—and there is a vast world of difference—nine times out of ten he is in a quandary as to whether he has found the true motive or a false one. Only the complex, mathematical system of analysis and deduction, as used by Sexton Blake, can decide that, and the amazing record of Blake's successes is proof enough of the efficacy of such a system.

This system he applied that night to the problem in hand. Thoughtfully his mind dwelt on the previous cases in which he had been pitted against Yvonne and her perfectly-organised system.

He realised that in planning her coups she was actuated, not by hope of personal gain or by criminal motives such as are commonly understood by that term, but rather by a misconceived and quixotic notion of revenge against the men who had swindled her and her frail mother in Australia, and who, keeping within the elaborate and comprehensive letter of the law, evaded the legal consequences of their acts.

As far as Blake's personal sympathies were concerned, he could not find it in his heart to blame Yvonne, but in the practice of his profession and the prosecution of his duty, he forbade the entry of any sentiment into the situation.

Moreover, he realised that his position regarding Yvonne was more delicate than would have been that of any other criminal investigator, for, in his heart of hearts, he knew the wayward young woman's love was his, and he even acknowledged to himself that, when she disappeared for months at a time, he felt a vague desire to once again experience the undeniable appeal of her subtle charm.

He smiled as he thought of her successful disguise as the Comtesse de Rastonet, and he smiled still more when he thought of their dinner together.

Certainly she had the advantage of him there, for, though suspicious of her, he had not the faintest idea that she was Yvonne, whereas he was not disguised, and it must have been hard for her to keep from indulging in a roguish smile.

As his thoughts reached this point, Blake roused himself, and began inspecting his surroundings in an attempt to discover what hopes there were of escaping. The very barrenness of the cabin told him it was only a temporary prison, probably until Yvonne's arrival; but, nevertheless, he got to his feet and began making a tour. The first thing he inspected was the porthole.

Gazing through, he could only see a vast stretch of starlit waters, and knew the land lay on the other side of the yacht. The porthole was of a fairish size, and after a critical examination, Blake decided, if he could get his hands free, he would be able to squirm through it. Leaving it, he closely examined the remainder of the cabin, but not a solitary article was there which, by the wildest stretch of the imagination could be used as a method of loosening his hands.

He returned to the bunk, and again cast himself down, this time with his face to the wall. As he did so, his bound hands came into contact with the sharp edge of the bunk, and with a jerk he sat up.

An inspection of the edge convinced him that it would take a long time at the very best, to sever the strong rope which bound him, but, even though he failed, any action was better than lying trussed up like a sack of meal.

Without a moment's hesitation he shifted his position, in order to bring the rope against the edge, and then he set to work, backwards and forwards, as well as the limited scope of his movements would allow.

Dawn found him weary and cramped, but still at it, and when the steward came at sunrise with his breakfast, Blake had desisted barely five minutes before.

He had no idea how much progress he had made, but, realising the folly of overtaxing his strength, he dropped off to sleep, and not until the steward returned with his lunch did he stir.

After lunch he was permitted a little exercise up and down the corridor, and the steward bathed his aching head in cold water.

After an hour of this he was led back, and, as the door closed, he heaved a sigh of relief, for only the gloom of the passage had prevented the man from seeing his frayed bonds.

All the afternoon Blake worked, but by evening the bonds still held strongly, and his arms ached with excruciating pain from the cramped action.

After he had eaten his evening meal and the man had gone, he got to his feet, and, half standing, half sitting over the edge of the bunk, he went at the monotonous work again.

He had been working some time when the sudden throbbing of the screw told him the engines had been started. Dumbfounded, he hastened to the porthole, and looked out.

At that moment the yacht began to move, heading out to sea, and Blake wrinkled his brows in puzzlement.

Had Yvonne arrived, and was she putting to sea at once? If not, what had happened, and what had developed on shore since his capture? Had Tinker arrived in answer to his telegram, and if so, what steps was he taking?

These, and a dozen other questions presented themselves to Blake; but as the yacht held steadily on, it seemed as though his efforts to escape would be too late, even if he did succeed in breaking his bonds.

Little did he know that it was Tinker and Roberts in a small boat which had caused the yacht to put to sea, and that even then the lad was gazing in futile anger at the swiftly-retreating yacht.

Blake, however, was determined, if possible, to discover what course was being taken, and, for that reason, he stood at the porthole throughout the night. As the yacht swung round on her way out to sea he saw a bald point off on the port side. Then the yacht swung further and steamed on for an hour or more.

Still he watched, and as she took a wide, sweeping curve Blake could see they were turning. On she steamed for what seemed about the same length of time until she took another wide sweep, and as they came round, Blake recognised the same bald point he had seen before.

His interest became roused at this, and he stood patiently while the yacht steamed on in her original line. Then again she swung and returned, and as for the third time Blake recognised the bald point, he knew she was cruising up and down the coast, apparently to put in time.

Dawn found him still at the porthole, but as the bald spot appeared for the fifth time, the yacht suddenly changed her course, and headed back into the bay. Twenty minutes later the engines stopped, and the yacht swung round as the anchor was dropped.

Blake glanced up at the paling stars, and from the fact that they were in the same position as when he had seen them at dawn the previous morning, he knew the yacht was at anchor in her old spot.

Greatly puzzled over the strange all-night cruise up and down the coast, he returned to his bunk.

That day was almost a repetition of the previous one for Blake. In the morning he slept. Then after lunch he exercised, and after that he tackled his bonds with renewed energy. He was compelled to desist while the guard fed him his evening meal, and in that moment Blake blessed the rule which had compelled him to eat with his hands bound, for, during the afternoon, he felt first one strand go and then another.

Inspired by his success, he forgot his aching arms, and once more set to work. He heard every hour struck, but still he kept on, and barely heard the last clang of eight bells die away when he stumbled forward free as his bonds snapped and dropped to the floor.

For five minutes Blake vigorously rubbed his aching wrists and arms, then he stooped and unlaced his boots. Discarding his coat and vest, he stuffed what papers he had in his oilskin wallet, and thrust it in his trousers pocket.

Then going softly to the porthole, he raised himself, and peered out. All seemed silent up above, and with a final look around, he began squirming through the porthole. The fit was tight, but by twisting and heaving, he eventually managed it.

Ten minutes later he was hanging by his hands from the bottom rim of the porthole, his stockinged feet braced against the side.

Then, judging the drop, he let go, and with toes pointed downwards, dropped into the water below with barely a splash.

He came up near the stern, and, swimming round into the shadow cast by its over-hanging bulk, he clutched a rudderchain and looked shorewards.

It was at least a mile, he knew; but to a man in good condition was not a long swim. The difficulty lay, however, in the fact that the water was phosphorescent, and were a good watch being kept, he ran great risk of being seen.

It must be risked, however, and he decided that, so far as possible, he would swim underwater.

With this decision, Blake dived silently and swam strongly, only his head showing black against the water as he came up fifty yards away from the yacht. Then he struck out, swimming steadily for the distant lights which showed on the shore.

He had been swimming for some time when suddenly a black shape appeared ahead. Treading water, he looked over the surface, and as it drew near, he saw it was a boatload of people.

Nearer and nearer it came, and still he could not tell whether they were friends or foes. They appeared to be rowing at a terrific pace, and Blake was puzzled until he heard the familiar sound of Hendricks' voice.

Then he took a long breath, and silently sank into the black depths.

When he came again to the surface, the boat had passed, and he was about to start once more for the shore, when another boat appeared, being rowed as fiercely as was the first, and treading water preparatory to sinking again, Blake watched its approach.

***

While Blake had been making his escape from the *Fleur-de-Lys* the exciting events had been taking place in the hotel which culminated in the terrific fall of Tinker, Yvonne, Pedro and Forsythe into the cove below.

While Tinker was endeavouring to stop Forsythe in his mad rush, Yvonne had been steadily slipping down the rope, and when the crash came, she had a bare ten feet to fall. The willing hands of her men caught her and swung her clear just as the others came dashing down.

Forsythe, in his madness, had hoped to avoid Pedro's spring in defence of his master. This leap carried him well out, and, as though his course were directed by some inscrutable force, he dropped straight as a rocket, his head striking the gunwale of the boat with a sickening crack, which told at once that he had been instantly killed.

Tinker's wild clutch, however, and Pedro's spring had left both the lad and the dog in near the wall when the rope parted. Together they dropped, and almost at the selfsame moment they flopped into the five feet of water in the cove little the worse for their experience.

Yvonne, though trembling from her own experience, and sickened by Forsythe's fate, watched anxiously until both the lad and the dog reappeared. Then she spoke in a low tone to her men, and they leaped to obey.

First they dragged Forsythe clear and laid him on the strip of beach; then they assisted Yvonne into the boat, where the drooping figure of another woman could be seen. After that, they piled in after and pushed off just as Tinker and Pedro landed on the jagged rocks to the left.

A moment later they were rowing madly for the yacht, while Tinker and Pedro took to the water again and landed on the narrow beach.

One glance sufficed to show Tinker that Forsythe was beyond any more worldly troubles, and he turned grimly to the men who were crowding at the window far above. It would have been easy to send a hail of bullets after the retreating boat, but the honeymooner had cried out that the drooping figure beside Yvonne was his wife. Consequently they refrained, though even with only Yvonne, Tinker would have forbidden firing. But something must be done, and done quickly, if he were to retrieve his position.

Suddenly his eyes lighted on the row-boat which he and Roberts had used so unsuccessfully the previous night.

From that they travelled to the door in the hotel which opened on to the little beach, and which Yvonne's men had so cunningly tied.

Then he dashed forward and shouted up to the under-porter, who was leaning out of the window:

"Down the stairs again! I will cut the rope! Hurry, or we shall be too late!"

As the heads above disappeared, Tinker jerked out his knife and attacked the rope which held the door. Slashing it through, he then turned and made for the boat.

Just as he shoved it along and it took the water, the under-porter, followed by the wild-eyed honeymooner and three others, opened the door and dashed out.

Not waiting for any laggards, they piled into the boat and as Tinker grasped the tiller-ropes, willing hands seized the oars and began rowing madly after the other boat.

Never was there a more earnest chase than that. Already the chase had cost one life, and the shock of that had made Tinker and his companions grimly determined to exact a reckoning. As for the honeymooner, he was half demented, and worked at his oar with the strength of two men.

Out of the cove they swept, and into the open bay. As yet the other boat was a good distance ahead, but Tinker hoped in the mile they had to cover that his men, spurred on by their feeling, would pull up.

Nor was he disappointed in his hopes, for gradually the leading boat began to assume a clearer-cut outline, and he shouted to his men to keep at it.

It was then, as the voice travelled over the water, that Blake had been preparing to sink for the second time into the depths of the bay, for Tinker's boat was the second boat which had caused Blake to pause.

Instead of sinking, however, he struck out strongly as Tinker's clear young voice floated over the water, and, swimming with a powerful overhand stroke, Blake cut across the course of the boat.

Then he raised himself up and shouted.

Tinker could hardly credit his senses as he heard the well-known imperative tones come from the waters of the bay, but as a second call came, he pulled his tiller-rope, and sent the boat in that direction.

Then a dark head appeared, and he shouted for joy as Blake's head and shoulders became visible against the water.

A moment later the wondering rowers had backed water, while Blake clambered in, and without word of explanation, he stood up and took command.

"On, on!" he cried out sharply. "There is no time to lose! Keep her head straight, Tinker."

As he stood there hatless and coatless, with the water dripping from him, he looked like an avenging spirit of the waters. His white shirt contrasted distinctly with his dark trousers, and his face, stern and clear-cut as granite, finished the impression of force which he gave, and inspired the men at the oars to greater zeal.

Ever the yacht drew nearer, but every moment was bringing them closer to the leading boat. Short as had been the pause in order to pick up Blake, it had consumed valuable time, and, where, before it had been almost a certainty that they would overtake the other boat, now it was only a desperate chance.

But, urged on by Blake, they laid to with a will, and if human effort could perform the feat, they must succeed.

When barely a hundred yards remained between them and the yacht, Blake saw his men would succeed in reaching the ladder first, and, bending down, he curtly demanded

Tinker's revolver. The lad passed it up to his master and then Blake, straightening up, levelled it and sent a stern command to the other boat to stop.

Yvonne's answer was to raise a white handkerchief, and Blake heaved an involuntary sigh of relief as he saw there was a chance of avoiding bloodshed while the two women were there.

Nearer and nearer drew the two boats, their respective crews resting on their oars until finally they bumped gently together and drifted on by their own impetus to the bottom of the ladder which hung from the yacht's deck.

"What do you want?" asked Yvonne faintly, and Blake drew a sharp breath as he saw the features of the real Yvonne, and not those of the Comtesse de Rastonet, for on that, the last night of her campaign, Yvonne had partly undone the work which had changed her appearance.

"It isn't a case of what I want," replied Blake sharply. "It is a case of what I demand. I demand firstly the release of the Duchess of Foreland, the Marquis of Rondel and Lord Cray, together with all their belongings."

"And my wife—my wife!" cried the honeymooner, pointing at the woman beside Yvonne, who was still under the influence of the vapour.

"Oh!" remarked Blake. "So you made another raid, did you, mademoiselle? Very well, kindly pass the lady over now. Then I will ascend with you and take formal possession of the yacht, when you can hand over your prisoners to me."

"Indeed?" answered Yvonne coldly. "You seem to have made your arrangements without consulting me. It would be interesting to know also how you happen to be in that boat, when, by all calculations, you should be in a cabin on the yacht."

"That is entirely beside the question!" snapped Blake. "Sufficient is it that I am here, and what I propose must be carried out. If not, I will use force, and as I have already been in contact with your men, I think they will know I mean what I say."

Yvonne's eyes softened as she thought of the fight on the beach, but though she recognised that Blake had the upper hand, while her men were divided between the yacht and the boat, still she did not intend to surrender until forced to do so.

"If I hand over this woman, and lead you to the others you mentioned, will you call a truce?" she asked, looking him in the eyes.

Blake nodded.

"Yes, I'll do that."

Then turning to Tinker, he said:

"Take charge here my lad, and see that there is no friction while I am gone."

With that he turned and made his way to the bow where Yvonne had already arrived. Both boats' crews watched in silence while Yvonne ran lightly up the ladder, followed by Blake, to disappear a moment later over the side, where Graves and the rest of Yvonne's men watched in trepidation.

"You certainly kept a splendid guard to permit Mr. Blake to escape," remarked Yvonne coldly to Graves.

"I give you my word," he protested. "I'm blest if I know how he got away. He was kept bound every moment, and was all right when the guard gave him his meal at seven."

"Indeed!" she replied, raising her brows, and with that swept on towards the saloon with Blake in her wake.

Closing the door after them, Blake sat down in the seat which Yvonne indicated, and as she did likewise, they faced each other in silence. For a long minute the stern man and the young woman with the wistful eyes gazed at each other until Blake leaned his head on one hand and spoke.

"Is either Bentley or Forsythe one of the men against whom you swore vengeance?" he asked abruptly.

"Bentley is, and Forsythe was!" she replied, in low tones.

"Forsythe was?" he echoed, "I don't understand!"

"Forsythe is dead," she said quietly. "He died through his own fault."

"How, please?"

Rapidly Yvonne told the details of the madman's act at the window, and Blake's eyes narrowed as he heard of the peril of Tinker and Pedro.

"And still he kept doing his duty," he murmured softly. "Good boy, he hasn't disappointed me!"

"Can't we come to some arrangement?" asked Yvonne, looking up at him. "Not for myself, but for my men."

"You ask me a very difficult question, mademoiselle," replied Blake slowly. "What you tell me regarding Forsythe's act in causing my assistant to fall to almost certain death alters matters. I was retained by them in this case, but such a treacherous act, even though prompted by madness, causes my duty to them to automatically cease."

Resting his head on his hand, Blake looked at her and said:

"Why don't you give this kind of thing up? I'll guarantee to get you a free pardon if you will. What do you say?"

Yvonne's head dropped, and her voice was very low as she replied:

"I can't! You know that is possible. One thing only will make me change and for that I would do anything!"

She looked up as she finished, her whole soul in her eyes, and Blake felt suddenly weak and helpless as he realised the full force of her love for him.

"I am sorry," he said a trifle huskily. "Let us discuss other matters. Will you give orders to have your prisoners released?"

"I have already done so," she replied. "I sent my uncle while you were down in the boats. They may even be aboard your boat by now. You didn't think I would keep their belongings, which I took did you?" she added, after a pause.

"Of course not!" he answered gruffly, in an attempt to hide his true feelings.

Again in her presence and experiencing the full force of her personality, Blake felt acutely the fact that some solution could not be arrived at which would cause her to change her ways.

Moreover, the feeling which only stirred him faintly while she was not near him, was making itself felt in no uncertain terms, and had Blake given in to it for a moment, it is hard to say what might have happened.

Deep, silent, and strong as was his nature, had he yielded to love, it would have gripped him with a terrific force that would have shaken him to the very depths of his soul. And no woman had ever appealed more to that side of him than did the girl sitting opposite him.

For several minutes he sat in silence, while Yvonne waited to hear her fate. Finally Blake spoke, and for him the tones were unusually gentle.

"You are free to go," he said slowly. "I will straighten matters out at the hotel and smooth over whatever comes up. If you have the duchess and the others put in the boat, and then call up your men, I will get away. All I insist upon is that you leave here at once, for I must inform Scotland Yard that you are here, and of what you have done. Had Forsythe not endangered Tinker's life, I would have acted differently, though, believe me, mademoiselle, it would have been hard!"

As Blake spoke, Yvonne's head drooped lower and lower, and as he finished, she began sobbing quietly.

"Oh," she said chokingly, you—are—good—to—me, and I don't deserve it!"

Blake looked at her bowed head, and then a sudden surge of emotion swept over him.

"Go!" he said hoarsely. "Go quickly!"

Startled by his tense tones, Yvonne lifted her head, but Blake's in turn was bowed on his hands. Softly she rose and moved round the table. Then she bent suddenly, and pressed her lips on his bowed head.

As Blake felt the warmth of her breath and lips, his hands clenched, and he started up with a half-smothered exclamation. For the bare fraction of a second his arms stretched out, and he swung round; but they dropped at once as he saw Yvonne disappear through the door.

He sank back wearily and muttered:

"It is best. It is best. I have done my duty. Anything else would be madness!"

Mechanically he drew out a cigar and lighted it. For ten minutes or more he smoked in silence, and then rising, he made his way out of the saloon and up the companion.

Walking to the side, he knew from the emphatic voice which came up from below, that the duchess, at least, had been released, and as he peered over, he saw the marquis and Lord Cray.

The other boat had already been hoisted up, and Yvonne's whole party, from Graves and Captain Vaughan down, glanced curiously at Blake as he strode through them, and passed to descend the ladder. And more than one of them, including Hendricks the mate, muttered:

"There goes a man!"

What had passed between Blake and Yvonne, they had no idea, but Graves had a shrewd notion, which in the continued non-appearance of Yvonne, became a certainty in his mind.

He said nothing, however, and a moment later Blake had disappeared.

The duchess desired to know what was going to be done about the outrage which had been perpetrated on her, but the marquis and Lord Cray seemed rather to be enjoying the situation than otherwise.

Certainly they had not lacked for attention on board the luxurious yacht, and, like Blake, they had been permitted almost continuously on the deck facing the sea.

When the silent man, who assumed command, made no comment, the duchess desisted from her ravings, and looked at him. The stern set of the jaw, and the sombre look in the eyes seemed to overawe her, for she subsided and spoke not another word.

Tinker, reading the danger-signals in Blake's face, asked no questions, and when his master curtly ordered the bow to be cast off, he did so.

A moment later they were turning, and already the water was being churned up by the propellers of the yacht as Captain Vaughan lost no time in getting under way.

As the distance between boat and yacht grew wider and wider, Blake looked upwards, and through the silent night he could see a lonely, white-clad figure watching the departure, and he knew a pair of great, wistful eyes would follow him shorewards.

Turning back abruptly, he rapped out a curt order, and the rowers bent to the oars with a will.

∗∗∗

On Blake's arrival at the hotel, he found Bentley had had Forsythe's body brought in and laid on a couch. He appeared very much upset at the fate of his partner, and his fat, puffy face looked flabby and lifeless.

Only Sexton Blake and Bentley himself knew what passed when Blake closed the office door and confronted the remaining partner. Only Blake's last words may be quoted, and as he spoke them, his voice was harsh and metallic:

"As I say, had I known the facts, I would never have taken the case for you. For the victims, yes; but it is needless for me to repeat my opinion of you. I will not judge Forsythe or you, for Forsythe has gone to a higher tribunal, and I think you have had a lesson. If you take my advice, you will dispose of this property and swallow your loss."

"How about pay for your services?" asked Bentley in shaking tones.

"You owe me nothing!" snapped Blake curtly. "And now you had better deal with your guests, who were kidnapped. The duchess appears to want compensation."

With that, he turned and left, but before going to meet his guests, Travers Bentley rose and raised his hand.

"I swear," he muttered hoarsely, "that I will never rest until I have had my revenge! Be it soon, or be it late, I will meet that woman who has brought this upon me, and then, let her beware!"

It never occurred to him at the time that the woman of whom he spoke had sworn an equally fervent vow to be revenged, and was as anxious as he to come to grips.

Then he opened the door and went out to meet his guests. It must be confessed that, with all his troubles, Travers Bentley rose to the situation with almost all his old suavity.

The Marquis of Rondel and Lord Cray were prepared to forget what had happened, providing their great curiosity as to the reason and the identity of their captor was satisfied. Bentley promised that on the morrow he would satisfy them fully, and, with a good-tempered smile, they retired.

Then came the duchess, who, as it happened, was an extremely shrewd lady, with an eye always open for the main chance. Consequently, she saw a magnificent action for damages against Bentley, but was graciously pleased to settle the matter on an amicable basis, providing the amount was large enough.

Bentley groaned as he saw there was nothing else for it, and after a strenuous half-hour's argument, they compromised on a thousand pounds.[23]

Then, with a weary sigh, Bentley closed the door and went back to his dead partner, and—his thoughts.

***

Here it may also be stated that the groan heard by Tinker as he was leading the way from the beach to the hotel earlier in the evening had been from Roberts, the reporter, as he went down with a sprained ankle.

When that pushing young man got the full story the next day, as Tinker had promised, and had wired it to his paper, he forgot the pain of his ankle in the frequent contemplation of a highly commendatory epistle from his editor.

***

Blake had heard from Yvonne about Tinker's grit and persistence in the chase, but there was much detail to be gone over. As they sat in Blake's room that night, with Pedro at their feet, Tinker told his story from the moment he had received Blake's telegram at Baker Street.

Blake's eyes lit up with pleasure as Tinker told how he had received the wireless telephone, and the use he had made of it. Then, when he told of how Pedro had guided him to the second beach by the links where Blake's trail suddenly ended, thus giving him his first clue to work on, Blake affectionately pulled the big fellow's ears.

When the lad had finished his tale, Blake rose and put his hand on Tinker's shoulder.

"I am very pleased with your conduct of the case during my absence. You have glossed over your peril when Forsythe cut the rope, but I have heard the story from other lips."

"From—her?" asked Tinker hesitatingly.

Blake nodded and turned away.

"Yes," he said softly; "from—her."

After some moments' silence Blake resumed his seat and satisfied Tinker's eager desire to know the details of his master's doings.

----

[23] £1,000 in 1913 is worth about £116,000.00 in 2020

"But I don't understand, guv'nor, how they got the honeymooner's wife. I can see how she got the duchess, and the marquis, as well as Lord Cray, but not the other."

"Very simple, my lad. She told me how it happened. She left her husband in the sitting-room of their apartments while she went along to the bath. She had completed it, and was returning to her room, when she saw another woman coming along the corridor.

"Naturally, she never dreamed of suspecting anything, and all she remembers is that some sort of spray was squirted in her face. She tried to cry out, but the stuff was overpowering, and that is all she remembers until she woke up an hour ago.

"Of course, it is easy enough for you to reconstruct the rest, since you yourself arrived on the scene shortly after.

"But to bed, my lad. We leave in the motor for London at daybreak."

Long after Tinker was asleep, Blake, with a fragrant cigar between his lips, descended to the terrace and stood in silence as the night waned.

Far out at sea, like, a tiny star, he could see a light which grew fainter and fainter every moment. Finally it disappeared, and when he could see it no more, Blake turned, with a heavy sigh, just as the purple east was changed to grey by the coming dawn.

BASED ON THE 'YVONNE'S VENGEANCE' SERIES
A <u>REAL</u> DETECTIVE FILM.
TO BE RELEASED APRIL 6th, 1914.

SEXTON BLAKE CONFRONTS YVONNE WITH THE NECKLACE.

A stirring scene from "THE CLUE OF THE WAX VESTA," the film which I want you all to see. It is far too good to miss, and I am giving you all the opportunity to have it at your local hall. See the form below.—THE SKIPPER.

FILL THIS FORM UP AND GIVE OR SEND IT TO YOUR LOCAL PICTURE PALACE MANAGER.

To the MANAGER,

_____________________ PICTURE PALACE, _____________________

    Sir,

        I am anxious to see "THE CLUE OF THE WAX VESTA"—the great Sexton Blake Detective Drama in three parts—at your hall. I should esteem it a favour if you would book it soon,

                And oblige,

                     ____

Yvonne's Last Revenge!

HERE IS SOMETHING YOU CANNOT AFFORD TO MISS! →

"THE DIAMOND DRAGON."

Don't forget that this 80,000-worder appears next week.

**Mademoiselle Yvonne,
Dr. Huxton Rymer,
Prince Wu Ling and
The Brotherhood of the
Yellow Beetle**

Prologue

MORE like a rich, unopened casket teeming with wealth and precious stones than anything else is the little-known and swamp-guarded Republic of Colombia, in South America. From the boundaries of Venezuela and the land of the cannibalistic Motillones Indians, past the Gulf of Darien and the threadlike Isthmus of Panama to the blue-foam-edged Pacific, she reeks with hidden wealth and disease.

The vast virgin jungle delta of the Magdalena is in itself a sea guard. The Motillones Indians—of whom little is known—permit entry into their land on the east, but fortunate indeed is the man who can get out again. The fever-ridden Choco district on the west, where the gold-divers hurry through their short span of life, each tend to keep at bay all but the most bold, the most reckless, or, perchance, the dodging fugitives from the law.

But, compared with the forbidding and unexplored expanse which stretches from the head-waters of the Magdalena to the vaguely-known source of the Amazon, these ramparts are like walls of cardboard.

From beyond Bogota, set like a white jewel high up in the green-lined mountains, there is nothing but dense jungle, fever swamps, a multitude of streams, deep, placid, and sinister in places, and merging into rushing, tortuous torrents. Guardian over all is the teeming deadly life of the tropics, from the giant boa-constrictor to the grey, slimy, loglike alligator.

Ranging between these are the millions of brilliantly-plumaged parrots and parakeets, the ibis, the stork, the flamingo, the humming-bird, and a hundred others. The mountain lion or jaguar skulks, lonely and savage, through the gloomy aisles of the great forest, and the wild pig crashes onward in savage herds.

Few men enter here, and fewer leave. But there have been adventurous spirits who have dared its forbidding confines, and some have emerged with mysteriously acquired wealth.

***

In a gloomy, rough sapling and palm-thatched hut on the bank of a jungle-lined stream, which was supposed to wind onwards until it reached the Amazon, sat two men, whose seamed, bearded faces and rough, torn garb indicated a long absence from the accessories of civilisation.

One was tall and thin and gaunt-looking, and his lacklustre eyes spoke of many fever-racked nights which he had known.

Not even the scraggy beard, however, could hide the forbidding set of the jaw, and when it was set, as at present, in an unyielding line, it was not a pleasant sight to see.

The other man, despite the ravages of the jungle, still bore traces of a once well-fed, well-groomed appearance; and, indeed, in the year which Travers Bentley had spent in the wilds of Colombia he had not quite lost the sleek air which had been his when Mademoiselle Yvonne had all but ruined him at the time of the well-known Traders' Bay Hotel mystery.

In the heat of his anger over that affair and his natural resentment at the home-thrust truths which Sexton Blake had deemed it necessary to give him, Travers Bentley had sworn revenge on Mademoiselle Yvonne for her audacious plot.

To this end he had re-entered the arena of doubtful promotion with the intention of replenishing his almost empty exchequer, and after a few months had done very well. A projected expedition after buried treasure in the Galapagos Islands had, however, lured him on with its fascinating promise of great wealth to come, and in that had his every available penny been sunk.

The treasure hunt had developed into a drunken orgy, followed by a mutiny and general free fight, and from the chaos Travers Bentley emerged penniless, and ready for the first thing that promised well for rejuvenating his fortunes.

From Galapagos he had got across to Buenaventura, and of his subsequent journey from there over the mountains and down the Magdalena to Bogota it is needless to relate the details. Sufficient is it to say that after spending almost his last peso in a clean suit of white and a shave, he had jingled his remaining coins in his pocket and betaken himself to the Calle de Simon Bolivar.

There at a small table in front of a garish café, with his eyes shaded from the white glare of the sun on the buildings opposite, he had found the next card which Fate intended he should play.

It came in the form of a tall, gaunt-looking man who, like all English-speaking adventurers in such places, was attracted towards his kind like the needle to the magnet.

One thing led to another. Bentley related the failure of his treasure-seeking expedition, and his new-found friend, who travelled under the obviously adopted name of White, detailed the particulars of a stillborn revolution in Ecuador which had made that unhealthy country still less healthy for him.

From that the two had put their heads together, and, with a courage and nerve which would have been laudable in a great explorer, they plunged boldly southwards into the unknown in search of wealth. And they had found it—found it beyond their wildest dreams.

Six months of heartbreaking days and fever-racked nights had brought them through a few wandering tribes of Indians into the depths of the jungle. Near where they had erected their hut they had passed a small body of forty Indians of the Arawak tribe, and it was the huge gleaming emeralds which this tribe wore as ornaments which roused their imagination and caused them to weave pictures of untold wealth which had at last been realised.

What mattered it if, by the use of their repeating Winchesters, they had terrorised the tribe and had driven them on to show where they had secured the emeralds? What mattered it if they worked them as slaves by day and tied them up like wild beasts at night? The mine had been found, and even their lustful eyes had been satisfied at the sight which met them.

Through the dim ages, from the time of the cultured and powerful Incas, had it laid hidden, guarded by the creeping jungle. Now, at the end of a year, with a magnificent hoard of emeralds in their hut, the partners had reached an impasse, and it was in an attempt to find a way out of the deadlock that they had tied the few remaining Indians up and sat down to consider.

"I tell you, White," Bentley was saying, "I've got enough of the ready stuff. If you won't come along I'll take my half and get out. I'm sick of this fever hole, and if we don't get out now it will be too late."

"Don't talk rot!" replied White, setting his jaw. "We've made a big haul, it's true, but are you such a fool that you can't see our finish if we leave now? We will never get another emerald out of the mine!"

"Why not?" asked Bentley querulously.

"Because do you think we can get this bunch of stones out of the country without taking all kinds of precautions? We will have to get them quietly to the coast, and while one lies hidden with them the other will have to get a boat at any price in order that we make a safe get-away. Then when these stones are put up on the market, don't you know any gem merchant will spot them at once as Colombian stones? What then? It will filter back here at once, and like everything else worth money in this country, the Government will grab them immediately.

"No, Bentley, our only chance is to get all we can now, for, rest assured, we'll never even see this mine again, much less get anything out of it."

"Well, why not be satisfied with what we have? Do you want to stay here and die of fever? Much good the stones would do you then! We must have well over half a million pounds'[24] worth by now."

---

[24] £500,000 in 1913 is worth about £58,000,000.00 in 2020

"It doesn't make any difference. There are more in sight, and we stay here until I say the word!"

"I'm hanged if I do!" blazed Bentley, losing his temper. "You can stay here and rot, if you will, but I'm going to take my half and go."

"Oh, are you?" said White coldly. "We'll see about that. You'll do just as I say, Bentley, and if you don't I'll put you to work beside the Indians. I guess that will cure you!"

"Curse you! Who are you, to say whether I shall or shall not leave? Haven't I played fair? Haven't I done my share? If I desire to leave and risk a safe get-away, why should you attempt to restrain me? I tell you I won't have it!"

"I should restrain you, my dear fellow," smiled White, "because if you attempt to get through alone you are bound to be caught, and if that happened it would bring them down on me. No! You must remain here until I say the word, which will be when I am satisfied."

For answer Bentley rose, and, with lowering brow, passed out through the doorway of the hut and struck off through the jungle. White watched him go with a cynical smile on his face; then, also rising, he pushed aside a grass door at the rear and made his way through a tangled mass of coffee-trees until he came to a small clearing.

It was encircled by a thick hedge of thorny shrubs, and on the farther side was a black opening indicative of a hole which went into the hedge but not through it. The grass had been trampled down as though a thousand feet had passed over it, but as White gave a soft whistle the cause of the trampling appeared.

From the dark leafy opening opposite the man a grinning head came into view, and as White moved forward the head was followed by the long, hairy arms and misshapen body of a huge reddish ape. It seemed to know the man well, for it hopped cringingly towards him, and, with many protestations of delight, submitted its head to his hand.

From his pocket he drew a packet of food, which he held out, and while the ape demolished it he coolly rolled and lighted a cigarette. Had Bentley seen him then he would have known that the domination which White exercised over him was inherent in the man and not assumed, for implacably, though patiently, he put the ape through a series of movements and performances which would have done credit to Consul.[25]

When he had finished he moved across the compound, followed by the huge ape, which was half as large as himself, and which seemed doubly as powerful. Then he pointed to a giant mahogany which reared its mighty trunk at the edge, and, with a grinning chatter, the ape mounted it and swung off through the forest for its daily exercise, from which it would return at nightfall.

With a smile of satisfaction on his face, White returned to the hut, and, slipping on a ragged coat, betook himself into the jungle.

"I suppose Bentley has gone along to the mine," he muttered, with a grin, as he puffed

---

[25] Consul was the name of a certain chimpanzee that, at the time of the genus's discovery, was on display in London. Consul was commonly used as a circus name for performing chimpanzees. ~ The Editor

a cloud of smoke into the hot, odorous air. "He's a fool, that's what Bentley is! If I trusted him to run things, he'd have half the Government down here on us in two twos, and then I'd like to know where we'd be with our stones. Besides, Mr. Travers Bentley, or whatever his right name really is, strikes me as being a slippery customer, and I intend keeping my eye on him until I get out of this infernal hole. When I shake the dust off my heels he can go and hang for all I care.

"I won't deny that he has been useful in a way, but certainly I have done all the hard work, and if I'd left things to him those Indians would have murdered us in our sleep months ago."

As he mused he turned mechanically along the path which led past the atrocious shelters termed huts, in which the Indians were herded like cattle and fed far worse than those animals fared on the pampas. On drawing near to the small compound and coming into view of the first hut, however, he pulled up, and his brows went down in black anger.

Talking earnestly with one of the Indians, and with many backward glances, was Bentley, his whole attitude indicating secrecy.

Though blazing with a sudden fierce anger, White was apparently unruffled as he strode forward to where Bentley and the Indian were speaking. As Bentley heard his partner coming, he jerked his head up guiltily and flushed under his beard. A look of defiance appeared in his eyes, and he made as though to speak.

But White, disregarding him entirely, kept on until he reached the Indian, who was looking at him furtively. Without preamble of any description, White raised his arm, and striking out, sent the Indian flying against the corner of the hut, where he lay still.

Then turning coolly to Bentley, he said:

"Come, Bentley, take a walk with me. I wish to speak with you."

For a bare moment Bentley looked mutinous, but the look in the other's face made him quail, and he obeyed. He took good care, however, that White led the way, and as the narrow forest aisle grew denser and denser, the mutinous look gave way to one of cunning, and his hand slowly fumbled at his belt for his knife.

He withdrew it stealthily, and increasing the length of his pace by an unnoticeable degree, he gradually drew closer and closer to the unconscious White, who strode on, smoking.

Bentley knew his partner was heading for the mine. When out of earshot of the Indians, he would take him—Bentley—to task for his conduct in talking with the Indian. He dreaded that moment, for he knew White could well imagine the subject of that conversation, and, indeed, he was right.

The moment White had seen him, he knew his crafty partner was probably promising the Indians reward and freedom if they would guide him to the nearest outpost of civilisation while his domineering partner slept. It was not any part of his plan to bow longer to White's will, and in the arrogance born of his new-found wealth he ached once more to feel the pavements of Piccadilly under his feet.

So obsessed was he with the distorted idea of White's injustice that his guilty feeling at being caught had given place to one of cunning, and the broad back of the unconscious man in front was a tempting invitation to plunge his knife in between the shoulder-blades, and, with not only half the stones, but all of them, make his way to the coast.

That White, though an adventurer of the first water, and though the logic of his course must have appealed to Bentley in his saner moments, his mind was warped and twisted by the long solitude of the jungle, and he saw with the eyes of the maniac.

For Travers Bentley was not made for Nature's virginity and the whispering solitudes of the jungle.

As the dense path began to widen slightly, and the clearing around the emerald-mine appeared to view, White spoke:

"See here, Bentley!" he said, over his shoulder, as he walked along. "Do you realise you have just made an unmitigated ass of yourself? Who gave you permission, I'd like to know, to untie that Indian? And what were the two of you whispering about? Answer me that, you,—Ah! You—cur!" he gasped, as Bentley, driven to a sudden anger by his cold, cutting voice, leaped forward and plunged the knife with all his strength between White's shoulders.

"I—might—have—known—you—were—a—cursed—coward!" whispered White jerkily, as he collapsed, and a great stain appeared on his coat.

Bentley, suddenly sobered by the consequences of his anger, stood looking in terror at his handiwork. Hot and heavy though the air was, a cold sweat broke out on his forehead, and he trembled like a spear of yellow straw in the wind.

Passing his hand across his face, he bent, shudderingly, but leaped back with a choking gurgle of terror as something appeared from the bushes on his left. Slowly thrusting its head through, came the writhing, supple folds of a giant boa-constrictor, and, guided straight by the scent, its great, repulsive head lowered in a growing arch over the prostrate man.

Bentley, rooted to the spot by fear, knew that the hidden coils of the great creature were wrapped about one of the towering trees, and that once its coils encircled its prey the man would crumple up like a pipe-stem and be drawn back swiftly to the serpent's lair.

As it turned its baleful eyes on him, however, his spell of terror was broken, and, with another gasp of fear, he turned and fled, leaving his helpless partner to his rapidly approaching fate. Nor did he stop until he regained the compound where were the Indian huts.

There he raced up breathlessly to the Indian with whom he had been speaking when White had come on the scene, and rapidly jerked out that his partner had been seized by a boa. The Indian, who had recovered from White's blow, regarded him in silence.

"Loki hears what the White Chief says," he replied, after a few moments; "but where is the chief's knife?" And he pointed to Bentley's empty sheath.

Bentley flushed, and his hand shot down to his belt.

"It—it dropped out as I ran," he jerked.

The Indian smiled the slow smile of the Arawak and shrugged his shoulders.

"The White Chief's sheath has a button. The button was fastened when he left here. But Loki cares not. If he has killed the cursed white devil who has beaten Loki, then Loki is his friend."

"Look here, Loki," said Bentley hastily, in atrocious dialect, "let us speak of what we were discussing when he came. I will repeat my offer. I will set you all free and not shoot any if you will guide me as you promised. You can bring all the men and leave the women and children here until you return. When we get there I will, as I promised, give you all the blankets, beads, and "bright cloth" (vividly coloured cottons, much prized by the Arawak Indians, as well as by the Motillones), which you can carry."

The Indian's eyes glistened greedily as Bentley spoke, and his gaze wandered slowly to the green top of a royal palm which reared its graceful head near at hand.

"How does Loki know the White Chief will keep his promise?" he asked slowly.

"Because you know I value the pretty stones we have been digging, and you can keep those until you get the things I promised."

"Then Loki consents," answered the Indian. "When will the White Chief leave?"

"At once," replied Bentley. "I don't want to spend another night here," he added, with a shudder.

"Loki and his men will be ready when the White Chief is," said the Indian, and Bentley, turning, hastened along to his own hut to gather together the precious emeralds which, when cut and polished, would be fit to grace the brow of an empress.

An hour later Bentley and twelve Indians started out in single file, and headed along the narrow path which led past the mines. As they drew near the scene of his attack on White, Bentley shivered and quickened his footsteps; but there was no sign of his late partner. He breathed more easily as they got past, and muttered:

"It was just as well, in a way. He would have been dead soon from the blow, but the boa's attack removes all traces; although, goodness knows, there won't be another white man through here in twenty years."

Again he shivered, and, as he hurried on, he never saw Loki stoop suddenly and pick from the bushes a knife whose red-stained blade was of the exact shape of Bentley's sheath. Nor did he hear the Indian's remark to his companions in native Arawakan as he surreptitiously thrust the knife inside his shirt.

"The White Chief will keep his word," was what he said. "If not, I'll show him this." And with that the little procession moved on.

Loki, however, had no need to use his find as a source of persuasion, for so relieved was Bentley to reach even the first primitive village that when they made Iraca he almost denuded the Spanish trader's store in payment of the promised reward.

The Indians gravely accepted the brilliantly-coloured cotton blankets, the cheap razors, the coloured beads and bright cloth which by their standards of value made them millionaires amongst their kind.

And when Bentley had secured burros for his packs and a mule for himself they saw him safely on his way for Honda and then began their return.

It was a long and trying journey which Bentley had before he made Honda on the Magdalena. Several of his stones had been changed to cash by the Spanish trader at Iraca, and only the prodigal use of this got him safely past the inquisitive departmental officers between Cundina Marca and Tolima.

They, poor wretches, had not been paid for months, and only by their legalised robbery of travellers did their positions return them anything. Rarely indeed was it that there appeared such a plump bird as was Bentley, and by the time he reached Honda his stock of cash was almost depleted.

But compared with the mass of wealth in his packs it was as nothing, and when at last he boarded the primitive flat-bottomed river steamer he breathed a sigh of relief.

"So far, so good," he muttered, as he paid the captain a fat sum from a new store of money which he had secured in Honda. "If I can get through Antioquia safely I'll make Barranquilla all right, and I know a German merchant there who will see me safely out of the country. Gad! It's been a heart-breaking journey, but thank Heaven the truth will never be known!"

Why he should thank Heaven in view of the facts seems puzzling, but Travers Bentley had a facile conscience, and even before he reached Barranquilla he had almost forgotten what happened back in the jungle.

Only the heap of precious stones served to remind him of it, and when he had disposed of them in Europe the last reproach of that reminder would disappear.

At Barranquilla he was not disappointed in his expectations. After much more judicious bribery he got past the department without an examination of his packs, and, on the day following his arrival, accompanied by his German friend, he climbed into the miniature train which runs to Puerto Colombia and boarded the Atrato.

As she left the long, fragile-looking pier at Puerto Colombia, and nosed the blue waters of the treacherous Caribbean, Bentley took off his hat and let the last flicker of the land-breeze play on his brow.

"Well, anyway, I've succeeded," he muttered, smiling grimly, and feeling a renewed confidence from the effect of his new clothes.

"It means close on a million[26] for these stones, and when I get rid of them it means the end of that episode."

With this he turned, and, smiling, with satisfaction, sought his cabin.

***

Speaking from Travers Bentley's point of view it is in a way a pity that his spell of terror before the approaching boa-constrictor broke so soon, and sent him flying on the wings of fear back to the huts, for had he paused a moment longer he would have seen a remarkable sight.

It seemed as though no earthly power would stop those great coils from being hurled

---

[26] £1,000,000 in 1913 is worth about £116,000,000 in 2020

forward and winding in a death embrace around the body of the man who lay so still in the narrow path.

But barely had Bentley turned and bolted when a lithe, supple, greyish body shot swiftly downwards from a giant branch above, and the aggressive head of the boa, which a moment before had been poised over its prey, turned upwards in a sharp move of defence as its old enemy the jaguar landed with a ripping, tearing of its claws, and closed its vicious, snarling jaws on the throat of the boa.

Then began one of those deadly forest fights which it is seldom the fortune of man to see. With a mighty heave the boa exerted every ounce of its strength, and, pulling desperately from its coils, which were wrapped around the tree behind it, the jaguar had perforce to follow it as it shot back to its lair.

Back and forth the battle waged, the jaguar watching his chance to slip his jaws along to the vital point in the back, and ripping with his powerful claws in order to escape the deadly coils.

The boa, on the other hand, gripped the tree with its coils, ever lengthening its great body, until only one twist was holding it to its anchorage. Then, with a lightning-like movement the long, powerful body between the jaguar and the tree curved, and, like a giant lariat, fell about the hind quarters of the mountain lion.

The jaguar leaped madly as the quivering coils enwrapped him, but he was too late, and with a sickening crunch the boa brought the coils tighter in that awful grip which invariably spells death.

When the jaguar's jaw dropped open and its body grew limp, the boa released its victim, and, leaving it lying where it fell, shot forward once more after the man in the path, which to it was a tit-bit. As its head pierced the bushes and it peered forth, however, it saw no sign of its intended prey.

Nor would the man who had lain in the path ever be its prey, for even as Bentley leaped forth and thrust the knife in his partner's back had White's strange pet been overhead on its way back to the compound which had been built for it by the man who wielded such power over it, and who held its savage nature in thrall.

All through that terrible struggle between the boa and the jaguar had White lain unconscious with the knife protruding from his back, but as the great serpent shot back with its prey to the shelter of its lair he stirred and opened his eyes.

Then it was that from far above swung a hairy, excited beast which dropped silently beside him and began whining softly. The familiar noise brought White's reeling senses back to the present, and, mechanically struggling to his knees, he put his arm around the ape's shoulders.

The ape at that moment seemed endowed with a mad frenzy, for drawing the knife from its master's back, it dashed it violently to the ground. Then, dragging slowly along, man and beast disappeared through a heavy, tangled screen of scarlet and green just as the boa returned.

It was well for the wounded man that the boa had sufficient to satiate its desires in the carcase of the jaguar, for his strength lasted barely long enough for him to reach the other side of the tangled screen when his senses again left him, and he dropped forward on his face.

For over an hour he lay there as one dead, with the ape squatting beside him. Then, as the dull sound of naked feet on hard ground broke the stillness, the ape peered through the bushes and saw a small party of men padding on in single file.

In the midst was the man who such a short time before had plunged his knife into the back of the ape's master, and little did Bentley dream as he went past on his forced march that he had made a savage, implacable enemy in the shape of the unreasoning beast which glared balefully at him. Nor did Bentley guess how close to him at that moment was the man whom he thought dead and destroyed in the lair of the boa-constrictor.

It was sundown before White again returned to consciousness and when he did, it was to feel the first chilling grip of a violent fever. He still had sense enough to realise that unless he gained a place of security he would never recover, and with that idea dominating his wavering senses, he dragged himself to his feet and sought the ape's support.

His terrible struggle back to the compound it is unnecessary to relate. Sufficient is it to say that the Indian women and children had long retired, the moon was just bathing the heavy jungle in its cold light, and the cry of the teeming night-life of the forest was sounding melancholy and discordant when man and beast stumbled through the compound and across to the retreat which was used by the ape.

White's last sane thoughts were that he must not remain in his hut in his present helpless condition, and, pausing only long enough to get a gourd of water, and dose himself with quinine, he kept on through the hut to the compound.

His back had stopped bleeding, but the pain was intense, for had he but known it, he had escaped death by the barest fraction of an inch.

On reaching the compound, White stumbled into the security of the ape's retreat, and with a whirling, beating insistence, delirium claimed him for its own.

For days did White lie in the grip of the fever, and when consciousness finally returned he was weak and helpless from lack of food and attention. All through his ravings the ape had sat whimpering at the opening, and when he finally looked about with reason in his eyes, his pet came cringing towards him with understanding.

Then it was that White dragged himself to the hut and gnawed at the remaining bits of food. After that the Indian women put down the mysterious disappearance of their supplies in the night to the evil spirits of the forest.

For nearly a month White lived in this manner until he was able to stand and walk with some semblance of his old strength.

Then things began to happen in that peaceful camp.

When he searched the hut and found that Bentley had taken every stone, White sat down with a slow, deadly calm, and cursed his fleeing partner. Then, feeling under his pile of blankets for his Winchester, which he found untouched, he started for the huts.

It needed all his old domineering nature to stem the panic which ensued on his appearance, for nothing could persuade the terrified women that he was not the ghost of his former self come for vengeance. In terror they tremblingly obeyed his orders, and, one by one, old and young, they proceeded to the mine, where they set to work as though the Evil One himself were driving them.

When Loki and his companions returned from Iraca, White had managed to gather together another small supply of stones. With these in his belt, and the terrified Indians leading the way, he started for Iraca on the trail of vengeance after Bentley.

The ape went with him, and all through the silent journey he spent his evenings in laboriously teaching the ape to do his every bidding.

When they reached Iraca, Loki, still in fear of the man so mysteriously come to life, tremblingly approached and handed him Bentley's knife. With a sudden gleam and a twisted smile White took it, and then driving the Indians to build a cage for the ape, he left on its completion for Honda.

All down the river he found traces of Bentley's passage, and on arriving at Barranquilla he discovered that Bentley had sailed on the *Atrato* for England. Then, and only then, did White permit himself to smile without restraint.

At a certain den in a little street that runs off Barranquilla's sandy apology for a plaza, he disposed of a few of his emeralds. Then he betook himself to the cable office, where he sent a cable to England. It was very brief, and addressed to a certain Perry, whom White remembered would do his bidding. It read simply:

"WATCH *ATRATO*. FIND PASSENGER BENTLEY. FOLLOW HIM UNTIL MY ARRIVAL ON *DARIEN*."

Three days later the *Darien* carried as a passenger from Puerto Colombia to England, a passenger whose name figured on the list as Henry Fairbanks, and not one of the ship's company knew that the taciturn owner of the name was to all intents and purposes lying dead in the Caqueta jungle.

End of Prologue

The First Chapter
Sexton Blake Buys an Emerald

SEXTON Blake leaned back in his chair and looked at the card which he held in his hand. "Señor Jose Manuel Sanchez, Attaché of the Colombian Embassy, London," was what he read. Then raising his eyes he looked at the little dark-skinned, dark-eyed man who was its possessor.

"You say you desire my assistance in a matter which it is impossible to place in the hands of the police," he remarked, slowly tapping the card.

"Exactly, Mr. Blake," answered the other, twirling his moustache nervously. "It is, shall we say, a matter in which, although your Government has no objections to our doing what we can, in order to succeed in our purpose, still, they can lend us no assistance."

"As long as it has nothing to do with diplomatic matters I am prepared to hear what you have to say, and then will give you my decision. If, however, it is a matter of diplomacy, and could in any way affect my own country's Government then I tell you frankly I must first consult with them, for, under an old arrangement, I have pledged myself to be at my country's service above everything else."

"Oh, it is nothing like that, I assure you!" exclaimed Señor Sanchez in almost perfect English. "It is purely a matter concerning my own country."

"Then you may proceed," said Blake. "Will you have a cigar?"

The Colombian accepted with a bow, and after they had both puffed in silence for some moments, the attaché leaned forward and said:

"I think, Mr. Blake, the best way for me to do will be to tell it in my own manner. Then, any question you care to ask, I shall be only too pleased to answer. Otherwise, while I can control my knowledge of the English language under ordinary circumstances, if I get nervous, through trying to think too quickly, I get mixed up."

"Proceed!" remarked Blake laconically.

"As you know, Mr. Blake," began the other, "the boundaries of my country extend technically over several large areas of territory which as yet are unexplored and consequently, unsettled. The only population they carry is composed of several tribes of nomadic Indians, chiefly of the Arawak tribe, although there are many more, such as the Motillones in the east, the Goajiras and several others.

"As you will understand, although these peoples are technically speaking, Colombians still, our authority over them is merely nominal, our officials rarely entering their territories and none of our laws reach them. Gradually, however, we are spreading towards them, and it is of one of these districts with which I have to deal.

"To the south of Bogota there is a vast stretch of practically unknown country, which embraces the sources of many large rivers. It has always been conceded that it is a place of great wealth and natural resources, and in fact, in the old records of the Spanish conquest of the Incas there are many references to it and its richness."

Blake nodded.

"I know. I have been in Iraca."

"Ah!" exclaimed Sanchez, "that is fortunate, for it is of that very district I wish to speak!"

"Then I can follow you intelligently. Proceed!"

"About a year and a half ago two Englishmen left Bogota for that district, and it was thought they had undoubtedly perished, until six months ago several things came to light which caused my Government to think very differently.

"As you know, the rich emerald mines of Colombia are mostly owned and operated by the Government, and you may be sure the disposition of every stone the country produces is known to it. But six months ago it was discovered that a trader, away back in Iraca, was in possession of some magnificent specimens, for he tried to dispose of them surreptitiously in Bogota.

"Inquiries were at once set on foot. That he had purchased them from any of the men working in the mines near Bogota was out of the question. In the first place, Iraca was too far away, and in the second place, the colour of the stones was deeper and richer than the Bogota stones."

Blake nodded.

"Good!" he said dreamily.

"Well, one of our officials was sent down to Iraca, and on the way discovered that some more stones had been sold in Honda.

"In Iraca he spent some time, but it was over a month before he got any definite information, and that he only succeeded in getting when he backed the trader up against the wall of his shack and threatened to shoot him. That information resulted in a description of a man who had passed through Iraca a short time before. He, with another man, had gone south a year or so previously, and it didn't take us long to discover that they were the same two who had left Bogota.

"The next thing we discovered was that the second man came through just before our agent got there, but beyond stopping long enough to build a cage for a huge brown ape he had with him, he kept on to Honda, and there are no indications that he disposed of any stones.

"The upshot was, we sent a small expedition south, and hit on a tribe of Indians there who conducted our men to one of the richest emerald-mines in the country. It was very evident that a large haul had been taken from it, and legally the stones belong to our Government.

"After that we traced the movements of both men. The first man who realised on the stones left as a consequence a trail which a child could follow. We trailed him to Barranquilla, and thence to Puerto Colombia, where he sailed on the *Atrato* for England. The other man left a month later on the *Darien*, but signs of either since they landed we can find none."

"What was the name by which the first man went?" asked Blake.

"He sailed on the *Atrato* under the name of Knox—Theodore Knox. At least, the description we had fitted that man. Previous to that, however, he went under the name of Bentley."

"Ah!" exclaimed Blake, sitting up suddenly. "Was his name Travers Bentley?"

"Yes," answered Sanchez, in surprise. "Do you know him?"

"Slightly," said Blake quietly. "And the other?"

"He was known as White in Colombia, but also sailed under an assumed name— Henry Fairbanks. He took his ape with him. Before he sailed, however, he cabled a man here in London to meet the *Atrato*, and keep track of Bentley's—or Knox's—movements until the arrival of the *Darien*. That, Mr. Blake, is where we have come to an impasse."

"Did you follow up the address of the man in London to whom the cable was sent?" asked Blake sharply.

"Certainly. We found, however, that it was only a newsagent's, where he received his letters, and here it is."

"And his name?" inquired Blake, glancing at the slip of paper.

"Perry."

"Ah! From what I can gather, Señor Sanchez, your claim against these men for the stones they got away with, while perfectly legal in Colombia, or within the walls of the Colombian Embassy, in London has no force."

"That is exactly the situation. If the stones were of a nominal value only, we would swallow the loss, but as we have reason to believe they represent a very large sum, we intend, if possible, to recover them."

"In a word, instead of 'possession being nine points of the law,' in this case it is ten points," remarked Blake.

Sanchez bowed.

"You see the case perfectly, Mr. Blake; and since you now have the facts, I should be glad to hear your decision."

Blake puffed silently at his cigar for some moments.

"What you ask, Señor Sanchez, although sanctioned informally by the British Government, is that I turn thief to catch a thief."

The Spaniard spread out his hands.

"Oh, Mr. Blake, it is hardly that! You see, the right of possession is ours."

"But the fact of possession is not," remarked Blake drily. "However, I grant you, were I in your place, I would endeavour to recover the stones. The policy of your Government in claiming such finds is, for the moment, beside the question. Still, I fancy if Mr. Travers Bentley is the Travers Bentley with whom I am slightly acquainted, then the balance of right is more liable to be on your side than on his. Furthermore, the fact that he is implicated in the matter rather inclines me to take the case up, although I promise nothing regarding results."

"I am satisfied to leave the whole affair in your hands," murmured Sanchez; "and if you recover the stones, you will find my Government not ungrateful."

"We will discuss that when I recover them," said Blake, with a curt motion of his cigar. "Now then, señor, a moment, until I jot down the names and particulars you have given me. This man White, or Fairbanks, seems to loom rather large in the matter, although we know less of him than the other."

For several minutes Blake wrote rapidly, then, tossing his notebook on the desk, rose.

"Very well, señor, you can consider the case as being in my hands from now. I will, of course, advise you should anything turn up."

"Thank you, Mr. Blake. It is very good of you."

"Not at all," smiled Blake. "The affair promises some interest, and if I should succeed, then your Government will have the pleasure of reimbursing me for the goodness you speak of."

He bowed the attaché out, and then returned to the consulting-room. Hardly had he picked up the notes on his desk, when the door opened, and Tinker hurried in.

"I got track of that man in Bloomsbury," he burst out, "and have put Tim on to watch him. I——"

"Hold on!" interrupted Blake curtly, holding up his hand. "Leave that report until tonight, as the matter is not urgent. Then write it out, and lay it on my desk. In the meantime, get into your regular clothes. I have work for you."

Slightly surprised, Tinker turned obediently, and made for his room, from which he emerged a few minutes later, dressed in his ordinary clothes. Then, approaching the desk, he waited in silence for Blake to speak.

"The case is this," rapped Blake. "A big haul of emeralds has been made in South America. There is reason to believe that they are in England. You are to go at once. Send cipher messages to our own agents in New York, Montreal, Paris, Vienna, Berlin, Amsterdam, Rotterdam, Rio de Janeiro, and Buenos Ayres. Instruct them to make thorough inquiries as to whether any emeralds, in small or large lots, have been put on the market other than those which come through the ordinary channels. Instruct them also to make a clean sweep of the pawnshops and fences, and find out if there are any parcels in those quarters. Then send off a code telegram to our London agents to do the same.

"Send this telegram which I have written to this man Perry. You will notice I have signed the name White. You had better send it the first thing. That is all. Report here at once as soon as you have done, and debit your expenditures in the ledger to the Colombian Government. Now go! Lose no time."

Without a word, Tinker turned and passed out, while Blake rose and filled his pipe.

"Six months," he muttered, as he sank back in his big chair and puffed thoughtfully, "six months, and Sanchez says they can find no trace of them. Unless they have been disposed of very quietly, Bentley must be too cautious to try and get rid of them yet. He may even be aware of the fact that the Colombian Government is after them."

"But who is this man White? Why didn't they come out together? And why did he cable to this man Perry to meet the *Atrato*, and keep track of Bentley? Six months is a long time, but if this man Perry is still in London, my telegram may reach him, and he may take the bait when he sees it signed White. On the other hand, he may not, and it is only a chance at the best.

"So Bentley has started his old tricks, has he? I heard his treasure-hunting expedition ended in smoke, but I didn't expect him to turn up again in just this manner. I'd like to know how the news would affect Mademoiselle Yvonne if she knew. That's a point to remember, too, for with the army of spies and agents about she is liable to drop on to the news. Nothing would please her better than to relieve Bentley of those emeralds.

"Query one, however, is—Who and what is this man White? I must settle that point. The next thing is to endeavour to get some idea of the movements of Bentley, or Knox, as he called himself after landing here. Heaven only knows what moves he may have made in the six months at his disposal!

"However, I can form no theory until I get further information. Let me see, it is now four o'clock. I'll just have about time to run down to the City and have a chat with Borwick. He ought to have his finger on the pulse of the emerald market in London as well as any man."

With this decision, Blake got to his feet and reached for the 'phone.

A few moments later he was holding a brief conversation with John Borwick, the head of Borwicks, the noted gem merchants. After that he made another call, this time to order the big grey car to be sent round at once.

Then, as he finished, he slipped into a pongee duster and grey cap, and barely had he adjusted his goggles when the car stopped outside.

Blake drove straight through to Borwicks, and on entering was asked at once into John Borwick's private office.

"Well, Blake, I'm surprised at your being in the City during this weather. Why don't you spend some of that haul you are reputed to have made on Steel Common last week, and take a month off?"

Blake laughed. The haul he had made in Steel Common was, had Borwick only known it, a drop compared to a neat little coup he was at that moment engineering, for though reputed in the City to be one of the biggest financial forces of his day, and though he gave away a fortune each year in charity, Sexton Blake found a keen delight in applying his mathematical genius and logical judgment to the intricacies of the Stock Market.

Every man has his hobby, but Blake had a dozen, of which this was one, and he threw himself into it with his usual thoroughness.

"I think you overrate the profit I made," he said, as he sank into a chair. "However, Borwick, I see you are busy, and will get to the point. It is a little matter about which anything you can tell me will be appreciated; and at the same time I shall be glad if you will, for the present, consider it as confidential."

"Certainly, my dear fellow! What is it?"

"I have got a consuming curiosity to know the exact state of the emerald market at the present time. How do the figures of supply and demand compare with, say, this month last year? How does that comparison go for the last six months? Are there any big lots coming on the market, or is the supply normal? Are big sales being made or not? Is the quality as usual, or have there been any particularly fine specimens offered lately? In short, Borwick, I want a complete resume of the emerald situation condensed into a half-hour's conversation."

Borwick laughed.

"It's a tall order, Blake, but I'm only too happy to oblige you, if what I know is of any use to you. To begin with, the market is, on the whole, about as usual. I think, if anything, it will show a trifle more activity than the same month last year, but that is solely attributable to natural causes. If my memory serves me rightly, the last six months— yes, the last eight months, will show a normal tone. You see, emeralds are about as stable and steady as any gem, not even excepting diamonds.

"As far as the Continent is concerned, its tone is, of course, about 'fifty-fifty'—if you will pardon the expression. If anything, it is the barest trifle less steady. However, in one way your questions are rather remarkable; or, I should say, a coincidence."

"Coincidence!" exclaimed Blake. "How do you mean, Borwick?"

"Well, firstly, during the past six months I have picked up a few emeralds which are as fine specimens as I ever saw. Their richness and depth of colour is perfect, and, although

I knew cutting and polishing would make them exceptionally fine stones, they more than fulfilled my expectations. Would you care to see them?"

"Rather!" smiled Blake. "That remark about their richness and depth of colouring makes me very keen to increase my knowledge of them."

Borwick smiled and rose. Turning to a big safe which stood beside his desk, he threw open the door, and, thrusting in his hand, drew out a small leather bag. He tossed it carelessly on the desk, and after untying the cord turned it upside-down.

Though he had in his long career handled hundreds of priceless gems, even Blake was compelled to lean forward in silent admiration of the regal stones before him.

"Gad! Borwick, you certainly haven't over-rated them," he said.

"Aren't they beauties?" remarked the merchant, as he lifted them caressingly. "See this one, Blake; fit for the brow of Cleopatra."

And there in the midst of business the fleeting thought came to Sexton Blake that he knew a throat of gleaming marble on which that same gem would rest with adorable perfection.

"You are right," he replied, dragging his thoughts back to the present. "By the way, you say you picked those up during the last six months. Did you get them through your regular channels?"

"Not much," smiled Borwick. "I picked them up through an outside source, and, between you and me, Blake, I didn't insist on their pedigree."

"I take it, then," drawled Blake, "that your source of supply was an individual?"

"Right, old man. I got 'em from a chap by the name of Knox—a big, prosperous-looking man, about fifty, I should think."

"Ah!" breathed Blake, lowering his lids and examining the tip of his cigar. "I think I have heard of him. If I remember rightly his first name is Theodore, is it not?"

"That's the man. You say you know him? Is he all right?"

"My dear Borwick, what a fellow you are!" laughed Blake. "Didn't I tell you when I came in that I was going to ask you some questions, and here you are asking them of me. However, don't worry about your stones," he added more soberly; "but let me give you a tip. Don't sell them to the public yet. Keep them in your safe for, say, the next three months. There is a history attached to them, but your possession will never be disputed."

"By thunder, Blake, that reminds me! There was a little dark-skinned fellow in here one day not long ago. Said he represented the Colombian Government, and asked all sorts of questions about emeralds—questions not unlike yours. Do you suppose he had any connection with these stones?"

"Possibly," answered Blake; "but don't answer any questions anybody may ask you. I'll tell you the full history some day; though, to tell the truth, I don't know very much myself yet. By the way, have you Knox's address? I seem to have forgotten it."

"I have it in the ledger. If you would like it, I can give it to you."

"Please; I should be grateful."

Borwick rose at once and left the office, while Blake leaned back and puffed at his cigar.

"It's not too well to let Borwick know any more than necessary yet!" he murmured to the empty air. "But what a fortunate thing I came on here! If, as he says, he has Knox's address, and it is Bentley, then it saves me several days of tedious investigation."

At that moment the merchant returned, and laid a slip of paper on the desk.

"There you are, Blake. It's a month since I've seen him, but I suppose he is still there!"

Blake picked up the slip and read:

"Theodore Knox, Esq., Carthorpe Hall, Carthorpe, Surrey."

"Thanks," he said, folding it up and thrusting it in his pocket. "I will communicate with him there. However, that's all I'll bother you today, Borwick. By the way, what do you want for that big emerald there? It looks like the 'daddy' of them all." And Blake's colour actually deepened the barest trifle as he asked the question.

"That," said the merchant, picking it up, "that, Blake, is, I think, the finest stone I have ever seen. Its purity is unrivalled, and its colour would defy any alchemist but Nature to produce."

"I believe you, Borwick," remarked Blake drily; "but I asked the price."

"Well, Blake, I'll tell you frankly what I paid. The price was fifteen hundred,[27] and cutting and polishing added. If you would like the stone I'd let you have it for two thousand,[28] although I had intended asking twenty-five hundred.[29] You can buy bigger stones, and pay more for them, but you can't excel the purity of this specimen."

"It's mine," said Blake laconically, drawing out his chequebook, and a few moments later the exchange had taken place. "I may bring it in later to have it set," he remarked as he rose, "but at present I'll have it in its pristine beauty."

On re-entering the car, Blake leaned back with a faint smile of satisfaction.

"I think I'll make a call at Carthorpe Hall at an early date!" he murmured. "It will be interesting to see Bentley playing the part of country squire. The information Borwick has given me sets one point at rest, however, and that is as to whether Bentley got away with the stones or not. The next thing is to ascertain if he still has the main part, and if so to relieve him of them. Then there is the question of this man White or Fairbanks. If tonight gives me the information I want on that point I may be able to follow matters up at once. In sending that wire to Perry, under White's signature, telling him to meet me at seven, at the first table in Rosaro's, I am in a way risking something. But when he sees that White doesn't turn up, if I am any judge of that element in human nature termed curiosity, he will go at once and send a wire to White, asking him why the deuce he didn't appear. And if things go as I hope I will endeavour to be right behind him when he sends it."

Then Blake's thoughts trailed off, and a smile flickered over his face as he thought of his purchase.

---

[27] £1,500 in 1913 is worth about £174,000 in 2020

[28] £2,000 in 1913 is worth about £230,000 in 2020

[29] £2,500 in 1913 is worth about £290,400.00 in 2020

"Heaven only knows when I shall meet her again!" he muttered; "but I can't think it will be never. In any event, I'll keep it until I do. She is jolly fond of emeralds, and, from what I remember, they suit her perfectly. Poor Yvonne! She will be surprised, but not so much as she will when she sees the folded slip of paper I have for her."

But what that folded slip of paper was has nothing to do with this story—just yet.

As Blake pulled up at Baker Street, ascended the steps, and entered he found on his arrival in the consulting-room that Tinker had returned, and was himself occupied in writing out his report of the Bloomsbury matter.

"Well?" inquired Blake briefly. "Did you fulfil all my instructions?"

"Yes, guv'nor," replied the lad, getting to his feet. "As you told me to do, I sent that telegram to Perry first, then attended to the other matters."

"Very well, my lad. Get into your dinner togs. We dine at Rosaro's, and it's now six."

Tinker obediently folded up his half-finished report, and put it carefully away, after which he hesitated for a moment as though to ask a question; but, seeing the abstracted look in his master's eyes, thought better of it and departed to his room.

Blake entered his dressing-room, and, after holding a one-sided conversation with Pedro, who had decided on that as being the coolest spot that hot July day, he began himself to get into his dinner-jacket.

At six-forty-five punctually, with the chauffeur fulfilling one of his rare calls to drive, the big, luxurious car glided away from the kerb, with Blake and Tinker leaning back in the tonneau.

***

If you have been in Rosaro's you will know the famous main room, where congenial spirits delight to do justice to the excellent cuisine and blend their laughter and conversation with the strains of the orchestra and the popping of corks.

You will also know, if you are a frequent visitor, that to the right, just inside the door, is a delightful little alcove containing half a dozen tables, where one can dine in an atmosphere of tropical verdure and watch unseen those arriving through the main door.

It was one of these tables to which Blake and Tinker were conducted after Blake had signified his wishes to Max, the undisputed emperor of the establishment.

For some minutes Blake was engaged in choosing a dinner which would have delighted the palate of the most fastidious gourmet, after which he settled back with half-closed eyes, wrapped in his thoughts, while Tinker confined his attention to the music.

Barely had they finished the hors d'oeuvre, when Blake carelessly stroked his chin with one finger; and Tinker, reading the signal, looked up just in time to see a man of nondescript appearance enter and approach the table next to theirs.

Blake knew at once that it was Perry, the man to whom he had sent a telegram in White's name, telling him to meet him—White—at the first table in the alcove at Rosaro's. The detective went calmly on with his dinner as the newcomer stood uncertainly for a few moments, and then, as a waiter approached, sank into a chair and ordered a dish or two.

While he waited for it to be served, he kept glancing anxiously at his watch from time to time, never realising that the man whom he had expected to meet would never come, nor that the well-dressed gentleman and lad opposite, though apparently wrapped up in the enjoyment of their dinner, were in reality mentally registering his every movement.

It was nearly eight when the newcomer, after a final frowning scrutiny of his watch, called the waiter and demanded his bill. Then, as he rose and departed, Sexton Blake leaned back and lit one of his favourite Penatellas, which he puffed luxuriously. Then he nodded at Tinker.

"You know what to do," he murmured. "Lose no time."

And as the disappointed Perry passed through the portals, Tinker slipped into his coat and moved carelessly after him.

For fully half an hour longer Blake sat there in dreamy enjoyment of his cigar; then, as Max moved up and informed him the chauffeur had arrived, he rose and slipped into the coat which the man held.

"I hope we shall see you more often, sir," murmured Max, as Blake lit a fresh cigar and handed him a substantial tip. "It is a pleasure to serve a man who can order as you can, sir. It must be three months since you were here."

"It is all of that," replied Blake, with a smile. "But I have been very busy, Max. However, I enjoyed the dinner immensely, and no doubt you will see me again soon. Good-night!"

"Good-night, sir, and thank you!"

A moment later Blake was leisurely settling himself in the car, and giving the order, leaned back as it moved off and headed for Baker Street.

The faintest flicker of surprise appeared in his eyes as, on his entry, he found Tinker had arrived.

"It didn't take you long, my lad," he remarked. "Did you succeed?"

"Oh, yes, guv'nor," grinned Tinker cheerfully. "He made tracks for the nearest post-office, and sent a telegram at once. I managed to get close behind him as he did so. Wrote one out myself and despatched it to a dummy name, as I saw that was the only way I could get close enough."

"Well," demanded Blake impatiently, "what was it?"

"He sent it to Henry Fairbanks, Esq., at Carthorpe, Surrey."

"Ah!"

Tinker looked up sharply as Blake emitted the long-drawn-out exclamation, for though he had received from Blake the bare details of the case in hand, and though he had deducted several things from Blake's orders of the afternoon, still he knew nothing of the man White nor Blake's reason for sending a telegram to the man Perry and signing it in White's name.

Had he known of the information which Blake had gained from Borwick, the gem-merchant, that afternoon, while Tinker thought his master at home all the time, he would have wondered still more; for even to Blake the news that the man White, alias Fairbanks, was living at Carthorpe village as well as Bentley, had come as a tremendous surprise.

"That means," he argued to himself, "that White and Bentley are either on friendly terms and are accomplices living at Carthorpe Hall together, or that one of them does not know of the other's presence in Carthorpe, which argues enmity between them. It would be interesting to know whether Bentley knows of this man White's presence there, or whether, on the other hand, White knows of Bentley's presence.

"Is it a case of both being friends and each aware of the other's presence, or one knowing the other is there while he himself is in ignorance? In that case it is safe to assume that the first one to arrive in Carthorpe is the one who remains in ignorance, and that being Bentley—ergo he is that one. Therefore, that being so, White has followed him down there. But for what purpose? That point must be discovered. I wonder if it is just possible that Bentley has in some way played the double-shuffle on this man White? If that were so, it might be possible to play one against the other."

While Blake had been thinking rapidly, as a consequence of the news he had just received, Tinker stood waiting for his comments. As he tossed away his Penatella, Blake spoke:

"You will be prepared, my lad, to make a night trip by motor into Surrey tomorrow night. We are going to turn burglars for a brief period. Now, as we have the balance of the evening free, come along! We will have a look in at one of the theatres."

And though Tinker's eyes were dancing with excitement at Blake's remark, he made no comment, but turned and followed his master back to the car.

Assuredly Tinker was coming along!

The Second Chapter
Bentley Has Two Severe Shocks

IN the morning following the events just related, a prosperous-looking, well-groomed man, who might have been any age between forty and fifty-five, walked briskly along Queen Victoria Street and turned down a side street near the Bank.

He was rather an isolated specimen in the resplendent glory of his immaculate morning-coat and gleaming silk hat, and, when the early hour was taken into consideration, he appeared just the merest trifle incongruous to the men who were hurrying along beside him.

It seemed not to trouble him, however, for his triple chin hung placidly over his collar, and his expansive waistcoat betokened the well-fed and the well-cared-for. Six months in London had made a marvellous change in Travers Bentley.

The wrinkled, dilapidated appearance which his jungle life had given him had given way to the triumph of the flesh-pots of civilisation, and in no city can that triumph be made more sweeping than in London, the Mecca of the gourmet.

Beyond a few fine lines in the corners of his eyes, which proved unyielding to his ideas of life, Travers Bentley looked as imposing as he had before his ill-fated hunt after buried treasure.

He had found that the surest way to make a treasure hunt fail was to mix champagne with a tropical proposition, but the knowledge had not deterred him from returning to the delights of his favourite vintage when he reached London with a fortune in emeralds in his luggage.

As he walked along this warm summer's morning, he moved briskly as a man with a definite purpose, which indeed he had. After turning several corners, and gradually getting into the confines of a disreputable looking district, he paused before a dingy pawnshop.

For a moment he gazed through the window at the varied assortment of cheap watches, cheaper rings, battered violins and other mementoes which represented the last reserve of the toiler, the drunkard, or the gambler. His very appearance proclaimed the fact that he had no material interest in the array, and had a careful gaze been directed at him it would have been seen that his interest in the display was assumed, the while his eyes furtively swept the street in either direction.

Then, bending as though suddenly interested in one of the battered violins, he drew out his pince-nez for a better inspection. Slowly nodding his head, as one who had made a sudden "find," he straightened up and boldly entered.

The Hebrew who came forward obsequiously at the sight of his unusually prosperous-looking customer, smiled an oily smile.

"Vot can I do for you, sir?" he asked, industriously dry-washing his hands.

Bentley smiled to himself as he slipped his pince-nez back in his pocket, for in the past he had done much business with Isaacs, and the man's non-recognition of him proved that his disguise was as good as he thought.

"I wish to speak with you—privately," replied Bentley, drawing out his card-case and tossing down a card, on which was engraved "Mr. Theodore Knox."

Isaacs picked up the card and peered at it with his near-sighted eyes, but the name told him nothing. Rapidly the old rascal's mind went back over many shady deals in the past, but the name seemed connected with none of them, and his customer certainly had not the appearance of a detective as Isaacs knew them.

"Vell, sir," he said, stuffing the card in his pocket, "if you vill come this vay, I talk in my private office."

Mr. Theodore Knox—or to use his real name of Bentley—bowed and followed the rotund man along the shop and through the dilapidated door into the private office. Waving him to a chair, Isaacs sat down at a littered desk.

"Now, sir," he said, "vot is it Isaacs can do for you?"

For answer Bentley reached up, and after a few moments' manipulation removed his luxuriant, closely-trimmed, grey beard, and as the Hebrew saw the real identity of his caller his eyes opened, and he started up.

"You!" he gasped. "I thought you vas abroad."

"So I was," smiled Bentley, replacing his beard. "I've been back in London for six months, however, and I've got some big business for you. Do you want it?"

"It all depends—it all depends," answered Isaacs, placing the tips of his fingers together and half closing his eyes. "Vat haf you got?"

"I've got the biggest bunch of emeralds gathered that one man ever had," replied Bentley, sinking his voice to a low murmur and leaning forward.

"Ah! And vere did you get them? There haf been no robberies lately."

"Fool!" snapped Bentley. "They're not stolen."

"Den vhy all this mystery?" asked Isaacs shrewdly.

"Look here, Isaacs," muttered Bentley savagely, "keep quiet until I tell you. I suppose you know that the Republic of Colombia produces magnificent emeralds?"

Isaacs nodded.

"Well, and I suppose you know that the Government have a monopoly of the production?"

"It iss my business."

"All right, in my case they missed that monopoly, for I found a mine and got away with the goods—See?"

"It iss risky to dispose of them," murmured Isaacs, looking down his nose.

"Oh, stow that!" answered Bentley. "I've been sounding things since my arrival, but beyond getting rid of a few big stones here and there in order to keep me in funds, I haven't dared risk disposing of the whole bunch."

"Vhy not?"

"Well, the truth is, the Colombian Government have got wind of the matter, and I hear are searching for the haul I got away with."

"It must haf been a big vun!"

"It will go to a million," whispered Bentley; and as he spoke Isaacs' eyes glittered greedily.

"Vat iss your proposition?" he asked with a show of indifference.

"This! I want you to dispose of them through your channels. You can get rid of them easily enough in Amsterdam, Rotterdam and Vienna."

"And vat percentage do you offer?"

"Ten percent."

"My dear friendt, I am a busy man. Goot morning!"

"You old robber!" growled Bentley. "Isn't that enough for you?"

"I might return the compliment, but I hope I am a gentlemans," replied Isaacs suavely. "No, my friendt, ten percent iss not enough."

"Then how much do you want?"

"Twenty-five per cent!"

"What!" gasped Bentley. "Why in blazes don't you ask a hundred while you are at it? I'll make it twelve and a-half. Not a penny more."

Isaacs shrugged his shoulders, and picked up a paper from his desk.

"Very well, my friendt. Good-day, I thaid."

Then began one of those haggling bargains which, though each knew the other would alter his terms, did not lessen the argument.

After half an hour, however, Bentley leaned back with a sigh, after compromising for seventeen and a-half per cent. Then drawing a cigar from his pocket he lit it and spoke again.

"Now that is settled, when can you handle them?"

"Any time," replied Isaacs. "The thooner the better. If the Colombian Government iss looking for them in London, ve must get them on the Continent at vunce. I myself vill take them to Amsterdam. I haf vays vich noboty knows."

"I don't doubt it," remarked Bentley grinning. "Very well, this is Tuesday. I'll bring them down Thursday night. Will that do?"

"Yes, that vill do."

Bentley rose.

"Is the way back in working order?" he asked.

"Yes, I vill let you out."

Isaacs moved across to a big fly-specked mirror which hung on the opposite wall, and, after pressing a nob on the bottom, it swung open to reveal a black hole and a flight of stairs.

Bentley evidently knew his way, for he nodded and strode through without guidance, and five minutes later he passed out through a clothing shop in the next street.

He had spoken the truth when he said the Colombian Government were after the stones, for in disposing of one magnificent specimen, the jeweller had jokingly remarked that he hoped it wasn't one of those for which the Colombian Government were making inquiries.

By judicious questioning Bentley had ascertained that cautious investigations had been set afoot, and since then he had not dared to dispose of any more. He knew Isaacs as a "fence" who could be relied upon to get rid of any shady stuff safely. How the old rascal managed it he hadn't the faintest idea, but it seemed the only way, and even had Isaacs stuck to twenty-five per cent., Bentley would have paid it gladly.

On reaching the Bank, he again entered a post-office, and after sending a wire, strolled along until he finally reached the Strand, where he lunched leisurely and well.

After lunch a taxi whirled him to Waterloo, and entering a train bound for Surrey he settled back well satisfied with his morning's work.

He had been thoroughly confident that, as in the past, his elastic conscience would soon forget all the unpleasant incidents attendant upon his last days in the jungle; but somehow of late a mental picture of his missing knife had been recurring with irritating persistency.

He laughed at himself for a fool, and brushed away the unpleasant thought: "What had he to worry about? White had only gone to a fate he deserved, for hadn't he bullied and dominated him (Bentley) unjustly? And why shouldn't he have his dead partner's stones as well as his own? Hadn't he worked and slaved for them too?"

It was most irritating to have these thoughts recurring to him so soon after his successful morning's work, and as the train pulled out, he closed his eyes in an endeavour to concentrate his mind on something more agreeable.

The warm sun, playing through the window, pressed on his lids until, from a pleasant, drowsy contemplation of the future, when he had disposed of the emeralds, he passed into slumber.

Into his sleep the pleasant thoughts strayed until suddenly a new element obtruded itself. The golden heap of sovereigns of which he had been dreaming changed to green, and with the green came a change of form until he saw a mighty sea of emeralds. Some resistless force dragged him nearer and nearer until he plunged headlong into their midst.

As he struggled madly to the surface, he looked up, and directly over his head was a great knife, whose blade gleamed reddish green over the emerald sea. His eyes widened with horror as the knife, held by no visible hand, slowly descended, and the horror turned to maudlin terror as he struggled wildly to throw off the embrace of the mire which held him.

Nearer and nearer came the knife, until it seemed that the point must pierce his heart, and as he looked up again he saw it was his own knife—the knife he had left in the jungle. With a shriek, he sank into the emerald sea, and as his senses reeled he gasped, and—woke.

As the blessed sun met his opened eyes, and the train pulled into his station, he laughed hysterically, with the relief of finding the terrible vision was all a dream; but as he entered the waiting motor which his wire had summoned, his face was still chalky from the effects of the nightmare.

Bentley had almost recovered his usual sangfroid by the time he arrived at the beautiful country place which his newly-acquired wealth had made possible, and as he entered the luxuriously-furnished library, which looked directly out on a wooded park of ancient oaks, he smiled.

"I'm thinking too much about those cursed stones," he muttered. "What I need is a change. As soon as Isaacs gets rid of them, I'll hit the Continent and forget things. A few months abroad will make me as right as a trivet again, and—— My heavens!"

Thus planning his future, he walked across the library to the desk, with the intention of going over his inventory of the stones. As he drew near, however, his thoughts broke off, and he gasped out the exclamation in terror, as there, lying in the very centre of the clean white blotting-paper, he saw a rough-looking knife, whose blade was stained a rusty red.

For a moment the blood of fear rushed to his face, and his mouth grew dry. Step by step, his fascinated gaze on the knife, he approached the desk. Was it another cursed dream? Was his mind beginning to conjure up visions, or, heavens, was it real?

Slowly his hand stretched out until it reached the edge of the desk. Then, inch by inch, it crept along towards the blotting-pad, followed by his dilated eyes. He was breathing in an agony of suspense, but as his fingers touched the handle and found it real, he trembled violently.

Slowly he drew the blade towards him, his fixed stare never leaving it until, with a cry, he saw beyond doubt that it was his own knife, which had been left in the jungle when he had raced for his life, leaving White to the tender mercies of the boa.

As the full force of it broke on his mind, he gave a second cry of fear, and, staggering backwards, collapsed in a heap on the library floor, the knife dropping with a metallic clatter to the desk.

And then, while Travers Bentley lay in a swoon born of the fear in his craven heart, a great hairy beast of a reddish tinge bounded through the open window, hovered with a chattering grin over the unconscious man, and, making as though to bury its powerful fingers in his throat, only desisted and turned as a shrill whistle came from outside.

With another hopping bound it turned, and, picking up the knife, leaped through the window, and swung off through the trees, only stopping when it reached a heavily-leafed oak some fifty yards away.

There sat a gaunt-looking, bearded man, a pair of opera-glasses in his hands, and a look of deadly hatred in his eyes. Even as, through the glasses, he discerned a manservant open the door of the library, and rush in in answer to his master's cry, the man in the tree muttered:

"He saw, and he knows fear. A month of this, you cur, and I'll have you in the asylum. After that, you won't dare dispose of the stones. Tonight I'll let you feel fear again. Yes, tonight!"

With that he snapped the glasses together, and, thrusting them in his pocket, turned to the ape, who still held the knife.

"Give me!" he ordered, and as the beast cringingly obeyed, he pointed back through the trees.

"Back, Caesar! You have done well. Tonight you will get plenty of sugar—sugar, d'ye hear?"

Obediently the ape turned, and, swinging from branch to branch, set off at a remarkable pace through the trees. When it had disappeared, the man in the tree put the knife carefully in his pocket, and, swinging cautiously downwards, landed easily on the soft turf below.

Then, slipping his feet into the leathers of what looked like a miniature pair of skis, he set off in the direction the ape had taken, with a long, sliding slither which left no print behind.

In the meantime, the efforts of the manservant within the house had succeeded in bringing Travers Bentley to his senses, and as he looked about the room, he gave a shudder of terror when returning memory cleared his mind.

"The knife—the knife!" he muttered excitedly, attempting to rise.

"There, sir, it's all right," answered the manservant cheerfully. "You have had a spell, sir—beggin' your pardon, sir—but if you keep quiet for a bit you'll be all right."

"Fool!" snapped Bentley, struggling to a sitting posture. "Where's that cursed knife? Look about, man, and see where it is!"

"A knife, sir?" asked the man in surprise. "Please, sir, what kind?"

"A big sheath knife," answered Bentley savagely. "It was on the desk, and I had just picked it up when I fainted. Look on the floor. It must be near where I fell."

The man obediently dropped to his knees, and began searching for the article his master described, but when he finally rose and said: "I'm sorry, sir, but it doesn't seem to be there," Bentley thrust him aside with a curse, and began himself to search.

His efforts were as fruitless as the man's, however, and after repeatedly searching every inch of the library without result, he arose, looking very pale.

Then, vainly endeavouring to keep his voice calm, he asked:

"How long was it after you heard my cry that you came in?"

"Not two minutes, sir. "I heard you call, and came at once. I knocked, but when you did not reply, I opened the door and entered."

"Nobody else came with you?"

"No, sir. All the other servants were below."

"And you touched nothing?"

"No, sir; indeed not! I picked you up, sir, and was with you every moment until you came round."

"That will do then, Barnes. You may go. Remember, though, you are to say nothing below about my seizure. It was merely a faint, brought on by—er—some bad news I heard. You understand, do you?"

"Oh, yes, sir; I will say nothing, sir!"

With that the man retired, but when he gained the privacy of the hall he muttered:

"Clean dotty. If I ever saw a man scared into a fit, he's that man, but it's none of my business. However, I'll just keep my eyes open, all the same."

When the door had closed behind the servant, Bentley stole swiftly across the room and turned the key; then, hastening across to the open window, he peered out, but, search as he would, he could see not the faintest trace of footsteps.

His brow was very puzzled as he returned slowly to the desk, and sank wearily into the chair. For a long time he stared at the white pad before him.

"My heavens! Am I going mad?" he muttered. "Was that knife only another vision, or—no; by heavens, it was real, as real as the peril which is threatening me! Who put that knife there, and who took it away again? I'll swear it wasn't Barnes, but who— who—who? Is there somebody who knows? Heavens! Who can it be? There was no-body there but White and myself and the boa, and it certainly isn't White. It must have been a vision; it can't be real!" he muttered brokenly.

But at that moment his eyes caught sight of a tiny rusty flake on the white blotter, and as he gazed at it with distended eyes and quickening pulse, a great fear filled the soul of Travers Bentley.

The Third Chapter
Yvonne Has a Narrow Squeak

JUST about the time Travers Bentley had somewhat recovered from his terror of the mysterious and unknown power which had placed the knife on his desk, and as mysteriously removed it, and when he had dragged himself into his dining room in order to force himself to go through what was usually the pleasantest hour of the day to him, a big, powerful magenta coloured car turned out of a driveway of a handsome old Surrey estate and turned to the left.

At the wheel was a woman whose youthful figure and features, partially visible through her motoring-veil, made her seem much younger than her actual years. Beside her was a bearded man in motoring duster, negligently smoking and gazing in languid enjoyment at the night-curtained hedges and trees, from which came the heavy, sweet scent of the country.

Not until the car was racing ahead at high speed did either speak, and then it was the man who broke the silence.

"How did you hear?" he asked.

"Captain Vaughan heard it through a man called Perry. It seems he watched Bentley's arrival for a man who followed on. What the other man's business is with Bentley I don't know, but since hearing from Captain Vaughan I went ahead and investigated matters. If you had seen the captain as you passed through London today he would have told you about it."

"I know, Yvonne," replied the man, whose voice, though not his appearance, was strangely like that of Graves, Yvonne's uncle. "As I told you, however, I missed him, and as your wire said come on at once, I came. Tell me the details, please."

"It's this way," answered Yvonne, settling down a trifle. "Bentley, as you now know, landed here a few months ago. I missed him when he went off on that treasure hunt, and I thought he had met his finish in South America. It turns out differently, however, and not only does he arrive back here safely, but he has returned wealthy.

"After Captain Vaughan sent me the news that he was back, I got busy. I cabled Santa Rita, our old Chinese agent in Puerto Costa, who is head of the secret society—the 'Source'—out there. He sent me the information that a white man had got out of Colombia by the *Atrato* with a fortune in emeralds, and that the Colombian Government had discovered the fact. He said, furthermore, that a man had been sent on to London to trace the stones and locate the man.

"Well, I put two and two together. Bentley, after the fiasco of his treasure hunt, was penniless. He landed at Buenaventura, and there is proof that he was later in Bogota. Then he disappears with another white man southwards. A year later a man leaves Colombia whose description, after making necessary allowances, would fit that of Travers Bentley. We discover that Bentley arrives on that steamer, and is very much in funds. Ergo, the man for whom the Colombian Government is searching is Travers Bentley, and he it is who got away with a fortune in emeralds."

"But what about the other man who went south with him?" asked Graves.

"The rumour is that he died in the jungle."

"Then who is the man who got this man Perry to watch Bentley's arrival?"

"I don't know. Captain Vaughan thinks it is the agent of the Colombian Government."

"Ah! That hadn't occurred to me. Then you think——"

"That Bentley got the emeralds, and, that being so, has them yet. I have had the most exhaustive inquiries made, but beyond the regular movement in that line no large batches of stones have yet come on the market. There have been a few exceptionally fine specimens, but up to now I haven't been able to trace those to Bentley.

"From what I know of the gentleman he will be in no hurry to dispose of them, and when he does you may rest assured that he will have arranged a minimum of risk. We must get those stones, however, before he does, and tonight I hope to do so. He has leased the Carthorpe Estate, and I think we will make it by ten o'clock."

"It seems risky to me, Yvonne," remarked Graves.

"What of it?" laughed Yvonne softly. "I've waited for this ever since his partner Forsythe went to his fate at Traders' Bay, and I don't intend that he shall slip through my fingers as he did when he went off on that treasure hunt."

"Well, of course, what you say goes; but at the same time I think it would have been wiser to send for Captain Vaughan and Hendricks in case of emergencies."

"Nonsense, uncle! I'll handle the matter all right."

"What is your exact plan?"

"This. When I pull up you are to wait an hour. If things come out as I have planned I shall be through by then. I have made a careful study of the grounds, and, after taking care of him, will get the safe opened as quickly as possible. If, as I think, the stones are there, I shall join you at once, but in case complications should arise, don't wait."

"But—but——"

"Wait! Hear me out. If things go against me I shall be able to take care of myself for tonight at least. If I haven't arrived home by tomorrow morning, wire to London for Captain Vaughan to come down, and bring Hendricks and half a dozen men. Then set a watch on the place, and at night force your way in. If he has got the better of me and is holding me prisoner, you will be in time.

"I prefer it this way, for I desire, if possible, to keep the thing quiet until we get away. This agent of the Colombian Government, or whoever he really is, may drop on Bentley's identity any day, and I wish to reach him first."

"What could they do to him?"

Yvonne shrugged.

"Oh, nothing much. It is a case to get them back as Bentley got them. The Government has the moral right to them, but they can't use the law in this case. If, however, they can take them by force or cunning from Bentley, then he can't recover them, for it is really a case of possession being ten points of the law. Of course, if they caught him in South America they would back him up against a wall and fill him full of lead; but England isn't South America. However, here we are, uncle. You understand exactly what you have to do?"

"Never fear, I'll do my part," drawled Graves. "If you aren't home by daylight I'll send a wire at once to Captain Vaughan and send Alec over at once to keep watch on the place."

"All right. Good-bye!"

"Good-bye, Yvonne, and good luck!"

With that Graves slid over and took the wheel, while Yvonne climbed easily over the boundary wall of the Carthorpe grounds, and set off cautiously through the wooded park.

In many ways a woman's mind is undoubtedly finer of perception and more capable of considering what seems an unimportant detail than that of a man. The highly-trained mechanism of the mentality of a Sexton Blake, or the finely-tuned perceptions of the most famous and therefore most successful criminals, are not included in a comparison of this kind.

But had it not been for mademoiselle's stern, almost austere mental discipline when she started on her campaign of vengeance against the men who brutally and remorselessly caused the financial ruin of her mother and herself, and had she not applied a really brilliant intellect in order to bend science to her will, she would, by neglecting these points, have failed to reach the pinnacle which the world called audacity, but which Sexton Blake called "the triumph of mental discipline."

And surely no better judgment of the young woman's nature could be obtained than that of the man who knew her better and understood her better than probably any other human being, not even excepting Graves, her uncle, or the members of her "circle."

Consequently the development of these faculties had resulted in her making a long and careful study of the grounds, the house, and the habits of Mr. Theodore Knox—or, as she knew him to be, Travers Bentley.

Nor did she stop there. She knew almost every detail of the internal and external arrangement of Bentley's house. She knew what time the servants were astir in the morning; she knew at what hour the stable-boy crossed the yard with his brimming pails of milk; she was aware of the hours set aside for meals, and the time allotted to each servant for their time off.

Also, she was cognisant of the hour at which they retired, and had a pretty thorough idea of Mr. Travers Bentley's habits while staying at his new home, which he did most of the time.

In addition to this, she had a mental picture of the interior, gained from an old plan of the Carthorpes'; and had it been necessary, she could have described in detail exactly what type of lock fastened the lower windows, at what moment each night the butler made the rounds of them, and, more than that, could have told you that the catch on the back drawing-room window worked more easily than any other, owing, possibly, to the fact that it had received some brief, though effective, attention.

She possessed a perfect mental photograph of the topography of the wooded park, and in view of these things, it is not surprising that, after slipping over the boundary wall, she moved forward with silent confidence until she stood in the friendly shadow of a tree which reared itself very close to the drawing-room window.

What Yvonne did not know, however, was the fact that the man she thought to be an agent of the Colombian Government had also located the whereabouts of Travers Bentley, and that during the afternoon had begun a carefully-thought-out plan of mental torture which was intended to bring Bentley to the verge of madness.

Knowing this, she would have known that, coincident with the mysterious appearance and disappearance of the sinister knife, deadly fear and cunning caution had been roused in her intended victim, naturally entailing a sudden change in her plans.

However, of these recent developments she was in ignorance, and, consequently, after slipping her small but potent automatic in the outside pocket of her coat, she drew out a tiny steel, spidery affair, and moved up to the window.

Darkness reigned supreme over the whole house, with one exception. That exception was where a light stood out against drawn curtains two windows down from where Yvonne stood.

She knew, as a result of her investigations, that the servants had retired fully an hour before, that the solitary light gleamed forth from the library, and she pictured Travers Bentley behind those drawn curtains fingering and gloating over his new-found wealth.

Curiously enough, her estimate of the man's nature was almost uncannily correct, for at that moment Travers Bentley sat at the massive mahogany desk—which was a legacy of the Carthorpes' furniture—while before him was a glittering heap of magnificent emeralds, which would have purchased a sultan's ransom. His forced dinner had been succeeded by a Magnum of 1900, and, from the courage born of the sparkling wine, he had been unable to resist his nightly enjoyment of toying with the stones.

At that moment the episode of the afternoon seemed far away, and where before he had considered finding a safe hiding-place for the gems and making no move towards their disposal until he had discovered the genesis of the knife's mysterious peregrinations, he had now almost regained his accustomed sangfroid.

To be sure, however, he had himself locked the library window, and when the butler had retired, he made a stealthy examination of the others, after which he secured the comforting companionship of a big service-revolver which lay reflected on the polished mahogany beside him.

Beautiful, seductive, almost baleful, were the great gems which threw back in a thousand multiplied facets the virgin rays of the light overhead. No wonder is it, therefore, that their lure seduced his mind from the past and present, and sent it careering on the wings of fantastic imaginings to roam with exquisite delight through the chimerical castles reared on his thoughts.

Nor was it surprising that his absorption should make him deaf to the very faintest click behind him as the well-oiled handle of the library door turned and a slim, veiled figure slipped through, to stand in the concealment of the heavy curtains which hung before it.

It was when, with a sigh, that Bentley looked up from the glittering heap before him that his eyes unconsciously rested on a beautiful specimen of seventeenth century art in the shape of an ebony-framed desk mirror; but as they did so, his beautiful dreams fled in disorder, his fantastic air-castles tumbled in ruins, and a sickly, chalky hue overspread his face.

For in that mirror, and framed by heavy curtains, was a veiled face and a gloved hand, and in that gloved hand, pointing with unpleasant certainty at his expansive back, was a small, businesslike looking automatic.

While the silver desk-clock ticked off a full minute, did Bentley gaze with distended eyes at the reflection in the mirror, and so tense was the silence of his fear, and the immovable, unwavering attitude of the veiled face and arm, that each tick sounded thunderously oppressive to his startled senses.

At the end of a minute the curtains were pushed aside, and, with the revolver still pointing steadily at his back, the slim figure of a young woman advanced into the room and stood close behind him, looking at his fear-stricken face in the mirror.

Bentley eyed the heavy service-revolver longingly, but as the point of his mysterious caller's automatic prodded him between the shoulder-blades, he jerked his eyes back, and a cold shiver passed down his spine.

"Good-evening, Mr. Bentley!" came a musical voice.

"Good-evening!" he managed to say, although his dry tongue had suddenly been stricken with a strong affection for the roof of his mouth. "To—to what do I owe the honour of this visit?"

"I'm glad that you have sense enough to realise that it is an honour," came the pleasant voice. "My primary reason, Mr. Bentley, is to have a short conversation with you, after which I propose to relieve you of that magnificent array of emeralds which seem to give you such pleasure.

"First, however, it would be as well if you understood that this automatic is quite capable of—er—sending you to join your late partner, Mr. Forsythe, shall we say, and also that it is fitted with a most effective silencer which, from experience, I can assure you does all its inventor claims for it. In fact, so excellent is it that he really deserves permanent recognition for such a successful production."

"Ah!" gasped Bentley, as Yvonne paused. "I know you now! You are the woman who, under the name of the Comtesse de Rastonet, ruined me and my partner at the Traders' Bay Hotel!"

"Really!" mocked Yvonne. "I am flattered! Your memory is excellent, and since it is now unnecessary for me to introduce myself, we will talk."

As she spoke, Yvonne moved around to the side of the big desk, and faced Bentley. As she stood there in the blended reflection of the light from the emeralds, her face looked almost ethereal in the purity of its beauty, and the heavy masses of her hair gleamed like burnished bronze before the red embers of the artisan's fire.

Only her straight, practical little nose saved the face from being too mystically beautiful, and the broad, white brow, around which little tendrils coiled distractingly, gave a grave dignity to the youthful face, which was enhanced by the faintest hint of weariness in the large, wistful eyes.

Even Bentley, in whom a terrible hatred had been born for her since the affair at the Traders' Bay Hotel, felt the compelling influence of her beauty; but as the weary look in the eyes changed to an expression of contempt for the man before her, he stiffened in expectation of something to come.

"I think," she said slowly, "that Mr. Sexton Blake dealt with you regarding my purpose and identity at the Traders' Bay Hotel, did he not?"

"Well, what of it?" growled Bentley, regaining some of his composure.

"Only this," she replied. "It saves me from going over in detail the reasons for my tracking you down in order to take the revenge which I propose to take tonight."

"Indeed!" he said sarcastically. "It might interest you to know that when my partner, Henry Forsythe, met his death, I swore vengeance on you; but as you seem to have the whip-hand at present, perhaps you will condescend to tell me exactly what you have against me. Mr. Blake was so occupied in justifying you and bullying me that I didn't gather exactly what your object was."

"Had you listened to what he said, my friend," replied Yvonne coldly, "you would have received all the information necessary, for when it comes to clarity of meaning and pointed expression, I think you will find Mr. Sexton Blake a master of both—as well as other things."

And Bentley never knew that, among the "other things" of which Sexton Blake was master, was the slim young woman seated so coolly on the desk, whose heart contracted with a spasm of exquisite pain in the proximity of the man who, though technically her greatest enemy, still held her in the hollow of his hand did he care to say the word.

"However," she continued, after a few moments' pause, "since you either wittingly or unwittingly have forgotten what he said, and since it is part of my plan that you should fully realise everything, I will make a few brief remarks which I think will clear matters up, but let me warn you, don't move, for this trigger is balanced to hair action."

"Since you seem to be in control of the situation there is nothing for it but to hear you out."

"I'm glad you think so. Have you by any chance ever heard of the name Cartier— John Cartier?"

Bentley's face contracted in a sudden twinge as he looked into the eyes of the girl before him, and saw there the feminine counterpart of John Cartier, the original controlling power of the Jig-Saw Mine, in Australia.

"Ah!" was all he said.

"I see that you do," went on Yvonne. "Perhaps, if you cast your memory back, you will also recollect the fact that on the death of John Cartier he left to his widow and only daughter his interest in that mine as well as a station home. Binabong was the name. I see it is unnecessary for me to elaborate my remarks. That being so, you will doubtless remember how the remaining eight men who were interested in the Jig Saw Mine cooked up what they considered a very worthy plot for the despoiling of a friendless woman and her child of all they owned, and so well was the taking done that not only did they succeed, but even the law technically sanctioned their perfidy.

"Neither you nor they, however, knew that after the shock had sent that poor frail mother to the grave, the daughter, insignificant and equally helpless in your eyes, swore a lifelong vengeance against the authors of all her misery."

As she paused for a moment, Yvonne leaned forward and continued tensely:

"How did she succeed, Travers Bentley? Do you know? I will tell you. What became of Vineburg, the wily originator of the scheme? What happened to Pearson, when he was at the very zenith of his power? For what reason did Mortimer Todd flee from Bournmill, his mill destroyed, and himself broken? What fate overtook Gorgon Kelly, the 'Money King,' whom fortune carried higher than any, only to cast him down? Do you know that Carfax Morton, once a Cabinet Minister, is now a babbling imbecile? And where is Henry Forsythe, your late partner at the Traders' Bay Hotel?

"Do you think the sequence of events which led to the downfall of each and every one was only the work of chance? Do you think ruin dogged them without an instrument to achieve its purpose? And who was that instrument? I—I, the 'helpless girl' whom you all considered not worth a thought. I—Yvonne Cartier, the daughter of the woman who was killed by the shock of your fiendish schemes! Do you think I hesitated or faltered? The result answers that!

"Do you think I have borne the name Mademoiselle Yvonne, the adventuress, from continent to continent, without a strong motive? Do you think I embarked on my vengeance without a preparation which fitted me for the work, and which lulled you all into a false security? You have only to remember the other seven to know whether I did or not.

"And now, Travers Bentley, you are the last of that despicable crew, and as sure as I sit here before you tonight so surely will this night see your ruin."

Yvonne's eyes were blazing fiercely, and her cheeks were pale with emotion as she straightened up and regarded the cringing man before her. As she went from point to point Bentley's face had grown a sickly green, which was not wholly due to the heap of emeralds before him.

As she dealt with the fate of his former associates, Bentley felt the same fear which he felt when Forsythe, his dead partner, had recalled the mysterious fate which seemed to have overtaken the other six.

He felt in his craven heart that the young woman before him was deadly serious, and even if she had to send a leaden messenger from that steadily-held automatic, that she would not count the cost.

He felt the force of her deadly calm, and in that saw more danger than in the ravings of a maniac. He knew that, unless he made some move very soon, that, as she said, this night would see his ruin. If he could only get hold of that revolver, so near yet so irretrievably far, he might turn the tables.

He knew, however, that his slightest move in that direction would, at the very least, cause his hand to be shattered by a bullet, and in that moment of his despair he cursed himself for not having taken more precautions, after his experience of the afternoon.

Yvonne, he reasoned, could have no connection with that occurrence, for if she had, she would undoubtedly have referred to it. But whoever it was, if after all it was not the figment of his fevered imagination, it had no connection with her, and he must confine himself to the matter in hand.

If Travers Bentley proved himself a coward when he stabbed his partner White in the back, he cleared up any question on that subject when he collapsed with fear at the sight of the knife on the blotting-pad during the afternoon, but he set the seal on his cowardice when he cringed with chalky cheeks before the self-constituted avenger of her mother's and her own wrongs, who at that moment stood before him.

But though Travers Bentley was craven-hearted, he was like all others of his ilk. He valued his life above all else, and, before risking that, he would fight with the hysterical courage born of fear, instead of the cool bravery of the naturally courageous. And it was that same hysterical courage which sent his pulses hammering with the force of the move which his reason told him must be made if he were to escape.

And once he realised that fact he dared not hesitate, for his frothy hysteria would evaporate and leave him inert, flabby, and helpless.

With this idea seething in his mind, he glanced up craftily at the girl who sat contemplating him with the contemptuous regard which she would have bestowed on a reptile.

Then, every nerve quivering with the battle between his cowardice and his hysteria, he leaped forward just as his muscles threatened to refuse obedience. So charged was his spring with the force of his almost frantic effort, that it carried him forwards to collide with terrific force against the young woman in front of him.

Startled by his sudden and unexpected move, Yvonne leaped backwards and pulled the trigger, but the bullet whistled past Bentley's head just as he struck her and grappled. As his hands touched her he lost the last vestige of his self-control, and, literally unbalanced by his mad hysteria, he struggled violently with the young woman as though she were a man.

Under his unrestrained attack Yvonne was helpless, and though his sickening brutality made him a thing instead of a man, his brain-storm drove him on, until with his fingers at her white throat, he forced her head slowly back until it finally sagged downwards and her body grew limp.

Then, as her mind sank into oblivion, the false courage of the man evaporated as suddenly as it had come, and as he held the inert body of his weaker antagonist, his flabby limbs trembled with the reaction. He stumbled across the room with her until he reached the couch.

As he laid her down something fell from her finger and thudded softly on the carpet. Not troubling to look, Bentley kicked it under the couch, but had he cast his mind back he would have remembered that he had seen on Yvonne's hand a big Egyptian scarab, which was now not there. Then he rose, and began moving back to the desk, when a slight sound behind him brought him up with a jerk, while his pulses beat madly.

For the second time that night Travers Bentley gazed into the ebony-framed mirror on his desk, and for the second time he saw therein something which sent the fear of death into his craven soul.

He watched, with fascinated gaze, while the curtains before the door parted, and a hand—a big, lean, brown hand—appeared, holding in its grip a knife whose blade gleamed rusty red in the light.

With horror-widened eyes, Bentley stared at the mirror, rooted to the spot and unable to move through sheer terror. Then, as mysteriously as the knife had appeared was it withdrawn, but the soft click of the door told Bentley it was no figment of the mind, but a deadly reality.

With this realisation he leaped for the revolver, and started for the door, but at that moment the silence without was broken by a scuffling sound, followed by a sharp exclamation. Then the door flew open, the curtains fell apart, and across the room sprang a great reddish-brown ape.

For a moment Bentley was too frozen with fear to act, and that lost moment was his undoing. Before he could pull the trigger the ape had landed on his shoulders, and as the beast's great hairy arms enwrapped his neck, and its fingers clawed his throat, the revolver dropped to the carpet.

At that moment the tall, gaunt-looking man who had sat in the trees earlier in the day, dashed through the door, and made for the ape. Quickly he grappled with it, all the time speaking sternly.

At first it paid no attention, but after a few moments the red light left its eyes, and its hold relaxed. It dropped to the floor, whimpering and cringing against its master, and as he turned and pointed at the door with a stern command, the ape hopped through quickly and disappeared.

Then the big, gaunt-looking man turned and knelt by the crumpled figure at his feet. It had been his intention to torture him to the verge of madness, and then deprive him of his ill-gotten wealth; but White—for the lean man was he—had never intended that Bentley's death should form a part of that vengeance.

When he had watched his former partner's terror in the afternoon, and when, by means of the ape which he had trained so laboriously, he was able to recover the knife and thus increase the tantalising terror of the mystery for Bentley, he had promised himself another visit that evening. It had been no part of his intention that the ape should accompany him, however, and just after ten he had started out alone; the ape, as far as he knew, being safely locked up.

Nobody knew but Perry, the man of whom he had made use in tracking Bentley, that on his arrival he had gone to Paris, and there borrowed several thousands on the stones he himself had brought home with him. He knew that at the present time to court publicity was to seek failure, and consequently the realisation had been in the form of a confidential loan, instead of an outright sale.

Thus equipped with the necessary ammunition, White, or Fairbanks, as he chose to call himself, returned to England, and set about his plan which would at one stroke break his treacherous partner and regain his stolen emeralds.

He had been hovering in the background when Bentley took the Carthorpe place, and though he had offered any price, together with persuasive cajolery, he had been compelled to wait until just a few days previous before being able to lease the one adjoining—the thickly-wooded slopes of which blended evenly with the park of Bentley's estate, and whose dividing wall formed no obstacle to White in the pursuit of his plans.

His gratitude towards the ape which had saved his life had taken tangible form in comfortable quarters for that animal, and White's months of patient training had borne fruit in the complete manner in which the ape obeyed his every order.

After his first surreptitious examination of Bentley's new home, he had located the library, and at his own place spent several days training the ape to leap from a tree through the open window, and, after laying the knife on a desk, return the way it came.

Then had come the next step, which was to send it back for the knife, and when he had attempted the terrorising scheme on Bentley that afternoon, the success of his efforts proved how well the ape had learned.

That night, however, after slipping his feet under the straps of his ski-like grass shoes, he had moved cautiously through the woods and over the dividing wall alone, for he knew it would be risking a discovery to use the ape too often.

As he drew near Bentley's house he pulled up sharply in the shadow of a tree, for against the blackness of a window he saw the dim form of a shadowy figure. Then the window had gone up and through it had disappeared the figure.

"Now, what the dickens does that mean?" he muttered, sliding forward several yards. "I'll swear that was either a woman or a youth in a long coat; and what can their business be with Bentley? I didn't know there were any other fingers in his pie, and if that is so I guess I'd better hump myself. The first thing I know, the stones and that cursed cur will be slipping through my fingers. I'll give that visitor fifteen minutes, and if he or she doesn't appear, then I'll take a hand in the game."

With this decision he leaned against the tree trunk and silently watched the black opening through which the other figure had disappeared. When he was quite satisfied that a quarter of an hour had passed, he slid ahead on his grass shoes until he was under the open window. Then slipping his feet out of the straps, he raised himself up and dropped with a soft thud inside the room.

All was silent as far as human presence seemed concerned, and only the slow ticking of a clock near at hand broke the stillness. With infinite caution White dropped to his knees and crept forwards until, by running his fingers along the wall, he felt the half-open door.

Squirming through, he crept along until his trained hearing caught the murmur of a voice—a voice pitched in a key which he knew instinctively to be that of a woman.

Then it had stopped, and as he drew nearer he thought he heard sounds of a struggle. Again all grew silent, and as his fingers felt the outlines of a door he rose and laid his hand on the handle.

Ever so softly he turned, and as it opened the heavy curtains which his hand encountered explained to him why no chink of light had filtered through under the door. He felt for the opening and peered through.

A man's back was towards him, and the familiar outlines told him at once that it was his treacherous partner. What had been going on he had no idea. What had become of the woman whose voice he had heard he knew not. He could see, however, that Bentley was white, breathless and dishevelled, and as his eyes saw the reflection of his late partner in the desk mirror he smiled grimly.

Then, swiftly drawing the knife which had almost been the cause of his death back in the jungle, he slipped his hand through and held it, steadily watching the while for the effect on Bentley.

He had not long to wait, for he saw Bentley's look of fixed horror as his eyes caught the reflection in the mirror. Then, not wishing to spoil the effect by giving Bentley time to collect his senses, he withdrew the knife and slipped through the door.

As he did so something came bounding along the dark hall and collided with him as he closed the door. As soon as his hands touched the new arrival, the truth flashed across his mind. The ape had escaped, and picking up his trail had at once followed him. Then, seeing where the trail led, his unreasoning nature had leaped out of bounds in the fear that peril threatened the master it loved. This frenzy had grown as it entered through the window, and not even its master's command could recall it for the moment.

To complicate the situation, as they scrambled on the floor the ape felt the knife which had fallen from White's hand, and its memory inflamed by the familiar touch, it leaped through the door where stood the man it hated.

How it hurled itself at that terror-stricken individual has been related; and quick as White was to follow, as he bent over Bentley's unconscious form, he saw that the treacherous, cowardly man had almost breathed his last, and would, unless he were revived soon, submit his case to a Higher Judge.

As he realised the full force of the situation, White started up sharply. Supposing somebody had been awakened by the noise and came in to investigate. What explanation could he give if he were found in the library with Bentley in such condition, and whose throat still bore the marks of the ape's fingers? What construction but that he had done it could possibly be put upon it? And the emeralds, some of which had been scattered to the floor, would prove a motive for such a deed which any attempt of his to prove otherwise would only aggravate. And—— Good Heavens! What was that?

For the first time his eyes fell on the unconscious figure of a young woman lying on the couch. Had there been not one death, but two deaths there that night? Who was she, and was her condition due to the struggle he had heard? What connection had she with Bentley, and did she still live?

He hastily crossed to the couch and put his finger on the young woman's pulse. Yes, it was steady, though weak. He glanced around for something which would serve to bring her round, and spied on a small table a syphon, a bottle of brandy and glasses. Evidently Bentley's night-cap—a night-cap he would never have!

White moved swiftly to the door and turned the key; then picking up the brandy, he poured out a small portion and held it to the lips of the unconscious young woman.

As the fiery spirit coursed down her throat, she gasped and opened her eyes, a puzzled look appearing in them as she comprehended her whereabouts.

"Who—who are you?" asked Yvonne, weakly struggling to a sitting posture. "Where is Bentley? Oh——"

The long drawn out exclamation escaped her as she saw the huddled up figure of her late assailant.

"Is he——" she asked.

White shook his head.

"No, not quite. It was unintentional. But who are you? Did he attack you?"

"Yes," she whispered. "He tried to kill me. Who I am makes no difference. He was my enemy and I sought revenge, but he managed for the moment to outwit me. How did you do it?"

"I didn't do it," replied White, gazing in amazement at the peerless beauty of her pale features. "It was an accident, I tell you."

Yvonne shrugged.

"If you wish to maintain that, it is immaterial to me. Only we had better get out of here at once. It would be awkward were somebody to come. What time is it? Ah, I have not been unconscious very long. Who are you, and what brings you here?"

"It is a long story, but this is neither the time nor the place for its relation. We must, as you say, get away, but I can't permit you to go until I know who you are, and what you were doing here."

A sudden light seemed to break in on Yvonne.

"Are you the agent of the Colombian Government who is after those stones?" she asked, pointing to the emeralds.

"No. All that I can say now is that I was Bentley's partner when he got them, and that half of them belong to me. He cleared out with the lot, and I sought vengeance."

"Ah, I begin to understand! What are you going to do about them?"

"I intend taking my half, but it would be sheer madness to leave the rest. As for me, I wouldn't touch his share, but if he is indebted to you, I would advise you to take them."

"That is exactly what I propose to do," replied Yvonne coolly. "He owed me a debt which they by no means cover; but I don't propose that they shall remain in his hands or those of the Colombian Government. There is bound to be a big hue and cry over this, and I think our best plan will be to keep in touch with each other."

"Er—yes, I think if you take my advice———"

Yvonne cut him short.

"It is not I who will take your advice, but you who will take mine. When you know me better you will understand. The first thing to do is to gather up those stones. Let us make haste. Do you live near here?"

"Yes—my place adjoins this."

"That is good. You will take the stones home with you tonight. In the morning come over to my place, the location of which I shall give you before we part, and there we can discuss future arrangements."

And White, dominating, overbearing man though he was, looked into her eyes in a battle of wills, and like others before him, bowed to her rule.

"You seem to be sweeping things along with a high hand," he said, with an attempt to laugh; "but, for the time being, I guess I'll agree."

"Very well," said Yvonne briskly. "Let us get to work."

They started at once picking up the emeralds, nor did they pause even to admire any of the peerless gems, which they bundled into the leather bag which had been used by Bentley.

When they had finished, White bent over the unconscious man on the floor, and, picking him up, laid him on the couch. Then, in a very methodical and very thorough manner, which evoked Yvonne's admiration, he tied his feet and hands.

"Shall we leave him here?" he asked, looking up at Yvonne.

"No," she replied, after gazing about. "I think the best plan is to take him with us, and keep him safe for a while. I have means by which I can ship him out of the country later, and land him on the other side of the globe. That will baffle any investigation, or will, at least, partly serve to do so. There is bound to be a hue and cry, in any event, although I am inclined to think it will be done quietly. From what I know, though the Colombian Government is morally entitled to the stones, still, they have no claim on them in England. They will undoubtedly succeed in tracing Bentley's movements, and will then try to regain the emeralds by force. They will find, however, that others have been before them."

"They won't get mine!" muttered White grimly. "I'd give a good deal to know who you are, though," he added. "You seem straight enough, but how do I know you aren't really the agent of the Colombian Government?"

Yvonne laughed softly.

"Because I intend trusting you with all the stones," she replied. "In addition, you must look after Travers Bentley for the present, but the question is—how are we to get him away?"

"I'll manage that," remarked White. "I guess I can sling him over my shoulders, and get him as far as my place."

"Very well, do so. We had better be getting away, and in the morning you can come over to my home, where we can have a general explanation, and arrange matters."

White leaned down, and wrapped his long arms about Bentley's body. Then, with a mighty heave, he swung the bound man upwards until he lay over his shoulder like a sack of meal. Signing to Yvonne to pass him the bag of emeralds, he stood waiting for her next move.

She gave a cautious look around, then, stealing across to the door, she unlocked it, and motioned White to go ahead. With his heavy burden on his shoulder he did so, and as they made their way through the drawing-room window neither of them knew that, in the general confusion and rapid march of events, a ring, whose setting was an Egyptian scarab, had been left under the couch in the library, while on the floor of the dark hall lay the knife with the rusty red blade which had caused Travers Bentley such terror.

When he reached the ground White turned to Yvonne.

"Won't you leave footprints behind you?"

"No, I have arranged for that. I came through only the thickest turf, and by morning there will be no sign. Those affairs of yours are worth adopting, though. However, you had better get started. I will close the window, and go off in the other direction. There will be a motor waiting for me."

"All right, I'll be over in the morning. I think I'm a fool to place myself in the hands of an unknown woman, but you seem genuine enough, and I'll have to risk it now. Good-night!"

As he slid off on his ski-like shoes through the trees, Yvonne turned back to the window with a smile.

"All in all, it was rather fortunate running into that man. If I am any judge of facial expressions, he hates Bentley worse than poison, and his very determination to hang on to his emeralds will make him a valuable instrument. I think, my friend, when you know just who I am, you will prove useful at least until I have finished with Travers Bentley and all that pertains to him. If the agent of the Colombian Government does get this far in his investigations, I think he will find he has reached a blank wall."

With that she closed the window, and stole off into the night, little dreaming what was the actual identity of the man who had now taken hold of the matter for the Colombian Government.

The Fourth Chapter
The Cablegrams—Blake and Tinker as Burglars

GET Inspector Thomas on the 'phone, Tinker."

It was the morning after their evening at the theatre, and was the same day on which took place the events in which Yvonne and White by choice, and Bentley perforce, played such leading parts. Blake still wore the loose smoking-jacket which seemed almost a part of the man who stood leaning negligently against the desk, smoking the old black pipe, waiting until Tinker got into connection with Inspector Thomas at Scotland Yard.

When the lad's conversation told Blake the inspector was at the other end of the line, he reached over and took the receiver from Tinker.

"Hallo, inspector," he said briefly, "I am in want of a little information."

"Right, Blake!" came back the inspector's voice. "What is it? It seems unusual for you to be appealing to us for information. Still, if there is anything I can do to assist you, just say what it is."

Blake smiled involuntarily at the inspector's self-important tone, which, after several years, Blake knew was unconscious on the inspector's part, and that underneath his harmless bombast was a brave, if slightly fatty, heart, as well as a really able official.

"It's this way, inspector," he replied. "I have been given to understand that an informal acquiescence has been made by Scotland Yard in the endeavours of a certain Government to recover property which they claim, but which cannot be regained through the instrumentality of the law. Is that a fact?"

"I don't know how you got your information, Blake, but it is correct. As far as we are concerned it is simply a case of possession proving ownership. We can't help the Government in question, and as long as they don't break any of our laws in its recovery, we have no objections to their prosecuting their endeavours."

"Ah! Does your ban include a little, shall we say legalised, burgling?"

"It all depends. Let us take a hypothetical case. Supposing such a case as you outline exists, and supposing you had been retained to recover the property; then, supposing in order to do so, you did what you suggest. That being so, as the articles in question are morally the property of your clients, and as you would be the instrument which adopted such apparently illegal means for their recovery, I should be inclined to say that nothing illegal had occurred. More than that I don't think I care to say."

"Thanks, inspector," remarked Blake. "No more is necessary. I shall govern myself accordingly. I didn't wish to go ahead until I knew at first hand if you had acquiesced in the recovery of the property as I had been given to understand. Yes, thanks, that is all. Yes, it is warm. Good-bye!"

Blake hung up the receiver, and sank into the chair at the desk.

"Sit down, my lad. As we shall go tonight on the burglarious expedition of which I spoke last evening, it will be as well for you to have the facts of the matter now. Briefly this is the case."

Blake then related to Tinker the main facts which Señor Sanchez had given him, after which he explained his reasons for wiring Perry under the name of White, the successful result of which move we have already seen. Then he detailed his interview with Borwick, the gem merchant, from whom he had, by dint of cautious inquiries, gained Bentley's address.

"So you see, my lad," he wound up, "it leaves us in this position. On the one side we have the Colombian Government, represented in the swarthy personage of Señor Sanchez, whose claim to the emeralds seems to me to be of the lot the most just. However, they are legally helpless to recover, and must meet their opponents on their own ground, or, in other words, use the same methods to get the gems which the present possessors used in acquiring them. That is where they appealed to us, and as we have taken up the case for them it puts us on that side as well.

"Then, on the other, we have Bentley, of whom we know something; the mysterious White, whose connection with the matter is still to be elucidated, and last, but not least, the stones themselves which, as far as we know, are in Bentley's possession. Now, then, my lad, since you know of the facts, let me hear what in your opinion should be the next move."

Tinker wrinkled his brows, and puckered up his boyish mouth while Blake watched him amusedly.

"Well, guv'nor," he said finally, "if you weren't here, and I had to make the next move on my own responsibility, I think I'd postpone my decision until some replies came in from our agents with reference to the matter about which we cabled them."

Blake smiled.

"Good boy! That is exactly what I hoped you would say, and as that is the rap of a telegraph-boy, now see what he has got, and we will at once put your plan into execution."

Pleased that his plan of action had met with Blake's endorsement, Tinker rose, and hurried to the street door, from which he returned a moment later, bearing several envelopes.

"Four replies, guv'nor," he said, taking them over to the desk.

"All right, my lad," replied Blake dreamily. "Just rip them open, and see what they say."

Tinker lifted down Blake's private code, and, opening the four envelopes, spread the messages out on the desk. For five minutes he transcribed busily, and then looked up.

"Amsterdam, Vienna, New York, Paris, guv'nor."

"Very well, my lad; read them in rotation."

"Amsterdam is brief," remarked Tinker, picking up the message, "and says: 'Nothing abnormal here. Have made closest inquiries. If any large lots are being held here they have not as yet been marketed. Neither can I get track of any having been placed as collateral for a loan. Will keep you advised fully.'"

"Vienna's is almost the same," went on Tinker, laying down the first one, "and our agent in New York is, as usual, very brief. He says: 'Nothing doing. Will advise at once should I strike oil.'"

"And Paris?" asked Blake, lazily watching the smoke curl upwards.

"Paris, guvnor, is different, and seems to be important. It says: 'No abnormal sale of stones mentioned been made. Large number very fine quality been placed privately as collateral for loan. Valuation roughly over half a million francs, or, in your money, over twenty thousand pounds.[30] Loan was negotiated five months ago by man bearing name of Henry Fairbanks. Believed to be in England at present, as interest was arranged quarterly, and first payment was made through London bank. Description—tall, bearded, gaunt looking. Age—roughly, forty-five. Eyes—blue. Evident, from appearance, has spent years in tropics, and looks malarial. Taciturn in manner. Any further details which arise will be forwarded at once.'"

For some moments after Tinker finished reading the message, Blake sat with half-closed eyes, his pipe held rigidly in his hand. Then he looked up.

"Well, my lad, now that you have read the replies, what is suggested to your mind?"

"It seems to me, guv'nor," said Tinker slowly, "that this chap White, or Fairbanks, looms pretty big in the matter. I've been wondering, since he has apparently disposed of a big bunch of stones as collateral in Paris, if, perhaps, he is doing that end of the business while Bentley looks after the safeguarding of them."

"Very well put, indeed, my lad!" remarked Blake. "Your surmise is given strength by the fact that both men are in Carthorpe, but I think, if you reflect a bit, you will see the odds against it are greater.

"For instance, we have, firstly, the fact that Bentley disposed of emeralds all the way from Iraca down the Magdalena until he reached the coast, proving that his journey was not only of a hurried nature, but urgent as well. Then we know he has regularly sold some fine specimens to Borwick, which point to the source of his money supply for living expenses. Were the Paris stones part of his holdings, it stands to reason he would not jeopardise his position by selling any here in London. That fact alone is proof that it has been done of necessity.

"Again, were he and White working in together, it seems to me that they would have taken different means of leaving Colombia, and, in addition, would have left together. Bentley's movements were about as baffling as those of an elephant would be in a jeweller's establishment. If he desired to advertise his route, he could not have done so

---

[30] £20,000 in 1913 is worth about £2,300,000 in 2020

better than he did. No; Bentley is not naturally such a bungler, and his flight from Colombia proves that caution was sacrificed to urgency.

"Furthermore, the fact that as soon as he reached Barranquilla, White cabled this man Perry to watch the arrival of the *Atrato*, on which Bentley was a passenger, is proof that he did not trust Bentley. Ergo, it argues strongly that Mr. Travers Bentley had done something which incurred the enmity of White, and I should not be at all surprised if I discover our old acquaintance of the Traders' Bay Hotel is unaware of White's residence in Carthorpe."

"By Jove, guv'nor!" exclaimed Tinker. "I see just what you mean now! It seems so simple, I can't understand why it didn't occur to me!" he added ruefully.

"Deduction always seems remarkably simple, my lad, until you come to apply it. It is because the results are so lacking in obscurity that one is tempted to exclaim— 'How easy! Anyone could do that!' Don't forget, though, that there is such a thing as false deduction, and the difficulty is that it usually wears truer colours than the genuine thing. That is where the illogical mind gets fogged, and the difference can only be weighed and regulated by mathematical proof. In that way we cast out the false results, and finally reach the bedrock of a true solution.

"You are doing well, though, my lad. Your idea was one which many a so-called logician would be very apt to assume. However, let us presume that my deductions are correct in so far as the main issue is concerned. What would you suggest as the next step?"

"Since the biggest question mark seems to be tacked on to White, I should think, guv'nor, we ought to make a few investigations regarding him."

"Exactly, my lad. That is what we shall do. To that end you will leave at once by train for Carthorpe village. Make judicious inquiries there, and find out what is known about both Knox and Fairbanks, as White and Bentley seem respectively known down there. I myself will motor down this evening, but any information you gain will have to be held until I arrive, for I will be out all day on that Bloomsbury matter. I expect I shall arrive at the inn in Carthorpe in the neighbourhood of midnight. Hold yourself in readiness for immediate action."

"Right, guv'nor! I'll get ready at once. Shall I take Pedro with me?"

"No. I wish to use him this afternoon, and will bring him along in the car with me."

"All right," answered Tinker, and, after carefully locking away the cipher messages, and burning his transcripts, he made haste to be gone.

Blake had an extremely busy time after Tinker's departure, for his investigations regarding the Bloomsbury matter had to be crowded into a very few hours. What that case was, or what was the result of his investigations regarding it, does not concern this story. Sufficient is it to say that when he hailed a taxi at eight o'clock that evening, and with Pedro headed for Baker Street, he had succeeded in laying his hands on a rascal who had been eluding him for some days.

With that marvellous capacity for concentration which was such an important element in the practice of his chosen profession, Blake had applied himself mentally and physically to the Bloomsbury case.

On entering the consulting-room, however, he jotted down the particulars for Tinker to enter in the "Index," and then, from the identical point where he had mentally left it in the morning, he once more took up the thread of the emerald case.

It took him very few minutes to complete his arrangements for leaving, and, by the time he had finished, the big grey car, which he had ordered to be sent round, stood panting at the kerb outside.

He picked up the bag which he had packed, put it in the tonneau and called Pedro. Then with the engine running beautifully, the big, powerful road-lamps blazing forth, and himself at the wheel, he started on the run through to Carthorpe, in Surrey.

As is well known, Blake liked nothing better as an accompaniment to his thoughts when analysing a particularly difficult problem, than the fresh night air rushing past him, the faint quiver of the car's vibration as it travelled, the black bowl of night with the golden shower of stars scattered prodigally within it, and the faint, steady purr of the powerful engine as, true and in perfect harmony, it responded, like the rakish body it carried, to every touch of the master hand on the wheel.

Nor was this night any exception. For him the conditions were perfect, and though subconsciously man and machine were one as they tore off the miles of that journey, still Blake's deductive faculties found perfect expression in the ideal atmosphere created.

It was close on midnight when familiar landmarks told him he was entering Carthorpe village, and barely slackening speed, he sent the car along the silent main street until he reached the inn. There he doused the road-lamps and swung the car into the inn yard, where he had hardly descended when a shadowy figure approached.

"That you, guv'nor?" whispered a voice which was unquestionably Tinker's.

"Yes; I'm glad you were on the watch. Any news?"

"Oh, yes, guv'nor. I found out several things."

"Did you engage rooms?"

"Oh, yes! Right at the back, where you told me."

"All right," jerked Blake. "Come along! You can make your report to me there."

Leading the way, Blake moved silently until he reached the side door of the inn. Then as he entered, he turned sharply to the right and kept on to the end of the passage, where were the rooms which Tinker had engaged. Blake had stopped there several times before, and knew his way about; consequently, it had not been without a reason that he told Tinker to engage those particular rooms which looked out on the fields at the back of the inn.

"Now, my lad," he said briskly as Tinker closed the door, "let me hear what you know."

"Well, sir, I found out that you were right in thinking White and Bentley don't live together, although they both reside in Carthorpe."

"Well?"

"Bentley, under the name of Knox, has had Carthorpe Hall leased for about six months, and rarely leaves it, although he went up to London by this morning's early train, and returned this afternoon. I saw him on his return, and, although he is disguised, it is Bentley, right enough.

"White, on the other hand, has only been here for about a month. He has leased a place which adjoins Carthorpe Hall, but although, after making sure of Bentley's identity, I spent several hours, I couldn't get a look at him. I have discovered that he and Bentley are never seen together, and that White encourages no callers of any description. People don't even know whether he brought many servants with him or not. The only two which have been seen are a man who looks after the stables, and a cook; though why he should have a stableman is odd, because, as far as is known, he has neither motors nor horses."

"Is that all?" inquired Blake briefly.

"Yes, guv'nor, practically all, except to say that I kept a quiet look-out at the driveway of Carthorpe Hall early this evening until I thought it wiser to return in case you arrived. I saw nothing, though."

"Lose no time in getting into your roughest disguise," said Blake after a pause. "I will do likewise. Make haste, we have much to do."

Tinker left for his room at once, and ten minutes later returned garbed as Blake had instructed. When, after turning out the lights, and putting several necessary articles in his pockets, Blake and Tinker, with Pedro at their heels, slipped through the window and started off across the fields, they were about as murderous-looking a pair as one could well find.

Tinker looked as tough as the most hardened specimen of criminally-raised youth, while Blake, if anything, was even worse. Had any policeman, village or otherwise, seen them, he would have arrested them at once on suspicion; but by keeping to the fields they evaded the street-loving arm of the law, and on reaching the boundaries of Carthorpe Hall, plunged into the wooded park, which formed one of the most valuable assets of that ancient estate.

Had Blake known the real object of Bentley's journey to London that day, or had he dreamed of the stirring events which had taken place that evening under Tinker's very nose, it is just possible he would have altered his plan of campaign.

So far, the elements on which he based his movements were those relating to three concrete facts—White, Bentley, and the emeralds. His chief desire was to settle at once whether Bentley had part or all of the stones, and if so to secure them surreptitiously, when Bentley could whistle for them, not daring to do more.

If, however, it eventuated that White had a portion, then, by settling with Bentley at once, he could strike quickly at White before the latter had time to fly.

A radically important element, however, had, in the person of Yvonne, obtruded itself into the matter, and of that fact Blake was as yet in ignorance.

Little did he dream when, back in London, he had wondered if Yvonne would get track of Bentley, and discover the facts of his new-found wealth, that even as the thought occurred, the young woman for whom he had bought Borwick's finest emerald, and for whom he had another pleasant surprise, was even then arranging to relieve Bentley of his haul.

As Blake and Tinker made their way along the boundary wall, a motor with all lights out, flashed by on the other side, and never for a moment did Blake imagine that it contained Yvonne and Graves, the former having just come from the Hall, after her stirring experiences and surprising discoveries which have already been related.

Nor did Yvonne, on her part, realise that barely an hour after she began was Sexton Blake creeping through the park of Carthorpe Hall, intent on the self-same mission as herself.

To say the least, it was, to both of their calculations, an important contingency, and considering exactly who they were, could result in only one thing—a complication of no small proportions.

One of Blake's theories was that, in order to follow up a clue successfully, or bring to book those who evaded the law, the criminal investigator must not only keep up to their latest methods, but rather exceed them in that knowledge, and in the scientific perfection of his burglarious campaign that night, he gave no indications that he had neglected to practise what he preached.

When they broke through the thicker woods, and came in view of the house, Blake pulled up and laid his hand on Tinker's arm.

"Steady, my lad! Let us make a survey of the place first. One light only, and from its position I should judge it to be in the library. Our friend Bentley keeps late hours. Three windows to the left, which are probably those of the kitchen and pantry. They are not sufficiently far apart to be those of the dining-room, nor is there room to include that room as part of them. It is unlikely that those two windows to the right look out from it either. I judge it to be at the other side of the house. Therefore, those two dark windows to the right must belong to a drawing-room of some sort. All dark and silent upstairs. Evidently the servants retired some time ago.

"I think our best plan will be to endeavour to force an entry through the windows of the drawing-room, and as there appears to be someone still in the library, we will choose the second one, which is the farthest from it."

"Will you enter while he is in the library?" whispered Tinker.

"Certainly," replied Blake. "If all goes well, we can discover who it is, and, if it is Bentley, I think we will enter the library boldly and play a hold-up game. It will save time if he opens the safe for us. Come along!"

Blake stole forward cautiously, with Tinker and Pedro following, and, using the trees as cover, reached the drawing-room window which, by chance, was the same one through which White and Yvonne, with the bound Bentley on the former's shoulders, had emerged half an hour earlier.

From his pocket Blake drew a tiny, spider-like steel instrument, which was almost a duplicate of the one Yvonne had used. It took him even less time than it had taken her to open the window, and, at the moment, the fact that the catch flew back so noiselessly, and the sash slid up so easily, awakened no suspicions in his mind.

Before slipping over the sill he drew out his pocket-lamp and flashed it about the room, smiling faintly as he saw his idea that the room was a drawing-room was correct. Then he slipped through and laid his hand on Pedro's collar as the bloodhound followed close on his heels. When Tinker had entered and stood beside him, the famous trio, with Blake leading, stole softly across and through the half-open door into the hall beyond.

Architecturally speaking, Carthorpe Hall was the sum total of the individual tastes of the Carthorpe family extending back for several centuries.

It embodied all periods of the building and decorative art, from the twelfth century onwards, and considering the generally "hotched-potched" ideas of the different ones who had tried their hand at alterations, enlargements, tearing down and rebuilding, it is a subject for wonder that the result was the dignified pile which it undoubtedly appeared.

Owing to these architectural changes, the hall into which Blake and Tinker emerged, broke off to the right into a huge rectangular space, more reminiscent of ancient hunting days and the yule log than the present, when luxury-loving young men not infrequently keep pace with the hounds while lolling at ease in a modern motor.

Straight ahead it continued between narrow walls, whose basic material was ancient stone, and had Yvonne and White only known it, they had little need for caution, since the peculiar construction of the lower floor served as a natural sound absorbent. Neither did Blake know this; but one would have gathered that he had, at least, an inkling of it, from the confident manner in which he moved.

The library opened off this narrow hall, and when his fingers touched a door a few feet along, Blake knew he had found the one he wanted. Then, after signing to Tinker to hold Pedro, he dropped flat to the floor and put his eye to the slit under the door.

The faintest vestige of light filtered through, telling him there was some obstruction on the other side, but this point faded from his mind for the moment as, on attempting to arise, his hand came into contact with a hard object on the floor.

As his fingers closed about it, he knew it was a knife, and, slightly puzzled, he thrust it in his pocket. Then, catching hold of the handle of the door, he turned it ever so gently, pushing inwards as, with the faintest of clicks, the catch was released.

He found to his surprise that it opened outwards, and, drawing back, saw the curtains as the door opened. He moved silently forward and peered through the opening between, but as his eyes swept an empty room he threw them apart.

"It's all right," he whispered to Tinker. "Come on!"

Tinker did so, taking Pedro with him, and when he had entered, stood beside his master in the middle of the room. Blake was standing rigid, his keen eyes darting first to the right, then to the left, then ahead, finally to fall on the overturned desk chair.

"It seems that our friend Bentley has either made a very hurried departure for bed or else we have arrived too late to witness a struggle, my lad," he murmured gently. "See if the safe is locked."

Tinker crossed over to that article of furniture, and bent down obediently. Not expecting it would by any chance be unlocked, he turned the handle, and heaved mightily, the result being that he made a graceful back somersault into Pedro as the small door swung open without resistance.

"I didn't say to wake the whole house," remarked Blake drily. "Get up, and try to be more quiet!"

Feeling rather sheepish, Tinker did so, while Blake dropped to his knees, and rapidly ran through the safe. Beyond a few unimportant papers, however, his search was unrewarded; but, just as he was turning away, he spied what looked like a roll of leather.

Lifting it out, he held it up to discover that it was an old, worn leather belt, with an empty, scarred sheath hanging to it. Instantly his mind recurred to the knife he had found outside the library door, and he felt in his pocket for it.

It did not surprise him, after glancing at it, to find that it fitted the empty sheath; but, as they seemed to indicate nothing at the moment, he tossed them on the desk beside the big Service revolver, whose presence there caused his mind to work rapidly.

To Blake the room presented every sign of having been the scene of a struggle. The very position of the chair indicated that it had been knocked over, and then kicked about, for it was some distance from the desk. Had it merely fallen over owing to its occupant rising too hastily, it would have been in a different position as well as nearer the desk.

Then, again, there were other signs, which, to the casual observer, would appear as merely a mild state of disorder—the turned-up rug, a fallen book, and a pencil on the rug.

Where was Bentley? If he were in bed, why had he retired, leaving the light on and the safe unlocked? Had he merely gone upstairs for a few moments, and would he return? It certainly seemed so at that moment, for barely had Blake reached that point in his thoughts when he and Tinker swung suddenly on hearing a quavering voice in the doorway.

There, standing between the parted curtains, with a double-barrelled gun held in his shaking hands, was Barnes, the butler, trying his best to appear brave.

"Hands up!" he said, with a voice in which the tremble still hung. I'll—shoot—you—villains!"

Tinker grinned unconsciously, and certainly there was some excuse, for the poor fellow was not an inspiring picture of courage.

"Drop that gun!" snapped Blake suddenly.

And, jumping in a startled manner, Barnes dropped the gun with a clatter to the floor.

"The next time you intend using a gun," remarked Blake drily, "I would advise you to cock it. Otherwise, you will have difficulty in discharging it. Come in here!"

Even through Blake's murderous-looking get-up the man recognised the ring of authority in the command, and meekly obeyed.

"Stand there!" ordered Blake, as Barnes reached the middle of the room.

And, beyond a few nervous movements as Pedro sniffed his legs, he managed to obey.

"Now then," went on Blake, "who are you?"

"The butler, sir."

"Where is your master—Mr. Knox?"

"Oh, please, sir, I don't know! When I locked up he was here, sir, and I thought he was yet. I got up to close my window, and saw you coming through the trees, and—and, sir, thinking you were burglars, I got the gun and came down. You are burglars, aren't you?"

Blake laughed.

"You say you don't know where your master is. Is he in the habit of retiring and leaving the light on as well as the safe unlocked?"

"Oh, no indeed, sir! He's most particular on that point. In fact, sir, he locks the library door as well."

"Ah! What is your name?"

"Barnes, sir, though why I says sir to you, I don't know! I never saw two such ruffians in my life! There, I've said it; and you can hit me if you want to!"

"You won't get hit," said Blake, making a few rapid changes in his appearance which brought a look of wonderment to the man's face.

"Now, Barnes, I wish to ask you a few questions, then I want you to make a thorough search of the premises in order to see if your master is about. First, let me tell you that if you don't do exactly as I say, and keep your tongue silent afterwards, you will fall seriously foul of the law. Do you absorb that fact?"

"Oh, yes, sir!"

"Very well. What time did you go to bed?"

"At ten, sir."

"And the other servants?"

"Just a few minutes before, sir."

"Your master was here when you retired?"

"Yes, sir. He spends hours in here every night, sir, though for why I can't say."

"You have no idea where he would be now?"

"No, sir; I haven't."

"Do you know if he kept anything of value in the safe?"

"I'm sure he did, sir, for he put it in new when he came, and was very particular about it, sir. If you look at the back, you will see it is chained to the wall."

"I know," nodded Blake. "I think that is all now."

"There is something, sir, which may interest you," said Barnes, not knowing who his interlocutor was, but reading in his changed appearance the man of authority.

"What is it?" asked Blake sharply.

"Well, sir, when he came home from London today he came direct here, as was his habit, sir. I was out in the 'all, sir, and he hadn't been here more than a minute when he cried out as in terror, sir. Twice he did that, and when I heard the second one I came at once. I knocked, but as he didn't answer, sir, I entered, and found him lying on the floor. He had fainted, sir, and when he came to, the first thing he said was, "The knife—the knife! I didn't know what he meant, sir; but as he told me to look on the floor for a knife I did so. When I couldn't find it, he looked himself, sir, and seemed very agitated when he couldn't find it. He sent me out then; but it was a very strange thing, if I may say so, sir!"

Blake's eyes wandered to the sheath on the desk. What did the man's story mean? Was the knife he had found outside the door the knife to which Bentley had referred? If so, what was its meaning, and if it had been on the floor when he fainted, how did it get into the hall, and remain there all that time unseen?

"I suppose you really didn't see the knife?" he asked suddenly.

"No, sir; I swear to you I didn't."

"Very well. Go with him, Tinker, and search the house for his master. See that you don't alarm the other servants. We don't want a panic. In the meantime I'll make an examination here."

As Tinker disappeared in the wake of the butler with Pedro padding along behind, Blake kicked the shot-gun aside, and drawing out his pocket-lamp and powerful glass, dropped to his knees.

Starting at the door, he blocked out the area for examination—which, in this case, was the floor—into the usual imaginary squares, and set to work. For some time he worked in silence, examining here, discarding there, until fully half the floor had been covered.

By this time he was working between the desk and the couch, and had almost passed from one point to a fresh one, when something suddenly came within the range of the glass.

Magnified by its power, he saw criss-crossed over each other three short hairs of a brownish-red shade. Not attaching great importance to them, but following up his theory that nothing must be passed, Blake picked them up, and laid them on the desk.

Again he went to work, and from that point found several scattered specimens of the hairs until, when he could discover no more, he had fully two dozen in the pile on the desk. Then, continuing his examination, Blake dropped flat, and squirmed half under the sofa, where he brought the lamp and glass once more into play. A slight cry escaped him as he saw something lying close in against the wall.

Dropping the glass momentarily, he thrust in his hand, and drew it out. As he saw exactly what it was his eyes grew grave, for it was an odd-looking ring, whose setting was a big, ancient Egyptian scarab.

"I think it will be a waste of time to search for Bentley here!" he muttered, as he thrust it in his waistcoat-pocket. "If I am not mistaken I can guess who owns this ring, but for the present I will keep that knowledge to myself."

The discovery he had just made brought to Blake's mind many new elements which would alter his theories and plans, and which, as a consequence, must be considered at once.

He moved swiftly over the rest of the floor, and one other thing he found which did not tend to lessen the gravity of his eyes. It was a small but perfect emerald lying almost hidden under the folds of the window-curtains, which fell to the floor.

Picking it up, Blake took it to the desk and laid it down, while he thrust his hand in an inside-pocket and drew out the magnificent stone he had purchased from Borwick. Then together he compared the two. Colour for colour, purity for purity, they were identical, and with a deep knowledge of precious stones Blake knew they had both come out of the same mine as surely as though he himself had dug them.

At that moment he heard the returning footsteps of Tinker and the butler. Hastily thrusting the stones into his pocket, and slipping the hairs into a small specimen box, he turned just as they entered.

"He's nowhere to be found, guv'nor!" exclaimed Tinker. "We've searched high and low. The housekeeper had hysterics when she saw me," he added, with a grin; "but Barnes got her quiet."

Blake nodded.

"That was what I expected. He will not return tonight. As for us, we will be going. Before I go, however," he added, turning to Barnes, "I want to warn you to do nothing and to say nothing regarding your master's absence. As you may have guessed, I am connected with the law, and I will explain what is necessary to you all in good time. Do you understand?"

"Yes, sir; I promise you I will keep quiet."

"And you will undertake that the other servants shall do likewise?"

"Yes, sir."

"Very well, Barnes. We will leave by the main door. Show us out."

Picking up the belt and sheath as he spoke, Blake signed to the man, and, with the puzzled Tinker following with Pedro, the burglarious trio departed, the moving spirit having found a good deal more in his nocturnal expedition than he had expected.

The Fifth Chapter
Blake's Little Present to Yvonne—The End

IT was a silent walk which Blake and Tinker had on their way back to the hotel. Blake was wrapped in his thoughts, endeavouring to resolve some semblance of mental order out of the chaos into which his previous theories had been cast by his discoveries back in the library of Carthorpe Hall.

Barnes, the butler, he felt positive, was safe enough for the time being, for his undoubted fear and vague imaginings would be sufficient to keep his tongue from wagging. As for the rest of the servants, they would undoubtedly follow the lead set them by Barnes.

Though his nocturnal adventure had been distinctly abortive, as far as the recovery of the stones was concerned, Blake could not help but feel that his discoveries were of prime importance, owing to the fact that he was undoubtedly the first to examine the library since Bentley, forcibly or otherwise, had left it earlier in the evening.

When he had started for Carthorpe it will be remembered that the three main concrete facts Blake had upon which to work, were Bentley's evident possession of the emeralds, White's unexplained association with the matter, and the actual existence of the stones themselves. True, there were many other details and half-shadowy points born of these three major facts, but to them he must now add the suggestions formed by his discoveries in the library.

First and foremost, there was the scarab ring which he had seen numbers of times on the dainty finger of Mademoiselle Yvonne. That proved at once that she had certainly not abated her interest in Bentley's movements the slightest jot, and that, in addition, she had wasted no time in moving once her plans had been made. Characteristic of her always.

But—and as yet it seemed folly to commit himself definitely—did she get the emeralds? If so, how came her scarab ring under the couch, and was its presence there the result of a struggle? Certainly, Mademoiselle Yvonne, mistress of every detail as she was, would not leave such blatant evidence behind her, except for two reasons—one, through force of circumstances; and the other owing to the fact that some stronger occurrence had taken place, which, for the moment, had driven everything else from her mind.

That argued that everything had not gone absolutely as planned. Would she return either surreptitiously or openly and contrive to regain possession of the scarab? Blake thought not, at least for the present, as probably she rested on the assumption that no one would know to whom it belonged, and were a hue-and-cry raised upon Bentley's disappearance, such a move would certainly court suspicion. She would hardly calculate on Sexton Blake's participation in the affair.

The natural question which then arose was the one relating to Bentley's apparent absence. Was his departure coincident with Yvonne's visit and a result of that? It unquestionably seemed so. That being a fact, what part, if any, did White play in the matter? Who was he in reality? Was he known to Yvonne? Had he any connection with her plans, and was he there that evening as well? What was the meaning of Bentley's attack during the afternoon? What did he mean by his reference to the knife, and what part, if any, did it play in the matter? Then, was the presence of those short, brown hairs on the carpet a matter for thought?

That they were not those of any dog which Bentley may have had was known to Blake, for on inquiry just before leaving, Barnes had informed him that there was no pet animal of any description whatever about the place. That they were not human hairs was obvious, but conjecture on that point was futile until he got them under the microscope. Lastly, the discovery of the small emerald which coincided in colour and quality with his own gem, proved conclusively that, although the stones were not now on the premises, they had been there only that evening.

The questions to be solved, and solved at once, were—into whose hands did they go, and where was their present resting-place. Certainly at present the arrow of suspicion pointed most strongly to Yvonne, but, to Blake's mind, that theory must remain a tentative one until he had solved White's connection with the affair.

As the detective reached this point in his thoughts they arrived at the back of the inn, from which they had departed such a short time before. As silently as they had entered Carthorpe Hall did they throw up the sash, and drop, with a soft thud, on to the floor of their sitting-room.

"Is it bed, guv'nor?" asked Tinker, as he lowered the blind and turned on the light.

"You had better lie down for a while, my lad," replied Blake. "I have some examinations to make, but if my calculations prove correct we shall have a busy day tomorrow, and you will need all your strength. Better take a couple of hours. I will call you at sunrise."

"All right, guv'nor; if you wish me to, I will. Is there nothing that I can do?"

"No, Tinker. It is just some tedious, microscopic work which is a necessary evil to the case."

As Tinker departed for his room, Blake drew from his pocket the belt and sheath in which he had placed the knife. Tossing them on the table, he pulled out the small specimen box containing the hairs, the emerald he had found, and the big scarab ring.

The latter received first attention at his hands, and it took barely two minutes' close scrutiny to convince him that it was the one belonging to Yvonne and no other. With a slight sigh he thrust it back in his pocket and turned to his bag. From its capacious interior he drew forth a small, but powerful, microscope, and, after arranging it in a satisfactory position, opened the specimen box. Then Blake set to work.

One by one he placed the hairs on the glass slide, and pushed them under the lens. Point by point he studied them, devoting particular care to the colour and texture. When he had finished he placed them back in the specimen box, and leaned back.

"No dog there!" he muttered, feeling absently for a cigar. "Besides, they are of too coarse a texture for a dog. Neither are they human. Are they by any chance a clue in this matter, or did they simply come there through some innocent cause entirely alien to the case?"

He lay back with half-closed eyes and puffed thoughtfully, going over every detail of the case in an endeavour to discover some point which, having been considered of a minor importance, might assume larger proportions, and perhaps form the keystone of the whole construction.

Back and forth went his mind, digging, probing, turning, with the skill of the surgeon striving to lay bare the hidden cause of the complication, for that the crux of the whole matter was to be found in the information he now possessed Blake felt assured.

The grey flood of dawn was breaking through the violet veil of night before Blake stirred, but as his eyes once more fell on the microscope, he sat up with a sudden jerk.

"Great Scott!" he muttered, reaching for the specimen box. "Why didn't that occur to me before? It's a hundred to one on."

Hastily opening the box, he turned out the hairs and once more placed them on the slide. This time his examination was very short, but as he finished, a grim smile was playing on his lips.

"It seems, Mr. White, that your connection with the case looms even larger than I thought. The details are certainly complicated between you and the charming mademoiselle, for, without doubt, your interest is not dependent upon hers. The fact that you followed Bentley from Colombia settles any doubt on that point. I wonder if you were there tonight, and if your visit was separate from or coincident with that of mademoiselle? Really, my dear Señor Sanchez, I never dreamed, when I consented to take this case, that I was in for such an interesting time. In view of the facts, I think a further examination of that knife might be worthwhile."

Following up the suggestion of his thoughts, Blake picked up the belt and drew the knife from the sheath. It was not unlike the usual hunting-knife which is used so extensively, being of a well-known make, though battered-looking from use. On the handle Blake discovered that two initials had been roughly cut, and he was not surprised to find that they were "T. B." The blade was discoloured by a rusty red coating, and Blake's eyes grew puzzled as he examined it.

"I wonder—I wonder," he muttered. "It is no doubt caused through being left dry after Bentley has despatched some animal—perchance a wild pig. At any rate, I shall determine exactly what it is. It seems that every point connected with my mysterious friends will bear investigation."

As he muttered to himself, he worked busily, drawing forth several phials and boxes from his bag. Finally, he discovered the one he wanted, and, laying the knife on the table, he went to work.

With chemicals and microscope Blake laboured strenuously for a half-hour, but when he finally desisted, there was a hard, dry glitter in his eyes, and he muttered just one word, "human!" Then he rose, and, sweeping everything into his bag, entered his bed-room.

The sun was just breaking through the window when he finally emerged, clad in fresh clothes, and feeling vigorous from a cold dip. Lighting a cigarette, he walked across and rapped on Tinker's door, after which he picked up his automatic, and spent some time going over it caressingly. When Tinker made his appearance, Blake thrust the revolver in his pocket and spoke.

"See what you can dig up to eat, my lad. I hear them moving about, but I suppose it is too early yet for breakfast. As soon as we have finished we will get away at once."

"All right, guv'nor," replied Tinker, looking refreshed after his sleep. "Anything new?"

"Some new complications, my lad. Make haste! I will tell you all about matters in the car."

Half an hour later, after Tinker had managed to make a successful raid on the kitchen, they were in the car, heading once more for Carthorpe Hall.

On their arrival, Blake ran up the steps, looking very different from when he had entered through the window in the night. Barnes, still rubbing the sleep from his eyes, opened the door, and, cutting short his remarks Blake asked curtly:

"Has your master returned yet?"

"No, sir. I have been sitting here in the hall ever since you left, and he hasn't come in."

"Very well, come to the library," ordered Blake. "Now, then, answer me one or two questions," he said, as Tinker closed the door. "Have you ever been in the library when your master's safe was open?"

"Oh, yes, sir, several times!"

"I presume, then, you have glanced at the contents?"

"Yes, sir, casual like."

"And did you notice this at any of those times?" And he held up the belt and sheath.

"Yes, sir, I could have told you that last night. One day it was lying on the floor just inside the safe door, but it had no knife in it, sir."

"Are you sure of that fact?" asked Blake sharply.

"Positive, sir, for I wondered why a belt and sheath was kept with no knife in it, sir."

"Have you seen at any time since you have been with Mr. Knox any animals about the grounds? An ape, for instance?"

"No, sir, never," answered the man decidedly.

"Very well, Barnes, that will do now. You might throw up the windows. I wish to make an examination of the ground outside."

Barnes moved at once to obey, and as the sash rolled up, Blake drew out his pocket-glass and hopped lightly over the sill. He saw at once, however, that if there had been any footprints outside, they had long ago disappeared owing to the springy nature of the thick turf. Not even the closest scrutiny gave any indications of such, and though there were several spears of grass lying flat, their appearance justified the opinion that they were in that position through natural causes.

Climbing back over the sill, Blake turned to the man.

"We will go along to the drawing-room. I wish to examine the catch on the window and the ground outside."

Barnes turned at once and led the way, while Blake and Tinker followed, with Pedro bringing up the rear. They had almost gained the door of the drawing-room, when Pedro stopped short and turned with a low growl.

Blake swung sharply, and watched the dog, who, after a moment's hesitation, turned and dashed back to the library. Tinker had closed the door as he left, but, quick as he was to open it, Blake was before him.

Right or Pedro's heels he dashed in, but to all appearances the room was in exactly the same condition as when they had left. Pedro kept on until he reached the window, where he stood with teeth bared and his great muzzle raised skywards.

Puzzled at his actions, Blake crossed and stood beside him; but nothing of a suspicious nature met his gaze. To right and left the ground was clear, while, though he could only see ahead through the trees for a short distance, there seemed no movement there.

He leaped over the sill to the ground, and called Pedro out. Then he put the hound at the ground in every direction, but Pedro refused to budge from the window. Just then Tinker's voice came from inside.

"I say, guv'nor, didn't you leave that belt and sheath with the knife in it on the desk here?"

"Yes, of course!" snapped Blake.

"Well, it isn't here now," answered Tinker.

"What's that?" exclaimed Blake, leaping back into the room. "Not here, you say?"

"No, guv'nor. I was positive I noticed it there as we left the room, too."

"So it was; but—— Ah!"

Blake swung as he broke off, and once more approached the window. For several long minutes he stood silently, then he turned to Tinker, and said:

"Take Pedro, my lad, and go through these grounds until you reach the adjoining place. Stick to cover, and get where you can command a view of the house. It may be hours before you can see anything, but I feel positive developments will take place in that direction sometime today. In the meantime, I shall watch from the front, and if the man we are after leaves, I shall follow him. Don't break cover under any circumstances, unless you should see me make my appearance. If I do so, join me at once. If he does leave, you can make your way back to the inn and get some lunch, for I will be after him. Then get back to your post. Do you understand?"

"Yes, guv'nor. I'll manage to get concealed in some place where I can watch unseen."

"Very well. Get along with you."

As Tinker and Pedro disappeared through the window and started through the woods, Blake called Barnes, who was in the hall.

"I want you to lock the window of this room as well as the door. Permit no one to enter for the present."

"Very well, sir. I'll do so," replied the man, and Blake turned at once to depart.

Half an hour later a grey car swung along the road past the thickly-wooded grounds of the estate recently leased by Mr. Henry Fairbanks. As it drew almost opposite the gates, however, there was an alarming explosion somewhere, and it came to a stop with a jerk.

The goggled man, who was the sole occupant of it, at once got to the ground and began making an examination. From the frowning look on his face one might have imagined that the breakage was of a serious nature—an opinion which would have been strengthened by the imposing array of tools which the man proceeded to lay out on the ground.

Then, getting into a suit of overalls, he began tinkering about the engine, stopping at intervals to turn the starting handle. All he managed to get out of it, however, was a feeble cough or two, and he had been labouring diligently for over an hour when a small gate beside the larger ones opened, and a man emerged.

With a casual look at the man working over the machine, he struck off at a brisk pace towards the village. Nor did he dream for one moment that, as he did so, every detail of his features, his walk, and his build, were being mentally photographed on the memory of the most brilliant detective living.

"So that is Mr. Henry Fairbanks, alias White," muttered Blake, as he continued his work on the engine. "I remember now that he keeps neither horse nor motor. I'll wager he would have jumped if I had shouted 'Perry' after him. I'd like to know whether he has those stones or not. The point is, where is he bound? If, by any chance, he and Mademoiselle are working together, then I wouldn't be surprised if he were on his way to a conference, possibly to divide the spoils. It seems to me that friend Bentley has his hands full at present. But since I have discovered the real nature of that stain on the knife blade, and since it has so mysteriously disappeared, I think, Mr. White, I'll stand in on this game."

With that Blake turned back to his engine, and unconcernedly tinkered away for another twenty minutes. Then, turning the starting handle, he closed the hood as the engine whirred rhythmically.

There never had been anything wrong with it, for the explosion which had caused its sudden stoppage had been a carefully planned bluff on Blake's part in order to have an apparent reason for pausing outside the gates of White's place.

After getting out of his overalls he climbed in, and, turning, headed leisurely for the village. His deductions had not been far wrong, for, as he expected, White was on his way there in order to engage a trap. Even as Blake drove slowly along and turned down the main street, he saw White far ahead in a trap, driving in the opposite direction.

Turning into the inn yard, Blake ordered a horse to be hitched up at once, and, himself taking the ribbons, started after. To follow slowly in the motor would be too risky, he reasoned, and White would be a fool, indeed, did he not recognise the same car which had been standing outside his gates.

When he had drawn away from the village Blake pulled up, and made a few rapid, though radical changes in his appearance. Then he shook up the horse, and bowled along after the other trap, which was just turning to the left. For well over an hour the chase continued until at the top of a long hill Blake pulled up, and smiled grimly.

"Horton village, eh!" he muttered. "If I remember rightly I had the pleasure of having tea just near there with Mademoiselle Yvonne during my chase after Cornelius Patterson, at the time I was trying out my aeroplane, the *Grey Panther*. She has evidently returned to that delightful spot, and another point in the case is settled. There is, undoubtedly, some connection between her and White. I shall drive on to the inn, and have lunch. If he returns he must pass there."

Suiting the action to the word, Blake started on again, not pulling up until he reached the inn. There, after having his horse seen to, and ordering lunch, he sat down in the shade of an elm, and smoked lazily.

After lunch he returned to his seat, from which he commanded a view of the village street, but not until three o'clock did he see the gaunt-faced White driving back.

When he had disappeared down the road in a cloud of dust, Blake rose, and after ordering his horse to be hitched up, started after. He did not attempt to keep the other in sight, however, but, taking a road which was a shorter, though rougher way, he put the horse along at a sharp pace.

On his arrival at Carthorpe he had left the trap at the inn, and was already walking briskly half way along the road towards White's place when that gentleman drove past him.

"That shortcut came in handy," smiled Blake, as he pulled up and glanced behind. "He'd never guess in a thousand years that I was at the inn in Horton when he drove past."

He had now reached the boundary wall, and, slipping warily across the road, climbed over the fence, and dropped softly to the ground.

With characteristic caution Blake began a zigzag course through the trees until they began to grow thinner, and finally the house came into view. He was just in time to see White leap out of the trap, and throw the reins to a man who climbed in and drove away, evidently to take the outfit back to the village.

Then White entered the house, and as he did so, Blake strode boldly forward, and whistled sharply. Not a hundred yards away Tinker and Pedro broke cover at once, and trotted across until they reached Blake.

"Anything doing?" asked the latter, without pausing.

"No, guv'nor, except that the chap who just got out of the trap left before noon."

"I know," replied Blake, "I followed him. Did you have lunch?"

"Yes, I went into the village after he left, just as you told me."

"Quite right, my lad. He did one of the two things which I thought possibilities. Come along. We are going to have an interview with him. It may be mild, or it may be stormy. In any case, have your revolver handy. He doesn't look like a milk-and-water customer."

On reaching the main steps, Blake led the way up, and rang the bell. At first no one answered, but after a second peal, shuffling footsteps sounded within, and an old woman appeared.

She was cautious enough, however, to keep the door on the chain, and through the narrow aperture Blake was compelled to speak.

"Is Mr. Fairbanks at home?" he asked curtly.

"Maybe he is, and then, again, maybe he ain't," replied the old woman, eyeing him sharply.

"You go at once, and tell him I wish to see him urgently," ordered Blake. "Tell him I come from Perry, and must speak with him at once."

"In that case you had better enter," came a cold voice over the old woman's shoulder, and a moment later the chain fell down with a clatter.

Without making any reply, Blake signed to Tinker and followed White along the hall to the library. As White entered he turned.

"Now, then, you say you come from Perry. What is it, and——"

He broke off, and his eyes narrowed suddenly, for as he turned completely, he found himself gazing into the extremely businesslike looking barrel of Blake's automatic.

"Sit down, Mr. White," said the latter softly. "You and I have a few things to talk over."

"Who in blazes are you?" jerked White, half starting forward.

"I'll tell you later. Sit down first; this thing might go off, and then I would have no opportunity of telling you."

Seeing that the man holding the revolver meant business, White sank into a chair, though with a very bad grace. Then, while Blake kept him covered, Tinker made short work of binding his hands and feet.

"Now, then," smiled Blake, lowering the automatic, and taking out a cigar, "we can talk. I am sorry to adopt these methods Mr. White, but until I have settled one or two points I think it necessary."

"Who are you?" growled White. "And how do you know my name? Are you the agent of the Colombian Government?"

Blake laughed cheerfully.

"Easy my friend, easy. It happens that I have a fancy to ask questions before answering them. By the way, how is the—er—ape?"

Blake's eyes dropped carelessly as he asked the question, but not before he had seen the lightning gleam spring into White's eyes, and fade as quickly.

"What do you mean?" asked the latter, unable to keep the hoarseness out of his voice.

"Merely curiosity!" drawled Blake, with a yawn. "Strictly speaking, however, I suppose I should have inquired first as to the health of that charming lady, Mademoiselle Yvonne."

White was speechless, and only glared, without making any attempt to reply. But suddenly Blake's manner changed and the drawl gave place to a steely ring.

"See here, White," he said sharply. "What have you done with Travers Bentley?"

"I don't see what business of yours that is!" growled White.

"No?" answered Blake. "It would be interesting to know, then, why you took such pains to recover a certain knife this morning on which was a stain of human blood? Look here, White, stop bluffing. One of two things has happened. Bentley has felt the cold touch of that knife from you, or—and to do you justice I incline to this belief—you have felt the touch of it from him. Whichever way it is, that knife plays a big part in your feud, for feud there is I know now. Stop hedging, White. You must produce Bentley, otherwise you are liable to get into a complicated situation. This isn't the Caqueta jungle, you know. Come, man, instead of being tied up there, you might be free, but I must have the truth of your connection with this matter. I can tell you Bentley's moves and yours ever since you left Iraca, even to the loan you negotiated in Paris. Come, now, do you intend to speak, and, perhaps, have my assistance, or must I go ahead on my own? If I do, White, believe me, you will not keep one of the stones you got last night."

"Who are you?" whispered White, with dilated eyes, as Blake unrolled facts which he thought no man knew. "How do you know all this? Are you an agent of Mademoiselle Yvonne's, and has she only gained my confidence to betray me?'

"Mademoiselle Yvonne is not that type of individual," replied Blake coldly. "I should have thought your common-sense would have told you that. There is no particular reason now, however, why you shouldn't know my name. Tinker, just hold one of my cards up in front of our friend's eyes."

With a grin, Tinker drew one of Blake's cards from his pocket, and held it before White, who, after reading it, looked over the top at Blake with astounded eyes.

"So you are Sexton Blake," he muttered. "I might have guessed it."

"At your service," smiled Blake.

"What are you doing in this case?" inquired White, with puzzled eyes.

"Merely a matter of a few hundred thousand pounds' worth of emeralds," drawled Blake. "But, come, White, do you intend making a clean breast of matters or not? Frankly, I am anxious to know the truth about that knife, and also Bentley's whereabouts. That move was unwise, White. It put you foul of the law."

"I tell you I only did what any man would do!" blazed White suddenly, while Blake murmured to himself:

"That roused him. Now, I'll get the truth, though he strikes me as being a pretty decent sort of a fellow."

Blake was right, for, boiling over with the long suppression of his anger against Bentley, and startled out of his reserve by Blake's bold move, he started talking at high pressure, pouring out all the details of his story from the time he had met Bentley in Bogota. He told how they had found the mine, and of Bentley's treachery in the Caqueta jungle, of the latter's leaving him to the mercy of the prowling denizens of the jungle, and of his cowardly flight, of his own long illness, and his enforced delay owing to the necessity of getting enough stones out of the mine in order to prosecute his campaign of vengeance.

Then he told of his following Bentley to England, and of his long wait before he could get a place adjoining that of his treacherous partner; of his intention to carry on a campaign of terror until he had driven Bentley to the verge of madness. Finally, how the coincidence of his night visit with that of a young woman whose identity he did not then know brought things to a head.

Then he related how Bentley had forcibly overcome Yvonne until she was unconscious, and of how he had at that moment entered.

"But, by heavens," he cried savagely, as he finished, "I've got Bentley in my power, and I intend to keep him until I have given him a taste of the torture he gave me! I don't care a hang for his share of the stones. I haven't got them, anyway; but my own share I keep. I've got a debt to pay to Travers Bentley, and I intend paying it, no matter what you say to the contrary. Then, when I have finished with him, I'll shake the dust of this country off my feet."

Beyond several silent nods of the head as the points of White's story fitted in with his own deductions, Blake had kept silent during the long recital, but now he spoke.

"I can't say that I blame you for your attitude in the matter," he said quietly. "I happen to know that Travers Bentley is a gentleman who is quite capable of defrauding his partner, though honestly I didn't think him capable of knifing a man in the back. On the other hand, there are other points to be considered which you seem to forget, and one of them is that I control the situation. That being so, and considering the fact that I am acting in the interests of the Colombian Government, I think you will see that the decision of the matter rests with me."

"I'm not a fool!" jerked White.

"Quite so. I thought not. Therefore, in my opinion, you would be wise to listen to my decision and follow it, for, frankly, if you don't, I am afraid you will fare badly."

"What is your suggestion?" asked White, who had cooled down, and was now looking at Blake with the look of a man who felt the force of a powerful nature and was compelled to bow to it.

"Simply this," replied Blake. "When I accepted this case from the Colombian Government, I made no comments one way or the other as to what my own private opinion was regarding their policy of claiming the whole of the stones. As far as I was concerned that was entirely beside the question. However, I gathered that they were worth a very respectable sum; otherwise, the Government would not have gone to so much trouble over them, nor would they have commissioned me in the matter, knowing that, in a case of this kind, my charges are not—er—shall we say microscopic?"

"They're worth a million pounds if they're worth a penny!" growled White.

"Quite so. I imagined they would reach somewhere around that figure. Very well. Since you discovered the mine and worked it, thus securing the stones which otherwise would have lain undiscovered for years, perhaps centuries, you are by all odds of fairness entitled to a share. In this case, I put it at one quarter, your partner Bentley being entitled to another quarter. The remaining half, in my opinion, belongs to the Colombian Government, and to them it shall go. As for Bentley, however, by his treachery in attempting to kill you, and his stealing of the stones, he automatically forfeits all claim to his portion which reverts to you, thus giving you one half, and the Government one half. Bentley, however, must be released, and I myself will see that he leaves the country. Whether he deserves punishment or not is outside your province. That is my judgment in the matter, White. What have you to say?"

"I say it's a fair one," muttered White slowly, "and I guess you are just enough. There are complications, however."

"What are they?"

"Well, I promised half the stones to Mademoiselle Yvonne, and, in fact, I took that half over to her today. She told me what she had against Bentley."

"I know all about that," answered Blake. "You may keep your share. I'll arrange with Mademoiselle Yvonne about hers."

"How about the Colombian Government?" asked White. "Won't they still keep after my half?"

"They will sign a full receipt, and undertake not to do so when I settle with them," answered Blake. "When I gave that judgment in the matter, I expected to see the terms of it carried out. Otherwise, I shouldn't have made it."

"I guess there's nothing for me to do but say yes," remarked White, looking up and smiling faintly. "If you'll untie me, I'll pass my word to do as you say, and then I'd like to shake hands."

"Good!" replied Blake heartily. "I thought you would see reason. Tinker, just release Mr. White, and then we can discuss details."

"I suppose you want me to free Bentley at once?" asked White, as Tinker freed him. Blake nodded.

"Yes. We will go along with you. I'd like a few words with him myself before he goes."

White rose and opened the door, and after him went Blake with Tinker following, a look of profound admiration in his eyes for the diplomacy of his master.

Blake's recent prisoner led the way along the hall, and had begun to mount the stairs, when at the top appeared the old woman with whom the two had parleyed at the front door. As yet she had not seen them, and with surprising agility for one of her age, she grasped the balustrade and hobbled down the stairs two at a time.

Not until she almost collided with White was she aware of his presence, and then she paused in her reckless descent, and looked at him with blanched cheeks and startled eyes.

"Oh, sir, he's gone—he's gone, and it hain't my fault!"

"Who's gone?" jerked White sharply. "Not——"

"Yes, sir, out of the window."

With a muttered remark, White thrust her aside.

"It's Bentley she means, Mr. Blake!"

"Hurry then," answered Blake, and pell-mell Blake, White, Tinker, and Pedro dashed up the stairs. White kept on down a passage which ran off to the right, and, pausing before a door half-way along, kicked it open.

"He was here!" he gasped. "But I had him tied safely. I can't imagine how he managed it!"

"There is your answer," rapped Blake, pointing to the mirror of the dresser. "He broke that with his elbow or shoulder, and cut his bonds on the edge."

Blake kept straight on to the window as he spoke, but on reaching it, drew up suddenly.

"My heavens, look!" he exclaimed, and as the others crowded forward, they saw a remarkable sight.

Just taking cover among the trees of the plantation was a flying figure which they instinctively knew to be Bentley's. The drain-pipe, which ran beside the window, showed how he had made his descent, and that it had taken place even while they talked in the library.

But that was not all. After him, and leaping along with great hopping paces, was a big reddish brown ape, all its human resemblance gone in a snarling look of bestial rage.

"He'll get Bentley, sure!" gasped White.

"Come on!" jerked Blake. "We can't have that! Follow me!"

Turning as he spoke, he dashed back through the door, and with the others at his heels, clattered down the stairs, and through the door. Drawing his revolver as he ran, Blake cocked it and broke into the cover of the plantation, where Bentley had disappeared. For fully two hundred yards he kept on, until, suddenly, the trees thinned away into a little clearing, and as he saw what had happened there, Blake levelled his revolver.

Lying on the ground was Bentley, while beside him sat the ape, a fiendish grin of satisfaction on its face, for even from where he stood, Blake could see that its vengeance which had been spoiled by White in the library at Carthorpe Hall, had this time been complete. Bentley would never more be affected by the laws or judgments of man, for he had taken his case to a higher court.

As he realised the truth, Blake muttered savagely, and fired straight between the eyes of the grinning ape. There is not the faintest doubt but that the leaden messenger which he despatched would have found its resting place in the spot he aimed at, but for a sudden jar against his leg which sent it wide. As he looked down, he saw the cause of the miss in Pedro, who was flying past, and before Blake could fire the second time, the great bloodhound was halfway across the clearing, covering the distance between it and the ape with great leaps.

Then the three human beings on the edge of that clearing watched a battle royal. Once Tinker, with a muttered exclamation, levelled his revolver and started forward, but Blake drew him back sharply.

"Let them alone!" he said sternly; and beyond that remark, they watched in silence.

On coming within a few feet of the ape, Pedro drew up sharply and crouched low. The ape, in its turn, chattered excitedly and leaped to the defensive. Then the great dog and the ferocious man-beast began circling around until an opening occurred, their eyes never leaving those of their antagonist.

Suddenly, and without the slightest warning, the ape dropped the defensive, and assumed the offensive. With a lightning-like spring it leaped, landing with marvellous precision on Pedro's back. As the bloodhound turned savagely the other's great, claw-like hands caught the dog's throat, while it bit savagely at his head. Then Pedro, with a giant heave, turned over on his back and, raising both hind paws, ripped savagely, the red streaks which appeared almost at once indicating that he had got home.

The pain maddened the ape, and withdrawing its "hands" from Pedro's throat, it wrapped its great hairy arms about the dog, and began a crushing, hugging pressure which rendered Pedro's feet powerless. Then, like an animated ball, the two straining animals turned over and over, the one trying to crush into insensibility while the other exerted every effort towards getting his powerful jaws to work.

White watched the battle with tense features. He probably had as great an affection for the beast which had saved his life, and had, after all, avenged him, as Blake and Tinker had for Pedro. He had been impelled by the same feeling which affected Tinker to leap forward and separate the two struggling beasts, but after Blake's stern command, he had desisted, and stood with clenched fists and rigid jaws.

As for Blake, he held his revolver ready, watching every move and counter-move of the fight—a self-appointed referee. If the ape did succeed in overcoming Pedro, he was grimly determined that it should hear from him afterwards; but since Pedro had taken the initiative, his master would let him fight it out himself, a decision which, to Tinker's younger nature, would have clashed most violently with his love for the hound.

A simultaneous decision to take a breathing spell seemed to suddenly strike the two combatants, for though their grip did not relax, they lay motionless for some time. Then the renewal came from the ape, who began rolling again, but that move was its undoing.

Pedro, a savage and wily beast when it came to a pitched battle, had been lying motionless, with half-closed eyes, apparently exhausted; but, as the ape moved, his head shot down with a terrible jerk, and came, jaw upwards, under the ape's head. The other's eyes literally blazed as it saw what was coming, but its own awful grip held it helpless to prevent it.

With a sharp, upward jerk, Pedro's jaws met in its throat, and then began a struggle compared with which the earlier part of the fight was a pink tea between a couple of fox terriers. Driven insane by Pedro's hold, and the knowledge that, unless it eluded those terrible jaws, it was done for, the ape leaped upwards and fought gamely.

Pedro was a big dog and a heavy one, but he was tossed about in the ape's struggles like a small pug, but his great jaws never, for the barest fraction of a second, relaxed their hold. Driven in its desperation to seek its native element for safety, the ape turned, and with Pedro hanging to it, dashed off through the trees, followed by the three watchers.

What happened in the shade of those trees, no man will ever know. Once, during the chase, Blake saw a flying figure leap from branch to branch high up in an oak-tree; then there was a crashing sound, followed by a thud, and he knew the ape had leaped to the earth in a death spring, which, if anything were of avail, would shake off the bloodhound's grip.

Then another crashing of branches sounded, followed by one short, screeching cry. They dashed on in the direction of the sound, and broke through the trees, to discover the ape lying motionless on the ground, while Pedro limped about, rubbing his muzzle in the long grass.

White regarded the dead beast sorrowfully:

"I feel tempted to shoot that dog of yours," he muttered slowly, "though it was the greatest fight I ever witnessed."

"I'm afraid if you shot Pedro, Tinker's bullet would reach you if mine didn't!" answered Blake drily. "You are right, though, it was a great fight. However, White, you must realise that even had Pedro not won, I should have been compelled to shoot the ape, regardless of the fact that it saved your life. Its fatal attack on Bentley sealed its death warrant."

"I know—I know!" replied the other. "But it was marvellously intelligent. What will you do now?"

"As soon as Tinker has finished his examination of Pedro," replied Blake, "we shall return to the house. It will be necessary to look after Bentley. I shall explain matters to the coroner, and it won't be necessary for you to remain."

"Why, do you wish me to leave at once?"

"You are to take your share of the stones and leave England immediately," replied Blake quietly. "In order that my decision may be carried out, that will be necessary. If you were here during the coroner's examination, the details of your history would come out, and in the complications which would ensue, you might find yourself in a decidedly awkward position, as well as running the risk of being jockeyed out of your emeralds. Don't forget the fact that Bentley was an unwilling guest in your house when he met with his fate."

"You are right, Mr. Blake, and deucedly good about the matter," remarked White. "I'll do as you say, and leave tonight. I'm not anxious to remain, I can tell you!"

"Very well, then, that is settled. How is he, Tinker?" asked Blake, turning to the lad, who came up, leading Pedro.

"He seems all right, guv'nor. He's got a few bruises here and there, and is bleeding in half a dozen places, but not seriously."

"That was to be expected," remarked Blake. "Let me have a look at him!"

He bent as he spoke, and made a rapid examination of Pedro's wounds. Truth to tell, Blake was secretly highly pleased with Pedro, and something of his pride must have been communicated to the dog in the very gentleness of his examination, for Pedro's great tongue came out and he slowly licked Blake's hand.

"Dear old chap!" whispered Blake. "I'd have skinned that ape alive if he had got the better of you. You are a battered-looking warrior, but I guess you are still in the ring."

And the energetic pounding of Pedro's tail indicated that that bruised, but victorious animal, was very much in the ring.

It was a silent party which took Bentley's body back to the house, and, after sending a message to the police, Blake and Tinker watched White take his departure.

"I don't know how I can express my gratitude to you, Mr. Blake," he said warmly, as he paused at the door.

"The best way is not to get into such a situation again," replied Blake, as he shook hands. "Try to remember, White, that it is not for us to take the law into our own hands and seek revenge. You know, had we not witnessed Bentley's fate, you would have been in a tight situation, for any jury would have been quite convinced that you drove the ape on to do it."

"I know," answered White, in a low tone. "I'll remember your good counsels. Give my regards to Señor Sanchez," he added, with a sudden smile, "and tell him I hope the mine pans out well."

"I shall," said Blake, also smiling.

After shaking hands with Tinker, the gaunt-looking man passed down the drive, and so out of this story, justice having been so strangely dealt out to him by Sexton Blake, who had been wise enough to see that the man's savage desire for vengeance was the growth of a genuine wrong—a growth which he had been able to root up by the application of a wide outlook and simple justice. For Sexton Blake knew what it was to pass long, lonely nights in the jungle, and he knew what fantastic creatures of the mind were born in man through such desolate and monotonous nights.

His thoughts had been following the retreating man down the drive, but as a blue-uniformed constable appeared in the distance, his mind came back to the present and the necessities of the occasion.

Half an hour later Blake and Tinker, having temporarily settled the arrangement of matters with the constable, betook themselves down the drive and struck off towards the village at a brisk pace, with Pedro padding behind, an extremely contented expression resting in his eyes as he did so.

It was just six when they reached the inn, and Tinker turned inquiringly to his master as they entered.

"Shall we be returning to London tonight, guv'nor?" he asked.

"Possibly, I can't say yet," answered Blake dreamily. "You'll have to kick your heels around the inn this evening, my lad. I am going to make a call, and shall be using the car. Later, we may motor through to London. It might be as well if you looked after Pedro's scars of battle."

"I can't come with you?" asked Tinker.

"Not this evening, my lad," smiled Blake. "It is not business."

Whatever was to be Blake's destination, it seemed evident that he considered evening clothes a necessary adjunct for when he finally emerged from his room he was clad in those garments and had a long coat over his arm. He had compromised on a soft cap as a necessity in driving the car, and when he finally drove out of the inn, it would have been difficult to guess that the capacious dust coat hid aught but a tweed suit.

He seemed thoroughly familiar with the way, for he showed no hesitation in heading along the same road over which he had followed White earlier in the day. He swung the big car around through a maze of narrow lanes unhesitatingly, until finally he pounded through Horton village, and kept on past the barracks, until he reached the plantation boundaries of a large estate.

Pausing only long enough to sound his horn and order the wondering lodgekeeper to open the gates, he glided through, and drove slowly up the elm-bordered drive, until he came to a stop opposite the main entrance. Shutting off the engine Blake leaped down and ran lightly up the broad steps which went over the terrace to the balcony.

As he paused for a moment at the top, drinking in the sweet air of the fragrant summer evening he saw, far down on the lawn, a white splash which stood out against the purple wings of the gathering dusk.

With a faint smile playing over his lips and an odd look in his eyes, he turned his footsteps and strode over the thick turf towards it. As he drew near, his footsteps noise-less in the velvety grass, he discerned a heavy mass of bronze-gold hair rimming the top of the low chair, while below was the white serge of a dainty gown.

Barely a yard separated him from the white patch ahead, when the faint rustle of his garments must have reached the ears of the young woman in the chair, for she stirred, and a sleepy voice asked:

"Is it you, Alice? Is dinner served?"

"I trust so, mademoiselle, for you are to have an uninvited guest," replied Blake quietly.

With a smothered exclamation the young woman leaped to her feet, her face flushing and paling, and her eyes looking like those of a frightened fawn at bay.

"You!" she gasped.

"You seem rather surprised to see me," said Blake, bowing.

"Oh, yes! I—— You see—it——"

"Exactly!" smiled Blake. "I understand."

"Why have you come?" asked Yvonne, recovering her self-possession, and dropping her lids to hide the fugitive gleam of pleasure which the presence of Sexton Blake always caused her.

"One reason was to tender you many happy returns of the day, mademoiselle."

"I am sure it is very nice of you, Mr. Blake, but how did you know this was my birthday?"

"I am afraid I must refuse to disclose such a secret," laughed Blake. "I have brought you a present. May I give it to you?"

"I—I am most happy to accept it," murmured Yvonne.

With deliberate movements Blake thrust his hand in the pocket of his coat and drew out a thin tube of paper which had been secured by thrusting it through a heavy gold ring. With a slight inclination of the head he handed it to her and smiled softly as he saw the puzzled look in her eyes.

"It—it isn't a——"

"A warrant?" finished Blake. "No, indeed. Please open it!"

Yvonne began to do so, but as she turned it over in her hand she saw the big Egyptian scarab which was set in the ring which bound it.

"My ring!" she whispered, with wide eyes. "Where did you get it?"

"Where did you leave it?" countered Blake.

"Then, after all you know about Carthorpe Hall?"

"Decidedly, mademoiselle. Also about a gentleman named White as well as our late friend Travers Bentley."

"Late! How late?"

"Mademoiselle, he is now beyond reach of any revenge either you or White might feel inclined to deal out. Travers Bentley was accidentally killed this afternoon, and White is on his way out of the country."

"And the emeralds?" exclaimed Yvonne involuntarily.

"White has been permitted to take his share with him. One of the reasons of my call is to recover the other share from you, mademoiselle."

"You didn't think I wanted them for myself, did you?" she asked.

"I felt such a supposition was hardly justified," murmured Blake.

"I only wanted to relieve Bentley of them. They would have been sold, and the money given to charity."

"Exactly; but it happens I have promised to return them to the Colombian Government, and I think you will grant my request."

"You know I will," answered Yvonne softly. "But you haven't told me what this paper contains."

"Suppose you look?"

Slipping off the ring Yvonne unrolled the paper and bent over it in the deepening dusk to decipher the writing with which it appeared to be covered. As she did so a stray tendril of her hair swept Blake's face, and as he gazed down at the graceful little head so close to him, he drew in a sharp breath and clenched his hands.

Suddenly she raised her head, and her face was very close to his as she whispered:

"Oh, you are good! A free pardon! No more haunting dread of Dalemoor Prison. Oh, I——"

Her voice trailed off into a sob, and as her shoulders heaved, Blake suddenly felt a wild desire to place his arm about them.

"I have been endeavouring to find you for some time," he said quietly. "I wanted to give it to you on your birthday, but until today thought it would be impossible."

"Why did you do this for me?" she asked, in a low tone, laying her hand on his arm.

"Mademoiselle," answered Blake slowly, "I give it to you with the hope that the future may never find us on opposite sides, as we have been in the past. It is a very dear wish of mine."

He paused for a few moments, gazing off into the coming night with sombre eyes, while the slim young woman at his side looked up at him with quivering lips. Then he spoke, and his voice was strangely metallic:

"I have for you something else."

He drew out the regal emerald which he had purchased from Borwick, and passed it to her.

"I half intended having it set," he said, with a faint tinge of embarrassment; "but I thought I would leave that to your own inclinations."

"You have made the day a very happy one for me," she said shyly.

As Yvonne spoke she looked up at him, and blind must Blake have been had he not seen the aching love which looked out of those wistful eyes, and felt the appeal of those soft, trembling lips.

"I think we had better return to the house," he said, looking down at her.

"Yes. You will stay to dinner?"

"With pleasure. Is your uncle here?"

Yvonne nodded.

"Yes; he will be very grateful for the happy surprise you have provided in securing me a free pardon."

"Don't, please," said Blake gently, as they paced side by side across the lawn. "It has made me happy that my influence was able to secure it."

It was a very astonished but still languid-mannered Graves who greeted Yvonne's unexpected guest on their arrival at the house, but on hearing the facts of the case, he quickly dropped back into his accustomed drawl, and did the honours to perfection.

He had an innate respect for the powers of Sexton Blake, and, though they had more than once been on the opposite side of the fence, and at daggers drawn, the clean sportsmanship and unruffled sangfroid of Blake had gained his secret admiration.

After dinner Yvonne played on her favourite violin with all her being for the man who sat back in a shadowy corner of the big drawing-room, and as he watched her his eyes grew dreamy, and his mind went back to those few moments on the lawn.

It was with a deep sigh that he rose to take his departure; and while he bade good-bye to Graves, Yvonne slipped away, to return a moment later with a package which he knew contained the emeralds. Then she followed him out to the terrace.

"Good-bye!" said Blake softly, taking her hand.

"I won't say good-bye," she answered, smiling at him through her tears. "I'll only say *au revoir!*"

The man looked long and silently into her eyes; then, turning, he ran hastily down the steps, and climbed into the car.

As he drove off into the night he did not see the yearning look of the white-clad figure on the terrace, as she pressed her hands to her heaving breast, and breathed:

"Some day—some day he must yield!"

***

Blake and Tinker were back in London again, and Tinker was looking at the remains of Pedro's wounds with a critical eye, the while he gave an ear to the conversation which was taking place between Blake and Señor Sanchez.

"It is remarkable, Mr. Blake!" the attaché was saying. "Such rapid results I would never have believed possible! We worked for months, and reached in the end nothing but a blank wall!"

Blake shrugged his shoulders.

"That is as it may be, señor," he said. "However, here are the stones, and, by the valuation of a friend of mine, I find they are worth, roughly, half a million!"

"So little," murmured the attaché. "We thought the original package must have been worth nearly a million!"

"So, they were," snapped Blake; "but what you see is all you are going to get back. In view of many points which I discovered after I took up this matter for you, I decided that half the parcel was all you were justly entitled to. I took it upon myself to sanction the retention of the other half by one of the men who found the mine for you. You would be well advised, señor, to look no further for that portion, for your efforts would be fruitless."

"I can only think the advice of a man who has succeeded so quickly in recovering them must be worth following," replied Sanchez suavely. "There is the little matter of er—remuneration for your trouble, Mr. Blake."

"In a case of this kind," remarked Blake, "my charges are based on percentage. Five percent of the value of the returned stones, Señor Sanchez, will fit the case."

"That is exactly twenty-five thousand,"[31] said the attaché, drawing out a cheque-book.

"Quite right," replied Blake, as he carelessly took the proffered cheque and tossed it on the desk.

"Thank you—and good-day!"

"Gee! That was quick money, guv'nor!" remarked Tinker, when, after much profuse thanks, Señor Sanchez had taken his departure.

"Exactly," said Blake succinctly; "but, considering the ethics of the case, my lad, Señor Sanchez can consider himself an extremely fortunate man. Burglary hasn't come our way for some little time; but I am glad, in a way, we took it up. It just happens that we managed to straighten out a tangle of injustice, and, by dealing out that quality to White, saved the world a good citizen and defrauded crime of a new recruit; for, had White been dealt with unfairly, he was exactly the type of man to avenge himself on society at large by trying to get back from them the hard-earned wealth of which he would feel himself unjustly dispossessed. A man saved from a life of crime, my lad, is worth more than the capture of a dozen men who are already criminals.

"In other words, in the stamping out of that festering sore on society's heart termed crime, an ounce of prevention is worth a ton of cure.

"And I think we may safely say White's prevention is permanent. Bentley has gone for good, and, as far as he is concerned, we suspend judgment. But come, my lad! It is a delightful afternoon. We shall take a run through to Henley in the car!"

And so ended the brief, though eventful, case which, through the instrumentality of Fate's decree, personified by an ape from the Caqueta jungle, Yvonne was avenged on Travers Bentley, who was the only one remaining of that octet of swindlers who had financially ruined her and her mother in Australia.

And she felt, in the depths of her heart, that she had gained something more than vengeance; for when, in the solitude of her room after Blake had departed, she looked into her mirror, her eyes dropped shyly and her lips trembled as she thought of those few exquisite moments on the lawn.

---

[31] £25,000 in 1913 is worth about £2,900,000.00 in 2020

YVONNE—A COMPLETE TRIUMPH.

Never was an editor's heart more gladdened than was mine, chums, when my first Yvonne versus Sexton Blake yarn appeared. The same week I was simply overwhelmed with letters and postcards crammed full with genuine praise, admiration, and complete satisfaction. Of course, I cannot reply to all, for I have received far too many for that, but I do sincerely trust that the thanks I convey now, from the bottom of my heart, will be taken by all individually.

There is no doubt of the absolute success of this series. They have taken the market by storm, and to quote from a reader's letter which I print below, they are a complete triumph.

The letters which follow are taken at random from the heaps in my office, and are, I think, sufficiently eloquent without any further remarks from me. Needless to say, I am hard at work on more Yvonne yarns, and they will appear at short intervals.

A FEW APPRECIATIVE LETTERS

"Liverpool. "January 23rd, 1913.

"Dear Skipper,

"I hope you will excuse me taking the liberty of writing to you, but I feel that I must say something to you about your new character, Yvonne. I have been reading the U.J. for a few years now, but none of the yarns come up to the one about the above-mentioned person. I am delighted with it, and shall tell all my friends about it, and try and induce them to read it every week.

"Your affectionate friend,

W. J. G."

"Limerick.
"January 23rd, 1913.

"Dear Skipper,
"I know that I am expressing the opinion of every one of the readers of the good old UNION JACK when I say that your first Yvonne yarn is going to score a complete triumph, and I heartily congratulate you.

"I have been a reader of the 'U. J.' for some years now, and I have always thought the Plummer yarns perfection, but you have gone one better this time.

"Once I got started, nothing would make me budge until I had finished, and that was midnight, and when I had finished, dear Skipper, I only wished you were near enough to take you by the hand, and tell you that I could never wish for anything better than your first Yvonne yarn.

"You have a good many readers here, fathers as well as sons, and I can safely say you will have a good many more very soon. I, for one, will do all I can to spread the UNION JACK'S fame, and I think I have something to attain my object with in this week's copy of the best detective-story paper in the world. I think you deserve that your readers should do something in return for the excellent reading you have taken such great pains to provide for them in the pages of the UNION JACK.

"I do not ask you to publish my letter, but if you should do so I do not wish it for my sake, but those of my friends here who, of course, would appreciate it very much, and would not forget it.
"LIMERICKMAN."

"4, Lansdowne Road, "Crumpsall,
Manchester. "January 25th, 1913.

"Dear Skipper,
"Having been for some years a constant reader of the UNION JACK, I take this opportunity to express my opinion of this paper. I think that of all papers the UNION JACK is the best, not only for its tales alone, but for the fact that any boy can take it home without any fear of being told not to buy such papers. This is, in my opinion, the best recommendation to the public that any paper could have.

"I, myself, take the paper home and read it, and my parents do not in the least correct me. I have given it to my friends after having read it, and they all express their opinion of it in glowing words, and I may say that the father of my particular chum sends him to ask me if I have any UNION JACKS to give him to read.

"Regarding the new series of tales dealing with the adventures of Yvonne, I can only say that they are, like all the other tales that appear in your paper, in one word, 'sterling.' Hoping I have not taken up too much of your valuable time, I will now, close by wishing you and your paper every success. "Your true reader and friend,
WILLIAM E. HOOLE.".

A LETTER FROM ABROAD

"Singapore,
March 22nd, 1913

"Dear Sir,
"As constant readers of The UNION JACK, it gives us a lot of pleasure to read about Mademoiselle Yvonne versus Sexton Blake yarns. We must say that we do admire the noble character of this female adventuress, who although belonging to the fair sex, yet can prove to those who have wronged her that her brains can work better and quicker than theirs, as far as criminality is concerned. It is true that she has gone against the law of a country, but in our opinion it is only right that she should fulfil her vow to have revenge on her enemies. We sincerely hope that you could bring Mademoiselle Yvonne to a peaceful end in your story, after she has had her revenge. The least you can do for her is that she can turn over a new leaf.

"We now suggest that she, possessing such skilful brains as has been shown in the stories, combines her skill with that of Sexton Blake's, who with her help certainly will bring criminals more cunning and dangerous than Carlac and Plummer to book.

"We hope a great success will befall to your valuable paper. We remain, dear Skip-per,
"Yours sincerely,
"Two SINGAPOREAN CHUMS.".

LAST—BUT NOT LEAST.

From a soldier chum at Lucknow, India, comes a very cheery letter, for which he has my sincere thanks. Please convey my cordial good wishes to all members of your company, Pte. W. D.

No. 6,238, C Squadron,
"8th K. R. Hussars,
"Lucknow,
"India.
"May 1st, 1913.

"Dear Sirs,
"Just a few lines in regard to the good old UNION JACK. I have been a reader now for five years, and can truly say that I have not missed a week. I have seen different letters from readers from all over the world, but I have not seen one from the Indian plains yet. My mother sends it out to me every week, and as I read them I pass them around the bungalow to my chums, who are all very pleased with them. In some of our readers' letters, some seem to think that the Carlac yarns are best; others the Plummer yarns.

"But in my opinion, I think that the Yvonne yarns are about the best I ever read, and

I have read a few, including Nick Carter, Dick Turpin, Claude Duval, Nick Winter, Spearing, and numerous other yarns. Let me say that the UNION JACK is best of the lot.

"Dear sir, wishing you every success and happiness, and may the good old UNION JACK live for years to come yet. Dear sir, hoping my letter will range amongst others on a page of the good old UNION JACK.

"I remain,

"Yours truly,

"PTE. W. D."

YVONNE!
How Do You Pronounce This Name?

F. W. has written to tell me that he has heard many different pronunciations of our new character's name, and will I let- him know which is the correct one.

Well, my chum, as you doubtless know, the name is a French one. Dividing it into syllables, "y" becomes one, and "vonne" the other. The "y" is soft sounding, and is pronounced exactly as you would pronounce the letter "e" saying the alphabet, and "vonne" is pronounced "von." Thus Yvonne (E-von).

OUR NEXT VOLUME BEGINS WITH: "THE DIAMOND DRAGON."

I have a rare treat for all my chums next week! I say rare of a truth, for candidly, I have never before read such a fine, stirring, true-to-life story drama, dealing with Chinese Peril, of dark intrigues, gambling dens, opium dens, Australian farm life, adventure in East Side, New York, in London, etc., as the yarn appearing in the *Union Jack* next week. Every chapter moves with a delicious ease, carrying the lucky reader along with it, marvelling at the versatility of the author, and at the absolute correctness of every detail of the yarn, until at last the end is reached-for there is an end of a Double Number, even and one leans back and whispers "What a marvellous yarn!"

Honestly, my chums, I can safely say that I have never before offered such a stupendous yarn to the reading public. When I say this, I realise what a statement I am making. But I DO say it, and will stand by it, too. If any chum, after he has read "THE DIAMOND DRAGON," can say that he has read a better yarn before in the "U. J.," well, I shall be surprised, that is all!

It introduces that grand character, Dr. Huxton Rymer, who appeared in that highly successful Yvonne yarn, *When Greek Meets Greek*. The yarn is by the same author, and that, I think, is enough recommendation for it.

My chums will recognise what a grand yarn it will be when I tell them that Rymer is fighting against a wonderful Chinese ring, whose tentacles seem to reach everywhere on earth, and Sexton Blake, at the same time. Blake is, of course, fighting Rymer, but at first does not know that he is also up against the Chinese ring, until he is nearly——

There I go, giving the game away. No, my chums, I cannot tell you any more about the yarn, but I rely, absolutely rely, upon all of you to push next week's double number all you can among non-readers. This is the first Easter Double Number the *Union Jack* has had for a long time, so please help me to establish a record! Order your copies now, chums, and take my word, you will not be sorry for it. Remember, I stake my word that it will be the finest yarn you ever read in the old U. J."

PLUS: INTRODUCING PRINCE WU LING THE WILIEST AND MOST DANGEROUS OF ALL OF BLAKE'S FOES

Imagine a man instilled with the wisdom of thousands of years, steeped in the writings of Confucius, educated at the best English, French, German, and American universities, a linguist of marvellous ability, a student and adept at every form of cunning conception and baffling mystery, shrewd, clever, unemotional, impassive, patient as the Sphinx, and as inscrutable.

Add to this an organisation with its tentacles throughout the world, and composed of members who would sacrifice their lives without the slightest hesitation. Then finish it off with unlimited wealth with which to carry on its operations, and you have the octopus-like organisation of which Prince Wu Ling was the ruling spirit.

It is a far cry from the ancient and sacred writings of Confucius to the present day, but Wu Ling was a modernised product of the mysterious past, and it is with his exploits we have to deal.

No human agency seemed able to stop or even locate the cause of the sinister and baffling operations of this powerful Celestial ring, until, spreading their tentacles further and further in the pursuit of their aim, they finally reached Europe.

There, that brilliant product of mathematics and science, Sexton Blake, the great British detective, was drawn into the fray, and the record of his struggle to locate the mysterious power, and to stop its threatening sweep, appears in our next volume. The title of the yarn is *The Brotherhood of the Yellow Beetle,* and it will be found one of the most extraordinary and startling stories of today.

Two great foes. Four great tales. *Sexton Blake: Rymer and Wu Ling.* Order now and avoid disappointment!

The Skipper

Grand Easter Double Number.
Dr. HUXTON RYMER EASTER 1913 V. SEXTON BLAKE.
The Union Jack 2d
SEXTON BLAKE
TREMBLING FROM HEAD TO FOOT RYMER ROSE AND PEERED INTO THE ROOM.
The DIAMOND DRAGON
A TALE OF CHINESE PERIL IN LONDON AND ABROAD.
Dr HUXTON RYMER
"OH! IS IT THAT TERRIBLE DRAGON?" SHE CRIED.
SPECIALLY WRITTEN FOR READERS OF ALL AGES.

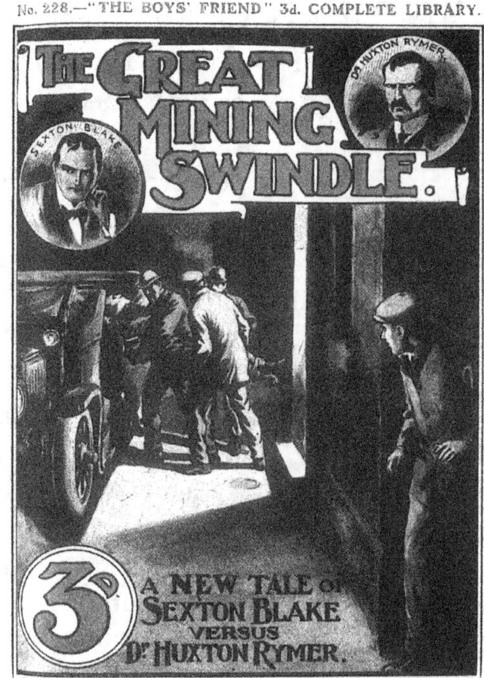

No. 228.—"THE BOYS' FRIEND" 3d. COMPLETE LIBRARY.
The GREAT MINING SWINDLE.
SEXTON BLAKE
DR HUXTON RYMER
3d
A NEW TALE OF SEXTON BLAKE VERSUS Dr HUXTON RYMER.

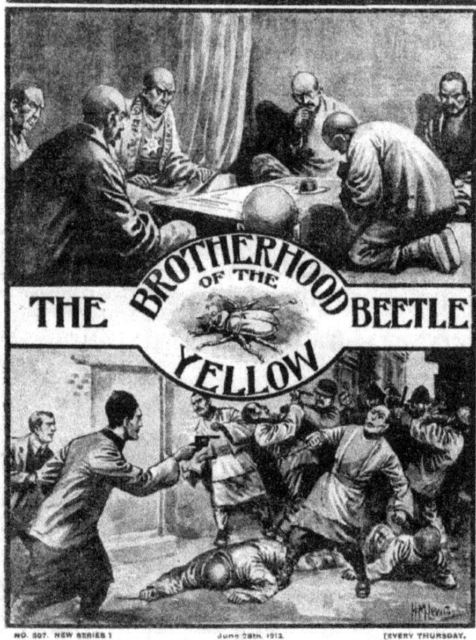

GREAT NEW SERIES TO-DAY.
The UNION JACK. 1d.
THE BROTHERHOOD OF THE YELLOW BEETLE
NO. 507. NEW SERIES 1
June 28th, 1913.
[EVERY THURSDAY.

A TALE OF THE BROTHERHOOD OF THE YELLOW BEETLE.
THE Union Jack. 1d
THE IDOL'S SPELL.
"YOU WILL OBEY—OBEY—OBEY!" CAME THE DEEP VOICE FROM THE IDOL'S MOUTH, AND ELAINE'S TONELESS VOICE REPLIED, "I WILL OBEY!" TINKER WATCHED FROM THE CURTAINS, SPEECHLESS WITH AMAZEMENT. WHAT WOULD HAPPEN NEXT?
No. 510. NEW SERIES.]
July 19th, 1913.
[EVERY THURSDAY.

THE TEED FILES #3: FIVE CLASSIC TALES

Detective, Intrigue, and Revolution.

Special Australian Yarn.

ALSO INCLUDES THE BLACK JEWEL CASE!

THE TEED FILES #4: FOUR CLASSIC TALES

DR. HUXTON RYMER, GRAVES & TINKER APPEAR.

THE LAST OF WU LING!

A TALE OF SEXTON BLAKE & WU LING.

We hope you enjoyed this Sexton Blake Anthology! If you have a moment, please help us out by leaving a review.

www.ingramcontent.com/pod-product-compliance
Lightning Source LLC
Chambersburg PA
CBHW081102300726
48976CB00011B/2699